TRUMP TOWER

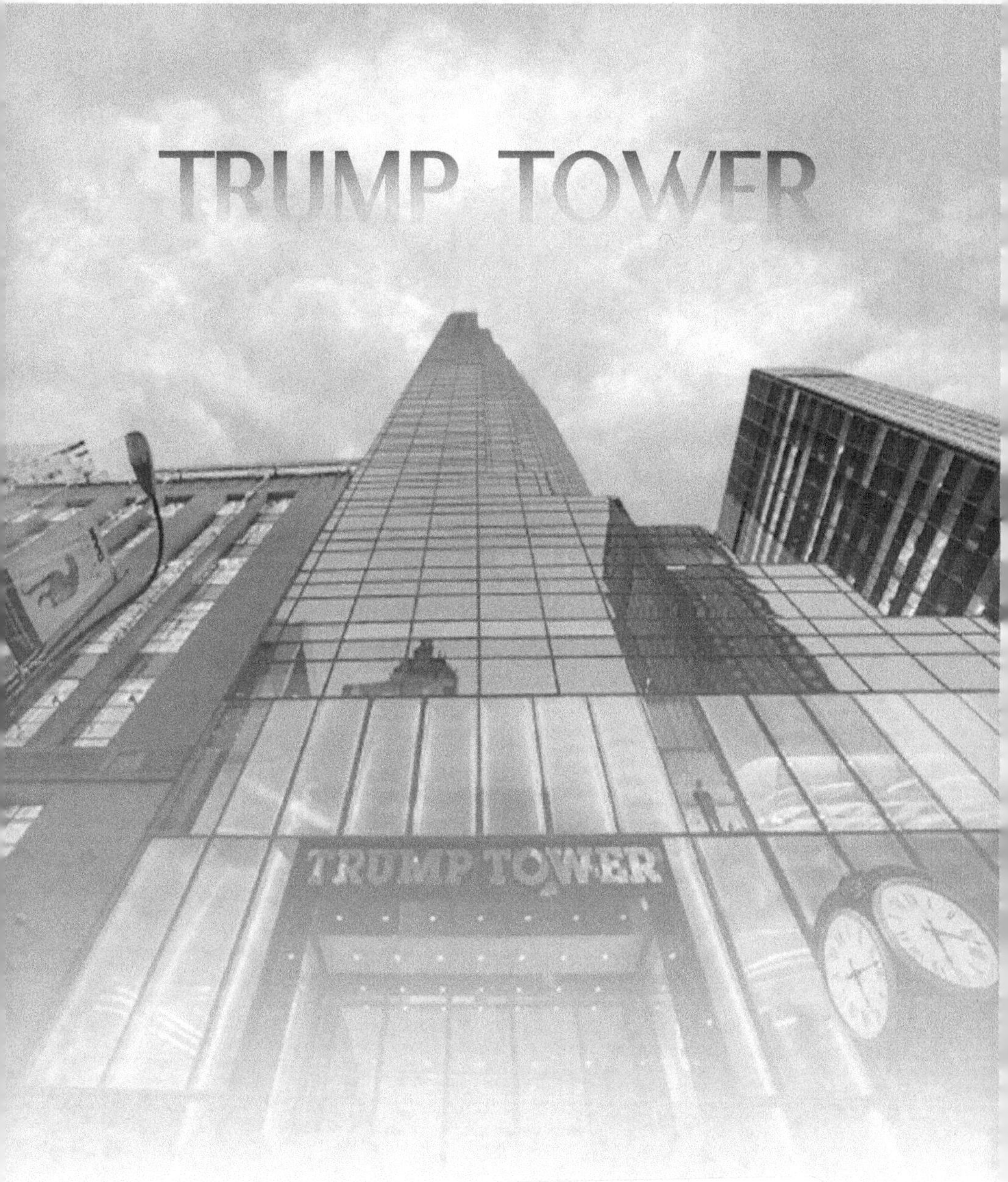

TRUMP TOWER

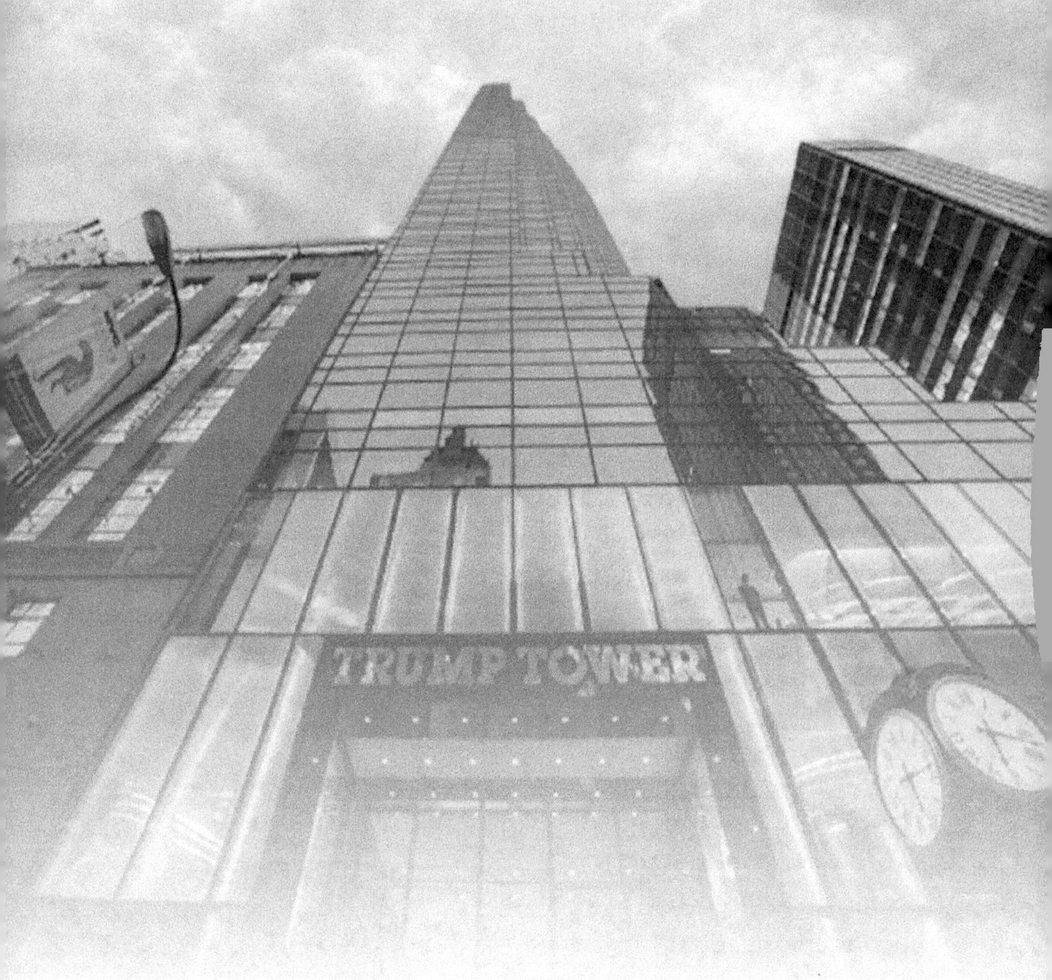

STEPHEN FRANCIS MONTAGNA

ARPress
45 Dan Road Suite 5
Canton MA 02021
Hotline: 1(888) 821-0229
Fax: 1(508) 545-7580

Ordering Information:

Quantity sales. Special discounts are available on quantity purchases by corporations, associations, and others. For details, contact the publisher at the address above.

Printed in the United States of America.
ISBN-13:   Softcover   979-8-89389-236-9
               eBook   979-8-89389-237-6

Library of Congress Control Number: 2024906317

TABLE OF CONTENTS

Prologue

President of the United States, Albert Cole, was visiting the Pentagon. He was being accompanied by General John White, the Chairman of the Joint Chiefs of Staff and Commander of JSOC. (United States Joint Special Operations Command) The President was followed by CIA Director, John Raincloud, the National Security Director, Norman P. Griffin, and the Secretary of Defense, Jerry R. Levenhagen. Others also attending the meeting with the President were the always troublesome and very argumentative civilian advisor Raymond P. Manning, along with the Secretary of the Army, Dominick (Bulldog) Tomasello, the Deputy Secretary of Defense, Harold B. Clifton and the Chief of Staff of the Air Force, General Luther (Nails) Claiborne. He was pushing the disabled Secretary of State, Maria Hernandez in her wheelchair while they were observing all the evidence being displayed before the gathering that was removed from the complex inside Iran during the attack of that country from the specialized soldiers.

General White was leading the way for some of the United States most powerful and influential politicians, explaining to them what they were viewing on the tables. The interested President clutched a thick stack of BBTSRs (Blue Border, Top Secret Reports) explaining everything that was located by the recently formed MNRRF (Multi National Rapid Response Force) troops sent to Iran. These elite soldiers were ordered to destroy the nuclear processing and production plant constructed in the sands of the Iranshahr Iranian desert, during the Operation Sand Storm mission some weeks before. Secretary of Defense Jerry Levenhagen stepped forward and made a motion of his hand, informing the President he was requesting permission to speak to the General.

General White paused for a moment and looked at the Secretary, and then nodded politely.

President Cole remarked. "Jerry, you seem to have something on your mind, what is it sir?"

"Yes Sir Mr. President, I certainly do at that sir." The Secretary replied calmly.

"Please ask the General anything you want cleared up for yourself, Jerry."

"Thank you very much Mr. President Sir. Err… General White Sir, I'm at a complete loss as to understand how come the Iranian Army had never challenged any of your specialized troops until they got into the complex center and started the mission, sir." The Secretary asked with concern.

General White smiled as he offered to the Secretary of Defense. "That was because Iran had no reason to expect a special operation attack on their supposed secret nuclear installation, Secretary Levenhagen. As far as the Iranian Command was concerned sir, we weren't even aware of this secluded complex's existence at the time we hit it, sir. This lack of concern for the security opened the complex up to our successful attack on the structure, sir. We also enjoyed the services of an undercover operative who was working under the direction of CIA Director Raincloud, and he was working inside Iran at the time of the event sir, ever since the attack on our American Embassy in that country. Armed with this new information supplied by the special operative.

"The Agent was able to enlist the services of a number of Persian Nomads who were unhappy with the present Iranian government running the country, and they assisted us in the preparation for, and then the carrying out of our attack, along with the complete destruction of the said complex, sir. With the combination of these forces, and the Special Agent and Persians, my troopers arrived at the complex undetected. With combined forces of ground troops, aircraft, and special support Units, we carried out our operation successfully, with very few causalities to our forces might I add, Mr. Secretary. The specialized troops brought out all this evidence you see being exhibited before you today, sir." The proud General waved his hand over the tables littered with equipment and machinery, and then he added to his explanation.

"We were lucky enough to get all this evidence out of the Iranian action in one piece, but this was because they weren't expecting us to attack the damn place from the beginning. On the other hand, if the Iranian's were aware we were coming for the complex, the outcome of the operation would have surely had a completely different conclusion, sir."

All eyes of the visitors went back to the tables littered with the items laid out on the tables in the NOR (Nuclear Operations Room) at the Pentagon building, along with a fully disassembled Russian constructed MIRV, (Multiple Independent Targetable Re-entry Vehicle) sold to the Iranian government by the Russian rebel Naval Admiral, Yevgeny Proushinsky. Each nuclear item was clearly marked as to what it was and how it operated. The plutonium core of the weapon of mass destruction was safely removed, and the warhead was thoroughly decontaminated of all possible traces of any radioactive residue, and the General explained the firing mechanism of the extremely lethal warhead. A fully assembled second warhead was resting at the other end of the table; its plutonium core was likewise completely removed and decontaminated, to avoid any possible radioactive contamination or accident.

Also sitting on the table were copies of the warhead blueprints, explaining the construction of the warheads and their delivery systems for the weapons. The long range, submarine launched, SS-N-23 ballistic missile, capable of carrying up to ten separate MRIVs on its nosecone.

General White droned unceasingly on over the hundreds of captured Iranian items and reports, displaying all the particulars of the items while moving some of them around on the table for better viewing by the President and his staff. The President drew in his breath, knowing in his mind the Iranian technicians were just a few days away from developing their own warheads of mass destruction, and the delivery systems needed to get the weapons to their targets.

The powerful Chairman of the Joint Chiefs of Staff carefully moved a few paces further down the long table, and then he showed a number of clear photos of the four destroyed, Russian built nuclear reactors also constructed in Iran. The Iranian technicians converted the reactors into breeder reactors solely for the production of weapons grade plutonium, along with the help of Russian technicians, who had deserted to the Persian nation in search of better pay and living conditions. The General took the time to display the many different pictures covering the destroyed development plant, and the destruction of the two major Naval Bases in Iran. One stationed at the Bandar Beheshi Port, with four destroyed nuclear powered submarines.

The pictures displayed the complete destruction of the Persian Port facility, including the submarine pens that were still under construction at the time of the attack. The next photos displayed the total destruction of the Naval Port stationed at Bandar-e-Abbas, which originally housed the submarines bought from Russia in early 1993. This Iranian Port was attacked mainly because it was Iran's major military port stationed right at the mouth of the Gulf of Oman. This port was geared to create sheer havoc whenever Iran decided to close the Persian Gulf waters down to all civilian shipping. Like Iran did during the war with Iraq back in the eighties.

The only civilian who went on the mission to Iran was Doctor Joel Russbinder, and he stood behind the table waiting silently, in case General White was asked a question by any of the visitors he could not answer for them. The nuclear research doctor's right arm was resting in a sling, and he was still in considerable pain from the bullet that had struck his body armor, when he accompanied the specialized MNRRF soldiers on their covert mission into Iran. He went along so he could help identify the evidence and papers the soldiers were ordered to remove from the Iranian complex, as evidence of what the technicians were doing.

As the concerned President and the rest of his entourage followed the General down the table, they carefully examined all the evidence laid out before them. The President suddenly noticed the doctor, and he nodded politely at him. When he realized his arm was hanging in a sling, his eyes narrowed and he turned to General White and then he snorted angrily at the military officer. "Why the devil is the Doctor's arm in that bandage, General White Sir?"

Before the General could explain about the wound, the doctor spoke up. "Mr. President Sir, it's not the General's fault I was wounded on this mission, sir. I was injured due to my own stupidity and ignorance of what I was doing on the mission sir. I was warned in advance by the troops not to take anything for granted while I was on the ground for this mission, Mr. President Sir. But I got so involved in what I was doing with checking the files and working on removing the hard drives from the many Iranian computers, and further collecting any other evidence; I completely failed to notice an enemy soldier moving until he got a shot off at me, sir."

"You were wounded on this damn mission Doctor Russbinder Sir! Arrr... I was so damn foolish to allow you to go along on that so dangerous mission, sir. I should've had my head examined before I ever allowed your superiors to talk me into that blunder. Doctor Russbinder, were you badly wounded during the operation sir? Despite what you might believe, it is the General's fault you were wounded, sir. Now don't go and get me wrong here Doctor, I really appreciate you sticking up for him, but the outcome can't be changed by mere words and loyalty, sir. Every one of his troops should've been destroyed before you were injured, sir. Arrr... never mind that shit for now, I'll speak to the General over this matter a little later on sir. Is that understood General White? I want you in my office at three thirty this afternoon, and we'll discuss this situation a bit further sir. I repeat Doctor Russbinder, were you badly injured sir?"

"Thank God, not at all Mr. President Sir. Though I must confess I thought I was dying when the bullet first hit my body armor though sir. I was stunned to find out the body armor stopped the bullet from penetrating the protective plating, sir. However, I received two broken ribs, and a bruise right in the center of my chest from the most memorable incident, Mr. President Sir."

"Is that why you're wearing the sling here , Doctor Russbinder Sir?" The upset President asked the doctor as he held him in his gaze.

"Yes Sir Mr. President Sir, it makes the pain a little more bearable for me to endure, sir." The smiling doctor replied politely to the President.

"How long will it be before you're back to normal again Doctor Russbinder?" The President allowed his weight to rest on one leg, as he waited for the doctor to reply to his question.

"I should be fine within the next two weeks or so I was told, Mr. President Sir. Give or take a few days I'd believe sir. Why do you ask me that question sir? It seems like you might have something more on your mind, sir. Am I correct Mr. President Sir?"

"It's strange you should ask me such a question, because I certainly do have something else on my mind for you, Doctor Russbinder Sir. I'm afraid we'll be having a little further need of your outstanding services and abilities as a constant that's continually involved with the MNRRF troops, and giving the physical condition that you're in, Doctor Russbinder Sir. I believe you're a natural for the chore at hand I put forth before you, sir."

"But Mr. President, I already do have a job sir. I wouldn't want to leave my position at the Institute, unless I'm really forced to do so, sir. I have many unfinished projects waiting for me to finish them, sir. To be quite frank with you Mr. President Sir, I was doing quite well over at the Institute sir. My name was placed right at the top of a few major projects that I'd give my left eye to be involved with, sir." The civilian doctor stopped speaking as he kind of stared at the concerned looking American Leader.

"Save you left eye Doctor, it's probably glass anyhow sir. I understand how you must feel about what I have planned for you, Doctor Russbinder. But I have taken the liberty of speaking with your superiors at the Institute, and I already informed them you'll not be returning to the Institute for the time being, sir. Before you go off on me sir. I understand you're obviously upset about my kind of shanghaiing you from the Institute, Doctor Russbinder Sir." The President announced with a grin as he raised his hand to stem the doctor's complaint, and then he added.

"Please sir, allow me to say if you join the MNRRF Unit on your own volition, sir. A raise will be issued and a place in the JCOS will be filled to personally..."

"Mr. President, I believe you mean the JSOC, sir." General White corrected him this time.

"Huh? What was that you said, General White?" The President snorted back at the General.

"Mr. President Sir, you made mention of the JCOS, it's the JSCO sir." General White tried a quick smile that fell like a rock in the room.

President Cole did not respond to the General's correction. Instead, he returned his attention to the doctor and then offered him. "You heard my General, Doctor Russbinder. I'm offering you a position of prominence you'll never be able to attain while working for the damn Institute, sir. All you have to do is agree to be a part of my JC, oh... whatever the hell the damn thing's called, and I'll carve a special position in it especially for you, Doctor. I'll give you five doctors for your personal staff, more if needed to work with by you, Doctor. Your picks, a nice office and unlimited funds to work with yearly, sir. Well, what do you say to the offer Doctor Russbinder Sir?" The President stretched out his hand while waiting for the doctor to shake it.

Doctor Joel Russbinder thought for a moment as he grasped the President's hand. A weak and unassuming smile followed the quick, firm hand shake.

"That's outstanding Doctor Russbinder Sir; I'm extremely pleased to have you on board with us sir. I'll give you a week to clear out your office over at the Institute, and to attend to any loose ends that you might have to take care of before you leave the place and linkup with my people. Then you'll move over to the Pentagon and your new office, Doctor Russbinder. The General will make an office available for your use, and he'll also help make your transition to the Pentagon much easier for you to carry out, sir. Doctor Russbinder, I'm afraid you might have to be rather quick on your feet for the next few weeks, sir. I'm allowing the General to organize his MNRRF for further action in the very near future, Doctor. You'll be hitting the ground running now that you're an active part of this specialized Unit of soldiers, Doctor Russbinder Sir."

"Mr. President, what will the next action be involving if I may ask, sir?" the doctor asked.

"Doctor Russbinder, it has come to my attention a number of days ago that Libya was secretly working on a pair of state of the art chemical weapons processing and developing plants covertly constructed in the deep desert of their damn country, sir. I'll not allow the Libyans to produce any this crap before I react to their latest threat aimed against the Middle East, and the rest of the world, Doctor Russbinder Sir. That's why I have the General's Special Units still being stationed in the Middle East at this time , sir.

"To avoid having to drag the soldiers all the way back to the States, only to be forced to turn them around again, and have them shipped back to the Middle East region. So the troops can settle the hash of the damn Libyans and this chemical crap they want to go playing around with, dammit. I'll have the soldiers train right in the Middle East to better prepare them for the next assault against these nuts who dream of world domination with weapons of mass destruction, Doctor Russbinder. Do you know anything about the chemical weapon's field and their terrible effects on a human body, Doctor Russbinder?" the President asked the doctor with concern.

"Yes, I know something about these terribly disgusting weapons of mass destruction, Mr. President Sir. I know these extremely dangerous weapons kill in most horrible of ways, Mr. President Sir. I even witnessed some of the injuries of these weapons and I hate the day the first of these weapons were ever developed, sir. I'm actually ashamed to be called a Doctor because of the doctor who developed them." Doctor Russbinder replied to the American Leader.

"Good, good and that's all you have to know about the damn things for the time being I assure you Doctor Russbinder, and that's all you're going to find out about this next mission at this point as well, sir. Keep this problem in the back of your mind when you're picking out the Doctors you'll need for your personal staff over at the Pentagon, sir. Please pick out only young and healthy Doctors who hopefully worked in this chemical field for at least a few years, Doctor Russbinder Sir. Try to find only young men or women, and pick out only Doctors you feel are in the best possible physical health, and hopefully not married also, Doctor Russbinder Sir."

"Why do you make such a request of me Mr. President Sir? Many of the Doctors I'd prefer to work with are much older than me, and many of them are happily married as well, sir." The doctor asked as he stared back at the President again.

"Because Doctor Russbinder, the Doctors you pick might find them running all over the world behind my specialized soldiers, much like you have done on this last mission inside Iran, Doctor Russbinder Sir. With these new Doctors trying to keep the blasted planet from blowing itself apart, that's why Doctor Russbinder Sir." The President smiled at the civilian doctor, he was waiting for another reply from the stunned looking doctor who seemed nervous and upset.

Chapter One

Doctor Joel Russbinder returned the President's smile weakly.

"Outstanding Doctor, I knew you'd understand the need I have of your specialized services, and you'd answer the call from your government, sir. Err... General White Sir, would you be kind enough to continue with this extremely detailed and interesting presentation you're offering us that I'll be placing on display before the United Nations members at the called for meeting err..." The President turned to Paul, and then he waited for him to respond to his concern.

Paul stiffened as he announced in a matter of fact tone to the American Leader. "Mr. President Sir, you're scheduled to address the United Nations meeting on Friday, November 20th, at nine a.m. sharp sir. The Vice President will leave for New York City a little later today, so she can get a jump on things over there, sir. Ms. Hirshfield has made plans to do a little shopping while she's visiting New York, sir. She also made it quite clear she was planning to visit her sister while visiting the City, sir. The Vice President told me personally that she'll be meeting with you at the United Nations building on Friday morning sir. Before you're scheduled to begin your address to the members of the meeting, Mr. President Sir."

"That's good to hear, she deserves a little time to herself, dammit. I've been working her to a frazzle lately, young man. Where's Ms. Hirshfield planning to stay while she visiting New York City, Paul?" the President asked his favorite young White House aide as he held him in his soft gaze, while waiting his reply.

"Mr. President Sir, I believe she plans to stay at the new Trump International Tower and Hotel, sir." Paul shot one of his best smiles at the President of the United States.

"Great choice if you were to ask me son. Do me a favor here Paul, I want you to get in touch with Donald. I want you to see if Mr. Trump has the Presidential suite available for the Vice President's visit. If he does, have him place it aside for Ms. Hirshfield's use. We might as well pamper her a might while she's visiting there. Maybe it'll help make up some for the crap I've been putting her through lately, young man." The President smiled again at his aide.

"Great idea Mr. President Sir. Will you be joining Ms. Hirshfield at the Trump Tower when you arrive in New York, sir?" The aide asked while flipping open his leather date book.

"Naw, I have made other plans, Paul." The President shook his head slightly while raising the side of his lip as he added to the young aide. "I don't think I'll be heading for New York City until the last possible moment. I want as much time as possible to go over these countless reports and other evidence I'm looking at here." The President held up a fist full of BBTSR's, and he then he waved his hand over the table as he added to his complaint. "I guess I'll head for New York sometime late on Thursday; I plan to spend the night at Ambassador Walter's private apartment, so I can keep a low profile before the meeting. I'll put him out for a change, and it'll also give my Vice President a little extra time to herself. I can spend the night bringing the American Ambassador up to speed on all this evidence and crap we have collected here, and I'll be that much closer to the United Nations building for the scheduled meeting, young man."

"Very well Mr. President Sir, I'll inform the Ambassador to be expecting you late Thursday then, sir." Paul mumbled as he wrote a reminder to himself to call the American Ambassador.

President Cole turned his attention back to General White, and he gave him a nod, informing the military officer he wanted to hear more about the evidence he had on the tables.

General White went over to a stack of satellite photos, and he passed them out to the President and the other dignitaries with him, along with the photos taken by the ground forces who had invaded Iran on this mission. He explained the significance of what was depicted on the photos.

ON BOARD THE NUCLEAR POWERED AIRCRAFT CARRIER WASHINGTON.
NOVEMBER 12th, 1998. 0433 HOURS IRANIAN TIME

The five troop carrying C-22 Osprey tilt winged aircraft hovered like a swarm of angry dragonflies over the massive Flight Deck of the nuclear powered Aircraft Carrier George Washington, before touching down lightly on the Flight Deck. The instant the first aircraft landed, its tail ramp slowly lowered, and the horde special operation soldiers came pouring out of the tail end of the aircraft. The soldiers stripped their filthy, grime covered body armor and uniforms as they moved out of the aircraft. The soldiers tossed the items down on the Flight Deck while waiting for the other soldiers to depart the landing planes from their last mission.

Most of the wounded and few deceased soldiers were placed inside the second aircraft. Lieutenant Robert Walker was one of the first soldiers walking on the Flight Deck, and he was already looking after some of the lesser wounded soldiers from his aircraft. He was waiting for the soldiers branded the Mutt, Lieutenant Frank Hall to follow Sergeant Barbara Meyerhoff's body down the tail ramp of the branded hospital aircraft that just landed. He did not like being separated from his closest friend, especially at his time of need.

The Lieutenant, who was better known to the rest of the elite soldiers as Road Kill, a name given to him by the soldiers because of the strong body odor that emitted from his body, whenever he was dressed in the body armor, or sweating. The young Marine Lieutenant stood about six foot four, and was twenty seven years old, and he started life in the service as a Buck Private in the Marine Corps at eighteen. He was forced to take a field commission because of his outstanding work and command ethics in Africa during the Operation Eagle One mission. Later, the Lieutenant was drafted into the elite Special Forces, which crossed over the other branches of the Army, Navy, and the Airforce for this Special Unit of selected soldiers.

Because of his outstanding leadership in the operation to Iran, and his government's need for the elite organization of specially trained soldiers. The Lieutenant was the natural pick for leadership of the Units. He had a barrel chest and a good set of arms. His long legs were thick and heavily muscled, and he had a bush of dark brown hair that he allowed to grow longer than was usually accepted by the service and his Commanding Officer. His facial features were finely chiseled, a sharp jaw, proud nose, and a deep set of steel blue eyes. His skin was dark, and many times he was mistaken for being Italian, even though his mother and father were both English. He was light on his feet and constantly moving, like he was always thinking and sizing everyone up he met or was around. He was highly respected by his troops and officers alike, and was usually sought after by both when the crunch time was at hand.

The exhausted and beat up Lieutenant was still dressed in most of his heavy body armor, and was a ratty sight to behold. One could pick up his aroma from ten feet away from the soldier. His armor was stained by sweat, blood, and in some places, urine, and was scratched up. His canvass fieldpack was ripped to shreds and hung helter-skelter off his back, much of its contents no longer in it. His side arm was in its holster, the rubber stock snapped off and the extra clip belt was empty, as was the clip holder for his MP-5 machine gun. His canteen hung a few inches below his behind by a tattered shoelace. Other items of need and luxury were also secured to his body here and there by shoelaces. His canteen was of no use to him, it was ripped open obviously hit by an enemy round. His armor was dented in a number of places where bullets and shrapnel had struck it, or from landing on it while fighting in Iran. His wrist was covered to his fingers by dried blood from the damage caused by a bullet striking the armor further up his arm.

A pair of ammunition straps used by soldiers to carry extra rounds crisscrossed his body in the center of his chest. They were mostly empty and looked like they were part of his chest plating. One of the ammo straps was nearly sliced in half below his left arm. Many of the rounds left in the holders were damaged one way or the other; their metal jacketed tips scratched, or otherwise marred or bent in some cases, and were no use as ammunition any longer.

The Lieutenant's face was covered with grime, dried mud, and some traces of what the troops referred to as their war paint. The camouflage paint was still slightly detectable under the layer of grime covering his face. The tip of his left ear had a nick by a bullet. He had a nastily cut over his left eye which stopped bleeding, but the blood remained and smeared down the side of his cheek where he swiped at it with his hand. His chin had a few days growth that looked sharp enough to be used as a weapon on its own. His left cheek, a scratch cut through the whiskers and the blood trail ran all the way down his chin to his neck, and then disappeared under the top of his armor.

A thick layer of filth was covering every part of his sweat stained body, what was once sand was mixed in with blood or other liquids, and had turned the mess to a thick, caking kind of mud mixture that clung to different parts of his body armor. He removed his Kevlar helmet with the field radio, and left it resting inside the plane, exposing his matted and filthy hair that had curled up, and stuck flat to his head. He took a few seconds and ran his hands through his filthy and matted hair, rubbing his itching scalp vigorously with his fingers as he growled over the sheer pleasure this action gave him. A cloud of dried skin, sand, and grime flew out of his hair, along with countless sand fleas, and whatever else that had taken up residence in his dirty hair. What remained took to the air to try and escape the ferocious scratching and growling coming from the young and extremely dangerous American soldier.

On the Pry Fly, or Primary Flight Control Center of the Carrier, was the domain of the Washington's Air Boss. The CAG Officer was responsible for the aircraft parked on the Flight Deck of the carrier or in the air, and he overlooked and controlled the Flight Deck operations. The Air Boss was rerouting his Carrier's Ready Air Cap and all incoming aircraft needing to land, while the C-22 Ospreys took up most of the Flight Deck of the Carrier while unloading what he classified as the scourge of the Armed Forces. The Special Operations Soldiers.

The Air Boss eyed the departing soldiers as they poured out of the tail ramps of the Osprey aircraft. He cursed himself for allowing these specialized soldiers to throw their crap all over his Flight Deck. He, like many other honorable soldiers, despised these specialized soldiers who operated well outside the realm of the usual military conduct and ethics. Everyone knew the soldiers did whatever they had to do, to complete their mission no matter what they had to stoop to. It was well known these soldiers sometimes resort to assassinations, rape, and torture, infiltrating government offices to create havoc, and laying down the seeds of revolt, while training soldiers of other countries to act like them. They separated families, using them as weapons against themselves, and remove children, never seen by their parents again.

Life as a Special Force's soldier left a lot to be desired in their troubling style, but no conventional soldiers gave much thought to the harsh and endless training these elite soldiers were forced to endure for their country's sake and need. It was known these soldiers would eat things that would make a normal person heave in disgust, and live in conditions that went against God and country, staying filthy for long periods of time, and lurking in the shadows of darkness while hunting their enemy. The faces of the soldiers were usually covered in striking patterns of war paint, and they always waited to kill anything alive, whether it be man or beast, or destroy the infrastructure of the host country they were operating in. The life of the Special Operations soldier was despised by many conventional soldiers from every country.

The angry Air Boss rose on his toes and stretched his neck out as he intensely watched the bulk of the filth covered Special Forces soldiers enter the main hatchway leading down to the auxiliary wardroom, and the briefing room three decks below the Flight Deck. The Commander allowed the soldiers to use this room, plus the visiting pilot's sleeping quarters for their use while being housed in the bowels of the Washington. There was a fully equipped head with showers to the left of the sleeping quarters, but there were no provisions allowed for the female members of the troops. The Commander was aware these soldiers bathed, ate, and slept together, and were fond of bragging they would die together. The Air Boss saw no need to make any special preparations for the female members of such a foul group of so called elite soldiers.

As the thoroughly exhausted group of soldiers began to disappear below deck, the Air Boss turned back to the C-22 Ospreys still taking up space on his Flight Deck. The aircraft were in the process of unloading the cargo of human trash, military equipment, file cabinets, and a number of heavy wood crates. It was then he noticed some of the soldiers were hanging around the tail end of the Osprey just starting to unload its cargo. The Air Boss reached for the speaker phone and then he barked as the first of the now unloaded Ospreys spooled up for takeoff, and then lifting vertically into the brightening sky from his Flight Deck.

"You soldiers out there at line Three, Four on my Flight Deck. Yeah, you guys. What the hell are you people doing hanging around like you don't have anything else to do for crap sake? Clear the Flight Deck so I can deck down my aircraft. You people were ordered in flight to report below deck immediately when you touched down. I have an Air Cap stacked up I have to worry about running out of fuel. I'm waiting to land my aircraft, and I need the Flight Deck cleared A-SAP. Get off the damn Flight Deck! Get a move on it people? Hustle out of the way, dammit!" The Air Boss growled in his radio intercom, and waited for the soldiers to obey his orders.

Lieutenant Robert Walker was fuming over the fact it was taking so long for the Mutt and the body of Barbara Meyerhoff to be offloaded from the aircraft, looked towards the Pry Fly of the Carrier in anger, not able to see who was angrily bellowing out orders at him and the rest of his troops. He was so angry that he raised his hand over his head, and then he gave the squawker the finger, and he barked back at the talker even though he knew the talker would never hear any of his words. "Fuck you Charlie, and the god damn horse you rode in on man."

The Air Boss jumped out of his chair as he actually choked the speaker phone locked in his hands. He was wild over the disrespect the filthy soldier just displayed against him. Especially before his flight and deck crew members. The pilots, airmen and deck crew stopped what they were doing, and now they just kind of glare at this one soldier disrespecting him.

For a moment, the Air Boss thought some of his more aggressive deck crew might take it upon themselves to try and seek revenge for the insult. He was suddenly worried if they did make a move on the soldier what these specialized soldiers would do to his people. He shuddered to think of a confrontation, and was about to react when he suddenly noticed what was coming out of the other plane. Then he realized why the soldier was so filled with anger.

The Air Boss calmed down when he noticed the stretcher with the body of a soldier covered to the neck by a blanket. The Commander thought this strange, because any soldiers killed in action, were usually stored inside the body bags called by the troops, mummy sacks. He checked the body using his field glasses, and noticed the female was dead just by the way her head laid resting on her chest. The group of soldiers moved up the ramp and took the stretcher from the Airmen. He could tell the dead soldier meant something special to one soldier, because he walked right by her side and he held her hand as they moved the body. The soldier who insulted the Commander rested his hand on that other soldier's arm and said something to him.

The Air Boss concentrated his view on the offending soldier's face, and focused in on him until he saw the soldier's rank. He checked his face again, committing it to memory for future reference and possible punishment. The Air Boss was no fool; he dealt with many troublemakers like this one during his twenty years of service. He knew who was going to give him problems, and this one was going to be the biggest problem he had ever come across. He felt bad for the exhausted soldiers, and allowed the minor act of defiance to go unpunished, taking into consideration what these elite soldiers had just been through in Iran on their last mission.

The soldiers and seamen milling about the Flight Deck instantly surrounded the stretcher, lining up respectfully behind it and then they all followed it as the strangely clad entourage made for the hatchway leading to medical bay below deck. The Air Boss smiled as he noticed his Airmen had recovered, and they were showing the proper respect to the dead female soldier, by removing their caps and remaining standing. Until the procession of elite but rag tailed soldiers past them and the lot of them disappeared into the bowels of the ship.

With one final look at the wild eyed young Marine Lieutenant before the group of soldiers disappeared below deck, he sighed as he turned back to the Osprey again. Flight deck forklifts picked up the cargo his deck crews secured on pallets. The equipment and boxes were being hustled over to the massive center Flight Deck elevator. When the equipment was stacked in the center, the elevator quickly lowered below deck. The deck crew knew they had a Ready Air Cap waiting to land, and they were aware if they did not get the planes down soon, they would be forced to refuel while in flight. The workers understood what would happen to the deck crew if that came about. The Captain would remove their film privileges for a week, plus other punishment. Once the elevator reached below deck, the crew unloaded the cargo with speed.

The Air Boss kept his field glasses trained on the hole in the center of his flight deck, tapping his foot while waiting for the elevator to return to position and completed the flight deck, so he could land his planes. He was still steaming over the fact he was forced to ignore his aircraft for the sake of these extremely disrespectful soldiers. The instant the Air Boss noticed the elevator rise, he notified the LSO (Landing Signal Officer) to deck down his Ready Air Cap.

'C' DECK, ON BOARD THE CARRIER GEORGE WASHINGTON

Lieutenant Robert Walker stayed real close by Lieutenant Frank Abbott, known as the Mutt. He was standing right by his side as they carried the blanket draped body of Sergeant Barbara Meyerhoff over to the sickbay. The doctor motioned for the body to be placed on an empty cot in the corner of the sickbay unit. Once this was done, he gave a quick inspection of the female's body, and then he snapped angrily at the young medic.

"What the hell kind of god damn medic are you mister? You know damn well any dead soldiers belong inside a body bag to avoid any unnecessary viewing of the body, and for sanity purposes and protection of the body, mister. Why the hell is this soldier's body covered by only a damn blanket, mister? A blood soaked blanket at that soldier. You screwed up big time on this one, and I'll be making a detailed report on this mistake to Command, and there's a good possibility that you'll lose the privilege of being a medic for this blunder. Well son, what the hell do you have to say for yourself sir?" the doctor growled at the Special Forces medic.

"Well Doc, the only excuse I have that I can offer ya is. I allowed the blanket because I kinda like the way I breathe sir." Blood Clot replied to the angry doctor's interrogation.

"What are you saying to me soldier? Do you want me to believe that someone has threaten your life if you placed this soldier's body inside a damn body bag, soldier?" the ship's doctor growled at the medic, and then added angrily at the soldier. "What's your name mister?"

"Corporal Richard Brumbach, Colonel. The troops call me Blood Clot sir; I'm the Unit's only medic sir." Brumbach snapped as he went to attention, and saluted the medical officer.

"Excuse me Colonel, the medic's right with his gripe sir. He was threatened, by me sir. Because it's our belief that none of us will ever be placed inside a stinking mummy sack no matter what, sir. Just as long as any member of the Unit's still alive to prevent the stinking insult to the dead soldier sir." Walker shifted his weight on his feet and then stared at the doctor.

The doctor cautiously eyed the second soldier for a moment, and then mumbled at the young military officer. "Err... Lieutenant, am I to believe you're the one who has dared to threaten this medic's life, sir? If you did Lieutenant, this charge could very well lead to you spending some serious time behind bars while making little rocks out of big ones at the Leavenworth facility, son. If you were foolish enough to dare threaten one of my god damn medics, your ass is going to be grass, and I'm going to be the lawn mower, mister. If what you say is true then I'll be forwarding criminal charges against you, and then Lieutenant you're going to find yourself..."

"Then mine is a lawn also Colonel." The Mutt hissed angrily as he clamped his fists together tightly, and then he glared at the Carrier's Chief Medical Officer. The angry look in his burning eyes caused the doctor concern and hesitation as he stared at this other soldier now.

"As is mine sir." Buckethead, (Sergeant Vincent Lombardo) growled as he took a step forward, and then he lined himself up on the Mutt's left side and he stared almost threateningly at the Naval Colonel and doctor.

"So is mine also Colonel." The equally as large and as angry No Neck, (Sergeant Robert Abbott) added as he moved nearer to the growing group of elite soldiers.

"Me also Colonel." Sergeant Dorothy Ramirez said as she also stepped forward and stood by the Lieutenant's side, she was followed by the three Russian women fighters, and then the French female fighter of the group also moved forward and nodded at the concerned doctor.

All the elite soldiers who crammed their way into the sickbay added their voices to those of Walker's and the other soldiers gathered in the sickbay area, and the soldiers speaking to the concerned looking Naval Doctor.

The doctor eyed the growing group of exhausted looking soldiers as more of them tried to squeeze their way into his sickbay. The doctor's glaze came to rest on Walker's again face. He slowly rubbed his chin as he stared into the steel blue eyes glaring back at him so intensely, displaying no care for whatever the doctor could do to him.

The surgeon suddenly let out a deep sigh and he waved his hand at the soldiers in disgust, as if he dismissed a troubling thought as he announced to the soldier. "I didn't understand how strong your belief was in this case, soldier. To tell you the truth sir, I hate the god damn things myself mister. I guess I can respect that much for you people, sir. Lieutenant, I have a question for you sir, now that you have forced me to go against the normal regulations of this ship, sir. What the hell do you expect me to do with this female soldier's body, sir? How do you want us to respect your fallen comrade while handling and processing her body, son?"

"No god damn mummy sack sir." The soldiers snapped as one at the medical officer.

"Calm down soldiers, I understand but there are regulations and precautions I have to follow."

"Colonel, if you can bend the damn regs just a wee bit sir." The Lieutenant said as he opened his index finger and thumb and then moved his hand before his eye as he added. "Why don't you do us a little favor here and step outside sickbay for a smoke, and take the rest of your blood suckers along with you sir. We'll look after Meyerhoff's body on our own, sir. We'll load Fun Bags into one of them damn freezers until someone from her family from Stateside tells us what they want done with her body, sir." Walker offered the doctor with a half smile.

"I'm sorry; I didn't get that last remark or what you meant by that comment, sir. Fun Bags, Lieutenant Walker Sir?" the doctor asked the grime covered soldier.

"That's her Unit tag name Colonel." The Mutt snapped hotly as he glared again at the doctor.

"I see none of you people will back down from this stance you have adopted until you people finally get your way around here. If you people feel so strongly about this, I can see my way through to overlooking a few of the normal regulations on your behalf. If you're willing to stick your dicks into a blender for your beliefs then I might as well join you people. Caporelli, you'll place the body of this female soldier in freezer Three, One, the way it's protected. Mark the body accordingly and treat her with the greatest of respect. I'll refrain from doing an autopsy and fill out her death certification, stating a bullet wound had caused her death. If her parents want an autopsy performed, they can always have it done stateside by the medics there. Will this do for you soldiers?" the concerned Naval Surgeon asked the group of angry soldiers.

Everyone of the filth covered soldiers nodded in thanks and slowly disperse.

Walker, the Mutt and Ramirez waited until the other soldiers left sickbay then Walker added. "Thanks a helluva lot there Doc, I knew you were a square peg when I first laid eyes on ya sir."

The doctor smiled, not knowing what the Lieutenant meant by his remark, he ignored it and turned to work on another wounded soldier. Sergeant Ramirez leaned forward and she kissed the old man's cheek, thanking him silently with her eyes. It was enough, because the

Colonel was moved by the affection displayed by the soldiers to their fallen comrade.

Outside sickbay a young Seaman waited, so he could lead the elite troops over to their sleeping quarters on board the Carrier. The Lieutenant was informed none of his people would be allowed to roam the ship unescorted. Upon entering the quarters, the Lieutenant noticed some of his people were lying on their bunks. He was angry as hell over this move and he spat out some orders. "What the hell's this crap all about, people? Haven't you slugs learned anything yet, god dammit? Since when do you shitheads get on your damn racks filthy and still dressed in your fucking killing gear? Where's the hell's Colonel Leadbetter and the other fucking Officers at for Christ sake, and how come they aren't eating you pack of shitbirds alive, dammit?"

"Hey Walker, since when does the hot shot brass bunk down with us stinking peons, man? What the fuck are you doing in no man's land yourself, Lieutenant? In case you don't remember man, you're fucking brass now buddy. The higher up pukes were given betta bunks at Club Med on this here damn tub, and you should be bunking down with them square wheels instead of busting our fucking asses like this in Grunt Land, Homes." The Ghost grumbled as he hoisted his feet up and then he plopped them defiantly down on his rack.

"I'm still one of you shit sacks until something betta comes along and I can be rid of you dopey shits, so you betta get offa them fucking bunks and shower before I skin you pack of shitbags a fucking live, dammit." Lieutenant Walker warned as he stepped a little closer to Casper and he angrily brushed his feet off the bed and added. "Hit the fucking showers before I really get pissed off at you fucking guys. Then we'll get something to eat and sleep for a stinking week. Anyone who needs medical looking after, stitches, or any other medical treatment, betta get your damn asses over to sickbay on the double quick. Get it done before eating or turning in." The new officer had to step aside as some of the troops past him on their way over to sickbay. A second Seaman lead the walking wounded for care. He noticed the soldier branded Stainless Private Alan Langworth who he knew had been hit in his neck by a round, and had a stack of bandages stuffed inside his chest plate, and he growled at the soldier.

"What the fuck are you still doing here, you asshole you? Do you need a special invitation or somethin', dopey. I saw you get tagged, and I was the one who stuffed the damn bandages on your fucking wound for you, Homes. Christ sake, aren't you smart enuf to go and get your slack ass over to sickbay without my having to look after you like a fucking little pussy, god dammit?"

"I ain't hurt bad enuf fur me to report to no stinking sickbay Walker. I was figuring to let the damn medics work on the badly wounded first, before I take up any of their damn time on them, Lieutenant." Private Alan Langworth griped to the Lieutenant.

"Hey hog in case you don't understand this crap yet, asshole. You're bad hurt, you damn fool you." Buckethead growled as he rested his huge paw down on Stainless' shoulder, making him jump from the pain his hand caused him and his hidden wound.

"Case fricking closed pal." The concerned Lieutenant shot back when he saw Stainless wince from the pain Buckethead just caused him. "You want someone to help you outta your damn armor, slick? You go down to sickbay while still dressed in that crap. The fucking Doc's are gonna cut the shit from your smelly ass body with a fucking bone saw, Home Boy."

"You mean them stinking meat hackers are gonna ruin my fucking body armor on me man? If they hafta remove the crap from my ass they're gonna just cut it off, Walker?"

"Yep, that's what they'll do alright to your damn armor, dickhead." He warned the wounded soldier as he held him in his angry glare until he replied to his last words.

"No way in hell any of those fucking body hacker's gonna ruin my stuff on my ass man. Hey guys, I gotta get this crap offa my stinking ass. You gotta help me out here people." Stainless cried as he tried to get out of his body armor on his own. He quickly realized how bad hurt he truly was when he could not snap the first clamp open on the armor.

Lieutenant Walker looked to Sergeant Ramirez and gave her a quick nod. He knew she would be the gentlest with helping Stainless out of his equipment. She moved in and unbuckled his shoulder pads then the chest plate protector. All the while she worked, Stainless cried like a baby, griping she was killing him. All the activity opened his wound, causing it to bleed again.

Walker gave a closer look at the injury and then he growled at the injured soldier. "Jesus Christ Homes, that's fucking real nasty, buddy. Hey Blood Clot, you betta get your ass over here and take a good look at this fricking mess. It looks much worse than before Homes."

The second Blood Clot took a look at the gaping wound in the soldier's neck; he jumped for the ship's intercom and then he called for a stretcher, coding the emergency as a flag red.

Stainless did not look so good suddenly, his color had drained from his skin, and he plopped down on the rack like a bag of potatoes thrown from the tail end of a moving truck. Blood Clot told the Lieutenant this was because the pressure on the wound was removed, and he was losing blood again, he was worried Stainless might go in shock on him. The concerned medic looped a number of blankets around the wounded soldier's back, trying to keep him warm while they waited for the stretcher to arrive for the injured trooper.

The Carrier medics appeared at the door. Buckethead moved over to Walker and Neck's side, watching the medics working on Stainless packing his wound with bandages, after they cleaned it of dirt and dried blood. Once they had the wounded man on the stretcher, they rushed by the concerned soldiers and the group quickly disappeared down the walkway. Some of the elite soldiers helped the medics carry Stainless over to sickbay.

He stopped Blood Clot from leaving by grabbing his arm asking him in an angry tone. "Hey Clot, how the fuck's he doing man? I didn't know how bad he was hit until now Homes."

"He's fucking dying on me man, that's how he's fucking doing Lieutenant. You couldn't see how bad hurt he was sir? Some hot shot fucking leader you are Homes." Blood Clot pulled his arm free of Walker's grasp and then followed the stretcher out of the soldier's quarters.

Lieutenant Walker glared angrily at the back of his medic as he followed Stainless. He was book ended on either side by the Neck and Buckethead. Road Kill found every soldier stopped what they were doing, and they were all staring at him and he snapped at the group. "Get in those fucking showers before I kick some fucking ass round here, dammit! That goes for the two of you slugs also." Walker shoved Buckethead hard who barely moved.

Tensions were mounting; many of the soldiers were highly concerned over Stainless' condition. At one point, Dago, (Corporal Leo DiStefano) accidentally stepped on Dock Rat's, (James McNulty) foot. With tensions stretching beyond the limit, this minor act usually overlooked by the close knitted soldiers, escalated from just curses to a hard shoving match. If it was not for the Lieutenant intervening, it would have gone even further.

Walker grabbed Dago by his neck and shoved him from Dock Rat, stepping between them and bitching. "What's this shit? We gonna start fighting between ourselves now? Christ sake, give it a fucking rest and hit the damn showers. I don't need any of this shit. In case you shits forgot who you are, I'll remind you. We're fucking brothers and sisters, and brothers and sisters don't fight each other. If you wanna fight someone, find the bastards who killed Fun Bags. I told you assholes to hit the fucking showers, and that's what you people are gonna do, or you're gonna hafta deal with me, and I'm in no mood for this crap." He placed his hands on his hips and then stared at Dock Rat; until he backed down and threw the towel he had looped over his shoulders to the floor then stormed off for the showers. He then turned to Dago and gave him the look.

Dago gave Walker a half assed smile while cocking his head to the side, and then he headed for his rack so he could collect his toiletries. He turned to the other soldiers in their temporary sleeping quarters, but did not say anything to them. He just stood glaring at them.

The rest of the troopers got the warning and made themselves look busy to get out of the Lieutenant harsh glare. Many of the soldiers headed for the showers or the head to relieve themselves, while other troopers crawled out of their body armor and placed it at the foot of their racks to be cleaned and looked after later. A few of the more innovative soldiers wore their armor in the showers, and after washing the equipment clean, they peeled the protective plating off their bodies and stacked it at the doorway. The soldiers assigned to look after the armor, picked up the equipment and they wiped it clean of water, and then they sorted it out according to the names printed on the inside of the equipment. It was then moved to the soldier's racks for them.

The four Russian fighters were kind of hanging back a little, they easily picked up an attitude being displayed against them from some of the other American soldiers. They were on loan to the United States from Russia, and were kind of getting the cold shoulder, and snapping replies to their questions or attempted jokes with the other soldiers. The Russian women chose to remain dressed in their body armor for more protection in case someone decided it was their fault for the Iran action. They leaned against a bulkhead while the lone Russian male known as AK, stood before them as if trying to protect the women from any possible attack. The Russian soldiers understood the bad feelings; because they knew it was one of their countrymen responsible for the action in the Iranian desert, and for the losses and wounded they suffered. But they were smart enough to know this snubbing of them would soon pass, and they would eventually be an accepted part of the elite group of specialized soldiers.

Many of the elite soldiers suffered from a myriad of sicknesses they constantly traded back and forth between themselves, because of their constant close proximity to each other. Some of the soldiers suffered from a stomach flu, others developed a hacking cough and runny noses, and as one got over his or her ailment, they were infected by another soldier who was or still sick. Most, if not all the elite troopers suffered from the same stomach problems brought on by consuming the MRE (Meals Ready to Eat) food packs loaded down with massive doses of carbohydrates and proteins, to help keep the soldiers going on the lighter food stuffs. Many of them were so bound up; taking a dump was on the same scale as giving birth through one's behind. But the soldiers accepted this as part of their duty and let it go at that.

The Carrier's medical crew worked on many soldier's problem, by making them take physics, and having them drink milk, and popping a ton of vitamins. The still grieving Mutt over the loss of his girlfriend in their last operation was given his space to get over Fun Bag's death. The group treated him with the greatest of respect; they were trying to engage him in conversations, while attempting to get his mind off her death. They chose to stay near him in case he wanted to talk, or cry. The soldiers watched over him as he suffered through his loss. When the Mutt headed for the showers, he was followed discreetly by half the other soldiers in the area.

The beautiful French Sergeant, Regina Raphael took it on herself to fill in the void created by Meyerhoff's death. She was following the Mutt everywhere he went while also giving him space to heal, she saw him get up and she followed him to the john. Regina smiled and wiggled her hips in his face while trying to speak with him, and striving to get him to eat something and rest a little and let go of his pain. She made a real pest of herself to the Mutt, but she always remained pleasant, or the other soldiers from the group would have surely stopped her from bugging him so much. The soldiers liked what she was trying to do, and they understood it and agreed with her efforts. She tried her best to get the Mutt out of his doldrums and depression.

After the soldiers showered and had something to eat, they felt much better and things started to get back to normal for the troops. Joking, laughter and the recital of recent war stories filled the ship's bowels where the Special Forces soldiers were bedded down. The Mutt enjoyed all the attention that was being paid to him by the beautiful young French woman. The lesser wounds and nicks on many soldiers were being aired out and allowed to heal, and the women fighters took to looking after the minor wounds for many male soldiers.

Lieutenant Walker cautiously eyed his troops and then sighed. Liking their reactions, he allowed himself to finally relax some, and he began to look for Sergeant Ramirez, who was busy speaking with other women fighters of the group. Baby Tee and Jail Bait were joking with Ramirez, when one of them noticed the Lieutenant, and she told Ramirez her man was in need. Without offering an apology, she left and she rushed to Walker's side.

"Hmmm... it took you long enough to come to your senses, where do you want to go?"

"Where else, the showers." Walker smirked as he grinned at his lover and soon to be wife.

"Of course Bobby." Ramirez purred as she led him to the stalls. Once in the shower area, she stripped him of his armor and filthy uniform and then bathed him. Paying special attention to the numerous cuts and abrasions everywhere she touched his body. Once he was clean, she made love to her man. First taking him in her mouth until he was ready, and then she mounted him while they stood. He supported her full weight in his arms while she wrapped her legs around his rearend, and she did most of the work for the two of them. They came together with Walker collapsing against the shower divider, while still holding her in his arms. She slowly slid down his body until she stood bathing in his wonderful gaze. A feeling struck her, and she spun her head around. She looked for Meyerhoff, who had always been behind her and protecting her back. Her air rushed from her lungs in a gasp, as if she had been struck in the guts by an unseen fist. Tears ran down her cheeks, mixing in with the water from the shower.

"What's up? You look white as a ghost." He asked, noticing the look of terror etched in her eyes then the tears. He did the only thing he could think of doing for his lover, he pulled her close to his body and hugged her for dear life and he felt her trembling in his powerful arms.

"I thought I felt Barbara standing behind me like she always was. Walker, I miss her so much."

"I know, so do I, so does everyone of the group. This crap sucks shit outta a dead dog's ass."

"Walker! It has to stop somewhere! I don't want to die young. I don't want to fight anyone anymore either. I'm really tired of it all my soldier. It seems this is all I do lately, there has to be more to life than fighting and killing, because some asshole thinks he's powerful enough to try and take over the damn world. I don't want to end up like Barbara, stuck in some freezer waiting for someone to send for my body. I want to live to be an old lady. I want a baby! I want many babies! I want a life of my own, a life with you and a real family Bobby."

Again, he pulled her close to him while kissing her on the forehead gently.

Chapter Two

THE PENTAGON, WASHINGTON DC. FRIDAY, NOVEMBER 13th ,1998. 0920 HOURS EST

The President listened to General White and Doctor Joel Russbinder as they droned on and on about all the evidence they had collected when the specialized troops attacked the complex inside Iran, and the color pictures until he could no longer absorb their words. Exasperated, President Cole raised his hand and then offered. "Please General White Sir, no more please; my head's spinning so fast I can't focus on anything any longer, sir. I don't see how I'm ever going to possibly remember all this crap you have here and telling me about, let alone try to explain it all in a coherent manner to the United Nations members. Christ Almighty General White Sir, I think I'm going to need a lot more help than I can possibly drag along with me to this upcoming meeting, sir." The President moaned in an exhausted tone of voice as he shook his head, and then he rubbed his eyes, dropping a few of the blue edged reports to the floor.

The ever hovering Presidential aide, Paul Woodworth, quickly moved in and he picked up the reports without being asked, and he handed them back to the waiting President.

"Mr. President Sir, CIA Director Raincloud and myself would be more than pleased to accompany you to New York City if you think it'd help you out any, sir." General White offered while waiting for the President to tuck the wayward reports back in his pile.

"I'm free to come along as well myself Mr. President Sir." Doctor Russbinder offered as he came around the table.

"That's three, four counting the Vice President who is supposed to address the meeting as well, General White Sir. She's a great narrator, passionate in her words and she's able to get her point across without screaming at anyone like I always end up doing might I add. I don't know how much time they'll allow me before cutting me off at the meeting, sir. I don't think the Secretary General will give us the full day to address the meeting, and with the five of us wanting to speak at the meeting, I see us going into the next day. No, I appreciate it, but I think I'm going to get stuck shouldering this mess myself. I wish there was one of you I can take with me who knows everything that went on, and could help me explain anything I get stuck on, dammit." President Cole grumbled as he placed his reports on the table, ordering Paul to gather them for him.

"Mr. President Sir, I believe the Doctor can fill in many of the missing blanks you might stumble over at the meeting, sir." Director Raincloud offered with a grin.

The President shifted his glaze over to the doctor. After studying his face for a few moments, he realized some members of the United Nations would be very happy to eat the mild mannered doctor alive if given the chance. Especially if they did not agree with the joint attack on Iran, and the rest of the action that took place inside Iran and on the waters of the Persian Gulf during that operation. The President decided against taking the doctor to the meeting.

"No Director Raincloud Sir, it was a good idea but I don't think the Doctor would do very well at the meeting. The Russian and Iranian Ambassadors would have a field day picking him apart, once they saw he was scared to death to be before the members."

"Err... excuse me Mr. President Sir, you might be making a slight mistake there sir. I think you're selling the Doctor a little short on this one Sir. Mr. President Sir, anyone who can survive a full day with my troops, will never be classified as scared of anything ever again in his life, sir." General White bragged while staring at the President of the United States.

"Hmmm... is this a fact Doctor Russbinder Sir? You really think the short time you spent with this pack of fruitcakes we call soldiers, changed you any, sir?" the now grinning President asked the doctor with a smile.

"I guess so Mr. President Sir." The doctor replied meekly to the grinning President.

"Zat so? Pray tell Doctor Russbinder, how come you feel so strongly about this situation, sir?"

"Well Mr. President Sir, I believe there's a very good chance that ther..."

"Let's hold it right there and come to an understanding between the two of us, Doctor Russbinder Sir." The President suddenly snapped as he raised his hand before his face and then he added to his words for the civilian doctor. "Please Doctor Russbinder Sir, Albert will do whenever addressing me, unless we're in the presence of others not part of this operation, sir. We're among friends here, and there's no need for formalities between us, sir."

"Only if you call me Joel, Mr. President Sir." The doctor offered back to the President kindly.

The President nodded wearily, pissed they were wasting so much time with this bantering back and forth like this. He wanted a simple yes or no answer from the doctor that easy.

"Well Albert, I learned how these fine young and highly trained soldiers live, and how they fight, and how they think and care for each other on a mission, and how they die sir. They have roughed up my edges a might on me I believe sir, and I have learned words I have never heard spoken, or dared to use in my life, and I belie..." The doctor was cut off by the President.

"I bet you did at that Doctor, I warned you in advance about these crazy ass soldiers of General White's beforehand, sir." The President smirked at the doctor.

"Yes sir, you certainly did sir, and I feel I have grown in both strength and stamina sir, and I have also gathered some very interesting knowledge with these young troopers during that mission, sir." The doctor remarked as he returned the President's smile with one of his own.

"You really think you can possibly handle the extreme arrogance of the Russian and Iranian Ambassadors at the meeting, Doctor? If they pounce on you like I'm certain they'll try to do at the damn meeting, sir. You have to understand sir, each of them were thoroughly embarrassed by this action, and you can believe they'll be head hunting anyone who was for or part of the attack at the meeting on Friday morning, sir. If I allow you to address the Ambassadors, I don't need you folding up on me if they pick your brains in ways you have never figured possible, Doctor Russbinder Sir. If the Ambassadors get under your damn skin, or make you stutter in the least, or they go against something you stated. The results would be disastrous for us, sir. You have to remember one thing whenever addressing these kind of people, sir.

"If you make the slightest mistake and say something that's foolish at the meeting, like the moon's made of green cheese then you better stick to that notion if you know what's good for you, no matter how much pressure's heaped down on your shoulders, Doctor. Or we're both going to end up looking like the south end of a north bound horse at the meeting, Doctor Russbinder. No matter what you say, no matter what you give any credence to, you have to believe in that commitment, and deliver it with conviction. Strength is the only thing these people believe in sir. If it's not being displayed every second that you're speaking to the damn members. If you're not absolutely confidant on everything you offer at the meeting, Doctor. No one's going to believe a damn word you say. Understanding this, what do you say sir? You still want to come Doctor?" the President stared at the doctor while waiting his reply.

"Yes Albert, I can handle the pressure I believe sir. Yes Mr. President Sir, I see no problem with it sir. I'd like to accompany you to the United Nations meeting, sir. I believe, no, check that Mr. President Sir. I know I can fill in any of the missing blanks that you might stumble into at the meeting sir, and I know I can state my convictions with absolute confidence, sir." Doctor Russbinder swallowed hard and then he shifted his weight as he gave a sigh.

"Doctor Russbinder Sir, I'm afraid that you have just named your own poison and bought yourself a ticket to New York City along with me and the rest of my staff, sir. But I have to warn you again Doctor, if you fuck up on me in the slightest at the meeting, it's going to be a one way ticket sir. You'll have to find your own way back to Washington, sir. I hope to hell you know what the hell you're getting yourself into here, sir. A United Nations meeting's a place that's better left avoided if at all possible, Doctor Russbinder Sir. What else can I say but, glad to have you on board with me Doctor... err... excuse me, Joel." President Cole offered pleasantly and then he turned his attention back to General White. Seeing the heated look on his face, he asked the military officer with concern in his tone.

"Uh oh, what's the matter with you now General White sir? You look suddenly upset at me I guess sir. Or do you have something on your mind you'd like to add to this conversation, sir? Please General, now is not the time to hold your tongue, sir."

"Well with all due respect Mr. President Sir, I happen to believe there is someone you might consider taking along with you to New York City who knows this mission inside out, and he can also fill in any missing blanks at the same time, sir. And, there's no question on his backbone, it has been proven many times during his stay in the service, Mr. President Sir. I know he'll have no problem whatsoever sparring with the hot shot Ambassadors in New York, sir. Quite on the contrary sir, he'll give them back everything he gets in spades while he's at it sir."

"Is zat so? Who is this missing marvel of strength you speak of General White Sir?"

"I don't know how else to put this without you going right for my throat Mr. President. I guess there's no other way to say this than out right and..." The General was cut off by the President.

"General White we're all supposed to be adults here, so spit it out will you please. I'm not patiently growing old while waiting for you to offer up the name of this person to me, sir. General White Sir, get it off your chest because I'm quickly becoming immune to the revelations that comes forth from the mouths of many of my military advisors lately, sir."

"Yes Sir Mr. President and please remember that you asked for this sir, I think it'd be a much wiser idea on your part for you to take Lieutenant Walker with you sir."

"Walker? Walker? Why the hell does that name ring a bell with me sir? Why is that General White?" the President mumbled more to himself, as he turned his gaze on General White again.

"It's because Lieutenant Robert Walker's the soldier who actually lead the mission into Iran, Mr. President Sir."

"Lieutenant Walker? Oh good Christ General White Sir, you don't mean to be offering me that wild fellow you people branded Road Work do you sir?" the stunned President said in an excited tone of voice once he realized who it was the General was speaking of.

"It's Road Kill Mr. President Sir, his tag name is Road Kill sir. Believe me sir, I had nothing to do with his nickname sir, or why it was given to him in the first place, sir." General White offered to the President on his own behalf while sort of defending himself.

The President goes up and he started pacing as he searched his mind for what was upsetting him so much about this one soldier. His pacing made the doctor and General White move a little to give the President more room to move. Lines of worry and concern covered the President's face as he continued to search his mind. He waved Paul over to his side and then he asked him some questions that could not be overheard by the others in the room with him. His back straightened and his face showed anger, and he was becoming rather animated with the young White House aide the more he spoke with his boss. Abruptly, the conversation ended between them.

"General White Sir, please allow me to tell you something you might not know, over the many years that I've known you sir. I have heard you offer up a number of crazy ass suggestions and precautions to me, sir. I thought some of them were way off the sheet of music we were singing from General White Sir. But this one really takes the icing off the damn cake I'm afraid, sir. Where the hell are your ideas coming from lately, General White Sir? I can't believe you're suggesting

I take one of the most unpredictable soldiers, one of the craziest human beings we have in the service. Leastwise, I believe he's a human being. Is he human General White Sir?"

General White smiled and he nodded yes as he watched his emotions get the best of the President who was suddenly staring at him so intensely.

"That's right mister, just stand there and allow me to make a first class fool of myself, sir. Jesus Christ Almighty General White Sir. I can't believe this suggestion actually came from your lips, sir. What the hell makes you believe for one second that I'd be able to control this wild wheel of yours in New York City, General? This man might be a damn good soldier, but he knows shit from shinola about addressing the damn Ambassadors of the United Nations, General White Sir. Many are our friends, and I'd like to keep it that way if you don't mind, sir. Christ, I could just see this crazy ass soldier of yours locking horns with the Iranian Ambassador."

"Yes Sir Mr. President, couldn't you though sir?" General White retorted with a smirk.

"General White Sir, I heard many stories about you in the past, sir. Some I didn't believe, others I chose not to believe even if they were true. But I see you're a real sonofabitch at that sir." The President added as he studied the General's face, and then he envisioned this young Marine Lieutenant locking horns with the Iranian or Russian Ambassadors at the meeting, as they tried to shake him up as the young soldier was speaking with them.

"Yes I am a sonofabitch Mr. President Sir, and I'm damn proud of it, and I can see Lieutenant Walker going at it with the Ambassadors at the meeting, sir. I don't see the sonsabitches shaking up my Lieutenant in the least sir. In fact Mr. President Sir, I'd be willing to give my left nut to witness him in action against them, sir. The Ambassadors aren't going to know what the hell they grabbed by the damn tail if they try shaking him up any at the meeting, sir."

"Interesting General, very interesting indeed sir. General White Sir, I can see this young Lieutenant of yours in action in my mind's eye, and I like what I see sir. What better answer to these blunders created by the Russians, than to have one of the soldiers who had to straighten out what their lack of vigilance had caused, sir. A word to the wise to you though General White Sir, I'm not saying I'm completely convinced on taking this loose cannon of yours to the United Nations with me, sir. But if I were to take him along, I trust you'll speak with him, and make certain he minds his P's and Q's while he's in the halls of the United Nations building, sir.

"I don't want him using any gutter language either, he has to know who he's speaking with at all times during the meeting, General." The President stopped speaking and he suddenly pointed his finger right at the General and then added to his words. "General White Sir, if I take this man with me, it'll be your left nut along with the right one, and the shaft that's on the line if this damn Lieutenant embarrasses me in any way, shape or form at the meeting, sir. Is this understood sir?"

"Yes Sir Mr. President sir, I'll have a little private chitchat with the soldier, and he'll understand what he's supposed to and not do while he's in New York with you sir. I'll let him know I'll be the one he'll be dealing with if he screws up any in New York, Mr. President Sir."

The President let out his breath in a rush; and then he turned his attention to the doctor and moaned at him. "Well Doctor, what do you say about the Lieutenant coming with us sir?"

"Am I to take it I'll be accompanying you to New York as well, Mr. President Sir?"

"Yes sir Doctor, you and this Lieutenant, if you think he'll be an asset to us, Doctor."

"Mr. President Sir, I think you'd be very wise if you were to bring this young soldier with you to the meeting, sir." Doctor Russbinder offered to the President of the United States.

"You really think so Doctor?" the President replied, surprised by the doctor's attitude.

"Mr. President Sir, I must admit that I have witnessed this young man in action sir. Nothing we went through on the entire mission shook him up in the least, and I don't think anyone could possibly do likewise with the soldier either, sir. He's very intelligent, and I don't believe anyone can box him into a corner where he wouldn't be able to esc..."

"But his uncontrollable attitude Doc, his mouth, his unpredictable and wild nature. I don't know about this idea, to be quite frank with you, Doctor. He scares the shit out of me sir."

"That's true Mr. President Sir, he scares the shit out of everyone who meets him, sir. But couldn't you just visualize this young and wild Lieutenant going off on the Russian or Iranian Ambassadors, sir? He'll say what we always wanted to say for so long, but being bound by the laws of ethics and political decorum, we always end up holding our tongues, sir. His youth will give him the privilege that escapes us whenever we're dealing with the Ambassadors from the United Nations, sir. Just think of it sir, if this man's played enough, through him, you can say everything you have held back in all these years, Mr. President Sir."

"Well, Doctor Russbinder sir, I do see my General was correct about you after all sir, his troops have rubbed off on you some, haven't they sir? I can't believe I'm hearing this coming from you sir. When I first met you Doctor Russbinder Sir, you were scared to death to dare open your mouth in my presence, sir. Now, you stand before me and you're ready to bite the Russian Ambassador right on his damn rump, sir. I'm no longer concerned about having you address the damn Ambassadors at the meeting, sir. Whoa, what I once believed was going to be a chore suddenly seems like a real pleasure for me. Ahhh... youth, where would we be without it?"

"Yes, quite right Mr. President Sir, and I'm remembering that old saying sir. 'The dreams of the youth are the nightmare of the old'."

"Yes quite right at that Doctor Russbinder Sir. General White, you seem to be right on target again sir. When will I ever learn to trust your judgments sir? I'm going to take this Lieutenant with me as you suggested, but not before you speak with him sir. I want you to place a screw in that boy I can turn to keep him under control while he's at this damn meeting, General White."

"Yes sir, do you want me to have Lieutenant Walker report here to Washington, or would you rather he link up with you while you're in New York City, Mr. President Sir?"

"There's no sense having him report to Washington, sir. Have him report directly to New York City, I want you there to help keep this wild card of yours under control, General."

"Fine with me Mr. President Sir, I'll have him put up someplace in New York, sir."

"I believe it'd be a better move to have this Lieutenant linkup with my Vice President, who'll be visiting New York City by the time the soldier arrives there, sir. This way she'll be able to speak to him directly, and help calm him down some and also brief him in on what we want from him at the United Nations meeting, sir. Yes General White Sir, I believe this is a much better course of action to take, sir. I want someone working on this kid before we address the meeting on Friday, General. Do you know any way to calm this kid down some, General White Sir?"

"I sure do Mr. President Sir, but most of them are illegal, or life threatening sir. I know one way to keep him down and happy though, Mr. President Sir." General White offered with a kind of smile on his lips, and evil flashing in his eyes.

"What might that be General White Sir?" the President asked of his military officer.

"Mr. President Sir, it'd be an extremely wise move on your part to allow his steady girlfriend to accompany him to New York City while he's there, sir. If there's anyone on the face of this earth who can keep him under some kind of control, it's surely Sergeant Dorothy Ramirez can, Mr. President Sir." The General offered the Commander in Chief.

"Where can we get hold of this Sergeant Ramirez, General White Sir?" the President asked.

"No problem Mr. President Sir, she's part of the elite soldiers with this Lieutenant, sir. She's likely with him I'd imagine right this moment, sir." The General offered with a grin on his lips.

"You mean to tell me this young soldier of yours is dragging his god damn girlfriend along on these extremely dangerous missions, General White Sir!"

"Yes and no I can say to that last question, Mr. President Sir. Sergeant Ramirez is quite the fighter in her own ranks, sir. This female

Sergeant can more than hold herself against the very best of any enemy forces, either male or female, Mr. President Sir. She's every bit as good a soldier and warrior as Lieutenant Walker is, and any of the other male soldiers of the specialized Unit at that, Mr. President Sir." The General offered proudly with conviction, and in his stance as he stared at President Cole while looking him in his eyes.

"Okay General, I'm going along with your judgment once again sir. It hasn't let me down this far General White Sir." The President smiled at his military officer.

"I'll have them both put up in a hotel near the Trump International Tower and Hotel, sir. If that's alright with you that is, Mr. President Sir." General White offered while he felt the President was in a good mood to hear his latest offer.

"I believe that won't be necessary in this case, General White Sir. Because I'll have two rooms set aside in the Trump Tower for these two soldiers, General. That way they'll both be closer to Ms. Hirshfield, and in this way she can work with Lieutenant Walker much closer, until I'm ready to use him at the United Nations meeting on Friday morning, General White Sir." The crafty and grinning President announced as he kind of got used to the idea of having this extremely dangerous soldier going with him in New York for the meeting.

"Why not make it one room then Mr. President Sir, and save the taxpayer's some extra money while we're at it, sir?" General White offered as he kind of smiled at the President who was still a little uncomfortable over having the Lieutenant address the meeting with him.

"You mean these two animals are intimate with each other, General White Sir?" the President asked with a surprised tone of voice.

"The two have been living together in the Florida Keys on an Island called Marathon for over a year now, Mr. President Sir. I understand they intend to get married in the very near future; I was informed of their intent by their Commander, Colonel Bruce Leadbetter, sir. They're well suited for each other at that Mr. President Sir." General White announced as he returned the President's concern stare with one of his own.

"Okay General White Sir, I believe you have convinced me on taking these two people with me, sir. I guess I'll handle things from my end, and I'll expect you to do the same from your end as well, General. Let's get some of these things set in motion, sir." The President announced as he slapped his hands together, and then he added. "Gentlemen, I believe I saw enough displayed before me today to last me a lifetime. Paul, have this stuff marked so I can read it then pack it up and have it all send on up to New York City for me, please."

THE PENTAGON, WASHINGTON DC.
FRIDAY, NOVEMBER 13th, 1998 10:35 A.M. EST

The traffic in downtown Washington D.C. was absolute murder at best, and General John White along with CIA Director John Raincloud, who remained at the Pentagon with the General during their meeting with the President and the rest of his staff. Made certain the President left the building before they both headed back for the General's office to communication with the USS George Washington's Commander.

By the time they both entered the General's office, they were laughing about the President's reaction to the idea of having Lieutenant Robert Walker accompany him to New York City for the United Nations meeting. General White plopped down heavily in his chair while still laughing over the thought of Lieutenant Walker attending the United Nations meeting along with the President of the United States as Director Raincloud spoke to him.

"Christ Almighty John, I thought the Boss was going to have a shit hemorrhage in the room when he realized who it was you were offering to go with him to New York City, General. Did you see how fat his neck got sir? His face was, Jesus Almighty." Director Raincloud snickered as he opened his jacket and then sat in the chair and grinned at the powerful General.

"I agree Chief." General White smirked; he was the only man in all of Washington who could dare rib the large Native American about his heritage as he went on with his words for the Director. "I'll bet the President's blood pressure must have climbed a few notches when he finally remembered who Lieutenant Walker was. I thought I was going to have to get him a paper bag to breathe into to keep him from hyperventilating on us John."

"I never saw him in such a state, General. You really had him going for a while there I can tell you sir. I never thought he'd be able to control himself without having to take a dump."

They shared another laugh at the President's expense, before Director Raincloud added. "Man, did you see the way the President rushed out of the damn room? Like his ass was on fire. Christ sake General, the President made the poor Doctor and his pencil neck geek of an aide run in order to try and stay up with him. I really hate to be the poor Doctor about now sir, or the President's dog for that matter, General White Sir. I can assure you sir, both of them are more than likely be sorry for being anywhere near the President for at least a week."

"I'd hate to be him and locked in the Boss' limo in this crummy traffic, in the state he's in. The bastard will be lucky enough to escape with his balls swinging between his legs." General White gave out with another laugh, and was joined by Director Raincloud again. Their laughter ended when Mary, his secretary entered the office and she shot a harsh glare at the two of them.

General White wiped his eye as he fought to control his mirth, and then he complained at his secretary. "For Christ sake Mary, I see by the expression on your face you overheard us talking about the Boss, and what happened at the meeting."

"Yes I did General White, and I really think you should be ashamed of yourself, sir. It's not good to laugh at the poor man, or upsetting the President until he's in such a rage, sir. You know how he gets whenever he's that disturbed, General. He's not a young man, and being so upset could cause him health problems. I don't know who this poor Doctor that you were speaking about is, but I feel terrible for him if he's trapped under the President's anger. That's not very fair to the poor Doctor if he has to deal with the President when he's this angry. Boy, you two are fast becoming a conniving pair to deal with lately." Mary picked up the ashtray and emptied it.

"C'mon Mary, cut us a little slack not flack here will ya please, you have to give John this one. He has out done himself this time, despite what you might think we done to the Boss. Lieutenant Walker's the best possible pick to accompany him on Friday to the United Nations meeting. The man has more balls than he knows what to do with, and he has no fear of anyone or thing. That boy will say whatever the hell is on his mind, no matter who he's standing before. This kid knows everything that happened on the mission to Iran, what they found, and what those finds mean to the security of the United States. He knows the damn workings of the nuclear warheads inside out, and he's more than capable of explaining this crap to the gathered Ambassadors.

"Whew, if you think the President's pissed off now, give some thought to how the damn Ambassadors are going to feel when they have to start dealing with this livewire. Sheesh Mary, I wish I could be a fly on the wall." Director Raincloud said as he laughed, and was joined by General White. Their laughter was infectious, and it made Mary fight to hold back a giggle.

"Is this Lieutenant you're talking about that good and strong, General White Sir? I seem to remember reading his 201 personnel files a while ago. I believe this soldier should be placed in a nut house, locked away from the rest of the civilized world for its own protection, General White Sir." Mary replied skeptically to the two grinning men seated in the room.

"Placed in a damn nut house you say Mary?" General White said mockingly as he continued with his words. "If this kid wasn't a damn soldier, I'd consider having him erased, or at least neutered so he couldn't be a future threat to the civilized world by spreading his damn seed around to the female population, young lady." The General said with a smirk.

"General please! You're speaking about one of our boys, one of our young soldiers, sir. He's what he is because of the training you have ordered him to go through, General White Sir. I can't believe you just said that about this poor soldier, sir. Shame, shame on you, that's a terrible thing to say about one of our soldiers, General. I'm shocked by your terrible words General White. I can't believe you're so heartless about this young man, sir. How would you like it if someone said such a terrible thing about one of your boys, General?"

"C'mon Mary, I didn't mean anything by it. You know I'd never do anything like that to one of our soldiers. Christ sake, I thank God everyday for Lieutenant Walker, and any soldier like him. I was just having a little laugh at remembering the Boss' expression, when he realized who it was I was speaking about, Mary. As far as him being a good soldier, this kid's one of the best. He's a natural born trooper, the kid has more balls that he…" General White looked at the Director and they both erupted in laughter again.

They laughed so hard this time that Mary lost it and she joined them in their laughter as she cried to the General. "The President was really that upset, General White Sir?"

"Upset? Gees Kriest Mary, the President was more than just upset young lady. I thought he was having a conniption fit right in front of the rest of us attending the damn meeting."

"An apoplexy is more like it Director Raincloud Sir. I thought the President was about to give birth in the room, and I was going to be forced to help him deliver." General White corrected as they continued to laugh like two kids who just took a peek into the girl's dressing room.

"Oh…you two are really impossible when you get like this." Mary retorted at them.

"You hit the nail right on the head Mary. We're impossible, but we're the guardians of the peace for the United States." General White snickered as he sat forward, he looked at his watch and then looked at Director Raincloud and added. "I think I better get hold of Colonel Bruce Leadbetter, and have him prepare the crazy ass Lieutenant to report to New York City, A-SAP. Christ Chief, the Trump International Tower and Hotel will never look the same once this one and his girlfriend leave the damn place in ruins, sir."

General White quickly dialed up the number for the Marine Commandant, while Mary finished messing around in his desk. Director Raincloud poured a cup of coffee then he waited while General White was on the phone. Once he got through, he was informed it would take a few moments to transfer his call out to the Aircraft Carrier Washington. It took a bit longer than first expected to make the connection work, but finally he was speaking with Colonel Leadbetter. "Ahhh... Colonel Leadbetter Sir, how was it in Iran sir?"

"So so I'd say General White Sir. Would it do me any good to gripe about it sir?"

"Nope, no good at all Colonel. Good job you did in Iran though Colonel, your people did real well, you got everything we wanted and a shit load more as well. Looks like the Boss is going to have himself a damn cake walk with making the Ambassadors understand his evidence your troops have collected for him. He's going to come out of this mess smelling like a fucking daisy at the United Nations meeting, sir. Did you receive any causalities during the action, Colonel?"

"Not as many as first expected sir. We lost five, one was Sergeant Barbara Meyerhoff, the only female to die..."

"Arrr... that's a damn shame Colonel. I didn't want anyone to die in this damn action, sir. I don't recognized the name, was she a good soldier, Colonel Leadbetter Sir?" General White asked with concern while trying to remember Meyerhoff's 201 report and who she was.

"One of the best we had General White sir. She was the pet of one of my other soldier's sir."

"Yeah? Which soldier was that Colonel?" General White asked the Marine Colonel, not really interested in the answer to his question though.

"Corporal Meyerhoff was dating the madman branded the Mutt, Lieutenant Frank Hall, sir. A close troublemaker and friend of Lieutenant Walker, sir." Colonel Leadbetter moaned as he lit up a smoke and then he sat back in his chair realizing there was more to this call from the General.

"Strange you should mention the Lieutenant's name. How did Walker take the hit sir?"

"Rough General, real rough sir. Evidently Meyerhoff was well respected by the troops, sir. We plan a special service in the ship's chapel tomorrow morning. Everyone plans to attend, we have word some of the damn Swabbies will be there as well, sir. I don't know if the Captain's putting them up to it or not, but I like the idea though, the move kinda makes us feel we belong to the service, General. I better ask you while I have you on the line sir. I know it's only a matter of time before Lieutenant Hall requests for permission to attend his girl's funeral, sir."

"He has leave coming, and it looks like there's going to be a short spell before we go hot against Libya, sir. Say Colonel, why don't you cut the orders and send him on his way, get me over the paperwork and I'll clear it from this end for you, sir. Supply him with transportation to the funeral and back out to the ship once it's over, sir. I want a full color guard at the ceremony, give it an eleven gun salute, and flag to the parents. Find out where she's being buried, and contact the nearest VFW post, and have them send their honor guard out. Do whatever it takes to make this thing right for this soldier, Colonel. Did you receive any wounded in the action sir? I know you filled out the paperwork, but I haven't seen it as of yet, Colonel Leadbetter Sir."

"No problem with that General White Sir, I don't have anything scheduled at the moment sir. We took fifteen wounded, many of them were walking wounded with numerous minor nicks or broken ribs, sir. I have three soldiers bad, one of them expected not to pull through. I have his name here somewhere General. Err... here we go sir, Private Jerome Rosenberger, his partners in crime branded him Short Cut, he stopped a round in the neck. The wound's bad sir. Excuse me; I have something to attend to General." The Colonel was interrupted by someone who just entered his room and handed him a report.

"Yeah sure go ahead and attend to your work Colonel, I have nothing but time on my hands."

The Colonel was back and reported to his Commander. "General White Sir, I was just handed an update on one of my people's condition sir. It seems another of my soldiers was just brought down to sickbay in critical condition, also suffering from a neck wound, sir. His name's Private Alan Langworth, his tag name is Stainless, General White sir. I was just about..."

"Jesus Christ Almighty Colonel Leadbetter, I never expected so many god damn wounded and killed on this damn mission to sand land, mister. You know I view all battlefield casualties not as an inevitable event of combat, mister. I see the casualties in the light of fucking mistakes, and gold bricking by the soldiers involved in the damn operation. These fucking mistakes were made out in the field in a bushel basket, and that means some of your people fucked up on the damn mission sir. You know me for a long time now Colonel, and you know damn well I'll not tolerate dead and wounded in any action we take, without looking for someone to hang.

"It seems there's a need for some further training by your pack of asses, mister. We have to weed out the weak, the fuckups, the I don't give a shit soldiers, and the leave it for the other guy to do types, Colonel. You know the old saying, 'if one soldier screws up, the entire outfit pays the price', and that's obviously what happened here, dammit. I'll get to the bottom of it or retire. Heads will roll, your people reacted like a bunch of god damn amateur's, and embarrassed the shit out of me over this last damn operation. The mashing of teeth will soon begin I tell you Colonel, even if I have to eliminate all the damn instructor crews, and put new people in there that can get the job done right for me. That changing might just begin with you, mister..."

"General White Sir, if you want a head to lop off, by all means take mine. I was in Command of this fucking operation, and if you think my people fucked up on this mission. Then I'm the one responsible for their damn mistakes, sir. The buck stops right on my fucking front doorstep, sir. I'm not going to blame the others, or anyone else for that matter, sir. If you don't like the way the damn operation was run then take it out on my ass, sir. I don't give a shit, all I know is I busted a fucking gut with training these kids, and they're the best we have to defend us, sir." Colonel Leadbetter growled, getting angry at how the General was dumping on his outfit.

General White ignored the angry Colonel's statement as he continued with his bitch at his lesser officer. "I can't tell you how embarrassed I am over the losses we suffered on this damn mission, and how disappointed the President is going to be when this report reaches his desk. He was making all sorts of noise that our MNRR Forces are nothing more than a glorified bunch of overpaid fuckups, and I have to change his mind, or he'll pull our funding, mister. The way he is, that might not be possible after this mess up. You know I'm uncompromising on battlefield losses Colonel, and your losses were accumulated as a result of someone sleeping on the fucking job, sir. If they were, I want heads on a damn platter, Colonel Leadbetter Sir.

"I'm holding you personally responsible for the injured and dead of this miserable operation, and there'll be an extensive investigation when you people return to the States. Didn't these assholes have their damn body armor on for God's sake? Those damn things cost the taxpayers a fucking bundle, and they were to be used to cut down on our dead and wounded, sir. No other services have the luxury of these damn protective devices because of their staggering cost. If the soldiers under your Command aren't going to use the shit we're supplying them. Then I'll going to pull the damn things out from under their asses, and then they can see how it feels butt ass naked working in the fucking field, Colonel Leadbetter Sir."

The fuming Marine Colonel cut General White off right in the middle of his complaint, and he snapped at his commanding officer. "General White Sir, my people had their damn body armor installed properly during the full duration of the operation. We ran a thorough inspection of the armor before we moved out sir. The wounded and killed were hit by enemy dumb luck rounds General, and there's nothing you or I can do about that type of wound, sir. Taking a round in the damn neck opening or through a soft spot in the body armor is just dumb enemy luck, that's all."

"Yeah Colonel Leadbetter I understand that sir. But they were tagged and killed, and I'm the one who has to answer to the Man for it, dammit. And, don't think for a moment I didn't notice how you were accepting blame, and I respect you for it. But nevertheless, it doesn't change the outcome of it one bit Colonel, someone's going to pick up the tab, and getting pissed on from above for the rest of his duty, if you catch my drift." General White warned the Colonel.

"General White Sir, I don't meant to be disrespectful sir. But this won't be the first time I was overlooked for a fucking promotion, sir. I ain't in this damn thing for more salad dressing on my damn chest, sir. Or prettier bars pinned on my shoulders, General. I'm in this to defend my country's interests. To teach my people how to best survive on the fucking battlefield, wherever they might be fighting." Colonel Leadbetter snapped defiantly at the powerful General.

Chapter Three

With a deep sigh, the General softened his stance against his officer as he remarked this time. "Yeah, right, okay Colonel, enough of this shit for the time being I guess, sir. We'll sort it all out later on when you're stateside, and we're face to face, Colonel. Anyway Bruce, I have two reasons for contacting you sir. After speaking with the Boss, we came to the conclusion there's to be no one in your outfit below the rank of Sergeant. The order crosses over to the soldiers on loan from other nations of the MNRRF as well sir. That means at least half of your crazed people will get a raise in rank and pay, sir. They deserve it for the job they just pulled off in Iran.

"Colonel Leadbetter Sir, I'll allow you handle the rate increases for your troopers. Use it as a club to beat them over their damn heads with, and send me the paperwork and I'll push it right through lickity-split for you, sir. Keep the loaners separate from the rest of our people, brand them clearly for me, sir. Mark Russians as such, French as French and so on and so forth, Colonel. Well, the other reason for this call and I'm sorry to dump this shit on you at this time sir, but Lieutenant Walker will have to miss the service for the female soldier, sir. I'm gonna draft his ass on ya. I know how tight he was to the female soldier, but this can't be helped, sir. I'll make sure he's back to your ranks well before your people go active against Libya though, sir. That's the best

I can offer ya, I don't want your people active without him on the job, Colonel." The General then leaned back, allowing the Colonel the opening to speak up.

"For sure? Why are you pulling Lieutenant Walker from me, General? He's going to be hot as hell over the fact of missing the service for Meyerhoff I can assure you, sir. I heard he threatened everyone in the outfit with bodily harm, to make sure they all attend Mass for her. I have word Lieutenant Walker's suffering from a number of minor cuts and scrapes himself, sir. I planned to cut him some slack, and maybe takeover his Unit for a little while for the soldier, General. Let him sort of lick his wounds if you catch my drift, sir." Colonel Leadbetter offered while biting his lip, he knew how the Chairman of the Joint Chiefs of Staff got when he tried to lay off his people. The Colonel received a rough tongue lashing from the General a few days before, when he tried to pull Walker's group from the lead Unit in the action in of Iran.

"He's not too bad hurt it might hinder him traveling over to New York City, is he Colonel Leadbetter Sir? I need the pain in the ass there even if he's still bleeding sir." General White snapped, sitting up and staring at the phone as if trying to see the Colonel's face through it.

Colonel Leadbetter was surprised over the General's reaction as he replied to his last question of him. "No Sir General, the medic believes he might have a broken rib or two. But there's not much anyone can do for that except wrap up his chest, and that won't stop him from traveling in the least, sir. I know he's got a helluva black and blue mark with an open wound on his right arm though General. Other than that, he's suffering from server exhaustion and lack of sleep and some good food to help him regain some of his strength back sir. I believe the medics gave him a clean bill of health already, or his ass would still be stuck in sickbay, sir."

"What about the female he's boffing (slang for fucking), Colonel?"

"You mean Sergeant Dorothy Ramirez, General?" the Colonel asked with surprise.

"Yeah, that one. What kind of condition is she in? If I want her, can she accompany this loose cannon to the States, Colonel? I might have need of her services with this other soldier, sir."

"Sure thing General White Sir. Far as I know she's in great shape, it's hard to tell she even just went through a military action now I'm thinking of her, sir. She's filthy yes, and I'm certain she has her own fair share of minor nicks and bruises from the operation, sir. But I'm positive she's been cleaned up and checked out by the Carrier's medics working wonders with my injured people, sir. I have no report crossing my desk on any injuries she might have received during the action, sir. I'm still waiting for all the damn fitness reports to dribbling in at anytime sir. I'm sorry they're taking so long to get, but we barely had time to take a dump, General White Sir."

"I need someone to accompany the President who won't go tit's up on me in the damn water, Colonel. Lieutenant Walker's the pick, and Ramirez will be used as a control over his hea..."

"Holy shit General White Sir, the United fucking Nations! Lieutenant Walker! You mean that lunatic's going to mingle in with those tight assed stinking pukes from that institution, sir? Holy crap, you're shitting me sir, what the hell's going on with the Boss over there in Washington anyhow, sir? Is he planning to go to war with the rest of the world to dare expose them stuff shirts to the likes of Lieutenant Walker, sir? Dammit sir, I don't think those screwed up blokes are ready for Lieutenant Walker and his nasty ass temper and..."

"Colonel Leadbetter Sir, every remark, every witticism you can think of, has been bantered about by us, sir. As weird as it might sound to you Colonel, Lieutenant Walker's the logical pick for this situation, sir. How soon can you have him ready to leave for New York, Colonel?"

"There's no problem getting his ass on a plane at this very moment, General."

"What about Sergeant Ramirez? I want her to tag along with Walker, Colonel."

"Same goes for her as well sir. I believe the only thing she's doing about now, is taking care of Walker one way or another sir. The troops are below deck working on themselves, General."

"Does that taking care of Walker include a box lunch and a soft pillow to lay his head on, Colonel?" General White snorted, imagining the two of them making love on the Carrier.

"Indeed it does I'm sure General." The Colonel retorted with a smirk stuck on his lips.

"Aw... the lucky bastard doesn't know how soft he has it in this Unit, dammit. Okay Colonel Leadbetter, I see no reason for pushing him that fast along, sir. The Vice President isn't planning to reach Manhattan until Thursday sometime for crap sake. Give Lieutenant Walker and his babe the rest of this day to lick their damn wounds, or anything else they choose to lick."

A slight snicker from Colonel Leadbetter, but the General ignored it as he went on with his words. "I'll have a Jetstar with in flight refueling capabilities and tail hook; touch down on the Carrier at exactly Oh, Three Hundred Hours your time, Colonel. I want them two cleaned up, repaired, well rested, and ready to go by then, sir. Inform Walker he's going to be bunking up with the damn Veep, so he's to be on his very best behavior at all times while he's in New York, sir. If not, I swear I'll skin his squeeze alive right before his fucking eyes, and have her tits tanned and hung from the flagpole right in front of the United Nations building if he fucks up in the least on this next mission I'm preparing to send this crazy ass soldier out on, Colonel."

"Walker and the Vice President are going to be bunking together, General? I heard she's a real wildcat to deal with, but shit, I believe I've heard just about everything now, General. I'm going to stay out to sea for the rest of my life. From the sound of it sir, it seems the brain thrust running Washington, is suddenly suffering from a brain fart, sir. Walker and Ramirez together, rubbing elbows with the VP then the Boss and United Nations Ambassadors. Man General White Sir!"

"Crazier things have happened in the world of politics I assure you sir. But I kind of doubt it. Colonel Leadbetter Sir, you have a good idea there, staying out to sea I mean sir. If Lieutenant Walker screws up in New York City, I just might join you out there, and keep my head low until the President cools off some, dammit. I like having my nuts swinging in the breeze, sir."

The two officers shared a quick laugh together over this last order, and then General White added to his words for the Colonel. "All joking aside Colonel, Lieutenant Walker and his lady will be ready to travel by Oh, Three Hundred Hours your time, sir. He's going to miss the funeral service, but them are the fucking breaks I'm afraid, Colonel Leadbetter Sir."

"I see no problem with that General White Sir. Lieutenant Walker's a big boy sir, and he knows when duty calls, he halls sir."

"Get it done for me then Colonel. Have a good heart to heart talk with the both of them before sending them on their way to New York. I want you to impress on the both of them in no uncertain terms, what I'll do to their damn bodies if they embarrass the President in any way, shape, or form while they're in New York City. You can warn them the punishment involves fire, a rusty nail, and a set of fucking nut crackers, Colonel. Inform them as long as they live, they'll never heal from what I'll inflict on their damn bodies if they screw up on this one, sir."

"Will do General White Sir, they'll be at their very best sir." The Colonel replied proudly.

"Err... by the way Bruce, don't forget about the rate increases for your people, sir."

"Err... General White Sir, I see a slight problem arising from that order, sir."

"Zat so? What problem do you see, Colonel?" the General asked his lesser officer.

"Err... I don't know how the other Strips (Sergeants) and Bars (Officers) are going to take half the damn Unit getting a buck up the ladder, while the rest of them have to stay where they are, sir. If half the group gets a rate increase, everyone in the outfit should get one, it's only fair sir. I don't need half my people getting left out in the damn dust, General."

"Hummmmm.... it seems to me you do have a slight problem on your hands at that, Colonel. Glad I don't have to deal with the damn problem though sir. Nice try there Colonel, but it didn't work sir. I can only lift the ones not Sergeants up the damn ladder, sir. It was suggested everyone get a buck up the ladder, but the President wouldn't hear of it, sir. Colonel Leadbetter Sir, in case you forgot about it sir, you're the big dick running the fucking Unit. If those pukes have a problem with your orders, deal with it sir. Don't take any shit from the pukes, unless that shit comes from me, mister. Understood sir?" General White growled harshly at the Colonel.

"Yes sir, I'll do that General White Sir." Colonel Leadbetter replied in the positive, fearing he might have pushed the General a bit too far by asking for everyone in the unit to get a rise.

"Expect the damn Jetstar arriving on the Fight Deck of the Washington at exactly Oh, Three Hundred Hours, Colonel. That'll put Lieutenant Walker and his main squeeze in the air and in New York City by Thursday morning, sir. I want him there at that precise time, because I have inside information that's when the Vice President's scheduled to reach New York, Colonel. I want to impress her I'm that efficient I can have my people anywhere in the damn world at any time I want them there, sir. And this will also give her a full week to work with Lieutenant Walker on a one on one basis, and sharpen his presentation for the upcoming United Nations meeting. He's to report to the Trump International Tower and Hotel where I have reserved a room for him and Sergeant Ramirez, Colonel." The General lied to the Colonel, he was not reserving the rooms. But he knew the Colonel was not aware of this fact, and he was trying to impress him with the power he wheeled in Washington.

"The Trump International fucking Hotel and Tower sir? Holy shit General White Sir, do you think you can get pissed off at me and order my ass to accompany the two shitbirds to New York city, sir? I never been in the damn Trump Tower, sir. What punishment for them to fuckup's sir, the Trump fucking Tower? I'm told Trump lives there with his entire family, General. Can you imagine him and Lieutenant Walker crossing swords together? Holy shit sir; there'd be hair in the air and blood on the ground on that one, sir. Two strong minded people living so close to one another for even a damn day could be a rather explosive situation, General White Sir."

"That's why I want you to have that little heart to heart with Lieutenant Walker, sir. I don't care if you have to pull his tongue out and stand on it until you can make him see how important this fucking meeting is for the President. He's not to screw up in the least on this one sir. I don't care if he has to eat shit out of a dead dog's ass; he's to remain cool all the while he's in New York City, sir. Explain to him if he gets angry, he can hang on to it, and wait until he crosses swords with the damn Libyans to clean his tubes out. That's when he can work out all his frustrations."

"Will do exactly that General. I'll take care of Walker from this end General White Sir."

"Fine Colonel Leadbetter, I'll speak with you off and on throughout the next few days, and I'm making plans to linkup with you and your troops in Egypt when your unit lands there. Colonel, I want Lieutenant Walker and Sergeant Ramirez dressed in civvies all the while they're stateside, sir. If they don't have them on board the ship, send them in uniform and cut a pay voucher for them, so they can buy what they need in New York, Colonel. I want the Ambassadors to know he's military, but I don't think it'd be appropriate to address the meeting while dressed in uniform. You know what they say, the uniform's intimidating, sir. Lieutenant Walker doesn't need his uniform to be intimidating, his presence alone is more than intimidation, Colonel."

"General White Sir, I know none of the troops have any civvies with them, sir. So I'll cut the voucher sir. How much do you want it for, sir? And I take it we're heading for Egypt sir?"

"Make it a thousand dollars apiece, they'll have to worry about food outside, inside they can charge everything to me at the Tower. To answer your other question, sir. Yes, you're heading for Egypt, Colonel. I'm not going to keep my damn ground forces cooped up on that ship, until you go active against Libya, sir. I sequestered an old military base for your bunch of screaming assholes in Egypt. I figure you'll spend at least a month there, if not more while recuperating and running out a number of selected scenarios to be employed against Libya. I don't know when we'll go active on the next mission sir, that's up to the Boss not me, Colonel. We don't have meeting one scheduled on this situation as of this time, sir. I want your shitbirds to know this next damn mission inside out, before jumping off against it. Some parts in Iran didn't run so smoothly, but the Libyan mission will run perfectly, or heads will roll Colonel Leadbetter."

"Understood General White Sir." Colonel Leadbetter replied into the dead receiver. He hung up and then sat back and rested his feet on the top of his desk built right in the bulkhead in the officer's quarters of the Carrier he shared with Colonel Joseph Salsiccia. He laced his fingers together behind his head and then he quickly collected his thoughts, and grinned to himself over his last orders before sending for Lieutenant Walker and Sergeant Ramirez. Colonel Salsiccia's snoring was driving him nuts, so he pulled a pillow off his rack, and threw it at the other sleeping Colonel to wake him and stop all his snoring at the same time.

With a snort, Colonel Salsiccia woke and glared at Colonel Leadbetter as he pitched the pillow back at him and complained. "What? What? What the hell did I do now dammit, Colonel?"

"You were snoring like a fucking thunderstorm, pecker. Get on your damn side and cut me some damn slack will ya, before I go fricking deaf on ya Colonel."

"Yeah yeah fine sir. You're starting to sound so much like my ex-wife you know, Colonel Leadbetter Sir." Colonel Salsiccia snapped at the other Colonel.

"Not for nothing Joe, but you might want to stay awake for this one sir." Colonel Leadbetter offered and then he added to the other officer. "I have Lieutenant Walker and Sergeant Ramirez reporting to our quarters for a special little meeting that'll knoc..."

"What the hell did the asshole screw up this time around, Colonel?" Colonel Salsiccia smirked as he got up on one elbow and then he smirked at the other military officer.

"Nothing yet, but I was ordered to have a little kind of heart to heart talk with the pain in the ass Lieutenant, that's all I can tell you right now Joe." Colonel Leadbetter replied at the other Colonel as he grinned back at him.

"Why the hell are you sending for him then, Colonel? Didn't you see enough of his damn puss in the damn desert, sir?" Colonel Salsiccia bitched, putting even more weight on his elbow while trying to blink the sleep from his eyes.

"I don't have the god damn time to clue ya in on everything that's happening right now, Colonel. If you want to know what the hell's up then stay awake and listen in on the damn conversation, Joe. I assure you man, it'll be well fucking worth it sir."

"It's going to be that good, huh Colonel Leadbetter Sir?" The still exhausted Colonel asked as he became more awake and more interested in what Leadbetter was talking about.

"Better than you can possibly imagine it being Joe. You're going to love this one I can promise you that much sir. I still can't believe the fucking orders I just received from General White, sir." The Colonel groaned as he sat suddenly forward, and he reached for the Carrier's inner communications mike. It was instantly answered by the on duty Boatswain's Mate stationed in the Command Center of the Carrier.

The Boatswain's Mate immediately knew where the call originated from below deck, and he replied to the special operations officer. "Yes Sir Colonel Leadbetter Sir, this is Boatswain's Mate Chief Petty Officer Richard Belluzzi, sir. What can I do for you sir? I've been ordered by the Captain to assist you in any needs and wants you might have, Colonel Leadbetter Sir."

Not thinking it odd the Mate knew it was the Colonel on the horn, he started with what he needed from the Petty Officer. "Yeah Chief," Colonel Leadbetter did not try to pronounce his last name as he went on with his words. "I need two of my people to report to my quarters ASAP sir. How do I go about getting this accomplished from my damn quarters, sir?"

"I can handle that from this end for you easy enough, Colonel Leadbetter Sir. All I need to know is the soldier's names you want to report to your quarters, sir. Once I have their names I can order them over to your wardroom for ya, Colonel Leadbetter Sir."

"Very Good then I want Lieutenant Robert Walker, and Sergeant Dorothy Ramirez to report to my wardroom immediately sir, I believe they're being stationed on C deck some place on board the ship. Have them report to my wardroom as soon as possible sir." The Marine Colonel smirked over the easy to get his people to report to him.

The Boatswain's Mate quickly wrote down the names of the two soldiers on a pad by the intercom, and then he added. "Very well Colonel Leadbetter Sir. If I remember right sir, you're currently stationed in wardroom Seven-A on deck Two, B Section sir."

"You got me by the short hairs there fella, alls I know is I'm on board the Aircraft Carrier Washington, sir. I don't even know what damn Ocean we're sailing in at this time sir, nor do I really care where the hell we are at this time sir. I went in the direction you guys pointed me and that was it sir." Colonel Leadbetter moaned at the Boatswain's Mate because he ready did not know where he was stationed on board the Carrier. All he did was follow a young Seaman who walked him over to these quarters and that was it.

The Boatswain laughed as he remarked to the Marine Colonel over the mike. "Take it from me Colonel Leadbetter Sir. You're where I just said you are on board the ship sir, and we're currently stationed in the Red Sea, sir. I'll have the two soldiers you have requested to come to your quarters, report to your quarters STAT, sir."

Colonel Leadbetter was bored with their conversation, and he made a masturbating motion with his other hand as he stared at the ceiling and shook his head. The moment he disconnected with the Boatswain, he bitched to Salsiccia while hanging up the receiver. "These tight assed Swabbies make me sick to my stomach sir. If the lousy fucker knew where the fuck I was on this stinking ship, why the hell did the lousy little prick make me feel like a stinking jerk by asking me where the hell I was on this damn thing for crap sake. I'd like to hop him in the damn ass."

"Whew, I guess Lieutenant Walker has really fucked up royally this time around, to have you in such a riled up state Colonel. What the devil did he do now to piss you off so badly sir? Get caught making love to his girlfriend in the showers again, Bruce?"

"Christ sake Colonel, when the hell are you ever going to ditch that Holy Roller attitude your ex-wife has instilled in your damn ass, sir. It's not making love man; it's fucking his ever loving brains out, sir." Colonel Leadbetter remarked to the other military officer.

Colonel Salsiccia smiled back at the obviously upset Colonel Leadbetter as he shook his head. Their conversation was interrupted by the ship's booming intercom system as the Boatswain's Mate nearly screamed into the intercom system.

"Now here this! Now here this! Lieutenant Robert Walker and Sergeant Dorothy Ramirez are ordered to report to wardroom Seven-A,

Deck Two, B-section immediately. I repeat, Lieutenant Robert Walker and Sergeant Dorothy Ramirez are ordered to report to wardroom Seven-A, Deck Two, B-section immediately. Seaman Second Class Gary Girgenti, will escort you two requested soldiers over to wardroom Seven-A."

'C' DECK, THE USS CARRIER GEORGE WASHINGTON

Lieutenant Robert Walker with a towel wrapped around his waist, just sat down on his rack after showering and put his feet up for a moment, when the Boatswain's voice echoed throughout the troops sleeping quarters. All eyes went right to Walker and Sergeant Dorothy Ramirez. She also had a towel wrapped around her waist, and she was standing by her soldier topless. Both soldiers felt a lot better after their shower and lovemaking session.

Buckethead bellowed at the Lieutenant. "Holy shit man, Walker fucked up again people."

Another voice called out. "Hey people, that's Officer's country. You see Walker; we told you didn't belong with us pack of sleazebags down here on no man's land on this tub, man. Someone musta found out you were still hanging around with us stinking Rift Raft down here, and they're gonna put a quick end to it on us by making you move up to Officer's land, buddy."

The Mutt remained as silent as death and was obviously locked deep in thought with his hands resting behind his head while he stared up at the bottom of the bunk above him. His foot moved a mile a minute while trying to work off some of the pent up anger in his body over Barbara Meyerhoff's death in Iran. To his right, the French soldier Raphael hovered over him like a butterfly over a flower while waiting for him to talk, or even recognize she was by him.

The Lieutenant swung his feet off his rack and then he cast a quick glance at the Mutt, and he sadly shook his head after seeing the pained look etched deep in his friend's sad eyes. As he dressed in a clean uniform, the other soldiers quickly gathered around him, not sure why he was being summoned over to officer's row on board the Carrier.

"Hey Walker, what the fuck's up with these people?" Casper asked as he lit a regular smoke.

"Beats the crap outta my ass, Homes. Maybe someone's upset over the saintly life I lead. As far as I know, I didn't screw up anything, yet. Maybe one of you pukes did something, and I'm being pulled on the fucking carpet over it. Who the hell knows and who the hell gives a fuck anyway. Alls I know is, I'm getting sick and tired of playing soldier all the damn time man."

The all soldiers gathered in the sleeping quarters began to chant 'Whoup, whoup, oorah', over the Lieutenant's last remark it might be their fault he's going up before the man.

"Hey man, you're not gonna scrub out on us, are you Home Boy?" Neck grumbled.

The Lieutenant slapped the big man on the back of his neck so hard that the sound made some of the troopers actually cringe a bit, because it sounded more like a weapon going off. Neck did not flinch a muscle as he continued to stare at Walker while waiting for his reply.

"Relax you gene experiment gone haywire. I can't scrub out of the damn Unit. Who'll look after you shits? Without me at the helm, you guys will crash in the rocks in three hours Homes."

"Why the fuck do you think the stinking brass is sending for your ass then, man? You know they never call for one of us unless they want to rip us apart, Walker." McNip, (Sergeant David Nirajima), the newest male member of the group of elite soldiers repeated.

"Your guess is as good as mine McNip. I know I didn't screw up anything this time around man. Maybe they want to pin a friggin medal on my stinking ass. I don't know, or care man."

Another chorus of 'Oorahs' rang throughout the troops sleeping quarters. All the bantering and joking back and forth was instantly cut off by the sudden appearance of a young Seaman who stopped right in the hatchway leading to the elite soldier's sleeping quarters.

"I'm waiting for a Lieutenant Walker and a Sergeant Ramirez, sir." He announced.

"Whoa." Someone called out as many of the soldiers pointed at the rather smallish looking man standing in the hatchway.

The others added "Dum, da, dum dum." Mimicking the old tune from the Dragnet show.

Sergeant Ramirez looped her arm in Walker's. She dressed and was already back at his side. The Lieutenant looked at her and saw the concerned look in her eyes and he grumbled at her. "C'mon, we're not the lambs heading for slaughter, baby. If anything, it's the uther way round; and we're the god damn wolves circling the fucking lambs as always baby."

The highly trained specialized soldiers laughed as they erupted into another chorus of 'Oorahs'. Then the soldiers parted ranks while continuing to hum the Dragnet theme. The group closed up and they followed the two soldiers towards the hatchway.

The young Seaman watched the soldiers suddenly closing in on him.

The Lieutenant barked over his shoulder at his fellow troopers. "C'mon people, you're scaring the shit outta the little Swabbie here man. Back off some will ya. I'll be back, and in one piece."

The soldiers broke up and they went back to what they were doing moments before the Seaman came to collect Walker and Ramirez as ordered.

"Lieutenant Walker Sir, I'm Seaman Second Class Girgenti, sir. I was ordered to lead you and the Sergeant over to wardroom C-Seven, sir. Stay close to my lead and don't wander off on your own on me, or we'll all be in a world of shit, sir. While we're moving, keep your eyes open for any knee knockers, sir. I don't want you guys getting hurt while walking around the ship, sir."

"Glad to meet you pal. But what the hell are you talking about? Knee knockers buddy?"

"Here sir, these things here are called knee knockers on board the ship, Lieutenant Walker Sir." The Seaman pointed to the stationary section of steel plating under the hatchway and he added to his warning to the Marine Lieutenant. "These babies here are referred to as knee knockers, Lieutenant. Every Sailor who ever walked around the ship at one time or another, tangled with one of these babies that don't give an inch when you smack into it with your lower legs, sir. I saw many a Sailors hit them so hard, they had to be air e-vaced from the ship, because of the amount of damage done by the hatch to their legs, Lieutenant Walker Sir."

"How come the Navy doesn't remove the damn things if they're so dangerous to the crew?" He snapped as he picked his leg up and over the steel obstacle without tangling with it, but not before he tested the bulkhead with his shin. Lightly bouncing it off the low steel wall twice. He realized how it could cause problems if he was not paying attention to where he was walking.

"Excuse me Lieutenant Walker Sir. But there's no way we can possibly remove the special walls, because without the lower section of the bulkhead, you can't keep the ship's water tight integrity intact, sir. The hatch creates a water tight seal with the bulkhead when the hatches are dogged down for action on board the ship, Lieutenant. Some Sailors branded them knee wackers, to give them another name to go by sir." The smiling young Seaman replied to Walker.

"Understood pal." He grumbled as he fell in line with the Navy man.

"All you have to do is pay attention and watch where you're walking on board the ship at all times Lieutenant. I'll call out each knee knockers when we come across them, sir."

He took Ramirez's hand and they both stepped over the next three heavy metal dividers. The three of them headed for a ladder leading to the next deck up. The Lieutenant listened to every word the Seaman called out. He watched when he said handhold, and then he grabbed a metal bar overhead to help him pull his weight over a divider where he had to stay closer to the wall, in order to avoid a large fuel valve sticking out into the walkway.

"Man, this stinking place has more fucking problems than most of the obstacle courses I ever danced through, buddy." He bitched at the young Seaman as he watched where he was going.

The Seaman looked over his shoulder and laughed while not missing a step as he called back. "You got that right Lieutenant Sir. Another knee knocker coming at ya sir."

He made it over this divider safely, but he heard Ramirez curse in a low voice behind him, and he immediately knew she just tangled with one of the metal dividers.

The Seaman suddenly stepped aside a closed door and announced. We're here sir. Your people are in this wardroom waiting for you and the Sergeant, Lieutenant."

"Fine, but what the hell am I supposed to do now buddy?" Walker grumbled angrily at him.

The Seaman looked at the door and then shrugged as he replied. "Beats the hell out of me sir. I guess you're supposed to bang on the hatch like we usually do, whenever we're ordered to report to one of the Officers of the ship, sir. Lieutenant Walker Sir, all water tight doors are ordered to be dogged down at all times when not in use, and that order includes all water tight wardroom doors at well, Lieutenant Walker Sir."

"Got'cha pal." He then pounded his palm down on the metal hatchway door. The latches were open and the door swung to the side as he heard the Colonel's voice. "If that's you Walker, you betta get your damn ass in here double quick, mister. You took your ever loving time with getting your ass here mister. I won't forget that next time there's any extra duty to be covered, sir."

He entered the wardroom wearing a fuck you look, followed closely by Ramirez.

Colonel Leadbetter cautiously eyed the two soldiers, looking for any signs of injuries on them as they stood at attention. It was then he noticed Ramirez was bleeding from the shin and he growled at the female soldier. "Shit, you still hurt Sergeant? You're leg's still bleeding."

Colonel Leadbetter hissed, angry his Sergeant did not have the time to be checked out properly by the slack assed Navy medics before he sent for them.

"I didn't think so Colonel Leadbetter Sir, I guess it happened when I tangled with one of those damn knee knockers the Swabbie warned us about on our way here, sir."

"Aw shit yeah... I tangled with one of the damn things myself, the first time I walked through one of the damn hatchways, Sergeant. Here you go Raz, put this on the damn wound will ya." The Colonel said to the Sergeant as he passed her a small band-aid.

The two officers waited for Sergeant Ramirez to lift the leg of her uniform, and then she place the bandage over the small scratch on her leg. When she was done, Colonel Leadbetter pointed towards the pair of metal chairs in the wardroom. Colonel Salsiccia was dressed, and he lifted his bunk and attached it to the side of the wall so there was more room in the tight narrow wardroom they were using for their private sleeping quarters. He sat down on another chair waiting for Colonel Leadbetter to begin his conversation with the young Lieutenant Walker.

He gave a half assed salute before he took his seat, but Colonel Leadbetter snapped hotly at him. "Skip that crap mister. That's only necessary when someone's watching Walker."

Walker sat down and moaned. "I give up Colonel, what the hell 's this shit about sir?"

"My friend, you're not going to believe what I have in store for your ass this time, Lieutenant."

"Another fucking mission already? Christ sake Colonel give me a fucking break will ya sir."

"You only wish it was another fucking mission I'm talking about, mister. It's not that simple this time around I warn you buster. At least on a mission, you'd know who your fucking enemy are out in the field, Lieutenant." Colonel Leadbetter said as he sneered at the Lieutenant.

Chapter Four

**NEW YORK CITY, 3:30 A.M. THURSDAY MORNING,
NOVEMBER 5th, 1998**

A young security guard from the Trump International Tower and Hotel, was meeting with his recent acquaintances, and he was telling them of the encounter that was to be held between some of the largest diamond dealers of the world inside the Trump Tower. The guard informed the group of the millions of dollars worth of diamonds to be inside the room with the dealers, and the lack of security surrounding them. The guard also told the others that the dealers did not want any extra attention drawn to them while trading diamonds, and bartered to set the price of diamonds for the upcoming year. There were seven men in the room with the guard, and they were all listening to every word he spoke, and writing down certain comments he made while talking to them. When the guard finished offering the group what he knew, the others were ready to go into action, but some questions had to be asked and answered by the guard first.

The leader of the group posed the first question to the rather excited young security guard. "Hey pal, how the hell are we going to get inside the building without having to fight our way in the place. If it has such good security surrounding it all the time my friend?"

"That's simple; all you have to do is come to the service area where I'll be working. I'll let you and the others in and get you up to the floor with the diamond dealers by the service elevator. Then, all you have to do is force your way into the apartment and scoop up all the glass and then get out." The guard announced proudly to the obvious leader of the group.

"How many diamond dealers are we going to be covering?" Another member asked.

"There'll probably be fifteen dealers scheduled to be in the room, but I heard a few more might be joining the others before they finish." The guard gave up the information happily.

"Fifteen you say, that means we're going to need at least twice as many helpers as we have. If we're going to make a move on them in this possible heist."

"Hey pal, how come we have to force our way into the room if you're going to be part of this scam, my friend? I thought you guards had the keys for all the rooms in the building, pal."

"That's true but I can't allow you in that easily, or the authorities will know right off that this is an inside job, and I had something to do with it. You have to make it look like a robbery, and you just happened to stumble over this room with the diamonds and dealers in it. Knock me over the head and slap me around a bit, and then take my keys and use my pass key to work the service elevator. I want you to kick me around and make it look like I tried to resist your attack against the building. I get extra pay for an encounter with any robbers. I don't want to be implicated in this robbery in the least. I have worked too many years for the company to be dump, and lose all my benefits that I have saved up."

"How much are you planning to get out of this robbery, if you're not going to be an active partner in this robbery?" A forth member asked the guard. No one used their names during the conversation, because they did not want the guard to know who he was dealing with yet. That way he would not be a threat against them if the police happened to arrest him after the robbery.

"An even split along with the rest of you." The security guard replied confidently.

"That's some shit there pal. We take all the risks while you step in and get as much we do."

"Why not? I'm holding up my end of the bargain with you guys. Without me you wouldn't even know anything about this deal in the first plac..."

"How much are we talking about being inside the building?" the third member asked.

"Nearly three quarter of a billion dollars of unset diamonds will be inside the room by the time you're ready to hit it I was informed in advance. I'll make certain the diamond dealers are inside the room before you hit in force." The guard for the Tower offered to his new found friends.

"Three quarter of a billion you say huh? Then we could dump the crap on the closed marked for half its worth without anyone detecting the deal. This thing's looking better to me all the time." A fourth man bitch with a grin, but a look from the leader quieted the excited one down.

"What else are you bringing to us that'll warrant you getting an equal share of the take along with the rest of us?" the one that the guard took to be the leader of the group, asked him.

"That's easy because I'll be giving you a very detailed map of the entire interior of the Trump Tower, marking out all the staircases, elevators, along with the special secret passageways commonly used by the ones who live inside the building. Simple."

"What do you mean by that? I thought the people only rented rooms in the place. Some of these people actually own the room inside the Trump Tower?" the leader of the would be robbers wanting to make certain he understood the security guard correctly.

"Yeah, the owners of the building actually sell some of the rooms for ridiculously and highly inflated prices to only the very rich of the City. Some of the rooms can go for up to like eight million dollars apiece for just a five bedroom, six bathroom suite inside the Trump Tower. The owners of these overly expensive rooms also have to pay over one hundred thousand dollars a year, just for the upkeep on the rooms on top of that. Then you have to add the taxes and other crap they still have to pay just to be able to say they live in the Trump Tower."

"So you want us to enter the building like we're a bunch of thieves just robbing the place, and we just kind of happened across the group of Jews with all the ice hidden in the room?" the leader asked the guard with a snap in his tone.

"Yes. That seems like the easiest thing to do in the heist." The security guard added.

"If that's it man then I want a lot more information than this little bit you offered me, if you want a full share of the take that is, my new friend. Can you get me the blueprints to the building, so I can study the full layout of the place before I make any decisions about this heist?"

"Yes, there's a layout of the entire place that's stored inside the security headquarters of the Tower. If someone makes a complaint, we have to know where that area is, so we can respond to the complaint properly. It's also used for fire purposes as well, and the prints are made available to the local police during all times of emergency." The guard reported to the leader of the group.

"Great, I want those blueprints in my hand before we even entertain going after the building. I want a complete list of all the apartments owned by the people living in the place, and who they are and what their net worth is, if you can get this information for me, my friend. See if you can figure out if any of them are loaded, and what they might have stashed inside their apartments, that would make it worth our attempt on the Trump Tower. I want to know if it'd be worth our time to tumble these apartments while we're going after the diamond dealers in the building at the same time." The leader snapped hotly at the security guard as he glared at him.

"I should have no problem with gathering this information for you. I know there's an itemized list of all valuables for each apartment we control, for insurance and police purposes at the security center. We have some stuff packed away on video tape for easy identification and..."

"Good, I want those tapes as well my friend." The leader interrupted the guard again.

"I can't take the originals from the room, I'll have to make copies of them, and then give you the copies." The guard cried as he looked at the leader with concern.

"I don't give a shit what you have to do to get them for me, I want them!"

"No problem, I guess. Oh, by the way something else to worry about. The room the diamond dealers are using for their meeting. It's built like a bank vault, when you try to get through the door, it'll stop you for several minutes. During that time, the dealers will have the opportunity to place the diamonds in seven different safes well hidden throughout the suite..."

"Are you telling me I'll need some heavy equipment to get through the damn door, friend? That's going to change things quite a bit for us. What about the safes? What kind of safes are they, and am I going to be able to break into them easy enough? You also have to find out where they are hidden inside the room we'll hit?" The leader glared at the guard from the Trump Tower.

"That's the way it has been set up by the original builders of the Tower. I believe you'll need something to help you get through the doors. Once inside the room, you can beat the dealers until they tell you the combination to the safes. I can get you the location of some of the safes, so that way they won't give you a lie about them. They're a sneaky bunch, and they might place the bulk of the diamonds in one or two safes, and hold their location from you. I'll make sure you have the position of each one of the safes clearly marked out in the apartment."

"You better get everything I need from you my friend. I'll have to pull in some more people so I can get inside this apartment. I want a full list of everyone who'll be inside the rooms when we hit the place, if we're going to hit the Tower that is. This thing's getting bigger than I had originally expected, my friend. I'm warning you, what you're telling me better be there, or I'll burn you. Okay, you know what I want, so get the stuff or it's no deal, friend." The leader waited for the dismissed security guard to leave. He was followed to the door by the second member.

Once the guard was out of the room, the second man took his seat, and asked the leader of the group. "What the hell are we going to do about this ass who wants to be part of the action? Yet, he doesn't want to take any of the risks that come with a full share from the take, Michael."

Michael Van Kirk stared at his second in command before responding to Richard Valentine's question. "That's really simply my friend, we'll just kill him! Once he lets us inside the place and gives us the keys we'll need, you'll simply put a bullet in his head and that will be that I guess. This should clear him of any of the blame of the robbery he's so fucking worried about, and it'll also cut him out of the picture at the same time for us." Van Kirk sneered at the others.

"Great, if you didn't order this I was going to suggest it to the rest of the group. He's a nothing who's trying to make it in the big time, while taking none of the risks that goes along with the effort. Michael, you seem like you already have a plan in mind about this supposed heist we're just starting to talk about? Do you mind sharing it with the rest of us, Mike."

Everyone from the group leaned forward, aiming their full attention towards the chosen leader of the group. This group concentrated on only high priced, easy to do white collar crimes in the big city where the return was great, and the risk even greater.

The leader stared into the cold, steel blue eyes of the beautiful Elizabeth Moulton, the only female member in the group. She was ruthless and cold blooded. Lizzie was so named because she could do with her legs, what Lizzie Borden done with her ax to her parents. She would gain access to any targets using her exquisite body. She was a rather tall woman of six foot, and she was thin and lanky with a good size bust, narrow waist and hips, and strong legs which she used very effectively as a weapon when needed. She also knew martial arts very well. Many times in her past, the men would stand by and watch her skillfully take apart an adversary with her outstanding fighting skills and ability. The leader of the group even witnessed her actually kill two men in separate hand to hand fights in one day a short while back.

"Yes Richard, I do have a plan in mind at that." He replied, not taking his eyes off Lizzie as he added to what he was intending to do about their attack on the Trump Tower. "We'll call in Alexander and the rest of his people, and let him set them in the Tower once we're in it. He has a good military mind, and the people needed to make our plan work out very well for ourselves."

"He's also crazy as hell Mike, and all he knows are weapons and killing anyone he doesn't like, or who gets in his way. The man believes in the old Russian doctrine of attacking in sheer force. The last time we used him and any of his people, he nearly brought the entire building down on our heads once if you. He's outright nuts and I really hate like hell working with him and any of his other people with him, Michael." The number two man complained as he shifted his weight in his chair over the thought of working with the Russian military type again.

"I agree with Richard, Mike. Why do we have to use him in this heist?" Lizzie added.

"We'll use him because we need him and that's that. We'll do most of the work, and we'll use his people to afford us the cover we'll need to carry out the rest of our plan inside the building. We'll hit the Tower as a pack of terrorists, take hostages and act like nuts while ransacking the entire building, and we'll take only the most expensive items and cash and leavin..."

"How will we get out of the Tower when we're done with our act, Michael?" Lizzie asked.

"That's why I want the blueprints for the building. To be honest with you Lizzie, I don't have all the details worked out just yet. But I do have a pretty good idea of what they'll entail and how to carry them out. Trust me, everything will work out just fine for us, and the seven of us will be wealthy beyond our wildest dreams evidently. If what this damn security guard says is true."

"What about Alexander and the rest of his pack of madmen you want to employ in our attack on the building, Michael? How are we going to end up so wealthy when we have to share the take with him and the rest of his people?" John Lavarack, the seventh man of the group asked.

"Who said we're going to share anything with him or his people? All I remember saying was we're pulling in Alexander and a number of his people. I don't remember saying anything about sharing, or getting him or any of his people out of the building." The leader allowed his face to turn into an ugly sneer and then he added. "What do you think of the plan so far my friends?"

"I like the sounds of this heist as it's shaping up, Michael! But what about the hostages we'll end up with in the building? Who will they be? How many of the hostages do you want to take and keep? How will we use them to make our escape from the building, Mike? The cops are good, and we'll be dealing with them in droves over this heist. They have those special hostage rescue and SWAT teams. If we go up against the Trump Tower, we'll be dealing with the entire NYPD, and who knows what else they might throw at us while they're at it, Mike. They'll get at us from the air, and from the surrounding buildings, and even from the rooftop of the Trump Tower itself I believe." Lizzie complained as she stood to stretch her cramped up legs.

The action of stretching her legs and the placing of her arms well over her head for a moment was enjoyed by the others of the group as he explained more of his plan to the rest of the group. Lizzie never wore a bra, and she was dressed in a tight fitting silk shirt. Her stretch enabled her breasts to easily be seen right through the thin fine almost sheer fabric.

"The hostages will be the pick of the litter, knowing who visits the Tower, and who lives there, adds to our picks. When we have the most important people as hostages, no cops will dare try and attack us. The hostages will afford us the time we need to ransack the penthouse apartments, open the safes and get the diamonds. We'll use the hostages as human shields if needed. Once we make our escape from the Trump Tower, the hostages will be killed. I don't care if we have the President of the United States as hostage, we'll kill them and then disappear for a few weeks before leaving the country. The way I feel, it'll be the last heist we ever do. I'm looking forward to being rich and living somewhere in South America for the rest of my life. If we play our cards right, the cops will never even know who we are or where we came from. That's why I want to use Alexander and his group of troublemakers. By the time Alexander is finished with the building and cops, not much of either will still remain in one piece."

"I see there's a reason behind your madness here, Michael. I'll repeat what I just said to you, I like your plan as you stated it to us. But I do have one question for you to answer for me, and then I'll remain quiet." She replied to the leader as she flashed a smile.

"What's that question Lizzie?" the leader of the group asked.

"Michael, how are we going to act once we're inside the Tower with the hostages?"

"What do you mean Lizzie?" he snapped at her, getting a little angry over her question.

"You said we're going to act like a bunch of terrorists attacking the building. What type of terrorists were you thinking about acting like?"

"I don't know, maybe a mixed bag of tricks this time. Some of us can act like Arabs; they seem to be getting all the blame for everything that's going wrong in the world lately. Some of us can even act like Cubans I guess, while others will act like the Russians they are. It doesn't matter how you act once we're inside the building. All I want you to remember, is no matter how we act, we have to be absolutely ruthless about ourselves and actions. We're going in like a pack of murderers, and we have to display that feeling to the hostages right off. If we plan to control them and the cops outside." The leader of the group menacingly warned the rest of them.

All the members of the group nodded in agreement to Michael's words.

WASHINGTON DC. 11:30 A.M. FRIDAY, NOVEMBER 13th, 1998.
THE PRIVATE LIVING QUARTERS OF THE VICE PRESIDENT

Vice President Mary Hirshfield just finished packing for her upcoming visit to New York City. For the past three weeks she was looking forward to nothing else but visiting the Big Apple and her baby sister, and this placed her in a great mood all week. It was two years since she last saw her sister, and there was plenty of shopping she had to catch up on as well. This was the first vacation she allowed herself, since first becoming the Vice President of the United States.

Her young female aide entered the room and Mary pointed to the suitcases lying on her bed.

"Very well Ma'am, I'll have them moved out to the car for you, Ma'am. Will the Vice President be reporting to the White House before leaving for New York City, Ma'am?"

Vice President Hirshfield took a second to think about it, and then she replied brusquely to her aide and also female bodyguard. "Naw, Albert knows I'm leaving today. If he wanted to speak with me before I left, he would've sent word to me by now. He has enough on his mind, without my distracting him any more than is absolutely necessary. I wonder how the meeting the other day at the Pentagon went for him." She asked absentmindedly of her aide.

"Forgive me Ma'am, but I know the President's at the White House, and the scuttlebutt around Ma'am, states he's in one of his not so pleasant moods..."

"Already back from the Pentagon you say, Cathy?" Ms. Hirshfield asked, concerned the meeting turned out to be a disaster for her boss and the others attending it.

"No Ma'am, I believe the President was placed in a foul mood, because of the terrible traffic he was caught in while returning to the White House, Ma'am."

"Whoa, ho, ho then for certain I don't have any intention of disturbing him if he's in that bad a mood because of the Washington traffic, young lady. You better get my bags out to the car then, my flight leaves in under forty minutes, Cathy dear."

"Will you be taking the full detachment of guards to New York City with you, Ma'am?" Cathy asked as she hoisted the two bags from the bed and then rested them on the floor.

"I'm tired of having so many men hanging around me all the time. I have five Agents reporting for duty. For once in my life I'd like to enjoy the luxury of stepping out of the shower, and roaming around the room naked for a change. I never thought being the Vice President would stop me from enjoying myself so much. I can't go out on a damn date without tripping all over them. It's driving me nuts trying to have a social life with them hanging around me all the time. Huh, my sex life is almost nonexistent, and it's showing no signs of getting any better for me in the near future either, Cathy." The Vice President complained as she folded a sweater.

"Err... if you want you can always use my apartment for a little tête-à-tête if you like, Mary. I can discretely arrange for anyone to come to my apartment for you, Ma'am. I'll have a great meal prepared and a bottle of wine chilling. No one will ever know about it, and I can work it out so only a few Agents will be involved, and none of them will be allowed inside the apartment to bother you. We can use the female Agents if they insist on someone being inside the apartment. I have a room where they can stay where they'll be well out of sight and mind, Mary."

"You'll do that for me Cathy?" Ms. Hirshfield replied while pointing at herself with a finger.

"I would Ma'am, we women have to stick together, and we have to break apart this lousy man's world while we're at it, Mary. Err... I know how I get when I haven't been with a man for a few days, Ma'am. I couldn't consider being without one of them pains in the ass for months..."

"Try a couple years my dear." Ms. Hirshfield replied meekly, thoroughly embarrassed.

"Oh sweet Jesus, a couple years? You haven't been with a man for over a year, Ma'am."

Mary shrugged at her concerned bodyguard, and sort of smirked at her aide at the same time.

"Oh boy then we have to do something about this situation in a fast hurry it up Ma'am." Cathy announced as her face blushed and she smiled at the Vice President.

"Hmmm... maybe when I get back from New York City, I just might take you up on that kind offer you just made to me, Cathy. Like you said, we women have to stick together."

"Do you have anyone in mind that you might have aimed your eyes on, Ma'am?" Cathy asked the Vice President of the United States as she shyly smiled at her.

"Edward Sweeney." Ms. Hirshfield replied just as shyly, feeling a bit like a school girl.

"You mean that nice young man from your Agent staff, Mary?" Cathy asked, surprised at her pick as she put her hands up to her face to hide her slight giggle from Mary's view.

"Did you ever notice his nice, tight buns Cathy? Oh God, every time he bends over, it makes me want to reach out and squeeze those little babies on him I tell you. To tell you the truth, I'm beginning to run out of excuses to make the poor man bend over all the time. The last time I dropped my pencil, I had all I could do to stop Frank from getting it for me, so Sweeney would bend over again." Mary Hirschfield said while she giggled along with her aide.

"Oh God, I couldn't imagine Frank bending over for any reason and enjoying it, Ma'am. If he ever did, someone would want to use his can for a billboard message, Ma'am. Mary, I was kind of keeping my eye on Edward myself lately, his buns make me swoon also. But I believe I'm one up on you though Ma'am. I once watched him coming from the shower over at the gym, Ma'am. God, he's so damn ripped..."

"The hell with his muscles, I'm only interested in one of his muscles that I want to enjoy." Ms. Hirshfield retorted with a wide grin, getting caught up in the heat of the conversation now.

"Oh, believe me Ma'am, it's there and it was wonderful at that, Ma'am." She remarked as she stared at the pretty female Vice President.

"Now you really have me going here I fear, Cathy dear. When I get back to Washington, I think I'm going to ask you for some help to jump start my love life running for me again, my dear. Do you think you can have everything arranged for me, err... let's say for maybe Sunday night at around seven I guess. I should be well rested by that time I believe, Cathy. I know the President's planning to meet with some of the more friendly Diplomats from the United Nations later on Saturday morning, and he wants me to attend the more important meetings with him. But they're scheduled to end by noon or a little after, well before one I believe, and then I plan to return to Washington later on the same day if I can get away that is, Cathy. I'll spend the rest of Saturday resting up, and then on Sunday I'll get everything ready for my err… little meeting with Edward, with your help of course my dear."

"Do you think there might be some interest from him for you, Mary? Has he ever made you feel like he was interested in you, Ma'am? Did he ever dare to make a pass, or anything like that at you, Ma'am? I really don't believe there is a romantic bone in his body, because every time I'm around him, he's always so stiff, so perfect." She dared to cautiously ask the Vice President.

"Oh boy is he interested in me Cathy. Let me tell you, I stepped out of the shower one day real accidentally like." Mary winked at Cathy and then she added to her story. "Leaving the bathroom door open just enough mind you, and I made certain the fool saw me in all my glory and boy did I enjoy his reaction, dear. Yes, he's definitely interested I can tell you alright Cathy."

The two young women shared another laugh at the unsuspecting Edward's expense, as Cathy left the Vice President's room with the luggage, and the Vice President went back to finishing her packing for her trip up to New York City.

THE AIRCRAFT CARRIER USS GEORGE WASHINGTON, ONCE STATIONED IN THE RED SEA, NOW STEAMING FOR THE SUEZ CANAL

Lieutenant Robert Walker and Sergeant Dorothy Ramirez listened carefully to Colonel Bruce Leadbetter as he quickly explained why the two soldiers were sent for, and where they would be going. The Colonel showered them with a flood of warnings on how to behave while in New York. They both laughed over the numerous threats, and how to address the Ambassadors and President when speaking to them. When Colonel Leadbetter was through, he handed the two young warriors the cash vouchers for a thousand dollars each, to be handed to the Carrier's paymaster. He further ordered them to charge their meals and other expenses to the credit card he just handed them. It was a military issued credit card used mainly by officers and the military VIPs on special duty, and was happily accepted by most stores and eateries spread throughout the United States. It was backed by the United States Treasury, which made it better than cash.

He took the credit card and then handed it right over to Ramirez for safekeeping.

"That won't be necessary Walker." Colonel Leadbetter handed a second credit card to Sergeant Ramirez as he told them both. "You two birds have carte blanche for eating and personal needs, and that's it dammit. I don't need to warn you two turds any foolish expenses will be your own responsibility on these orders. All your bills will be gone over with a fine tooth comb, and any bills deemed a waste or not authorized, with be sent back to you for payment."

"Such as what Colonel Leadbetter Sir? I need to know this so I know what I can charge to the damn card, sir." He grunted as he placed the special plastic card into his wallet.

"Such as any of them damn sex shows in the City, any prostitutes, cars, like buying one for yourself, or purchases bought on the taxpayers money that wasn't absolutely necessary for survival while you two are in New York, mister. The taxpayers treat us well, but don't try to overdo it, or you'll have me to answer to. Now get out of my fucking office so I can accomplish something today." Colonel Leadbetter picked up a pencil and began to thumb through a stack of papers lying on his desk. He stopped and then glared at Walker and barked. "What?"

"Colonel Leadbetter Sir, are you sure you got the right people for this fucking mess, sir? You know I was bred for killing, not sucking up to some soft bellied sonofabitchs, who makes the decisions to send in us kids out to carry off their stupid fucking ideas, Colonel. I'm a soldier, not some damn politician, Colonel Leadbetter Sir." The concerned Lieutenant offered, both confused and angry as to why he was being picked for such a shit filled mission.

"Whatsumatter with you mister. You don't like hobnobbing with the higher ups of this stinking world, Walker?" the smirking Colonel grumbled at the young warrior.

"Colonel Leadbetter Sir, I'd much rather be smacked right square in the stinking nuts with a fucking baseball bat, than to be forced to deal with any of these stinking stuffed shirts from the United Nations, sir." Walker moaned as he put a frown on his face.

"And, that's exactly what will happen to your ass if you fuck up on these damn orders, mister. I'll slam you right in the nuts with a baseball bat if you embarrass me on this order. Arrr… I guess I'd also rather take one in the damn nuts than be forced to deal with these fucks, mister. But you and the Sergeant's stuck with the fucking orders Lieutenant, and to answer your other question for you at the same time buster. Yeah, you're the right pick for this damn mission sir. There's no way out for you this time around buster, so put a damn lid on it and be ready to shove off at exactly Oh, Three Hundred Hours. The General's sending out a special jet for you two shitbirds. Remember Lieutenant Walker, this is not a military mission, so there're to be no uniforms worn by you two birds while in New York City. Civilian clothes are the word for the day. Now get the hell out of my office, so I can do something done around here, dammit!

"By the way Walker, take a shower and brush your damn teeth and do something about your damn BO while you're at it will ya. You should see a Doctor about that shit. I don't think a healthy man's supposed to stink like you do, buster. Lieutenant, you better remember who the hell you'll be dealing with in New York City, and I don't want anyone offended by your damn stink." Colonel Leadbetter stopped complaining and then stared at Walker as he added. "And get a damn haircut also. You look like a wild man with that damn mop of yours buster. I've been meaning to discuss your hair with you soldier. You're a fucking soldier, not some damn beatnik who's sliming his worthless way through life; you're hair's too fucking long mister."

"Yeah yeah, and my dick's too short, and leave time is never long enough for my ass either, Colonel Leadbetter Sir." Lieutenant Walker shot back sarcastically at his Commanding Officer as he turned to leave the Colonel's wardroom.

"Bitch, bitch, bitch. All the time bitching, Grunt. If you don't get yourself a fucking hair cut, I'm gonna buy you a pair of tits to go along with your damn long hair, mister." Colonel Leadbetter growled as he threw his pencil at Walker, striking him in the middle of his back as he offered. "Remember to mind your fucking Ps and Qs while in the Big Apple mister, or you'll wish your papa never porked your mama by the time I'm through with your damn asses if I get a shit report on you two turds. Sergeant Ramirez, it's your responsibility to keep a leash on this damn soldier of yours to keep his stinking ass out of any trouble on these orders, dammit."

"Yeah Colonel, talk about bitching all the time, huh Homes." He bitched at the Colonel.

"And get a fucking haircut while you're at it before you shove off for New York fucking City mister!" Colonel Leadbetter added as he turned to Colonel Salsiccia, only to find the military officer staring with a wide, shit eating grin plastered on his Italian face.

"What the fuck's up your damn ass now, mister? You look like the damn cat that swallowed the stinking bird. I could've used some of your help with that one you know. Why did you just sit back and allow him to drive me fucking nuts like he was doing, Colonel? Some fricking help you were. That sonofabitch is never at a loss for words, and he drives me crazy all the damn time."

"Huh Colonel, I wasn't going to touch that conversation with a ten foot pole. I have to hand it to you Bruce. When you told me this conversation was going to be worth my staying awake for, you weren't kidding me sir. You sure the President knows what he's doing, bringing that one to the U.N.? I don't think the Ambassador's are ready for him." Salsiccia stood and stretched.

"I don't think the world's ready for that one, but they're about to be introduced a fast fucking hurry to the sonofabitch. Christ sake Colonel, I'd give a week's pay, to see their damn faces when Lieutenant Walker gets going on them. Talk about wishing your papa never porked your mama."

Both Walker and Ramirez headed right for the paymaster of the Carrier. They were being lead there by the Seaman who was waiting outside the Colonel's room until they were done with their conversation. After filing out the paperwork, they each left with a fist full of cash in their hands. They allowed Seaman Girgenti to lead them back to the troop's sleeping quarters and as they entered the area. The soldiers immediately surrounded the two to find out what the visit to Colonel Leadbetter was all about. The Seaman left without saying a word any of the soldiers.

"What's the Colonel gonna do with ya ass, man? Stand you before the wall and take a coupla pot shots at ya, Walker?" Buckethead asked as he went to Walker's side and grinned at him.

"Gather round me boys and girls, because I'm not gonna repeat this shit for a second time to you turds. If you slobs snooze, you lose. You guys aren't gonna fucking believe this shit for one stinking second, but it seems the friggin Pres wants, no, check that shit, he needs my help."

"Whoa man, you gotta be shitting us, Homes. Since when do the hot shots back in Washington need the help from us stinking peon's types over here, man? Those shits can buy and sell anything they want with the damn taxpayer's money." McNip called out from the group.

"Beats the shit outta my ass man, alls I know is me and Raz are gonna be leaving tomorrow for New York fucking City at Oh, Three Hundred Hours, heading for Mackintoshville, and a special meeting of the United Nations with the Pres himself, people. If you think I'm shitting ya, cast your evil eyes on this stack of shit." He held out the bills he just received from the paymaster.

"Holy shit man, Walker musta robbed a fucking bank along the way to the Colonel's quarters. Look at that stack of damn cabbage." Neck griped as he tried to snatch some cash from Walker.

"Hey man, come to think bout it, when the hell are we gonna get fucking paid around here? I heard some bullshit that we're gonna get some leave time when we get to wherever the hell this stinking tub's taking us to. There's some bitches out there somewhere just waiting to have some fun and games with my black ass, and they can take a ride on space mountain at the same time man." Dock Rat called out as he grabbed his crotch and then shook his dick through his pants.

He ignored Dock Rat's bragging as he pushed a few of the guys out of his way, and then he headed for his rack as he replied to the concerned looking group of elite soldiers. "I don't know what this shit's all about yet, but Colonel Leadbetter gave me the fucking word I hafta stand on my stinking tongue while in New York or he's gonna do it for me."

"I bet he will at that Homes. That fuck will hurt you anyway he can, man." Mother Flanagan offered as he took a joint and lit it, and then he passed it around the group of elite soldiers.

"Yeah, I got the stinking word to watch myself over there all the while I gotta be with these damn stuff shirts." He added as he took the cooking joint and took a good pull from it.

"I can't believe you're gonna give these hot shots a stinking break at the damn meeting, Walker? That seems like it goes against your fucking grain a little there and it's sure not like you, Homes?" McNip remarked as he took the joint from Walker and took a hit from it.

Walker smiled at McNip as he smirked at him. "Don't be such a fucking asshole, man. You know me much betta than that. I plan to take full advantage of these stinking asses now I'm gonna get a chance to get at them. I'm gonna get a shitload of stuff offa my damn chest. By the time I finish with them fools, they're gonna be scratching their heads saying, 'What did he say'?"

"That's a lot betta there Home Boy. I didn't think you were gonna allow them big shots to keep your spirit in check on you man. For fuck sake, I wish I was going with ya. I have a load of shit I'd like to get offa my chest. What a stinking place to dump on the pencil neck geeks, the United Nations. You're luckier than a turd floating on saltwater, Homes." Buckethead replied as he stared at the Lieutenant packing what he thought he would need to take with him.

The Lieutenant turned to the big man and shook his head because he was unable to figure out what Buckethead meant by a turd floating on saltwater remark. He took a quick glance over at Sergeant Ramirez and then smiled, because he noticed a number of the women warriors from their Unit were helping her pack up the stuff she would need in new York. Some of the women gave her money to buy them some stuff from New York, while others gave her perfume and lipstick and other crap like that to use for her trip. Road Kill watched her and the girls, he had to admit the three female Russian fighters were a good addition to the elite group of soldiers, and they had earned the respect of the other troops. He felt real bad it took him so long to trust the three female

Russian fighters. He shrugged while in thought about the reason. Just about every action the group was involved in lately, was created because of damn Russians.

The young Lieutenant did not care a bit about the political end of his work. He always said he was a soldier and enjoyed accepting this as fact, but he found himself mired in the middle of what he did not care for. He gave a last look at the three Russian women hovering over Ramirez as if she was a queen bee, and then he went back to packing up his own stuff.

The soldiers relentlessly hounded him with a flood of questions about what he was going to do while they were visiting New York City, but the Lieutenant completely ignored most of their questions. By the time he finished packing, the other troops grew bored with questions going unanswered, and they drifted away from him, and then went about their own business. Jokes and bantering replaced the questions. Pillows flew as the guys picked on the women of their group. They were working off the adrenaline still coursing through their veins from the Iran action.

The Lieutenant, as well as the other soldiers knew the first time they allowed themselves to rest; they were going to sleep for a week. A few of the beat up soldiers gave in to their needs and exhaustion, and were asleep. They had no idea nor did they care what was going on around them.

When he was done packing, he looked for the Mutt who was always usually standing by his side and making a constant pest of himself. His heart broke when he picked up the Mutt still lying in the rack in the same exact position he had been in ever since they were given the quarters on the Carrier. He shook his head sadly as he saw the Mutt's staring but non-seeing eyes. The Lieutenant did not know what to do for his closest friend, but he closed his case and decided to try and get the Mutt out of his doldrums. He shoved the soldier branded the Neck out of his way to get around the large soldier. It was then he realized Sergeant Raphael had moved her stuff over to the bunk right next to the Mutt, and she was trying to speak to him. She sat down on the edge of her bunk while leaning over the Mutt ignoring her.

As he neared the Mutt's bunk, the beautiful French Sergeant saw him coming, and she stood but was immediately waved back to her bunk by Walker. He punched the Mutt in the armor plated arm as he griped at the soldier. "Hey dude, didn't you hear me when I told everyone to get outta their damn body armor before getting on the stinking racks. Besides man, you must be dying of the heat in that crap. C'mon friend, get up and I'll help you outta it and then you can take a shower. You'll feel a helluva lot betta once you showered and had something to eat. The food on this tub's pretty good, man. Plenty of steak and potatoes and shit like that Homes."

The Mutt barely moved, but his eyes drifted towards Walker's face for a brief moment. But he never said a word or reacted to any of his words.

The Lieutenant glanced at the Frenchie who shrugged and said. "That's more than I was able to get out of him. He didn't even react when I called him White Chocolate, sir."

He nodded as he turned back to his friend and added. "C'mon pal, this ain't doing you any fucking good you know, man. You gotta eat something, get out of that fucking carp and talk to me or anyone buddy. C'mon man." He shoved the Mutt for a second time.

"Leave me the fuck alone before I break your fucking arm, sucka. I don't wanna speak to anyone, everybody can go to hell as far as I'm concerned, dammit." The Mutt hissed nastily.

"C'mon man, when did you ever know me to leave you the fuck alone? C'mon pal and get out of that crap and head for the damn showers. You wanna talk, I'm here for ya man."

"Talk about fucking what!" the Mutt snapped as nasty as his other words at him. "What the fuck's left to talk about man? Barb is fucking dead, she left me alone, man."

"I know this shit hurts like hell, it hurts all of us as well man. But you hafta remember Fun Bags was a soldier, and she understood one day she could wake up dead. It's all part of the suck ass job we got ourselves involved in, buddy." The worried Lieutenant had to bite his lip when he realized what he just said to his best friend.

The Mutt turned until his eyes locked on Walker's and he snarled at the Lieutenant. "Yeah, a fucking soldier alright. If only she could wake up fucking dead. At least I'd still have her. Aw... what the fuck am I talking about for crap sake, she's dead and nothing's gonna bring her back in this fucking world or the next to me, dammit."

He moved his leg up against the Mutt's shoulder, and he used it to shove him as he grumbled at the soldier again. "C'mon buddy, you're not alone you know, everyone on board this damn bird's nest is suffering along with ya, man. Hey, I gotta go and I'm not gonna leave your stinking ass until I know for certain your stinking head's screwed on right again."

"Going? Where the fuck are you going on me Homes? You're not leaving me like Barb did, are you buddy?" the Mutt growled as he glared at Walker while waiting for him to reply.

"Well my crazy ass friend, if your head wasn't in outer fucking space somewhere, you woulda heard me and Raz are going to New York fucking City to address the damn United Nations assholes along with the President of the United States, man." He boasted to his friend, but it was wasted because his words drew no further reaction from the terribly suffering Mutt.

"You're not leaving the Unit for good are ya man?" the Mutt protested as he turned and got up on his elbow, and he stared at him. His face showing fear at losing another friend.

He rested his hand lightly on the Mutt's head as he offered him barely over a whisper. "Naw buddy, you're not gonna get rid of my stinking ass that fucking easy, man. I should be gone a week at the most; the damn meeting's supposed to go off sometime on Friday morning so I'm told, buddy. Then I'm coming back to the rest of you damn slugs to keep the lot of ya outta any stinking trouble. C'mon buddy, get up and I'll help you get outta that fucking body protection crap." The Lieutenant grabbed his hair and pull the Mutt up by it.

The Mutt followed the pressure he was putting on his body, he felt better after speaking with the Lieutenant. Once he was on his feet, he unlatched the lock down clips on the shoulder pads of his still filthy body armor. His actions was stopped by Raphael who put her hand on his and she said to the Lieutenant. "Walker, I'll be pleased to handle that for you if you don't mind, sir. Leave White Chocolate in my hands, and I'll take good care of him while you're away from us sir. I'll do this and I'll return him in better shape than he's in, Lieutenant. Please sir."

He bowed slightly to the beautiful young female French fighter, and then he gave way as she started to work on the Mutt's armor.

The Mutt leaned closer to Raphael and complained barely over a whisper at her. "Hey bitch, how many fucking times do I gotta tell ya stinking ass my fucking name's the Mutt. Stick this White Chocolate shit up your purdy little ass. I'm not gonna tell ya again bitch."

"What are you going to do to me if I keep calling you White Chocolate, sweetie?" Raphael retorted sexily as she continued to work the latches free on the rest of his armor.

"Keep calling me White Chocolate, and I'm gonna stick my black dick down your fucking throat on ya until you remember my stinking name right." The Mutt warned her angrily.

"Go ahead." Blind Date replied, opening her mouth and running her tongue over her lips.

"Keep it up bitch, and you're gonna find out what I'm saying is true to your stinking little ass, baby. You're now one of us and you betta respect me, or I'm gonna make you pay big time for your stinking mistakes, bitch. I'm not the one to go fucking round with my feelings you know." The Mutt warned the beautiful French warrior as he allowed himself to be shoved back on the bunk by her. The female soldier branded Blind Date smiled as she worked on the armor shin and thigh guard, after she removed the loin plating that covered between the Mutt's legs.

Walker saw Lieutenant Hall was in good hands and he left him to Raphael's care. He turned and headed back for his rack. He stopped moving when he realized the entire Unit was standing behind him, and they were all watching him and the Mutt speaking together. He smiled and said to the concerned soldiers. "I believe we just got the dog man back on our fucking turf, people."

Many of the worried soldiers slapped the air with their fists. The mood improved dramatically as the bantering resumed in the living quarters of the elite soldiers. Ramirez finished packing and she was waiting for Walker to come over to her.

"How's the Mutt doing? I'm really worried about him you know Bobby."

"You and me both baby girl, but I think he's gonna be just fine in a coupla days at the most, baby. I believe he's in good hands right now little sister." He said as he glanced over his shoulder and then smiled when he saw a naked Mutt showing no interest while being led by Raphael, who was undressing as they continued towards the showers. The other soldiers gave them both room to get by them. Even the soldiers in the head already showering or taking a dump, left the area when the two entered the head area.

"Yeah Raz, I believe the stinking Mutt's gonna be just fine, take a look at the lousy puke will ya. I never saw him so damn happy to be with someone ever since he first linked up with Barbara." He announced as he smiled at Ramirez a second time.

Sergeant Ramirez looked over his shoulder, and when she picked up the Mutt and Blind Date entering the shower area. She was happy he was showing some signs of life coming back to his battered body as she smiled at the two soldiers entering the shower area.

Some of the specialized soldiers gathered around Walker's bunk, taking note the Mutt was up and moving around for the first time since he entered the quarters. They suggested a celebration in his honor. Others wanted to have a sex party with the women of the Unit like old times, before there was another death of one of the female soldiers in the elite group.

He allowed the soldiers to talk and get excited, and then he interrupted them. "Okay, here's what we're gonna do. First things first you guys. We're gonna get something to fucking eat. Then we're gonna catch up on some of our rest. Then, if you people are still able to, I'll see if any of the girls are ready to take some of us on for some fun and games. We'll instigate another Fun Night, if everyone agrees to it that is." Walker grinned at the staring faces staring at him.

Fun Night was a claim of the Sergeants of the elite group, where they would indulge in sex with the female members of the specialized soldiers. The women took on as many as three and four men at a time during party time. The soldiers slapped each other on the backs in anticipation of the fun and games about to take place on board the

Carrier, when they returned from the mess. The women soldiers were just as equally as excited about the party as the men were. They were going to get some attention paid to them from the males of the group.

Chapter Five

SHOWERS, 'C' DECK, ON BOARD THE CARRIER,
USS GEORGE WASHINGTON

Sergeant Regina Raphael carefully guided the Mutt over to the shower, taking special notice of the many nicks and bruises covering his rock hard body, he received in the action in Iran. Blind Date was stunned as she deposited the Mutt up against the metal wall of the shower, and then she turned on the hot water. She adjusted the water until it was the proper temperature. She then moved the Mutt under the soothing water flow. A soft moan escaped from the Mutt as he enjoyed the soothing warm water washing over his exhausted and hurting body.

Those in control of the water on board the Carrier, were kind to the new arrivals on the ship. Usually, the water was cut off in two minutes, so the bather had to soak himself quick and then shut the water then lather up. Then turn the water on to rinse off and hope it would still be there for your use. Sometimes, the bather was left covered with soap and no water to rinse off with. This was known as the waterless GI shower on board the Carrier.

The second the water ran over his head, the Mutt groaned with pleasure as he leaned against the wall and looked into the streaming steam of water. Raphael rubbed some soap all over the Mutt's body, carefully checking the many damaged areas. She made her mind up she was going to force him to go visit the sickbay once they finished showering. She was not sure, but she thought the Mutt might have a broken rib or two. The area around the injury she was concerned about the most, seemed to move wrong under her light pressure while she washed his chest. The Mutt even flinched when she lightly touched the damaged spot.

Once she had the Mutt soaped up, she attacked his body with a face cloth, scrubbing the filth and grime and sweat from his body. When she finished scrubbing him, she moved him under the water until the soap washed from his body, and then she turned him until his back was up against the metal divider. Raphael looked at his eyes, seeing no response in them she slowly slid her exquisite body down his, catching his dick between her breasts and using them on his member. When the Mutt was rock hard she continued to slide down his body until her face was even with his crotch. She played with him with her hands until she knew she was not overstepping her bounds with the soldier. When the Mutt finally responded to her touch, she knew she was in control and she drew him in her mouth. She worked over his shaft with her tongue, teeth and lips. The more the Mutt responded, the faster she increased her tempo on his throbbing shaft.

Regina Raphael was really starting to get into it herself, and the more she got into it, the more the Mutt responded to her manipulations. The Mutt came, shooting over her face and chest, and then he collapsed and used the wall to slide down until he sat on the tiled floor of the shower in a heap. Raphael ended up resting between his legs while still stroking him with her hand, waiting for him to open his eyes and look at her again. The water cleaned her face.

With closed eyes, the Mutt softly called. "Barbara. Where the hell are you girl, god dammit?"

Raphael fought back tears as she took the Mutt's hand in hers and gave it a squeeze.

He opened his eyes and when he saw it was Raphael, she replied. "Barbara's gone."

"I fucking know that!" the Mutt snapped angrily at her and his face contorted into a mask of pain and anger. The water hiding the tears from his eyes. "I loved her you know."

"I know Frank." Raphael replied tenderly as she pulled the Mutt to her, and they silently cried in each other's arms. The Mutt struggled back to his feet and pulled her up. He looked in the water to erase the signs of tears; he pulled her close and gave her a breath robbing hug as he held on her for dead life for several long seconds.

"I really needed that, I needed to feel the warmth of a woman. I'm over her for now, I'll continue to mourn her but in my way, I'm back." The Mutt announced barely above a whisper.

Raphael kissed him, he returned it as eagerly, but when she tried to pull away from his grasp. He stopped her by increasing his pressure as he asked her with concern. "You're not gonna tell the rest of that shit out there know I cried like a fucking baby?"

Raphael struggled from his grasp and slapped him across the face to show she was insulted by the thought she would ever betray the special moment they had just shared together, as she bitched bitterly at him. "What the hell type of person do you think I am mista? I'm honored to share your memory of Barbara with you privately, Frank. That was between us, and no one deserves to know what we did to remember her in here. I'm angry that you would ever think I'd let any of those crude bastards out there know about this. Besides, you cried, and that shows me you're human, and a man. It shows me you're more a man than any of them. If you allow me, I'd be honored to share more memories you have of her. I'll never intrude in her zone, but I hope you'll allow me to share your life a little. I really need someone, I need you, Mutt."

The Mutt stared at the beautiful face. She was a beauty any man would give his left nut to be with. The Lieutenant's mind was confused, and the last thing he needed at the moment was to get involved in another relationship so soon after losing his love of life as he groaned at the female soldier. "You're right, I need someone, but now's not the time for that need to be filled by another. You're pushing too hard right now, give it some time and if it's meant to be, it'll happen soon enuf. C'mon, I don't want them getting the wrong impression."

Raphael allowed herself to be led out of the shower area by the shaking and still upset Mutt. She picked up a towel from a rack and dried herself. But when the Mutt took a towel and tried to dry himself, she pulled it from his hands. She wanted to do it, and she dried his body.

"You're okay for a stinking frog you know, girl." The Mutt smirked with a grin.

It was the wrong time for the Mutt to say such a crude remark to the female French fighter, she was drying him between the legs. She grabbed his balls and gave them a tug and then complained angrily at him. "Frog, I'll show you who's a frog around here, mista. How would you like it if I called you nigger? Oh God... that's a terrible word I just used, I'm so terribly sorry Mutt."

"Hey baby, you can call me anything you want as long as you smile at me baby girl. But you can only call me half a nigger, on my father's side little sister." The Mutt grunted proudly as he took the towel from her and he finished drying himself. Then he looped it over his shoulder and went to move out of the bathroom.

"White Cho... Err... I mean Mutt; I don't want to call you that terrible word ever again in my life. I'm so sorry I ever used it against you, Frank." She moaned as she wrapped the towel around herself, and then she helped the Mutt do the same thing. She was still mumbling at herself over the insult she just fired off at the Mutt when he grumbled at her.

"Fuhgedaboutit will ya baby, it's no big fucking deal sister. I've been called a helluva lot worse than that in my stinking life I assure you, baby."

Together, they came out of the shower with Raphael heading for her rack to change in her uniform. It was no longer the French Regiment Etranger de Parachutistes, the French Foreign Legion Paratrooper's uniform. She now wore the uniform of the MNRRF, with the shoulder patch depicting a shrunken head and snake resting on top of the skull.

It was the sign of the elite Unit of soldiers who had adopted the Head Hunters as their banner.

The Mutt walked over to his rack naked except for the towel looped over his shoulder. The Lieutenant nodded as the Mutt headed back to his bunk. He did not move to allow the Mutt to sit down as he grumbled at him. "How the fuck you doing now dog face?"

"Betta, a whole lot betta now Homes. I think I'm getting over it, it still sucks though."

"Life always sucks the fucking big one Mutt. That's why we gotta take all we can whenever we can get it, my friend. I really hate to say this crap to you man. But Barbara's not the last grunt who's gonna die before our hitch is over with man. I fear we're gonna keep losing some of our people, until everyone can get along with each uther in the stinking world, man."

"Yeah, and that's why I decided to leave this Mickey Mouse outfit fur good. I'm through taking risks, only to lose the only thing I ever loved in life, Walker." The Mutt looped the towel around his waist, and tried to get around Walker, who was still blocking his way on purpose.

He slapped the Mutt on his back, and then he added to his words aimed at the other Lieutenant from the outfit. "I wish to hell I had a stinking dime for every time you told me you were leaving the damn outfit, dog man. C'mon friend, this stinking Unit would be nothing more than a shit float without ya ass in it buddy." He tried his best to ignore the Mutt's angry words.

"I know I threatened to leave the damn Unit before, but this time I really mean it man. I taken all I can take and more, and I have eaten enough stinking shit to last me a fucking lifetime, brother. I wanna do what Barbara wanted, I wanna settle down and raise a bushel basket of stinking kids, and screw my ever loving brains out in the damn effort, Walker. I'm done playing god damn soldier for people who don't give a stinking rat's ass if I live or die man. I'm gonna take some time for myself and get an honest job, do some fishing and enjoy life for a change."

"Look Mutt, now isn't the time to make any stupid or rash decisions. You're fucked up in the noggin from losing Barb, and the heat of the fights still in your stinking gut, man. I'm sure once you had time to clear your damn head, you'll realize we're your only family, buddy. Let's get ourselves something to eat, once you're full and had a dump, you'll feel a helluva lot better about yourself." He turned to leave but he was stopped by the Mutt who grabbed him by his arm.

He allowed himself to be turned by the Mutt's pressure and he continued his bitch at Walker. "I'm not shitting ya this time man. I'm really done with this stinking shit, Walker! Losing Barb has opened my damn eyes fur me good and wide. I'm gonna get me another woman and settle down and raise a bunch of stinking ankle biters, and then enjoy stinking life for a change."

"Yeah, yeah dog man, I know what you're saying now buddy. But what woman in her right mind would ever think about sharing a life with the likes of you, buddy? You about fucked every woman in the damn States, so they all know bout ya lousy ass and the way you are with any woman. I think you're gonna hafta leave the stinking States if you wanna find another woman to settle down with who doesn't know anything about ya yet buddy."

"In case you don't know Walker, I think I have already found myself one, old friend."

"C'mon Homes, you didn't even get over Barb yet, and now you're trying to make me believe you have your evil eyes set on the next poor woman you're gonna corrupt, dog face." He groused to his closest friend as he cast an eye at him.

"It's okay, really Homes, and I do, I swear it man." The Mutt offered with a smile on his lips.

"Okay asshole, who is this young beauty you have already locked your evil eyes on, dog man?"

"You can't tell yet Walker? It's Blind Date man. I know she likes me a helluva lot man." The Mutt cried as he looked over his shoulder back at the beautiful young French female soldier who was sitting on her bunk and speaking to the female soldier branded Baby Tee.

"Blind Date! You gotta be fucking shitting me, dog man. She's only pity fucking your mixed breed ass for ya if you couldn't figure that move out for yourself, stupid. You betta step back some and take a deep breath and let your head get settled down some, before you go making any stinking decisions that are only a stinking make believe dream in your mind, buddy."

"You watch my fucking smoke man. I'm gonna do it chum." The Mutt cried to Walker.

"I'll do that buddy." He snapped as he shook his head and smiled at the Mutt.

Sergeant Dorothy Ramirez moved over to Walker's side, and she took his arm in hers as she nodded at the Mutt, who smiled up at her as she told Walker. "Hey Bobby, I'm afraid I'm starving. I want to go get something to eat before I pass out on my feet."

She knew what she was doing; she was trying to break up the conversation she knew was heading for an angry confrontation between the two strong headed elite soldiers.

"Yeah, me too, I'm hungry enuf to eat a stinking salad for once in my life baby. You coming with us pig head?" Walker growled at the Mutt.

"As soon as I get my stinking uniform on, I'll be right wit you two guys. You betta think about what I just told you Walker. I wasn't shitting you in the least, I meant everything I said, man."

The Lieutenant glared back at the Mutt as Ramirez pulled him away from the other Lieutenant because she was that hungry. The meal was strained at best, the Mutt sat with Walker, Ramirez, Neck, Buckethead, Mother Flanagan and Raphael. There was little if any real talking going down between the soldiers, giving the Mutt private time he needed to get over Barbara's death.

The elite soldiers ate at the ship's mess opened to them all the time they were stationed on board the Aircraft Carrier Washington. The soldiers started to calm down some from the adrenaline they were feeding from their last mission. The more they ate, the more tired they became until most of them were having trouble keeping their eyes open any longer. One by one, they drifted from the mess, stumbling back to the sleeping quarters. Many soldiers still dressed in their uniforms, laid down on their racks and quickly dropped off to sleep.

Gone were all thoughts of partying with the girls from the group. The few soldiers still able to keep their eyes open, could barely move their battered bodies. The troopers laid on their racks exhausted while staring at the gray painted ceiling, and allowing their minds to wander over the recent hard hitting action in Iran, and the painful losses they had suffered. Their troubling thoughts went to their loved ones waiting for their return back to the States, or the soldiers daydreamed about nothing, and allowed their bodies to rest for the first time in quite a while.

Lieutenant Walker was one of the last soldiers still in the mess, he was flanked by Neck and Buckethead. Ramirez was there along with the Mutt. Raphael long ago gave into her body's need for sleep and she left with the other soldiers. The Mutt announced he was turning in. He gave Walker a look which he thought was maybe to blame him for Barb's death. He nodded as the Mutt growled at them. "I'll see you people tomorrow morning, right Homes?"

"Only if you get up early enuf to see us off, dog man." He said to his lifelong friend.

The Mutt grinned as he gave in to his body's needs for sleep and left the mess.

The Lieutenant kept his eyes glued to his friend until he was almost out of the mess. Ramirez broke the trance by taking Walker's hand and she offered to her lover and soldier.

"I agree with the mad dog as well, Bobby. I believe I had enough of this bullshit playing soldier all the time, honey. I want to settle down and have some kids before I'm too old to enjoy them. Walker, I don't want to end up like Barb. I want out of this crap Bobby."

"So you said in the past baby." He hissed at Ramirez, trying to keep his false manly guard up.

"What the hell's that supposed to mean Bobby? What the hell's wrong with you, mister?" she hissed at him as she stared into his eyes.

"Look baby, I got my stinking hands full with the fucking Mutt driving me crazy right now. We'll discuss this shit on the plane while we're heading for New York." The Lieutenant allowed his eyes to wander towards the Mutt before he disappeared from the mess. He did not tell the Mutt he and Ramirez were going to be gone before the service for Barbara took place. He was crushed, but there was nothing he could do about it, the plane was scheduled to land on the Carrier and they would be gone by Oh, Three Hundred Hours.

The Sergeant thought she could tell what her man was thinking, and she backed off him. The other soldiers still in the mess, were kind of picked and nibbled at their food, but they did not want to give into their need for sleep. One after the other though, the exhausted soldiers gave into nature's call. Walker and Ramirez were the last two to leave the mess, and he allowed her to lean against him as they both headed back for their quarters. She was about out on her feet, and he had to pour her on her rack, and then he covers her with the blanket.

Road Kill looked around the quarters; everyone was out sound asleep or settled in for the night. The room was filled with snores, grunts, moans and farts. Without knowing he searched for the Mutt, seeing him lying on his rack he headed for him out of habit. He tapped him on the shoulder, sensing the Mutt was not asleep.

The Mutt looked in his eyes, and The Lieutenant stared at him for the moment.

"You all fucking right buddy?" he asked, concerned for the Mutt's psychological health.

"Yeah, I'm just stinking dandy buddy, thanks for letting me get it offa my chest, man. I really needed that Walker." The Mutt offered as he smiled up at his friend and fellow soldier.

"I know. Say Mutt, you're not really gonna scrub outta the damn Unit, are ya man?"

"Naw, it's like you said, you people are the only family I really got. I'd be outta my mind to think of leaving you stinking fools and go off on my own." The Mutt smiled weakly at Walker.

He reached his hand out and allowed it to float over the Mutt's face.

The Mutt reached out with both hands and he locked Walker's hand between his.

"Good to have you back with us Mutt." Walker said with compassion for his friend.

"Yeah, you're coming back to the group when you finish with this load of crap they dumped on your stinking ass, right buddy?" the Mutt asked, worried someone was pulling Walker away from the Unit. He did not understand why he and Ramirez were going to New York on the government's dime though. He really did not pay very much attention while Walker was explaining it to him why he was leaving the group, and he was not going to ask him to repeat it either. It was not his style, if the Lieutenant wanted him to understand what was going down, he would explain it more to him.

"You bet'cha ever loving ass I'm coming back to the fucking Unit, stupid. So be a cool dude until I return. I'll not see you in the stinking morning unless you're up when I leave for the damn big city, Homes." He held his breath, fearing the Mutt was going to realize he was telling him he would miss the service planned for Barbara tomorrow afternoon. He was really worried that the Mutt might fly off the handle when he realized he was going to miss the service.

"I got no problem there man." The Mutt grunted, he understood Walker and Ramirez was going to miss Barb's service, but he decided not to beat them over the head with it.

"Hey Mutt, I need you to hold the rest of the group together while I'm gone, buddy. I really need you on this one, man. I'm depending on your ass to make sure none of these uther slugs get in any trouble on this stinking tub while I'm gone man." He told the Mutt as he stared at him.

"You got it. Hey man, you betta be real in New York fucking City buddy. I hear it's a pretty tough place to hang out in, especially at fucking night Homes." The Mutt warned him.

"Yeah, tougher than where we just came from, right dog man?" Walker retorted to his friend.

"Yeah, maybe so man." The Mutt responded as he reluctantly let go of Walker's hand.

"Don't fucking worry bout me and my lady man. We'll be fine hanging out in the Big fucking Apple for a few days. This shit's a piece of cake, man." The now excited Lieutenant replied as he turned, and then headed for his rack. He did not know it, but two other people were listening to their conversation, and they were silently crying in the darkness of the ship.

Raphael tossed and turned all night long as she cried. She was so worried about the Mutt, Sergeant Ramirez, Lieutenant Walker and the rest of the soldiers who made up the elite Unit and thought of them as her friends. She did not know what was going to happen to them in the future. She was deathly in fear the future was going to violently rip some of her friends from her. She folded her arms across her chest to draw up her inner strength. Nothing she did allowed her to sleep. Sergeant Ramirez also cried herself to sleep, at least she knew her soldier was going to be there for her, and that was all she was concerned about.

AVIANO AIR BASE, ITALY. 1210 HOURS
SATURDAY MORNING, NOVEMBER 21st, 1998

The Aviano military airbase stationed in Italy was the home for the American 31st fighter wing F-16 Falcons, of the 510th fighter squadron. Today a civilian type of Jetstar aircraft screamed down the tarmac, and then shot up in the black sky heading for the Aircraft Carrier Washington, steaming the Red Sea on its way to the Mediterranean. The Carrier was scheduled to port in Egypt to disembark its cargo of elite soldiers.

Aviano control tower was in contact with the Flight Boss of the Carrier, informing the commander the Jetstar flight was airborne and on its way out to his ship. The Air Boss moved his decked aircraft around on the flight deck, to make room for the Jetstar about to land on the Carrier. He had the White Shirts that controlled of the movements of all the aircraft on the flight deck, lower five of the aging F-14 Tomcats to below deck storage, and they also move two F-18 Hornets to the sideline of the flight deck. The Flight Boss ordered the launch of a fuel tanker to refuel his ready air cap hovering over the Carrier at all times while she was on station.

It was the Carrier's air defense against a possible plane or missile attacks on the ship. The Air Boss informed the ready air cap of the incoming Jetstar, and allowed the pilots to run an attack scenario on the small inbound plane. Two F-14s broke off and charged after the unsuspecting aircraft. Within an hour, the two F-14s closed in on their target, attacking it from below and above. When the fighter pilots made the suggested kill, they closed in on the Jetstar's wings, and they then escorted the plane to the Carrier. The leader assured the Jetstar pilot they were just running a mockup attack against him.

The Air Boss watched the progress of the inbound friendly Jetstar on the radar scope as it rapidly closed in on his Carrier, and when the plane marshaled off the fantail, and the pilot requested permission to deck down on his ship. The Air Boss barked orders at his deck crews. He wanted everything to go smoothly, because this was the second time they landed a VIP plane on his flight deck. When the Jetstar was near, he turned his flight over to the LSO (Landing, Signal Officer) who commanded the craft until it was decked down on the Carrier.

The Carrier's Air Boss stared at the deck as the Jetstar started its final approach for landing on his flight deck. He held his breath as the small plane came in at full power, allowing a smile when he saw the modified tail hook grab the third arresting wire on the deck. The aircraft's engines shut down, and the fire control teams rushed out in their fire protection, checking the plane for any signs of fire in the engine wells, or the exhaust section of the Jetstar. He watched as the two pilots climbed out of the plane, and the Jetstar was hooked up to the Turtle, and then dragged from the landing area of the deck. The Jetstar was deposited on the deck sideline, out of the way of any incoming military aircraft. The aircraft was checked out by the Carrier's engineers, refueled then made ready for flight.

NEW YORK, 7:10 P.M. SUNDAY NIGHT, NOVEMBER 8th, 1998

At the second meeting of the team planning the diamond heist at the Trump International Hotel and Tower. The leader of the group waited not so patiently for the turncoat security guard to arrive for the meeting. The guard called earlier to inform Michael he had the blueprints for the Trump Tower he demanded. They marked out the position of elevators, stairwells, walkways and private stairwells used by the elite who own or rented the expensive rooms inside the Tower.

Michael was with Lizzie and his second in command, Richard Valentine. The leader decided not to allow the others of the group to meet with the security guard for fear of possibly scaring him off. He wanted the guard to forget about what the others looked like, in case their action went sour on them and the cops discovered their plan and caught some of his people.

He intended to meet with everyone the following morning, including Alexander for the first time, the wild Russian ex-soldier so he could lay out his plan for all of them concerned over this robbery. He worked out how they were going to leave the building after they had the diamonds in their possession; but that escape was going to cost Alexander and the rest of his people their lives, while the rest of them made good their escape from the Tower. All he really needed was the Trump Tower blueprints to make certain his escape would work for him. He was pissed the guard said nothing about getting him the list of those who lived in the Trump Tower. He wanted to know who they were, so he could pick and choose his hostages from the lot. Hostages that would force the police to hold their fire until they were gone from the Tower.

The soon to be leader of the terrorists was positive there were going to be a few VIPs in the building at the time of their attack, and he intended to grab the best of the lot, and let the rest out of the Tower. But not before taking anything of worth from them and their apartments. He only needed a few hostages, in case the cops tried and block his escape before they could get out of the building. Once outside, he would kill the hostages he dragged along with him. He was a firm believer of not leaving any witnesses behind who could possibly identify him or the others.

The late Trump Tower security guard banged on the door. Michael did not want to meet in the same place twice, to keep any possible surveillance by the police off step. He pulled the prints out of the guard's hand and quickly unfolded them on the table. Together with Richard, they both went over the blueprints, while Lizzie occupied the guard by playing with herself.

Without a word, he ran his finger over the prints, silently showing Richard where their escape route was. He smiled, because he knew they would get out of the Tower unobserved. Richard punched Michael in the arm, knowing in the next few weeks, they were going to be rich. The leader refolded the blueprints, and then he tucked them under his arm as he turned to the security guard who was busy staring at Lizzie's breasts dangling just inches away from his face.

"Okay pal, you done good enough to make you a full partner in this heist. But I need more than just these blueprints, friend. I asked you for a list of the people living in the condos, and a list of names of those renting rooms on the day of our attack. I wanted a list of the wealthy, condo dwellers. Where is it friend?" He reached out and wiggled his fingers impatiently at the guard.

"I have them with me, but I was holding them back until I was absolutely sure I could trust you and the rest of these people." The guard replied to Michael's words. Then he handed a sealed envelope he removed from his coat pocket.

Michael glared angrily at the security guard as he opened the envelope. He whistled as he read the wealth in the Tower. "Jesus it's better than hitting the bank of Switzerland. Will you look at the stuff? Okay Richard, I'm going to leave you with this list, pick out the hostages, and what we're going after in the Tower. I want a list by tomorrow, ten copies so everyone has…"

"Will I be getting a copy of that list as well?" the worried security guard asked.

The leader glared as he snapped at the man. "Now why in the hell would you need a copy of the list? You're not going to be part of the robbery, unless you might have changed your mind my friend. Did you change your mind and you're going to help with the heist?"

The security guard thought for a moment, and then he announced. "I want a copy so I'll know what I'm entitled to, after the heist is over I mean."

"Don't you worry about that my friend, you'll get everything you're entitled to and more. I'll not cheat the one who brought us this information out of what he deserves from our actions. Don't concern yourself with this part, I want your head clear when we attack the building. You just worry about getting us inside the Trump Tower and leave the rest to us, you have to show us to elevator E-Three. We'll take it from there once we handcuffed you to the pluming after roughing you up a little as we agreed. We'll meet in two weeks after the robbery, and split the shares up evenly then. I promise you'll get yours and maybe more if we get what we're expecting from this heist. There's a section of the building I have to go over with you yet. I want to know how many other security guards will be on duty on Sunday when we hit the Tower. I want to know where the security headquarters is located inside the building as well."

The Tower guard hesitated for a brief moment before informing Michael there were seven guards on duty in the Tower both day and night. If there was a special event planned for the Tower, or a visit from some VIP. The security guards could be increased up to threefold, depending on who the visitor might be. He offered at times, new security guards were walked through the security of the Tower, to show how they work, and some were trainees to their unit. Others were guards getting transferred to the Tower security force to make certain they had enough security guards to cover the Trump Tower at all times.

"What's the shifts the guards follow, and how do your people relieve each other when their shift ends?" Michael asked as he jotted down notes once the guard answered his questions.

This time the turncoat guard did not hesitate, the fear was gone with the offering. No longer did the guard feel he was betraying a trust as he said. "The shift change occurs three times a day, the first at seven a.m., then at four p.m. and then at midnight. At these times there's generally fourteen guards inside the building. The other guards show up a half an hour before their shift is scheduled to begin. The seven security guards to be relieved, can't leave their post until they're relieved by their replacements.

"Michael, each security guard has to punch in a special small time clock always carried by the guard on duty at all times with their key, to show where they were and when they were there on their watch. This is so Command knows the guard was walking his rounds faithfully, and not sleeping on the job. When one guard's relieved by the other, each guard punches in on the clock. The one reporting to work punches in first; the one leaving his position punches out by turning his key in the opposite direction. The number on the edge of the electronic key shows up inside the clock on a small paper disk, and when two key numbers show up in one place on the disk, it means one guard was taking over for the other..."

"How often do the guards have to punch in on this clock, and what is it?" he asked.

"It's a time clock that measures seven inches in diameter, by two inches thick. It has a place to insert the key. There are a number of keys spread throughout the guard's area of responsibility, and he has to go to each station and punch in with the key, and then follow up with his key. So his number shows up on the location at the time he was supposed to check in with the clock at that station. No one can sign in for him, unless he has the other guard's key. This way Command knows he's carrying out his duties all times he's working on his shift." The security guard paused, not sure if Michael wanted to hear more about the security system of the Tower.

"Enough, I don't care about this stuff at all. Where's the security headquarters stationed in the building? Give me everything you know about the station, and don't make me ask you twice for any needed information from you, my friend." He warned the security guard angrily.

With a deep breath, the guard explained. "The Security Center is located on the first floor of the basement of the building, there's five floors that make up the basement. The builders dug this deep to make the foundation strong enough to hold up the fifty two floors of the Trump Tower. Two levels are put aside for the private parking for the residents and visitors. A sub level is where the Tower supplies are usually stored, and the last sub basement levels are set aside for common storage for the tenant's use, and what extra storage is needed by the Tower staff. In the Command Center, there's two secured phone lines linked directly to nearest police stations..."

"I want you to disable those two lines before we make our hit on the Tower. I don't want any alarm going out to the police until the last possible moment, my friend." The leader of the group demanded of the worried security guard from the Tower.

"That's impossible, if I do that everyone I work with will know I'm part of this damn thing." The security guard cried at the leader of the group.

"I don't care what anyone thinks about you, pal! I want those two lines down before we attack the place, pal. I'm going to have one of our people enter the building through the service area, and he's going to make his way over to the security center and take it out, along with any of the security guards manning in the center. That's why I want those communication lines down before we go in action against the Tower. I don't want the security guards calling the cops on us before we're in and ready to deal with them. How many guards are usually manning this Command Center at any one time, buster?" He almost roared at the guard this time.

"Two!" The scared guard replied.

"Good, Three, I want you to enter the building. It's your responsibility to get to the Command Center and take out anyone inside the security center no matter who they are. Kill all the guards and then destroy the structure so no one can use it against us. Make it easy on yourself, just lob a grenade we'll get from Alexander in and wipe it out, and then I want you to go to the..."

"I think that would be a very foolish move on your part, One." The security guard interrupted, getting in the habit of not mentioning anyone by name, even though he knew only a few of them.

He took his attention from Suarez, and then he glared as he snarled at the security guard who was staring at him now. "Why not buster! Why was that a bad idea my friend?"

"Because One, if you kill just the guards and not destroy the entire Command Center, you'll be able to use the security cameras to assist your own security of the building, until you're ready to leave the building. The security cameras cover every entry and exit of the entire building, as well as the main hall and the massive reservations desk area. There's a camera stationed on the roof of the building, and another one stationed outside that covers the approach to the large parking area. It scans the outside parking lot and entry to the underground parking lot. There's another security camera stationed below that also covers this parking area from a different direction. The main approach to the building is covered by a pair of revolving security cameras, and there's another camera mounted in each of the stairwells leading to the upper floors of the Tower."

After thinking about the guard's words for a moment, Michael replied. "Hmmm... you might have a good point there, I'm glad you opened your mouth. Three, you hear that? Never mind the grenade, just make certain you get to the Command Center and take out just the security guards, we'll move in force and secure the rest of the building. Is there anything else I should know about the security systems of the building?" he asked the guard.

Originally, he had planned to destroy all the telephone lines going in and out of the Tower, but after going over the papers from the last meeting. He discovered the Trump Tower offered free cellular phone, along with fax services to their elite clientele. He knew there was no way he could possibly secure the entire Tower from all outside contact world. Besides, he did not care what the police knew about their attack, once he and his group was inside, and the building was secured by Alexandra and his extremely dangerous crew. When they had the entire building and hostages in control, it would take nothing short of an invading Army to get to his people. His thoughts were interrupted by the security guard as he offered.

"Yes, there are a number of special lockdowns built in on the main floor of the building that locks everyone in or out of the building. These metal doors are controlled by the Security Command Center, Number One. The doors close off all entry to the building, stopping anyone who wants to get at you, or away from you. The fire doors are located on every floor controlled by the security center. It's an easy way to close off certain floors, by releasing the fire doors once we're sure everyone is off that floor, and we're finished. I warn you though Number One, once you activate the fire doors, alarms will be automatically transmitted to all surrounding fire and police stations. There's no way I can possibly disable this system, it's not controlled by our security force. So you should activate these doors, only when you no longer have any concern or worry of the police discovering you in the building, Number One."

"That's it?" Michael grumbled, his mind made up to follow the advice of the guard.

"Yes Number One, that's all I have for you, unless you ask for more information about the Tower you might want or need from me." The guard replied to Michael.

"Are you going to be able to disable the secured lines leading from Command Center to the police departments before we hit the building?"

"Errr..." The security guard started to speak, but he was immediately cut off by the angry acting leader of the group as he barked at the security guard.

Chapter Six

Errr... nothing! I need a direct answer to my question, dammit. I must know that these damn communication lines are disabled before I go in action. If you won't do it then I'm putting an end to this heist, and you can go to hell my friend." He hissed at the security guard.

"Yes! I'll do it." The guard offered with hesitation.

"How are you going to accomplish disabling the damn lines for us, pal?" He demanded.

"It's easy enough for me to accomplish I guess, Number One. I can just place something sharp against the lines, and when you're about to enter the building. I can just shove it, cutting the lines and putting the security center completely out of commission to the outside world. This way, all they can accuse me of is being stupid, and not being part of the gang, Number One." The security guard moaned at the leader of the soon to be attackers.

"You will do this for us when we hit the building my friend!" Michael asked the guard.

"Yes I will, Number One." The scared guard replied.

"Err... is there anything else that'd stop the security guards from going to their regular lines to notify the police, if they discover their normal lines are disabled on them?" Lizzie asked, fearing the men were overlooking the obvious.

Michael looked from her to the guard as he waited for him to reply.

"That's why the lines were installed in the first place, Number One. Over the past few years, the police had been repeatedly called to the Tower by countless wackos giving false reports and alarms, and causing the police to respond in force, only to discover everything was okay at the Tower. These lines removed this problem from happening and no one knows about them, so they can't be tampered with by any of these nuts. If someone calls in a report over any other line but these two, the police would be suspect, and wouldn't respond in force, unless confirmation came from us manning the Command Center. At the most, the police would respond one or at the most two squad cars only, and by the time they do that, we should be well inside the building, and the building secured and we're locking it down."

The leader turned to Lizzie and then asked her. "Are you satisfied with his rely?"

"Yes, but this seems too simple to me. Something has to go wrong with it on us."

"That's what I like about it, keep it simple and confuse the other guys, Lizzie. Anything else you can think of I should know about the security systems of the Tower?" he asked the security guard as he turned back to him.

"No. That's all of it, Number One." The guard replied confidently.

"Fine, that's it then." His mind raced, he worked these gates into his plan. Once Three killed the guards manning the Command Center, and the gates were down and locked in place, and his people were in complete control of the security. He was going to order the destruction of one gate to the outside. The gate he chose was the one leading to Broadway. He planned to use this door to get rid of the hostages he did not want trapped inside the building, adding to the mass confusion he knew was going to be running wild on the streets of midtown Manhattan.

He turned to the guard once again and barked at him. "We're done here, if you don't have anything else to add. Leave so we can get down to the business that concerns us..."

"How will I know where and when to meet you next?" the guard interrupted, remembering Michael said they would be meeting at different times around the building before the attack.

Michael sharpened his harsh glare at the turncoat security guard as he replied to him. "We'll meet a number of times more before we finally go against the Tower. I'll tell you where and when we'll meet in advance, so you can attend the meeting. I promise you I'll not cheat you on anything due you from this heist, pal." He smiled at the security guard.

The guard could do nothing more but nod in agreement to Michael's words.

"That's better, now, are these the only people who'll be at the Tower when we begin our robbery?" he waved the paper containing the names handed to him by the guard.

"No, there's always someone who checks in or out at any time of the day or night, and we find only out about them after we get the computer updates sent down to the security center. Who knows who might be there when you finally attack the Trump Tower, Number One. I can't even be that certain the ones on the list will be there on Sunday when this attack goes down. I thought this over and came to the conclusion the ones on the top of the list are more than likely the ones who'll be there when you hit the building. As you go further down the list, the less likely those people will be home. If you want, I can always update the list on Sunday morning before you start your attack, that way you'll have an up to date list to work from, Number One." The security guard announced, feeling a little more like he was part of the gang now.

"That's good, I want you to do that. Okay pal, that's it for now. The next meeting will take place on Tuesday, November 10th, at ten a.m. I want an update on the residents at that time. I also want a continuing update of any residents in the Tower at every meeting. You can go now, pal." The leader did not bother to look at the guard when he rudely dismissed him.

When the security guard was out of the room he looked at Lizzie, and then he ordered her. "Lizzie, get out there and make sure the pricks gone, and then I want you to scout out the area and make sure no cops are lurking around out there or following that asshole. Better yet, trail the jackass back to the Tower, and make sure no one's following the fool there. I'll make contact with Alexander and bring him up to date on this latest information we just amassed from our friend." He waited for Lizzie to leave before addressing Richard.

"Two; I want you to kill that asshole when we no longer have any further need of him. But for now, I want you to go over the list of hostages he just gave us, and make a separate list up of the ones you give priority to make hostages of. We'll grab them first and allow the rest of them to dribble out of the building, to keep the cops off stride on us. It's good these heavy fire doors are on every floor of the building; we can close them and trap the ones who won't leave their apartments, peacefully. If this goes off without a hitch, we'll never have to pull off another heist for the rest of our lives. This is the one I've been looking for all my life, I can't believe this piece of shit just delivered it into my hands." He smiled at Valentine.

"Michael, who's going to control Alexander and the rest of his group of crazies? Someone from our group is going to have to keep him from going off and killing everyone in the building."

"Don't worry about Alex, I'll handle him through this heist. We're going to meet tomorrow, and I'll bring him up to speed and make sure he has everything he needs to hold off the cops with him, while we rip apart the Tower." He let out his breath in a rush.

"Fine, I'll be glad to leave him up to you Mike. I don't like working with that crazy one, he's too damn unpredictable and dangerous for my likes." Richard warned cautiously.

Michael ignored the warning from his Number Three member, as he started to thumb through the many pages of information just delivered to him by the security guard. He began to read over the countless amenities offered by the Trump Tower to the ones who own the apartments, and the others who visit the Tower that opened to the general public on January 20th, 1997. He smiled as he read the building was a fifty two story high mostly glass structure, and a concrete and steel complex offering many luxurious, condo type apartments at prices that would choke a horse, if he was forced fed the paper the numbers were out written on. One of the large apartments was actually selling for eight million dollars, along with a ten thousand dollars a month upkeep and taxes added to the price. The paper also stated the Trump Tower was blessed with bronze mirrored glass reaching from the floor to ceiling windows, and richly polished stainless steel and brass fixtures throughout the building.

The pamphlet further bragged of the countless accommodations unparalleled and unique to the industry that went along with the uncountable amenities and services. The Trump Tower had successfully redefined hotel standards of midtown Manhattan. The structure was positioned right on the crossroads of Manhattan's elite West Side, and Central Park West at Columbus Circle, overlooking the Central Park steps from the main doors of the structure. The Trump Tower's prestigious shadows cast across the front of Lincoln Center, and was well within walking distance to the Tavern on the Green and Cafe des Artistes. Located on the third to seventh floors of the building, the Trump International Tower and Hotel offers over one hundred eight apartments, including thirty eight stimulating Parlor studio dwellings, ninety exhilarating one bedroom Salons, and forty, two bedroom, breathtaking Gallery apartments, decked out with magnificence from floor to ceiling of every apartment.

A one of a kind marble bathrooms with European style kitchens to bring out the very best in every cook. Many beautiful apartments were drenched with spectacular views spanning Central Park, Columbus Circle, Broadway, the Hudson River and its many bridges, and the famous Manhattan skyline. At night one is mesmerized by the constant fantastic light displays of the many buildings and other breathtaking sights of the city that never sleeps. Each room of the Tower was equipped with remote control TV, VCR, stereo with CD player, fax and cell phone services, two line telephone with a data port terminal thrown in for good measure.

As he read the pamphlet for the Trump International Tower and Hotel, his smile grew as the pamphlet went on bragging about the outstanding accommodations waiting for anyone visiting, or chose to live at the magnificent Tower and Hotel. A special Trump Attaché was assigned to each guest reserving a room in the Tower, and this Attaché happily provides a comprehensive service, no matter how particular, how demanding, before, during and even after the guest's visit concluded. This private Attaché would contact certain Fifth Avenue boutiques, to have specially ordered clothes delivered on spec to the potential buyer.

This highly attentive and polite Attaché, will anticipate pre-arrival needs, and has his pick of the very best seats to many of the local Broadway, and off Broadway hits and shows. He's also instrumental in organizing private dining at exclusive clubs or restaurants throughout New York City, while making certain every request of the guest is fulfilled, leaving no details overlooked or ignored. The Attaché is well versed, and he'll follow up on any arrangements and transactions completed on the guest's request, even after he or she has checked out of the hotel, becoming the guest's ears and eyes while visiting Manhattan. He further maintains an up to date network of most art galleries, and he'll search out for particular artist's work, or arranges for the client gifts to be sent out, maintaining the commitment of providing unsurpassed customer service to their discerning guests and visitors to the Trump Tower.

The Trump International Hotel and Tower enjoys an outstanding restaurant constructed within its walls, the Jean Georges restaurant offers room service twenty four hours a day to all guests and owners of the apartments. For an exceptional one of a kind experience in Suite Dining's available, which brings the hotel's acclaimed restaurant right into the guest's rooms. With little notice, an in room chef can be arranged to personally prepare culinary delights in the guest's private kitchen, and then present the offering of a gourmet meal course by course, while the guests continues to enjoy the luxury offered by the marble whirlpool bath of their room.

A one of a kind health spa, and all the amenities that goes along with it, are also offered at the Trump Tower along with a lap pool, private pool and personal trainers for owners and visitors alike. You can even learn how to roller blade at the Tower if you are interested in that type of fun. Nothing was left out, or overlooked or neglected. He let out his breath in a huff as he bitched at his Number Three member of his gang. "With all the money floating around inside the Trump Tower, it's a wonder someone before us has not gone after it."

MONDAY MORNING, NOVEMBER 9th 1998, NEW YORK CITY

Michael called for another meeting to take place with the other members of his group, leaving Richard to explain what they had so far, while he pulled Alexander aside and spoke privately with him. "Alexander, have you given any further thought as to what you might need in the way of weapons and supplies to carry out your part of this heist?"

"Da, I have everything I need at hand now." His heavy Russian accent made his words very hard for Michael to understand as he went on with his words. "I get me hand on poor and inferior American made M-60 machine gun, I also get hand on pair superior Soviet made AGS 17 30 mm grenade launch, and every people in group arm 9 mm RAK PM-63 machine pistol made Poland, and 9 mm good Germany made Glock 17 pistol, some of fool carry 9 mm German made Heckler & Koch gun. Every weapon carry on attack be 9 mm, so same ammunition fit each weapon carried by my people. I have grenade plus three LAW 80 anti armor weapon. Two Russian made shoulder launch SA-7 Grail surface to air missile if try assault Tower use aircraft or helicopter against us. I have best men arm 7.62 mm Soviet built Dragunov SVD sniper weapon, in case dom police shoot from other building at us stationed on rooftop of our building."

"From what I can see of the Trump Tower, there are no other buildings near enough to this structure, to enable the cops to get any shots off at us when we station some of our people up on the roof. I think it's much better to be safe than sorry. It seems like you have thought of everything that was needed to be covered by you my friend, and I'm sorry I poked my nose into your business Alexander. Something you know a lot more about than I obviously do." He bowed slightly to the grinning and rather large Russian ex-soldier.

Alexander came from Russia around the same time the Berlin wall came crumbling down. In Russia he was Mafia, but when he went against his boss, he knew he had to flee Russia to save his own life. Leaving his wife and children to their own fate. Since coming to the United States, he made a living dealing in Russian weapons he was able to get from his country. He also supplied gang members from New York to LA with them. His contacts were still active inside Russia shipped anything he requested for a third of what he was paid for them.

Business was good for the Russian soldier, he offered some of the members of his gang for outside work. He supplied warriors to run protection for bank robberies throughout Los Angeles, for an equal share of the profits. He put one hundred of his warriors in the field. These warriors would do whatever was necessary to carry out his orders. None of them were afraid to die, nor were they very worried about killing anyone who happened to get in their way.

The large Russian grinned as he ran his mind over the words in his mind. He enjoyed putting his warriors out in the field to do battle with any gangs, police, and American soldiers, if his people came up against the military. He suffered from the mentality that plagued most Russian military leaders of the past. The United States was the enemy, and he thought it was his duty to harass and harm anything American if he possibly could. His eyes clouded over as his forehead creased with furrows of confusion for a quick moment. The leader of the group noticed the lines of worry etched on his face and asked him. "What's wrong with you Twenty Seven?"

"I sudden concern over matter you just speak of moments before to me, Number One. Your words have caused me some concern and I need to hear them again and clear the words up more for me to understand much better, Number One." He grumbled at the leader of the group.

"Why is that Alexander?" he asked the extremely dangerous Russian fighter.

"Moment go you said me seem I cover everything protect you people in build we attack. You no mention any of my people. I cover everything I should thought on own, and then I feel I…" His words were suddenly cut off when Michael spoke again.

"That's correct Alexander then what has you so worried now?" he asked the Russian.

"I big dumb stupid fool you believe Michael. I thought everything be important to attack please. I no thought how we make escape from god dom Tower once have what want from dom build. I big stupid fool for miss this worry, so I ask you how we get out build with skin still on bones, please?" the angry Russian glared hotly at Michael.

He laughed as he replied to the Russian. "Alexander, don't you worry about how we'll get out of the Tower. I have everything under control from my end there my friend, and we'll be sitting in South America sipping pina colata's while we're at it, my friend."

"Huh, somehow word does not make brain comfortable in seat, big shot leader you. If you have everything work out so perfect for you say please. Perhaps you kind explain this to big stupid man how get out dom build alive please." He glared a second time at Michael, showing him he was deeply concerned about the escape once they were done inside the building.

"Here is how we'll escape from the Trump Tower nice and easy once we have everything we wanted when we attacked the building, Alex. Once we opened all the safes and we have removed all the diamonds from them, we'll then ransack a number of the apartments of the VIP's living in the building. We have a complete inventory of the worth inside the building. We'll stuff what we can carry, taking larger bills in backpacks which will be hidden by our over shirts. The diamonds should be able to be carried by just one or two persons. I figure each man should hide one million dollars in cash in the backpacks, while able to keep the fact we're carrying something on our backs a secret. The building's stuffed with rings, expensive pins and necklaces worth thousands of dollars, which can easily be hidden in our pockets and elsewhere on..."

"Ahhh... this very good I know is great worth in American fooking build all time Number One. If I no believe this, I no be with you on this attack, Number One. I no that concern with worth inside fooking Tower. I more concern how make escape from god dom once we have all want take from place, please." Alexander again glared angrily at

Michael, this time his stare was more on the threatening side, than just concern.

"Relax big man, I'm getting to that point if you allow me to finish my thoughts. I was sayi..."

"Get point quick you do please for me. I grow old wait you explanation, big shot leader." The Russian interrupted, as he placed his hands on his hips, and shifted his weight, while continuing to stare into the non blinking eyes of the leader of the group, as he waited for him to reply.

"Okay my very apprehensive big Russian friend. I'll explain it to you how we'll get out of the building, once we have everything we want, and the hostages we want to take with us, my friend. We'll change clothes with some of the hostages, and then we'll supply the hostages with empty weapons, and order them to escort us to the buses we'll demand from the police, to take us to the airport as if we were the hostages, and they the criminals. My plan's good, because if the police open fire on the hostages who'll supposed to be guarding us, we'll use the ensuing mayhem to make our escape away from the Tower. Like any other hostages who'll be running into the park for their own safety. Once we're in Central Park, we'll quickly disappear in the streets of midtown Manhattan, while carrying what we have on our backs.

"Alexander, we'll stay away from each other for two weeks, and then meet at a designated spot and split the take evenly between all of us. The reason I want everyone to fill their backpacks is if they feel they have enough loot to be happy for the rest of their lives on their backs. They don't have to show up at the meeting place and split the rest of the loot with the others and..."

"Who carry billion dollar diamond worth on back, mister big shot leader you? This I demand to know myself of, before I agree with you foolish plan as you told me of please." The concerned Russian smirked at Michael as if he already knew the answer to his last question.

"You're right my rather large friend, I'll carry most of the diamonds. So if you want more than what you have on your back. Then you'll have to meet me after the heist, to get your full share of the spoils, Alex." Now it was Michael smirking at the angry looking Russian.

"It see have thought out well plan my friend, have force everyone marry you, no? But one more question no answered by you fool words, mister big shot leader Michael."

"Yes? And what's that one more question Alexander?" he snapped at the Russian.

"What happen you plan if police do no wait us rob safe and apartment as you say to me we do please? What happen police rush god dom Tower and they say hell with hostage we keep, big shot leader you? There still too many question unanswered with you fool plan for my like of operation you say, please." The Russian glared again at Michael while waiting his reply.

"That's where you and the rest of your people come in to play during the heist, Alex. If the police attack the Tower before we have completed our plans inside. Your people will have to react against their attack, my friend. I'm glad you have a good supply of hand grenades and heavy weapons at your disposal for this attack, Alexander. If the police attack us, you'll have your people rain down the grenades and bullets on them from the roof area of the building. You'll pour it on until the police finally back off their possible attack against us. Alexander, I have no doubt in my mind whatsoever that the police will try something against us, until we prove we can fight off all their attempts to get at us inside the building. I know if I was in Command of the police, and something like this took place on my watch. I'd do something about it; until it was proven all my moves could be countered by the terrorists I'm trying to get at..."

"So I guess we terrorist now, no big shot leader you?" he hissed, despising the sound of the word. He knew he was many things in life, but he never once thought of himself as a terrorist.

"We're whatever the hell we have to be in order to carry out our plan, my big Russian friend. We'll be successful on this heist Alexander." The leader announced proudly to the big Russian.

"Huh, I see! What you think police do get at us, fearless leader you?" the Russian asked.

"Alexander, I'm quite certain the police will most likely try to land a helicopter on the roof. Their first move would be to get their SWAT teams inside the building to counter our attack, my large Russian friend. It's SOP for most police actions. That's why I want you to secure the roof area of the building as soon as we attack the place. I want you to put some of your heavier weapons up on the roof for our protection. From that position, you can easily protect the roof, while also defending the street below at the same time, Alexander. If the police make a frontal attack on the building, you can have your people lob the grenades at them from the roof.

"Yesterday, I made a series of quick drive bys around the Tower. From what I was able to see of the building, there's no way to attack the structure without using tanks and armored vehicles to get it done. If the police try that, they'd have to understand many of the hostages would be killed, before they can possibly breach our security, and they have to be willing to accept that fact. Not even the police are stupid enough to try something that costly to the hostages, Alexander. Besides my friend, there's going to be concern for the building itself. To destroy such an exquisite building as this one, would severely harm the police image in New York City, Alexander."

"This very good me understand please, I know my people easy fend off possible attack mount by inferior American police department against us. Perhaps you would explain build structure and location me more, so I better formulate plan of defense for me self, big shot leader you. I like study print of structure too please, so you see I overlook something by accident maybe yes, Michael." The large Russian moaned at the chosen leader of the group.

"I have no problem with you seeing the blueprints of the building my friend, you can never be too sure of your plans. The more you go over them, the safer we'll be during the heist, Alex." He replied as he unrolled the blueprints of the Trump Tower. As they both looked the plans over, he went to the twentieth floor; this was where the diamond dealers were scheduled to be staying, according to the Tower security guard. He found the room marked Two One Four Five on the prints, and checked the side number that described the apartment layout on the prints. Then he went over to the ledger of the blueprints, and found the page describing the apartment in much more detail. He thumbed through the pages until he found the one he was looking for.

"Here's the room layout I was looking for Alexander. It borders the West 61st Street and Broadway on the corner of the building, the living and dining room measures fourteen foot by thirty foot, and that's probably where the diamond dealers will be carrying out most of their transactions, and drinking. The apartment has two bedrooms to it, Alexander. I see a walk in closet and six smaller closets, and you can bet the bank they'll probably hide at least one of the safes inside them. I also see five corner sections that look like support columns inside the apartment; we have to check these out also my Russian friend.

"I'd bet one or two of the safes are hidden inside one of these columns. Dammit, there are too many small nooks and crannies to hide a safe in to find them, Alexander. We're going to get stuck ripping the entire apartment apart piece by piece. Look Alex, there's also two bathrooms, one with a tub and shower stall, and the other's smaller, with only a shower stall and kitchen. Christ sake, this damn apartment's bigger than my whole house is." He complained as he checked the ledger of the prints again, giving him the specs of the apartment.

"Damn, there's almost sixteen hundred square feet to this one apartment, Alexander. See how thick the damn wall containing the front door is." He moaned as he pointed at the wall laid out on the blueprints, and then he traced it with his finger. He checked the side ledger and found out the wall was poured concrete sixteen inches thick, with two separate layers of reinforcing bars, that were wove throughout the thick cement wall.

"I think we'll need a cannon to penetrate a wall that thick my large Russian friend. I hope you can blow that door off its hinges for us Alexander, if we can't get the diamond dealers to open it up for us. Hinges!" He suddenly growled at the Russian as he went back to the ledger. He checks the hinge specifications and read with anger. The hinges were designed with special air pressure locks, to hold the reinforced door closed, and once the door was closed and locked down, the hinges were activated. He looked at the Russian with concern in his eyes.

The ex-Russian soldier could hear the unasked question resounding in his ears, and he offered to the leader of the group. "Do no worry one minute about it mister big shot leader you please. I get through any door easy for you if you want door opened that is. No door made ever in the world I no can destroy if want destroy it, please. I carry enough equipment accomplish my part job for you please. LAW weapon pop any door off hinge, big shot leader you."

Michael was a little familiar with the weapon Alexander was talking about, and he scanned the narrow confines of the hall on the blueprints of the building, which looked like it was less than five feet wide. He went back to the ledger of the blueprints and smiled when he found out the hall was eight feet wide, and he pointed that out to the Russian soldier. The leader of the group noticed from the floor to the ceiling was nine foot high. This meant if they tried to go through the floor of the apartment above, it was going to be a good drop to the apartment below. He checked the width of the concrete floor on the ledger, and immediately dismissed that idea as foolhardy. When he read the concrete was two feet thick, and had two layers of reinforcing bars mixed in with the concrete, with a line of mesh wire for added support.

The ex-Russian soldier checked the number, and realized it was going to be extremely dangerous to fire off a LAW rocket launcher in such a tight area as the hall. He searched his mind and decided to allow Fritch to fire the weapon, if he was going to incorporate this type of approach against the heavily reinforced door. He was the most expendable and least liked of all his fighters. Losing him would be no big deal. In his mind, the Russian knew he was not going to use the rocket launcher to breach the apartment. But he was not going to tell Michael. He wanted to keep him worried about the door, and smiled at the leader as he mumbled at him. "I see no problem with god dom apartment door stop me long to get in apartment room please."

"Fine, will you fire the weapon at the door yourself, Alexander?" he asked the Russian.

"No big shot leader you, I give Fritch that honor do. He earn worth to heist if he want money."

The chosen leader of the group nodded at the Russian, knowing what he meant, and then he asked the Russian the most important question of them all. "Then it's a go for the operation I take it Alexander? You see no problem with what we have planned as it is laid out before you so far my friend? You know this entire heist rest mostly on your shoulders

Alexander. If you can't get us inside that god damn apartment. Then there's no sense for us to even begin this heist in the first place. I have no intentions of getting myself involved in a heist that I can't pull off successfully my friend. I have to be absolutely positive that you can get us inside the apartment before I commit myself to this deal, and the rest of my people to this heist."

THE AIRCRAFT CARRIER CVN 73 GEORGE WASHINGTON.
O210 HOURS SATURDAY MORNING, NOVEMBER THE 14th, 1998

Lieutenant Robert Walker was awakened by the young Seaman who had escorted him and Sergeant Dorothy Ramirez over to Colonel Bruce Leadbetter's private quarters on board the Carrier the day before. He told the Sailor he wanted to be up before the VIP Jetstar landed on the Carrier's Flight Deck, but Colonel Leadbetter changed his orders without informing the Lieutenant, and had the Seaman wake him later. He knew Walker and Ramirez needed their rest.

The Seaman allowed Walker to wake Ramirez, because he did not like walking around the quarters of mixed men and women soldiers. In reaching his bunk, he passed two women's racks, one was naked and her breasts were out of the covers. It was not his fault for being embarrassed; it was the law on the Carrier strictly enforced by the Captain of the ship. Any women on board the ship were always given privacy for dressing and showering.

The young Seaman was scared he was going to be pulled before the Captain for punishment over seeing this woman half naked. The Seaman immediately diverted his eyes, but months at sea and the need to see a woman's breasts outweighed the fear of punishment. He took a good look before waking the Lieutenant. He could not wait to get back to his crew to boast about how great the female's breasts were. There was some scuttlebutt about the women of the Special Forces, it was said they were more man than woman. But seeing the softness of her breast made him realize it was all bull, and they were every bit as female as the Navy Waves were.

Lieutenant Walker opened his eyes, blinking them rapidly as the Seaman lightly shoved him on the shoulder and whispered to him. "Lieutenant Walker Sir, it's time to get up now sir."

The young military officer stretched and then he moaned. "Man, I slept like a stinking log last night, buddy. What the hell time is it anyway, Seaman?"

"Zero, Two Ten Hour's sir." The Seaman replied with a snap in his tone.

"What the fuck? I thought I told you to wake my ass up at Oh One hundred Hours, fucker."

"I understand Lieutenant, but Colonel Leadbetter countermanded those orders last night sir. He told me it was important you catch up on sleep, rather than walking around like a Zombie, the Colonel called it sir. I'm sorry sir, but a Colonel outweighs a Lieutenant on board this ship, sir."

"Those orders outweigh mine where I come from also pal. Arrr... sorry I bit your head off a moment ago fella. Did you wake Sergeant Ramirez yet?" He asked as he swung one leg off the rack, he was naked and did not care who knew it as he scratched his balls.

"No sir on this ship sir, we're ordered to respect a woman's sleeping quarters at all times, Lieutenant. Usually, another woman would wake a female sleeping on board the ship, sir. I didn't want to invade her privacy sir. I chose to allow you to wake up the female Sergeant if you don't mind, Lieutenant Walker Sir." The Seaman snapped back as he shot a quick smile at him.

"Man, you're getting to be a real pain in the ass, buster. You people have more stinking regs and uther crap than you guys know what the fuck to do with, man. Damn, it's a wonder how you people ever get anything done on this here tub, Mac. In our world, there's no such thing as privacy and niceties. You eat, sleep, and shit where you are, and you don't give a shit who's near ya when you do it either, fella. You people betta get with the damn program man. You're putting your women fighters in a closet, and I'm sure they resent it buddy. You guys betta respect your women warriors for what they are, rather than who you think they are.

"You guys will get along with the woman warriors a helluva lot betta when you do. Ever since we started to treat our women like fighters, it's been a lot better for all concern. Occasionally we get a stuffed shirt who gets crazy because someone glanced at her tits, but they're few and far in between. As long as we respect the women, we get along just fine with them. This is the Twenty First Century man, and the women of our country burned more than their bras, they can kill with the best of us. Tell your nosy ass Captain he betta wake up and smell the damn roses, before he has more problems on this tub than he knows what to do with..."

The first time the Seaman allowed the insult aimed against his ship to slide, this time he was angry and snapped at the soldier. "Lieutenant Walker Sir, this is a proud ship in the United States Navy sir, she's not a tub sir. I resent your remark about our ship, and I request you refrain from using that word whenever referring to the Washington sir, or I'm going to have to react."

While he stuffed his leg in his pants, he stopped and then looked up at the angry talking Seaman out of the corner of his eye, and then he smirked at the man. "React huh punk? I'd give a month's fucking pay to see one of you guys react to anything that goes on around here, buddy. Arrrr... why the hell am I dumping on your ass for man? You're right to be pissed off any me, buddy. Sorry for the nasty slur against your ship, I'll watch it next time."

The Seaman nodded and then waited for the Lieutenant to finish dressing. When he was dressed, he went over to Ramirez's rack and shoved it with his leg, waking her.

"Oh, it's you, what's up Bobby?" She asked in a sleepy voice as she sat up and then stretched her arms over her head, making her breasts point upwards. The Seaman swallowed hard.

"It's late Raz, you gotta get a move on it, the stinking Swabby woke us late baby."

"What time is it Bobby?" She asked as she swung her legs off the rack and stood naked.

"Zero, Two, Eighteen, Raz." He replied to the yawning Ramirez.

"Christ, the plane must have already landed on the ship by now, Robert. I was hoping to take a quick shower before departing for the City."

"Take your shower, I'll have the cooks pack us something so you can eat on the damn plane, baby." He offered to the beautiful rearend of Ramirez.

"I'd like that, will you do that for me Bobby?" She asked as she wiggled her behind.

He did not reply, instead he started off for the mess, coming face to face with the Seaman still staring at Ramirez's beauty. The Lieutenant laughed as he slammed a hand on the Seaman's shoulder and then he remarked to him. "I know what you're staring at my friend, it's what drew me to her in the first place, buddy. Then her inner beauty captured me like a stinking puppy. She's a real beauty inside and out man. C'mon, I gotta get some food in my ass, I'm fucking starving pal." He applied pressure, turning the Seaman who snapped out of his trance.

"Say Lieutenant I think I see what you mean by the twenty first century sir. I'll take you to the mess; the cooks were making up a load of scrambled eggs and crap when I left it earlier, sir."

"Lead the way. It's been..." He checked his watch. "Over twelve hours since I last ate any real food, and I can't remember when I last had a square meal before that." He did not bother to glance at Mutt. If he had, he would have realized his friend was already awake. His mind was racing over the many memories of Meyerhoff, and all the fun they shared together over the years.

The Mutt had not slept much last night, he used the solitude of the darkness along with the quiet of the sleeping area to pay a remembrance to his girlfriend who the troops branded Fun Bags. He cried, smiled and cursing the countless memories flooding in and out of his mind. He placed the memory of Barbara in one of those special closets in the back his mind that saved his sanity. He knew he would visit it every now and again, when he wanted to feel sorry for himself. Or when he wanted to share a special moment with the memory of his dead girlfriend.

Sergeant Ramirez came out of the shower while still dressing. She glanced over at the Mutt and realized he was up. She went over to him and leaned over his rack and kissed him on the forehead, and then she smiled at him warmly.

Lieutenant Frank Hall immediately looped his arms over her back and pulled her near, hugging her and breathing deeply, needing her warmth. She could not help it and she sobbed over the moment, locked in the Mutt's protective arms she was brought back to Barbara's memory.

"It's all right, I'm back and well honey, I'm okay, I really am Raz. You gotta relax and back offa me and let things go until we're all over her death, baby sister." The Mutt tried to reassure her, but Ramirez was having none of it from her long time friend.

Chapter Seven

Don't give me any of that crap, mister. In a pig's ear you're alright Frankie. You'll never be over her, just as Walker and I will never be over her…" The Sergeant's words were interrupted by someone calling out to her from the darkness of the sleeping quarters.

"Don't stop there Raz. None of us guys will be over losing Barbara either, honey."

"He's right; no one here will ever get over losing Barbara. We all loved her you know, she was one of us, and she'll always be one of us. Never forgotten, Raz."

A number of Aye's filled the sleeping quarters of the elite soldiers.

"I didn't mean I'm over losing her you slugs. I meant I'm handling it alright and beginning to live with it." The Mutt retorted, feeling much better many soldiers cared for her, and him.

She looked in the pained eyes of the Mutt, and kissed him on the cheek and rubbed her chin against his face. She pulled back and ran a hand down the side of his face as she said in her softest tone. "Frankie, Walker and I are going to miss the service for Barb. I'm sorry Frank, but we can't do anything about it. We have orders and the plane's waiting topside for us already." She ran a finger over his lips, and fought desperately to stop herself from crying in front of him.

The Mutt let out his breath and mumbled back at her. "Do you think I'm an asshole I didn't realize you were gonna miss the service for Barbara, Raz? I'm smarter than anyone gives me any credit for you know, sister. I just act the fool, but every now and then I know what I'm doing."

"Mutt, I never thought of you a fool in the least, never. I know how smart you are, it's just that Walker thought you might be so caught up in your grief over losing Barb that your head was coming loose on you. That's all Frankie."

"Hey baby, my head's always on a swivel, but level! Honey, I'm really starting to get a handle on losing Barb, I getting to the point of getting my life going again, baby."

Sergeant Ramirez gave a shiver, and the Mutt pulled her closer, enjoying her warmth, her nakedness. Reluctantly, he let her loose and warned. "You betta get dressed before you catch a chill. I don't want you battling a cold while enjoying New York, and the slug you're wit."

She sat down and wiggled into her shirt and stuffed the tails in her pants as she purred. "Mutt, you don't have a problem with us missing the service for Barb? It was driving me nuts."

"I'd rather have you standing by my side as always. You know you and your slug are the closest thing I have to real family, baby. But I understand when duty calls; it's our lifestyle that forces us to answer the call. I'm really okay with you and Walker missing the service, I know you'll be there in spirit, and that's all I need to keep me sane, honey."

"Thank you so much for that Frankie, you're making this much easier for us. You know we miss Barb dearly, she'll never be replaced in our hearts, in our thoughts." She sighed deeply.

"I hope that's not written in stone you know baby." The Mutt offered with a slight sneer.

"What the hell do you mean by that remark mister?" the female Sergeant suddenly snapped at the Mutt, sharpening her senses, just in case he had no intention of explaining his remark.

"Raz, you have to leave some room in your heart for someone else to step into my life, baby."

"Why you lousy little sonofabitch you. Don't tell me you have your eyes already locked on another woman's ass, mister? How dare you, I have a good mind to…" Sergeant Ramirez growled as she rapped him in his stomach.

"Natch baby." The Mutt retorted with a grin and a grunt from the blow she gave him.

"Who's this poor girl you got caught up in your filthy sights already, pig man?" she grunted at him as she grabbed a hand full of his chest hairs and then she pulled on them while she waited for him to answer her last question of him.

"Yeeeaaaooowww, wow, wow. That's hurts like hell girl. I hate when you do that kinda shit to my ass, dammit. One of these days I'm gonna grab your damn nipple and give it a good twist on you, sister. Then you'll know how that crap feels when you do that carp to me, girl. Let go will ya for God's sake, I'll tell ya baby." The Mutt pleaded with her.

She was not giving into the Mutt's threat as she retorted. "Promises, promises. You men are all alike mister. Who is this other hen you have your sneaky ass eye on, Frankie baby?"

The Mutt lifted up to take the pressure off his chest hairs as he whispered. "Blind Date."

"The French bitch, Mutt?" she snapped, angry he was going after a foreigner this time.

"Yep, you got it baby." The Mutt grinned broadly as he added. "She's hot as hell for my ass."

"Christ Almighty Mutt, couldn't you have at least picked out an American girl to aim your evil intentions on, mister? That one's not going to take any of your usual shit you always dump on us ladies you know. You go and screw around with her like you did Barb, and she's liable to cut your balls off on you, asshole." The Sergeant mumbled as she looked around the sleeping area until her eyes found the French woman sleeping two racks away from the Mutt's.

"Raz, she made it so much easier for me to get over Barbara. She stayed with me when I needed someone the most, and she let me cry on her shoulder. I like her a lot, and I'm sure Barbara wouldn't mind about her Raz." The Mutt pleaded again with her.

"Yeah, I think you might be right there you know, and if it'll help you like you said it will then I like her also Frankie." Ramirez said as she gave into the Mutt's bragging over Blind Date.

"Thanks for understanding my needs baby; I really need your approval for this one, little sister. When are you and that pain in the ass soldier of yours coming back to the damn Unit, honey?" The Mutt asked with concern in his tone as he stared into her eyes.

"We shouldn't be gone no more than a week at the most, Mutt. I'll find a way to call you if it's only by radio to let you know, dog man." She offered as she kissed him again on his forehead.

"I'll be waiting for your call with bated breath baby. You know I'm gonna miss you guys, sister." The Mutt replied as he enjoyed her warmth a second time.

"Mutt, I have to shove off right away. If you know Walker, he's probably having a cow by now. You know how he gets whenever he's ready to shove off, and he has to wait around for someone else to catch up to him. Whew."

"Oh brother do I." The Mutt turned serious and asked. "You'll call me baby?"

"I'll definitely find a way to call you while we're in New York, Frankie. I promise, and I'll have Walker there too. So you can speak to him at the same time." The Sergeant said as she straightened up and then she prepared to leave the Mutt's side.

"You two are coming back, right? You guys are not using this as a way to get out of my sight, never to be seen again? I couldn't go on if I lost you pukes, not so close after losing Barbara." The Mutt moaned as he got up on an elbow, and he looked deep into her beautiful eyes.

"Boy, you dare to ask me that after you just handed me a piss and moan story about how smart you are, mister? I should plant a smack right on that mixed breed granite knob of yours you call a head, fella." She smiled at her dear friend.

"I'm scared to death honey. For the first time in my life, I'm scared to death of what the future might bring. I don't like losing any friends like I have Raz." The Mutt offered.

"I know what you're saying Frankie. Don't worry about it. Before you know it, you'll have us back busting your horns again, honey. Then you'll complain, 'don't you two slugs have someplace else to go' at us Frankie?"

The Mutt made a quick head movement as he grumbled at the female soldier. "You betta get going before the nut comes down here looking for something to gnaw on, sister. I hate it when he tries to eat my leg off because I screwed up something again. Thanks for being there for me when I needed you the most Raz. I love you and that nut you're dating, baby."

"I wish I and Walker could be with you at the service for Barb. Standing by your side as always." She had to fight tears threatening to overtake her emotions.

"I know you and Walker will be there in mind and that will be all I'll need to get myself through this mess, Raz. You gonna say good-bye to that thick headed, crazy assed Irishman of yours for me honey?" the Mutt asked her seriously.

"You bet I will Frankie. We're going to miss you like hell Mutt."

"I know, but you betta get a move on it before Walker gets pissed off at ya, I love ya Raz."

"I love you too, and I'll see ya real soon and stay safe for me please, Frankie." She kissed the Mutt again and with one last look at the Mutt, she pulled free of his grasp. From out of the darkness, a lone voice cried out to the two soldiers.

"I'll look after him while you're gone Raz. He'll be okay, I promise." Blind Date said softly.

"Thanks." Ramirez replied, she did not know for sure, but she was pretty certain it was Regina Raphael. With a thought to Barb, Raz felt she was pushing the Mutt and Frenchie together. She vowed if Barbara did not mind, she would welcome her to the group of close friends.

When she got out of the troops quarters, she ran right into Lieutenant Walker, and the young Seaman returning for her as Walker bitched at her as soon as he bumped into her. "What the hell were you doing in there this long for carp sake, having a stinking baby on me? Or waiting for Christmas for fuck sake, I had to come back to see where the hell you were at?"

"Awwww... poor little baby." She purred as she ran her finger down the side of his face.

"Don't give me any of that stinking bullshit, Raz. What the hell were you doing in there so long, dammit? We gotta get going, the stinking plane's waiting for us on the Flight Deck."

"Well grouch if you must know what I was doing, I was talking to the Mutt."

"He's up?" Walker moaned as he tried to look around Ramirez and see into the unlit quarters.

"Yes, and we had a good talk also Bobby. I think he's going to be fine, really Walker."

"I guess I betta go in there and tell him we're not going to make the Mass for Barbara."

"I already done that Walker." She offered with a half smile.

"Yeah? And how did the pain in the ass take it?" the concerned Lieutenant asked her.

"You know how he is Walker; he's a helluva lot smarter than we give him any credit for, honey." Ramirez offered as she stuck up for the Mutt.

"Zat so? You must know a different Mutt than I do all of a sudden Raz."

"Yeah wiseguy, he knew we were going to miss the service, and he was cool with it Bobby."

"And that makes him smart huh? Even someone who can't count up to fucking ten woulda been able to figure that much out all by himself that we're going to miss the service. It ain't scheduled until nine, and we're pulling the hell outta here three in the stinking morning. Seems like a stinking no brainer if you were to ask me, pretty girl."

"You're impossible when you get like this you know, Walker. That's supposed to be your best friend in there who is really hurting you're talking about."

"And this means what to me?" he shot back with a smirk, not giving into Ramirez.

"And nothing thickhead. Shall we get going? I want to breathe some fresh air for a change."

The Lieutenant turned to the Seaman and snarled at him. "To the Flight Deck, Watson."

The two Special Forces soldiers followed the young Seaman up the ladders and through hatchways leading up to the massive Flight Deck of the Carrier. Walker tangled once with one of the knee knockers, cursing while taking a second to rub the pain away. Deep in the bowels of the Aircraft Carrier, the air was warm to almost hot, but the second the two soldiers stepped foot on the Flight Deck, they were immediately sorry they did not have much warmer clothes on. It was freezing, with a strong wind force hard enough to blow you right off the Flight Deck if you were not careful about yourself.

Sergeant Ramirez moved closer to Lieutenant Walker's side, trying to steal some warmth from him as he searched the Flight Deck for the Jetstar aircraft. To his surprise, he picked up Colonel Leadbetter on the deck, and he was busy speaking to someone. Seeing them emerge from the hatchway, Colonel Leadbetter immediately waved them over to him.

The Lieutenant growled at the Seaman. "Who the hell's the big cheese with the Colonel?"

"That's Captain Collins, he's the Boss of the ship so watch your mouth with him, sir."

"Got'cha Swabby. I'm a cool dude when it comes to the big brass asses round me."

When they reached Colonel Leadbetter, he announced. "Lieutenant Robert Walker, Sergeant Dorothy Ramirez, this is Captain Robert Collins, Commander of the Washington, sir."

He reached out his shivering hand and shook hands with the likeable Captain.

"Ahhh... Lieutenant Walker, I have heard quite a bit about you son. I feel like I'm standing in the presence of real Royalty. How have my people been treating you and yours on board my ship, sir?" the Captain asked the Lieutenant pleasantly.

"Just fine Captain Collins Sir, I have no possible complaints I can offer you, sir. I'm glad to be aboard this here... err... ship of yours Captain Collins Sir. Your people really have their shit together and know what they are doing at all..." He was enjoying speaking to the Captain.

"Lieutenant Walker!" Colonel Leadbetter said hotly as he took a step toward him, in an effort to try and stop him before he said something that might insult the Captain.

"Sorry sir, I guess I still have some battlefield mentality stuck in my craw, sir. Christ sake sir, it's as cold as a witch's tit out here, Colonel." He complained as he crossed his arms over his chest. Ramirez moved a bit closer to Walker, again trying to get some warmth from him.

Captain Collins turned to Sergeant Ramirez when she moved towards the other soldier to keep warm, and said to her to get her involved in the conversation that was being carried on by the officers. "Yes, and this must be Sergeant Dorothy Ramirez. I'm sorry the accommodations below deck for women weren't better equipped for your short stay with us, Ma'am. You must be aware that space is a commodity on board an Aircraft Carrier, Ma'am. I tried my best to supply some minor comforts for you and the other female fighters of your Unit, Ma'am. I'm sure it could have been a lot more to your liking though but that's the best I have to offer, Ma'am."

"No problem Captain Collins Sir. The accommodations were outstanding, sir. Better than we're usually accustomed to, sir." She purred as she cast a wary eye at Colonel Leadbetter.

"Hmmm... I must say that you and the other women brought the woman's cause in this man's Navy to a new heading, young lady. I heard about your military exploits in Iran, Sergeant. Err... I must say I'm sadden by the death of the young woman fighter we're still holding in sickbay, Ma'am. She's the first woman warrior to have ever lost her life on the battlefield as far as I understand, Ma'am. In case you're wondering, I intend to visit the service personally later today, with all free hands on board the Washington, Ma'am." The Captain slightly bowed to Ramirez.

"Thank you for that Captain Collins, she meant a lot to me sir. She was my friend. She meant a lot to everyone from the outfit. I'm sorry I can't attend the service, but I have to be in Ne..."

Lieutenant Walker shifted his weight on his feet, and then he interrupted their conversation by saying to the Commander of the Carrier. "Captain Collins Sir, have you heard anything from any of her stinking relatives, sir? Is anyone gonna claim her body sir? When are they coming for Barbara? Or are we going to be allowed to bury her in the massive Field of Honor in Washington, sir?" the Lieutenant was referring to Arlington National Cemetery.

"Yes Lieutenant Walker Sir, I'm glad you asked me about this, sir. We heard from Miss Meyerhoff's relatives, sir. Her brother and he wants to bury her in Ohio, sir. He's not a very friendly person to deal with, and it didn't impress him I had arranged for transportation for him to retrieve the body. All he kept asking me about was if there were any death benies due him from the service, sir." The Captain took an angry breath in and held it for a moment.

"Sounds like he's a real dirt bag to me, sir. No wonder Barb never talked very much about her family, sir. If they're anything like that one, I can't blame her not talking bout them, sir. Shit, I hope the guys are gonna arrange transportation for the funeral, sir. Ohio is a helluva way out there sir. The Mutt's gonna be really pissed off being cooped up in a plane for that long a time sir. Captain, is the Mutt gonna get leave to enable him to attend the funeral in Ohio, sir?"

"Err... Lieutenant Walker Sir, I'm sorry to be the one to be forced to inform you of this, sir. But the funeral's going to end up a real shit pie, and the Mutt and the rest of you are going to be forced to choke it down, sir. Who is this one you call the Mutt, Lieutenant Walker Sir?" the Captain asked, never hearing this name mentioned before to him.

"He's Lieutenant Frank Hall, and the dead soldier was his main squeeze, Captain." He could tell from the Captain's expression he did not know what he meant and added. "Barbara Meyerhoff was his girlfriend, and they were planning to marry after this last mission, sir."

"I didn't know that Lieutenant Walker Sir! That really sucks the big one then Walker." Colonel Leadbetter replied. "That adds more crap to the shit pie we have to eat Walker."

"What's all this crap about a shit pie, Colonel?" the Sergeant snapped as she moved before Walker, and then she glared first at Colonel Leadbetter, and then at the Captain.

Colonel Leadbetter suddenly cleared his throat but was immediately cut off by the concerned Captain of the ship as he spoke to the other military officer. "I'll take this one for you Colonel Leadbetter Sir; it's my ship, so it's my responsibility to dump shit on anyone on board her, Colonel." The Captain then turned to Walker and added. "Son, Sergeant Meyerhoff's brother made it absolutely clear that he doesn't want any military types to attend her funeral, sir. He plans to make it a small funeral, inviting just a few of her relatives. You know her mother and father are dead, and this brother's the only one surviving her entire family, sir. I don't mind telling you he's a real bag of shit to deal with, sir."

The Lieutenant spun around with anger locked in his heart, as he turned his eyes towards the heavens and hissed. "Shit, if I wasn't stuck going to New fucking York, I'd show you how the soldiers from my Unit would show up at the stinking funeral. And if this bro didn't like it, I'd plant him in the fucking ground with his sister. Fuck sake sirs, this worm isn't worthy of looking at Barb's body. Let alone entitled to anything Barb has coming from the Gov. God dammit, I wish to hell I wasn't going to New York, sir. I'd like to show the little fucker alright. I'd dragged everyone's ass out to Ofuckinghio and leveled the damn place, after I skull fucked the lousy little prick who calls himself Barbara's brother, right through his missing eye sockets sir.

"Who the hell does this stinking scumbag think he is not to invite us, the ones she died with to her stinking funeral, Captain, Colonel? Christ sake Captain Collins Sir, Colonel Leadbetter. Can't either of you guys do anything about this can of crap we're forced to chow down, sirs? If anyone's entitled to attend her damn funeral, it has to be all of us she died with, Colonel." He pointed at his chest; and he did not notice Ramirez was crying.

The Captain of the Carrier put up his hand in order to silence Lieutenant Walker's bitch and calm him down a little at the same time, as he offered to the young and extremely upset officer. "Lieutenant Walker Sir, I completely agree with your gripe and I'm on your side with it as well, sir. You can believe I was on the damn horn the moment I heard this lousy little shit of a person was going to be a real dirt bag about the funeral, sir. I spoke to everyone from the Pentagon on up and down the damn ladder, sir. I even griped to the White House, and anyone else I could get on the damn phone to even speak to me over this matter, sir. Everyone told me the same damn thing though Lieutenant. If the brother doesn't want any military at the funeral, it's his prerogative and we're helpless to do anything about it, Lieutenant."

"What about the stinking President sir? He owes us big time, he should be able to order us there sir." Walker complained at the two Commanders.

"Hey cus, in case you don't know it yet mister. The President doesn't owe you or your people jack fucking shit. But I did speak to him about the situation, and he has assured me he was going to looking into it. He even told me he was planning to speak to the brother personally. That's the best I can do for you and the rest of your soldiers, Lieutenant." The Captain growled as he looked at the deck, pissed that he was unable to do more for the soldiers and their dead comrade.

Colonel Bruce Leadbetter stepped in on the conversation and warned his officer. "C'mon Lieutenant Walker, that's it sir. You have to board the damn aircraft and get in the air if you intend to make it to New York City on schedule, sir." Colonel Leadbetter then stepped aside and waved his hand towards the Jetstar aircraft that had maneuvered its way to the Catapult One System, and it was hooked up to the steam slide car in the flight deck. The Jetstar's engines were spooling just above idle speed, while waiting for permission to be launched from the ship.

"Fuck that damn bullshit Colonel Leadbetter Sir, I'm needed by my fucking troops here, sir. What about the stinking Mutt? How do you think he's gonna react once he's told he can't attend the funeral for Barb, sir? He's gonna tear this stinking ship apart with his bare hands, starting at its rearend and ending up with the bow of the ship in his hands, sir."

"You're getting on board that fucking plane, Lieutenant! One way or the fucking other, in one piece, or in puzzle form buster." Colonel Leadbetter snarled at Walker as he pointed towards the small plane. Then he assumed a much more threatening posture towards the

Lieutenant and added to his angry words. "The President said he wants you two shitbirds in New York City, and that's where you two are going, dammit! Get on board that fucking plane and leave the damn Mutt and the other soldiers to me, mister. He'll be alright Lieutenant that much I can assure you. Now get on board that god damn plane and get the hell out of my sight, Lieutenant!"

"Colonel Leadbetter Sir, I don't want him ending up being thrown in the stinking brig, or worse sir. Getting a fist full of bad paper, sir." He complained as he stepped forward and headed for the plane's ladder. Bad paper was military slang for a dishonorable discharge.

"Don't worry about him, I already told you that the fucking Mutt will be well taken care of, and as for any bad paper, the only bad paper he'll receive is shitty looking wallpaper, mister. Put your mind at ease Lieutenant, I swear to the good Christ Child I'll look after him personally, and he'll be waiting for you when you get back to the Unit, sir. Walker, get going, now, dammit!" Colonel Leadbetter rested his hand on his back and applied some pressure.

Unseen by either Walker, Ramirez or Colonel Leadbetter. Captain Collins made a number of subtle but quick hand movements, after Walker growled at the Colonel that he was not going to board the waiting plane. Ten Shore Patrol Seaman swiftly moved out of their nooks and crannies while taking up a loose protective ring around surrounding their Captain. Captain Collins heard many of the very upsetting stories about these special operations soldiers, and how they were extremely uncontrollable, and how hard they fought. The Captain was not taking any chances with these two obviously extremely dangerous soldiers going off on him. If Walker was going to act like a nut, he was going to be treated like a madman and placed in handcuffs. Then shoved on board the Jetstar one way or the other. Captain Collins could not wait to get these crazy ass soldiers off his ship, the faster they left, the better he liked it.

The Captain watched as Colonel Leadbetter ushered the two young soldiers towards the waiting aircraft, only relaxing when Lieutenant Walker finally climbed the ladder, stopping to look back and give the Captain a slight nod and weak salute. Walker was followed by the female soldier. The second Ramirez was on board, Colonel Leadbetter slammed his palm on the side of the aircraft. The ladder folded and disappeared while forming the outer wall of the aircraft.

The Jetstar aircraft had worked its way through the chain of handlers on board the Carrier, beginning with Blue Shirts responsible for the chocking and chaining the plane down to the Flight Deck while the engines were down. Once this was completed, the Jetstar was turned over to the Purple Shirts, responsible for the fueling and maintenance of the aircraft while on the Flight Deck. When the Jetstar was ready for launch, the aircraft was turned over to White Shirts, responsible for the final inspection of the plane. While the idling aircraft was on the deck, it was under the control of Yellow Shirts, the directors of aircraft movement on the Flight Deck.

Once the Jetstar went that far up the Chain of Command, the aircraft was then turned over to the last of the Flight Deck handlers. The Green Shirts, responsible for securing the plane's nose wheel toe bar arm, to the head of the steam driven catapult cart. It was at this point the plane was deemed ready for immediate launch from the Flight Deck, and the jet blast defectors were already raised out of the deck, to direct the heat raised from the powerful engines of the aircraft, away from the other planes or the crews working on massive Flight Deck.

Captain Collins waved his hand at the Air Boss as he gave way to the plane building up launch power. The Captain waited until Colonel Leadbetter was by his side. They hung onto their caps as the plane's engines spooled up, building speed to take off power. The plane would not be allowed to launch until it reached its full power, and the engines were screaming raw power.

Captain Collins turned to Colonel Leadbetter, grunting over the roar of the engines. "I didn't have the heart to tell your young Lieutenant and Sergeant that the brother had even refused to allow the VFW Honor Guard to show up and pay their respects to the fallen soldier, sir."

"That was very wise on your part Captain." Colonel Leadbetter screamed into the Captain's ear while he was still hanging onto his cap and then he added. "If you allowed that information to slip out, I know Walker would never have boarded the damn plane in one piece, sir."

"He's a rather excitable young chap, isn't he Colonel?" the Captain offered with a smirk.

"I'm afraid that's the way we breed them and want them in our line of work, sir. We need people who can reach the peak of savagery at a moment's notice, and be ready to challenge any threat leveled against them or this nation, sir. If Walker didn't react the way he did, I would've been concerned about his state of mind, Captain Collins Sir."

"Do you really think it would've gotten that out of control on us with the Lieutenant, Colonel Leadbetter Sir?" the Captain of the Carrier asked the Commander of the specialized troops he had on board his ship.

"Sure, but only if I lost control over the damn situation, sir. If I displayed any possible weakness with that wild one, you can rest assured he wouldn't be on that damn plane at this time, Captain." The Marine Colonel offered also with a smirk on his lips.

"Huh Colonel Leadbetter Sir, I had some of my security people move up, just in your Lieutenant Walker caused a problem for us, Colonel. They would've made certain the two soldiers boarded that aircraft, sir." Captain Collins announced with a snap in his voice.

"Yeah, I picked them people up moving steathfully around on the damn Flight Deck sir, and they wouldn't have been enough to control my two soldiers, Captain."

"You picked up my people moving around on the Flight Deck Sir? I'm stunned Colonel, usually no one sees them getting in position until it's too late to react against them, sir. Do you think those two soldiers noticed them moving also, Colonel?" the Captain asked with surprise.

"If I saw them, you can bet the bank on it those two noticed them moving as well, Captain."

"Hmmm... and you say my people wouldn't have been enough to control your people, sir?"

"Damn right Captain, those two would've handled the ten you had moving to intercept them."

"Colonel Leadbetter Sir, you even counted my security people moving around on the damn Flight Deck, let alone picking them all out of the crowd so easily, sir. I'm very impressed sir, but you said they wouldn't have been enough personnel to stop your two soldiers from creating a scene, sir. Would they have reacted violently towards my people, Colonel?" the Captain asked, deeply concerned over the fact these two soldiers might have killed a few of his people.

"Bet your ass on it Captain Collins Sir. My soldiers are trained to act, and to react against any possible threat leveled against them in an instant, and they only know one way to do it sir. That's with extreme malice aimed at their attackers, Captain. I'm afraid the ones who would have survived their attack, would never be the same for the rest of their lives, Captain Collins Sir." Colonel Leadbetter warned the Captain of the ship about his troop's abilities.

"And you would've allowed these two animals of yours to get out of control and attack my people, Colonel?" the Captain growled, angered his men were threatened so by his soldiers.

"No sir, not in the least..." The Colonel offered, but he was cut off by the Captain.

"That's much better Colonel..."

This time it was the Captain who was cut off by the Colonel as he added to his warning he just leveled at the Commander of the Carrier. "I would've been helping my troops, Captain Collins."

"What the hell kind of animals do you have under your Command, Colonel Leadbetter? And, I use the term command cautiously in this conversation, sir. I can't believe you would've killed or otherwise injured other soldiers of the United States Navy, just like that Colonel Leadbetter. Christ Almighty, we're on the same god damn team you're threatening my people like this, sir."

"We're the worst fucking nightmare conjured up to go against any of our country's enemies, no matter where they come from or who they might be, sir. If anyone's foolish enough to dare attack any of my people, they better have a damn good supply of mummy bags with them. Or their damn asses are going to be lying out in the open where they fell, Captain Collins Sir." The Marine Colonel retorted angrily, refusing to back down an inch from the Naval Captain.

The change of the Jetstar's engines broke the stalemate, and the two officers turned their attention towards the aircraft waiting to be launched from the flight deck. The Colonel grinned as the plane built up power. The Navy Captain glared at the back of the Marine Colonel, fuming he would have allowed his fighters to hurt his lesser trained people. The Captain planned to send a steaming memo to Naval Command, stating under no circumstances would he ever allow any other Special Forces soldiers to be a part of his Carrier Group. The little the Captain was involved with these extremely dangerous soldiers, was enough to last him for a lifetime. He ripped his eyes off the Colonel's back, and then allowed them to drift towards the plane.

The Captain watched the signal officer raised his hand overhead, and then rapidly twirled his fingers in a circle, to make certain the Jetstar's engines were at their maximum takeoff power. Then he looked at the nose tow bar before turning the plane over to the CLO (Catapult Launch Officer). Once he had the aircraft, he signaled the catapult operator, giving him the thumbs up signal to the pilot of the Jetstar, and then he waited for his salute. Once receiving it, the Green Shirt gave the signal as he dropped down to his knees on the flight deck, and allowed the plane's wing to pass just inches over his head, as the steam powered catapult dragged the Jetstar aircraft down the flight deck at breath robbing speed.

With an ear piercing roar, the catapult cart whipped the small aircraft down the Flight Deck in just under two seconds, until it released it with the catapult head dropping below the Flight Deck to allow the nose tow bar to be released from the slide car and clear the aircraft. The Jetstar shot in the air, its increased speed giving the aircraft the needed lift to become airborne. Slowly, the plane climbed until the wings grabbed the air, and then the aircraft soared into the heavens.

Colonel Leadbetter was the first one to let out his breath as he smiled at the Captain, still steaming from their heated conversation, as he offered. "Well that's that, shall we go, Captain?"

"Not until we come to a much better understanding about a few things that bugging the shit out of me, Colonel Leadbetter Sir. From this point forward sir, I want all your damn special troops restricted to their fucking quarters, the mess, and the showers below the deck. All other areas on board this ship are to be considered off limits to any of your extremely dangerous soldiers for the duration they're stationed on board this ship, sir. I want you to inform your troops they're not allowed to go anywhere on this ship without a Seaman escort from one of my crew, and a written request signed by me, or my EO. (Executive Officer)

"I'm terribly sorry to inform you of this order and demand Colonel Leadbetter Sir. I'm also planning to have armed escorts surrounding your people at all times while they're on board this ship, Colonel. To be quite frank with you Colonel, I don't have any god damn intention of allowing your troops to hurt my people on board my Carrier while I'm still in command of this ship, sir." Captain Collins glared at the special operations officer for a long and tense moment.

Fighting to control his mounting anger, Colonel Leadbetter fired right back at the Naval Captain. "Suit yourself, I'll also be making a report to my superiors myself as well, Captain. Informing them how you're treating my forces trapped on this ship, sir."

"That's fine with me Colonel Leadbetter Sir, and your report will cross mine I assure you, Sir. Complaining about how threatening your damn troops are to the safety and security of my ship and her crew, Colonel. As for these so called troops of yours belonging to the Armed Forces, sir. I seriously doubt they understand what that truly means to them, sir. Because no member of the Armed Forces would ever threaten another member with death, as your troops have obviously just done here today, sir. Shall we go below deck Colonel Leadbetter Sir?" the Captain waved his hand out before him, allowing the Colonel to lead the way for the both of them.

Over his shoulder, the extremely angry Colonel Leadbetter growled at the trailing Captain. "Are we still going to be allowed to hold the service for Sergeant Meyerhoff, Captain Collins?"

"Under armed escorts, Colonel Leadbetter!" the Captain fired off as he stared at his back.

"Will you be attending the service as offered, Captain?" the Marine Colonel asked.

"No, not on your life Colonel Leadbetter Sir. I have to make damn certain that my security people control your pack of obvious wild animals all the while they are stationed on board my ship, sir." Captain Collins snapped as he followed the Colonel.

"That's fine with me, Captain Collins Sir." Colonel Leadbetter shot back at the angry Captain as he entered the hatchway before the Captain entered it.

ON BOARD JETSTAR AIRCRAFT ONE, ONE, SEVEN

Lieutenant Robert Walker let out with a howl as the small aircraft shot up into the air with breath robbing speed. He loved the feeling of the rapid acceleration and speed.

Ramirez held his hand in a death grip fighting to keep her stomach down. Only when they were airborne, and the aircraft leveled out in flight, did she finally relax her grip on his hand.

He smiled as he wiggled his fingers, trying to get circulation going again as he piped up. "We're up Raz." Just as he said that, the pilot's voice came over the plane's intercom.

"Please feel free to release your seatbelts, you're free to move about the plane while in flight. There are refreshments stored in the tail section of the aircraft for your pleasure, feel free to help yourself. But remember, when you're in your seat, keep your seatbelt fastened. Thank you."

Lieutenant Walker unhooked his seatbelt and then he stood and stretched his arms the best he could in the rather confining interior of the small aircraft because there was little headroom above him. Once he accomplished this, he headed for the refreshments, seeking a cup of coffee to keep him awake, while there he poured a cup for her. He returned to his seat with two donuts stuffed between his teeth, and he handed a cup and donut to Sergeant Ramirez.

He then plopped down in the seat next to Ramirez, but he did not fasten his seatbelt as he sipped the hot brew. It was strong and he needed it that way, he gnawed through the donut then retrieved another. He did not realize how hungry he was until he took time to eat; he forgot the food he wanted to take with him back on the ship. She did not eat the cake, she was troubled over Meyerhoff's death, and content to stare in the blackness of the night for answers to her dilemma.

"A penny for your thoughts Raz." The Lieutenant offered to his lover and fellow soldier.

"Awww... I was just thinking about that pain in the ass Frank Hall and Meyerhoff, Bobby, that's all." She replied as she glanced at her soldier staring at her intensely.

"C'mon baby, you gotta let it go for crap's sake. Hey hon think of it this way, we're off to the Big fucking Apple, and we have a pocket full of stinking cash to boot. All compliments of the stinking government, and we're gonna be hob knobbing with the fricking big shots of the damn town. Man, what a stinking country we live in, huh baby?"

The Lieutenant sighed, he was sorry he was unable to get Ramirez out of her dilemma and he continued trying to get her to lighten up. "Shit, I shoulda got me some damn chips while I was back there." He pulled down the seat table and then placed the food he took for her on it.

Raz slid the food to her table and picked at her donut. He immediately snitched a piece.

"Gees are you still hungry Walker?"

"Yeah why?" he snorted, figuring she was going to get on him.

"Here, eat this thing then will you please. I'm not in the mood to eat anything anyhow."

"You sure? I could sure use it, I'm still starving you know baby. Travel always makes me hungry as hell all the damn time, sister." He grinned as he took the donut then dove into it.

"Eat it Bobby." The female Sergeant said as she turned to look outside the plane. She smiled when she noticed the lights from a ship below them.

Chapter Eight

The Vice President of the United States, Mary Hirshfield arrived at Joint Andrews Air Force Base a few minutes ahead of schedule, and she was immediately seated in the plush Air Force One aircraft nick named Eagle's Nest by the President. Waiting for the massive aircraft to be secured and then cleared for liftoff for their flight out to New York City. There seemed to be some sort of a problem with the runway. The small group of security guards had not finished their usual walk through to make certain there were no bombs, or other obstructions hidden along the tarmac that could cause damage to the specialized aircraft. Mary's aide was by her side as always, and she was working on a memo issued by the Vice President.

Vice President Hirshfield stared out the window, watching the special agents dragging their feet along the full length of the runway. They were always checking something, and she felt her life was not her own because of their constant presence around her both day and night. Air traffic into and out of Andrews was stacked up, or held back while waiting for Eagle's Nest to liftoff. She let out a deep sigh that immediately got the attention of her aide.

"Does the Vice President have a problem Ma'am?" her concerned bodyguard asked as she stared at the Vice President of the United States.

"When are those damn fools out there ever going to finish whatever the hell they're doing out there? I'm bored to death sitting on my rump while waiting for those pains in the can to play Secret Agent all the damn time around me. We should've been halfway to New York by this time, Cathy." Ms. Hirshfield complained at her female bodyguard and aide.

"Does the Vice President want me to check with the pilot, and see how much longer it'll be before we finally get permission to liftoff for New York City, Ma'am?" she asked as she turned to look into the eyes of the pretty Vice President.

"No! I'll keep myself amuse watching the damn Agents playing with themselves out there. I wish to hell for once in your sweet life, you'd stop calling me Vice President and call me Mary, or Ms. Hirshfield. Anything but Vice President, Cathy." Ms. Hirshfield griped at her aide, as she continued to stare at what the agents were doing outside the idling plane.

"Very well then Ma'am, I'll do as you have just ordered, Ma'am." Cathy replied while wearing a mild smile, and then she went back to what she was doing before Ms. Hirshfield asked her a question. But she was interrupted for a second time by the Vice President as she complained again in a disgusted and sharp tone of voice.

"Huh, that's just as bad Cathy. Look honey, I'll make a pact with you. Either you call me Mary, or I'll call you aide. How do you like that idea, dear?" Vice President Hirshfield complained as she let out her breath in a rush.

"Yes Mary, it'll be my pleasure to call you by your first name, if that's what you want, Ma'am." Her bodyguard placed a pleasant smile on her lips as she looked at Mary.

"That's much better Cathy dear. Thank you so much for the kind consideration." Ms. Hirshfield smile back just as pleasantly at her aide.

The 747s four massive engines went from idle to full take off power in an instant. As a number of Special Agents quickly scurried away from the aircraft.

"It's about time they're getting underway. I'm bored to death over this unending wait." Mary bitched as she leaned back in her seat and then she closed her eyes. She wanted to rest a little during the short flight, so she would be able to remain awake when they landed in New York.

Air Force One pulled onto the runway and waited for full military power to be reached by the engines. When they did, the plane shot down the runway, and in seconds was airborne along with its four heavily armed F18 attack aircraft escorts. A light mist was falling, making it feel colder than it was in Washington this time of year. It was no better in New York, the high was expected to be forty, and light rain or snow showers were forecast. She was wearing her silver fox fur coat that she loved dearly. She was very proud of her coat, and she did not care what the fur dogs from Pita were going to say about it while she was visiting New York City.

The now well pleased Vice President pulled the thick and fluffy collar of the exquisite and expensive coat around her neck and then she nuzzled in the soft fur with pleasure as she tried to get some rest during the flight.

The aide and special agent assigned to protect the Vice President at all times, smiled when she noticed Mary making herself comfortable. Seeing this, she finally allowed herself to relax a little since she first set out with the Vice President on their trip to New York City. Cathy leaned back in her seat, and she closed her eyes while allowing her mind to wander over the many duties she was responsible for while visiting the Big Apple for the meeting at the United Nations.

She was looking forward to visiting the City, it was a number of months since the last time she was in the City, and she wanted to see if it changed during her time away. She did not hide the fact she loved the greatest City in the world. She loved New York better than anywhere else on the earth, and she enjoyed the interesting people who lived and worked in the City. They were great people, fun loving, active, and always looking for a challenge to conquer, or fun to enjoy.

ON BOARD JETSTAR ONE, ONE, SEVEN, HEADING FOR NEW YORK CITY

Lieutenant Robert Walker shifted his weight in his chair, he just could not get comfortable in the aircraft seat no matter how hard he tried, and parts of him were on pins and needles. Sergeant Dorothy Ramirez was getting angry at his constant fidgeting around and she finally snapped at him. "Would you pleaseeee sit still for a moment dammit. You're keeping me awake Walker."

"I hate this shit, I'm a ground pounding mud loving grunt, sister. I belong on the ground, not dangling my ass in the air. How much longer before we touchdown in the Big Apple, baby?"

Sergeant Ramirez checked her watch and then replied. "Walker, we've only been in the air for an hour and twenty minutes. We have a long time to go before we reach New York. Will you sit back and relax, please. You're becoming a real pest with all the movement you're doing. Will you relax for once in your life? I really need some rest, Robert."

"That's all it's been? Damn, I wish I had some lousy candy or something to eat."

"Here take this, but only if you'll behave. I'd like to catch up on sleep if possible during the flight. I'm exhausted, and all you want to do is bug my ass." She complained at her soldier.

"Whoa shit, where the hell did ya get this from, baby? It's my favorite candy bar, you holding out on me girl? You got anything else hidden under your shirt I should know about, baby?"

"I picked it up from the Gedunk (Gedunk was the junk food store on the Carrier) before we left the ship. I have two more and one sugar titty if you get out of hand on me, big boy."

"Sugar titty? What the hell's that Raz?" he asked as he stared at her.

She let out her breath and then she pulled open the front of her shirt to allow her breasts to pop out. Then she pulled the melting candy bar from his hand and she smeared some over her erected nipple and snapped at him. "There you big baby you. That's a sugar titty, and it's something we women do for babies to keep them quiet when we're trying to sleep, Bobby. Now I want to sleep, are you going to let me sleep, or do I have to smack you on the back of your noggin, mister?"

"Sure thing, but only if you allow me to clear up that nasty little mess you just made." The excited Lieutenant smiled as he fingered the melted chocolate smeared on her breast.

"That's why I did it for Bobby. What the devil are you waiting for stupid? Clean it up for me will you please." She smiled as she waited for him to do what she told him to.

He bent his head over and then he licked away at her candy covered nipple. He was quickly getting carried away with assaulting her breast with her tongue, and Ramirez had to push him away when he began to fumble around with the front of his pants.

"Hey, hold on a minute there big boy. I'm not going to make love to you on this damn plane mister. I like a little kink in my life as much the next person does, but this is pushing it a little too far for my likes, Bobby. Back off a little and save some of that for when we're alone in New York, please Walker." She said as she enjoyed what he was doing to her breast.

"C'mon, I'm stiff as a stinking board now baby. I gotta do something with the damn thing or I'm gonna bust the damn thing off my stinking body, and you'll end up with Walker all over the plane's interior, honey." The extremely excited now Lieutenant complained at his girlfriend as he tried to get her in the mood to make love with him.

"Slap it down and think about something else so you can get out of the mood, Bobby." She moaned as she tried to pull her hand free of his grasp. He grabbed her hand and shoved it down the front of his pants, and she wrapped her fingers around his rock hard shaft. She thought better of it and she pulled her hand free before she got carried away with the moment herself.

"C'mon that's not gonna do me any stinking good this time baby. Why don't you slide down there and give me a little stinking head. You're so damn good at it and the way I feel right now, it wouldn't take you very long to pop me off, sister. I swear baby I'll be real easy for you to do your act on me, Raz." He flashed his butter melting smile at her.

"Forget it fella, I'm not going to suck you off in the plane, and that's that. The pilot could come out of the cockpit anytime, and I'm not going to get caught with your dick in my mouth again for nothing." She snapped as he tried to guide her head to his crotch with his free hand.

"No, I said so forget it, and that's it, mister. If you want some head, give it to yourself because I'm not going to do you this time so there, buster. I want to be in a room in a bed before we do anything." She growled, actually getting a little angry at him for pushing her like he was doing.

"Oh good now you did it to me sister. There, look at this Raz. Look at what you just done to me girl. You hurt my stinking feelings, and I'm outta the stinking mood now, thank you very much, sister. You wait; I'll fix you good and proper Raz. The next time you want a little sugar from my ass, you're gonna have to beg my ass from your stinking hands and knees I tell ya." The teasing Lieutenant complained as he pointed towards his softening dick.

"Huh, that'll be the day I'll ever have to beg you for some sex, Bobby. You're way to easy to say that to me, buster" She retorted with a smirk as she opened her eyes and stared at him.

"I'm telling ya Raz, you just wait, you'll see. I'm not screwing round with you this time in the least, sister. I'm really pissed off at you this time, and the next time you want some, you're gonna have to beg me for real for it, Raz." He repeated as he stared back at his lover.

"Oh yeah, and how will I have to beg you to make love to me?" she smirked back at Walker.

"On your hands and knees like I just told you, Home Girl. I'm not fooling around with ya this time Raz." The smirking Lieutenant was trying to keep the smile from his lips as he looked at her, and hoping she was going to do him on the plane.

"Ha, that'll be the day when I have to beg you on my hands and knees for some sex, buster. You have to come up with something better that that threat." She replied as she gave him one of her looks that would have melted the hardest of hearts, and a twinkle in her beautiful eyes.

"I swear I'm not joking around with you this time, Raz. I'm gonna be strong, you wait, you'll see. I'm gonna be the fucking Rock of Gibraltar, a real hard ass man this time, girl. I can do things like that because I'm big and strong, sister. Once I set my mind to do something, you know damn well nothing this side of Judgment day will ever change it." He snapped, trying to show her he was angry as he puffed up his chest and took a steadfast stance against her.

She was up to the challenge as she rubbed her breasts against his arm; she then ran her tongue erotically over her lips and even fluttered her eyes at him, while not saying a word to him.

"Well, that's enuf fucking begging from you little sister. I told you I was gonna be the rock of Gibraltar. Let's say we do it right here, that should be thrilling Raz." He snickered as he pushed her back, and then he buried his face between her breasts and lapped at her nipple again.

"Yeah Walker, I admit you're the Rock of Gibraltar, the stone of ages, a hard assed man, lover. Yep, you really made me beg ya big boy. I don't know how I'll ever live with myself what with the way I had to beg ya for sex, mister ass man." She was really enjoying all the bantering she was doing with her soldier, as she shoved his face away from her chest and buttoned her blouse.

"Hey Raz, I swear, you're getting to be a big tease lately there you know, baby. I guess you like it when I walk round with my tongue hanging out, and my dick hard as a rock, girl."

"Ha... that really turns me on to see your tongue hanging out like a dog I tell you, mister. I'm warning you buster, you wait until we get to the apartment and I had a chance to rest up a little, bathe and oil myself up good and proper. Then I'll show you what real teasing is all about, mister. I have a special little present tucked away in my suitcase for your enjoyment, mister."

"Yeah? What the hell is that Raz?" he begged as he sat up and looked at her.

"You have to wait until we get to the Trump Tower then you'll see, Bobby."

"C'mon Raz, tell me what it is. If you don't, I'll look for my fucking self honey."

"Just try it buster, and it'll take you days before you ever get to screw anything but your own damn hand, mister." She snapped her teeth and he picked up the warning she just issued as she added to her words aimed at him. "I won't show you what it is, but I'll give you a little hint to wet your appetite though, mister. It's something for me to wear to put you in the mood, baby."

"Hey baby I'm always in the stinking mood to see something that'll make making love to you that much betta, baby. I wanna see, please Raz." He cried as he panted, allowing his tongue to dangle like a retriever dog and he asked her between breaths. "Where didja get it from, huh baby? We weren't anywhere near where you coulda brought that kinda stuff from, Raz."

"If you must know where I got it from you pain in the backside, Jail Bait gave it to me to wear just for your pleasure. She had it with her all along. She was planning to wear it for Shot Gun when they went on leave, and they hooked up for some fun and games together."

"Huh, talk about being knocked over by a stinking pubic hair, baby? I didn't know McNutty (Private James McNulty) was playing around with Soloman (Sergeant Michelle Soloman). If that don't take the damn cake. Hey Raz, if she was saving it for him, how didja get your hands on it?"

"That was easy Bobby, when she found out we were going to New York for a week and sharing a room together, she offered it saying I was going to need it more than she would."

"Man, if Jail Bait had it, its gotta be a gem. She's a firecracker, sister. C'mon, lemme see it."

"You're getting a little gross again Bobby. Don't tell me you're getting the hots for her now too? And, you're not going to see it, not until we get to New York City and we're in the apartment they rented for our use there like I told you, and if you keep busting my horns like this about it then you'll never see it on me, mister. Believe me lover; I assure you that you'll lose out big time if that happens to ya. You'll really love it and I'm sure it fits me to a tee, and I'll look great in it." The Sergeant stuck out her tongue and then she touched the tip of it with her finger. She then turned in the chair and placed her fingertip on her hip and made a hissing sound as she added. "It's hotter than hell, and if you think you're drooling now, you just wait till you see me dressed in it. Then you'll really be drooling all over yourself, Bobby."

TUESDAY, NOVEMBER THE 17th, 1998, NEW YORK CITY

This was Michael's fourth meeting with his group of thieves, and he considered it their last one before they went in action against the Trump International Hotel and Tower. He knew he would be holding other meetings throughout the coming days to make certain their preparations were all in order for his attack against the building. As far as meeting as a group, it was out of the question. This meeting was the last one between all of them. He wanted as little contact with the group as possible, because he could not be certain if the cops were aware of their future plans or not. Or if someone might have ratted him out to the cops, and they set up an ambush against them before they reached the Tower and target.

The day before, he met one on one with the turncoat Trump Tower security guard. At that meeting, the guard handed him an updated list of the important people scheduled to be at the Tower when they planned to attack the structure.

At the last meeting, he read the long list of names of the civilians, and he picking out the ones he wanted to control for hostages from the Tower. He assigned certain hostages to each member of his group. They were to search and bring the civilians he wanted to keep down to the assembly area on the East Wing of the 20th floor. There he planned to use the diamond trader's room as their headquarters while ransacking the rest of the Tower for any valuables the rich kept in their rooms. It was two floors below the Presidential Suite, which according to the security guard's list, was to be unoccupied for the next few weeks in a row.

He and the security guard had no idea the suite was soon to be occupied by the Vice President of the United States. For security reasons, there was no paperwork filed with the security personnel of the Tower on her upcoming visit. Once the Vice President was in the building, she became the problem of her special agents to protect, and the Tower personnel would not be concerned who knew she was there. In fact, the manager was planning to make a big deal over the Vice President's stay at the Tower, to draw attention to the greatness of the Trump Tower.

He passed out copies of Tower's interior of the room with the diamond dealers. He was given an update on room 2145. It was built like Fort Knox. The door to the apartment was two inches thick, and it had a quarter inch steel plate sandwiched between the laminated wood sections of the door. The solid door frame made of reinforced steel, with bolts from the hinges going deep into the concrete wall to give added strength and security to the room and front door.

Getting through the concrete floor from above the apartment was out of the question, and he wanted everyone to know this. He was hoping to gain access to the fortified room, by allowing Alexander's man to attack the door with the rocket launcher. He went over this with the other members of his group, because he wanted them to be aware of what they were going up against.

The leader of the group did not want to have much to do with Alexander's crew, they were controlled by the Russian, and if anyone did not need watching, it was him. He spent most of his life fighting his parents, police then military officers when he did his duty for the Russian Army. Then he spent his time fighting gangs of Moscow once he was out of the service. He knew if anyone was prepared for a fight, he was. He was going to let him worry about the hostages.

Checking out the new Tower blueprints the security guard just handed him, the group discussed the known location of five of the seven safes inside the targeted room. Five of the safes were marked out clearly on the new prints. Two safes were hidden in end tables on either side of the couch in the living/dining room. Another safe was concealed in a support column surrounded by two closets, and the door to the spare bedroom. A forth one was hidden in the walk in closet, and the fifth safe was concealed in the oven. That meant there would be only two other safes they would have to locate on their own.

When He asked the guard where the other two safes were located, he could not answer the question. The guard informed him the traders did not trust everyone. So they were allowed to move in their safes, and hide them according to their likes in the apartment. Hearing this he turned to their safe cracker, Geofferson Prochaska, and asked him if he was going to have any trouble opening the seven strong boxes. Prochaska studied the picture of the safes and then bragged. "I know of these safes and I see no trouble with opening them, Number One."

"How long do you think you'll need to work on each safe, before you can open them for us, Prochaska?" the leader of the group asked the new Russian member of his group.

"Hmmm... I see at least ten minutes on each safe, if I'm able to figure out their combinations that is. Less time if they're easy, but there's the possibility I might damage the items inside it if I have to resort to the use of explosives on them." The Russian grumbled back at him.

"I don't want you using any explosives on the safes, resorting to them only if there's no other alternative left to open them for us. I want the safes opened by their combinations if at all possible." He snapped, allowing his anger to rise a bit with the Russian.

"I to would also like nothing better in life than to open the safes by their combination, Number One. But I'm unsure if they might have some kind of extra safety precautions installed in the safes that might make this impossible to achieve, Number One." The Russian responded to Michael's anger, by becoming excited himself, and when he was excited, his Russian accent surfaced. Making his words harder to understand by the group who were not Russian.

He stared at the Russian for a long moment and then he growled at him. "Look friend, when you first came to me, you bragged that you were the best safe cracker to ever walk the face of the earth, and there was no safe you couldn't open with your fingers. Now you sit on your damn arse telling me you might not be able to open these store bought cheap safes by their combinations. Let me tell you my friend, if you can't open the safes, I don't need you on the heist. If they have to be blown open then I can have Alexander do it, and I won't need you at all, my friend."

When Alexander's name was mentioned, all eyes went over to the extremely dangerous and unpredictable Russian ex-soldier. He remained seated, but he allowed a leer to cross his lips. He did not like Prochaska in the least, mainly because he came from the Ukraine, and any Muscovite worth his salt. Did not like the lowlife's who lived in the armpit of the earth according to him.

Geoffweson Prochaska glance at Alexander, and when he noticed him grinning at his dilemma, he was all the more angry with him and Michael.

"I just asked you the question Prochaska, Alexander didn't my friend. You're not going to find the answer on him." He snapped as he stabbed himself with his finger, drawing Prochaska's attention to him. Geofferson was one of his men, the fifth member of the group.

"I know you asked me god dom question about the safes you demand I open, One." Prochaska roared in anger, as he leapt to his feet and assumed a threatening stance against Michael.

Alexander was on his feet in a flash along with Lizzie, and they both held a pistol in their hands. Lizzie was the more threatening of the two, just daring Prochaska to make a move on Michael. So she could eliminate him and get on with the meeting at hand again.

Michael knew the Russian was no threat as he said. "Elizabeth, put up your weapon. He's angry, but he's not stupid." He stared at Lizzie until she relented and lowered her weapon at the floor. She never did put it away, she held it at arm's length while aimed towards the ground.

When he was sure Lizzie was under control, he glanced at Alexander who nodded at him, and then he holstered his weapon. He turned back to the steaming Prochaska who looked foolish standing the way he was, and feeling threatened and offered. "I believe I asked you a question?"

"I open the god dom fooking safes by their cursed combination for you Number One!" Prochaska hissed angrily at Michael as he openly glared at him.

"Or you forfeit your part of the take from the damn heist, Prochaska." The leader of the group added to his threat against the other member of his group.

Prochaska's eyes narrowed more as they held him in their angry glare. For a few tense moments, the two stared at each other. Then Prochaska's shoulders noticeably sagged as he mumbled. "Then I shall forfeit my share of the take if I no open god dom safes."

"Then you're still part of the group my friend." He then turned his attention to Alexander, and grumbled at the huge Russian. "Alexander, I want you to make certain you have something with you that'll knock the door off its hinges, if it has to go down that way for us. Oh, and make certain you have something that'll pop the safes opened, just in case Prochaska can't open the damn things for us. I don't want to destroy the safe, just open the door Alexander."

The Russian turned to Prochaska before replying. "I always more explosive open dom door on worthless American made safe. Unlike stupid Ukrainian dog standing here, I prepare anything for that comes at me way, Number One big shot leader you. Err... I even have another man who note for ability open cheap lock be safes, or gates. This how we get hand on inferior American made weapon I use time to time in me line of work, big shot Number One Leader." He allowed himself a quick laugh at Prochaska's behalf.

"That's great, just make sure this man's part of your unit, Alexander."

"Guastavino always part of unit no matter what, hot shot Number One big man. He trust and tried fight and action need soldier part and good friend also, if is to succeed no? Besides, never know when force open lock see what hid from one view in god dom safe, Number One."

"Good Alexander, but we'll only use him if Prochaska runs into any trouble with the safes." He knew what he was doing, first he ripped Prochaska apart before the other members of his group, and then he gave him face by letting him know he was the man. Both of them knew Michael was not going to hold back his share of the job if he could not open the safes as he bragged. He turned to Prochaska, and noticed the anger draining from his face.

"This is it for the meeting, I'll speak with each of you during the next week. At the meetings, I'll tell you where I want you, and when you'll go into the Tower. I don't want anyone linking up with the other until we're within one block of the Tower. I want everyone to make sure they're not being followed by the police or FBI. Make sure you keep your noses out of trouble when we make our move on the building. I don't want anyone drawing attention to themselves. If you screw up, or you believe you're being followed by the police, here's a pager number

I'll activate on the last days before we attack the Tower. Leave three numbers, one, two, three and hang up.

"If these numbers appear on my pager. I'll send out a hold warning to the others, by calling everyone and backing you off our attack on the Tower. If the call comes on the day we're going to hit the Tower, and it's too late to get hold of everyone to stop them from their orders. I'll fire off a red boater's flare. If you see a red star, break off your action and disappear in the crowd sure to be out and about when we hit the place. Remember, don't draw any attention to yourselves, and make sure your movements are smooth, like you're Joe visitor to the City. Alexander, you'll move your people and equipment out on Saturday, get it in position and then sit tight..."

"What time day we attack this fooking Tower place, Number One?" Alexander grumbled.

"You'll find that answer out at the last meeting, Alexander. Along with everyone else who's part of this heist. I'm going to stagger each person, and I'll keep my eyes on them. If someone doesn't show up when he's scheduled. I'll put the brakes on the attack until I'm certain there's no danger we've been discovered by police. Everyone knows what they have to do for this attack, and where they have to be at the time of the attack, and when they have to be there to begin our action on the Tower. Leave one at a time and get out of the area as quickly as possible. If anyone has to get in touch with me, just dial the first number I gave you and tell the woman who answers your call you're looking for the Chinese restaurant, and you dialed the number wrong.

"Then leave your first name with her, and I'll get back to you as soon as I can make contact with you. If anyone's taken prisoner by the police, give this woman up. She won't be much help to them, because she has no idea what she's involved with. She doesn't know me, so if you're taken by police, give her up and I'll know our plan was discovered, and I'll warn the others off the attack." Michael looked at each member of the group, and then he waited until they all nodded, and then he added to his words. "Very well then, I believe it's time to leave. Remember leave one at a time, and look like you're a tourist. Richard, you, Elizabeth, and Alexander will remain behind for a few moments. We have a few other things to discuss. The rest of you will make sure the items you'll need are in order, and then sit tight and wait my call."

He stopped speaking and waited for the others to file out of the room.

ON BOARD THE JETSTAR AIRCRAFT

The Jetstar flew for four hours and was less than halfway to New York City. Lieutenant Robert Walker allowed Sergeant Dorothy Ramirez to catch up on her sleep, and he took a quick catnap. He was awakened when the co-pilot came through the plane for a cup of coffee. As the co-pilot passed him, he got up and went to the rear of the plane with the co-pilot.

The co-pilot smiled at the Lieutenant as he asked him. "You want a cup? It's hot sir."

He nodded as he put out his hand. "Hey man, I'm Lieutenant Robert Walker buddy."

The co-pilot took the offered hand and replied to the military officer as he shook his hand. "Glad to meet ya Lieutenant. I'm Major Joe Rossie, sir. Why is the brass shipping your ass over to New York City, Lieutenant? It seems important to all concerned with this aircraft, sir."

"Dunno fur sure sir. It seems they want to show my ass off to some of the stinking hot shot brass for some reason, Major." He thought if this Major did not know what his mission was about, he sure was not going to brief him in on it.

"Yeah, and I'm little Red Riding Hood, Lieutenant. If you didn't want to cue me in, it would've been easier for you to say just mind your own business, sir." The co-pilot grumbled.

"You got it sir, mind your own business, Major Rossie Sir. If you were supposed to know they woulda told you why they wanted me, sir." He snapped at the Airforce Major.

The co-pilot glared at Walker then growled. "I have to admit, you got some balls Lieutenant."

"Hey man, you asked for it sir. Where you going? I wanna talk to you some more Major." The Lieutenant pressed as he grabbed the co-pilot's arm and stopped him from walking off.

"Sorry Lieutenant, I have to get back to the cockpit double quick, sir. We're scheduled to fuel in flight any moment sir. The pilot's looking for the guiding lights of the tanker now sir. I don't have time to engage in an extended conversation with you at this time, Lieutenant." The co-pilot shook his hand free, and then he rushed up the aisle and quickly disappearing inside the cockpit.

The Lieutenant watched Major Rossie leave and then he shrugged and strolled back to his seat. As he sat and buckled himself in, Ramirez eyes opened and she immediately complained at him again. "You have to bug the shit out of everyone near ya, don't cha Bobby?"

"Keep riding my ass and don't cut me any stinking slack, baby sister. I was just trying to find out what the hell's going on, that's all Raz. But that's your lot in life, nag, nag, nag, that's all you've been doing lately on my ass Raz. Want some coffee? It's hot, but tastes like shit. I think it's over perked. I wonder if we're gonna get something to eat on this damn thing, honey?"

"Sure Bobby, you're going to be served a three course meal and all the beer you want. Next, you're going to want a female flight attendant and movie." She tried to get comfortable again.

"Hey, you're right baby. There should be a few of them good looking hens on this damn thing. It'd give me something else to look at. You're no fun, all you wanna do is sleep and bitch at me."

She reached out and pinched his arm.

"Owe! Hey, what the hell was that for? I didn't do nuthin baby." he bitched at her.

"I told you I wanted to sleep and I can't do that if you're talking to me all the time, Bobby."

"Well pardon my stinking ass I wanna talk. I'm bored to death on board this damn thing, Raz. I wish they had a stinking movie on this damn lawn dart. Some VIP plane this damn thing is, no good looking flight attendants to look at, no stinking food to chow down on, and no friggin movie on this thing. I got a good mind to demand my money back for the damn flight, baby."

She did not respond, instead she pinched him on his arm for a second time.

"Arrr, I guess I'm not going to get any stinking sympathy around here from you I see, baby sister." He griped as he rubbed his arm, and then he looked at the smiling Sergeant lying against his shoulder. She looked like an angel the way she was curled up leaning against him.

"You know what they say Bobby. You want some sympathy, you know where to find it..."

"Yeah look in the dictionary between shit and syphilis, right girl?" his moaned cut her off.

She laughed and then closed her eyes and snuggled tightly up against his powerful shoulder, and in seconds she was breathing heavily, sound asleep.

The excited Lieutenant fidgeted around in his chair, making it impossible for her to sleep. Giving in to his constant pressure and moving around, she sat up and rubbed the sleep from her eyes and then she glared angrily at him. She suddenly slugged him in the arm.

"Hey, what the hell's that for?" He complained again at her.

"You know damn well what you were doing here Bobby. You didn't want me to sleep, and you sure got your damn wish mister. What the devil's bugging you anyhow Walker? I never seen you act like this in an aircraft." she grumbled as she sighed deeply.

"I couldn't help it Raz, I'm hungry as hell baby girl and they really have nuthin good to eat on this damn lawn dart for crap sake honey."

"You're always hungry all the time Bobby. You must have a tape worm or something, you want another candy bar? You big baby you."

"Only if you do what you did with the uther one then I'd love another candy bar, baby. I like my candy served that way and I never had it served to me that way. Was that your idea, or didja see it done somewhere and you remembered about it, little sister?"

"Forget that mister, I'm not in the mood to make you happy that way right now, Bobby. Maybe, if I was allowed to sleep a little bit I would've been in a much better mood, and you might have gotten your wish, Mr. Walker."

"A little head?" he asked with a wide grin plastered on his lips.

"Yep, a little head to keep you nice and quiet Bobby.

"Then go back to sleep honey. I'll be as quiet as a church mouse I swear it baby." He offered while trying to get her to put her had back on his shoulder.

"Nope, you missed the boat big boy. I'm wide awake and I'll never fall asleep, baby." She gave him one of the smiles all the women gave me when they were teasing them.

"Aw C'mon will ya Raz, I could sure use a little stinking fun and games on this damn thing, honey." Walker was really begging now for her to go back to sleep.

"If you want some fun and games, do it with yourself mister. I'm too tired to perform for you right now, Robert. Now you can see why it was so important I caught up on my sleep, mister. If I wasn't still so tired, I would have been more interested in having a little fun with you, but you wouldn't get off my back for a minute, mister. The next time I tell you to let me sleep, I'm certain you'll allow me to sleep." She retorted with a smirk.

Chapter Nine

KENNEDY INTERNATIONAL AIRPORT, NEW YORK CITY
4:20 P.M., FRIDAY, NOVEMBER 13th, 1998

Air Force One or code named Eagle's Nest by the special agents, landed at the John F. Kennedy International Airport, and the press had not been informed the Vice President of the United States was arriving in New York City. A lucky few reporters picked up the Presidential aircraft as it came out of the sunshine and landed, and was quickly moved off the tarmac over to the penalty box area of the airfield. The plane was instantly swarmed by a gaggle of heavily armed special agents usually assigned to the protection of the President or Vice President. A good number of New York City police officers added to the protective ring surrounding the plane. The time of departure and arrival was kept secret, the need to know people were kept out of the loop for as long as possible. In an attempt to try and avoid unneeded attention drawn to the Vice President's visit to the Big City. It was unintentional, but the Vice President's staff failed to inform the police of the correct times of their departure and arrival at the city.

General John White, the current Chairman of the Joint Chiefs of Staff, thought the Vice President was scheduled to be arriving in New York City around the same time as Lieutenant Walker and Sergeant

Ramirez were to arrive. If he known the Vice President was going to arrive early, he would have made certain Walker and Ramirez left the Carrier earlier. It was that important the soldiers arrived in the Big Apple at the same time the Vice President did.

The security for the Vice President was as tight as when the President visited the City. Her guards in the plane got up first; three left the aircraft while the other three agents stayed close to Ms. Hirshfield, surrounding her as the agents checked the security outside the aircraft. One Agent, Edward Sweeney, her personal aide Cathy Williams made certain he was part of the squad accompanying them to the City. She hoped to find a way to have him and the Vice President end up together to see if they could come to a romantic understanding between them.

Once the special agents were positive everything was in the proper order outside the aircraft. The limousines were allowed to pull up alongside the aircraft, and were quickly gone over by the same group of special agents. After the vehicles were cleared, the signal was sent to the agents still inside the plane, escorted Ms. Hirshfield and her aide out to the cars.

Special Agents Sweeney and Porter climbed into the lead limousine, while the remaining agents climbed into the other vehicle. New York City police cars pulled out before the Vice President's car, while two other squad cars pulled up to the rear of the soon to be convoy, and then the caravan pulled into the flow of the city traffic. With sirens blaring, the police cars cut off all civilian traffic, carving the way for the Vice President's car. The limousines turned off the FDR (Franklin D. Roosevelt) Drive at West 57th Street, and then headed uptown, while the police blocked all dissecting side roads and avenues that lead onto and off of West 57th Street.

Cathy enjoyed pointing out all the famous buildings and historical landmarks of the city as they drove up West 57th Street. For half a mile, the two women acted like school girls, looking at all the familiar and famous sights of the city. The car stopped at a sidewalk frankfurter vender, and the ladies ordered one each. It was quite a scene to see a stretch limousine parked on the corner blocking the street as two agents piled out of the vehicle, followed by Cathy who ordered the franks for her and the Vice President. They ate them as if they were gourmet specialties. They both laughed and pointed to places of interest and Ms. Hirshfield considered ordering the driver to turn down a number of other roads, so they could enjoy a few more of the sights of midtown Manhattan. But she knew this was impossible, so she quickly dismissed the thought.

The traffic of midtown Manhattan suffered drastically from the unannounced visit from the Vice President of the United States, causing sheer chaos during the Friday afternoon rush hour traffic. Without warning, the workers and visitors of Manhattan found themselves locked in bumper to bumper heavy traffic, while the police vehicles forced the civilian cars off the roads. Many side roads and avenues were also closed to all civilian traffic by the police. First, Second, and Third Avenues were closed down while the Vice Presidential motorcade past. But when the limousine stopped for the franks, havoc was created with the police working on rerouting city traffic to other avenues, to get the pressure off the upper roadways.

Madison Avenue turned into a major problem for traffic and police; it was closed only for the shortest of time. But the Vice President ordered the driver to slow down when the limousines entered Fifth Avenue at the mouth of Central Park. Both women drew in their breath as they enjoyed the Grand Army Plaza. The sight was absolutely breathtaking, and it made the two women aware of why New York City was always called the place to visit in the United States.

When the Vice Presidential motorcade slowed to a crawl to enjoy the views of the city a while longer. So did the traffic of Manhattan stuck behind the pair of limousines making up the motorcade. At Sixth Avenue, and Avenue of the Americans, and an entry to the Park, the motorcade slowed down even more. After viewing this grand entry to the park, the cars slowly increased speed until the caravan came in view of Columbus Circle. Both women were thrilled to death at the breathtaking sight, but when the driver pointed out the Trump International Hotel and Tower to them, they both clapped because they were so thrilled by the beautiful sight.

The building was so breathtaking in its own right. The Trump Tower was the tallest structure in the entire area. The four hundred and eighty acres of Central Park bordered the very edge of the building, with Columbus Circle on the other side of the structure, along with the old New York Coliseum building. It was also bordered by other grand and old buildings on the other sides, and the main entrance to the Trump Tower actually overlooked the Circle.

The limousine driver enjoyed the excitement the two women were displaying, so he turned left and took a right and then drove right through the center of the Circle for the two women's enjoyment. He drove up Broadway and parked the vehicle on the side of the Tower nearest the main entry. Ms. Hirshfield remained seated in the car as the special agents poured out of the vehicle, and they quickly secured the entire area and entrance of the Tower. New York City's finest deployed three SWAT teams for added protection as the civilian traffic rerouted. Every building in the surrounding area had a number of police snipers in position inside them.

Once the horde of special agents were certain everything was in order, the Vice President was finally allowed to leave the vehicle, and she was quickly whisked inside the Tower. She was greeted by the always elegant and polite Donald Trump, who shook hands and introduced her to his beautiful wife, and to other members of the staff who would be waiting on her hand and foot during her stay at the Tower. Once this was accomplished, Mr. Trump walked side by side with the Vice President and gaggle of special agents as they quickly headed for the elevators.

The lobby of the building was completely void of any civilians, and the only people there were police and special agents. Ms. Hirshfield and her aide was ushered over to the elevators. Mr. Trump made his excuses and he left the Vice President as her personal entourage entered the elevator after the special agents checked it out first. Ms. Hirshfield kept watching as the elevator clicked off the floor numbers. The car stopped with a slight hop, and the doors silently opened on the twenty second floor. There were three apartments on this floor, one the Presidential Suite.

Vice President Hirshfield allowed herself to be guided to the set of beautifully carved thick oak double doors with a Star and Three on it. This was the first time she ever saw the room, and she never informed Cathy that they were going to stay at the suite. She realized the number and knew what it meant, and excitedly tugged on Mary's coat and smiled at her at the same time.

Mary whispered to her. "This is the President's room reserved at the Tower, Cathy dear."

Ms. Hirshfield nodded as the doors were suddenly flung open. Already waiting inside the large apartment where a number of other special agents Mary did not immediately recognized right off. This group of agents were sent ahead to check out and secure the apartment and rest of the floor, before the Vice President arrived at the Tower. The special agents bowed slightly as Ms. Hirshfield and the others entered the room.

Mary's bags were carried by other special agents. Sweeney took the lead and explained the room layout for the Vice President. "Ma'am, we're giving you the master bedroom that overlooks Central Park. Cathy will have the bedroom next to yours, and we'll occupy the last bedroom on the same side of the apartment, Ma'am. We took the liberty to set up a number of motion detectors in the apartment, so warn us before you or any of your people move about the apartment, once everyone turned in for the night. We decided to set up the special QR-7 tanks..."

"What was that you just said to me, Agent Sweeney?" Ms. Hirshfield interrupted the man, showing her ire at the agent using numbers to describe something obviously important to her.

"Sorry about that Ma'am, the QR-7 canisters contain a special and very powerful knockout gas incorporated into the security system installed at the White House recently, to guard it against a possible terrorist attack on the building, Ma'am. It was decided in event of a terrorist attack on the White House, and the protective Special Agents found themselves trapped in a no win situation that would compromise the President's safety and life, this gas is to be released, Ma'am. The gas will put everyone to sleep for an hour or so. By that time, the backup Special Agents would get inside the White House, and then take custody of the sleeping terrorists. It was thought a better scenario to remove a sleeping President with a helluva headache, than to remove a dead President, along with everyone else visiting the White House at the time of the attack..."

"Are there any other side effects besides a headache from this knockout gas you think I should know about, Agent Sweeney?" Ms. Hirshfield snapped, but was relieved the security was moving in the direction of non-lethal means, to discourage any life threatening situations.

"There are no other side effects from the gas that I am aware of Ma'am, all the gas is supposed to do is put you to sleep, and although you wake up with one helluva pounder, nothing more than that is supposed to happen to you, Ma'am. We're informed the effects of the gas is completely out of your system within several hours at the longest, Ma'am. However Ma'am, the first signs of the gas is a rapid heartbeat, this is what leads to the passing out I believe and then..."

"How fast does the gas react once it's released against any invaders, Agent Sweeney?" the highly concerned Vice President asked, because she learned a long time ago not to trust what any of her special agents told her. They had been known to lie to her every once in a while.

"The moment the first breath of gas is taken in the body, the brain's prevented from any further acting in a coherent manner, to the extent the terrorists would be unable to pull the trigger of his weapon against anyone, Ma'am. Besides the rapid heartbeat, your ears will feel like they have to pop. This is why the gas is so effective, and where we believe the headache comes from, Ma'am. The brain feels something's happening to it, and it goes into a protective mode. That's why the experiments we conducted involving this gas, the host was unable to pull the trigger before passing out. It's a foolproof way to control a terrorist situation involving the President, or any of his staff, Ma'am. The canisters are small, but there's enough gas to knock out a small Army in a confined area such as this apartment is. Ma'am, the gas will reach into every room in less than a heartbeat, so there's no place a terrorist could possibly hide from the effects fro..."

"Does that go for us as well Agent Sweeney? We'll not be able to hide from the gas, sir?"

"Errr... that's correct Ma'am. But why would you want to Ma'am?" Agent Sweeney took a quick breath and then added. "There's another option this systems offers us, mobility Ma'am. We carry two, twenty five pound canisters, and with a simple press of a button we can secure any area from attack almost immediately, Ma'am. We can quickly end any hostile situations we feel is a serious threat to the President or yourself, Ma'am. Without the loss of lives, might I add."

"And you have this system already set up inside this apartment, Agent?" Mary asked.

"Yes Ma'am, it's simple to incorporate in any such situation as this Ma'am, a simple push of a button and the gas is dispersed so rapidly there's no possible defense or place to hid against it."

"What happens if these supposed terrorists attack while wearing gas masks, or whatever they use to try and protect themselves from the effects of the gas, mister?"

"That would put us in a different situation I'm afraid, but we see no reason for any terrorists to try that act, unless they use gas themselves in their attack aimed against us, Ma'am. We have worked this scenario into the equation Ma'am. If the terrorists employ gasmasks, then our system's placed on standby mode, and when the terrorists remove their protective devices, the gas can be then triggered by an outside source, putting us as the controlling factor in a terrorist situation we're faced with, Ma'am." The young special agent offered to the Vice President.

"Who ordered this system to be employed here, Agent Sweeney?"

"It was ordered by President Cole himself, Ma'am. He pointed out he was concerned about the Iranian's doing something in response to the attack on Iran that was just carried out by a group of our Special Forces, Ma'am. Killing the Vice President of the United States would be a helluva coup d'état for them, Ma'am." Agent Sweeney offered the Vice President politely.

"Hmmm... I understand and agree with the use of this gas. I'm pleased someone's using their head and came up with an easier way to put an end to terrorist attacks, by putting everyone to sleep peacefully. What other precautions do you have set in place inside this apartment I need to know about, Agent Sweeney?" She asked and smiled at her future lover, hopefully.

"Well Ma'am, we have room to room communications, and a number of motion detector sensors set up, so you'll have to beep us before you or any of your personal staff leave the rooms at night,

Ma'am. That way you won't be bothered by our coming out to see who's moving about the apartment room, Ma'am. We're taking over another bedroom overlooking the door and hall of the apartment. So we can secure the hallway leading into the apartment, and the bedrooms at the same time, Ms. Hirshfield. Ma'am, I'd like it if you woul..."

"You do understand I don't want to be tripping over any of you guys while I'm visiting here, mister. I want it to be like you people aren't even here, Mr. Agent. I like my privacy, and the less I see of you people, the better I'll like it. Do you understand my wants, Agent Sweeney?" the Vice President warned as she removed her fur coat and suit jacket, draping them both over the back of a chair. She stretched, raising her arms over her head, and forcing her breasts to press against the tight fitting fabric of her blouse. This did not go unnoticed by Edward or Cathy, who observed Edward's reaction to Mary's move. She smiled as she thought, 'Ahhh... that's what I wanted to see from you Sweeney, I think you better swallow before you hurt yourself, fool'.

"Yes Ma'am, I gave orders for all agents to act like furniture when you're in the apartment."

The agent carrying the luggage rushed it to the master bedroom. He placed the bags on top of the oversized, raised bed and then he disappeared, so he could set up the communication center needed by the special agents to link them with the police, FBI and Washington. The other agents made themselves scarce, and silently disappeared into the bedrooms designated for their use, following their orders by Agent Sweeney to make themselves as inconspicuous as possible.

"Are you hungry? I'm starving Ma'am." Cathy asked and announced to Ms. Hirshfield.

"No, I want to take a bath and warm up first, and then I'll have something to eat I guess, dear." The Vice President replied to her personal aide and bodyguard with a slight smile.

"I'll run your bath for you if you'd like Ma'am." She offered pleasantly.

"I'll handle it for myself if you don't mind, Cathy. I know you're dying to check out the apartment, why don't you do that while I bathe and fix myself up? I'll send for you if and when I want anything, enjoy yourself please Cathy." The female Vice President offered, knowing each room had a private intercom system for communication throughout the entire apartment.

"Really?" her young and pretty female bodyguard asked the Vice President.

"Really, I'm fine Cathy. It's not every day we get to trash the Bosses private place and I'm going to take full advantage of this opportunity." She laughed then headed for the bathroom, stripping as she walked away and leaving Cathy and Edward staring at her back.

"Wow, she's a real beautiful woman, Edward." She purred at the gawking and good looking special agent standing by her side still watching Mary walk away from them.

"Yeah, she sure is Cathy." The agent offered before he caught himself and he snap his mouth shut, turning away from Mary to Cathy, thoroughly embarrassed by his absentminded words.

"Well, she is Agent. But I wish she would take to wearing a bra if she's going to wear white, sheer blouses like she enjoys. You could see everything she has when she stretched her arms out like that, Mr. Sweeney." She purred, continuing to feel the special agent out, trying to get his feelings for Mary before she tried to get them together for a night of love making and romance.

"Err... is that a fact, I'm afraid I hadn't noticed Ma'am." Sweeney offered in his defense as he began to break out in a cold sweat, thinking of Mary's outstanding figure.

"Really, I don't know about you Agent Sweeney." She purred again as she pulled Sweeney's tie free of his suit jacket, and then she allowed it to slide seductively through her fingers as she turned her back on him. She then went over to the Broadway side of the apartment where two bedrooms, three bathrooms and the kitchen was situated. The bedrooms were long and narrow. The special agents used one room for their second headquarters with two closets, and a bathroom. The second bedroom was somewhat smaller, but the bathroom was larger than the other one. Each room was a wash of pastel colors and fine marble. The kitchen was vast, with a small breakfast nook. It had a microwave, an island stove, and plenty of cabinet space. Whoever designed it and the bathrooms, kept a woman's needs and wants in mind, everything was perfect.

Cathy moved out into the living/dining room, which was more than vast. She ran from one end of the large room to the other and then she checked out the TV, stereo system, and computer terminal, it was an IBM machine, none better in the world in her mind. She then ran up the hall branded the gallery because of the many fine paintings and other artworks covering the walls. She turned in the hall off the main one, and entered her designated room. The first thing she noticed was the bathroom, the door was slightly open. It too had a beautiful marble bathtub with a heat light for drying her body after taking a quick shower or bath.

She had a large walk in closet, and her room had a queen size bed that she jumped on like a child, bouncing her rearend off the hard mattress then kicking her feet in the air. The bodyguard looked at the light blue ceiling above her, and she could actually see tiny stars shining, star dust was mixed in with the paint when the ceiling was painted. She could not believe how relaxing the effect was. She moaned. "Boy, I could easily get used to this kind of living in New York City." She stretched out on the bed and then got up and looked at the exquisite furniture. Her bags were placed before the large oak armoire. When she grew bored with her exploring of the apartment, she flung open the curtains and was struck by the breathtaking view of Central Park.

When she had enough of the stunning view and exploring the rest of the apartment, she headed for the kitchen area, avoiding the special agent's bedroom and headquarters as she went down the hall. She passes right by Agent Sweeney who was standing in the hall, he was preparing his other agents to their proper posts. Once she was in the kitchen, she removed a bottle of Dom Perignon, popped the top and then poured a glass for her, and then one for the Vice President.

She then headed for the room and tapped lightly on the bathroom door after she checked out the rest of the Vice President's bedroom for security and curiosity, which was the largest of the three bedrooms in the apartment and also counting the three walk in closets and two bathrooms.

"I was wondering when you were going to pay me a little visit, Cathy dear." The Vice President called out from the bathroom, then she added. "Come in honey."

She entered the bathroom with a bidet and water closet off to the right, before the shower stall. Mary enjoyed the raised whirlpool tub, steam rose gently from the hot water surrounding her body as Cathy sat down on the edge of the tub, while offering the champagne to her ward. Mary reached out, her breasts rising just above the water level, showing no concern because she saw her naked more than once since assuming her office.

"Why don't you come in and join me, the water's wonderful Cathy." Mary offered kindly.

"Naw, I'm too excited right now to stop and take a bath now, Mary." She moaned as she looked over the entirety of the huge bathroom.

"You don't know what you're missing here, it's delightful, Cathy." Mary grumbled contentedly as she sat back and enjoyed the whirlpool. The motor could barely be heard.

"I happen to know your target's pretty interested in you, Mary." Her bodyguard announced as she flashed one of her best smiles at the beautiful Vice President.

The Vice President's eyes instantly flew open as she stared back at her grinning aide and she offered. "I trust you're not going to make me ask what you observed about him, young lady."

"Did you see his face when you took off your jacket and stretched like you did, Mary?"

"Yes, I was worried he was going to hurt himself, dear." She replied with a smile on her lips.

"I thought he was going to come in his pants. He surely would've if you hung around outside the bedroom any longer than you did, Ma'am." Her bodyguard offered with a giggle.

"Me too, I was subconsciously trying to tell the fool to breathe before he ended up hurting himself. Did he say anything to you, about me I mean?" she asked with wonder as she leaned forward and Cathy out of habit, put down her drink and rubbed her back with the louffa sponge.

"Well, I made the comment I wished you'd wear a bra and he said he hadn't noti…"

"I can assure you that'll never happen. I hate them damn things designed by a stuffy old man, for us women to hide our femininity with. What did Sweeney say about me, Cathy?" Mary asked in an excited voice as she interrupted her, allowing her excitement to raise a little more.

"Oh… he gave me a politically correct responses he hadn't noticed your sexy display. As he wiped the salvia from the corners of his mouth with the back of his sweat coated hand, Mary."

Both women enjoyed a giggle at the special agent's expense as Mary slid back in the water, and rested against the tub. She picked up a face cloth and ran it over Mary's chest and breasts.

"Hmmm… I wish those were Edward's hands washing me right now Cathy. I can't wait until we get back to Washington, and you set up that little tête-à-tête we spoke of earlier for me, Cathy." Ms. Hirshfield murmur dreamily, as she enjoyed being washed by her aide.

Her bodyguard replied shyly, her eyes displaying the devilment held within them. "Well, why wait until we get back to Washington to set up that little tete-a-tete with Sweeney you Ma'am."

Mary stared with wide eyes at Cathy for a long moment as she sat slightly forward again and then she asked her female protector. "What the devil do you mean by that remark Cathy?"

"Why wait till then Mary. Everything we're planning in Washington is already set in place in the City, Mary. Edward's here and you have a private bedroom, and what's better than here and now? We're out of the backdrop of Washington, and the ever present eyes of those pain in the ass reporters and news hounds always following your every move. All I'm saying is, why not take advantage of the moment now, Mary? You know what I keep telling you. 'Never say I should have, always say I shouldn't have'." She smiled at the interested and beautiful Vice President.

"Hmmm… I see you're wise beyond your young year's young lady. You have a good point there Cathy. Why not take advantage of the moment at hand and that way I can find out if he's really interested or not in me. I'd hate to waste my time on him if he's not going to be ready to…"

"I swear, he'd be a damn fool if he's not drop dead interested in you Mary."

Mary looked her in the eyes as she offered. "Now who's being politically correct my dear? Do you really think I have a shot at landing him? You know this old body's not what it once was." The Vice President snickered as she ran her hands over her breasts and then down her body.

"Huh, with the equipment you have at hand, I believe you can land any man you set your eyes on, Ma'am." The pretty and young bodyguard replied to the Vice President pleasantly.

"You're way too kind to me you know Cathy." She moaned as she shut the whirlpool down. Then she stood and Cathy automatically picked up the towel and held it out before Mary, and she immediately wrapped it around her exquisite body as she carefully stepped out of the tub. Leaving behind her champagne, as Mary tucked the ends of the towel between her breasts.

She picked up her glass and sipped it as she followed the Vice President to her bedroom.

She dropped the towel on the floor as she slipped into an exquisite red and black silk kimono she brought while visiting Japan the last time she and the President were there for a political meeting. She tied it with a gold Obi tie, and then she slipped her feet into the opened sandals that matched her outfit perfectly. When she was dressed to the tee, she turned to Cathy and asked.

"Do you really think you can arrange this meeting between him and I, Cathy? Oh what the hell am I doing, I feel so cheap. I feel like I'm using you to arrange a man for me, pimping I believe it's called in the world of the streets." She moaned, her face red from embarrassment.

"Don't be so damn foolish Ma'am; you have to stop thinking like that Mary. Look at the world you live in. Do you think it's possible for the Vice President of the United States to go out on a romantic date, without a horde of pain in the ass reporters trailing, and reporting on your every move you make to the rest of the world? How else do you think you could be intimate with the opposite sex, unless someone helps you set it up, Ma'am? As for pimping for you, how the devil do you think I got a lot of my dates, someone helped set me up." Cathy offered with a smile.

She shook her head and replied. "I don't know what I'd do without you at my side, Cathy."

"Remember this when I get lucky and request a weekend off for some of my own pleasures, Ma'am." She offered as she smiled warmly at the Vice President.

"I will Cathy, I promise dear." Ms. Hirshfield purred and added cautiously. "I don't know, do you think we can pull this off without the world finding out about it on us, honey?"

"I not only think we can pull this meeting off between the two of you, but I intend to carry it out for you, Ma'am." The pretty bodyguard announced proudly to her lovely female boss.

"When are you planning to approach Edward?" the Vice President asked her aide.

"Hmmm... you're bathed and your hair looks great, and your horny as hell as far as I can see." Cathy offered, knowing she was the only one in all of Washington who could dare speak to the Vice President in this manner, and live to tell about it later on.

"Boy, am I ever horny at that Cathy. I told you I can't even remember the last time I was with a man, my dear." She retorted, completely ignoring the crude remark from her aide.

"Then why the hell are we wasting any further time with talking about what you want to have happen, Ma'am? Are you suffering from any jet lag, Mary?"

"No. Not really, the flight was way too short to get any jet lag I believe Cathy." She replied as she drew in a quick breath and then let it out slowly as she shifted her weight on her feet.

"Then let's set it up for a little later on tonight and see what happens. If he wants you, this is the perfect scenario we have set up before us, Mary. You have the room and the bed and opportunity to enjoy yourself with him. Why not put the situations to work for you, Mary?"

"Tonight, I can't possibly do it this early, I have to be better prepa..."

"Don't go and chicken out on me now you big baby. Tonight's the night to let it happen, take it from me you'll really enjoy yourself tonight if I have any say in it, Mary. If you don't bed him then I'm going to step in and do him. It's up to you honey." The bodyguard warned her ward.

"There's no way in the devil, I just can't do it tonight dear. I'm expecting that foul tempered young soldier and his girlfriend who are scheduled to arrive at the Tower later on today, dear. I planned to have my first meeting with him and his girlfriend later on today sometime. I have to make contact with the soldier today to make certain he's okay, and he and his female friend has everything they might need for their visit to the Big City, the room, some spending money, food, stuff like that I believe, Cathy." The Vice President moaned as she got up from the bed and started to pace around the bedroom for a few moments while she went deep in thought.

"Sounds like you're just fishing around for a cheap excuse to put off this meeting with dear old Sweeney tonight if you were to ask me, Mary. Please excuse my French, but fuck this soldier where he breaths from, what the hell's more important to you anyway, Mary? Your love life or you sitting in some stuff room with some ugly and foul smelling soldier who doesn't care one bit what you have to or offer him and his girlfriend, Mary." She retorted as she flashed another one of her well known smiles at the stunned looking Mary.

"That's a no brainer, my love life is more important, what there is of it I'm afraid, Cathy." Mary replied in an excited voice while she allowed a wide grin to quickly spread across her lips.

"Fine, then the hell with this smelly soldier and his girlfriend, he'll keep on ice until tomorrow when it's better for you to meet him. If you're so concerned about him and his comfort, I'll meet with them, and I'll make certain they have everything they need, once I'm certain you're enjoying Sweeney's fine treasures, young lady. Mary, I won't take no for an answer, I know the last time you shared your time with a man. Take it from me; it's not healthy to go so long without sharing sex with a man..." She was really on a roll now, but she was interrupted by Mary who offered.

"It's so hard to land a good man who'll put up with a woman constantly on the go, honey."

"That sounds like another lame excuse to put off this meeting with Agent Sweeney, Mary. What can I tell you, if you can't land a man then land a woman. You have to do something to get your sex life back in gear." She actually growled at the female Vice President this time.

"A woman, whoa... I don't know if I'm quite ready for anything like that, Cathy."

"When you're in the state you're in, you'll try anything once, even a god damn cucumber I would, Mary." She smirked at the Vice President as she stared at her.

"Let's be a little more careful with our poor choice of words when speaking to me if you don't mind, please Young lady." The stunned Vice President warned her with a sharp snap in her tone of voice, not liking the direction the conversation was heading off in.

"I'm just kidding around with you Mary, but putting everything aside. What do you say; I can setup your meeting with Mr. Sweeney for later on tonight?" she smiled at the Vice President.

"Yes, why the hell not." Mary said as she gave into the pressure from her aide.

"Outstanding, I'll have the big jerk primed and ready to enter your room at ten, with a chilled bottle of wine, dish of shrimp and who knows what might happen after that, Mary. I want you to dress in your finest nighty, I'll get some candles and backup bottle of wine for you two to enjoy. You be on the bed when the jerk comes in, he'll do the rest if he's half the man I think he is. If not I'll swat him in the ass with a damn paddle to get him in gear for you, Ma'am. I want you to really get bombed to erase any inhibitions and enjoy the hell out of yourself tonight, please."

"What about the other Agents hanging around in the damn apartment? Won't they know what's going on in my room Cathy?" the Vice President asked her aide with concern lacing her voice.

"More French, fuck them where they breath too, Ma'am. What the hell do you care what they might think is going on in your bedroom? Its they who have to worry about what you think about them and the way they're protecting your life. But I'll make certain the Agents are well occupy, so they don't have any time to pay attention to what you two consenting adults are doing in your bedroom. I promise you Mary, your visitor will arrive in secrecy for your pleasure tonight if I have anything to do with it Ma'am. All I want you to concern yourself with, is all the fun you'll have with the big dumb jerk tonight. I'll worry about everything else for you, Ma'am."

"Okay you win, I'm leaving myself completely in your very capable hands my dear. I only hope everything will work out the way you see it, Cathy." Mary offered to her young aide.

"It will I promise you, are you hungry yet Ma'am? I want you to keep up your strength for tonight's festivities, Ma'am. I can't have you falling off to sleep with Sweeney in your bed with you because you were weak from not eating enough to sustain you for the night's fun and games." She repeated, trying to get Mary to eat something for her own good.

"Yes, but I'm in no mood to go to the kitchen to eat something, Cathy. I'm afraid if I happen to bump into one of these pain in the ass Agents walking around out there, I might take a chunk out of them, they upset me so much all the time dear." The Vice President replied in a upset tone.

"We can always order something from room service, or we can send Edward downstairs to get us something to enjoy." She winked at Mary and then added. "Or I can just rustle something up in the kitchen for us to enjoy; I believe the refrigerator's well stocked with all sorts of food. I checked it out a little earlier and there's plenty to eat. I believe it's compliments of Mr. Trump."

"That one really knows how to put on the dog when he wants to, Cathy." Mary replied.

The special agents set up their communication center for the Presidential apartment and arranged for relief to arrive the following morning. Two of the six agents, turned in for a nap so they could stay up all night. The agents knew they were banished to the bedrooms whenever the Vice President was in the room, unless they were needed by anyone else in of the apartment.

It was left up to Agent Sweeney to venture out of their rooms every once in a while, to keep an eye on Ms. Hirshfield when she was roaming around the apartment. The special agents assigned to protect the Vice President's life could easily tell there was a special bond developing between the two, and the Vice President favored him. No agent realized it might be of a romantic interest. The agents knew Ms. Hirshfield was in a good mood whenever Sweeney was in sight. They picked up the Vice President's aide moving around the kitchen, and motioned for Edward to find out what she was doing. The curtains in the outer rooms were drawn for security reasons, and to stop anyone from shooting through the windows at whoever was inside the large apartment.

Chapter Ten

THE JETSTAR AIRCRAFT RAPIDLY CLOSING IN ON NEW YORK CITY

Lieutenant Robert Walker was finally able to get comfortable in the aircraft just before landing, but he so worked up Sergeant Dorothy Ramirez before falling asleep, she could not nod off again herself. She amused herself by watching Walker curled in a ball in the chair snoring away. A few times she ran a piece of thread over his nose, making him swat at the fake bug he thought was bothering him. At first, she felt like stopping him from sleeping like he did to her, but she was not like that for she loved her soldier to death and would never be nasty to him.

She leaned her shoulder against his broad back, enjoying the warming feeling of the close contact, and it gave her the comfort needed and she relaxed. She smiled as she listened to his deep breathing; she could feel the strength pent up in his body even though he was asleep. As long as she was by his side, she feared nothing in this world. She remembered when he drifted off to sleep. It was after the co-pilot returned and offered them some cold turkey sandwiches. She was amazed the small plane had anything substantial to eat on board. She knew when his belly was full; he would quickly nod off, even though it cost her half her sandwich to fill him.

The second in flight refueling went off without a hitch. As she stared out the window of the aircraft, she noticed a soft glow way off on the horizon. While the plane headed for the glow she thought it was the sun rising, but when she checked her watch, she realized it was going to be between seven and eight o'clock when they finally land in the Big City, and knew it could not possibly be the sun rising. She concentrated her vision on this glow raising towards the aircraft. Sergeant Dorothy Ramirez' concentration was suddenly interrupted by the pilot when he loudly announced over the aircraft's intercom system. "Err... you have to secure your seatbelts, we should be landing in New York in less than fifteen minutes. The co-pilot will be back in a few moments to secure any loose items and coffee for landing. If you want a last cup of Java, I suggest you better get now it before he closes it up on you. Thank you."

 She glanced at the coffee urn in the back of the aircraft; she did not dare entertain another cup as she secured her seatbelt. Then she looked at Walker sleeping peacefully by her side. She checked his seatbelt and moved his chair in an upright position, knocking the magazine he was reading on the floor. She scooped it up and smiled when she noticed the cover. It was a Playboy magazine. At first she wanted to slug him with it as she wondered where he ever found it on board the Aircraft Carrier. She knew it was his favorite tit and ass magazine, and she had to admit she also enjoyed reading and looking at the beautiful women on the many pages.

She flipped right to the triple center page; she could not believe a woman could look so gorgeous. There was an article where Madonna was interviewed then she knew why Walker got the magazine. He loved her, he loved seeing her body and loved reading every word she said, and really enjoyed all her records. Her soldier always said Madonna was one of the smartest and ambitious women he ever saw. He pointed out she would not take no for an answer, and she truly enjoyed ripping the doors to a man's world off their hinges. She knew he respected her, and she could not blame him in the least, for everything he pointed out about her was true. She placed the magazine down by her side so she would not forget it for him.

The co-pilot came out of the cockpit, she raised her hand and made like she was going to get up so she could speak with him. He leaned over the Lieutenant to see what it was she wanted.

"Say friend, for the past fifteen minutes or so I noticed a light way off to the west. At first I thought it might be the sun coming up, but after checking my watch I realized that was impossible, sir. What am I seeing out there sir?" She asked the co-pilot with some concern.

"That light's from New York City, Ma'am. Sort of brightens up the entire night for us no, Sergeant?" The co-pilot offered with a pleasant smile.

"It sure does sir, I can't believe the lights from New York City are bright enough to make me believe it was the sun coming up." She replied as she watched the co-pilot move away.

"Just wait Sarge, you haven't seen anything yet Ma'am. We're still flying some twenty miles away from shore yet. The closer we get to the City the brighter the lights will get for you, Ma'am. I can't blame you for mistaking it for the sunrise though, Sergeant. I sometimes get confuse by the two myself. Would you care for another cup of coffee before I wrap it up for landing?"

"Naw, I'm floating as it is sir, but I think I'll visit the head before landing sir."

The co-pilot helped Ramirez climb over the sleeping military officer as he complained at her. "Gees, this guy can sleep through a bloody war can't he, Sergeant. I thought you guys from the Special Forces always sleep with one eye open all the time, and your hands on your weapon."

"Don't count on it sir, if you were the enemy you'd be dispatched by now, and he'd be out looking for any of your friends after that, sir. He sleeps like he's dead while safely in the arms of his own country. But put him out in the field of battle, and he's the best possible weapon our government has to offer up against our enemy anywhere in the world." Sergeant Ramirez offered with a trace of warning in her tone of voice, while straightening up her uniform.

"I'll take your word for that Sergeant. I heard of your troop's actions in the past, Ma'am. You better make your visit to the head quick now,

Sergeant. We're a few minutes away from landing, and the Captain wants everyone and thing well secured when he lands, Ma'am."

"I'll be quick about it sir. Say Major, do you know if anyone will be waiting to meet us when we land, sir? Or are we going to have to find our own way through downtown Manhattan, sir?"

"We were briefed before leaving Italy for the Carrier, there's supposed to be a vehicle waiting for you when we touchdown, Sergeant. Now that doesn't mean a jeep or HUMVEE will be your transportation. If I was to place a bet on it Sergeant, I'd say an officer's staff car will be waiting for you guys when we touchdown, Ma'am. I know the government has no tact when moving her officers around the town, but I seriously doubt they'd transport you two through the streets of downtown Manhattan in a Humvee, Sergeant." The co-pilot offered with a grunt and a grin.

Sergeant Ramirez entered the head as the co-pilot emptied the urn; and then he slid it in the wall and secured the doors. Next, he walked up the plane while checking the seats for any loose items that might become airborne during a rough landing. The only thing he found was a pillow. He tucked it in the retaining pouch of the chair in front of where he found it. As he worked his way to the cockpit, he checked the Lieutenant, seeing nothing out of place except for a magazine, he headed for the cockpit. When the co-pilot entered, he made sure he secured the door for landing. Taking his seat, he reported the aircraft was secured for landing to the pilot.

The Sergeant brushed some cool water over her face, the coldness instantly reviving her. She used her finger and water to brush her teeth and then she ran her damp hands through her hair, shaping it the best she could, cursing for packing her hairbrush in her duffle bag. When she was satisfied with her appearance, she left the head and went back to her soldier and her seat. As she climbed over him, he reached up, putting his hand between her legs and giving her a squeeze.

"Hmmm..., I see we're up and already making a pest of yourself. How did you sleep Bobby?"

"Like more I'm afraid baby." He moaned as he shifted his weight in his narrow chair to make some room for her to pass him to her chair.

"I told you to sleep before you nodded off, mister." She replied indignantly to her soldier and lover. She was still tired, but the thought of landing in New York City and seeing all there was to see in the Big City, erased any thoughts of trying to sleep any further on the aircraft.

"Well, I told you to try and sleep long before you fell asleep. I told you to nod off before you did. Yada, yada, yada." He said mockingly as he made his voice sound like a woman, and he used his hand to simulate a nagging mouth going off right in his face.

She laughed as she punched him in the arm for a second time and then she stared at him.

"Owe, hey take it easy sister. I don't have my stinking body armor on, and you're stronger than you think you are, sister." The Lieutenant complained as he rubbed the spot she punched him.

"Oh, you poor little baby. Did I hurt your itty bitty arm on you big boy."

"Keep it up Raz; I'll remember this crap when you next want some good loving from me."

"Oh brother, what a helluva threat that is Bobby. You seem to forget big boy, as long as they keep growing cucumbers, you men have a lot to be worried about, fella." She smiled as she winked, and then she took her seat and quickly buckled up for the landing.

"Cucumber? What the hell good are those damn things for? You gonna eat a stinking salad?"

"Watch your step Bobby. They're a lot better than any man I know, they're always ready for immediate action when we are, and they never go soft on us, and they always make sure we come. And the best of all is, after making love to a cucumber, we women don't have to sleep in the wet spot for the rest of the night like we do when you pigs come and go on us, mister."

"Oh you think! In a pig's ear they are, at least I'm warm and alive Raz."

"Yeah! Big deal that offer is to me mister." She replied as she put her forehead right up against his and then she stared him dead in his eyes.

"You know what you are Raz?" he growled, trying to act like he was getting angry at her.

"No! What am I Bobby? Please tell me and be kind my darling." She retorted.

"You're a you, that's what you are Raz. One of these days, pow, zoom straight to the moon Alice." He growled as he stuck his tongue at Ramirez and then he licked the end of her nose.

"Oh pew you, you big pig you. That was disgusting mister." She chuckled as she pulled back from him and wiped her nose with the back of her hand.

"We landing?" The Lieutenant asked as he tried to look around Ramirez out of the window.

"We should be touching down in ten minutes." She replied as she glanced out of the window.

He shifted his weight again and then offered her. "I can't wait till we're finally off this jet age stinking sewer pipe. Didja find out if anyone's gonna be waiting for us when we land?"

"Yep I asked the co-pilot and he said a staff car should be waiting for us when we land, Bobby. He was informed while we were on the Carrier." The Sergeant offered to the Lieutenant.

"Out fucking standing, I can't wait until we get a stinking room under us, and I can take a good dump for myself in comfort and then have me a hot shower, and use all the fucking hot water I wanna use for a damn change sister. No more of that having the water cut off on us when..."

While he was complaining about everything on the plane, the landing gear lowered. Hearing this, they knew they were about to land. He stopped talking in an effort to hear what the pilot was saying to the control tower. He loved listening in on the speed jocks messed up lingo. But he could not hear a word the pilot said to the traffic controller, asking for permission to land.

"Shit, I wish I could hear what the sonofabitches are saying in the cockpit, dammit."

"I don't know about you Robert, can't you for once in your life just sit back and enjoy the scenery. Christ sake Bobby, didn't you have enough of this crap in Iran..."

"You're nagging my ass once again I see Raz." He warned her with his waving finger.

The pilot's voice interrupted their conversation. "Be advised, we'll coming in for a landing at John F. Kennedy International Airport in the next two minutes. We're locked in on our final approach and cleared for landing. Please make certain your seats are set in the upright position, and your food trays are secured in their proper place, and your seatbelts are fastened and any loose items are stowed away properly for our landing. Prepare for landing people."

He glanced at Ramirez which prompted her to bitch back at him. "Don't look at my chair Bobby. I know what the devil I'm doing all the time. I'm fine, what about you mister?"

"Keep nagging my ass like this, and you're gonna end up finding yourself alone on the moon, Raz." He aimed a fist right at her chin as he repeated that famous phrase. "Pow, zoom."

"Who the hell are you aiming that damn thing at mister? You aim that at me again, and you'll draw back a bloody stump, mister." She offered as she actually stuck out her chin, just daring him to take a swing at it so he could see what he gets for his foolish actions.

"Huh, if you think I'm gonna be fool enough to take a shot like that, I have a bridge leading to Brooklyn I wanna sell ya sweetheart." He toyed as he leaned forward and kissed her.

They were still kissing when the wheels of the plane lightly touched down on the tarmac. The jolt breaking them apart with him adding. "Whew, that must be the first time in aviation history two people kissed while landing. What a fucking rush that was, I'm as hard as a rock honey."

"You are always hard as a rock Walker. Huh, I believe you can find sex right in the middle of a Hurricane, Bobby. I don't know what I'm ever going to do with you buster." She smirked at him as she unbuckled her seatbelt and then she stood up and prepared to leave the aircraft.

"Hey baby, we're still moving, are you supposed to be moving about like that, baby?"

"What are they going to do? Fire us? Take my birthday away? I seriously doubt that. Send us home? Well, I for one don't know about you, but I for one miss our home, Bobby."

The plane came to a rolling stop as the pilot warned over the intercom. "Please remain in your seats while we're holding on the runway. We're ordered over to a certain section of the airfield, and have to wait until two jumbos get the green light for takeoff. The tower stated it shouldn't take five more minutes before we can proceed to the terminal. That is all."

"You wanna screw around a little Raz?" the smirking Lieutenant offered as he reached for her.

"Let me tell you something Bobby. The next time we screw around a little, I promise you it's going to last a helluva lot longer than just five minutes, mister. Besides, it'll take me that long to get out of my uniform and make you ready for action, Robert." She complained at him.

"Don't bet your little ass on that last remark Raz. It won't take you but a few seconds to get me ready for action baby." He replied as he took hold of himself through his trousers, and then he shook himself to show her he was already ready for work.

"Jesus Walker, isn't that the way I left you when we first began this damn flight mister?"

"What the hell can I tell ya, you know it's always hard, baby. I'm locked, cocked, and always ready to rock all the time, sister." He bragged to his lover as he gave her a wink of the eye.

The plane jolted as it moved forward to the designated position on the airfield. At a snail's pace, the aircraft slowly walked across the tarmac to park in the penalty box area where Air Force One was usually resting in the cloistered area of the airport.

The special agents assigned to guard Air Force One drew their weapons, and they kept the moving plane under constant surveillance. Even the 30 mm cannon was trained on it as the small Jetstar aircraft stopped some fifty feet away from the President's parked aircraft. When the Jetstar stopped moving, Sergeant Dorothy Ramirez moved over to the door with Lieutenant Robert Walker. But it did not open, and they were forced to stop. The co-pilot came out to check on them, and when he noticed them standing by the door he said in an angry tone of voice. "What the hell are you two doing out of your damn seats? The pilot didn't give you permission to move around the aircraft. You two better get back to your seats before the Captain reams you two new assholes dammit. He's not one who takes his orders being disobeyed very lightly you know."

The Lieutenant was not moving, but when she pushed him, he allowed himself to be led back to his seat. Once seated, the co-pilot snapped at them a second time. "We're stuck until the Special Agents outside give our aircraft the once over, and then we'll open the ladder and they'll check the interior of the aircraft. Once they're satisfied we're not a threat to the aircraft in the secluded zone, we'll get clearance and be allowed to disembark the aircraft. I suggest you two make yourselves comfortable as possible until we get the green light to deplane from the Agents. It shouldn't take more than ten minutes for them to clear us." The co-pilot shrugged, because he did not know what else to say to the two soldiers he knew wanted to get out of the plane.

He watched out the window as team of special agents from the President's detail went over the outside of the aircraft with two dogs. For what seemed like hours, the agents walked around the plane, and then the door opened. Two agents rushed in, each armed with Heckler & Koch MP-5 machine guns. One agent aimed his weapon at the two soldiers as the second one rushed in the cockpit, and aimed his weapon at the pilots. They were motioned out of their chairs and then pushed towards the rear of the plane. The second agent made them sit by the two soldiers.

The agent scanned the interior nerve center of the plane, when he was certain everything was in order, he let the third agent with the dog enter the plane. The dog went from cockpit to the tail of the aircraft, while the agents checked the pilots and soldier's IDs. When they were certain everything was right, the four occupants were finally allowed to leave the aircraft, but not the area. Outside, they were held in a bus while the dog continued to check out the interior of the jet.

Once it was determined everything was ship shape with the aircraft, the searching agents allowed themselves relaxed and be a little friendlier. The two pilots of the Jetstar were allowed back in their aircraft with an agent escort, while they ran through their check off list while Walker and Ramirez were allowed to roam around the area waiting for their ride to reach them.

One agent engaged the Lieutenant in conversation. He knew the soldiers were part of the special operations group, and he was longing to be a part of their group. He ignored most of the questions from the agent; only answering the few needing to keep the agent's attention peaked.

Sergeant Ramirez kept her eyes glued to the gate. She was waiting to see if the staff car arrives. She checked her watch, it was twenty past eight, their ride was late. Angrily, she let out her breath in a rush, she was tired, dirty, and cooling off in the slight night breeze, and she needed a bath in the worst way and she was also starving. She was suffering the major let down military action usually gives one whenever it was over. Every muscle in her body ached, every nerve cried out to be relaxed, her neck ached from all the tension of the hard hitting action just completed in Iran. She was in one shitty mood, and she was looking for something to take it out on.

The Lieutenant easily sensed the anger building up in her tone, and he pulled her close to him and he gave her a squeeze. She automatically wrapped herself around him trying to steal some warmth from his body, she was freezing. The temperature was below forty degrees, and she was dressed in her light summer military uniform, and spring jacket. It was the only clean uniform she had in her duffle bag. She shivered as her teeth chattered as she complained with anger. "Where the hell's this damn staff car at? I'm freezing my tits off standing here like this Robert."

He looked at her with a grin and then he offered to her. "Why Raz, I believe you've been hanging round me a little too much lately sister. You're starting to talk like me you know."

"Fuck you wiseguy. I'm freezing my tits off Bobby. Where's this sonofabitch at, dammit?"

"He's gotta be on his way, maybe the traffic's running against him baby."

"If I get any colder, I'm going to be holding my body against his to get warm, Robert." She snapped as she started to jump up and down, while blowing on her hands then rubbing them together. She tried stomping her feet to try and warm them up, but the stomping only hurt them.

He glared at the young special agent still bugging the hell out of him about the service, searching his mind on how to escape his unending questions. He came up with a solution and offered. "Hey pal, why don't you give me your damn name, and I'll see what I can do bout having your stinking ass transferred out from this fag outfit, and get you into a real man's Unit for a friggin change, Mac. Write it down and I'll give it to my Commander, and he'll draft your ass out of this chicken shit outfit, man." The Lieutenant smiled, calling the agent's bluff.

Without hesitation he replied. "You'll really do that for me sir, holy shit Lieutenant; I can't thank you enough for this offer sir. Not a night goes by that I don't dream about becoming a Special Forces soldier, sir. Do you have any paper on you sir?"

He gave a sigh as he offered to the young agent. "Now why the hell would I be carrying any stinking paper on my backside for, bright ass? My friggin business is shooting, not writing shit down. Killing, and words don't fucking kill mister. Words are for stinking turd pushers who don't wanna get any stinking blood on their damn hands, buddy. If you want me to take your name with me, you're gonna hafta get yourself something to fucking write it down on, if not, stop bugging my stinking ass will ya fella. I'm freezing my fucking nuts off here man."

The agent spun around and shot off to the command unit parked at the point of Air Force One.

Sergeant Ramirez leaned a little closer to Lieutenant Walker and mumbled barely over a whisper. "A real man's Unit huh Bobby? Brother give me a break. Do I look like a thick headed, non thinking, always farting, balls scratching, inconsiderate, ugly, self centered, egotistical, meat eating, beer guzzling, knuckle dragging perverted rutting pig faced ugly man to you, mister."

"Hey Raz, whaddaya mean by that shit, I ain't ugly sister." He complained back at her.

"I said it before and I'll say it again Bobby. You're impossible Mr. Walker. I hope our kids take after me and not you for their sake. Or there's not going to be any hope for the rest of the world." She growled as she shot an elbow out, jabbing it in his ribs and making him grunt.

"Hey, you don't think I'm a man, Raz?" Walker grumbled at her this time as he stared at her.

"Oh, you're all man alright mister. I can't believe how much of a man you truly are Bobby. It oozes out of every smelly pore of that body of yours, mister. It makes me swoon, oh I need you Bobby, take me stud, take me right here right now Mr. Man. Oh baby do me right in front of all these stupid ass Agents standing all over the place." She offered as she leaned up against his warm body, and then she flung her arms out wide and closed her eyes and put her head back, as if she was waiting for him to kiss her on the neck and then take her right on the tarmac.

"Really, you really want me to do you right here and now, sister? Man, that's fucking great Raz, let's do it. Hmmmm… Yeah, you don't wanna do it; you're just screwing around with me again. You keep teasing me like that and you'll see what happens to your little ass, Raz."

"Huh, you would screw me right in front of all these men, wouldn't you, you pig you?" she asked, stunned he would ever consider having her remove her clothes in this freezing cold.

"Only if I thought you were really serious about the offer, and I can get away with it at the same time that us, sister." He retorted with a wide grin on his face.

Another short elbow jabbed him in the ribs, backed by an icy cold stare was his answer.

Their conversation was interrupted by the black Chevy station wagon turning in the side gate.

"It's about time the dumb shit finally got his stinking ass here Walker." She hissed through her chattering teeth as she picked up her duffle bag, and then hoisted it over her shoulder.

The Lieutenant heaved his duffle bag over his shoulders as if it weighed nothing, and then he pushed her and said at the same time. "Looks like we're in the Army, be all you can be baby."

"Don't shove me like that Bobby. You know damn well I really hate when you do that to me, mister. You better knock it off if you know what's good for you!" She growled angrily at him.

"Hey baby calm the hell down a little huh? You just looked like you needed a little jump start that's all. I'm sorry huh. Christ, you do get in a bad mood when you get cold, don'tcha?"

"I'm not cold, I'm past fucking cold ten minutes ago. I'm freezing my ass off now Bobby." She shot right back between chattering teeth as she rushed her pace towards the waiting car.

The two soldiers rushed up to the car and quickly piled in, with Walker grabbing her bag from her and he tossed it in the rear of the wagon as she sat in the back seat of the vehicle.

"Hey driver, I hope you have the damn heater on full." Ramirez warned as she folded her arms across her chest and she squeezed herself, trying to find warmth anywhere she could steal.

"Yes Ma'am, sorry I'm late Sergeant. But the traffic's really fucked up on the City's streets. There must have been some bigwig come in for a damn visit to the City I didn't know about, dammit. They had more roads closed off than opened for traffic, and the damn cops were writing bad paper (tickets) on any drivers for any reason. Shit, I even saw them tag a parked UPS truck. I hope most of the crap's over with by the time we finally reach the center of the City, or it's going to suck shit." The Sergeant Major complained to the two soldiers in the back seat.

"Yeah, we all got some heartaches and pains to deal with?" Walker bitched at the driver then added. "How long before we get wherever the hell we're going, buddy? By the way Sergeant, where the fuck are we going, man?" He closed the door of the car and noticed the special agent who was busting is horns was now running after him. "Hold on a second, I gotta get this piece of paper from this stinking punk ass kid before he drives me over the fucking falls, Sergeant."

"I thought you were already briefed on where we're heading for, Lieutenant. We're heading for the Trump International Hotel and Tower, sir. It's really someplace to stay I hear, Lieutenant. I get a damn hardon just passing by the damn dump whenever I'm driving in the City."

"Yeah, I was making sure things didn't get change on us while we were in flight, Sergeant. It never seems to fail, every time I think I'm gonna end up in one fucking place, by the time I finally get there, I'm already heading in a different direction, man." The Lieutenant griped as he opened the window and took the slip of paper from the excited young special agent.

"Hey Lieutenant, I'm glad I caught you before you shoved off on me sir. This is the first break I caught while hoping to join the Special Forces, and I don't want it to slip through my hands on me, sir. Thanks a helluva lot for all your help with my dream, sir. I won't forget this for a minute sir. If I get in the Special Forces, I'm going to try and link up with your Unit, Lieutenant."

The Lieutenant took the paper and read the name. Special Agent Frank Farraro and offered. "Hey Frank, how come you never tried to get in the forces on your fucking own, Homes?"

"I did try Lieutenant, but I had a broken toe and it never healed quite right on me, sir. When I tried to enlist, they were real asses about it, dumping guys for any reason whatsoever sir. My toe was enough to get me bounced from the Unit I was trying to get into, sir. It's not going to stop me a second time will it sir?" The suddenly concerned agent questioned, showing serious worry he might have just blown his chance to get into the specialized group of soldiers.

"Naw, I'll make sure the stinking Docs overlook the toe thing for ya, fella if you do try and get in my Unit, pal." He offered as he folded the paper and then stuffed it in his pocket. For some reason, he kinda liked this kid and he decided he was going to do what he could to get him in his Unit. He had already settled on a name for the kid, if he made the mark. He was going to tag him 'Four F' because of his toe thing. Looking at the kid, he realized what he liked about him, his enthusiasm. "Yeah, you got the heart to make it in the damn Unit. I'll make sure fella."

The agent's hand shot out and Walker shook it. "Enough, we're freezing, let us go dammit."

The agent smiled as his head bobbed up and down, and he pulled his hand back. The vehicle pulled off the tarmac with the agent slapping the fender. Then he hopped to Air Force One.

The Lieutenant zipped the window closed and then he bitched at the Army driver. "Hey Sarge, you got any fucking blankets hiding in this here wreck looking to happen, man?"

"Yeah, I believe there are a few stowed in the back of the car somewhere, sir. You should find a few of them stuffed someplace back there Lieutenant. Probably under your gear you just pitched back there sir. Say Lieutenant, mind clueing me in on why a Special Forces Lieutenant and Sergeant, gets picked to spend a day staying at the damn Trump Tower, sir? I've been thinking about it since giving this detail, and it's driving me crazy trying to figure it out, sir."

He reached behind him and searched until he located a couple blankets. He pulled them forward and he quickly covered Ramirez with both of them. She immediately snuggled in, straightening the blankets until they covered every part of her shaking body. Try as she might, she just could not stop shaking and get warm because of the chill she had set in on her body.

"Just lucky I guess pal." He bitched back at the driver.

"Lucky my black ass, Lieutenant. All the time I've been hauling and damn VIP's asses through the heart of downtown Manhattan for three years. I never once dragged one of them over to the god damn Trump Tower dump, sir. What the hell's going on here, you can be square with me Lieutenant? I'll never tell anyone if you be square with me sir." The Army driver offered.

"Fuhgedaboutit Homes and keep your stinking eyes glued to the damn road, will ya for a change man. You're not on the fucking list of people need to know. Besides Sergeant Major, if I tell you then I'll have to kill and eat ya black ass, buster." The military officer retorted as he leaned against her, trying to add his heat to help stop her from shivering so badly.

"C'monnn, you can be square with me Lieutenant." The driver moaned again at Walker.

"Forget it Homes, you betta keep your eyes on the fucking road, and forget about why I'm here man. Or I'm gonna smack you right in that damn black gob of yours, pal." He warned the driver.

"It must really be something for the big shots back in Washington to send me out to pick up your honky ass and then dump you two birds off at the Trump Tower building, sir. But if you guys have to be buttoned lipped about it then you're right sir. I don't need to know the reason why you're in the damn City, sir. Thinking about it some more sir, I don't believe I want to know why you two are here in the City, sir." The driver said as he stared out the window at the slow flow of traffic, and then he added at the Marine Officer. "At least this crap's finally starting to move a little quicker for us, Lieutenant. I really hope that it's going to be the same way when we finally reach the very heart of midtown Manhattan, Lieutenant."

He looked at Ramirez, who was finally starting to show some signs of thawing out a little, and she whispered the driver was trying some reverse psychology on him, he was trying to pull the information from him by the back door politics. The Lieutenant nodded; and then he turned back to the driver and growled at him. "Nice fucking try there, Top Sarge but if you really wanna know then join up then you'll get all the stinking information first hand."

"Err... no thanks sir; I heard all the stories about you fucking guys. I'm quite happy where I am sir." The driver announced as he gunned the engine, and then zipped in the speed lane.

"I didn't think so, you chicken shit. All mouth and no fucking guts, huh Sarge?" he growled low, but it was enough for the driver to hear, and he chose to ignore Walker's last remark.

The trip to midtown Manhattan went smoothly, but when the car hit the FDR, the traffic slowed down to a crawl again. The New York police were in the speed lane, forcing traffic over to the slow lane. It was the police job to keep the cars moving as quickly as they keep them moving. Many one way streets leading to midtown were turned the other way to help with the traffic heading out of Manhattan for the weekend. It was sheer mayhem on the streets, with countless fender benders, stalled cars, and extremely angry drivers cursing everyone clogging the roads. Twice, the staff car was bumped by the trailing car. The last time the Lieutenant nearly jumped out of the window to get at the other driver who just tapped them. He was pulled down by Ramirez, who shook her head no and stopped him from going after the other driver.

"This traffic's nuts on a good day in Manhattan, Lieutenant." The driver announced as he suddenly changed lanes, and then he beeped his horn at by the other car he just cut off recklessly.

"Well Sergeant Major then get offa this parking lot, and get on some damn side streets of this dump, if you wanna make up time, buddy." Walker complained, showing all this traveling was starting to get under his skin. All he wanted to do was to get a New York strip steak cooked the way he liked them, rare, still bleeding and smothered in brown gravy, mushrooms and onions. Then he wanted to grab a night's sleep after making serious love in a soft bed with his lady.

"Hey big mouth!" The driver snapped, getting angry with Walker's constant backseat driving. "I know the damn side streets are in worse shape than this mess is in, sir. I'm sticking tight, it'll break soon enough." The driver was anything but right. The traffic did not break, instead, it grew worse, with the staff car doing about five mph for the full length of the FDR drive.

"Hey Top Sarge, how about putting on some stinking music for us? I need something to break up the stinking boredom of this damn ride." He bitched at the driver.

"No can do Lieutenant, there's no radio in this here jalopy, sir. This here thing's a military machine and is subject to the same rules and regs as the other machines. No luxuries sir."

"An Italian car I take it Top Sarge. A no thrills sardine can, Sergeant Major?" the Lieutenant added with a smirk as he shot the driver a quick smile.

"You understand good for a killing machine back there, Lieutenant." The driver replied.

"Yep, you got that right." He remarked as he turned his attention outside of the window.

Ramirez tugged on his arm, and then she pointed to his wrist and the Lieutenant grumbled at the driver and he growled. "Christ, it ten after nine already. Hey Top Sarge, if you don't get me to the damn apartment in the next ten fucking minutes, pull off the damn road and get us over to a stinking restaurant so we can eat something for crap's sake man. We're starved to fucking death here." The female military officer roared back at the driver.

"Sorry, no can do that either, Lieutenant Sir. I'm not cleared to pull off the road for any reason other than death or an emergency situation, sir. If I did as you just requested, it'll be my ass placed on a tray, and I like the way my ass is hanging, sir."

"How much further is it then to this damn place you're taking us to, Sarge?" he asked of the driver with anger in his tone of voice.

"We're on Seventy Second Avenue, and we have to get over to Fifty Seventh West. You can do the math yourself, Lieutenant." The driver snapped, allowing the stress of the traffic get him.

"Relax, you're starting to get worked up over this traffic, Hoss." Ramirez shot at the Sergeant.

"Boy, I wish I had one of those damn candy bars you had to gnaw on, Raz." Walker offered, hoping Ramirez was holding out on him again, he looked at her out of the corner of his eye.

"Here you go you big baby you, I should've known you'd cry for another one of these things. I was saving this one for myself to enjoy later on today, Bobby." She snapped hotly as she opened the wrapper and then offered him the last Butterfinger bar she had.

"Christ sake Lieutenant, the damn traffic's starting to finally open up a little for us sir. We're turning onto Fifty Seventh Street sir." The Sergeant spun the wheel hard and then he laid on his horn as the car shot out of the heavy traffic right in front of him. Traffic was moving here, but still at a snail's pace. There was mass confusion due to the roads like Lexington and Fifth Avenue turned the other direction.

Instead of being a one way heading downtown, the roads were now one way heading out of town. The NYPD done this in an effort to try and get some of the bottled up traffic moving a little quicker for them. The attempt was making it a real madhouse on the City roads, trying to drive down side streets the police were leading everyone on.

The Sergeant Major picked up the Trump Tower off in the distance and he pointed it out to the two young soldiers in the rear seat. "There's the big hardon of a building Lieutenant."

Both Walker and Ramirez sat forward to see the size of the building. The fifty two story building stood out like what the Sergeant Major just called it, its lights making it a sight to see.

"That's where we're staying here in the City, Sergeant Major?" Sergeant Ramirez asked as she stared at the building out the car window in awe.

"Yep Sergeant, that's the Trump International Hotel and Tower alright, Ma'am."

"Sarge, you betta cool down a little before a cop gets a hardon about you, and he pulls your ass over just for the stinking hell of it, and he tap dances on your fucking head for ya, man."

"Fuck them where they breathe from Lieutenant. If it wasn't for them doing all this crap to us damn drivers, this lousy traffic would be flowing like it usually does in Manhattan, sir."

A police officer glared at the stalled car beeping its horn, and then he made his way for it.

"Uh oh, now you fucking did it Sarge. The stinking heat's coming over for your fucking ass Homes." Walker warned the upset driver as he watched the cop heading for them.

The cop leaned over the window and he stared at the Sergeant as the driver zipped down his window. "What's your problem, buddy? Did your mummy use some starch in your undies?"

"I'm sorry fella, but I've been stuck in this damn traffic for over an hour now. Earlier today I spent two hours going the other way. What's happening up there? The President come in?"

"Naw, but I heard his Veeps visiting the City. Look fella, you better get a move on it, and keep it cool. If I didn't have so many cars driving over my feet today, and you weren't military, I'd make an example of your ass, Sergeant. Move on mister." The cop tapped on the windshield with his nightstick, and then he waved his hand at the traffic, opening it up for the military driver.

"Jesus H. Christ!" The Sergeant roared as he laid on the horn then cursed at every vehicle in front of him. Letting it go on the Vice President now he knew she was the problem for the traffic.

After what seemed like a short lifetime, the staff car stopped before the main entrance of the Trump Tower. Lieutenant Walker was the first out of the car. The still angry Sergeant Major climbed out of the vehicle and opened the backdoor and pulled their baggage out, depositing the two duffle bags down on the sidewalk. Ramirez moved over to Walker's side and she stared at the Trump Tower in awe of the magnificent building.

"Looks like the stinking Sergeant Major called it right after all Raz. That's one huge ass friggin hardon there Raz." The Lieutenant grumbled as he stared at the building.

Ramirez struck Walker in the ribs and then complained at him. "Gees Walker, you're getting worst than ever lately with that foul mouth of yours, mister. You better start watching it while we're meeting with the Vice President and the rest of her staff, Bobby."

"And you fucking love it sister." He retorted with a grin as they lifted their bags and he looked at the Sergeant Major as he gave him a half hearted salute.

"I can't say this was one bowl of cherries Lieutenant, because it wasn't, sir. You guys are home, and I gotta get through this damn traffic for a third fucking time, before I calls it a night, sir." The driver complained as he returned the salute of the Lieutenant.

"Thanks for getting us here in one piece, Sarge. If you get any grief about those coupla little dingers, get in contact with me and I'll do my best to try and straighten things out for ya, Sarge."

"Yeah, it was nice meeting ya sir. Good luck tonight, Lieutenant. Keep them hot and ready to rock sir. Sure wish I knew why I was forced to drive through this mess tonight for you guys."

"Still trying it I see huh Sarge?" he taunted the older driver, not giving in to his questions.

"Yep, my mama always told me my nose was way too damn long for my face, Lieutenant."

"Nice try again Sarge, but it's still not gonna work for ya here pal."

"You can't blame this old fool for trying, can ya Lieutenant?" the driver shot back.

"Nope, not at all Sarge, but it's not gonna do you any fucking good though, pal." Walker said as he turned on his heels, and then he headed for the building with Ramirez in tow. Unlike the greeting the Vice President had received earlier in the day, no one was waiting to meet the two soldiers. The concierge cautiously eyed the young pair as the soldiers struggled in the lobby with their over packed duffle bags. He hoped the two made a mistake, and they entered his building by an oversight. The concierge stared at them while holding a number of envelopes in his hand.

He dropped the military bag as if it was a sack of garbage. Then he smiled at the bald headed man. With a grin he grunted at him. "Hey Q ball, I believe you have a room for us in here man."

The old man's eyes open wide as he cried. "I beg your pardon sir, are you certain you have the right hotel, sir? Our rooms might be a little out of your, err... price range, young man. There's a fine hotel I'm certain that's more within your price range, a few blocks to the east sid..."

"Will you stop begging, for crap sake you're fucking old enough to steal man." He fired back at the old man as he shot him one of his smiles and then a slight nod of his head.

Ramirez pulled on his arm and she whispered in an angry tone at him. "Please Bobby; keep a civil tongue in your mouth for once in your life. These guys aren't used to the likes of us staying here, Robert." Then she turned to the concierge and offered in a polite voice to him. "I'm sorry we started off on the wrong foot with you sir. We were told there was a room being held in reserve in our name by a General John White, sir. Are we right with that assumption sir?" she offered as she put on one of her finest smile for the old and stunned looking man.

The elderly concierge was not to be appeased so easily by her beautiful smile and eyes and kind words; he was still fuming over the crude remark made by the male soldier with her leveled at his losing his hair. He decided he was going to make the two wait for as long as he could before giving them the room. At the mention of the General's name, the concierge knew right away the soldiers were in the right place as he replied to the female soldier. "What is your name young lady? The name of the General you just mentioned sounds a little familiar to me, but I'll have to check my records to see what room was err... set aside for your use in the Trump international Tower and Hotel, Ma'am. I'm sorry, but this might take me a few moments."

"Our names are Lieutenant Robert Walker and Sergeant Dorothy Ramirez, sir. Please try to hurry it up a little for us sir, we're starving and really exhausted sir. We have been on the move ever since three o'clock this morning, and we want to sleep for a week if we can, sir"

"I'll do my very best for you to try and hurry young lady. Please wait here while I check my reservations list and find out what room was set aside for the two of you, please."

Chapter Ten

Lieutenant Robert Walker leaned a little closer to Sergeant Dorothy Ramirez and then he bitched at her just above a whisper. "This lousy prick's gonna dick us around until he's good and ready to give us the stinking room. Didja see the fricking look on the old fart's puss when we first walked into this fucking dump, I thought he was gonna shit himself right then and..."

"Walker please! You're embarrassing the shit out of me again Bobby" She grumbled as she tugged on his arm, and she tried to stop him from being so nasty to the older man.

"Yeah I know, what say we dick the stinking dicker for a change around here, and we get ourselves something to eat while the old fart's still busy looking up our damn room fur us, baby?" Walker asked and then he quickly scanned the interior of the marble and brass lobby looking for someplace to eat. He noticed a fine looking restaurant with the name, The Jean-Georges Vongerichten printed on the outside of the restaurant, and he snapped at her. "C'mon sister, I'll buy ya supper in that stinking dump there. It looks clean enuf and it comes with compliments of the government and we're gonna enjoy the freebees as long as we can, baby."

"Walker, I think you'll need a tie and a suit jacket to even enter a restaurant like that. It looks like a real classy ass and expensive place to chow down in I'm sure Bobby."

"What the hell do you call this thing I'm wearing baby? A stinking feather boa honey?"

"It's not the same thing I believe Bobby. By tie I mean you need a jacket also, preferably black and a matching tie, mister." She snapped at him as she stared at him for a long moment.

"Hey baby, I didn't fight in a stinking foxhole fur half my fricking life, just to be told I'm not good enuf to eat wherever the hell I wanna eat here in the United States, sister. If these stinking pissants wanna keep my ass outta that fricking place. Then they betta get a small fucking Army of cops to help them keep me outta the stinking place. I'm going in there, and I'm gonna fricking eat something in there, or I'll rip the damn place apart good and proper, baby."

"You know I'm behind you Bobby. But if you ask me, I'd be just as happy eating one of those frankfurters they sell on the street corners. I heard they're pretty good Robert to eat. My mouth's watering for one of them little babies. C'mon, let's go out and get franks and sodas, Bobby."

"Fuck that shit, I didn't travel all the way over to New York fucking City just to eat on a damn sidewalk like one of the bum's that are always hanging around this damn City. I want a New York fricking strip steak and that's what I'm gonna have, and in that there restaurant as well, dammit. If this shit filled stuff shirts refuse to serve my ass then them bastards are gonna find out how good their hospitalization coverage is. C'mon baby, we're gonna getting us something to eat in there little sister!" he snarled as he tugged on her arm, and they both charged through the stained glass doors separating the restaurant from the rest of the lobby area of the hotel.

They were greeted by an overly polite Madre De, who eyed them cautiously and whispered to Walker. "I beg your pardon sir, but I'm afraid you'll need a suit and tie if you'd like to dine with us tonight, sir. Perhaps you might like something sent up to your room. If you're staying at the hotel, sir? I'd be pleased to arrange it for you sir." The Madre De flashed a quick smile at them.

Walker glared at the grinning concerned older man, his look made the waiter actually step back as he growled at the man. "Hey pal, they're hunting down my stinking room for us right now man, so there's no place to send my fucking food to. Look chum, I just came from fighting a pack of crazy ass sand fleas in the stinking desert and I'm dog ass tired. I was wounded and got myself enough cuts and scrapes to last me a fucking lifetime and then some. I'm not only exhausted, but me and my lady are starving as well, and all I want is a fricking steak to sink my damn teeth in, and then catch up on some of my sleep. Whaddaya say pal? You gonna keep busting my stinking horns, or are you gonna seat us so we can eat and then we'll leave your place as we have found it, in one fucking piece and we'll all end up smiling at each other, pal."

The older man did not respond to his threat as he eyed the soldiers for a long moment. Then he announced politely to the upset acting soldier. "If you'd be so kind as to follow me sir. I'll be happy to show you over to one of our finest tables in the restaurant, sir. There's no smoking in the restaurant sir. Everything is served ala mode as well. We accept both Master Charge and Visa credit cards, or you can just charge it to your room if you prefer to do that, sir."

"I don't smoke anything but fucking grass my new friend." Walker snorted at the man.

"Walker please!" She snapped as she tugged on his arm and then glared at him again.

"I beg your pardon sir. I'm afraid I did not understand what you just said to me sir." The polished and extremely polite old man asked and then he offered as his eyebrows arched a bit.

"Nuthin man, just get me a damn steak before I pass out from stinking hunger, Homes. Hey Raz, that was the first time someone called me sir without adding I was making a friggin scene." The Lieutenant smirked as he turned and looked at the still angry looking female soldier.

"In case you don't realize it mister, you were creating a scene in here Bobby."

Amidst the many stares and quick looks coming from many of the high class snobs eating in the posh restaurant, the two soldiers were proudly led over to a table overlooking the Park. He did not know if this guy was using them to rub someone the wrong way in the restaurant, and he really did not care either. The Lieutenant was too hurt and tired to care about anything but eating.

The old man politely pulled the seat out for Ramirez and then he asked the couple. "Would you like something from the bar while you wait for your meal to be prepared for you please?"

"Yeah, now you're talking my language, a Bud in a bottle will do fine for me, Mac!"

"I'll have a glass of chilled red wine please, and you can place the Bud in a glass please, sir." Ramirez added as she corrected Walker's order for the man.

"Very well Ma'am and I was planning to place his beer in a glass, we don't allow any bottles on the table unless they're wine, a waiter will be with you shortly to take your order for you, Ma'am. I hope you'll enjoy the meal we'll prepare especially for your enjoyment Ma'am."

They ignored the politeness of the man as they glanced over the menu. Walker kept looking over the top to see how the other people in the restaurant were taking to them. He was stunned at the prices of the meals. He smiled when he saw two people approach the Madre De, and they seemed to be obviously complaining about something. He knew right off they were griping about them being served in the restaurant, and he did not have a suit jacket on.

"Hey Raz, it looks like we just got the old bugger's ass in a little scrap on him."

The Sergeant looked up in time to see the two older people leaving the old man, who shot a quick smile at her and she told him. "It looks like he can handle himself pretty well. Bobby, I wish you'd be a little more friendlier while we're visiting the Big City. Relax and enjoy yourself, let yourself go will you please Robert. I want to have some fun here, I don't want everyone we see angry at us just because you pissed them off somehow with that mouth of your, mister."

The Lieutenant liked they were being served in the restaurant, even though they did not conform to the usual stuffy rules of the place. It proved someone appreciated the efforts they were putting forward for the sake of the United States. After eating an outstanding meal, they both walked back to the lobby of the Trump Tower and saw the concierge looking for them.

"I'm terribly sorry it has taken me so long to locate your room for you, sir. Where did you disappear to sir? I looked all over the lobby for you, I was afraid you might have decided to try another hotel for your stay in New York, sir." The old man offered kindly to the soldiers.

"We had us something to fucking eat in that dump over there, Homes." He shot a quick thumb towards the fine restaurant some twenty five feet away from where they were standing.

"You mean to tell me they seated you in the restaurant dressed as you are sir?" the surprised concierge asked, stunned the soldiers were served the way they were dressed.

"Yeah why, we the wrong fucking color or something man?" he snarled combatively.

"I beg your pardon sir?" the concierge asked as he placed a stunned look on his face again.

"There he goes again. Everyone round here keeps begging my fucking pardon for something. All I want is a stinking room where I can put up my damn feet up and watch some TV for a change. Hey pal, do we get any of them fuck and suck channels piped into our room?" Walker was trying to be as crude as possible because he felt this guy was still trying to bust his horns.

"I beg your pardon sir?" the stunned concierge repeated his words as he stared at Walker.

"Walker pleaseeee! Can't you be nice for a few moments in your life, mister? I just told you to be kind to these people and will you please." The Sergeant hissed at Walker in a growl.

"There you go a fucking gain pal. Begging my fricking pardon for something I don't know you did pal, just gimme the fucking key and I'll be gone lickity-split from your stinking puss, pal." The upset Lieutenant grunted as he put out his hand and then wiggled his fingers.

She took the key, fearing Walker was in such a mood he might hurt the old man's fingers. She hated when he got in an aggressive mood where he wanted to take on the world and win.

"Your room number's Two, Oh, One, Two sir, and it's on the twentieth floor on the east side of the building, young man. Do you want me to have someone help you with your luggage, sir?"

"Do we see a view of the Park?" the Sergeant asked, getting excited over the apartment.

"I'm sorry young lady, but not every room overlooks the Park. I'll get someone to help you."

"No need fur that man. I'll handle my crap for us Homes." Walker snapped at the old man.

"Very well then sir. But someone will show you to your room sir. I beg your pardon sir, but no one visiting the hotel is allowed to wander around the building unescorted, sir."

"Why? You think we're gonna steal a fucking apartment on ya ass, buddy?" he snickered as he headed to the elevators. The Special Forces soldiers were being lead by a smiling young bellhop.

Once the soldiers were inside the elevator, she really laced into Walker as she yelled at him. "You better lighten up some if you know what's good for you Bobby, or I'm not going to hang around you all the while we're in New York mister. You want to act like a big jerk then you'll do it without me watching you. I have a good mind to hop you right in the can because of the way you're acting against everyone we met so far. Walker, not everyone's your enemy, we're visiting New York City, the finest City in the United States, with that comes unending sights and things to do. I want to visit the Statue of Liberty and Empire State Building. Times Square, oh God, we're near Times Square you know. I want to see where the ball falls. Walker, the sights we'll see are limitless, and I intend to see them all before we're shipped off to sand land again."

"Yeah, I guess I am acting like the south end section of a north bound horse at that, baby. I'll lighten up some and start enjoying myself, why don't you make a list of what you wanna see..."

The elevator stopped at their floor, and the soldiers were quickly ushered to their room. He lead the way following the bellhop. The young bellhop opened a wood carved door and Walker announced at the same time. "I can't wait to see the shithole the lousy bastards rented us. I bet this place is a stinking dump they couldn't rent if their lives depended on it, baby."

"There you go again Bobby; you're looking for problems where there aren't any. Who cares what the place looks like as long... Oh my God will you look at this place Bobby. Jesus Robert, do people really live like this? Looks like you're going to have to eat your own words, Bobby. This place is wonderful, it's beautiful." She said in awe as she added. "This place is like a castle, look at how high the ceiling is. Walker, we can have a game of basketball in here if we want."

The bellhop stared at Ramirez, afraid she was serious about playing basketball in their room. If the soldiers were going to do that, he would have to report this to the front desk on them.

The Lieutenant slammed a hand on the hotel worker's shoulder as he snapped at him. "Relax chum, she's just pulling your leg on ya man. She can't shoot hoops for love or money, Homes."

She stripped where the bellhop called the gallery. "Where's the bathroom at?" She asked.

"The bathroom's this way Ma'am." The bellhop opened the door, as the now naked Ramirez rushed past him and headed for the marble tub.

"Oh God Walker, it's a whirlpool bath! It's bigger than my pool was back home, Bobby." She turned on the water and steam instantly rose. "Oh God, it's hot! I love this place, Bobby."

He tried to look over the bellhop's shoulder at the beautiful woman naked as the day she was born, waiting for the tub to fill. Both men looked at each other and smiled over the sight.

"How do you get the motor on this thing running? I want to try the whirlpool out sir. I never had one before in my life." She asked as she pushed all the buttons and turned all the dials.

"Beats the shit outta my stinking ass baby. The only time we ever had a whirlpool when I was a kid, was when mom let the water out of the tub and it swirled around the damn drain as the cold water went out." The Lieutenant offered with a grin.

"If you'd like Ma'am, I can show you how the whirlpool operates Ma'am."

"Welllll don't just stand there like you are get it done for me mister." The excited Ramirez snapped while placing her hands on her hips and then she stared at the bellhop.

The bellhop moved a little further into the bathroom and set the dials properly for her, and the soft whine of the motor was heard as the water whipped up into a soft white froth.

She actually pushed the young bellhop aside and she nearly jumped into the steaming water and then she let out with a yell when the water hit her battered, bruised and exhausted body. "Yeeeaaaooowww, this is wonderful Robert." She cried as she sank below the water, and closed her eyes as she allowed her body to absorb the warmth assaulting her body with great pleasure.

The Lieutenant tapped the bellhop on the shoulder and then he warned him. "C'mon pal, I think you've seen enough, you betta leave before you hurt yourself buddy."

The two men left the bathroom, with the hotel worker closing the door behind him.

"Do you have anything to drink hidden in this stinking dump, buddy?"

"Yes sir, there's a well stocked bar in the kitchen, sir. All you do is pay for what you drink when you and the lady are checking out of the Hotel, sir. They keep a running tab for you sir." The bellhop offered as he got around him and then started to lead him towards the kitchen area.

"Where the hell is the damn thing located pal? I need myself a stinking drink if you know what I mean, buddy." He asked as he stared to look around the place for the bar.

The bellhop happily showed Walker to the bar at the beginning of the kitchen.

"Well, that's it for me I guess, I got what I wanted now get the hell out of here buddy."

The bellhop left without a word, or a tip for that matter from the angry young soldier.

He poured Ramirez a chilled glass of wine, he did not really enjoy wine all that much. But nevertheless, he poured the second glass for himself. He entered the bathroom and then sat down on the side of the bathtub and handed a glass to her.

She heard Walker come in the bathroom and she lazily opened her eyes and stared dreamily at her lover and soldier before taking the wine and saying. "Robert, do you think people really live like this in New York? I can't believe the luxury this place offers, there's even music in here. If I didn't know any better, I'd swear to God the bathwater was scented as it came out of the faucet. I forgot how many beautiful odors there are in the real world, Robert. All I smelt lately is spent gun powder mixed in with burning flesh and body odors and camel dung. This dump's sheer Heaven Walker, sheer Heaven. Why don't you come in and join me? There's plenty of room for the two of us in this little pond here you know." She sipped the wine and smiled at him.

IN THE VICE PRESIDENT ROOM

When the two highly trained soldiers checked in the hotel, the Vice President was immediately notified of the fact. Cathy put off greeting the two young soldiers until she was sure Agent Sweeney was going to pay a visit to Mary. She hung around the kitchen waiting for Sweeney to return, she made a remark earlier to him that he smelled of body odor and cigarette smoke, and he rushed off to shower and change his clothes. It was the only way she could think of, to make him take a shower without telling him outright to do so. She lightly tapped her foot on the floor while waiting for him to come out of the room. All the while she was thinking of how easy it was for a woman to manipulate a stupid man. All a woman had to do was just wiggle her hips and show a little cleavage, and the man was immediately eating out of her hand.

Agent Sweeney came charging into the kitchen with his hair combed neatly but still slightly wet. He smelled good, and Cathy could tell he was clean, and his teeth was freshly brushed. She poured him a cold beer while she sipped her champagne, she smiled as she circled the poor agent like an animal circling its wounded prey, running her hands over his shoulders, and pulling his tie out from inside his jacket again, and even jabbing him under the arm lightly with her elbow.

"Hey, what the hell gives with you anyway Ma'am?" Sweeney suddenly barked angrily at her, thinking Cathy might be making a play for him in the kitchen.

"You know something Mr. Agent Man, I was thinking about you lately, and I think I'd real..."

"Yeah? You were thinking about me how Cathy?" Sweeney asked the pretty lady with a snap.

"Never mind that fearless. Do you mind if I ask you a few questions Mr. Agent?"

"Sure, why the hell not Ma'am. Shoot away if you want to take a shot at me, Cathy. I've been hit on by the best of people I was protecting, Ma'am." The concerned agent offered sarcastically, waiting for her to get to the bottom of this little game of hers she was playing on him.

"Don't tempt me big boy. Err... Mr. Agent Man, I was wondering how you felt about Mary?" She was one of the few Presidential and Vice Presidential aides that was always armed, and she knew how to use a weapon and her arms and feet as added weapons.

"She's an extremely smart and a great Vice President, and she always has her head above the water, Cathy. Ms. Hirshfield really knows what she's doing at all times she's in office."

"Good looking too, right mister?" she asked the more concerned looking agent shyly this time.

"Yeah, very good looking at that Ma'am. Why you say that to me Cathy?"

"Sexy." She purred at the now sweating agent as she stared at him.

"Sorry Ma'am, but I hadn't noticed that Cathy." Sweeney replied correctly.

"I'll bet you didn't notice it buster." She snipped at him and then continued her interrogation of the agent. "Sweeney, how would you feel if I was to tell you Mary was interested in you?"

"What do you mean, interested in me Ma'am?" the agent was beginning to put his back up over the course the conversation was heading in.

"Interested in you in a romantic way, stupid." She allowed herself a slight giggle, but she put her hand to her lips to hide her smile from him, as she enjoyed his uncomfortable feeling.

"Huh, I'd say you had a little too much of that there shit there to drink, Ma'am." The upset special agent snapped hotly at her as he tried to leave the kitchen area, not liking the direction the conversation was heading more than ever now.

She reached out and grabbed his arm with surprising strength, and she stopped him from leaving the room. She was well versed in a number of different Marshal Arts Disciplines as she added to the uncomfortable looking agent. "I'm not kidding you Mr. Agent. Right now she's waiting for you in her bedroom, stupid. She's an extremely lonely woman Mr. Agent, and she's really interested in you for reasons I am unaware of, mister. I told her I'd find out if the feeling was mutual from you tonight. Is it, Agent Sweeney?"

Sweeney stared back at her with a dumb look plastered on his face and saying nothing to her. He was stunned, his wildest dreams seemed to be answered for him. For years he followed Mary around like a puppy during her career, longing for her to notice him. His responsibility for her welfare spilled over to where he developed some romantic feelings for her. He tried to be near her, look after her every needs, but the one need he sought the most was a romantic one. And now, he was hearing she felt the same way about him. His mind raced wildly, he was confused and even scared to death. He did not know what to say, or how to react to her words. His thoughts were brought back to the present by Cathy, who suddenly cleared her throat loudly.

"Agent Sweeney, I believe you feel the same way about her. Am I right Edward?"

Sweeney's first thought was to keep protecting the Vice President's reputation to his last breath of his body by denying any romantic feelings about her. But his heart spoke before his mind did. "I do, for years I felt this way about her, Cathy…" He wanted to immediately bite his tongue when his mind registered what his mouth just said to the female agent.

"That's wonderful Mr. Agent Man. That's why I made you take a shower tonight, stupid. I swear Mary's waiting for you to come into her bedroom, Sweeney. All you have to do is knock lightly on the door and you're home free, stupid."

"What about the other guys in the apartment, Cathy? What will they think if they know I'm bedding the Vice President in the next room, Ma'am? Holy shit, I can't believe I just said that."

"Don't worry about those other fools, stupid. I'll handle them. Besides, what the hell do you care about them or what they have to say about anything? They know if they say anything about what happens in the room of the Vice President, I'll have them roasted alive over an open pit, Agent Sweeney. All I want you to worry about tonight is making Mary happy, stupid. She's a good woman, and she deserves a little pleasure out of life. Heaven knows her position demands too much from her, robbing her of all her private life. That's going to stop on this night mister. Mary's going to enjoy herself one way or the other, with you." She pointed her finger at him.

"She sure is, what do you want me to do Cathy?" Sweeney asked while getting excited.

"Okay Mr. Agent, bring this chilled bottle of wine to her bedroom, along with this basket of fried shrimp I had sent up for her to enjoy. Take off your damn tie and loosen your top button and relax a little will you please. Then go in there like a real man, not as a stupid agent and hopefully nature will take over for you, stupid." She said as she stared at the stunned looking man, hoping he was going to treat Mary in the way she deserved to be treated by any man.

"Suppose I'm not good making love to her? You know, clumsy."

"Don't be stupid, stupid. Take it from me and relax and you'll do just fine Sweeney."

"But suppose I am, dammit? I'm scared to death about screwing this up on her, Cathy."

"Look Eddy, you're a big boy right? I don't have all the answers in my crystal ball for you, mister. But I do know all you have to do is relax and let things happen naturally like, and I'm sure you'll do just fine with Mary tonight, stupid. Don't sell Mary short Sweeney, she's all woman and she knows her way around the bedroom very well I tell you, mister."

"I don't know I'm scared to death about this, Cathy." He started to sweat as he took the tray from her and turned towards the Vice President's bedroom, as if he was walking his last mile.

"Hold on for a minute stupid, you're forgetting what I just told you to do, mister. Come back here and listen to me and do all I tell you to do for her tonight, stupid."

Sweeney turned around and she loosened his tie and then slipped it over his head. She undid the top button of his shirt and even messed up his hair a little on him. She then slapped his shoulders with her hands, forcing them up and then she moaned at him. "Jesus Mr. Agent, will you relax a little please. You're acting like you're about to have your head lopped off your damn shoulders, stupid." She covered her mouth as she thought about what she said then giggled.

Sweeney did not catch what she was laughing about as he stared at her, almost shaking now.

"Look stupid, go in there like you were visiting any woman you were trying to bed. You do date women I mean? You do like women don't you, Agent Sweeney?" the female bodyguard had to ask the question, what with the way he was acting was causing her some concern.

"Huh? Hey whaddaya think I am, of course I like women! I'm no god damn tail gunner."

She placed her hand on his shoulder, turning him around and aimed him at Mary's bedroom and then she gave him a little shove forward to get him moving.

He dragged his feet painfully while heading to the door, reaching it he gently he knocked.

"Come in please." Mary sexily purred from inside the master bedroom.

Cathy had to laugh over the way the foolish agent was acting, she thought he was never going to reach the door before he died of old age. Let alone have the guts to go into the room with Mary. She saw his knees actually buckle slightly when he opened the door to her bedroom. "Finally!" She said barely above a whisper as she watched the door close behind him.

The worried and confused special agent swallowed the instant he saw Mary resting in the bedroom lying on the bed, her head was up, held by her leaning on her elbow. She was dressed in a beautiful black nighty, her right breast just about escaping from the soft silk expensive fabric. Her long hair was fixed up in a bun, and her makeup was absolutely perfect. The beautiful female Vice President held out her glass, her breast sneaking out of the fine fabric and almost making Agent Sweeney wet himself as he stared at it and Mary.

"Err... Edward, my glass is empty, do you mind filling it for me please."

Agent Sweeney's eyes were wide as saucers as he stood with his mouth hanging open, and he drank in all of Mary's stunning beauty and outstanding treasures. When she spoke to him, his mouth snapped shut and Mary found herself happy he did not accidently catch his tongue between his teeth, or it would have been bitten off. This would have been unacceptable to her, because she had a number of rather interesting plans for his tongue on this night.

Seeing him shaking like a leaf, Mary knew she had to make the first move on the poor man if she wanted to get on making love to him. She looped her nighty off her shoulders, exposing both breasts to his gaze as she purred. "You can come here; I won't bite you, at least not right away."

Like a mindless robot, Sweeney cautiously approached the bed and she sat up and then swung her legs over the side of the bed and she pulled him close to her. "Come here Edward."

ROOM 2012, THE TRUMP INTERNATIONAL HOTEL AND TOWER

Lieutenant Robert Walker stripped out of his uniform and joined Sergeant Dorothy Ramirez in the oversized bathtub. They drank and ate cheese and laughed. When everything was gone, they turned to each other's needs. He made love to her for the first time in three months. The both of them almost forgot how wonderful it was to be held in each other's arms, and be alone. No sooner did he finish making love to his lady then he was ready to go for a second time.

Neither one of them paid very much attention to the time, or what they were supposed to do after they checked into the hotel, or noticed the water was cooling off around them. When they finished making love for a second time, she whispered in his ear that she wanted another glass of wine, and something more to nibble on while he was at it.

Without thinking about it, he got out of the tub and headed for the kitchen naked as the day he was born, and dripping wet from the bath water. She watched her soldier as he left her in the bathroom. She laughed because he looked so funny, his powerful back, strong arms, and shoulders were delightfully well tanned. So was his legs from mid thigh down to his feet, but his rearend was as white as the driven snow. She could not get the old song she once heard a soldier singing when Blind Date stripped down for the doctor to examine her.

"Boom, boom, boom, boom, I see your hinny, it's bright and shiny." She could not help but laugh as the song kept repeating in her head. He heard her laughing and stopped before the tub and he griped at her. "What? What's so god damn funny all of the sudden to you, Raz?"

She had to wipe a tear from her eye and she looked at him again and laughed harder. He was as white in the front; his dick looked like a bleached white snake hanging between his legs. He looked funny because most of his body was black with tan, except for this one area of his body.

The Lieutenant spread his arms out, spilling some of the wine and as he repeated. "What?"

"Walker, I'm afraid I have some bad news for you, honey. When we get home I'm going to make you tan your white ass and front, you look so funny like that baby." She smiled at her lover.

He looked down at his dick and then he joined her laughter. He realized he looked ridiculous half assed tanned like he was. He suddenly shivered because he was still soaking wet and she yelled at him. "You better get back in this tub before you catch a cold, shiny hinny."

"What?" he growled as he crawled back into the hot water tub with his lover.

"Never mind what I just said, it's a private little joke I'll take to my grave." Once he was back in the water she quickly wrapped herself around him to help warm his body.

He was getting bored with staying in the tub so long. He wanted to watch some TV, but Ramirez was not letting go of him that easily, she was not finished with him just yet.

ROOM 2250, STAR 3, THE TRUMP INTERNATIONAL TOWER

Cathy waited in the Presidential Suite until she was certain everything in the Vice President's bedroom was going well with the two soon to be lovers. Then she checked her watch, it was ten thirty five p.m. and she checked the phone memo, which informed her that the two dangerous Special Forces soldiers had checked in, and they were in the hotel and staying in room 2012. She drew in a breath and let it out as she finished her glass of wine. She picked up her purse with the Colt, 9 mm pistol in it, and clocked in with the special agents before she left the Presidential apartment. She told the three agents in the room that Sweeney was helping Mary get settled in, and she was going to visit room 2012, to make sure the two soldiers arrived and had no needs.

The agent gave her a simple wave of his hand as he wrote the apartment number on his pad.

She started to leave the room and thought for a second, and then she stopped as she looked in the agent's bedroom and added to the agent who looked like he was bored to death. "Agent Sweeney's helping the Vice President with some of her important paperwork, and they're not to be disturbed for any reason less than a national emergency. Right Mr. Agent Man?"

"We have no problem with that Ma'am." The controlling agent replied.

When she was out the door, the second agent smirked. "Well, whaddaya think Sweeney's doing in there with the Vice President? Do you think he might be porking the old Iron Lady?"

"Sweeney, that'll be the fucking day, he doesn't have the balls to try that with the Iron Lady. You better get your head out of the damn gutter if you know what's good for you, if Number Two Mama hears you talking like that, she'll take your nuts and use them for earrings, buddy."

She headed for the elevators, her legs aching from lack of use, so she decided to take the stairs. She headed for the stairwell, passing an older police officer stationed there to complete the security ring weaved around the Vice President all the while she was visiting the Trump Tower. Cathy nodded to the officer, but he stopped her and demanded to know where she was going, and he wanted to check her identification card before he allowed her to leave the floor.

She produced her White House staff photo ID card and offered it to the concerned police officer as she told the officer she was going down to floor twenty, so she could visit with the other part of the Vice President's personal entourage. The elderly police officer smiled as he handed her ID back to her when he was satisfied who she was. He even opened the door to the stairwell for her, and then nodded as she darted down the stairs. The officer kept a close eye on the young lady until she turned the stairwell and then she disappeared from his view.

She took the cement steps two at a time; she was enjoying the exercise and making the best of it. She read the floor number printed on the side of the concrete wall in black paint, telling her she reached her destination. She quickly caught her breath as she slowed down and then walked the rest of the way to the apartment door, and she used the knocker to announce her presence.

The Lieutenant was starting to get excited all over again, he took her glass of wine from her and dribbled it over her nipples, and then he lapped the wine up with his tongue and mouth, causing her to roar with glee and excitement. Walker was so involved in what he was doing to his lady that he did not hear the light knocking on their door. But she did.

"Walker, what was that?" she asked while trying to sit up in the bathtub, and listen as she pulled his head from her breast and growled. "Stop that will you please so I can hear, Bobby."

"Hear what I didn't hear nuthin sister. What the hell was what, baby? I think you're fucking hear things baby. Leave it alone will ya and sit back and enjoy what I'm about to do to your lovely body, little sister. I can't help it; this place is making me hornier than I was in my entire ever loving stinking life, baby." He grumbled as he started to lap at her nipples again.

"There it is again Bobby. I think someone's knocking on our front door. You better go out there and see who's there." She warned him as she tried to wiggle out from under his weight, causing a small wave of water to rush over of the tub edge.

"Fuck them where they breathe, no one knows we're in New York City. So whoever the hell's out there will come back later on if they really wanna talk to us, baby. It's probably the old dick face from downstairs, and he wants to put our asses out in the cold, sister. You know he was plenty pissed off that he hadta give us the stinking room in the first place. So you see, it's betta we don't answer the damn door for him. Besides, I'm having too much fun attacking your tits to stop now, baby." The Lieutenant again buried his face between Ramirez's breasts, and he made god awful slurping noises as he continued his assault on both her breasts and nipples.

"I swear you're getting to be worse and worse lately with me, mister. It can't be the old man from downstairs; he's not the least bit interested in us any longer I assure you, Bobby. Maybe it's the Vice President? We know she's already in the building." Sergeant Ramirez offered, getting excited at the prospect of maybe at long last meeting with the Vice President.

He lifted his head from her breasts and looked in her eyes and grumbled. "That's all bullshit and bad manners. First off honey, the stinking Veep wouldn't waste her precious time coming down here to see us poor peon shits. She woulda sent some other peon to get us for her."

"Maybe like whoever might be standing outside the door to our apartment knocking on our door, Walker?" she interrupted him with a smirk and a look that warned him to answer the door.

"Give it a stinking rest for fuck sake will ya Raz. Look at the damn time it is baby! The Veep and the rest of her stinking crew are long time asleep by this time, baby girl. The damn Veep needs all the fucking beauty rest she can possibly get, all women need their beauty rest, baby doll." The Lieutenant grinned until she reached down between his legs, and then she grabbed him by the balls as growled and held him under her evil eye.

"Err... excuse me mister? What did you just say to me Bobby? I hope I didn't hear what I thought I heard you say, mister. Was that a male chauvinist statement from your stupid lips, and was it aimed at me? You know how I feel about any sexist remarks, especially from you, mister soldier man." She gave a slight tug on his nuts as she glared and looked him dead in the eyes.

"Err... Me? No... owe... way in hell baby. I know not to go there on you. I might be stupid, but I'm not dumb little sister." He moaned as he wiggled out from under her slight pressure to relieve the feeling of her tugging on him.

"Well Mr. Walker, it sure as hell sounded like that to me, mister. I don't believe after all we have been through together, you'd dare use that low class crap on me, Bobby." She gave another slight tug on his balls as she smiled at him.

"Whoa, whoa, whoa, I know Walker for a long time now little lady, and I don't think he would ever be stupid enuf to say anything of the sort to you, Raz. You musta misunderstood what Walker just said to you." He offered with a smile as he slid his hand between his legs, and held on to her hand to hold it still so she could no longer hurt him with what she was doing to him.

She smiled again and they kissed, but it was interrupted by another knock on their door. Much louder this time, making even Walker hear it and he grumbled at whoever was knocking on the door. "Arrr... for fuck sake, someone's really at the damn door." He carefully climbed out of the tub, and then he headed for the front door while still dripping wet and naked.

"You see, I told you someone was out there, thickhead." She called after him.

"I told you so, I told you so. I told you someone was at the door." He grumbled as he tried to mimic Ramirez's voice. He even wiggled his naked reared back at her as he left the bathroom.

She threw the face cloth at him as she called at her soldier. "Aren't you going to put something on before you answer the door mister? In case you don't know it, you're still naked Bobby."

"Why? Anyone coming to my door this late at night, gets me the way I come and that's that."

"You better put something on before answering the door, stupid. With your white ass beaming like it is, you might drive our visitor away in horror, or at least blind the poor soul by your shine, mister." She retorted as she smiled to herself and she shook her head at him.

The Lieutenant turned around and picked up the wet face cloth, and he draped it over his semi hard dick and then he bitched back at her. "There, is that betta? Are you happy now baby girl?"

"Oh yeah, that's going to do it alright I see, mister." She laughed as she sank back down a little deeper in the warm water while still shaking her head at her lover and soldier.

He stomped to the door mumbling all the way as he unlatched the chain, and flung the door open. The breeze sent the face cloth flying from covering him. He suddenly found himself standing naked before a good looking young woman standing in the hall, looking right at him.

Cathy's back straightened at seeing this strange apparition standing before her naked. Quickly regaining her composure, she shot a witty come back at Walker as she snapped at him. "Is this the way you usually answer the door, soldier?" she reached out and tweaked the end of his dick with her finger as she pushed past him as if he was not standing there, and she entered the apartment uninvited as she added to the good looking naked soldier. "I thought you soldiers were always standing at attention, mister? I think you need improvement with your little soldier there."

He allowed himself to be pushed aside by the pretty woman, and then he closed the door after her and placed his hands on his hips and barked at her. "Yeah, I always answer the fucking door in the stinking buff after ten o'clock at night, baby. You got a fricking problem with that, whoever the hell you are? It's because I never expect any stinking company this late. But if someone does comes to my home and he's my friend, he don't gotta knock on my fucking door for nuthin. My friends know where I put the extra key, and they open the door themselves, baby. So I guess that doesn't make you my fucking friend, now does it lady? Who the hell are you bitch? And, what the fuck do you want with me this stinking late at night, sister?"

"If I were you, I think I'd take a little greater care when addressing me like you are, mister. Bad things can happen to your body if you were foolish enough to get me angry at you, soldier. Especially if you're the one who's stupid enough to be standing butt ass naked in front of me like you are and pissing me off. That makes my job all the easier to accomplish against you mister."

"Just try something that stupid against him bitch, and you'll fucking end up with my foot sticking outta your damn ass on you." Sergeant Ramirez snarled savagely at the pretty young stranger from behind her soldier. She came out of the bathroom when she heard him speaking angrily with someone he just allowed into their apartment.

She looked around Walker and picked up Ramirez behind him, and she was naked as she remarked. "What the hell did I do walk into a nudist colony right in the center of Manhattan?"

Neither soldier laughed, with Walker repeating harshly at the stranger. "Hey bitch I just asked you once, and I'm asking you again. I'll not repeat it for a third time. You sure ain't the damn Veep, so if you don't give me a straight answer who you are and what the fuck you want from us, you're gonna find your ass naked and pitched outta the fucking window, lady. Who the hell are you, and what the crap do you want with us this late at night, sister?" he growled angrily while assuming a threatening stance against the young woman as he continued to glare at her face.

"Relax before you blow a head gasket and end up with a nosebleed, soldier." She warned as she fished around her pocketbook, she removed her ID and flashed it at Walker's face.

He did not even glance at the ID, but Ramirez did and she complained at her soldier. "Walker, I told you it was someone from the Vice President's group, stupid."

She ducked in the bathroom and quickly wrapped a hotel bathrobe around her. Once she was covered up, she came back in the main room. She swatted Walker on his butt and warned him. "Go get something on, you're embarrassing me standing before someone as important as she."

"Please, he doesn't have to put anything on my account. I don't mind the show he's giving me, Sergeant Ramirez." Cathy smiled as she enjoyed the display the soldier offered. It had been a few years since she last seen a man like Walker in great shape and naked. She noticed the black and blue marks marring his body, along with healed scars and old wounds. The worst was the one on his leg where he was wounded in the Cuba action some years back. The wound was so bad that the soldier branded the Mutt, Lieutenant Frank Hall, was actually forced to stick his finger in the wound, or Walker would have bled to death before the medics reach and gave him assistance.

Chapter Twelve

That's fine with my ass, cause I ain't got no fucking intention of getting in any stinking clothes this late at night, not even for the Veep herself. My days over a long time ago baby, and I'm on my own time now, little sister." Lieutenant Walker snapped at the good looking lady.

"You're going to put on a bathrobe they gave us from the hotel, or I'll cut the damn thing off and put it in my pocket to cover it up, mister." The angry female Sergeant warned her soldier while shoving him back, she did not like him standing before this woman naked like he was.

She turned back to Cathy and then asked her in a pleasant voice. "Can I fix you a cup of coffee, or something to eat?" She saw Walker dip back in the bathroom to hopefully get dressed. "Coffee would be fine. How was your trip to New York?" she asked the pretty female soldier.

"Not bad, we're exhausted though. We didn't have much time to even breathe, coming out of the desert and then being shipped right here, Ma'am." Ramirez complained as she fixed coffee.

"Oh…that's right, you soldiers came here right from a battlefield I understand, am I right honey? How was it Ma'am?" Cathy asked the Sergeant with genuine concern in her voice.

"Terrible, terrible, it was one of the worst operations I was ever sent out on, Ma'am. I lost a very dear and close friend in the action." Sergeant Ramirez drew in a breath as a tear rolled down her cheek, and then she added. "But if we didn't stop them there, we would've been forced to stop them with nuclear weapons sometime in the future, Ma'am. It was a necessary operation we were sent out on Ma'am." She bit her lower lip, remembering Barbara Meyerhoff's smiling face.

The Lieutenant made a noise, and the two women looked in that direction, and Cathy added. "He's really good looking, and he's in great shape as well. It's easy to tell he's all man…"

"And, he's all mine Ma'am." The Sergeant warned the woman so interested in her lover.

Cathy laughed as she asked if he always answered the door naked like he was.

"Just when he's trying to be a real pain in the ass. Look Ma'am, I don't kno…"

"Cathy." The Vice President's aide interrupted, and she informed Ramirez mater of factly.

Without skipping a beat, she continued with her words to the female bodyguard. "Cathy, he's been through a helluva lot lately, more than any one person should ever have to go through in two lifetimes. I don't want you hurting him just because he's being such a shit tonight. He's normally a loving and very caring man, but he's hell on steroids if he feels he's been crossed, and he feels like he has been crossed over being ordered to report to New York City like this, Ma'am. He doesn't like being pulled away from the rest of his troops or rubbing elbows with the higher ups of the world, and he's scared as hell about mistakenly insulting the Vice President. That's all he talks about, he's worried about slipping up and cursing in front of or embarrassing her. He doesn't like to have General White hanging over his head, knowing the General will fall on his shoulders like an old house if he screws up any on this bullshit order he's stuck with. I don't know how many times I heard him say he's a soldier, not a politician..."

Cathy held up her hand to silence female soldier as she said. "Sergeant Ramirez, I can't see Walker being scared of anything in life. I assure you the Vice President's no prude and as long as Lieutenant Walker's speaking for the United States and her people, he has nothing to fear from her. The Vice President heard every word in the book, and a few so bad they can't even make the book, and she put them to use from time to time herself, so please tell Walker..."

"So tell Walker what?" He growled nastily as he appeared in the bathroom doorway with the guest bathrobe wrapped around him like it was causing him some pain. He was so broad in the shoulders and chest that the hotel robe barely closed around his wide body and every step he took, he was exposed to the two women again.

The Sergeant shook her head and had to stifle a laugh when she saw him sticking out of the robe and she snapped at him. "Jesus Christ Walker, you might as well be naked again."

"Might as well be. Hey, I didn't invent the damn thing, so why are you pissed off at me for, huh? The shits who made the damn thing, musta made them for the damn gooks in their country where the damn thing was made. They don't fit any real fucking American men, baby."

"Not everyone's as big as you are buster." Both women snapped at the same time, they both laughed, already forming the bonds that tied working people together throughout the world.

"Ha fucking ha. Now I got me two bitches dumping on my stinking ass here I see." He grumbled as he disappeared and then quickly returned with a towel wrapped around him.

Cathy could not hide the displeasure in her eyes at having him covered up, even though she stared at the heavily muscular upper body of the well tanned and good looking soldier.

The Sergeant knew what Cathy was staring at and she decided to get her mind off Walker's body by saying to her. "Err... Cathy Williams, is that right Ma'am?"

She turned and nodded yes to Ramirez's question.

"Do you mind my asking you why you have come down to our room this late at night, Cathy? We thought you people would've all been sound asleep by this time, Cathy." Sergeant Ramirez questioned while staring at the good looking female special agent with questioning eyes.

"Normally, I would've been sound asleep by this time, but the Vice President was extremely concerned about you two solders, and she wanted to connect with you A-SAP. She was actually intending to come down to your apartment herself, but you arrived later than was first expected, Sergeant. It seems Ms. Hirshfield's presently involved in meetings with her security staff, so I was sent down here in her stead to meet with you and welcome you two to New York City, and see if you need anything while I was at it, Sergeant Ramirez."

"That's all fine, well, and good, but why did you have to bother us tonight? We were just getting ready to turn in ourselves Ma'am. As I said, we're pretty exhausted Ma'am."

"The Vice President wants the first meeting with you two to take place over brunch tomorrow morning, and I was sent down here to arrange the meeting for her with you, Sergeant. Ms. Hirshfield's intending to have the brunch meeting set at eleven o'clock sharp. The apartment's Two Thousand and Fifty B, but you'll recognize it by the large brass star and number three on the door to the apartment. If you can't find the apartment, just ask anyone in the building for room Two Thousand and Fifty B and they'll tell you where it is Sergeant. You're to be expected at that time Sergeant Ramirez. The Vice President's a real stickler for promptness, so don't be late please. I don't want you two starting off on the wrong foot with her Sergeant. Is there anything you'd like specially prepared for breakfast tomorrow morning for either you or Lieutenant Walker? If so, please tell me and I'll make certain I have it at the room when you arrive."

Ramirez glanced at Walker, and noticed what he was doing and she snapped hotly at him. "Walker! Stop that will you please! We have company you know dammit."

He actually jumped at the force in Ramirez's voice as she yelled at him. He stared at her, not knowing what he done that was so wrong.

He sat across from her and arched his eyebrows as he stared back at Raz and then asked her. "What the hell did I do now, dammit?"

While the women were talking amongst themselves, a very bored and exhausted military officer, absentmindedly slid his hand underneath his towel, and he was picking away at his nuts, exposing himself now and then as he picked away on them.

Cathy turned and saw he was doing nothing out of the ordinary.

"You know what you were doing, and you better stop it right now mister. So don't play innocent with me, Bobby. We have company, and I don't want to see you doing that in front of her again." She snapped angrily again at her soldier and lover.

The Lieutenant shrugged back at her, still not knowing what he had done so wrong, and he cared even less about it and let it rest. He was sure she was going to dump on him later on when this one left their apartment. Then he would find out what got her so pissed off at him. He felt he could wait until then to find out why she was so angry at him.

The bodyguard knew she had to break the tension between them, and she stood and look down the hall leading to the bedroom and remarked. "My, this seems like a beautiful apartment."

Ramirez stood, her robe glued in place as she offered her visitor. "I don't know, I haven't had a chance to check out the rest of the place, Cathy. I'm dying to see the apartment though."

"You haven't check out the apartment yet? Well, what were you doing since you arrived here, oh, never mind. I think I know the answer to that question, Sergeant. Shall we check out the rest of the place together then?" Cathy said as she smiled at the female soldier and then she turned on her heels and started to explore the apartment.

Ramirez looked back at Walker who made a motion like he was masturbating back at her.

"Stop that will you please Bobby!" She hissed in a low whisper at him.

He stuck his tongue at her and made a funny face as he got up and followed her as she chased after Cathy, who was charging through the apartment like a child at her first day of school. There was not much to see of the apartment, there was a small kitchen off the bathroom near the entry door. A small walk in closet off the kitchen which stood before the master bedroom with a TV in the room. A king sized bed sat in the center of the bedroom, with a love seat and wing chair to one side by the double wide window, which overlooked Broadway and part of the Circle.

In moments, all the excitement ended with all three of them found themselves sitting on the end of the bed. He got up and strolled over to the TV and snapped it on.

Sergeant Ramirez tried to get the Lieutenant's attention, but he was having none of it this time. An HBO movie with Madonna playing the part of a female killer was playing, and she was doing some dude on the floor good and proper on the screen.

"Oh wow man, it's her!" He explained as he stared at Madonna's swaying breasts on the set, he hopped up on the bed and laid back while staring at the tube.

Ramirez leaned over to Cathy and mumbled to her. "It looks like we just lost him for the rest of the night I see, Ma'am." She formed bonds of friendship with Cathy already.

"Is he worth it?" the female bodyguard asked her seriously as she stared at her.

"Is he worth it? He makes my teeth sweat. Would you like another cup of coffee please?"

"That makes him worth all the trouble he obviously gives you most of the time, sweetheart. Sure. Why not, I'd love another cup of coffee please, Sergeant Ramirez." The two women got up and they left him staring at the TV like it was the first time he ever saw one, and they both headed to the kitchen laughing and joking together.

Cathy engaged the Sergeant in conversation while sipping her coffee, she wanted to know how it was like being a female soldier in this man's service. Being a highly trained weapon herself, she was very interested if she and the other women who suffered the same discriminations she was exposed to, while trying to make it in the so called man's world. She was very surprised when the Sergeant told her she went through no such discrimination with the soldiers as she did with the men of the agency. She was surprised Cathy had so much trouble with the male agents. She was proud to say she and the other women soldiers were treated with the greatest of respect most of the time from the male soldiers of the specialized Unit.

The Sergeant believed it was because the male soldiers knew their lives were in the female's hands, as well as their lives were in the hands of the male soldiers during any military action they were involved in. Once this part of the conversation ended, they women both talked about their sex lives, making nasty jokes and generally enjoying themselves and getting to know one another better. Sergeant Dorothy Ramirez went over the extremely intense training she went through when she was trying to make the grade for the elite band of soldiers of the Special Forces.

Cathy listened attentively to all her words, and when she was through speaking, she went over her special training for the agents. Both women were surprised their training was so close alike. They both were in great shape, and could do any man as easily as taking out a woman determined to be a threat to either of them. When the ladies grew bored with this part of the conversation, they drifted to love making talk, and she told Cathy about Fun Week on the base. Which came to be after what the soldiers branded as Hell Week, the first and hardest week of special training, was completed for the soldiers who past the tests of that week. It was during this first week anyone who wasn't going to make the grade, scrubbed out of the harsh training program. It rooted out the weak of body and mind; only the motivated soldiers finish the course.

Cathy never heard anything about fun week, so she listened attentively as she told her how on the night of the last day of hell week, the women NCOs, (Non Commissioned Officers) took care of the male NCOs in the showers any way the male soldiers wanted it done. The bodyguard asked how many men there were in the showers the girls had to take care of on that night.

Sergeant Ramirez told her there were ten women and thirty three men in the elite Unit.

"My God that meant you girls had to take care of at least three men apiece." Cathy exclaimed finding herself a little excited over the prospect of making love to so many men at one time.

"Huh, if only it was that easy. We each took care of the men, many coming two and three times. It was great; the fun lasted long." She bragged to her new friend as she smiled at her now.

"What the hell did you have to do to them to make them come so many times in one night, Sergeant?" she asked Ramirez as she stared her in the face, waiting her to reply.

"Ha, we sucked and fucked them until they couldn't rise to the occasion for us again, girl."

"It didn't bother you the other soldiers was able to see what you girls were doing to the guys in the showers, Sergeant?" she asked, amazed the elite soldiers were so close to one another.

"Care if they saw what we were doing to the guys in the showers? Hell girl, we were taking care of two and three of the damn fools at the same time, Cathy. Believe me, no one cared to watch, why should they when they could be part of all the action. The way it should be between good friends. Believe me, it was one helluva gas to live through. It was the second Fun Night I went through, and I'm looking forward to going through another one real soon." The Sergeant grunted, smiling as she remembered all the fun and great friendship she and Barbara Meyerhoff made doing the guys from the group on that night. The thought of Barbara made her sad, and she had to force Barbara's memory out of her mind. Now was not the time to grieve for her.

She stared at the Sergeant before allowing herself to smile and say. "Sergeant, the next time you girls are going to have one of these so called Fun Nights, you have to invite me to it. I'd love to be part of this kind of thing at least once in my boring life. I always wondered how the male soldiers were getting along with the female members of their units, ever since our government allowed you women to fight alongside the male soldiers in a combat situation, Sergeant."

"Are you quite certain you know what you're asking to get yourself involved in Cathy? Some of the pigs can be awful crude when they really want to be you know."

"Yep. I know men but I'd like to try some of that action on for myself, Sergeant Ramirez."

"Okay, consider yourself invited to the next Fun Night then, Cathy. We girls can always use another hand taking care of them jerks. It won't take place until the other troops return to the States I'm certain. Then I'm positive the guys will be looking to party out by that time, girl. Do you mind coming to my place if that's where we're going to schedule our next party out, Cathy?"

"I have no problem with that." Cathy offered pleasantly to the female Sergeant.

The two women had a giggled so long they lost all track of time, and before they knew it they talked to each other for over an hour and a half, before Cathy stood and stretched her back. Then announced she had to get back to her apartment upstairs to see what was going on there.

The Sergeant also got up and she happily walked Cathy to the door while still talking together.

"You'll remember to be at the Vice President's apartment at eleven o'clock sharp tomorrow morning, right girlfriend? Please remember what I told you about the Vice President, Sergeant Ramirez. The only thing that sets her off in a real bad mood, is someone late for a schedule meeting, Sergeant." The special agent bodyguard said and warned the female warrior at the same time as she leaned over, and then she gave Ramirez a friendly kiss on the side of her cheek.

"We'll be there with bells and a smile on our lips, Cathy." The excited Sergeant purred back at the pretty lady who worked for the Vice President.

"Ahhh yes, I see we're going to get along together just fine, Raz." Cathy said as she allowed herself to relax with the Special Forces female soldier.

As soon as the door was closed, the Sergeant rushed at her soldier, jumping on top of him while he was lying on the bed staring at the TV. He tried to look around her to see the TV as she quickly stripped her robe and then she mounted him.

"You like that woman, don't you my big dumb American soldier?" she asked, mimicking one of the Russian soldiers who always addressed him that way, as she looked at the TV to see Madonna smoking a cigar, and snapping nastily at a couple of police officers questioning her.

"C'mon baby, how about paying a little more attention to me, I'll make you forget about her, the movie, and all the political crap we've been through tonight, Bobby. Why don't you sit back and enjoy, and allow me do all the work for you this time. Then see if you can remember what we were complaining about, mister." She took his hands and placed them on her breasts.

They made love nice and slow, loving and long and enjoying the wonders of their bodies. The excitement of meeting the Vice President tomorrow morning gave her a new passion and daring, and she was taking full advantage of the emotions on this unending night. The beautiful Latino Sergeant was looking forward to meeting with the Vice President tomorrow morning. She respected the female politician much the same way Walker respected Madonna. Ever since she was first elected Vice President, she followed whatever she did for the United States.

Ramirez truly believed the Vice President was a very strong lady and great political leader. The dangerous female soldier watched a number of meetings the Vice President was involved in on TV, and she felt she took over the meeting on the other politicians. It was great to see another strong woman in a powerful position, and pulling it off so well while she was at it. The Sergeant believed in a woman trying any post opened for a man in this crazy, mixed up world.

THURSDAY, NOVEMBER 19th, 1998 8:30 P.M. EST

It was the final meeting being held between Michael and the others of his group, before they made their move on the Trump International Tower and Hotel. The gang was going over the last minute details of their upcoming heist while waiting for the security guard to arrive. The leader was pleased with the way everything was shaping up for him. The Russian located every piece of military hardware he felt he would need for the operation. He had most of his weapons stored inside the rented truck, waiting for the time to pass so he could move the truck over to the target.

Alexander's men were assembled, and he went through their part of the attack, until his people knew exactly what was expected of them, and they could carry out their orders in their sleep.

The only female member of the group was angry to the point that she became uncontrollable, because they were depending so much on this turncoat security guard who worked in the Trump Tower. No one liked or trusted the man, because they all felt he was betraying a trust, something these soon to be terrorists believed heavily in. Michael had some of his people do a quick drive by of the Trump Tower and surrounding area. To get themselves acquainted with the structure and their intended target. Lizzie and Valentine actually went inside the building, and made like they were interested in renting a room. All the while they spoke to the help, they scouted out the lobby area of the hotel, checking out the elevators and security guards hanging around the lobby.

She easily located the Trump Tower guard working with them, he tried to take no notice of them as they left the building. She had to restrain herself from beating the crap out of the man she hated so much. Once outside, Lizzie and Richard took a walk around the Tower, checking the outside security arrangements. They walked three blocks in each direction, using the Tower as their center point. The future terrorists looked for any possible areas where they felt the police would most likely set up their headquarters, and where their snipers would probably roost.

It was a warm day for the middle of November, and the streets of midtown Manhattan were overflowing with hordes of people heading to and from work, or shopping in the countless stores of the City. The street vendors were out in forces hawking their wares no matter what the weather was like. They pushed everything from watches, to ripped off copies of expensive pocketbooks and handbags. Richard had to shove a beggar out of his face, as the guy pester him for a buck.

When the two terrorists thought they saw everything there was to observe around the massive building, they returned home and made their report to Michael. Richard pointed out a number of places where the police would surely set up their sniper teams they would have to pit against them. Lizzie kept a close eye on his report, and interrupted him a few times in order to correct where a sniper might be set up during their attack on the building.

The large Russian ex-soldier watched and listened to their report over Michael's shoulder, and when the leader turned to him, but never asked the question he knew he was about to ask. The extremely dangerous and uncontrollable Russian grunted nastily at him.

"Michael, I have AGS 17 grenade launch work area over thoroughly when time react against police come. I order both grenade automatic launch open up suspect area of sniper activity, until no longer perch for sniper work from. I make clear to big shot police that they go up against superior Russian force, and fruitless wage any further war against and hope success..."

"A helicopter can get a good angle on the Tower using the park for its approach against us, Alexander. If they use helicopters to attack us, they can keep us pinned down until the police can figure out a way to get in the building. Michael, the longer we stay in the building, the odds of the police getting at us successfully increase dramatically on us." Richard offered as he traced a flight path through the park with his finger, to prove his point to the other members of the group.

"Mudnya! (Shit!) Let fool police try use god dom helicopter us against! Let fools come at us if dare, they no get in strike zone before they knock out of god dom sky with superior made Russian built SA-7 shoulder launch missile system. This why I god dom sure I took along with us for use. I aware well police resort use of feared attack helicopter at least against us."

The leader of the group was hot and got in Alexander's face, this was the first time he heard mention about the use of police helicopters against the people he wanted positioned on the roof of the Trump Tower. All the pictures he ever saw of what these terribly deadly war machines did during the Desert Storm action. Came flooding back in his mind as he barked angrily at the large Russian. "God dammit Alexander! Are you that certain you can keep the damn police helicopters off us while we're working over the inside of the Trump Tower?"

"Michael, Number One big shot leader you. Is simple feat accomplish yes for you please. All have do is take out god dom aircraft, and police immediate change tactics they employed against us. Think about second for you please, can imagine you the mayhem create by helicopter crash in middle New York? Imagine dead and injure such catastrophe cause in street below the god dom Trump Tower, and public cry out after action is carry out by us against the police. Yes, with one aircraft knocked out dom sky, police no dare use second time against us I assure you."

"Hmmm... I see what you're driving at here, Twenty Seven. (Alexander's number) Thinking about this a little closer, I agree with your assumption of the police attacking us my friend. Are you certain you can hit a helicopter in the air with your missiles, Twenty Seven? I remember the helicopters were awful hard for the Iraq Army to locate, let alone knock any of them out of the sky, or destroy even one of them, Twenty Seven." He replied, concerned the Russian was bragging to hear himself talk, than being positive he could destroy a helicopter in the air.

"Yes Number One big shot leader, I get police helicopter easy before attack god dom Tower. There is big difference between this action, and one take place in Iraq please. Here, fool police helicopter force attack at slow speed, much less angle with room for helicopter to maneuver between build of City to attack us please. The police no expect missile attack placed against them once they approach god dom Trump Tower. And, is one difference big with attack and defense when United States attack Iraqi, fool. This time, United States pilot come against high trained good Russia defend soldier, no some fool svinaya (fucking) Iraqi chicken shit soldier.

"Get back to god dom helicopter, knowledge no expect missile attack aim against them make income America police pilot sloppy take attack approach, and sloppy will stupid fall. Number One big shot Leader, you worry you part of god dom plan and defense of you own people, and leave god dom Trump Tower and defense of us to me and my well train people. I be at time and successful too, no one get you ass Number One you, no until we gone from god dom Tower thing, and can no they find where we disappeared to in the Big City. My people no Iraqi fools, we Russian train soldier and we know what we do against police if dare attack us, god dommit."

The leader stared at Twenty Seven for a few long moments, he smiled cautiously as he returned to the plans and corrections Richard and Lizzie placed on the blueprints. Their conversation was interrupted by the security guard who just strolled in the meeting fifteen minutes late.

"You're late buster!" Michael growled angrily at him as he looked up from the prints.

"Calm down a little Number One please, I was stuck in traffic, that's all and I was forced..."

"Why was that? Has anything changed over at the Trump Tower, mister?"

"I don't know Number One, but it suddenly seems like we're expecting a visit from some unknown VIP to the Tower in the very near future. But as of yet, the Command Post hasn't been informed on who is checking in, or on their way to visit the Trump Tower. I noticed a good number of plain clothes Special Agents suddenly walking around the lobby area lately, and..."

"And, you don't know why these plain clothes people are suddenly hanging around the damn building, my friend?" he snarled as he turned his attention on the security guard.

"I don't!" the security guard replied, displaying his temper at his interrogator, and then he continued with his concerns. "Usually, when we see plain clothes types hanging around the lobby, it usually means someone important is about to check in. Like I just told you Number One, there has been no mention of any VIP checking in has crossed the desk in the Security Center. If someone's scheduled in, we'd be the first ones to know about it. Once I get any information on about who it is, or if anyone out of the ordinary checks in, I'll inform you instan..."

"Can there be any other reason for these type of people to be hanging around the hotel?"

"Could be a number of different reasons for them to be in the Trump Tower, Number One. It could be as simple as they might have heard something about the Tower, and they were interested in checking it out. Sometimes, the FBI Agents run some defending attack scenarios on the building, to sort of sharpen their skills, or when they get some new recruits to train. On other occasions, sometimes the Don himself invites certain other protection agencies in the building. So as to get their staff used to their presence for those special occasions when they have to be part of the hotel staff, and he doesn't want them sticking out like sore thumbs in the building. There could be some other reasons for these people to be inside the building..."

"Like them finding out about our plans to attack the damn building maybe!" the leader of the group suddenly roared at the turncoat security guard.

"That's impossible Number One. If anyone knew of our plans to hit the Tower, there would be so many plain clothes guards showing up and working inside the building that no one else could possibly enter or leave the place in peace. No Number One, that's totally impossible I'm telling you. It's completely out of the question, and I'll stake my life on.."

"You just have my friend." He hissed nastily back at the excited security guard.

The guard ignored the warning from the group leader. He was certain no one stumbled over their plans as he continued with his words. "If anyone knew about us, we'd be doubling and even tripling our security presence inside the building, Number One. A ton of special precautions would also be set in place, and no one would dare enter or leave the Trump Tower without being really checked out first, and that'd involve us. As I already told you Number One, no one has increased our security alertness in the building. No Number One, I believe these precautions are set in place, because someone special will be checking in the building pretty soon. I read nothing more into the presence of these men in the building all of a sudden. To tell you the truth Number One, I don't think they're FBI, they're acting much too professional for..."

"Then who the hell are they buster? You have to find out who the hell they are for me. I don't want to start an attack on the building, without knowing who might be inside and will attack us as we come for the building" He asked in a much calmer tone this time.

"I don't really know the answer to that question at this time, Number One. The new Agents could be members of a private security firm someone might have hired for themselves, or they could be members of the President's personal staff. But if he's planning to visit the Tower, we'd know about it well in advance I'm telling you, Number One."

"You better not be fucking around with me, because you won't like the outcome if you are, my friend." The leader warned the security guard as he opened the papers the guard just handed him. It was the latest update on who was scheduled to be in the Trump Tower when they attacked the building. He glanced over the list of very impressive names. Then he compared them with the other two lists he already had, noting the few changes on the list. He handed the new list to Lizzie in charge of adding and subtracting the names of hostages they were going to take. She changed two names Number Seven, John Lavarack, was to stop from leaving the building.

The turncoat security guard stood all the time he was meeting with the rest of his group because he had not been offered a seat. He waited as Michael went over all the precautions for their operation. He felt slightly snubbed by the leader, but he really did not care. The less he had to do with any of these people, the better he liked it. Besides, everything Michael was going over, did not concern him in the least. All he had to do to become filthy rich, was to let these animals inside the building, and then take a few raps in the chops and fake like he passed out. The security guard smiled as he watched Michael working on his last minute plans.

When he was satisfied that he had covered all the loose ends for the upcoming attack on the Trump Tower, he grumbled at his group. "Okay, that's it for the time being I guess. The next time we meet, it'll be inside the lobby of the Trump International Hotel and Tower. You can all leave now, and I'll be back in contact with all of you ten minutes before we attack the Trump Tower." The leader stared at the young security guard until he finally left the room. He then turned to his Number Six person, and with a swift head movement, Lizzie immediately followed the security guard to make sure he was not being trailed by the police.

Michael went over a few still nagging items with the other members of his group because they all knew Michael only wanted the security guard to leave the meeting. Afterwards, he ordered everyone to leave one at a time once he had finished speaking to each of them. They each were to take a different direction while leaving the meeting. He ordered his crew to look over their shoulders to make sure none of them were being trailed by the police. He even went over the procedure to be followed if they believed the police were on to them. Each member nodded in agreement, and the leader allowed them to leave, holding the large Russian back. He wanted to make certain his people were positive about what was expected of them during the operation.

THE TRUMP INTERNATIONAL HOTEL AND TOWER

Cathy rushed back to the Presidential suite to check on how it was going between Ms. Hirshfield and Agent Sweeney. When entering the apartment, she had to be let in by the agents who, even though they knew her well, they checked her ID. The agent disappeared as she rushed down the hall and made a left and cautiously opened the door to the master bedroom. The Vice President's bodyguard then tip toed as silently as she could into the dark room past the bathroom. She stopped where the hall ended, and she saw the bed and two sleeping figures. Mary rested on her side with Sweeney's arm looped over her side and resting on the sheet by her breast.

She looked a little closer when her eyes adjusted to the darkness of the room, and she noticed Mary was topless, both her breasts were out of the covers. She looked at Sweeney and knew he was naked, because his left leg and rearend were out of the covers. What she did not notice, Sweeney was awake and eyeing her every move while making it look like he was asleep. Earlier, he hid his pistol under his pillow, and his hand carefully worked to the weapon. He kept his eyes glued to the figure in the darkness, and breathed normally again when his fingers finally felt the steel of his weapon. His fingers gripped it and pulled the weapon down to his side.

He then fumbled around with it until the weapon was properly in his hand, and then he concentrated on the figure moving around in the room, trying to recognize it before he sprang into action against the person. He began to blink his eyes rapidly a number of times until he saw well in the dark. It was here he realized it was Cathy, and she was only checking on her boss. But nevertheless, he did not relax his posture again until he saw the figure leave.

She smiled at the cozy looking couple, she turned and then headed out of the room before startling them. On her way out, she closed the bathroom door silently, a soft light cast a glow over the floor, and it made it look like someone was in the bathroom with them.

Sweeney got up on an elbow and he watched Cathy as she silently left the room. When she was gone, he put his weapon away and relaxed. To his surprise, Mary said in a sleepy voice.

"Edward, I knew it was Cathy who came in the room just by the way she walked in. She's been doing the same thing ever since I hired her on to my personal staff. I was afraid you were going to scare the poor thing to death by leaping at her with your gun. It would've been an awful funny sight to see a naked wild man waving a gun at her. She would've more than likely died laughing at you, Edward. But I warn you, Cathy's a well trained bodyguard on her own right, who knows that stuff with the hands and feet, and she carries a gun. I feel safe whenever she's around me. I'm glad you were able to tell it was Cathy, before you reacted against her. I didn't know what I was going to do if you went in action against her as you planned, Edward."

Sweeney replied as he smiled at the Vice President. "I know all about Cathy and her abilities and weapon, Ma'am. I read her personal file when I took over your security, Ma'am. You realized I hid my weapon under the pillow, Ma'am?" Sweeney asked as he cupped her breast.

"Of course I did Edward, what do you think I am, stupid? I notice everything that goes on around me." Mary wiggled her rearend into Sweeney's belly, and he pulled her closer.

Cathy headed for the kitchen while humming in a great mood. She wanted a glass of orange juice before turning in for the rest of the night. She forgot to inform the special agents on duty before she walked around the apartment. Two agents threateningly appeared at the door to the kitchen, their weapons held at the ready and one agent complaining at the other.

"You see Joe, I told you it was probably Cathy moving around out here, dammit." It was the special agent who just let her in the apartment a few moments ago, speaking.

"Yeah Ralph, but we had to check it out just in case some damn wacko might have found his way into the place." Ralph said and then he turned to Cathy who was frozen in place while still holding the container of orange juice and empty glass in her hands.

"Cathy, I thought you were informed in advance to notify us if you, or anyone else in the god damn apartment decided to raid the damn ice box in the middle of the fucking night, Ma'am. You could've been shot by us you know if we didn't realize who it was moving around out here. I'll have to make a complete report on this mistake of yours in my dailies, and I wouldn't be a bit surprised if you got a yellow flag stuck in your damn file jacket for this serious infraction to the usual rules, Ma'am." The special agent growled as he shot her an angry glare.

"I'm really sorry about this mistake, that order had completely slipped my mind. But I just returned from visiting the two young soldiers and it was late and my mouth felt like someone had marched through it with mud covered boots on, Ralph." She tried her best smile on the angry special agent, but he was oblivious to her attempt to try and smooth out his ruffled feathers out a little as he continued to stare at her with an angry scowl plastered on his face.

Joe picked up the conversation as he offered. "I'm sorry Cathy, but your movement had set off two of our detectors, and they registered on our security equipment. Once it's registered on our equipment, it's then out of our hands and we have to make a full report on the cause of the security alarm that was set off in the Vice President's apartment, Ma'am. It's our ass if we don't follow orders to the tee, that's why we tried to impress on you and the others in the apartment, it's absolutely essential you notify us first before you march through the apartment at night, Ma'am. I hate like hell to write a yellow on any agent who's a part of our security team, Cathy."

"Then don't do it Joe. What's the big deal anyway?" she bitched at him while pouring some orange juice in her glass. She dreaded getting a yellow flag placed in her 201 file. It would stay with her for the rest of her entire career. It was like getting a black eye, no matter what you did to it, you could never cover it up, and everyone who looked at her file would see it right off.

"Like I said, I'm sorry, but you can't say you weren't warned about this, them are the breaks Cathy." Ralph spoke up, angry he was forced out of the bedroom where he was starting to relax.

Joe leaned over and spoke with the other agent. After a few moments of speaking the two agents he offered. "Of course there's a way we can work around writing any yellow on you Cathy. We can always put it down the Vice President was the one who was moving around the apartment, and she forgot to notify us first before leaving her room, that'll be okay. No one in his right mind is ever going to dare write Ms. Hirshfield a yellow, and hope to keep his or her job for long afterwards, Ma'am." Joe looked at Cathy as if he is seeking her permission to file his way.

"That's a good idea you just came up with Joe, write it up that way and I'll straighten it out with Mary tomorrow morning. I know she's back me and agree with the excuse. She doesn't want anyone from her entourage to get in any trouble on her account, Joe." Cathy growled as she turned her back on the two agents and then sipped her juice, dismissing them with her back.

"Excuse me Ma'am, are you intending to stay up much longer tonight, Ma'am?" Joe asked kindly as he stared at her while waiting her response.

"Yes, why, Agent Man? I'm not allowed to do whatever I want to do in this apartment, mister?" she snapped without turning around to face the two agents in the kitchen with her.

"I asked you that question, because we'll have to turn off the few motion detectors operating in this section of the apartment while you're still moving about the apartment, Cathy." The special agent said as he moved a little forward and he also poured himself a glass of juice, and then he joined her as she drank hers as he again waited for her reply.

"Yes I am going to stay up for a while, I'm planning to watch a little TV, if that's alright with you two guys that is." She replied in a kind of nasty reply to the agent speaking with her.

"Very well then Ma'am, I'll turn down the detectors while you're staying up watching TV. When you're going to turn in for the night, just give me two light taps on my door and I'll reactivate the motion sensors in this area of the apartment, Cathy. Don't stay up long though if you don't mind Ma'am, we don't like keeping the detectors off line too long at night Ma'am."

"Then why don't you stay up with me, that way I don't get myself in anymore trouble for the rest of the night walking around in the apartment with you two guys."

"Hmmm... that seems like a plan to me, Cathy. That way I can keep the living room fully secured while the detectors are on the down mode. Good deal Ralph?" He turned to the other agent as he kind of asked his permission to stay up with the female agent.

"Joe I don't give a damn what two consenting adults do on their own time, as long as this apartment's secured for the rest of the night, and the Vice President's safe in her damn room." Ralph growled as he headed for the bedroom the agents were using for their headquarters.

"Whew, what a grouch he is. What's the matter with him, Joe? He's not getting any lately?" She grumbled as she headed for the living room. "You want to put a little charge in that juice of yours, Joe?" She added as if an afterthought as she smiled pleasantly at him this time.

"Sorry, no can do I'm still on duty, Ma'am." Joe offered as he fell in line behind the shapely and beautiful young woman. He sat down on the sofa while Cathy screwed around with the channels, she was looking for something interesting to watch. She was looking for the same show Walker was watching downstairs. She like Madonna as an actress and entertainer as much as the young soldier obviously did. But the program must have already ended. Finally, she checked the guide that came up on the screen to pick something out to watch for the two of them to enjoy.

Chapter Thirteen

THE TRUMP INTERNATIONAL HOTEL AND TOWER,
ROOM 2012,
SATURDAY, NOVEMBER 14th, 1998. 6:10 A.M.

Sergeant Dorothy Ramirez was the first one up, and she carefully crawled out of bed without waking Lieutenant Robert Walker up. She looked at him and smiled before leaving the bedroom. Their lovemaking was something to be remembered for the rest of her life. She was sticky and wanted to take a quick shower before he woke up and he took over the bathroom and messed it up on her. She knew she would have to wait for at least an hour before using it after he finished with the bathroom. The hot water was marvelous and rather refreshing, and she swore she would never allow herself to take hot water for granted ever again. She washed her hair, it was matted from their lovemaking and rolling around in the bed. After she showered and felt much better, she put on a pot of coffee for them. She heard a noise from the bedroom and saw Walker stumbling around while still rubbing the sleep from his eyes with the palms of his hands.

"What the hell's wrong with you Raz? I thought you'd sleep until we had to visit the damn Veep in her hot shot stinking apartment baby. You sure you're okay kid?" the naked and complaining soldier grumbled as he placed his hands on his hips and then he looked at his lover.

"Look at you Bobby. Who are you trying to impress already this morning mister?"

"Nice try but you didn't answer my question, little sister. Why are you up so early in the damn morning Raz?" Walker bitched as he moved in on her, and he gave her a breath robbing bear hug, while lifting her off the floor with his arms. Then he rubbed her breasts through the robe.

"I'm warning you, don't go and get my motor running on me mister. We have too much to do this morning before our scheduled meeting with the Vice President. Walker, I don't think it's a good idea for you to keep referring to her as the Veep you know. One of these times you might forget and slip and call her that to her face, and she might not dig the idea too much mister."

"Whadda we gotta do that's so damn important before we meet with the damn Veep? I don't hafta do nuthin' but stay white and fucking die, sometimes pay some fucking taxes. Is the coffee ready, my mouth feels like someone pissed in it for crap sake." The military officer grumbled as he ran his tongue around the inside of his mouth and grown. "Uck. What a foul taste baby."

"You're a crude dude Bobby! You better get out of that gutter talk before we meet with the Vice President. I don't think she'd like to hear it." The Sergeant warned then she added. "I just started the coffee, honey. You're going to have to wait for a cup. Why don't you take a quick shower, by then the coffee should be ready. We have to get going right after the coffee, Bobby."

"I repeat, whadda we hafta do to be prepared for this damn meeting with the stinking Vice President this morning baby? I don't see why we can't meet with her in our damn uniforms anyway, baby. If our stinking uniforms are good enuf to die in, then they're good enuf to meet her in, dammit." The Lieutenant grunted sarcastically as he scratched his eye with a finger.

"We have to buy some civilian clothes honey. Remember, Colonel Leadbetter told us he didn't want us hanging around New York City in our uniforms, or meeting the VP in them Bobby."

"Yeah I know that for crap sake sister. Where we gonna get a stinking store open this early in the damn morning. Any juice left baby?"

"You're forgetting where we are, Robert. We're here right in the middle of New York. The City that never sleeps. I'm sure someone downstairs will direct us to a store open this early."

"Whew, that's a little betta I say. Hey girl, you were dynamite last night, I can't remember when the last time I enjoyed making love like that." He smiled as he cupped he breast again.

The Sergeant swatted his hand away from her breast as she bitched at her soldier again. "I just told you you're not going to get my motor running on me this morning, at least not until after the meeting with the Vice President went down. Then I'm all yours Bobby for the rest of the day. We have to get going, I'm a little self-conscious about walking around Manhattan in our uniforms Bobby. Especially with our field badges on our shoulders. You know what they represent."

"I sure fucking do girl, they tell all these little shits that we're the elite of the best, the Special Forces soldiers of the Marine Corps. If any of these stinking slugs in this damn dump has a stinking problem with it, let them bring it up to my fucking attention, and I'll relieve them of that misconception real fast like, little sister. I'll stomp a fucking mud hole right in the middle of their stinking chest and then I'll walk it dry if anyone bugs us about our Units, sister."

"Calm down a little Captain Killer. That's what I'm trying to tell you Bobby. Do you see how you were so easily brought up to a fast boil. I don't want that happening outside where it's much harder for me to control you some." She tried to warn Walker about his snapshot temper again.

"Control me? Whatsumatter with me all of the sudden? Am I some kinda stinking jerk I need someone to look after my fucking ass so I don't get into any damn trouble, girl. As if I were some kinda baby, little sister?" the Lieutenant growled, getting upset over the thought she felt she had to watch over him like she offered, and he added angrily. "I ain't no fricking little puppy dog who has to be watched over so I don't make a stinking mess on the friggin floor on my owner."

She stared at her soldier and lover, she was really enjoying seeing him so riled up, and yet not flying off the handle like he usually did. He glared at her, but the loving expression refused to leave her face until it softened his anger. Giving into the look, the calming down Lieutenant grumbled. "Huh, I guess I'm a stinking puppy after all. In that case baby, I think I'll take a stinking piss on the damn floor right at your purdy feet, little sister." He took a hold of his dick and then he made like he was fixing to take a pee on the floor right in front of her.

She stepped back to give him room, and then warned. "If you take a piss on the floor you better clean it. You might be a puppy at that, but I'm not going to wipe your ass for you, mister."

"Look out, here it comes!" he yelled and then he began to chase her through the apartment while barking like a dog and holding his dick in his hand. The two laughed as they ran around the room, with him continuing to bark and wiggling his dick at her until he tackled her on the bed. He kissed her as she complained she thought she left the Mutt back on the Carrier Washington.

She purred as she enjoyed his kissing and wildly roaming hands, she forced herself to push him off her and bitched at him. "C'mon, we're running out of time, and we have shop before the meeting. Why don't you, stop that and take a shower and I'll get dressed. You're impossible, stop that will you please." She snapped as she tried to get his head out from between her legs.

"Well, I might as well take a stinking shower now. It doesn't look like there's gonna be any stinking action round here." He moaned as he rolled off her, and then sat on the edge of the bed.

"You might as well shower then, mister. I just told you there'll be no nick nick until after the meeting with the Vice President, and that's the way it's going to be, Bobby. Now be a good little boy and take your shower before I slug ya right in that mush of yours, buster." The Sergeant kissed her soldier on his shoulder and then slid her hand to his rearend and gave him a pinch.

"Yeah, I'm nothing but a sex object to be toyed with at will, but only when it pleases you, huh? Other than that, I can take my pen in hand, and take care of my fucking self. Right baby?"

"That's right you little old sex object you. Go and take a shower so I can get dressed please."

He continued to bark like a dog all the way to the bathroom and showered, he had to admit he was looking forward to wearing something other than a military uniform. When he was done showering, he struggled into his tight fitting uniform, and grumbled at himself because it was not smelling right. He hated getting dressed in dirty clothes after he took a shower. He fixed his tie and dogged down the buttons on his blouse, and then left the bathroom to be with his lady.

She was sipping on her coffee and sort of daydreaming while waiting for him to finish with his shower. When he saw her sitting on the chair dressed in her uniform, he shook his head.

"What the devil's wrong with you now Bobby? You look angry all over again mister. Are you going to be like this all day long, you better not act like this before the Vice-President and the rest of the people with her, Robert. She might not want to put up with you when you're like this you know." She groaned, thinking she might have upset him when they were fooling around.

"Nuthin's wrong with me baby. It's just you're the only woman I know on the face of the stinking earth, who looks great no matter what you're wearing. You make my dick hard even wearing olive fricking drab." The Lieutenant grunted like an ape as he scratched under his arms, and jumped from side to side while making his legs bowled and grinning like a nut at her.

She sexily swayed her way over to Walker and kiss him passionately. He immediately responded by reaching for her breasts and she shove him away and bitched at him again. "I should've known you had something evil up your damn sleeve on me, mister. You never give a compliment without looking for something in return do you mister? C'mon big boy, let's do some shopping and have some real fun for a change. The last one to the elevator has to please the other with his mouth when we get back to the apartment." She suddenly yelled out as she shoved Walker, and made a mad dash out of the door running towards the elevators laughing at him.

He was running a few steps behind her. But he stopped dead in his tracks when she yelled over her shoulder back at him. "Hey stupid, lock the damn door, you big dummy you."

The Lieutenant slid on the polished floor then ran back for the door, pulling it shut and locking it. Then he ran after Ramirez who reached the elevator and pressed the button first.

"Hey, now you have to go down on me until I'm well satisfied when we get back, Bobby."

"No way in fricking hell, I'm not doing you because you cheated me little sister."

"Hey, I never gave any rules to this little game we were playing, mister. I called it the way I see it. I won the race as far as I'm concerned fair and square and that means you have to do me tonight right and proper with your tongue, Robert. You're not going to sneak out of this one on me are you, lover? Besides, I was the last one to satisfy you with my mouth, mister. So it's only right you do me right this time Bobby." She gave him one of those butter melting smiles of hers.

"Big fucking whoop, I wish every time I lose, I get the same fricking punishment as this one is, little sister." He complained with a huge grin on his lips and then he ran his tongue over his lips.

The elevator door slid open and they quickly piled into the cab, two other people stood in the cab. The Lieutenant made like he was angry at her for cheating him, and she looked at him from the corner of her eye and then smiled. He did the same thing, and when they noticed each other looking at each other, they both laughed. She even bumped him with her hip and whispered. "You lost the bet, are you going to live up to your end of the bargain with me, Mister?"

"Yeah, I'll do you good and proper later on tonight as you have requested, sister. I intend to teach you good for cheating my ass, Raz." He warned her, he then stuck his tongue at her.

The elevator stopped in the lobby of the Trump Tower and Walker cut Ramirez off and came out first. Without knowing it, his training was working on overtime. He scanned the interior of the lobby for any sign of a possible threat against him and Ramirez. He picked up the agent hiding near a large planter. The agent scrutinized the four people getting out of the elevator.

The cautious military officer watched him as the agent put his hand over his ear to hide the fact he was wearing an ear phone, he said something in the palm of his hand. He looked pretty stupid speaking in his hand like he was doing, and he committed the guy's face to memory. He then scanned the rest of the lobby, which was overflowing with tons of people going in all directions.

She caught up to him and put her hand in his and bitched at him. "Thanks a lot for waiting for me mister. Don't allow anyone to tell you you're not a real gentleman to us women, buster."

He ignored her complaint as he warned her. "We got a fucking spook hiding over by that damn planter by that archway. It looks like another jerk is lurking around near the main doors of the dump. The first guy gave us a quick once over, and he's reporting us to his control right now baby. These flaming assholes should try a little harder to betta fit in with their stinking surroundings for crap sake. They stick out like a pair of sore thumbs. Raz, if I wanted them, I could own their asses before they even realized I was making a move on the two dopey bastards."

She squeezed his hand as she told him. "Let it go will ya please, you're not on a mission here Robert. You're in New York City, and it's in the United States, and there's no one looking to hurt you here in the States Bobby. Relax a little, we're going to have some fun today. Soon, we'll be wearing civilian clothes, and eating real food on real plates, instead of the cold shit we always get stuck eating of out plastic bags I wouldn't feed to my dog. Fun Walker, fun, not a mission. Enjoy and let it go, it's a beautiful day and we're going to have some serious fun today mister. Get that military crap out of your mind for a change, there's plenty of time later to go military."

He nodded but continued to allow his training to guide all his actions. His eyes focused in on a security guard standing by a window in the large lobby. The guard did not do very good with his attempt to look like he was a visitor as he stared at them. Walker had no way of knowing, this guy was the one working with the terrorists about to hit the Trump Tower.

She had to pull on his hand and complained at him. "You're doing it again Bobby. Trust me Robert, none of these people are a threat against you, so let it go for once in your life, please."

"Trust you, yeah sure, trust you and you won't come in my mouth, right?" the Lieutenant smirked at her as he moved forwards in the lobby like the soldier he was and was on the hunt.

"Hey, that's my line to pitch Bobby. You have to think up a different one if you want any credit from me, big boy." She replied and then bumped him lightly again with her hip.

"If I wanted any stinking credit, I'd deal with fucking Sears baby sister." The ever alert Special Forces Lieutenant remarked as he continued to scope out the lobby area of the hotel

Sergeant Ramirez tried her best to ignore his dark mood as she looked around the lobby. Unlike him, she was not looking for any possible threats aimed at her, she was only interested in looking for someone who might be able to direct them to an opened store near the Trump Tower. Searching the huge lobby area, she located the person she was looking for, and then she pulled on his arm so he would follow her lead. She headed right for the elderly concierge they met last night walking around the lobby, trying to be helpful to the other guests in the hotel.

"Excuse me sir, but I was wondering if you could help me out a little, please sir."

The concierge stopped walking and he bowed slightly to the two soldiers. Then he waited for them to catch up with him. Once they were near, he smiled warmly as he nodded at them.

"Excuse me sir, we're new in town and we want to buy some clothes while we're here, sir." She asked as she flashed one of her best smiles at the elderly man, trying to make up for the terrible insults Walker aimed at him last night when they checked into the beautiful Tower.

"Yes Ma'am, there's a Tj's clothing store just two blocks north that sells fad jeans and tee shirts and clothing like that, but if you're looking for a better line of clothes, Ma'am. I suggest you try Macy's, three blocks south of the Trump Tower, Ma'am. I think you should go there before trying Tj's, unless that's the type of clothes you're interested in buying, Ma'am."

"Three blocks south, right sir?" She asked, making sure she heard him right.

"Yes Ma'am, three blocks south, one block down. They'll have what you're looking for."

"Are you sure the store's open this early in the morning, sir?"

The concierge looked at his watch and then replied. "Yes Ma'am, I'm quite certain the store is open at this time of the morning, Ma'am. Well, they're sure to be open by the time you get there, Ma'am. Shall I hail a cab for you, or would you rather walk over to Macy's, Ma'am?"

"No cab I think we'll walk to the store thank you very much sir. It's such a beautiful town to see and the only way to really see it is on foot I believe, sir." Ramirez offered with a smile.

"Yes it certainly is young lady, and it's a bright and beautiful day, but a little too cold for my liking I'm afraid, Ma'am. But the sun's up and it's promising to be a warm day later on for the middle of November, Ma'am." The elderly man offered pleasantly to the female soldier.

Walker was bored to death waiting for Ramirez to finish speaking with the old man. He tugged on her arm to get her moving again. She got the message and smiled at the older man and then she left him in the richly decorated lobby, as they rushed outside like two kids who just got out of school. It was pleasant out, but colder than it looked and in a few seconds her teeth were chattering away, and she was again trying to use his body to block the breeze, she was freezing.

The Lieutenant did everything in his power to try and give some of his body heat to his pretty girlfriend, increasing his pace while heading for Macy's. But her teeth continued to chatter. He stopped and looked her in the eyes then asked her. "What do you say, you wanna get a stinking cab and drive the rest of the way to the stinking store? It'll be warm in the cab little sister."

"No way! I walked this far, so I intend to go all the way to the store walking there. Keep walking, I'm freezing my tail off." She told him as she hugged herself to try and keep warm.

Although they were more than halfway to the Macy's department store, the rest of the trip seem to take the two soldiers a lifetime to get there. They ended up running the final block to the store. They charged through the main doors and spotted a wall heater, and they both hovered around it until the chill left their bodies. Inside the store, countless racks of fine clothes appeared wherever she looked. She was thrilled to death to see so many different styles of clothes as she thumbed through the first rack. She pulled out an arm full of clothes, and then she asked the sales girl where the dressing room was located on the floor. She informed the saleswoman she wanted to try on some of the clothes she held before buying any of them.

The Lieutenant looked at the racks of blue jeans and plaid shirts, but before she disappeared in the dressing room, she warned him in no uncertain terms. "Don't even try to consider any of them clothes Bobby. I want you to pick out a nice suit for the meeting, get a white shirt with a collar and matching tie, or I'll pick it out for you when I'm done here, mister."

"Yeah, keep it up if you wanna win the medal for nagging baby." He barked like a dog again.

"Remember what I told you Bobby, I think I might be forced to change your name from Road Kill to Pooch or Fido, if you keep barking at me like this. No more fooling around mister, we have to buy proper clothes for our meeting with the Vice President." She warned her soldier.

"Keep nagging me little sister. Don't you have some clothes to try on, baby?" he grumbled as he left the blue jeans rack, and then he headed for the suit racks. A salesman helped him pick out the suit and then he watched him as Walker headed for the dressing rooms.

The Sergeant came out of the dressing room with a light blue long dress on that could double for a full length gown. Her shoulders were bare, and the saleslady offered her a beautiful scarf to drape over them. It finished off the outfit perfectly. For the first time in months, she felt like a real woman. She looked for Walker to see what he thought about her dress. She had two other picks of clothes set aside in the dressing room. She headed for the suit section and the salesman informed her the soldier was trying a suit on. He pointed her to where he was dressing.

She took up position right outside the male dressing room. He came out still wrestling around with the suit that looked like it was fighting him all the way, and he was grumbling to beat the band to boot. But he shut up when he realized she was decked out in a fine looking dress.

"Whewwwww wee lady. Now I know why I love you so much. You look outstanding. When the Veep lays eyes on you, she's gonna wish she was a man, so she could enjoy your sexual pleasures. You look hot enough to eat where you're standing, baby girl." He gave her the look that warned her he was madly in love with her, and he loved the way she looked in her new dress.

"Now that's the response I was looking for from you, mister. You look damn good too, did you pick out this suit all by yourself Bobby? Here, let me help you with the tie, you have it tied all wrong, butthead. You surprise me, I never thought you'd pick out a suit like this one. Looks like I'm going to be forced to change my mind a little about your taste in clothes, mister."

"I didn't pick out the damn monkey suit on my own Raz. I'd never pick out something this lame. The jerk over there told me this suit was just made for me. Sure is, the damn thing costs nearly five hundred dollars. So I had no choice but to look good in the damn thing." He complained as he tossed a nasty look back at the salesman who helped him pick out the suite.

She smiled at him and then she nodded to the saleswoman who helped her pick out the dress, she headed back to the dressing room to try on the second dress she picked out. When she returned dressed in a long black dress, she was even more stunning than before.

He stared at her with his mouth hanging open. The saleswoman showed her the finer intricacies of the dress. "Here, if you wear the collar that's really a flap this way, you can wear this dress to church if you pleased Ma'am, and be conservative while you're at it, Ma'am."

When the wide collar was flipped over, it covered over her fine cleavage completely.

"When you finished with church, and you want to be a little more daring without being forced to change your clothes for the rest of the day. All you have to do is unbutton the collar here, and then just flip the wide collar over like this, and then you simply button it right here Ma'am." The saleswoman secured the collar for her as she continued to explain the workings of the dress, and the Sergeant suddenly found herself open practically to the naval.

"Whew, I like it that way much betta Raz." Walker offered with a grin to the ladies.

"You would, you like it when my breasts are hanging out, you pig you." She complained with a smile as she told the sales help she wanted the dress. They both laughed then shopped for some leisure wear, settling on a pair of blue jeans, some shirts, and a set of sneakers. By the time they picked out what they felt they needed or wanted for their stay in the Big Apple, the bill was over a thousand dollars. When he produced the military credit card, the worker had her manager give the okay for the transactions. The manager saw the military card used before, and he knew it was used when a VIP General was visiting New York City. She thought these two were every bit as important as the others, and she treated them with the greatest of respect and politeness.

The military officer wanted to wear the blue jeans and plaid shirt out of the store, because the clothes were comfortable and warm. But Ramirez argued they were out of time, and she forced him to wear the suit. She warned him if they had to return to the apartment in order to change their clothes, it would make them both late for the meeting with the Vice President. They left the store and headed for the hotel, but they decided to wait outside the lobby of the Trump Tower and Hotel, until it was time to meet Vice President Hirshfield in her apartment.

Sergeant Dorothy Ramirez was so looking forward to meeting the beautiful and very powerful Vice President. She wanted to see if the youngish woman was really like she acted whenever she saw her on TV, and she was speaking to the press, or someone she was meeting with. Sergeant Ramirez thought Ms. Hirshfield was an extremely intelligent woman, and she was the right pick to be the second most powerful leader of the United States.

SATURDAY, NOVEMBER 14th, 1998, 10:35 A.M.
THE TRUMP INTERNATIONAL HOTEL AND TOWER

When the time neared for their meeting, both Lieutenant Robert Walker and Sergeant Dorothy Ramirez hurried in the Trump International Tower and Hotel. They boarded the express elevator and pressed the button for the 22nd floor. When the door opened on the requested floor, they were immediately greeted by two angry looking special agents, and they were demanding to know in no uncertain terms who they were, and what they were doing on the floor.

The Lieutenant told them they were there to meet with the Vice President, but the cautious special agent demanded to see his identification card. Once he checked it out, he cleared the way for them both to enter the Presidential Suite. The agent even escorted them to the door after expertly padded them both down for any hidden weapons. The agent then banged on the door, and another agent from inside the room cautiously escorted them into the apartment and then he hovered over them. The two young soldiers were lead over to a table and told to wait there.

Seconds later the Vice President strolled into the room, and she was flanked on either side by Special Agent Edward Sweeney, and her personal secretary and bodyguard, Cathy. The Lieutenant went to stand, but he was immediately waved back to his seat by Ms. Hirshfield, who sat and spread out the napkin on her lap. The bodyguard began speaking as she introduced the two soldiers to her boss. "Vice President Mary Hirshfield, I'd like to take this time to introduce you to Lieutenant Robert Walker and Sergeant Dorothy Ramirez, Ma'am. They're both members of the recently formed Multi National Rapid Response Force connected with the JSOC, err... pardon me Ma'am. That's the United States Joint Special Operations Command Unit, which carried out the low intensity action to eliminate the manufacturing plant designed to mass produce nuclear warheads and submarine launched long range missiles in Iran, Ma'am.

"These two brave young soldiers were both wounded in the hard hitting action, but nothing serious I'm pleased to report, Ma'am. The action cost the United States three soldier's lives, and we suffered ten seriously wounded troopers in the Iranian action, Ma'am. The other soldiers of Lieutenant Walker's elite force are at this moment, steaming their way to Egypt via the United States Aircraft Carrier George Washington, Ma'am. There, the soldiers will begin their training for the upcoming attack presently not scheduled against Libya's two secret chemical weapons factories in the near future. I believe, and please correct me if I'm incorrect on anything I have just offered to the Vice President, Lieutenant Walker Sir. The code name for the upcoming operation to be carried out in Libya had been branded 'Bio Level Three' Ma'am." She looked at Lieutenant Walker to see if she was right, and he nodded and then he added in a snit.

"That's correct lady, and I'm surprised you know so fricking much about my upcoming operation, missy." His anger was building, and he did not know this woman from Adam. Yet she knew he was planning to head for Libya, and he did not like it one bit, and if she knew that much about his upcoming operation. How many other people knew about his mission. The more people who knew about it, the harder the security for the operation would be to control.

"Will Lieutenant Walker and Sergeant Ramirez be part of that future action scheduled to take place inside Libya, Cathy?" Vice President Hirshfield interrupted as she stared at Lieutenant Walker for a moment, who looked terribly uncomfortable while dressed in his new suit, his body looked like it was painful, and it was about to explode on the young soldier.

The military officer took the initiative and answered for Cathy. "Yes Ma'am, my fuc... err... outfit doesn't go anywhere in the world without me and Raz tagging along for ballast, Ma'am."

When they sat down at the table, she maneuvered her chair nearer to his, until she could rest her hand on the top of his. This way she could pinch him if he allowed his mouth to get away on him. Ramirez pinched his hand when he almost said the word fuck. The action cut off his word in mid-sentence, and it saved them from suffering the Vice President's well noted wrath.

Ms. Hirshfield saw the pinch from the female soldier and knew why it happened and she smiled, but she was also saddened the woman had to resort to physical pain against the rather excited male soldier, to keep the one she convinced herself was a sick twist, in check. Ms. Hirshfield stared at him, carefully sizing him up and wondering what kept him from wigging out, before snapping angrily at him. "I wasn't asking the Lieutenant that question, sir. I was asking my secretary for her comments. When I want to hear from you, I'll ask you a question directly, Lieutenant Walker Sir. Do you understand your position in this conversation, Lieutenant?"

The Lieutenant could not hide his rage over being rebutted by the female Vice President. He was sure she was trying to get his goat as his face turned red, and he had to force himself to actually maintain control over his mounting anger. He hated with a passion being forced to play the part of a politician, it went against his grain and everything he believed in.

Sergeant Ramirez sensed his anger mounting, and she pinched him harder this time. Walker jumped and stared angrily at her, before calming down enough to sit still again.

"Would you like to have something to eat Lieutenant Walker Sir?" Ms. Hirshfield asked as she looked at the special agent hovering over Walker's shoulder. The agent nodded and left and spoke to someone in the kitchen. Cathy took the seat to the right of the Vice President, while Sweeney continued to hover over the left shoulder of Ms. Hirshfield. His jacket open and once in a while Walker picked up the stock of the Colt 9 mm automatic pistol hanging under the left arm. He knew this guy was right handed, and made his attack angle out of force of habit, and his training against the agent. A moment later he smiled, knowing if he wanted the guy, the agent would not stand a snowball's chance in hell against his attack, if he chose to work against him.

A wicker wheel cart was pushed into the large dining room of the Presidential Suite, covered to overflowing with a mountain of scrambled eggs, bacon, sausages, ham, waffles, hash browns, coffee, tea, and even a flask of cold orange juice. Everything was packed in special heating trays to remain warm for the members of the meeting enjoyment.

The Lieutenant greedily eyed the food, not knowing what he was going to take first. Ms. Hirshfield took the slight hesitation as his not liking anything on the cart. She offered politely to the confused looking soldier. "Lieutenant Walker, if there's nothing to your liking on the cart. Please tell me what you desire, and I'll have my chef prepare a meal especially for your likes."

"Chill out a little Ma'am, I like everything that's on the stinking table..." Another pinch from the Sergeant made him nearly bite his tongue as he turned and almost barked at her for hurting him this time. He then looked at his hand and wiggled his fingers, it was oozing a slight trace of blood from the painful pinch he had just received from his lover and soldier.

Ms. Hirshfield smiled, wondering how much more this young soldier was going to take, before exploding before her. The Vice President gave orders to all special agents in the room, to maintain a close eye on the male soldier named Walker. She knew of his wild and extremely uncontrollable reputation, of keeping his temper hanging on a hair trigger, and the Vice President wanted to control him. But Ms. Hirshfield did not want to stifle him during their conversation either. If she wanted an honest answer from the young soldier, she would have to put up with a momentary slip of the tongue every now and then during their talk. She watched as he rested his hand on the table after rubbing the pain away from it, and it was immediately covered again by the Sergeant's hand, trying her best to hide the fact she was causing him any pain.

The man servant placed a dish before Walker and then he moved the serving cart over to him, so he could get at the food a little easier. He stabbed his fork at the stack of sausages like they were his enemy. Then he shook them off his fork while making grease fly on the fine tablecloth, as he scooped up a heaping mound of scrambled eggs. He was acting like he was in the mess of the base, rather than sharing a table and meal with the Vice President of the United States.

Vice President Hirshfield looked to Sergeant Dorothy Ramirez, and noticed her face was a red with embarrassment, as she tried desperately to get Lieutenant Walker's attention. The Vice President smiled at her when she looked at her, and she returned the smile politely then she shrugged. The Vice President mouthed the words, "I understand, and it's alright Sergeant."

Both women watched as he piled enough food on his plate to feed a small army, it was his way. He ate what he could when he could, because he never knew when he was going to eat another square meal in the service. When they were on alert, the soldiers of the special operations group ate on the run, standing and never eating enough to satisfy their hunger completely.

He ignored the glances coming his way from the women, as he continued to pile the food on his dish until he could not get more on it. He then held up his cup, and the servant poured him coffee. The Lieutenant slurped the coffee loudly, making God awful noises as he drank it.

The mortified female Sergeant took a small amount of scrambled eggs and two sausages. She had a cup of tea and sipped it watching the Lieutenant shoveled the food in his mouth as if he had not eaten in a week. She picked at her rapidly cooling food, thoroughly mortified over Walker behaving like a knuckle dragging Neanderthal at the meal with the Vice President.

Ms. Hirshfield had a cup of coffee, she ate long before the two soldiers arrived.

Agent Sweeney moved a little closer to Lieutenant Walker's side, and he actually bumped him in the head with his elbow to serve as a warning, and to make him look at the special agent. Once he had Walker's attention, he growled in a low and extremely threatening voice at him, warning him in no uncertain terms that he was thoroughly embarrassing himself along with his fellow female soldier in front of the Vice President and others in the room with them.

The Lieutenant put down his fork and he placed his other hand flat on the table, and then he curled all his fingers under his palm but one. When he was sure the special agent got his message, he went back to shoveling the food down his throat without changing his manners.

Agent Sweeney's eyes narrowed to mere slits as he tried to burn a hole in the back of the male soldier's head. He made a mental note to look up this crude bastard later, and teach him a lesson in manners.

All the while he watched the soldier eat, he was desperately trying to control his temper. His action did not go unnoticed by the Vice President who got his attention, and then she made a movement of her fork, pointed him away from the extremely dangerous soldier.

Ms. Hirshfield ignored the Lieutenant's terrible manners until he finished eating, she turned to Ramirez, and offered in a friendly manner. "My, but don't you look stunning this morning. If I knew you were going to dress so properly for our meeting, I would have slipped into something a little more appropriate for the occasion." Ms. Hirshfield was dressed in a silk lounging suit.

"Nonsense Ma'am, you look exquisite as always. You always look stunning Ma'am. Every time I ever saw you on TV, you look awesome Ma'am." The female Sergeant offered politely to the powerful female American Leader of her country. She really liked the Vice President, she even felt Ms. Hirshfield reminded her a lot like herself, not willing to take any shit from anyone, especially a man. The female Sergeant happily followed the Vice President through the past years, and liked how she always carved out a wide path, right though the center of the man's world, and she inserted her will on them all the way.

"Ohh... you're so kind. Please, you can call me Mary, or Ms. Hirshfield. I must insist on it Sergeant Ramirez." The pleasant Vice President offered the warrior.

The military officer began to speak with a mouth full of food, even though the Vice President was not through speaking to his girlfriend. "You see Raz, I told you we didn't hafta dress up in these damn high priced rags for this stinking meeting. I'm sure we coulda come here dressed in our stinking blue jeans and been a helluva lot more comfortable." He growled as he stuck a finger in the collar of his shirt and he tugged on it and then grumbled. "I really hate these damn monkey suits, they stops a man from breathing right. Err... Hirshfield, that's Jewish, right Ma'am?"

Sergeant Ramirez went to say something back to her soldier, but she was silenced by the Vice President, who put up her hand and then she snapped at the male soldier. "Err... Yes Lieutenant Walker, it is. Why do you ask if I'm Jewish, Lieutenant? Do you have a problem with my being a Jew, mister?" The Vice President eyed the angry looking soldier cautiously now.

"Naw I ain't got no problem with that, as a matter of fact I know some Jewish, Ma'am."

"Is that a fact Lieutenant Walker Sir." Ms. Hirshfield replied skeptically while staring at him coldly, not knowing where this conversation was heading with this soldier.

"Yeah, Manischevitz Ma'am." The wise Lieutenant laughed at his own remark, now it was he who was trying to get the Vice President's goat. He succeeded beyond his wildest dreams.

"Now you look here Lieutenant Walker. I warn you, don't go messing around with me, mister. I assure you Lieutenant Walker, you won't like the outcome of your little head game you're trying to play on me. I know all about you young man. I was warned in advance about your terrible attitudes, and I guarantee you Lieutenant. I'm not going to take any of your guff for one moment. You screw with me, and you'll live just long enough to pay dearly for your sins, mister. All I want from you is to show up, shut up, and wear beige so you blend in with the background, Lieutenant Walker Sir." Ms. Hirshfield snapped as she glared at him, knowing he was doing nothing more than probing her, to see how much she would take from him before she reacted.

The Sergeant's pinch cut his next words off, as she glared at him out of the corner of her eye. But he was in one of his dark moods, and nothing short of her screwing his brains out, was going to make him behave like the gentleman she knew he was. She never broke eye contact with Ms. Hirshfield as she replied to her. "I'll call you Mary only if you call me Dot, or Raz."

"I'll be most pleased and honored to call you Dot, young lady.".

He shook his head then went back to eating, his hand hurt like hell and he was becoming bored with the whole thing. His black mood and actions were driving the agents around the table nuts. Most of the agents wanted to take his head off of his shoulders. Sweeney, and two other agents near the table were extremely nervous. They did not know how this young nut was going to act, or react, and they had to stay on their toes in case he went over the line. The group of special agents were briefed on his military training, and they understood he was an expert in hand to hand combat, and knew the ways of making his body an extremely lethal weapon to deal with.

Agent Sweeney was prepared and chosen to arm himself with a stun gun also. He was ready and just itching to use it on the arrogant bastard sitting at the table with the Vice President. Every time he moved an inch, Agent Sweeney move a little closer to him, paralleling his every move while sliding his hand under his suite every now and then, and cautiously fingering the stun gun while waiting to be used on this extremely dangerous and nasty acting soldier.

The highly trained soldier caught the secretive action of the agent twice, and when Sweeney moved his hand a third time against him he reacted. The Lieutenant waved him over to his side with his fork and hissed at the agent with a mouth full of food. "Go for it man if you got the fucking balls, and you don't like the way you're living, Mac. I swear, your stinking neck will be snapped in two fucking places before you can get the damn thing outta your damn pocket, buster. So why don't you be a good little fricking spook, and make yourself fucking invisible, huh pal?"

xAgent Sweeney's hand slid on the back of Walker's neck, and then he squeezed it as he hissed angrily at the soldier. "When this thing is over with, you and me are going to have a nice little talk buster. Then I'll see if your dick's as long as you brag is, soldier. You should be ashamed of yourself over how you're acting in front of the Vice President of the United States, sir."

"Hey dog breath, no fucking fear man. You feel fucking Froggy, leap for it pal. But your feet will never hit the fucking ground before I stomp you in the god damn gro..."

Chapter Fourteen

"Err... excuse me Agent Sweeney, is there a problem between you and Lieutenant Walker, sir?" Ms. Hirshfield asked with concern lacing her tone, noticing the intense confrontation taking place between the two men, amidst many whispers and sharp stares and hand movements.

Agent Sweeney straightened up, releasing his neck as he answered the Vice President. "No Ma'am, the soldier just wanted to know if I had the right time, that's all Ma'am."

Lieutenant Walker ignored the remark from the agent, he knew the special agent was just protecting his backside. Besides, he had no interest in checking out the agent's combat skills. He merely went back to eating so intensely that Ms. Hirshfield was able to speak with the Sergeant without him butting in on their conversation. The women spoke pleasantly between themselves.

"Is he always like this? I must admit, I find him very refreshing. Honest." The Vice President asked, she was aware the two soldiers had a thing for each other, and she respected that.

"I'm afraid he's like this whenever he's around Politicians, or preparing for an action for his country, Ma'am. Usually, he's a very well mannered and pleasant man to be around, Mary. I intend to have some words with him after this meeting, Ma'am. He'll be on his best manners the next time we meet I promise you Mary." She flashed her best smile at the Vice President.

"Oh... I have no doubt about that young lady." Ms. Hirshfield chuckled softly at her.

The Lieutenant finished eating and sat back in his chair, and the Sergeant was scared to death he was going to burp, or even worse. But he did not commit the worst sin of farting she feared.

Ms. Hirshfield relaxed along with the small group of agents. The tension dissipated as the Lieutenant smiled at her and then he grunted. "Man, that was a meal fit for a King." He wiped his mouth and then looked at Ms. Hirshfield, waiting to find out the reason why they were ordered to meet with her. He did not mistake it for a second, it was an outright order they were issued.

Ms. Hirshfield was not about to waste any more time, as she offered when she knew the Lieutenant stopped eating. "Lieutenant Walker Sir, I'm certain you're wondering why you were ordered here sir. It was because I want to know everything that went on during your mission in Iran sir. I want to know everything that was discovered in the Iranian warhead and missile factory, and what Russian equipment and workers were employed there, and the reaction by the Iranians to your presence in their country uninvited, sir. I want to know this information, so I'm well prepared when I address the United Nations members before the President and yourself, Lieutenant. I especially want to be able to speak with a complete understanding of all the items you brought back to the United States from Iran from that attack, Lieutenant Walker Sir."

"I didn't know you were gonna address those bunch of fucking stuff shirts, alls I was told was... Owe, god dammit that hurt now Raz!" He barked as she pinched him for cursing.

The Sergeant knew she had to say something, because of the way he cried out when she pinched him. But before she could speak, the Vice President cut her off as she warned the angry soldier in a harsh manner. "Now you look here Mr. Walker. I know you're in possession of a mouth that would make the devil himself blush and it's salty enough to cure bacon. But I'll not stand for that kind of gutter mouth crap in front of me and the rest of my staff's presence. If you're not more careful while attending this meeting, Lieutenant Walker Sir. I'll have a Vee chip installed in your rearend, so it'll control that depraved mouth of yours, mister. I have a number of fine young women workers here, and I'll not subject them to these types of words. If you can't control yourself much better that you have, I'll have you cut so you calm down and speak civil."

"Hey Lady I don't need this stinking rigmarole either, Ma'am. I lost the stinking hood a long time ago, Lady. So you're a little late for the stinking job, Ma'am." He growled angrily, referring to the fact he was circumcised, and he was not willing to back down from the angry Vice President, knowing it was she who needed him and not the other way around. He was not afraid to address anyone in the way he felt. What was the worst they could do to him, dump his ass out of the service or take his birthday away? That would break his heart, and set him to moping all over the place. Besides, he was getting tired of traipsing all over the world while engaging his country's enemy, and losing his close friends like Meyerhoff in the process. He was willing to say whatever was on his mind at the time, and allowing the chips fall where they may.

Ms. Hirshfield glared rather angrily at Lieutenant Walker, knowing what he just meant by the crude remark about his losing the hood, as she warned him in no uncertain terms this time. "I wasn't thinking about circumcising you, Mr. Walker. I was thinking more on the terms of castrating you, if you don't get control of that filthy mouth of yours, mister." The Vice President stared threateningly at him, showing him that she was more than willing to carry out her threat against him as she added to her angry words.

"Now you will keep a civilized tongue in that filthy mouth for the rest of this meeting. Or I'll carry out my threat by employing a pair of dull scissors, personally. You see Lieutenant Walker Sir, you're not the only one who has a foul temper around here, mister. I've been dealing with knuckle draggers like you all my life Lieutenant Walker, and I know how to handle them I assure you. So you'll sit there and answer my questions to the best of your abilities, politely might I add. And, you'll remember the fact I have female aides present, and I don't like anyone cursing in front of them. Unless it's me that is mister. Do you understand me loud and clear soldier!"

The Lieutenant could not help it and he smiled at the fuming Vice President. Suddenly, he had a new attitude towards the female politician, one she was cool and would give him all she got and he liked that. He locked his fingers together and then he nodded as he continued to smile.

The smirking Sergeant leaned a bit closer to her soldier with the devil shining in her eyes as she remarked to him. "If you're looking for you testicles Bobby, I think I saw them rolling out the door a few seconds ago mister. Hey big boy, it looks like you finally met your match here."

The tension in the room immediately lessened. He smiled at her, knowing he might have stepped a bit over the line, and he decided to back off and see what happens next.

"I must say that's much better Lieutenant Walker Sir. I knew we could come to a mutual understanding if we really tried to get there, sir." Ms. Hirshfield offered calmly as she sat back, and then she stared at the strikingly good looking young soldier and then went on with her request of the soldier. "Lieutenant Walker Sir, I'd like you to remember this warning while you're addressing the Ambassadors at the United Nations meeting as well, sir. I don't want you embarrassing the President or myself, by using your filthy mouth in the presence of the Ambassadors. Is this understood Lieutenant Walker?"

"Yes Ma'am." The grinning Lieutenant replied, feeling smug he got such a raise from her.

"If you chose, you may call me Mary as well, Lieutenant. But only if you're going to act civilized that is, sir. Another thing I want you to understand Mr. Walker. I don't want you eating in the presence of the President or the Ambassadors for that matter. I just witnessed the spectacle and I don't think they're ready to witness such a vision." Mary nodded at the grinning soldier.

"Does that mean you're gonna call me Robert, or Road Kill, Ma'am?"

"No thank you sir, I think I'll stay with Lieutenant Walker if you don't mind, sir. Now Lieutenant Walker Sir, I want you to explain everything that had taken place in Iran, and I'd like Sergeant... err... pardon me, Dot, to correct you if you happen to omit something, or she might want to add something to your explanation, Lieutenant. I'll help me make up my presentation for the Ambassadors after I have judged everything you will tell me today, sir."

Walker shrugged and then he began to tell her everything they had discovered in Iran, making certain he did not leave out any of the very boring details. Ms. Hirshfield seemed uninterested with his narration of their training, and what lead to their covert invasion inside Iran, and she perked up when he told of how they engaged the soldiers in their country. The Lieutenant was extremely careful when he came to Meyerhoff getting killed, and he glanced at the Sergeant and noticed she was fighting back tears. He went over the inventory they removed from the Iranian factory. The two complete nuclear warheads, and the three that were still under construction.

He went over a number of the papers and reports they removed from the complex, detailing the process of extracting the weapon's grade plutonium from the converted breeder reactors. He also informed her how the SEAL teams had successfully destroyed the five nuclear powered Iranian submarines at their home port in Iran. He even went over how the soldiers were extracted from Iran, leaving most of their military equipment behind, but not before mining and destroying the Bradley Fighting Machines, and the AAV-7A1's, Amphibious Assault vehicles.

The Lieutenant omitted talking about the sand sleds they used for extra vehicles in the Iranian desert, and also used to remove the Iranian equipment before completely destroying the building as the soldiers pulled out of Iran. By the time he finished with his presentation, the wise Vice President had a very good idea of what she was going to say at the United Nations meeting. Only twice did Sergeant Ramirez have to correct something Walker said.

Ms. Hirshfield turned to Sergeant Ramirez and then she asked her if she wanted to add anything more to Walker's rather long winded explanation.

She shook her head no, but her tears overwhelmed her and the Vice President wanted to know what was suddenly wrong with her. Once she began to speak, she could not help herself and she admitted she was crushed over having to miss the service on the Aircraft Carrier for Sergeant Barbara Meyerhoff, who was killed in the invasion of Iran. She also cried about the funeral, and how Barbara's hateful brother would not allow any of the soldiers to attend her funeral. The female Sergeant went on, telling the Vice President of all the fun she, Barbara, the Mutt, and Walker had together, and how tight they were, and how they loved each other.

As she went on, Ms. Hirshfield grew angry over the fact the soldiers Barbara died with, were being kept away from her funeral, and she lost it when Ramirez told her the brother even stopped the honor guard ordered for her from the VFW hall. The Sergeant admitted she found this out from Colonel Leadbetter, who took her in his confidence before they left for New York.

Ms. Hirshfield turned and she growled at Agent Sweeney, ordering him to dispatch one of the special agents to the brother in Ohio, to see if they could explain the errors of his foolish ways of thinking to the brother. She even suggested Sweeney use some rather persuasive means, while informing the brother if he continued with these extremely outrageous demands, the IRS just might be paying him a little visit. Along with anyone else who could cause the nasty brother any grief and serious problems, including the FBI if needed to get her point across to the brother.

Sweeney grinned, offering he was sure he could show the brother how stupid he was acting.

The Lieutenant was pleased the guys might be allowed to attend the funeral after all, as he took her hand. She fought desperately to control her tears, but they betrayed her. When Ms. Hirshfield thought she took everything from the soldiers she needed, she ended the meeting. She told the soldiers to rest over the weekend, and the next meeting between them would take place on Monday morning, November 16th, at ten a.m. She took the Sergeant's hand and told her everything was going to be alright, and she would make certain the soldiers attended Meyerhoff's funeral. Even if she had to have a second one for them, when they returned from Operation Bio Level Three. The Vice President handed her two tickets for the Broadway play, Cats.

The Special Forces soldiers were then escorted from the Presidential Suite by the agent at the meeting. In the elevator, Ramirez rested her head against his shoulder, exhausted after bring out everything about Meyerhoff's death. The Lieutenant hit the button for their floor, and after they entered the apartment, they both stripped down. Naked, Ramirez open the boxes of clothes from Macy's, she was looking for one of Walker's heavy flannel shirts, finding one she threw it on.

"Hey, C'mon Raz, find one of your own stinking shirts, will ya please." Walker complained as his girlfriend like he was really upset with her suddenly.

"Ohhh... whatsumatter with my baby now? I'm not sexy enough for you in one of your oversized shirts mister?" She retorted smartly as she sexily wiggled her hips at his back.

"Naw, it's not that at all little sister. If you keep wearing my stinking shirts all the time, you're gonna get some tit bends and nipple bumps in the damn thing on me, and they'll never come out no matter how many times I get them ironed."

The Sergeant smiled, knowing he was only joking around with her as she yelled at him to get a haircut as he was ordered by Colonel Leadbetter before they left the Carrier for New York. It was late afternoon and there wasn't anything on the TV, so they made love and then they took a nap. They were still suffering from the hard hitting action in Iran, and the jet lag getting to New York.

They ended up sleeping for the entire afternoon and into the night. The only reason he woke was because he was starving, and he had to take a leak. He crawled out of bed and raided the icebox after taking his leak. He remembered they could get room service, finding the menu he ordered double helping of fried shrimp and crab claws then he tried to wake her. Finding that impossible, he returned to the kitchen, he was pissed the only TV in the apartment was in the bedroom, and he decided to wait for the food before turning it on to catch up on the sports news.

While he was eating, a pillow suddenly struck him on the back of his head, and then he heard her bitching at him. "What the devil are you doing now mister? I want to sleep more you prick."

The Lieutenant ignored her and when she realized he was eating something, her hunger got the best of her and she crawled over to his side of the bed and looked over his shoulder. "What are ya eating there my darling?" she asked him in a very sexy tone of voice.

"What the heck does it look like I'm eating to you? Food." He snapped while not bothering to look back at her he continued to stuff the food in his mouth.

"I can see that for myself dickhead! Did you get anything for me to eat?" she asked again in a sexy voice as she ran her hand over his hair and the back of his neck.

"Yeah, right here." The Lieutenant grumbled as he wiggled his dick inches from her face.

"Oh no, does this mean I have to work for my food again, Walker?" she groused at him.

"You got that right little sister. You gotta work if you want any of this crap to eat, baby." He retorted, he wiggled as she drew him in her mouth. She worked him over and spat him out and growled. "That's all you get for now, I'll finish you off after I had some real food to eat."

Walker shifted his rearend to the side to give her some extra room to sit beside him on the floor, and they finished their meal while roaring for the Knicks kicking the hell out of the Miami Heat, and their old coach. The happy Sergeant opened a bottle wine, and he made a real thing out of the food, the basketball game, and their sexual games and love for each other.

When the two lovers finished eating and watching the basketball game and making love, they slept for the rest of the night and did not wake again until eleven Sunday morning. Sergeant Ramirez woke excited, because she was really looking forward to her second visit with the Vice President of the United States. Walker was excited as well but for a different reason, today there were four football games scheduled, and the best game was going to be between Dallas and San Francisco. He checked the icebox and saw a six pack of Bud, and felt that should be more than enough to last him through all the games. The only drawback was the Mutt was not with them.

The Sergeant knew what he was planning for the day, so she decided to cook him up a mess of fried shrimp and serve them to him topless, and remain that way for the entire day's lineup of football games. She knew how he liked to look at her when he was watching the games, and what would come at the end of the day, whether or not his favorite teams won. Football, or anything that showed any violence, always got his blood moving, and when he was excited he was a hell of a bed partner. He moved the bed to one side of the room so he could lay down flat on the floor, he took the stack of pillows and settled down to watch the pre-game show.

Sergeant Ramirez ordered a stack of shrimp, bread crumbs and eggs sent to their room, and she started the oil cooking while waiting for her order to arrive. She loved putting everything on the card, but adding it up in her mind, she realized she was saving the taxpayers a small fortune by cooking for her soldier in their room. Besides, Mr. Trump knew the soldiers were in his building, and they were part of the President's special party. So he made certain more than enough food and other items were sent to not only the Presidential Suite, but to room 2012.

The day was slowly dragging on, while the Lieutenant waited for the first of the football games to finally begin. Sergeant Ramirez kept teasing him with her exquisite body dancing in front of the TV, while he waited not so patiently for the games to start.

THE LAST MEETING BEING HELD BETWEEN THE GROUP OF FUTURE TERRORISTS

The leader of the group called the would be terrorists to order, to make sure Alexander had everything he was going to need for the attack, and everything was set in place. Although the dangerous Russian ex-soldier told him he was ready, he wanted to hear the words from the Russian's lips before going into action. There was another reason for this meeting, because he decided on the time to attack the Trump Tower, and he wanted to go over it with the rest of his people. He was aiming at ten p.m. on Sunday night, November 22nd for the attack. He settled on ten p.m. with the help of the Trump Tower security guard, who told him this was the so called slack time where most of the security guards were thinking about getting off work. At this time, the security guards were just stumbling through the remaining parts of their duties for the day, using habit rather than senses for work. This time would give his group an hour of time, before the relieving security guards showed up at the Tower for the start of their duty.

The leader and soon to be terrorist would have time to not only secure and seal the Trump Tower, but to prepare for the relief security guards if they showed up before he locked down the Tower on them. The security guard working with him was the only one who was not at the meeting, he told him they were coming at the time he told Michael they would be the most vulnerable for attack. The leader looked at Suarez while gathering his thoughts.

"Suarez, you and Four take Five with you. But make him stay out of harm's way, or we're fucked before we get started with this attack. I don't want anything happening to him until we no longer have any need of him. You better take Number Six with you as well, I guess. That should be enough fire power and help with you, to prepare for the arriving relief security guards..."

"What are we supposed to do with the guards when we take them in control, Number One?" Suarez interrupted his words as he stared at the leader of the group.

"What do you think you should do with them, Suarez. You just kill them!" he replied without hesitation while still looking at Suarez, who barely nodded in response to his last words. No one was surprised at how easily Michael just gave seven men and women the death sentence.

Seeing no complaint from the other members of his group, the leader going by Number One continued with his orders. "Good, I'll have the rest of the group secure the Tower, and then take the hostages we want. The other civilians in the hotel will be herded together in the lobby area, and then let go through the front door we're going to leave unsecured. But the hostages will be released after we have full control of the Tower. Alexander, you'll be responsible for getting the equipment up to the roof, and setting up our defense of the building. You're free to fire on anything you want eliminated, or anything you don't want anywhere near your position, Twenty Seven (Alexander). You're our safety net for this entire operation Alexander, and if you screw up on us in any way, shape or form, everyone's going to die. Getting back to the hostages now.

"If anyone we want held as hostage gives you any sort of trouble, is to be shot no questions asked. I don't care if it's one of the chosen few we want to keep, waste them plain and simple without hesitation. You can't hesitate for nothing, I want all the hostages to understand we're not fucking around with them, and they're not to fuck with us. If they don't do as they're ordered, they'll be shot, period. We don't need any of them giving us any problems, or giving backbone to any of the other hostages we want. I don't want any leaders in the hostages, if anyone's forced to take out one, we can keep his death a secret and bluff the police until we escape the Tower.

"I don't want any of you giving the hostages any grief either, I want the hostages as mellow as possible while we control the fools. Once we're out of the building, we'll kill them. We have to do whatever we have to do if we intend to pull this thing off successfully. We have to get to the safes, grab what we want and then be gone before the police mount a counterattack against us."

"And, there's been no change on the security guard's situation with us, Number One?"

Michael smiled at Lizzie who just asked him the question about the fate of the security guard as he replied to her angry words. "He's dead, and I'll leave that solely up to you Lizzie."

Lizzie smiled at the leader of the group as she lightly patted the weapon lying in her lap, and then she finally relaxed so Michael could finish his orders to the rest of the group.

When he was certain everyone was ready to act, and everyone knew what was expected from each of them to ensure their mission's success, he finally called the last meeting to an end.

THE PRESIDENTIAL SUITE, THE TRUMP INTERNATIONAL HOTEL AND TOWER

Time passed slowly for the rather excited Vice President. She went over her long list of notes and memos taken by both her and Cathy during their meeting with the two elite soldiers. She ordered her secretary to listen in on the conversation with the Special Forces soldiers, and to take down notes at that meeting. She had a number of audio tapes secretly recorded everything that was said during the entire meeting, and she was going to listen to them once she finished her speech from the notes. Ms. Hirshfield wanted to be well prepared for any questions she was certain would come at the meeting, once she finished her speech to the Ambassadors.

For a brief second, Ms. Hirshfield allowed her mind to wander a bit, remembering what happened in her bedroom with Sweeney the night before. She smirked fondly remembering how clumsy he was with her, to the point of shaking he was so scared of being with her in bed. She remembered all the trouble he had getting hard, and it only happened when she took him in her mouth, and she worked him over for a few moments that way. She chuckled as she saw his stunned expression when she did it, and how he tried to stop her. She could not believe Edward did not think a female Vice President would give oral intercourse to her lover. She was amazed he did not think of her as a whole woman, just a Vice President and that belief did not extend to the most natural ways of making love to a man, with her mouth or hands or body.

Mary shook her head while looking forward to being alone Sweeney again. She went back to her notes scattered out before her, once she was certain she had everything in the proper position on her pad, she listened to the audio tapes. Mary heard the soldier growling about his manhood, and her threat to castrate him. She grinned as she remembered him asking if she was Jewish, and the remark that followed. She could not do anything but come to the conclusion she liked the two elite soldiers. She enjoyed his honesty, fearlessness, and willingness to say whatever was on his mind, no matter who he was speaking with, or was in ear shot of him. She decided Lieutenant

Walker was very refreshing, and she admitted she really enjoyed his witty and pleasing remarks.

Ms. Hirshfield looked to Cathy sipping tea while waiting to see if she was needed, and she offered her. "Cathy, take a memo please. I want to visit the troops in Egypt the first chance I get. I want to see if they're like the crazy and wild one we met yesterday. He was some shit Cathy."

"Yes Ma'am, but I like him and his swift lady. They're what makes this country what she is."

"Good commercial there Cathy. You're learning fast hanging around me you know honey."

She overlooked the jab as the Vice President went back to the audio tapes, taking down a few more tidbits of information, and jotting them down on her pad. The Vice President was amazed she forgot so much of their conversations. It seemed anytime Walker said something on the tape, it made her giggle or roll her eyes over his remarks. When she completed her notes, she snapped off the recorder and then took in a quick breath. Ms. Hirshfield used the bed as her work table, and she was dressed in a loosely fitting silk lounging outfit, enjoying the freedom the garment offered her body by the fine thin and very pleasing fabric engulfing her entire body.

While she sipped her tea and waited to be asked a question by the Vice President, Cathy kept looking at Mary and expecting her to say something to her about last night.

Ms. Hirshfield noticed the many quick looks, but she totally ignored them for the most part, until she finally noticed that Cathy was outright staring at her now. The Vice President folded the pad closed and then she looked at Cathy and snapped at her at the same time. "What?"

Her secretary did not move a muscle as she merely smiled at Mary mischievously.

Mary let out her breath and then she shook her head as she repeated to her bodyguard's look. "What? What seems to be bothering you all of a sudden, Cathy dear?"

"What, what?" Cathy remarked and added. "You know very well what, Ma'am. I want to know how it went last night with Sweeney, Ma'am. Was he as good as he looks, in bed I mean Ma'am? I want to know everything that went on in your bedroom last night with him, Ma'am."

"Oh that, it went well enough I guess my dear." She blushed as she diverted her eyes.

"Well that wasn't very thrilling I dare say. I didn't see any rockets coming from your eyes when you spoke about last night, Mary. That's all you have to say about your lovemaking session with Agent Sweeney, Ma'am? After not having sex for so long, I thought I'd see the wallpaper peeling from the walls, and the windows still fogged over and dripping with sweat. I'm dying to know what happened last night, Ma'am. I'll make it easy for you to tell me all the details. If you could sum up last night in one word, what would it be?" the concerned bodyguard held her cup, her elbows resting on the chair arms. She stared at Mary while waiting for her response.

After waiting for what seemed like a short lifetime, Mary finally responded thoroughly embarrassed. "I guess that one word would have to be clumsy, maybe two words, very clumsy."

"Clumsy! Clumsy! You have to be kidding me Ma'am. How the hell could you possibly be clumsy with him after abstaining from sex for so long a time, Ma'am? What the devil did you do that was so clumsy last night?" the secretary roared with laughter at Mary.

"Whoa, whoa, back up the laughter train there. It wasn't me who was the clumsy one, it was him. He couldn't raise the flag until I gave him a helping, err... hand." She giggled as she covered her face and then laughed after not admitting she had to use her mouth on the poor agent.

"Sweeney couldn't get hard? Didn't you try alternate means on the dummy, Ma'am? I can't believe he had a hard time getting hard. Wow!" she laughed knowing she used oral on him.

Mary knew what Cathy meant and she replied while trying to control her laughter. "I did that, that's what I meant by a helping hand. When I tried to get him in my mouth, I thought he was going to have an apoplexy on me. He kept telling me no, and trying to stop me from giving him pleasure that way, the damn fool he is. He was so scared of me all night long, Cathy."

"What's wrong with the dumb ass anyhow? Could he possibly be that stupid, Mary? Doesn't he think you're a woman like any other women he might share his bed with for Pete's sake? That you have the same needs and wants as any other woman in the world? Boy, talk about living a sheltered life he's the poster child, the damn fool. It looks like we'll have to loosen this one up a bit, before he gives you some oral pleasure in return. Oh God, he did return the favor, didn't he?" Cathy asked in shock that Sweeney did not try and bring Mary to a climax.

"Huh, try as I might I just couldn't get his head maneuvered properly for him to get the job done properly with me. But we did make the best of it, after his heart stopped pounding so rapidly in his chest. I must admit Cathy, I had a good time last night, even as clumsy as he was. The poor fool came almost as soon as he got home. Typical man, when we women have to deal with men, we always get the short end of the stick when it comes the art of making love."

Her secretary's eyebrows arched as she stared at Mary, hoping she was not getting the meaning by the Vice President's last remark. The smiling Vice President easily picked up the expression on Cathy's face and she laughed as she added. "No, he was all there when it came to length and width okay. It's just that he was so damned clumsy. I wondered how he made it this far in life, not knowing what to do or how to do it for the lady he was with for the night, my dear."

Cathy wiped a tear from her eye as she admitted. "It looks like I'll have to have a little, pardon me Ma'am. I know how men react when they hear that 'little' word used. But it looks like I'm going to have a word with this dumb fellow, if you're ever to be pleased by him Mary."

"Do you think it'll help out any Cathy?" the smiling Vice President asked her pretty aide. The bodyguard nodded yes, and then she put on a mischievous smile as she looked at her.

The Vice President joined her as she held out her hand, and she gave her the new stack of notes and said. "Would you be a real dear and have these papers typed up for me please?"

The aide took the notepad and tucked it under her arm as she replied. "Sure." She said then she looked at the Vice President again. They both broke out in laughter as the two enjoyed the moment, and Mary reliving her night of making love to the foolish Sweeney.

Special Agent Edward Sweeney was trying his best to avoid being seen by anyone working in the secured apartment, as he struggled with himself while trying to figure out the night before and what went wrong on him. Over and over, he kept kicking himself for not treating Mary like any other normal woman like he treated women he was with. He cringed when he remembered her trying to guide his head down between her legs, and how he fought off her pressure and he did not share that part of their lovemaking. He could not believe he was such a prude with her. The agent sat up straight and shook his head at himself as he remembered his stupid reaction to her giving him oral sex, and how quickly he came once he mounted her. He cursed as he smacked himself on the forehead with the palm of his hand, calling himself an amateur and he threatened to cut off his dick, if he was not better the next time he shared the bed with Mary. He found himself admitting he loved her, and he always had since first coming to work for her.

With a chilling thought suddenly striking him like a thunderbolt, he found himself hoping he would get another chance at making love to Mary. Now he had something to prove to her, that he was a man and he knew all the special ways to please, and to make a woman squirm under his sexual skills. He vowed to himself he was going to make her come twice by using his mouth on her, before mounting and showing her his skills of lovemaking. Sweeney began to pace the room the agents used as their headquarters, as his mind continued to curse him. He stormed in the bathroom and looked at himself in the mirror, and went so far as to stick his tongue at his reflection as he made a disgusted face at himself as he was so angry with himself.

The other special agent sharing the room with Sweeney, gave the obviously upset agent the space he needed to get whatever was bugging him out of his system. One agent told Sweeney he was going to get something to eat, and he was to hold the fort down for him until he returned to man his position again. He did not hear a word the other agent said to him, as he continued to stare at his face in the mirror and still making ugly faces at himself. He had to fight to stop his hand from picking up something to write on the mirror, making his face look like he felt. An ass. He heard the women giggling in the other room a little while ago, and he could not help but feel they were laughing at him and his love making abilities. This served to upset him further, and he found himself making even more ugly faces at his reflection in the mirror.

The three other agents controlling the security of the interior of the apartment, were in the kitchen of the Presidential Suite having a cup of coffee and a little private time for themselves, and to get something to eat before returning to their normal duties. Although none of the agents expressed it, they all seemed to know Sweeney spent the night with the beautiful Vice President. The agents taking their break in the kitchen, had been on duty since the night before, and they were certain they heard the sounds of lovemaking coming from the Vice President's bedroom. The only thing stopping them from being positive about their thoughts, was the fact the noises ended almost as quickly as they had started. None of the agents would dare believe that Sweeney, or the Vice President was not that good in bed, or with their lovemaking abilities.

The agents looked at each other, and smirked over the fact of knowing something they were not entitled to know about their ward. They dared to take time on their extended coffee break. As if they had a right, because of what they believed they knew about their boss and lead agent.

Agent Sweeney kept hammering away at his reflection in the mirror. Over and over he kept telling himself he hated his image in the mirror, and if he ever got another chance to share Ms. Hirshfield's bed. He was going to make her fingernails melt, and her heart burst in her chest from all the pleasure he was going to deliver to her body and mind on their next coupling. He stood before the mirror shaking his head, upset over the fact he had failed to bring much pleasure to Mary she so richly deserved. Or anyone else he was with for that matter, and he knew he could deliver for her, if he had his head screwed on right, and had another chance with Mary in bed. He now wanted to make her so happy and want to be with him for the rest of her life.

The still upset special agent continued to stare at his reflection as he started to calm down a little. His driving force now, was to make love to Mary in a most loving and tender manner, and to make her know he loved and truly respected her.

Chapter Fifteen

EIGHT O'CLOCK EASTERN STANDARD TIME,
SUNDAY EVENING, NOVEMBER 15th, 1998.
THE TRUMP INTERNATIONAL HOTEL AND TOWER

Lieutenant Robert Walker was getting comfortable while sitting on the floor of the apartment in the Trump Tower, just as the last football game for the day was about to start. First, he had to sit through a very boring commercial for Bud Light. This game did not promise to be very exciting or interesting, the night's game was going to be played between the Washington Redskins and the Buffalo Bills, who were still laboring with their new quarterback. Without Jim Kelly at the helm, the Bills 1997 year was less than expected, but the young dude was trying his best, and that was all anyone could want from the young man in command of the team effort.

The Lieutenant was enjoying himself, it was the first time in many years he took time off to relax like he was doing in New York. Since he enlisted in the service, it's been one military action after the other, the Cuba mess then the Middle East situation, followed by Taiwan action. He barely had a chance to catch his breath, before the soldiers were shipped off to Namibia so they could beat back the white assholes who wanted to retake power in South Africa. He just made it back to the

States, before he was packed up and then shipped out to North Korea, to hunt down the nuclear tipped missiles stolen by a pack of Russian rebels. That action took some time to accomplish, because the Rapid Response Force soldiers had to actually cross into Russia so they could aid the badly depleted Russian forces in search of the rebel Colonel who was responsible for the theft of the short range missiles and deadly nuclear warheads.

It took two weeks to locate him and the rest of his rebel forces. But not before they took over a major missile installation inside Russia, and the rebels threaten the world with the long range multi nuclear warhead tipped missiles. It was by just sheer luck his group of elite troops was able to weed out the rebel Russians, before they were able to launch the missiles at the United States. The bad part of this operation was, he and his troops did not have a chance to settle down, before being shipped out to the Middle East, this time to invade Iran and rid that country of its latest ambitions to develop their own long range ballistic missiles, and nuclear warheads.

This time things were far worse for the group of specialized soldiers, because his group of elite soldier was not going to be brought back to the United States, before going into another mission for their country. The soldiers were scheduled to go against Libya, and their twin chemical and biological weapons plants. But today, the young Lieutenant put that crap out of his mind, and he happily settled down to enjoy the four football games of the day, and to catch up on the new players and what they were capable of doing for the teams.

The Lieutenant sat on the plush carpeted floor surrounded by the TV changer, a couple of cans of suds, and an overflowing basket of deep fried shrimp. He loved them, and when he could get them, he could not get enough of them to fill him. The Sergeant was in the kitchen, humming away as she fried up another batch of shrimp for the both of them. She truly loved cooking for her man, she loved doing anything for her soldier and lover.

The commercial was going on for so long that it seemed like it was never going to end, so he pulled a New York newspaper over to his side, and went to put the basket of shrimp on it. Moving the paper he noticed a story printed on the front page, on how someone won a judgment against another person, and the winner was overjoyed about his victory. This set him off, and she moved nearer him, so she could see what was suddenly bugging her soldier. He flashed the article in front of her face and then he barked over the article.

"Anyone who thinks the fricking laws are working for them in this twisted up country, betta wise up in a fast fucking hurry it up, and rethink his damn believes. Just try and get someone who ripped you off in fucking court and see what that move gets you. The damn criminals have so many rights that by the time you finally get the lousy little prick to court, it's you who always ends up feeling like the damn criminal. If the stinking courts would do one tenth of what it does to protect the damn criminal to help the victims out first then there might be some help and things might start getting straighten out for us. But that crap's not gonna happen until someone gets a damn handle on some of these fricking lawyers making a living using the ACLU as cover for their stupid actions. The ACLU's becoming too powerful in the States, and it's no longer protecting anyone's civil fucking rights. It's now a form of job security for the damn lawyers, by finding stupid things to gripe about and sue over, dammit.

"Then the stinking lawyers get the ridiculous things dragged into court. The people running that thing have it made in the shade. Get short on money? Find something to gripe about no matter how stupid it is, and then drag it to court. There's a new way to get medical coverage and schooling sweeping this country, get yourself sent to fucking jail and you're entitled to this crap at the taxpayer's fucking expense. Yet the poor slob stuck paying for this shit for the criminals, can't afford to send his own kids to college, or have fricking medical insurance for him and his family. Something's seriously wrong with this stinking picture I tell ya Raz."

"Enough Bobby. You have to let it go, you're not going to change the system by allowing it get to you like this my lover." Sergeant Ramirez tried her best to calm down the increasingly agitated Lieutenant, before he really went off on her, but he was having none of it.

"Yeah, it's like I just said Raz, the stinking ACLU's a job security thing, and the damn lawyers involved with it change the laws or read them to suit their own damn needs. So they have a reason to drag someone's ass to court, and spend the taxpayer's money while doing it. They keep pushing, and soon there's not going to be a clear way to get the criminals to jail. We'd rather place the police, the stinking labs and doctors on fucking trial. With this 'what if' defense, there's no working laws anymore. The criminals pay doctors and labs to go against good solid evidence, and they create that shadow of a doubt and walk away scot fucking free.

"Think about it baby, one stinking Doctor says the criminal did it, and the defense Doctor says no he didn't do it. How the hell could you convict anyone on that kinda crap? Things got so bad, murderers are set free, and some poor cop ends up getting busted and finds himself with a police record, because he was too embarrassed to own up to using that terrible epithet. Now that asshole cop can't vote, or hold office, or carry a fricking weapon, and he's disgraced before the entire world, while a double murderer's walking around with all his rights still in fucking tact.

"Don't get me wrong here Raz. I'm not sticking up for this fricking bigot ass cop, but we have a question we have to ask ourselves. What the hell's worse, murder, or using the stinking 'N' word? It doesn't make any fucking sense to me, and we're starting to take into consideration personal experiences too. They're taking them into the damn jury room with them, and allowing that uther crap to outweigh good, hard evidence against the damn criminals. If that's a fact then we might as well chuck the whole fucking legal system right into the damn shitter and be done with it, and allow the stinking criminals and lawyers to run the fricking country for us. Now there's a contradiction in terms. Look at what the ACLU's trying to do, go after some damn judge just because he's displaying a personal, hand carved plaque he did himself of the Ten Commandments." The upset Lieutenant took a breath, and then went on with his angry words.

"Instead of saying wow, what a cool fucking job the dude did carving it. The ACLU's dragging his ass to court, spending a shitload of taxpayer's money on this crap while they're at it. What's next? Soon, you're not going to be allowed to wear a cross, or the Star of David around your damn neck, if some asshole can see it. It's all bullshit and bad manners if you were to ask me. Huh, instead of trying to block

God and His great wisdom from us and our court, maybe we should take a second look at the overall picture here, and start relying on God and his Commandments like back in the good old days. They worked pretty well in the past for us.

"It didn't fucking hurt us before, but now we have to be ashamed because we believe in God, any God. Oh yeah, win a judgment in this country, don't make me fucking laugh. You might as well wipe your stinking ass with the papers, because the only ones who come out the winners in the suite, are the damn lawyers. We allow a lousy prick who ripped off the old, hungry and disabled for some forty million dollars, to plea bargain it down to where he spends only three years in jail, and doesn't have to pay back the stinking monies he stole. Shit, I'd go to jail for three years for forty million stinking dollars, and do the time standing on my stinking head. And, to know this is what I'm putting my fricking ass on the front of the dime for, makes me sick to my friggin stomach, dammit. Look at this crap about controlling guns now, if you take the guns outta the hands of good civilians, you're depriving them of the right to defend themselves against any damn criminals. Everyone's looking at the guns as the problem, it's not dammit.

"If we go after the real problem facing us in the damn States, we're starting to do something about the lousy situation. What the hell does the damn criminal have to fear? They commit a crime and by the time it's brought to fucking court, it's not anywhere near what it was. Christ sake, the way things are going, soon, the damn victim will be forced to apologize to the stinking criminal for making him mug the guy, because the lousy bastard was deprived of love when he was a fucking kid. If we wanna stop the fucking violence, we have to go after the stinking criminal like he's the criminal, and take his rights away from him, not the damn victims. It's not the automatic weapons or hand guns, it's the damn criminals, stupid. If they can't get any damn guns, they'll use knives, pipes or cars to carry out their profit of living offa the victims.

"It goes back to the stinking lawyers changing the fricking laws, and getting the criminals off for their stinking crimes." He suddenly threw his hands in the air and then added to his bitch. "Everyone's dumping on the damn police, but we have a serious problem on our hands. What would we rather live in, a police state or a fucking criminal state? We allow an asshole who savagely killed twenty seven people, along with his cult on the internet. Yet Congress is busting their fucking horns to stop stations such as Playboy, from being broadcast over the damn internet. I guess our leaders believe it's better to have savage violence in the States, rather than love on the internet. I'm telling ya, it doesn't make any fucking sense to me, baby." The Lieutenant griped and then he calmed down and stared at the TV again. The game started a few moments before.

"What do you think we should do with the damn criminals then, Walker?" the concerned female Sergeant asked him calmly as she shot him a warming smile.

"Kill the sonofabitches that fucking quick!" the angry military officer snapped his fingers and then added. "If they use a stinking gun in a fucking crime, they rape, or dare molest a child, they die nice and slow. If they do a white collar crime without violence, they go to jail for the full term of their conviction, none of this plea bargaining crap, and they hafta pay the money back to their victims. There's a simple solution to the gun problem. Use a fucking gun for any reason but hunting, you die, fuck that year in jail crap, that's all bullshit and bad manners. Dead is the only thing a fucking murderer understands. And, I'm not saying just kill the rotten bastards. I mean they should lose their damn lives in the same fucking way that they took a life. Kill with a gun, and you die with a fucking gun and it's that simple to solve.

"Beat someone to death, and you get beaten to death. Rape someone, you get fed to the old wood chipper, the same goes for any damn puke child molesters, the wood chipper comes out again. But they get lowered in the damn thing nice and slow. Let them think about their crime before they die, dammit. Revenge, that's the name of the game, an eye for a fricking eye, Raz. Deal out death to the criminals in the same fashion they gave it out. It's time to stop the fucking stinking bleeding hearts from giving away our god damn legal rights, just to soothe the damn criminals and their damn lawyers and bleeding hearts. We have to start getting control back over our country before our country disappears on us." He was really pissed, and he was on a roll.

The concerned Sergeant did the only thing she could think of doing, she allowed her soldier to blow off steam. He was much better off once he finished his griping. She came back in the bedroom topless with another basket of shrimp for her angry soldier to enjoy, but he was now too involved in the football game to even noting she was still topless.

The Lieutenant took the basket and said. Ahhh... baby, you're the greatest." He already forgot all about what was making him angry just minutes before.

The football game dragged on because of so many penalties and commercials, and it was nine forty five by the time the game reached halftime with the Redskins leading by just seven points. She laid on the bed reaching over Walker's shoulder, so she could get at some shrimp. Her beer resting on the floor by Walker's rearend. When the game entered halftime, Walker attacked, placing his head between Raz's legs, and causing her to roar with laughter as he worked her over good and proper. The two got so involved in their sex game that he forgot about the football game. He truly enjoyed making his lover laugh, and knew the right buttons to push to accomplish it. Soon, they were rolling all over the bed, laughing, joking, and doing their thing. She sat on his face, and then she moaning to the rhythm of his very skilled tongue.

THREE RENTED TRUCKS ON THE STREETS OF NEW YORK CITY, 9:35 P.M. SUNDAY (EST) NOVEMBER 15th ,1998

It was pitch black by the time Michael finished loading the last of his group, and their weapons and equipment into the trucks. The group was lucky to get their hands on a covered parking space to park the closed in trucks, until they were needed. He had Lizzie rent the vehicles the day before for two weeks, stating the reason for the rentals was to move her mother down to Florida. She did everything above board, except for using a fake driver's license, and a credit card that was not going to be reported stolen until Monday morning as agreed.

The card belonged to a close friend respected and beyond reproach. All she had to do was make love to the older married man while his wife was out of town, and the guy did not care what she did with the credit card, or what she might have charged to it. Because he was going to have all the charges erased, once he reported the card stolen. Everyone from his group checked in, and no one reported being trailed by the police. Even the Trump Tower security guard checked in, and he informed him nothing out of the ordinary was occurring at the Tower.

Although the Tower guard knew someone special had obviously checked in the Tower Friday night, everything about the guest was being kept closed mouth from the guards. He could not find out the identification of the new visitor. He tried to get on the twenty second floor, but he was stopped by the police who demanded to know what he was doing on the floor. After checking his ID, the officer ordered him off the floor, telling him not to return until further notice.

The security guard heard some scuttlebutt floating around the guards about the stranger visiting the Trump Tower in secret, might be the President of the United States. But this was quickly blown out of the water, when he saw a news program showing the President was still in Washington and he was preparing to pay a visit to New York City on November 20th. The reporter stated the President planned to address the United Nations members on a number of very pressing global concerns. The security guard had no other choice but to let it lay, because he knew he would find out who this secret visitor was when his friends arrived at the Tower and took it over. He did not mention this visitor to the leader, because he was worried he might want to call off the attack until they knew who this stranger was. He did not want that, the guard wanted to be a millionaire, and he had to take daring chances to accomplish this feat.

The three rented Rider rented trucks slowly and cautiously pulled away from the curb on their way towards the Trump International Hotel and Tower constructed at the very mouth of Central Park. Traffic was rather light at this time and day, and this was another reason for Michael picking this day and time to get things going for their planned attack on the building.

The drivers of the trucks moved out one after the other, paying close attention to all the traffic laws and stop lights. Because the soon to be group of terrorists did not want to call any special attention to themselves by the police, by breaking the traffic laws. It seemed wherever the three vehicles drove, the traffic was flowing pretty well for them. In no time, the small caravan of vehicles turned from 54th Street, and slowly made their way towards Central Avenue, heading right for Columbus Circle at just twenty five miles an hour.

Michael was riding in the lead vehicle, and a slight smile slowly crossed his lips when he picked up the massive building they were going to attack being bathed in a million bright lights, completely filling his entire windshield. He lightly tapped Lizzie on the shoulder as she kept a close eye on the two trailing vehicles in the rearview mirror. Once she turned to see what he wanted from her, he pointed towards the magnificent Trump Tower and Hotel.

She looked at her watch and discovered it was still too early to begin their attack, and she quickly pointed this fact out to the leader of the group, who told her they were going to split up after leaving the Circle. Then the three trucks were going to move to the scheduled positions much closer to the Trump Tower and then wait for the time to pass for them before they went into action against the building and everyone in the structure.

Lizzie gave the leader a queer look, forcing him to smile again as he quickly explained his thoughts to her. "Lizzie, the reason why we left to begin this ting a little early, was because I wanted everyone within striking distance of the Trump Tower when we're ready to go into action. Just in case some nosey cop happens to stumble over us before we hit the damn Tower. The second truck will park on Central Park West, right by the mouth of the Park. The other truck will park as near as possible on 61st Street behind the Tower, while our truck is going to park right on Broadway, like we're making a late night delivery to the building, so no cops come snooping around and they discover us and what we're doing tonight."

"I think we should've stayed where we were, at least until it was much closer to the time to begin our attack on the Tower, Number One. What happens if we're challenged by a police vehicle?" She replied to the leader of the group of robbers.

"What do you feel would happened to any police officer if we're discovered miles away from our target? They would have no idea what the hell we might be up to and they can only let us go after they give us a ticket for whatever reason they stopped us in the first place." He snapped at the only female member of the group nastily.

"The police probably would stop our plan from going ahead as was expected by us, Number One." She replied with a little concern in her tone as she stared him in the eyes.

"Yeah, that's another thing they can do to us Lizzie, but if we're parked already within just running distance of the Trump Tower. If some cop does happen to stop one of the other trucks, and we charge out of our vehicle and we head for the Tower while firing at the cops challenging the other vehicle. What do you think the police first action would be, Lizzie?" the confident leader of the group did not like referring to Lizzie by a number.

"The officers would most likely turn their attention against us, thus giving the other vehicle being challenged, their chance to attack the police from their backs. Hmmm... now I see what your madness is about, Number One. It's a wise plan indeed if you ask me, my friend." She replied as she smiled pleasantly at the leader of the group.

"I'm glad you agree with my plans so far, Lizzie. I figured it was the wisest move to make. I'd much rather be waiting nearer our target when we begin our attack against the building, Lizzie." Number One offered with a grunt in his voice, as he stopped the truck for a red light at the opening to Columbus Circle. Then he waited for the three way light to turn green before continuing on towards his intended target.

Chapter Sixteen

THE TRUMP INTERNATIONAL HOTEL AND TOWER,
ROOM STAR #3

Vice President Mary Hirshfield was exhausted after correcting her speech for the United Nations meeting scheduled for Friday morning. Her speech was to be delivered before the President of the United States took the podium for his speech for the gathered Ambassadors. Then this would be followed by Lieutenant Walker's question and answer session.

Ms. Hirshfield was to be the ice breaker for her country. Cathy, did a fine effort with getting everything properly typed up for her. The Vice President pushed to get the speech completed so she knew what she was saying at the meeting. As Mary read over the final draft of her speech for a second time, she noted a few minor changes to be corrected or deleted. She knew some additional information was more than likely going to be added, as well as some other changes and omissions made, once she had another chance to meet with Lieutenant Walker and his fellow female soldier. She felt sorry Cathy was forced to retype the entire report for a third time. What she did not know was, Cathy's machine had instant memory, and all she did was make the corrections on the print and press copy, and the machine automatically did the rest for her.

Although she was still fatigued, the Vice President had no interest with turning in for the night. Her mind was too active to give in to her body's need for some sleep. Because of her activity, she kept her entire entourage motivated and hopping all night long. The five special agents stayed awake watching TV, and her aide copied the report over for her, and she made some small talk with the Vice President. Agent Edwards Sweeney paced the apartment, hoping he was again going to be invited into Mary's bedroom for the night.

THE TRUMP INTERNATIONAL HOTEL AND TOWER

Michael's team parked their vehicles well within view of the Trump Tower. Everyone waited for the time to come in their trucks, so they could begin the assault on the building. The leader of the group armed everyone with a closed circuit FM radio, making it impossible for other radios to pick up his broadcasts. Unless they happened to have the same type radio, and had it tuned in to the same frequency they were using. This was the only way he could start his people in motion, while still controlling the assault teams to the very last minute of the attack. He wanted complete control over the situation to call it off at the very last moment, if he did not like what he saw around the Trump Tower. So far, everything looked like a go to him.

Michael checked his watch for the umpteenth time, before he gave the okay to begin their attack. He tapped Valentine on the shoulder, and then pointed at the Tower. The Number Two man started the truck and headed for the loading area of the Tower. He glanced at Alexander's truck riding behind his, it was moving forward. He never looked at the third truck, knowing it to was heading for the building. His truck was the first to pull up to the loading dock, and he and Suarez piled out of the truck, with Suarez ringing the bell for admittance into the Tower.

The Tower Security Command Post instantly picked up the vehicle entering the loading dock area on their monitors when it entered the property of the Tower. One guard mumbled to the other. "I wonder who the hell's not following procedures, these rick pricks think they can have anything delivered any time they damn well choose. One of these days they're going to learn."

"Yeah, one of these days they'll learn alright." The second security guard grumbled as he contacted the guard working with Michael. "Hey Ray come in, this is Command."

"This is Ray. What's up?" Ray shot back over the radio unit knowing what it was all about.

"It looks like someone's having something delivered to their damn apartment unscheduled, you better get over to the loading dock area and see what's up with this delivery, Ray."

"I'm there." Ray said in the radio as he headed for the loading dock.

"Let me know what's up when you get there Ray." The other guard said.

"Sure, do you want me to allow the delivery to go through, or should I send the truck and workers away and make them return during the day and regular delivery time for the Tower?"

"That's entirely up to you Ray. If you want the extra paperwork then allow the delivery. It depends on who the package is for. Handle it, if you want to accept the delivery, send the driver down to the center, and I'll give him a temporary pass to the building, after I bust his horns."

"Sure will, take the alarm off the dock doors Three and Four while you're at it for me." Ray asked his Commander as he smiled to himself, knowing his friends were in now.

The guard in the Command Center moved a pair of switches and then announced in the radio. "They're clear and down Ray, do you want backup? You can never be too sure about anything."

"Naw I see the driver, he looks cool, he made a couple of deliveries to the building before. I recognize him, yeah, that's him alright." Before he opened the garage door, he shoved the sheet of metal and it fell across the phone wires leading from the Command Center to the local police departments. A flash of sparks destroyed the communication lines, and now the Security Center had no way of knowing they were cut off from police reinforcements coming to their aide.

The security guard opened the loading dock door and smiled as Michael and Suarez rushed by him and he immediately pointed towards the overhead camera. Suarez handed the guard a paper to make it look like a real delivery and made like he was getting hot, while the guard made a big deal out of accepting the late day delivery to the Tower. The radio was being monitored by command, and he was following the usual procedures, he left his radio key open so the other security guards could hear everything being said in the loading dock area.

The first guard positioned inside the Command Post complained to his partner. "It looks like another furniture delivery to me. Don't these pricks ever get tired of buying this crap?"

The security guard spoke to Command in a very bored sounding tone of voice. "Hey Bob, it looks like McKinney has done it again to us, man. He ordered a new living room set, and this was the only time these guys could possibly deliver it for him. They want to know if we'll make an exception for the late time delivery, and allow them to deliver the crap to McKinney's apartment. They say if they can't drop it off now, they'll lose their profit by bringing the stuff back to the warehouse, and then reschedule it for delivery sometime later on tomorrow morning. I checked out their paperwork, it's a McKinney deal alright Bob."

"You going to accept the damn delivery then Ray? It's entirely up to you like I told you before man. One thing you should keep in mind Ray, McKinney's a helluva tipper you know. The last time he did this to us, he took good care of us for allowing the afterhours delivery."

"I think I'll let it go through then, Bob." The guard offered with a smirk.

"Great, but I want you to make a big deal out of excepting the late delivery in front of the two drivers. So they report the fact we allowed them to make the delivery to McKinney's apartment after hours. You know the procedures you need to follow man. Send one of the drivers down to the Center so we can bust his horns a little to. Who is the other guy with the driver, Ray?"

"That's his helper Bob, you know there's three truck loads of this crap in this delivery man. He must have brought out the whole damn store this time. The driver says he has help he needs in the other trucks to make the delivery."

"I picked up the other trucks when the other two pulled into the loading area on my monitor. I figured they were all part of this delivery to McKinney. Do you know what they're going to do with McKinney's old stuff, Ray? I saw some of the crap in his apartment a few days ago, it's good furniture in great shape." The second guard asked Ray to find out this information.

He made it look like he was speaking with the driver for the benefit of the security camera watching their every move in the loading dock area. Then he reported to the Command Center. "Hey Bob, they say he's paying them to remove the old stuff from his apartment. They said they're going to have to find a home for the crap, or dump it off someplace where they can get rid of it. They said it's a pain to get rid of used furniture anywhere in Manhattan these days."

"Ray, ask the driver if we can have the stuff." The guard told his fellow worker.

He spoke to Number One this time and then reported back. "Bob, he said sure, he even offered to deliver it wherever you want it dropped off free of charge, because we're allowing the late delivery for them. But they'll just dump it off on the sidewalk. Are you going to split the take with the rest of us as usual?" the security guard asked like nothing was wrong with the delivery.

"Always, I'll take what I want from the stuff first, and then I'll sell the rest and split the profit between us. Hey Ray, send the driver down to the Command Center like I said, and we'll make it easy now they're taking care of us. Who are the other ones coming in with this delivery, Ray?"

"The driver states they're his helpers for this delivery and pickup. One of them is a chick man. She's a real good looker Bob." The security guard reported to his Command Center Commander.

"Better send them down to the Center, so we can check them out before we allow them to roam around the building this late. I'll have Paul and Eddy come up and help after we checked them out. Tell the driver you'll watch them while they're making the delivery in the building."

The guard informed Number One what his boss just told him, and then he pointed to a staircase leading down to the Security Command Post stationed in the basement of the Trump Tower, and Suarez, Purvis, Prochaska, and Moulton headed for the center. When the robbers entered the stairwell and were certain the security guards working in the Command Center could not see what they were doing, they removed their weapons from under their work coats. They left the outerwear in the hall and then continued down towards the Command Center.

Suarez was in the lead, followed by Lizzie and Edwin. Geofferson brought up the rear for the small group. Five staircases later, the soon to be terrorists were on the security level. Lizzie was shoved to the front of the group, with her shirt hanging opened on her shoulders. When the group entered the security camera area, they closed ranks so the guards could not see their weapons. The first security guard saw Lizzie, and noticed her breasts nearly popping out of the front of her shirt, and he called it to the attention of the other guards stationed with him.

"Holy shit will you look at this? Why the hell can't we get help like this?" the three security guards gathered around the screen and gawked at her treasures. They were so busy staring at Lizzie's breasts that they did not notice Suarez and Purvis peel off from the group, and come at them from the blind side of the Command Center. Suarez got between a support column and the window, and he carefully aimed his weapon right at one guard, while Purvis caught the other one up in his sights. Prochaska got the third security guard lined up using Lizzie's back as cover for his weapon. Once he was certain he had the guard covered he was going to tap Lizzie, and she would then drop down towards the floor while clearing his shot for him.

Suarez nodded to Lizzie, Geofferson tapped her on the back and she dropped to the floor.

"Hey, she must have just tripped over something man. I sure hope she's alrig..."

The guard did not get the chance to finish his remark, his life was cut short by a bullet that ripped into his neck. Suarez fired as the man who moved nearer to the window to check on Lizzie's condition. The second guard stared as his friend went flying back with blood pouring from his mouth, and his hands clutched at his neck. The second guard did not have a chance to react before a bullet smashed his skull. Geoffferson hit the third guard. Suarez then rushed in the Center and hit each guard a second time to make certain they were dead then reported to Michael.

"One, Three. We're in the pool and the water's just fine." Three reported to his leader.

"That's great Three." He broke off the connection with his Number Three man, and then he ordered Ray and Valentine, his Number Two man, to throw open the other garage doors. The remaining trucks were parked in place, and Alexander heaved open the doors to his truck, and screamed at his people to unload the weapons and other equipment they needed, and get them to the service elevator. He took off with Ray, and they both headed for the elevator master panel.

The security guard pointed out the elevator controls, and Number One cut the power wires with insulated bolt cutters. In seconds, the elevators were useless to anyone inside the building. Both he and Ray then headed back to the loading dock area. Once there, he told Ray to show Alexander to the service elevator, and help him with their equipment and weapons.

The security guard's adrenaline was pumping as he ran before Michael beaming, because everything was going off so well for them so far. By the time the attackers reached the loading area of the building. Lizzie was standing alongside Valentine and she was grinning at them.

Number One nodded and then asked her. "How did it go down there for you Lizzie?"

"Great, we killed all three security guards in the Center, and Three and Four are waiting for the other security guards to show up for work, so they can take them out as well. Lavarack intercepted the guards coming to assist Ray with our supposed delivery, and killed them two." All the while she spoke to Michael, she kept staring at the rat guard helping them. She was looking for any kind of reaction from him over the death of his fellow workers. When none came, she rolled her eyes and looked forward to killing this back stabbing jackal all the more.

"Where's Five at, Lizzie? I don't want anything to happen to him. We need him most of all of us for this heist. He has the important work for this thing. Without him we can't get in the damn safes." Number One asked the others as he looked for the man they branded Number Five.

"Five's in the truck checking his equipment, One. I was lead to believe we had other backup, in case Five was unable to crack the safes, or he was injured during the attack on the building."

"Right, one of Twenty Seven's men is a whiz with combinations to most safes, and he's with Twenty Seven. We'll use him as a last resort though. I want to get the job done. We disabled all the elevators, but the ones we'll use to get around in the place. I want everyone to round up the hostages we want, beginning with McKinney. Let's move, we have a lot to accomplish. Jurado, I want you and Jaureque, Twenty Seven's Ten and Eleven men, to get up to the lobby and take that area over for us. Settle down and take Command of the lobby, lockdown the security doors and put up signs the hotel is in the midst of a special clean up because of a recent water leak.

"Ask anyone trying to get inside the building to come back tomorrow. Stop anyone trying to get out and tell them the same thing, but tell them the busted pipe is outside the front door, and it's not safe to leave the building. We'll send down the ones we want outside when we get to them, stack them up in the lobby until I open the door so we can get rid of them. We have to keep things moving people." Number One keyed his radio and then barked. "Three, One. Talk to me."

"This is Three, what's up One?" Number Three reported in as he was ordered.

"Three. Have you been able to figure out the security console mess for us?"

"Easy One. This thing is a piece of cake, even my son could work it it's so easy."

"Fine, close down the security gates by the entrance doors to the damn Tower."

"Closing them down now Number One." Three reported to Michael with confidence.

The group of soon to be terrorists watched from the raised platform of the loading dock as the heavy steel gates slowly closed on the overhead doors as the leader offered to his group and the ones in the Security Center. "That's great Three, everything's working out real fine for us down here. I want the gates locking out the loading area from the rest of the building closed when we're done down here." Number One ordered his man to carry out these orders immediately.

"It's done Number One, as soon as you're done with unloading the vehicles, One."

He looked at the staring faces of his people and then he smirked at them as he offered. "We done it, we're in complete control of the entire building. We have three other security guards we still have to eliminate, so let's get it done. Everyone knows their hostages, once the guards are out of our way for us, get your targets under control. Remember people, anyone who gives you any grief, kill them and we'll use their names as live hostages then. Let's move it guys."

Lizzie got in his face, and using just her eyes and head movement, she made it known she was interested in the fate of the security guard helping them get in the building. Number One looked at Ray and then he replied to his fellow female partner. "We have the elevators we need working, and everyone's in the building. Ray has served us very well, and he should be well paid for his services. Lizzie, show our friend how you're going to reward him for the work he did for us."

The security guard nodded as he grinned back at Number One. Not knowing what was about to happen to him for the help he gave Michael and the rest of his group.

Lizzie sexually unbuttoned the last two buttons of her blouse as she informed the security guard. "I've been chosen to pay you especially for your services for this robbery." With her breasts out of her blouse, she lifted her arms and aimed her pistol right at Ray's face.

The guard's smile instantly left his face as he stared at the pistol, he turned to Number One and pleaded. "What this? I did everything you asked of me and more. If it wasn't for me, you guys wouldn't even know about the diamonds. It's because of me you guys are going to be rich. You can't kill me! I helped you. You can't kill me! I... you need me. I'll take less for my shar..."

She grew bored with the guard's begging and she fired one round at the sniveling man, striking Ray in the forehead. His body pitched back until it came to a tumbling rest before Michael.

Number One tapped the twitching body with the end of his foot as Number Two mumbled at the female. "Wow that was cold blooded. Lizzie, you must have really hated that poor bastard."

"I hated the bastard's miserable face. If he betrayed his own people then he would think nothing of sticking it to us as well, Number One." She offered to the leader of the group.

"Lizzie, you killed the sonofabitch, so you have to get his body out of the way of Twenty Seven's people, before he bitches if they have to work around it." He grumbled at the only female member as he headed for the elevator packed with Alexander's equipment and weapons.

She cursed him under her breath as she struggled, dragging the guard's limp body to a off side room in the loading area of the Tower, and she roughly shove it inside the room and then she rushed back to Number One's side, while he waited in the elevator for her. He checked his list of names for the hostages he wanted, and what floors they were on, so he knew where his hostages were in the building. He hit the buttons of each floor he wanted the elevator to stop at.

The large commercial elevator rose slowly and as the huge cab stopped at each floor, one terrorist got off on each floor, and headed right for the apartment and hostage he was responsible for. Sixteen hostages were being searched for inside the Trump International Tower and Hotel. The men were going to be kept, the children were going to be let go, and the wives kept if their husband was killed, or they gave them any trouble during their capture.

The hostages Michael was responsible for, were staying on the twenty first and second floors of the Trump Tower. Lizzie's hostages were on the next two floors up. The leader of the group got out of the elevator cab next, and he walked down the long hallway. Finding the door he was looking for, he knocked on it and then he waited for a response from inside.

"Yeah? Who the hell's out there?" A gruff voice from inside the apartment called out.

"Room service sir." Number One replied as he prepared to fire through the door.

"You must be mistaken young man. I didn't order any damn room service." McKinney replied as he opened the door, only to find himself staring into the barrel of an automatic pistol.

"You didn't order a gun, McKinney? I could have sworn they said you did." He smirked as he shoved the older man back inside his apartment. Seeing the gun McKinney raised his hands and offered no resistance to the invader pushing him in his apartment with the barrel of the weapon.

"Where's your wife at old man?" Number One demanded from the much older man.

"What do you mean sonny?" McKinney asked as he allowed himself to be handcuffed.

"Where's your fucking wife at wiseguy! Don't screw around with me, or you're not going to live long enough to enjoy your little head game! I don't have the time to waste on this kind of bullshit from you, McKinney." He roared while striking the old man on the side of his head with the butt of his pistol. The blow staggered McKinney, but he did not go down from the blow.

McKinney rubbed the side of his head where he was hit then looked at his hands and noticed the trace of blood from the wound the blow opened and he said to the man with the weapon. "I don't want to die, I'm sorry, I didn't understand your question, that's all sonny. She's off visiting her sister in Jersey who just had a baby. She won't be back for a week. Don't tell me that's what this is all about? What the hell are you after my wife for? You're not going to kill are you? She's a good woman who wouldn't harm anyone, or hurt a bug. Why do you want her for, mister?"

"Why, do you think she deserves to die McKinney?" Number One replied as he opened the handcuffs, and then he yanked his hands down and locked them behind his back, after realizing his mistake of cuffing his hands together in the front of his body.

"No she never did anything worth being killed for to anyone, young man."

"Good then relax McKinney. We're not after your wife or you. We're here to do something, and if you do as I tell you. There's a good possibility you'll live long enough to see that new kid your wife's visiting in Jersey, McKinney." He growled as he shoved the old man down to the floor, using a second set of cuffs he chained McKinney to the oven door in the kitchen area.

"I assure you, you'll have no problems with me sonny. My cash is in the top drawer of my dresser, along with my watch and some other crap my wife brought me, young man."

"If that's true, you'll surely live through this mess McKinney. I have to leave you for a few moments, but I'll be back to you as quickly as I can return. Fuck with me and you'll never see your wife or this new kid. If you fuck around with me, I'll toss you out of the damn window, and then you'll end up as a blood splat on the damn sidewalks of New York City, McKinney."

Number One patted the old man on the shoulder, and then he was on his feet and checked out the rest of the apartment, to make sure no one else was hiding in the room. He left and ran for the staircase leading up to the next floor. He held his MP-5 at his side as he rushed up the stairs two at a time. Looking up as he ran, he suddenly noticed a shadow staring down at him. He stopped running in time to see a police officer looking down at him. He slid his weapon to behind his back, and then he smiled up at the cop as he took the remaining steps slowly.

"You're in quite a hurry there aren't you young fella? Where are you heading young man?" The older officer smirked while his hand rested threateningly on his side arm.

"Yes sir, I have an urgent message for Mr. Carroll who's in Suite Star Two, sir. The elevators are out of service for the moment, and I was forced to leg it up here from the front desk."

"Whew, you must be in fine shape to be able to run up all them steps to this floor, young man. I trust you have a photo ID on your person, sonny. You do know you're not supposed to come near this floor except for an emergency, son." The officer seemed like he lowered his guard a might, and was trusting Michael as he removed his hand from his weapon and relaxed.

"Yes sir I have my hotel ID with me someplace, Officer." Number One winced at calling the Tower a hotel as he started up the remaining steps as he made like he was looking for his ID.

The officer held out his hand with a grin as he waited for his ID.

When the leader felt he was near enough to the cop, he suddenly whirled his silenced weapon around his body and then he pointed it right at the stunned officer. The smile left his lips as he went in action. The officer went for his pistol with surprising speed as Number One fired at him. He went down in a heap, hit three times in the chest and was dead before he hit the floor.

He jumped the last two steps up, and skillfully checked the cop's body out, he was dead. He hesitated, trying to figure out why a cop was stationed in the stairway on this floor. He moved a little closer to the door and looked in the small window. He saw a second man standing in the hall, and it was obvious he was guarding an apartment. When the man in the hall saw Number One's face through the window, he instantly assumed the stance of a soldier. He had a pistol locked in his hands in a blur and aimed it at his door. The guy also looked like he was speaking in his hand to someone else who must have been working with this one.

He keyed his radio and yelled. "Hey Lizzie, I need your help on the twenty second floor. Someone's guarding a room, and he's armed and looking to blow me away. Looks like he's got some friends, he's talking in a radio around his wrist. You have to enter the floor from the north side while I keep this one busy. Something's up, and I'm sorry we killed Ray. He would know what's going on up here. I think he fucked us by not telling us someone important was in the building. Uh oh, my friend just got some extra company. You better get Two to help you out."

"We're on our way, One." Lizzie offered as she called Valentine to help her. They joined forces and headed for the north staircase, they made their way to the twenty second floor.

He hovered by the window cut into the heavy fire door while waiting for help to arrive on the other side of the floor. He ducked down when one of the men spotted him, and he aimed his pistol at his image in the reinforced glass panel and fired twice at him. The rounds shattered the small wire reinforced window. He ducked behind the concrete wall out of breath as he mumbled in an excited voice. "Shit, shit, shit. Who the hell are these two fucking guys for Christ sake, and why the hell are they fucking with me?" He was scared at being shot at as his body shook, and he leaned up against the wall. The coldness of the concrete wall felt good, actually reviving him.

Both Lizzie and Richard heard the gun fire and they increased their pace. She was the first one to enter the floor from the north side. She quickly worked her way to the south staircase using the doors to the other apartment and service closets as cover. As she turned the corner of the hallway, she immediately spotted the two men aiming their weapons at the other stairway. She signaled Richard who came up behind her, and he crossed to the other side of the hallway until they had a clear shot at the two men from their backs. When he was ready, he nodded and they singled out their targets. She held her breath as she aimed her weapon at the back of the agent guarding one of the doors. She fired twice at the same instant Richard did, and both agents went forward as the bullets tore into their bodies, both dead before they hit the ground.

Michael was on his feet the instant he heard the gun fire go off from his people from the other side of the hall, they did not have silenced weapons. He looked though the shattered reinforced window as Lizzie and Richard closed in on the strangers now lying on their faces in the hall. He rushed out the staircase and looked at Lizzie who was busy digging through her target's pockets.

"Who the hell are these two fucking guys and what the hell were these two guarding, Lizzie?" Number One roared at her as she quickly checked the body for their identification papers.

She found the man's wallet and she flipped it open, she stared at the Special Agent's ID, and gold shield and then announced to her leader. "His name's Joe Disbrow, and he's a Lieutenant, and he works for the President's personal security staff, Number One."

He turned to the pair of thick, heavy red oak and highly carved and polished doors, and then he mumbled in disbelief. "You don't think he's really in the fucking room do you?"

"I seriously doubt that Michael." She offered and then she added. "I think if he was in there, this whole floor would be crawling with a ton of cops and special agents by now, Number One."

"Who do you think is in there?" Number One asked as he stared at the pair of heavy oak doors.

"You got me, but we might as well find out who's in there." She offered as she moved a little closer to the set of heavy doors, and then she knocked on one of them.

Sweeney, lying on top of the stunned Vice President after he forced her to the floor the instant the agents inside the apartment heard the gun fire go off in the hallway, called out. "Yeah!"

"You better open this damn door if you know what's good for you, or we're blow it open, and anyone inside is going to die when we do it, mister. Your VIP isn't going to make it through this mess if you don't open this door right this moment. I assure you Agent, we're coming through the damn door one way or the other. So you better be smart about it and open it nice and easy."

Agent Sweeney tried his best to move Mary out of the way of the line of fire, but there was no place safe for her to go. Cathy moved close to them, her pistol locked in her hands and her knuckles turning white from the pressure she had on the grip of her weapon.

"What do you want to do about this fucking shit, Sweeney? Your call." Cathy demanded.

"We have to get Mary the hell out of here before these assholes come through the damn door on us. How long do you think the doors will keep them out of the damn apartment?"

The scared to death Vice President went to say something, but Sweeney placed his hand over her mouth so he could hear Cathy's response. "That depends on what they hit the doors with, Edward. They're a set of double doors, and that's makes them very weak in the center and easily breached. But they're also thick and heavy to boot, Sweeney. But I don't think the doors will keep them out of the apartment for very long. What about the damn knockout gas?"

The special agent looked over his shoulder to the other agent behind him and he responded. "I'm ready Sweeney. Give me the word and we're all going to sleep for a couple of hours, sir."

The Vice President pulled Sweeney's hand away from her mouth and then she snapped at him angrily. "It's too damn tight in here to get involved in a gun battle with these people, Sweeney. I want you to put up your guns and let whoever's in the hallway into the apartment."

Sweeney stared at Mary in stunned disbelief and growled at her. "That's bullshit Ma'am!"

"That order wasn't open to discussion by you or anyone else, Mister. I gave you an order, and I expect you to carry it out, mister. Call out to them, or I'm going to do it for you and tell them we're opening the door for them. I'll not have anyone dying on my account inside this apartment. Do I make my wishes perfectly clear to you, Agent." Ms. Hirshfield hissed at the stunned agent.

Sweeney looked at Cathy who shook her head. Then he turned to the agent manning the radio and he demanded from him. "Did you get anything out yet? We need some fucking help here!"

"Yes sir, I'm in contact with CIA headquarters in Washington as we speak, Ed."

"You better tell them what's going on in here, and what we're up against, and the Vice President wants us to give up to the attackers. I have no choice but to follow her orders. I don't want her life placed in any more danger than it's in. It's too damn close in here to get involved in a sustained shoot out with these guys. I'll stall them for as long as possibly before allowing them inside the apartment. I heard automatic weapons fire, but these jerks sound like Americans. You better figure the outside Agents are down and out of it. Tell them in Washington to get some fucking help to us fast, or we're going to be history in here!" Sweeney roared at the other agent.

Sweeney then turned back to Mary and questioned her. "Are you absolutely positive you want us to give up to them, Ma'am? We could hold out long enough for help to arrive, Ma'am."

"And what if you don't hold them off until help arrives for us, Edward?"

"Then we're dead Ma'am." Sweeney replied in a flat, dead pan tone.

"Exactly, then we're all dead and I'll not stand for that option, mister. Give up Sweeney, I don't want any bloodshed in this damn apartment. Did you hear what I just told you to do mister?" The Vice President turned to Cathy and repeated her words. "Give up Cathy. Please."

The Vice President's bodyguard let out her breath in a disgusted sigh, and then she rolled over on her back and hiked her skirt up and slid a small 32 automatic pistol she always carried in her pocketbook, in her panties and then dropped her dress down again. Then she picked up her 9 mm Colt pistol and got ready to defend the Vice President's life again.

"I said to give up Edward, Cathy, and if you don't do as I ordered. I'll do it for you two!" The Vice President warned her two bodyguards as she glared at both of them.

As if to take the question out of the agent's hands, Lizzie pounded on the oak double wide doors with her machine gun stock again. The door did not open so twenty five rounds tore into the hard, finely carved wood doors, sending splinters and lead flying, making everyone duck in the room. Some items in the room were shattered as the rounds found and smashed into them.

Sweeney pulled the Vice President back down to the floor, and he covered her body with his again. Cathy added her weight on top of the Vice President, to the point where Mary was having some serious trouble trying to breathe properly as she struggled underneath the both of them.

"How soon before any help can arrive over here, dammit!" Sweeney suddenly bellowed to anyone listening to him, while he was looking for an answer from someone in the apartment.

The agent manning the long range radio called out to Sweeney. "No one knows for certain Sweeney, they're trying to locate CIA Director Raincloud, but it seems no one knows where he might be. The guy I'm talking with is giving me the run around here. Don't count on any help arriving until after the fact, Sweeney. You better do something and you better do it real soon."

"Didn't you tell the jerk the Vice President's life is on the line here? Jesus, what's wrong with them people?" Sweeney roared as he looked over his shoulder at the agent speaking to him.

"Sure did, and he's alerting CIA New York, but he doesn't know how fast anyone will get over to the Tower. This guy seems like he's a new guy afraid to take a dump without someone holding his damn hand, Ed." The shook up agent reported to Sweeney as he continued to talk to the guy.

"Okay people, what do you want to do? Call out your ideas, I need some fucking input."

The agents standing behind Sweeney growled in a confidant tone at him. "Fight!"

Sweeney looked at Cathy and she nodded in agreement with what the other two agents just offered and then Sweeney growled to the other agents. "Then we fight the bastards."

Ms. Hirshfield grabbed his wrist and complained at Sweeney. "Didn't you just hear what the fucking I said to you! I told you to give up to the bastards, mister. If you don't do as I tell you, I'm going to stand up so you can't fire at the people in the hallway. Then I'm going to open the doors, Sweeney." The Vice President glared at the agent as she waited for him to do as ordered.

Chapter Seventeen

ROOM 2012, INSIDE THE TRUMP INTERNATIONAL
TOWER AND HOTEL

Lieutenant Robert Walker and Sergeant Dorothy Ramirez were so involved make loving to each other, they did not hear the first rounds of weapon's fire. The TV helping to drown out the short burst from the weapon, when the cop was killed on the Presidential room floor. When Lizzie and Richard killed the two agents, Walker thought he heard something, but he credited it to the TV and continued making love to his lady. But when Lizzie emptied her clip in the oak doors of the Vice President's room. There was no mistaking the sound, or the soldier's reaction.

The Lieutenant jumped off the bed, landing on the floor on his shoulder and rearend, and he rolled over to a defensive position, ready to defend himself and his lady against any harm. He heard a noise and looked to his left and noticed Sergeant Ramirez was at his side, and she was ready to go with him. Without thinking, his hand searched for his weapon which was not there.

"What was that shit? The last thing I knew, I went to bed in New York fucking City. Now I find myself smack fucking dab in the middle of another god damn war zone for crap sake." The Lieutenant complained to his upset girlfriend as he quickly checked on her condition.

Sergeant Dorothy Ramirez noticed he was hunting for his weapon and she reminded him. "That's no good Robert, we have no weapons for this mess. Sounds like someone just opened up on someone, maybe it's the cops or Agents doing all the shooting outside the room, Bobby."

"In a pig's fucking ass it's a stinking police or Agent response. If they were cops doing the fucking shooting, you woulda heard a shitload of bullshitting before they opened up on someone. I think someone's trying to rob the lousy dump. Remember the training we had back at Lejeune. I wish I had my damn weapons. I'd straighten things out in a damn hurry it up, little sister."

"What are we going to do about it, Bobby?" the Sergeant asked while keeping her eye on the front door, fearing someone was going to come busting through it any second and attack them.

"Beat's the fuck outta my stinking ass what the fuck I'm gonna do about this stinking shit. I want you to follow me and stay real low to the damn floor until I figure this shit out some for us. We gotta get us some god damn weapons to work with, if we're to stand any kinda fucking chance against the flaming assholes doing all the fricking shooting round here, baby."

Before moving out, Lieutenant Walker flipped over an end table and then he ripped off a pair of legs. He tossed one to Ramirez and ordered her. "Keep your eye on the fucking door. If anyone comes through it, crown him good with the damn table leg and then take his stinking weapon. We hafta find out what the hell's going on inside this dump before we fucking react against it."

Sergeant Ramirez took the table leg and then watched her soldier move low and fast along the floor as she called out to him. "Err... don't you think we should get something on first, Robert. I don't think anyone's going to be too afraid of a naked crazy man wielding a table leg, Walker."

"Not until we get better armed then we'll dress." He snapped back at her as he slid forward on his belly toward the kitchen area. All he knew was someone was using an automatic weapon and he was unarmed, and he needed a weapon in a hurry if he was going to survive this one.

Sergeant Ramirez followed him along the floor, she knew they needed better weapons to defend themselves with, or they were going to end up like sitting ducks to whatever was happening inside the Trump Tower.

When he was alongside the kitchen, he leaped to his feet and made a dash to the kitchen. He pulled a drawer open and fished around until he located the largest knife in the drawer. He pulled it out, examining it for a second and when he was satisfied, he pitched it to the Sergeant who was still lying on the floor behind him checking the front door to the room as he ordered her to do.

Once she was better armed, she felt a lot better about herself and their situation, as she pitched the table leg aside, and then she got up on one knee and prepared to defend their position. Lieutenant Walker also felt a little better about his situation, and he cautiously stood and the he looked for a second weapon to arm himself with. He found a heavy butcher's knife in the drawer and took it to defend himself with. Once he had the blade in hand, he smiled at Ramirez, proud he was ready to work. He kept the table leg in his other hand as a backup weapon in case it was needed, adding to his satisfaction.

Sergeant Ramirez took her eyes off the door and looked at Walker and the knife in his hand held at the ready. The table leg was in the other hand and she laughed at the sight she was looking at. She could not get used to seeing him so well tanned on the upper and lower parts of his body, and so white in his crotch area.

He knew what she was giggling about and he snapped at her. "Fuck you, you got fricking white spots too you know, sister."

"Nowhere near as bad as yours are, Bobby. What do you think is going on out there?"

"No fucking idea. But something heavy's going down inside this stinking dump. Automatic weapons fire means only one thing to my ass, fucking terrorists must be trying to hit the dump." The concerned Lieutenant grumbled hotly as he moved a little closer to Ramirez, his military mind formulating a defense against whatever was going down in the Trump Tower. Just as he reached her side, the automatic weapons fire returned in all its anger.

FLOOR TWENTY TWO, THE TRUMP INTERNATIONAL HOTEL AND TOWER

The leader of the group ran out of patience waiting for the splintered doors to be opened from inside the apartment for him. He slammed a clip in the 9 mm Heckler & Koch machine gun, and then he opened fire after he removed the silencer from the weapon. A second wave of twenty five rounds slammed into the heavy oak doors. The thickness of the doors stopped many of the rounds from getting through the door, but some of them penetrated the wood and they create an extremely dangerous situation inside the once plush suite, and to the Vice President's life.

Again, Agent Sweeney pulled Ms. Hirshfield's head down, and Cathy covered any part of Mary's body not covered by Sweeney's larger frame. When the firing stopped, the fuming Vice President wiggled out from under the two agent's bodies and then she hissed at them nastily. "God dammit Sweeney! I told you to give up to them sonofabitches, and I'm ordering you to do it again. If you don't stop this foolishness, I'm going to stand up and put a stop to it myself, mister." The angry Vice President looked into the determined green eyes of her bodyguard, and then she added. "Do it before someone loses his life in here, Sweeney."

Special Agent Sweeney's head noticeably sagged as he let out his breath in a disgusted sigh and his strength quickly drained from his body. He knew they did not have any other choice but to give up to whoever was shooting at them from outside the apartment. If they were to wait until the terrorists went nuts out in the hallway and blew apart the doors before releasing the gas. So much fresh air would get into the apartment, it would dilute the gas, rendering it to a state that would only make the intruders slightly groggy. He looked back at Mary and then asked her. "Are you quite certain about this request of yours, Ma'am? We can always use the damn gas. Possibly hold them off until help finally arrives for us. At least we'll keep you safe, Ma'am."

"At what cost Sweeney? Your lives? Mine? No, I'm quite satisfied you have done everything in your power to try and keep me safe during this situation, Edward. You have done your job perfectly, but it's too late for any heroics here. Besides Sweeney, what happens if some of the terrorists remain out in the hallway after you use the gas? All they have to do is wait until the gas disperses, and then they can come walking in here and take us prisoners. No Sweeney, I'd much rather know what's going on about me, than find myself waking up in an hour, trying to figure out what they might have done to me, or what was going on around me. Sweeney, it's far safer if we give up to them. I'm certain once the idiots find out I'm the Vice President of the United States, they're going to wet their pants and run like the cowards they are."

"Okay Ma'am, if you're positive about this, you're running the show for us Ma'am. I'll do as you ordered, but you might as well know. I completely disagree with your decision to give up to these people, Ma'am. I say we fight them off until hel..."

"I understand how you feel Sweeney, Edward. You have my utmost respect and admiration to be willing to die for my sake. But this is the United States, and no one would be foolish enough to dare harm the Vice President in her own country, no matter who we're dealing with out in the hallway. There wouldn't be a place small enough on the face of the earth for them to hide in if they did. No Edward, I don't want anyone dying for my safety. Enough! Give up, please. I'm begging you to do as I say. Don't die on my account Edward." The Vice President looked deeply into Sweeney's eyes, begging for the agents to give up before anyone else died.

Sweeney put a disgusted look on as he shook his head and called out. "Hey, you guys in the hall, don't shoot! We give up, there are women in the apartment, so don't fire anymore huh?"

Number One smiled, knowing he was about to find out who was inside the apartment, and who was going to end up as his ace in the hole. He called back in a threatening tone to the man speaking at him, proud he was going to take whoever was in the room as hostage, no matter who that person was. "Inside, I'll hold my fire, but only until I count to ten. If the doors aren't open by then, everyone inside the room will die. You hear me in there? I don't want any tricks from your side.

We know who you are, and how you react. Screw with us, and I assure you that you'll all end up dead in there. Your time's running as of this moment people, you have until the count of ten to open the damn doors for me, starting right now. One! Two!"

Sweeney jumped to his feet and then he rushed for the set of damaged double doors.

"Three!" Number One called from the hall in a commanding voice as he stared at the doors.

Edward flipped the broken lock up, and then tugged on the all but destroyed doors with all his might. The heavy oak doors were too badly chopped up, and too much debris was lying about on the floor, to allow the doors to swing freely open no matter how hard he pulled on one thick door.

"Four." He called out loudly, adding to the stress on Sweeney's shoulders.

The doors would not move even though Sweeney pulled harder, actually using his foot on the destroyed mess for some added help. Nothing the agent tried, worked for him.

"Five." Number One called out louder as he continued to stare at the set of heavy doors.

Pulling harder on the doors while kicking the stalled doors, Sweeney cursed. Finally, the door gave way and began to swing. The door was so heavy when it started moving, it would not stop, sweeping the debris from the floor. Sweeney then came face to face with Michael and Lizzie standing out in the hallway. He aimed his weapon right at the agent's face as sneered nastily.

"Six! Put your hands over your head and drop your weapon. Then get on your knees and you might live through this." Number One moved the weapon and then he trained it right on the center of Sweeney's chest as he glared at the disheveled looking young man.

The Vice President saw what was happening and was scared the man with the gun was going to kill Sweeney just for the hell of it, and she went to rise while calling out to him. "No! Don't!"

The two agents positioned behind the Vice President, mistook her sudden movements and thought the gunman was going to kill her. Their years of training instantly took over their reactions, and they made a move with their weapons, trying to get a bead on the gunman standing in front of Agent Sweeney, and aiming his weapon right at him. The two agents were going to fire, even if they took Sweeney out in the process of killing the two terrorists standing out in the hallway, and protecting the Vice President's life at the same time for her.

Lizzie kept her eyes glued on the remaining people still inside the apartment. The sudden movement by the two agents instantly caught her eye, and she went right in action against them. She saw what they were intending to do and she fired first at them, killing both agents before they even had a chance to fire on Michael or herself. She watched as her bullets chopped down both agents as if they were nothing to her.

Vice President Hirshfield spun around, and when she saw the two agents go flying back, and roll along the floor as the rounds continued to rip into their helpless bodies, she held up her hands and waved them frantically at the two terrorists shooting at the agents. Her stomach turning, she was getting sick from the sight of so much blood, she never saw anyone get slaughtered in cold blood like this. She called to everyone who could hear her words.

"Don't shoot, I'm the god damn Vice President of the United States. I have issued orders to my people not to resist you any further. I don't know who you people are or what you want, but I'm sure you're not going to slaughter unarmed and unresisting people in this room. I want to stand up, dammit." Mary announced in an extremely angry tone at everyone around her.

Lizzie leaned over to Michael and she whispered to him. "I thought I recognized her. She's not lying to us Number One. She is the Vice President of the United States. Oh my God, I'm going to allow her stand up and see what she has on her mind, One."

Michael nodded while keeping his eye trained on Agent Sweeney as Lizzie called out to the almost crying female Vice President. "You can stand up, but if anyone tries anything stupid against us, it'll cost you dearly, Ma'am." She warned as she leveled her weapon right at Ms. Hirshfield's chest, as Mary struggled to stand up. The shaking Vice

President glanced back at the two dead agents and almost threw up from the sight of them.

When the two other special agents made their move, Sweeney went to react, but he frozen in place when Michael raised his weapon and pointed it right at his face. He stood before him, just daring Agent Sweeney to try anything against him. Sweeney realized he was going to be forced to wait for a better time and place to react against the two terrorists.

The second Mary started to move Cathy wanted to act, but she knew if she drew her hidden weapon at the angle she was on. It would draw the terrorist's fire at the Vice President in their attempt to get at her. She understood it would be nothing short of fool hearted to try anything while she was in a kneeling position with her hands locked behind her head. Her training told her as long as they were alive, there was a chance they could live through this, or find the proper time to go into action against the terrorists. Instead of reacting, Cathy reached out and she tried to stop Mary from getting up by grabbing her hand. She was unable to grab Mary's flailing arms, and when Cathy saw the two agents crumble to the floor, anger instantly filled her body. Her mind screaming out for revenge, but the Vice President's presence stopped her from tasting it.

Vice President Hirshfield put her arms over her head, this action removed the steam from the remaining agents and her secretary and bodyguard trapped in the room with her.

When Lizzie noticed the agent on his knees relax, she relaxed as she pushed her way deeper into the room, and she roughly grabbed the Vice President by the back of her hair. She then shoved Mary towards an overturned chair, she flipped the chair back on its legs and then shoved the Vice President roughly in it, ordering Mary not to breathe as she went after Cathy. She pulled Cathy up to her feet by the hair, and she shook her head violently by it, disorienting the female bodyguard momentarily. Her hands were all over Cathy's body, looking for any hidden weapons on her person. Her weapon buried between her legs was so small, Lizzie completely missed it while she padded her down so rudely. Once she was satisfied the woman had no weapon on her person, she swung her towards a second chair right next to the Vice President by the hair.

Lizzie slammed Cathy's body in the seat so hard, it almost knocked the chair over in the process. She had to swing her legs apart to stop it from overturning. When she was seated, Lizzie smashed her across the face with the back of her hand, and then warned her while pointed her finger in her face. "Try something stupid bitch! Try something and see what happens to you."

Cathy lowered her eyes, looking contrite and scared to death before the angry woman.

"I didn't think so bitch. Just another tit sucking secretary." Lizzie hissed as she turned her attention to the surviving agent kneeing in the doorway. She pulled him back by the hair, not allowing Sweeney to get to his feet, she frisked him while he laid on the floor. She then dragged him across the floor to the third chair placed away from the other two, and she pushed him in it.

Agent Sweeney was acting like a wet rag, not offering any resistance whatsoever against what was happening to him. Lizzie handcuffed Cathy's hands behind her back, and then Number One tossed a second pair of handcuffs to her, and she secured Sweeney's arms behind his back. Then she fished around until she located her other set of handcuffs, and she dragged Cathy's chair over the highly polished floor towards Sweeney's chair with her still sitting in the chair, and used the second pair of cuffs to link the two agents hands together through the back of the chairs, she did not want to handcuff the Vice President, she just could not do it to the woman.

Michael pointed to Mary and then he asked Lizzie with concern lacing his tone of voice. "What do you want to do about her, we have to secure her as well, Six?"

"Jesus Number One, she's the Vice President of the United States. I'm not going to handcuff her, I just can't do that to her Number One. One, do you know what this means to us? We actually have the Vice President as a hostage, no one's going to dare dream of storming the Trump Tower while we have control of her. We did it, dammit, we did it Number One."

"You going to keep your eyes on the big time fucking bitch then for me, Number Six?" Number One grumbled as he looked at Mary, not allowing Lizzie's words to excite him any.

"Yes, I'll take care of her. She's my responsibility now, Number One." Lizzie replied to him.

"That's great Six, we don't need any other hostages taking up our time. I'm going to change our plans, we'll keep the hostages we have so far, and we're going to lock the others inside the building on their floors by means of the fire doors. I'm going to call downstairs and order Three to secure the fire doors on all floors except for the floors we want access to. Floors Twenty Two, Twenty One, Twenty, Seventeen and Fifteen. Seventeen and Fifteen are where Sawler and the Stackpoole's apartments are. That'll give us eight hostages not counting the damn Vice President, and the other two we already have, Lizzie." Number One relaxed his stance.

"What about the others we planned to take hostage? Their apartments are supposed to be packed with cash and valuables, One." Lizzie inquired from him as she waited his reply.

"We'll get the diamond dealers first and collect all the diamonds they have control of then we'll clean out McKinney and Carroll's place. If we don't feel we have enough crap to be satisfied by then, we'll start on the other apartments of the building we want to search. Once we're finished with them, we can then have Number Three open the floors with the other people we once planned to take hostage, and we'll rip apart their rooms. We can pick this building clean, floor by floor from top to bottom if we really want too, until we have enough loot to make us happy for the rest of our lives. Then we can take the Vice President along with the other hostages we have and get out of here, long before the police can put together a plan to get at us."

Lizzie did not ask about the fate of the two other people handcuffed together in the all but destroyed apartment the Vice President was using on her visit to New York. She knew they, along with the Vice President and other few hostages, were as good as dead.

The leader of the group went to call Suarez on the radio, but Lizzie stopped him by asking him another question. "Number One, what about the fire and police departments who'll respond to the building, the second you break the electronic lock on the fire doors?"

"Fuck them where they breathe, Six. As you just said, we have the Vice President hostage. All we have to do is keep the emergency responders locked out of the building, and let them know who we got control of. I assure you Number Six, the police and Agents will sit on their thumbs, until someone comes along and takes control of the situation for them. By that time, we should have everything we want, and concentrating on our escape. No one is going to push their way in the building, not while we're holding her as hostage. This is better than I had dare hoped for."

Lizzie moved away from the leader, turning her attention on Mary and the other two hostages, she aimed her weapon right at the Vice President's chest to keep the others under control.

Number One placed the call to Suarez, and ordered him to secure the fire doors on every floor of the Trump Tower, but the five floors he wanted left accessible to them. Without questions, Suarez flipped the fire door toggle switches from the Command Center. Not before warning the others working with him, so they did not end up trapped behind the heavy fireproof doors. The specially treated doors closed automatically, trapping the residents and renters on their floors until his people were ready to set them free, and then raid their apartments.

The instant the protective doors broke their electronic locks, a series of alarms automatically went off in the surrounding fire and police departments throughout midtown Manhattan. Fire doors were flung open on firehouses, and fire trucks screaming out of their resting places. Police cars joined the roaring lines of fire trucks, as they rushed for the Trump International Tower and Hotel at breakneck speeds, and a possible skyscraper fire inside the magnificent building.

ROOM 2012, THE TRUMP INTERNATIONAL TOWER AND HOTEL

Lieutenant Robert Walker, and Sergeant Dorothy Ramirez remained as quite as possible while kneeling on the floor as they prepared to attack anyone who stumbled through the door to their room. Sergeant Ramirez noticed the Lieutenant armed with the table leg still locked in hand, and she retrieved hers and took the same stance he had assumed. Road Kill gave a slight shiver and realized he was still naked, he turned to her and told her to go get something on while he secured the door. When she returned dressed in blue jeans and tee shirt, he told her to stand guard while he went and got dressed. He came out dressed also in blue jeans and tee shirt as well. Dressed, they both felt a little better about themselves as they stood pat and waited for what was coming their way next. The last gun fire they heard, was the short burst that killed the two agents inside the Vice President's apartment. Since then, everything was quiet and peaceful.

When she went to dress, she shut the TV and lights, their apartment was now bathed in silence and darkness, only their own heartbeats could be heard breaking the silence.

THE WHITE HOUSE, SEVERAL MINUTES BEFORE THE ATTACK ON
THE VICE PRESIDENT'S APARTMENT

The second the agent heard the weapon's fire in the hall, he placed a call to CIA-SOC (Special Operations Center) at CIA Headquarters in Langley Virginia. He alerted them as to what was taking place in the Trump Tower in New York City. The agent on desk duty, placed an emergency call out to CIA Director John Raincloud. But he was afraid to do anything more than alert the CIA office in New York City, being manned by a lone agent at this time of night. The agent there informed CIA Headquarters it would take the agents at least thirty five minutes to arrive at their stations from their homes in New Jersey and surrounding areas of the tri-states.

The phone rang three times at his home before the sleepy CIA Director answered it. All the agent on the phone said, was. "Director Raincloud Sir, we have a Red Flag Two situation sir."

Director Raincloud's eyes flew open as he sat upright in bed, and he flipped the table light on. The sleepiness instantly fled his body, and he was immediately ready for action as he replied. "Understood your message as received, I'm on my way over to Headquarters. Has the President been alerted to this present situation?" Director Raincloud knew what the Red Flag Two warning meant to him. It meant the Vice President was believed to be held hostage by unknown forces. Red Flag One was the alert given if the President of the United States was taken hostage.

"No, not at this time Director Raincloud Sir." The agent replied in a flat tone of voice.

"Okay, I'll handle that notification myself. You better alert everyone that needs to be involved in this damn mess. I want a total news blackout of the event, until we know for certain what the hell we're going up against, and who these possible terrorists might be and what they want from this situation. I trust we're talking about the Trump Tower in New York City over this alert?" The Director asked as he started to get up then he sat back down and finished his conversation.

"Correct as stated Director Raincloud Sir, the alarm was transmitted from radio Seven, Four, Six. Those numbers belong to the Special Agents protecting the Vice President, sir."

"I'm on my way. Hmmmm... I want the Chairman of the Joint Chiefs of Staff, General White in on this mess. No telling if we'll need the use of his special troops over this possible situation. Better make sure the FBI Director's alerted about this crap as well. Have him report to my office the moment he can get over here. We'll use it as HQ, (Head Quarters) until we know who's going to run the damn show for everyone else. Get going mister, I'm leaving for my office."

"Yes sir." The communication ended swiftly from the agent on the phone.

Director Raincloud got out of the bed and went over to his dresser. His wife asked as she rested her hand lightly on his shoulder. "Trouble dear?" as she watched her man move as if he had the weight of the world pressing down on them and he started to get dressed.

"Yes, but nothing you have to worry about my love. I have to place a call to the President, excuse me for a sec please, sweetheart." Director Raincloud then dialed the number, and it was immediately answered by Waters, the President's White House aide.

"Yes good evening Peter, this is Director Raincloud, son. I need to speak to the President, STAT young man." Director Raincloud said in a commanding tone to the aide.

"Good evening Director Raincloud Sir, and how are you tonight, sir? I'm sorry to inform you sir, but the President has turned in for the night, and he has issued strict orders not to be disturbed by anyone under any circumstances but for a national..." The aide's words were cut off in mid-sentence by excited Director Raincloud as he growled at the stunned aide.

"Well then, I want you to get a message to him, tell him we have a Red Flag Two situation on our hands, and inform him that I need to speak to him over this matter immediately, mister."

"A Red Flag Two, what's that alert about Director Raincloud Sir? I don't recognize that code warning sir." The aide asked, wanting information if he had to disturb his boss.

"You don't need to know anything more than what I just told you, mister. Give the man the damn message for Christ sake will you please. We don't have time to start a dancing game."

"Yes Sir Director Raincloud Sir, please hold the line while I inform the President of the Red Flag Two alert you just told me about, Director?" The aide replied regaining his composure.

"That's right, and you better get a hop, ship and a jump on it while you're at it, mister. This alert is that fucking important, mister." Director Raincloud demanded angrily.

Peter laid down the receiver and rushed up the marble staircase leading to the President's private sleeping quarters in the White House, and ever so lightly he tapped on the closed door.

"What? Who's that out there dammit? This better be important, disturbing me like this!" the President grumbled from the room as he fished around in the darkness, looking for the overhead light. Finding it he snapped it on and angrily stared at the door as he reached for his bathrobe.

"Mr. President Sir, I'm terribly sorry for disturbing you this late at night sir. But Director Raincloud is on the line and he has asked to speak to you STAT Mr. President Sir."

"Well what the hell does he want at this time of night, dammit? I told you I wasn't to be disturbed by anyone unless it was a national emergency tonight, Peter."

"He told me to inform you we have a Red Flag Two situation, sir. Whatever that means sir."

The President was out of bed in a flash, and he covered the distance from the door in three strides. He yanked the door open with such force, it actually scared Peter who took a step away from the door. The President screamed as he pulled him inside his bedroom. "Peter, some nut has just taken the Vice President hostage on us! What else did Director Raincloud say to you?"

"Nothing much more than that sir. He's still on the line waiting to speak with you sir."

The President's screaming at the young aide woke everyone else in the White House. A horde of special agents rushed in all directions half dressed with weapons drawn, looking for any signs of trouble in the building. Slamming doors and taking up defensive positions while locking down the entire building, not knowing what was happening. Until the special agents knew, they were going to follow standard orders and secure the entire building, and all occupants.

The President's wife was at his side helping him with his bathrobe, and offering to make him a cup of coffee. The President ignored her offer as he rushed for the phone in the LBJ library, he picked it up and barked. "Director Raincloud, what the hell's going on sir? I go to bed thinking Mary's safe and sound in New York City, and now I find out she's been taken hostage by some nuts. You better have some positive answers for me, or you'll be looking for a new job by tomorrow morning mister. Do you hear me for the love of God, Mr. Raincloud?" the upset President roared in the receiver so loud, it forced the director to move the phone from his ear.

"Yes Sir Mr. President Sir, I hear you loud and clear I assure you sir. I'm afraid the Trump International Tower and Hotel has come under attack by a group of unknown purps at this time, Mr. President Sir. We're still trying to ascertain what's happening in New Yor..."

"The Trump International Tower and Hotel under attack, by who Director Raincloud Sir? When did this shit take place on us, god dammit? Did they know the Vice President was visiting the Trump Tower and she must be caught up in this mess? Oh Christ, of course they knew or you wouldn't be giving me this damn Red Flag alarm warning sir. Do you know if the attackers are Arabs? They wouldn't dare hurt the Vice President of the United States. I want you and anyone you need, to get their asses over to the White House as fast as you can get here, sir. I'm not fucking around on this one Director, someone dared to take Mary hostage and that's bullshit, and I'll not stand for it for one god damn moment, do you hear me mister?

"Not for a god damn second will I allow this to take place, dammit Director Raincloud Sir. Get your people assembled and here by the time I hang up this fucking phone. I'll get the ones I'll need on their way from my side. I won't stand for this shit, no sir! Not for a miserable second will I stand for this shit to take place, mister. I'm about to teach someone some god damn manners in a fast hurry." The angry President slammed down the phone on the Director.

Peter moved over to the President's side and he tried a smile on the American Leader, but it was totally ignored as the President roared at the aide. "Pete, send out for police escorts to get Director Raincloud and the others I need here, PDQ, son. Then notify the National Security Director, and the Secretaries of Defense, State... Arr... you know who's on the need to know list, get them all here ten minutes ago. Make damn sure the FBI Director's coming also. I don't want any lip from anyone. If they give you grief, don't argue with them, back off and send the police to arrest anyone who balks, and have them dragged here in handcuffs if necessary. Get moving on this order." The President turned on his heels and went back in his bedroom to dress.

Director Raincloud ignored the President's angry mood as he checked his where book, and located General White. The Director quickly dialed the number written next to the powerful General's name, and he waited for the Chairman of the Joint Chiefs of Staff to answer the phone for him. It was answered by the sleepy sounding military officer.

"Yeah, General White here. What can I do for you sir?" the General offered in the phone. "John, Raincloud sir. General, we have a serious situation rapidly developing and you're ordered to report to the White House STAT, for a meeting with the President and his staf..."

"Are you fucking around with me or what Chief? Our boys just finished off Iran, and there's nothing else on the threat board that we're currently concerned about sir. Outside of the damn upcoming Libya crap, Director Raincloud Sir. But that's not to happen for some weeks yet. What else could have blown apart this quick on us, to get you so excited and the President sending for his troops tonight? I'm too fucking tired for one of your little head games, John. Have you been nipping on the firewater bucket again?" General White complained as he sat up in bed.

"General White Sir! This is no joke in the least sir, we have a Red Flag Two situation developing on us, and the President's angry as hell about it, and he calling for all his troops, General." The Director inform the Chairman of the Joint Chiefs of Staff over the phone.

General White bolted out of bed while holding the cordless phone locked in his hand, as he offered. "Someone has taken the fucking Vice President hostage, John? Where? When did this shit happen? I'm on my way for the White House, you have the FBI Director alerted, right?"

"Not as of this time General, but I'll get his ass moving as soon as I hang up with you, sir. He should be arriving at the White House at about the same time as us. You have a ride in sir?"

"Hold on a second John, someone pulled up outside. It's a police car with his lights flashing. That's going to really piss off the fucking neighbors a might, Director. I have my ride in, see you at the White House when you get there." General White hung up and dressed. He ran to the waiting squad car that took off the second he was inside the vehicle with its siren blaring.

Director Raincloud next dialed up the FBI Director, who was reported attending a special fund raising function in downtown Washington. It took a few seconds for him to reach the phone. After identifying himself to FBI Director, Director Raincloud added the words he was certain would make the FBI Director go nuts once he heard them said. "We have a Red Flag Two."

"Where? When did this happen Director Raincloud Sir?" The FBI Director demanded hotly.

"New York City, the President wants everyone at the White House A-SAP, Director. I'll see you there I'm certain sir." The CIA Director informed the lead FBI Agent.

"I'm on my way there now sir." The FBI Director announced into the phone calmly.

Director Raincloud then checked his important people list, and once he was satisfied with the ones he alerted, he dressed and picked up his suitcase and left home, with his wife escorting him to the door. The children were up and waited for their father to leave. The Director bolted from the house and rushed to his car, he got there at the same time a police squad car pulled up in front of his home. Director Raincloud waved the officer back in his car and pulled out behind him, allowing the police to clear his way for him. Traffic was light on Sunday night in Washington.

It took Director Raincloud seven minutes to reach the White House. General White and FBI Director Wilford Hedemann, were already waiting for him to arrive outside the President's mansion. Director Raincloud joined the others and together they entered the building. The three were greeted by a rather disheveled looking Presidential Aide Peter, who was a sight to see. The aide informed the three leaders the President was waiting for them in the Oval Office and warned them the President was not in a very good mood and he was pacing the office.

They fell in line behind the fast walking Peter as he led them down the corridor to the office.

Inside the Oval Office, the President was busy pacing in front of his antique desk, trying to control his rage while Marie Hernandez, the Secretary of State addressed him from her wheelchair. The President's hair was a mess as he half listened to his secretary. "Mr. President, Albert, we can't react to shadows until we find out what the terrorists, if they are terrorists, are up to, or what they might want in return for the freedom of the Vice President, sir. There's too many questions that needs answering, before we can possibly start formulating a solution on how to deal with whoever they are and get the Vice President out of this while she's still alive and..."

"Like what?" the President barked as he stopped pacing long enough to look at his favorite.

"Like, if the Vice President was the target of their attack and the only reason for their assault on the Trump Tower, Al. Are these people who took her hostage, Americans, and if so, can they be reasoned with sanely? You know, there's that possibility these terrorists, and I shall refer to them as such, until we know otherwise. Didn't even know the Vice President was in the building at the time of their attack. Besides, from the little we know about this present situation, we don't know for certain if the Vice President was taken prisoner by these terrorists..."

"Or if she's still alive for that matter, dammit. We don't know very much about this fucking mess as yet I guess, Maria." The President interrupted angrily.

"Yes, you're correct, if she's still alive Albert. I'm terribly sorry to say, just because we lost radio contact with the special agents assigned to her security, doesn't mean we have to assume the worst about this situation. For all we know, the Agent's radio could be merely suffering from a mechanical malfunction, or their own knock out gas sir."

"I guess you have asked a very good question there, and it seems we'll have to sit tight and wait for Director Raincloud to finally get here to get the answer to that question and then we... Ahhh... speak of the devil and he pops up his evil head. Director Raincloud Sir, I believe you know everyone here, so I won't waste any of my time with introducing you to them sir. I trust you heard what Maria was just saying to me, sir. Is she right with what she was saying Director? Could it be a simple radio malfunction that's stopping us from communicating with the Vice President, or the rest of any of her security staff, sir?"

Director Raincloud nodded politely to Maria, and then he replied to the American Leader's question. "With all due respect President Cole, I believe that's not the case in this situation, sir. From what we were able to pick up at headquarters. The Special Agent responsible for manning the radio at the time of the supposed attack, reported the apartment was being assaulted by person, or persons unknown with automatic weapons. Before we lost contact with the Agent who was stationed inside the Presidential Suite at the Trump Tower, sir. No number was attached to the perps (Perpetrators) involved in this possible action, Mr. President Sir."

"Dammit to hell! What the hell are you doing about this god damn situation then, Director Raincloud Sir?" the President growled hotly at the powerful CIA Commander.

"I'm doing all I can to solve this situation Mr. President, until I receive useful information on the situation at the Trump International Tower. I placed my people in New York, New Jersey, and Connecticut on full alert. But this is more of an FBI situation than a CIA one. Mr. President Sir, I'm not saying I don't want to be an active part of this damn thing sir. But I believe the Chain of Command prescribes FBI Director Hedemann, must be in charge of any actions taken against a possible terrorist situation taking place within the Continental United States, sir."

Chapter Eighteen

The fuming President ripped his eyes away from Director Raincloud's face, and then he aimed them right at the FBI Director, standing to Director Raincloud's left, as if they were weapons as he snarled at him. "Well Director Hedemann Sir, what do you have in store for these bastards holding my fucking Vice President their hostage? It better be damn good or else mister."

"Well Mr. President Sir, the second I was alerted to the Code Red Flag Two situation taking place up there in New York City, sir. I immediately notified and placed all our HRU teams on standby ready alert in the eastern seaboard region, and I have ordered them to report to New York on the double quick sir. Mr. President Sir I also have the new..." The FBI Director was cut off in mid-sentence by the angry President as he growled at him again.

"What's this HRU shit you just mentioned Director Hedemann Sir? Am I going to have trouble with you now? I broke General White of the habit of speaking in confusing numbers and letters to me. I don't want fucking letters aimed at me, if you have something represented in letters, you'll tell me what those letters stand for!" President Cole glared at the FBI Director.

The tall black man shifted his weight uneasily on his feet, because all the time he had known the President, he never saw him so riled up and angry as he was on this night as he responded to the American Leader. "I'm terribly sorry Mr. President Sir, the letters I just mentioned stand for Hostage Rescue Units, sir. They're highly trained professionals..."

"I don't know what this crap is about, but I intend to find out. General White, am I led to believe you're loaning some of your elite soldiers to the FBI? And if I'm correct then why the hell are you doing this instead of using your troops to get my Vice President free."

"No sir, these are not my people at all Director Hedemann's speaking of, Mr. President Sir." General White replied to the words the President just snapped at him.

"Then how come this is the first time I'm hearing anything about this so called FBI Hostage Rescue Unit? Is it something new that has been added in our ongoing fight against terrorism? When was this special Unit of FBI Agents sanctioned for being an active Unit?"

"Mr. President Sir, my Paramilitary Hostage Rescue Units have been in existence for a number of years now, sir. Ever since the terrorists hit the bank in Los Angeles back in early 90' was when we created this specialized Units sir. Well as I was saying Mr. President Sir, these FBI soldiers are a group of highly trained people who..."

"How come you keep referring to these Agents as soldiers, sir?" the President interrupted.

"Mr. President Sir, that's because my Agents go through much of the same type of specialized training schools as does many of our highly trained special unit soldiers do. These Agents who are part of the FBI, continue their special training every day, and they run countless different hostage situations covering every possible scenario we believe could face the United States, or any of our interests abroad, Mr. President Sir."

"I don't know anything about this hostage training stuff, Director Hedemann. Do your Agents go through the same type of training as does General White's Rapid Response Forces do?" the President asked while leaning towards the General's soldiers, rather than those of the FBI Agents. At least he knew what those soldiers were capable of accomplishing when ordered.

"I'm not certain to the answer to that question Mr. President Sir. I'm not very familiar with the General's training courses, sir." Director Hedemann offered as he cast a quick glance at the General, to see if he was going to offer anything about his training of his elite soldiers.

The President turned to General White and asked him. "General White Sir, would you mind giving the Director a quick rundown of your command structure, and all of what your specialized soldiers have at their disposal, and some of their training crap as well, sir."

General White moved a step away from the FBI Director, so he could see him a little better as he offered. "Director Hedemann Sir, as you're well aware of I'm certain sir. I'm in Command of the USJSOC, which was formed to take command of the MNRRF that stands for the Multi National Rapid Response Force. These specialized soldiers operate under the COD, or Cover Of Deniability orders sir. So our actions can be easily denied by the President of knowing we were set out on a mission, if we screw up on the missions we go out on, sir. The defense department has classified my troops as quiet professionals. The Liberals have branded my soldiers a pack of blood thirsty mercenaries, developed by the past Republican President, as a means to forward the ideals of the Right Wing Agenda..." The Chairman of the Joint Chiefs of Staff was just getting going when he was cut off by the President as he snapped at the General.

"Now is not the time for any grand standing, just keep to the facts of the matter, General White Sir." The instantly upset President moaned, because he knew he was going to use the General's soldiers for this situation, all he had to do was convince the FBI Director that the General's troops were much more suited for this type of action, even here in the States.

"Sorry Mr. President Sir, I'll keep it as brief as possible. Mr. Director Hedemann, my MNRR Force breaks down in this manner, sir. We have developed a three task forces, consisting of seventy to eighty highly trained and experienced men and women soldiers in each task force. Each task force is made up of between four to six separate squads, breaking the troops down further to a four to seven personnel specialized assault teams. These teams or units as we like to refer to them, are separated into independent working teams of certain specialties covering just about anything from close quarter combat, to snipers and control weapons fire, along with long distance marksmen and snipers. Any one of my troops are marksmen in their own right, easily converted to sniper duties, and all of them remembering the SSSK law." General White turned and looked at the President and offered before the American Leader asked him to explain.

"Pardon me Mr. President Sir, the SSSK represents the Single Shot, Single Kill theory. These men and women soldiers from my squads, these warriors, can enter a room packed with hostages, and have the ability to recognize, and single out their targets, and take them out without putting the hostage's lives in much danger. The Smash and Bang crews covers mainly the stun weapons, they can pick locks, enter terrorist controlled rooms, aircraft, ships, subways, just about anything that carries, houses, or otherwise transports human beings around the world. These specialized and highly trained soldiers can free the bulk of the hostages trapped therein, while taking out the terrorist subjects with extreme malice at the same time sir.

"We also have scuba divers for shore insurgencies, low altitude controlled parachutists and hang gliding experts, mountain ranging experts, helicopter pilots, heavy weapons experts, and explosive planting and disarming teams, covering anything that can explode, burn, or freeze, Mr. President, Director Hedemann Sir. Some of these elite soldiers are structural engineers, and they know the insides of most buildings like the back of their hand, sir."

The Chairman of the Joint Chiefs of Staff took a quick breath before continuing with his explanation of his troop's combat abilities. "Many of my people can read and understand blueprints of buildings or structures they're handed, and they can locate working passageways, possible escape routes, and other assault angles, to get to, or at their assigned target. These elite soldiers can hide weapons on their bodies a dog couldn't locate. They're well schooled in the art of dealing with terrorists, paying them, negotiating with them, and or killing them. All my people are masters at anything they're assigned to accomplish out in the field.

"Any one of these soldiers can stand in for any other member who finds him or herself wounded or killed, or otherwise out of the loop, and they can carry out the disabled soldier's part of the mission to a successful conclusion. Every one of my people are experts when it comes to dealing with any insurgencies, counter insurgencies, coup d'etats, terrorism, and short and long intensity conflicts, and also economic and psychological warfare, with surgical operations, and low intensity conflicts and terrorism situations. We have studied and know our OPFORS, Opposition Forces, and the soldiers know what they are, and aren't capable of carrying out. Each squad carries the firepower on their backs to go up against any forces, no matter how well armed or trained the opposition forces might be. We'll never allow to happen to us, what happened to the Los Angeles Police Department dealing with the bank robbers in early 97' sir."

General White shifted his weight and then went on with his explanation to the FBI Director. "My squads come equipped with their in place command structure and Commanders. So there's never any waiting for the brains to arrive on scene for the soldiers. In this case, the Commanders are Colonel Bruce Leadbetter, and his Seconds in Command is Lieutenant Colonels Joseph Salsiccia, Robert Wilson, and a third to be named when that Officer becomes available. Each squad is further lead by a Captain or Major, and has a Senior Sergeant Major as their Second in Command. Right now the squads are being lead by Lieutenants, until we can get that situation righted. The main man in my Unit is the best in his field, Lieutenant Robert Walker. I think after this meeting concludes, he'll be lifted to the rank of Major at the best, or Captain at least..."

"Now is not the time to try and blackmail me into offering one of your Officers a buck up the damn ladder, General White Sir! I wise to your many ways of getting something out of me, sir."

The Chairman of the Joint Chiefs of Staff totally ignored the President's remark as he went on. "My forces are backed by other specialized Units and services of the Armed Forces, that aren't available to your Units, Director Hedemann Sir. We have the backing of the Navy SEAL Team Six recently converted to the NSDG or the Naval Special Development Group based in Norfolk, Virginia. With their main headquarters stationed in Coronado, San Diego, with the United States First Special Forces Operations, Detachment Delta Task Force out of Fort Bragg. These forces are also stationed on the supposedly closed Fort Campbell in Kentucky, along with the special Commando outfit Rangers of Fort Benning, Georgia. We do little if anything with the Tenth Special Forces stationed at Fort Devens, Mass, their Units are the Green Berets, sir."

Even though the General was ordered by the President to inform Director Hedemann on his command structure, the General was aiming his explanation mainly at the President as he added. "Mr. President Sir, we use these highly motivated forces to draw from, when we have a need of a few more people for a specific operation. We're also being backed by the Twentieth Special Operations Squadron based at Hurlbustfield Air Force Base, in Florida. We further employ the 23rd Air Force, along with the 2nd and 3rd Air Division Military Airlift Command, which covers 1st Special Operations Wing and 160th Aviation Regiment for long range transport and support and supplies transportation for our troops. These special Divisions maintain the MC-130E Combat Talon Units, with the MC-130H Talon II cargo transport aircrafts, AC-130H Specter gunships, along with the HH-53 H Pave Low, and MH-60G Pave Hawk helicopters, and MH-53 H/J Super Jolly Green Giant, and the Apache fast attack helicopter units, Director Hedemann."

General White took another quick breath for himself, and then he went on explaining more of his special command structure. "Unlike your outstanding FBI Agents, there's no reproach with any of my specialized troops, Director. When they go in, all talking's over with, and people are going to die plain and simple, sir. Hopefully, those deaths will only occur mainly on the other side. No one is going to check my troops, not Congress, the ACLU or any damn bleeding hearts, and no one will get away with complaining my soldiers went into a certain situation heavy handed, or the elite soldiers were guilty of overreacting, or were sent out hunting bear.

"That's what my people are trained for, to overreact, to get in there and get the job done flat out Mr. President Sir, while saving as many hostages lives as possible. My soldiers operate under the orders to save hostage lives or DIP, before you ask me Mr. President Sir that means Die In Place. Of course, Director Hedemann, everyone knows not all hostages can be saved in any one terrorist operation. Some as always happens in situations like the one we're facing here, will have to pick up the tab for the more important hostages such as the Vice President in this case.

"Our motto's very simple and right to the point Director Hedemann, Mr. President 'Overkill to win at all costs'. My soldiers are not trained to lose, good or otherwise and they are highly trained to save who we want saved, and the hell with the rest in any military operation or response. Now I know this might sound a little harsh to the civilized world and to everyone in this office, and it could go against your grain as well, Director, Mr. President Sir. But we have to be realistic in any possible military operation, or response we're involved in where hostages' lives are on the front of the dime. There's rarely the possibility of getting all the hostages out of most of these types of situations safely, during a terrorist or military action, sir.

"Usually, we operate at a fifty percent bases, lose one hostage for every one we can save, and that's why we pick and chose the hostages to be saved in any situation, and we count ourselves lucky at our success rate of saving those hostage's lives. When my troops go into action, the enemy's time has ran out on them sir. If you want the Vice President out of the Trump Tower alive? Then Mr. President, Director Hedemann, I suggest you get my people back here to the States, and let them lose inside the Trump Tower and allow them to do their act against whoever has invaded the Trump Tower. My people will get the Vice President out of this situation, alive. Lieutenant Walker's people are intensely patriotic, and are trained to win in every situation they're engaged in." General White turned his attention away from the FBI Director, and he looked in the President's eyes as if he was demanding the President to send his people in.

Director Hedemann reared on his heels; feeling threatened by the General's revelations he stated to the other members of the meeting, and he shook his head while complaining at the General. "Now you hold on there for a minute, General White. No, no, that's completely out of the question General. First off General White, do you think my people aren't as every bit as patriotic as your soldiers are, sir? Each of my Hostage Rescue Team members, will do what's necessary to get the bulk of any hostages out of any situation they're assigned to, alive might I add to you, General White Sir. My Agents will die trying to accomplish their orders, without thought or hesitation. Besides General, everyone here understands the FBI Hostage Rescue Unit has complete jurisdiction over any possible terrorist attacks or hostage situations occurring in the bounders of the United States borders concerning any Federal personnel, General White Sir.

"I warn you in no uncertain terms General White Sir. I have no intention whatsoever of capitulating my jurisdiction over these such matters under any circumstances to you and your troops, or to anyone else who might be involved in this god damn hostage situation involving the Vice President of the United States and her staff and my Agents, sir. I swear to the good Lord above that I'll fight you tooth and nail on this one, sir. I went through too much organizing these Hostage Rescue Units. Begging for the funding from Congress for their training, bending knee and bowing head to any and all who could possibly help me.

"Eating their shit just to get the god damn funding I needed, and to allow my Agents to be forced to the sidelines on this situation when I feel my Special Units will be needed the most by our government. No way in hell will I step aside for you or anyone else, General White Sir. This mission's far too important to accept anything but absolute total control over this situation involving the Vice President with my specialized HRU's, General White Sir."

The FBI Director angrily placed his hands on his hips, and then he glared angrily at General White for daring to suggest that his specialized troops be given command of this obvious civilian situation taking place right in the heart of the United States, and in the greatest city in the world. The Director was so upset over the fact he might love command of an action his agents should be in control over. The fuming FBI Director continued to stare at General White, before allowing himself to finally relax a little, and waited for the General to reply to his angry words.

THE TRUMP INTERNATIONAL HOTEL AND TOWER.
NEW YORK CITY.
10:10 P.M. SUNDAY, NOVEMBER 15th, 1998

Michael had his people send one hundred and fifty residents, visitors, and renters down to the huge lobby area of the building. Lizzie had the civilians assembled while waiting for him to allow them to leave the building. Outside the Trump Tower, the scene was sheer mayhem at best. The streets of the City usually empty at this time of the night, were teeming with tens of police cars and fire trucks, all rapidly converging on the Trump International Hotel and Tower.

When the first alarm came in to Manhattan's main fire station, the Chief checked the location of the structure reporting the alarm. When he discovered it was the Trump Tower, he did not wait to find out what was happening, he immediately raised the warning up to a three alarm structure status fire. He was not willing to be caught short handed if there was an active blaze at the skyscraper. The moment the Fire Chief raised the alarm status, he ran for his car and he turned on the lights and siren then he lead the way for his trailing fire trucks.

As the deeply concerned Fire Chief plowed through the streets of midtown Manhattan at breakneck speed, he heard a number of sirens converging on the Trump Tower from different areas of the city, and he felt a chill run down his back. Fearing one of his trucks might collide with a second responding vehicle. He took his receiver and screamed in it. "Chief Addams Sir, I want you people to be god damn careful out there, sir. We have other emergency vehicles responding to this present emergency, I don't need you people ramming into one another."

The elderly Fire Chief spun his wheel and his car shot onto Amsterdam Avenue from 68th Street, his car was being trailed by three fire engines, two pumper trucks, and ladder truck used for skyscraper structure fires. The scream of sirens was deafening, but the Chief refused to look in his rearview mirror as he stomped on the gas pedal, urging his speeding car forward.

Once Michael was certain the Vice President and her entourage were secured, he decided to do something with the crowd rapidly assembling in the lobby. Twice, Jurado called on the radio, complaining there were way too many people for him to control in one place. He rushed for the slow moving service elevator, and he waited to be delivered to the first floor. Leaving Lizzie and Valentine in charge of the Vice President and the others with her until his return. When the doors slid opened, and he was surprised by the size of the mob of civilians huddled around in the lobby. He had to fight his way through the horde of people, women crying, children confused, and men looking to pick a fight with anyone. Only his weapon kept the horde from attacking him.

Number One pushed his way through the center of the unruly horde of civilians, working his way towards the lobby desk. Once there, he jumped on the counter and fired his weapon at the ceiling, making everyone duck and cover their ears. Shouts and crying quickly filled the lobby. He fired his weapon again as he bellowed at the scared civilians. "Shut up! I want fucking silence! I'm not going to allow any of you people out of this damn building, until I have absolute quiet, so you can hear what I have to say to you people. Shut up before I shoot people." Michael raised the weapon over his head, but this time he did not fire. It was more than enough of a threat to wave his weapon in the air, to silence nearly everyone trapped in the lobby area.

Hearing the sobs and crying from the confused civilians, he began speaking. "Listen close and you'll live through this nightmare. I want everyone to line up in an orderly fashion, and head for the door in the corner of the lobby." The leader of the group pointed towards the door with the barrel of his weapon, and then he continued to speak. "I'm putting everyone on their best honor. You screw with me, and you'll die that simply, any heroes will cost the lot of you your damn lives. Everyone is going to be released and once you people are outside this damn building, get out of the area as quickly as you can. There's going to be plenty of gun fire when the police arrive, so the sooner you're safely away from here, the better off you people will be.

"Don't allow the police or anyone else out there try and stop you from running away from here for any reason, until you're well away from this god damn building. Remember you people, when you're outside, anything can happen so be quick about yourself, and leave the area as quickly as you can move and let no one stop you from leaving the area."

Number One nodded towards the three men he stolen from Alexander's group, and two of them immediately fired short bursts of rounds into the suspended ceiling, and then he ordered the screaming horde of civilians to line up where they were just ordered to assemble. He then jumped down from the lobby desk, and he walked over to the emergency door like he was God, as the civilians quickly moved out of his way for of this man with the weapon in his hands.

The tightly packed civilian horde made a path for lead terrorist to get through, fearing his wrath and their deaths. The leader of the terrorists reached the door, and he looked at the roughly forming lines of shoving and scared civilians behind him, and snapped at them. "Remember you people, the second you're outside the building I want you people to get far out of the area as fast as you can run. If I see anyone hanging around outside this building, I'll shoot you plain and simple. Don't fuck with me, I don't care if I shoot male or female so get the hell away from here quick." Number One flipped the emergency lever down, and he flung the door open. He unslung his weapon and aimed it at the bulk of civilians, causing everyone to step away from him.

A good number of the civilians fell to the floor, others stepped on the downed people rather than help them back to their feet. It was what the leader wanted all along, what he predicted. He wanted pure mayhem and mass confusion outside the building when the fire trucks and police arrived at the building. He looked outside and saw the first sign of flashing lights reflecting off the building across the street from the Tower. It was time to get the civilians in motion.

The Fire Chief turned his car onto 60th Street, and gunned the engine. He could now see the Trump Tower filling the windshield, reaching towards the heavens in front of him. From where he was on the street of midtown, everything looked normal at and around the Tower, and for the first time since receiving the alarm. He allowed himself to take a relaxing breath for himself.

He waited until he saw the first emergency vehicle coming down the street. He mistaken the Fire Chief's car for a police vehicle, as he announced to the scared group of civilians. "Okay, everyone who wants to live, better move out of here fast, now! Get going!" He moved away from the front door and at first, he tried to control the wave of civilians trying to get out of the Tower. But too many of the people hit the door at the same time, causing a bottleneck at the doors.

He stared as unconcerned men stepped on women, and children left their parents to get out of the building. It was terrible sight to witness and he had enough fired at the ceiling, stopping everyone dead in their tracks. He slung his weapon, and then grabbed some of the people by the arms and started to actually fling them out of the way until he was standing right by the door. He shoved other people in a half assed controlled manner, and began to push them through the door. The flow of humans leaving the building was going well. He kept a watch on the civilians outside, and smiled when he noticed they ran helter-skelter in all directions away from the Tower. The civilians ran in the streets making traffic stop, and causing emergency vehicles to swerve in order to avoid the other skidding vehicles, and wildly charging civilians.

When the elderly Fire Chief noticed the civilians pouring out of the Tower like they were scared to death. He went to his radio and bellowed into it. "All Units responding to the Trump Tower alarm. I see no flames or smoke, but I'm certain we have an active fire inside the building somewhere. I have a horde of civilians rushing around in the streets like a horde of crazy people. Be advised, keep your eyes open for the fleeing civilians. Chief Addams to Central Command."

"Central Command, go ahead Chief Addams. Whaddaya got going on out there sir?"

"Judging by the number of crazy ass civilians fleeing the god damn building. I'd say we have an active fire at the Trump Tower. Let's push the panic button here and go to a Seven Alarm Status immediately sir. Under the circumstances, I'd rather have too much firefighting equipment on the damn scene, rather than not enough responders and emergency equipment on site. What's the situation with our police shadows? I could sure use their help over here to try and get some kind of control over these damn civilians running all over the place, dammit."

"Going to Fire Status Alert Seven, Chief. The police are responding with their emergency squad, and should be arriving on scene momentarily, if not already on scene, sir. I'll notify Air Rescue to standby and prepare for possible airlift from the roof of the Tower if needed, sir."

"Roger that, better get more of our people down here. I have many panicking civilians dropping like flies out here. It must be a helluva mess inside the damn Tower sir. I hate these damn sky high buildings for Pete's sake. I hope the fire's low, and not way up there... Jesus..."

The Fire Chief have to let go the radio, and then he had to swerve hard to his right to miss a running and scared woman who just darted out right in front of his speeding car without looking where she was running, while carrying a young child in her arms at the same time. Her face was a mask of fear and terror, as she nearly ran over the top of his car.

"Chief! Chief Addams Sir! This is Command Center come back Chief! What's happening out there sir? Are you okay? I lost communication with you Chief Addams Sir. Come back Chief. Over!" The dispatcher bellowed in his radio, scared over what might have just happened to make Chief Addams break off his communications. The dispatcher flipped two switches on his console, and in three other firehouse's alarms went off as the overhead doors automatically opened, and the stop lights outside the firehouse for blocks around flashed to stop approaching traffic near the firehouses. A traffic light in front of the station went to a constant red.

Stopping all traffic on the block of the firehouse in all directions, so the emergency trucks could get out of the building without waiting, or fearing an accident with other vehicles. Firemen and women woke, and quickly dressed and then they slid down poles, and manned the lifesaving machines. In less than a heartbeat, the first fire trucks responded to the new alarm calls. On board computers inside the fire trucks, flashed the location of the suspected fire on their display boards. When the Commanders realized where the fire was located, they reacted with haste.

"Come back Chief Addams!" the dispatch bellowed again in his radio.

"I'm here, I'm here, I'm dropping down to a crawl speed, dammit. Christ, I almost smashed right into a dopey broad who ran right out in front of my car with her eyes up her damn ass, and she had a young child with her for Christ sake. It scared the hell out of me, shit. There are so many god damn civilians running around out here, I'm ordering all emergency responders to approach the Trump Tower at a slower speed. It looks like everyone in New York's running around like a pack of crazy ass nuts around here. It's got to be a bad one in there Command."

"You want to go to a ten alarm at this point Chief?" the dispatcher asked the old Chief.

For a brief second, the Fire Chief considered going to a ten alarm status for the compromised building. Going to a ten would place all fire stations as far away as Brooklyn, Bronx, Long Island, and even Staten Island on alert status. In case they had to respond to cover any fire calls that come in Manhattan, because he could no longer cover with his firefighting equipment. While every piece of his firefighting equipment on the Island was involved in the Tower emergency. Thinking about it for a few moment, the Fire chief replied.

"Naw, we'll hold off on that alarm status until we know for certain what the hell we're facing inside the damn Tower. It might be good to alert our outer stations, just in case we have to go to a ten status on this one. Christ, I have civilians running all over the damn place out here. What a god damn mess this one is already. Dispatch, put a rush on the damn police cars will ya, I can sure use their help with getting a handle on some of these damn people running around here. They're pouring out of the building like a swarm of bees for the love of God. I can just about get through them myself. If they get any thicker, I'm not going to be able to get my damn equipment anywhere near the building. Get a chopper in the air, and have him give me a bird's eye report on what the hell they can see around the Tower. I still can't see any sign of flames or smoke."

"Can do Chief Addams Sir, I was notified the police just dispatched one of their helicopters to the scene, sir. It should be arriving over your position within the next five minutes to seven or so, Chief." The operator reported to the concerned sounding Fire Chief.

"That'll do me a hell of a load of good, sonny. I'll be at the damn building by that time."

"Understood last as reported Chief Addams Sir, and I'll report same to the Command Center at the police department, Commander. Chief Addams Sir, Air Rescue's just been alerted, and the helicopter's waiting to respond to the incident, in case they're needed on scene, sir."

The Fire Chief shook his head as he dodged a few more people wildly darting out in the street, disregarding the flood of responding emergency vehicles.

INSIDE THE TRUMP INTERNATIONAL TOWER AND HOTEL

Michael smiled as he watched the fleeing civilians stop the fire car from reaching the Tower. He wanted this, in fact he was actually relying on this to happen. He wanted all the mayhem he could possibly create outside the Tower. He was going to keep releasing the civilians still trapped in the lobby area of the building, to make sure the mayhem continued outside. He knew he could count on the male animal to do what was expected of them, acting like he thought they would when they were released. The leader of the group moved to the other side of the door, giving the civilians more room to get out of the Trump Tower. He motioned them through the door using his gun. Behind him, one of Alexander's men fired at the civilians, giving a new charge to their fears. The new hordes bolted through the doors like wild people in fear for their lives.

The old Fire Chief was just yards away from the Trump Tower, and for a brief second he could swear he heard automatic weapons fire going down inside the Tower. But this thought was lost as he slammed his car in park, and then he tried to get out of the vehicle to access the condition of the fire in the building. The Chief was trapped in his car by the countless horde of civilians rushing past his vehicle like crazy people. He grabbed his radio and barked into it angrily. "Where the hell are those damn cops at for the love of God? I can't even get out of my fucking vehicle to assess the fire condition. I got civilians running all over the place, dammit."

"Chief Addams Sir, this is Command Center South sir. I just spoke with the Police Tactical Sergeant in the field, he's stating he's having the same problems with his people trying to make it through the fleeing masses running around on the streets around the Trump Tower. The Tactical Sergeant reported he should be arriving at the building at any second now, Chief."

"Get him on my Tact Unit Three, I want to speak to him. This way we can help each other in this mess by setting up a command and communication and control center to handle any injured."

"Will do, hold on for a second Chief hang on sir. Chief, I have a call coming in sir. Christ Chief, it's from the FBI sir. What the hell's going on over there? What do they want with us?"

"Find out what the hell they want and then get back to me Command Center. Out."

THE WHITE HOUSE, WASHINGTON DC
10:15 HOURS EST

Even before FBI Director Hedemann could continue his gripe against the Chairman of the Joint Chiefs of Staff, he was interrupted by Peter Waters, the Presidential aide who rushed into the Oval Office while carrying a slip of paper in his hands. The upset President held up his hand, silencing the Director for a moment and then the President waved Peter over to his side, and he took the memo from him. His eyes flashed with anger, and he handed the memo over to General White, as he began to explain the contents of the memo to the FBI Director, along with the other members of the meeting.

General White read the paper then handed it to CIA Director Raincloud as he listened to the President. "Director Hedemann, we just received a communiqué from one of your people in the field, who responded to the Tower situation, sir. He's reporting masses of civilians pouring out of the Tower, creating many problems for the responding emergency equipment and their personnel. It seems someone has sent out a fire alarm on the Trump Tower. That action has caused the local fire and police departments to become involved in this situation, even before your people could get in position on the terrorists. I'm afraid your people lost the element of surprise on this one."

Before the FBI Director could reply to the President's words, the General spoke up.

"I think it was someone from inside the building who sent out the alarm, Mr. President Sir."

"Zat so? Why do you believe that General?" the President asked, confused by his words. He felt the terrorists would want to keep themselves on low key for as long as they could. Before being forced to deal with the police or firefighters, and the rest of the emergency first responders.

"Mr. President Sir, you have to think like a terrorists. If you were one of them, what would you want to have happening outside the building. Especially as the police and emergency responding personnel started to show up at the damn scene, sir?" General White asked the President.

"Hmmm... I'd want to keep a low profile for as long as possible, before being forced to deal with police or special services that'd surely be arriving on the scene, General White Sir."

"Exactly Mr. President Sir, that's the civilized way to look at this situation, sir. But if you were a real bastard, and I believe these birds are just that. You'd want to create as many problems as humanly possible for the responding police and firefighters and any other emergency responders. Thus, dumping hostages you don't want out of the Tower, so they're no longer a problem to you, but they instantly become a serious problem to the police taking up positions outside the structure, sir. The police now have to deal with the crazy acting civilians, even before they can set up a working Command Center to start dealing with the terrorists, Mr. President Sir."

"I see what you're driving at, those sonofabitches, I want their asses hanging from my door, General White Sir. I want them bad, placing civilian lives on the line like this just to cover their damn asses from our police." The President hissed with anger emanating from his tone.

"With all due respect Mr. President Sir, I don't think for one second they're done just yet, sir. I do believe the terrorists are dumping only certain hostages out of the Tower, sir. It's not only freeing up the men they'll probably need to secure the rest of the hostages they intend to hang on to. But I also believe whoever the hell's running this god damn sideshow, is smart enough to hold some of the hostages in reserve, and only when they're about to make their escape from the damn Tower. Will the rats use the rest of the hostages as their cover, by forcing them out into the streets before them. I know if I was one of the bastards, I'd do the same damn thing, Mr. President Sir. I think if some of my people were able to work their way into the bui…"

"Excuse me Mr. President Sir, we seem to be getting a little ahead of ourselves for a second time here, sir." Director Hedemann replied as he moved forward and stared at the President.

"How's that Director Hedemann Sir? We should all be working for a common cause here, sir." President Cole snapped, taking his eyes from General White, and then resting them on FBI Director Hedemann's face as he moved a little forward in his chair.

"With all due respect Mr. President, we seem to be taking it for granted that General White's Special Forces soldiers, will be the Units responding to this situation, sir. I already pointed out to everyone at this meeting that his forces do not have jurisdiction in this manner. My Hostage Rescue Unit and mine alone, is the only force that has jurisdiction when it comes to dealing with a terrorist situation committed on United States soil, sir. Any terrorist, or hostage situations in the States pertaining to Federal personnel will be handled by my units, period Mr. President. As I stated, I'm not planning to relinquish that jurisdiction to any forces, military or otherwise sir."

"I beg your pardon Director Hedemann?" the President snapped at the Lead FBI Agent as he rose from his chair, and rested his hands on his desk. The President resented Hedemann telling him what he was going to allow. The fuming American Leader puffed up his chest and warned him in no uncertain words. "Director Hedemann Sir, I'm not the least bit concerned over whose responsibility it is to handle any situation anywhere on the face of God's green earth. It's not up to you to decide anything. You better realize your position in this conversation. It's my Vice President held hostage by these terrorists." The President pointed to his chest then continued.

"So that makes it my decision alone on how I plan to handle this present situation, sir. It's I who am going to pick to place in Command of that decision, Director. I'm not taking anything from you or any of your outstanding Agents. Believe me Director Hedemann Sir, I completely understand how hard your people have trained for this type of situation, Director. If I think the General's people are going to be a better Unit to pit against the terrorists. Then that's who'll do the operation, Director Hedemann Sir. That's plain and simple, and I don't want any crying about my decision, if I choose to go in that direction, sir. We're Americans, we have fellow Americans in trouble, and that means we work together to draw this situation to a conclusion sir."

The President then turned his attention back to General White and said to his military officer. "General White Sir, you just stated your operation would get at least half the hostages out of the building safely sir. Is that not correct as stated General White Sir?"

"Yes Sir Mr. President Sir, that's what I stated sir." The General replied confidently.

"You can't give me a little better percentage of surviving hostages in your assumption than that, sir?" the President asked the powerful General.

"Not if I want to be perfectly honest with you that is, Mr. President Sir. Fifty percent is the least of the hostages my people will get out of any terrorist situation safely, sir."

"That's a fair enough reply General White Sir. That's what I want from everyone, total honesty. Director Hedemann Sir, can you offer me any better numbers, if your people go in, in instead of General White's troops?" the President wanted to hear the Director's reply.

Director Hedemann's face distorted into a mask of confusion, as he was forced to admit to the American Leader. "No I can't Mr. President Sir, if you want me to be as honest as the General is, sir. I can't come up with any better numbers for you, sir. Of course Mr. President Sir, I'm quite certain of the outcome of the situation. There'll always be more survivors than we plan for sir."

The President looked at the General who nodded in agreement with the FBI Director.

"That makes me feel better about this situation. Director Hedemann, I'm afraid I'm going to insult you. I think I'd have General White's soldiers go against the bastards who attack the..."

Director Hedemann went to speak, but he was kept silent by the President who raised his hand and spoke over the Director's unspoken protest. "Believe me Director Hedemann Sir, I fully understand how you must feel about this decision. I have witnessed General White's people in action more times than I care to admit. I know what his soldiers are capable of accomplishing, and how they're going to act against this terrorist situation, sir. I'm terribly sorry to say Director Hedemann Sir, I have never saw your people in action, sir. Until today, I didn't even know your Hostage Rescue Unit's even existence. Please indulge me for a moment longer if you don't mind, Director. I want Mary, and I want her back alive. I know I'm hurting your feelings here, but I don't care. Feelings can be repaired, but a human life once gone, is gone forever sir." The worried President smiled at Hedemann and then turned his attention back to the General.

"General White! Do you think your people can get the job done? And don't promise what you can't deliver, General. I know how your military mind works, and if your people can't carry out this action safely for my Vice President's sake. I want to know so I can make other arrangements for this situation." President Cole stared at the powerful General while waiting for his reply.

"President Cole, my Special Forces personnel can accomplish anything I send them out on..."

The Secretary of State, Maria Hernandez moved her wheelchair a bit closer to the couch. She nodded to the President who replied while cutting the General's answer off in mid-stream. "Yes Maria, do you have something you want to add to this conversation please, Ma'am?"

"Yes Albert, I'd like to speak to the General for a moment if you don't mind sir."

"Not at all young lady, please, go ahead. He's all yours to ask any questions you have of him, Ma'am." The President smiled warmly at the terribly crippled female secretary.

Maria nodded to the military officer who smiled. "Err... General White Sir, correct me if I'm wrong, but aren't your special soldiers half way to Port Said in Egypt at this moment, sir? I know my body's betraying me, but I assure you sir, there's nothing wrong with my mind, leastwise, not I'm aware of. If I'm not mistaken, when we gave you permission to begin your attack on Iran, you committed all your forces to the operation. I don't remember my being informed you held any of your elite soldiers in reserve, General White Sir. Am I correct with my memory sir?"

General White cocked his head to the side and then he admitted reluctantly to the Secretary of State. "You have me dead to right with that one, Ma'am. All my specialized troops were committed to the operation accomplished in Iran, and at this moment they're nearing Port Said in Egypt, Ma'am. This is so they can begin their preparations for their upcoming operation in Libya, Ma'am. What's the point you're making here Ma'am? I don't see it I'm afraid Ma'am."

"My point being General, how long will it take you to get your people shipped back to the States, sir? You may consider the time element necessary to brief the troops and get them to New York, which we have to believe is nothing short of sheer madness now. You also have to equip the troops with weapons needed for them to carry out their rescue attempt of the Vice President. I see a lot of time and effort wasted by that decision if it's made in your favor, General White Sir."

"Hmmm... I see what you're driving at..." The General started to offer to the Secretary.

"Does the Secretary have a valid point there, General White Sir? I want to know how long it'll take for your troops to be prepared to make their first entry into the Trump Tower, General White Sir." President Cole growled at his military officer as he began to pace behind his desk for a second time, fearing what he might hear next from his military advisor.

"It's going to take me a few seconds to figure this time schedule out, Mr. President Sir." The deeply concerned Chairman of the Joint Chiefs of Staff offered to the President.

"A few seconds is way too long when we're dealing with my Vice President's life and her becoming a hostage, General White Sir!" the

President steamed as he pounded his fist down heavily on the desk in frustration, and then continued with his angry words. "I want to know how long you're going to need to get your damn people set position, General White Sir!"

"It's going to take me seven hours to get my troopers to the States, and another two so we can brief them on the situation. Maybe another hour or so to arm and get them set in position for..."

"Does that include the time your soldiers will need to secure their equipment they need for this operation in Egypt?" the Secretary of Defense asked, trying to put his nose in the conversation.

"No, I didn't take that time element into consideration in my estimate Secretary Levenhagen Sir. I'd have to add at least another hour or so needed to get my troops out to New York City! That's where I'd have them sent directly to over this matter, Secretary Levenhagen Sir."

"What type of transportation will you need to get your troops here in seven hours, General White Sir? I'm afraid I don't know of any aircraft that could make it here from Egypt in that short amount of time, sir. The only aircraft that can do it I believe, is the French made SST supersonic aircraft, General White Sir." Director Hedemann inquired, fighting hard to keep the smirk from crossing his face, knowing there was no way they could wait that long, before mounting an offensive against the terrorists in the Trump Tower. If they were forced to wait for nearly twelve hours before going in then it would more than likely be over by that time.

"That's exactly what I'm planning to commandeer for my troop's need over this matter, Director Hedemann Sir." The General snapped while displaying his obvious anger.

"Whattt? For the love of God, General White Sir. How the hell can you possibly plan to take over a civilian aircraft that doesn't even belong to us, sir?" the excited President cried, stunned at the nerve the military officer just displayed before him as he added. "How the hell do you plan to get your troops on board that plane, as well as their military equipment, General White Sir?"

"Mr. President Sir, I'm not really planning to haul all the troops' equipment back to the States, sir. I can have their backup equipment shipped up to New York, while my troops are in transit for this site. As far as getting the soldier on board the SST aircraft sir. I don't care if I have to stack them in the damn thing like cord wood one on top of the other, Mr. President Sir. I'll do whatever the hell I have to do in order to get them here in time, and my troops will endure anything I expect from them, without complaints if they know what's good for them."

The President nodded as he offered. "General White Sir, as much as I'd like to have your troops operating on this situation, I'm going to be forced to agree with Director Hedemann here on this one and go against you at this time sir. There's no way I'm going to wait for half a day, before I have something mounted against the terrorists holding my Vice President their fucking hostage during this situation, sir." The President turned to Director Hedemann and said.

"Okay Wilford, it looks like the balls in your court and you're getting your way. Only if you can prove to me beyond a shadow of a doubt, it'll be a better move to use your people for this rescue of my Vice President. Rather than waiting for General White's troops to pack their equipment, and get their asses to the States for the mission, Director. I'm waiting your reply."

"I think I can convince you if I get half a chance to explain about my people, Mr. Pres..."

"Don't gloat about it either Mr. Hedemann Sir. Get down to the bare facts and I don't want to hear any boasting from you either. Tell me how you're going to get your people inside the Trump Tower, and have the Agents free my Vice President." The President badgered the FBI Director, coming to a slow boil with his mounting temper he was trying so desperately to control.

"With all due respect Mr. President, when I was informed about what was taking place in New York. I placed my entire HRU teams in the Northeast sector of the country on ready alert. As of this moment, my Units are carrying out their orders to assemble their people at the old Brooklyn Navy Yard across the River from Manhattan. From this position Mr. President, my Hostage Units will be no more than fifteen minutes from the Trump Tower. I have the entire Unit assemb..."

"Exactly what type of transportation are you speaking about, that'd get your troops, excuse me Director Hedemann Sir, your Special Agents in position?" the National Security Director, Norman Griffin asked the FBI Director.

The FBI Director nodded to Secretary Griffin as he started to speak again. "Mr. Secretary, I have a pair of EH-60A Blackhawk troop transport helicopters stationed at the Brooklyn Navy Yard." The Director stopped speaking and checked his watch then added. "The helicopters are on loan from Camp Smith stationed in Peekskill, New York. Before I left my office, I spoke to the Commander of Camp Smith, and he assured me by the time I reached the White House, his helicopters would be waiting for my people to show up at the Navy Yard. He informed me he was going to place at my disposal, a pair of heavily armed AH-64 Apache fast attack helicopters armed for bear, just in case things get a out of hand, and we need the heavier firepower for assistance. My Special Agents are more than likely on board these helicopters as we speak, and are by now waiting orders to set them in motion." Director Hedemann took a quick breath.

When no further questions came from the other members attending the meeting, Director Hedemann continued with his words. "I have a number of marksmen on board these attack helicopters. They're more than capable of killing any terrorists hiding on the roof of the Trump Tower at the time of the insertion against the building takes place. Once my Agents have successfully secured the roof area of the building in question. They have orders to work their way deeper into the building, and down to where the hostages are being held inside the building. I'm quite certain, just as General White's soldiers are highly trained, my Agents are likewise highly trained and ready for anything that comes their way during any situation, sir.

"My Special Agents will enter the room and take out terrorists holding the hostages with orders to give the Vice President top priority. Once they get the Vice President away from the terrorists and secured and move her to the roof. The Vice President will then be placed in one of the helicopters, and she'll be taken out of harm's way. My Agents will then reenter the target, and work their way to the other hostages still being held in the Tower. I'm certain my Agents won't move as fast as General White's troops would during this situation, sir. But I feel my people might get more of the hostages out of the building alive, by moving in a slower and more precise manner during their second insertion into the Trump Tower, Mr. President..."

"Your teams plan to make two separate insertions into a compromised building, Mr. Hedemann? Don't you think the terrorists would be lying in wait for your Agents to return to attack them? I never heard of anything so foolish as to carrying out a double insertion against an armed terrorist held position with hostages involved in the situation." General White scoffed.

"What other choice do I have with this situation, General White Sir? I have to get the Vice President out of the line of fire first before we go after the damn terrorists General White, and I feel this action is the only way to accomplish this feat safely, sir." Director Hedemann pleaded to the staring military officer, feeling rather uncomfortable under his harsh glare.

"Director Hedemann Sir, I suggest splitting up your forces for the insertion. Have two of your Units remove the Vice President from the scene, while your other forces continue on with their assault against the terrorists inside the building. In this manner, your assault teams will keep the damn terrorists off balance, thus assuring the possibility of getting more of the hostages out of the damn building alive, Director Hedemann Sir." General White grouse, feeling a lot better he believed he was helping Hedemann's Agents pull off this operation. In his heart, he knew the Hostage Rescue Unit was in a better position to help the hostages, but he was damned if he was going to admit it before the President and the others attending the meeting.

"Hmmm... I see what you mean and I'll do just that, General White Sir. I agree with your remarks and I'll have my Agent's do as you have just suggested, sir. I thank you for that most useful bit of information, sir. Yes Sir General White Sir, that's what I'll have my Agents carry out during their assault of the building in question sir. Do you think two Agents will be enough to protect the Vice President's life, until I can get her the hell out of there in one piece, General White Sir?" Director Hedemann asked the military officer with concern on his voice.

"Two Agents should be enough to carry out that part of their operation once they have successfully freed the Vice President from the terrorist's control. I'd use two if this was my operation," The General offered as he nodded and then added to his words. "that way they can move faster getting the Vice President out of the god damn building. A small group of attackers might not draw as much attention as a larger group during the assault, Director Hedemann Sir."

"Err… excuse me General White, Director Hedemann Sir. So far, I haven't heard anything offered by either of you as to why the terrorists, or whoever the hell they are, or what we're calling these damn people, went after the Tower in the first place for. We heard nothing in the way of any demands from them, and try as I might I just can't come up with a logical reason for them to attack the Trump Tower. They can't carry the damn thing away with them for Christ sake. The damn jerks couldn't have known the Vice President was visiting the Tower, sir.

"Besides gentlemen, if the damn fools were going after one of the heads of our government, wouldn't it have been a far wiser idea for them to wait for the President to arrive in New York City before they attacked the damn building? Heaven knows, you made it well known that you're planning to arrive in New York City Thursday morning for the United Nation's meeting, Albert. If these people were after anyone from our government, I'd think they would've waited, and gone after you when you arrived in the City, Mr. President Sir." Maria offered, slightly confused by her own troubling thoughts as she said to the people in the Oval Office.

President Cole's eyes left Maria and shot to CIA Director Raincloud, as he bitched at him. "God dammit Director Raincloud Sir! How come this god damn subject wasn't breached with me before this time, mister? Someone should've floated their damn opinion by us by this time. Before the Secretary had brought up the subject to our attention. God dammit, I'm relying on you people to save my Vice President's life and get her away from these fucking terrorists."

Director Raincloud let out his breath in a rush as he spoke quickly to the extremely upset American Leader. "As of yet Mr. President Sir, I haven't given the reason for the attack on the Trump Tower, or the Vice President for that matter very much thought, sir. To be quite frank with you Mr. President Sir, I was more concerned with getting the Vice President out of this damn situation alive, more than worrying about what was the reason for…"

"I completely understand that and that was what you should've been doing all along ever since the start of this damn situation, Director Raincloud Sir. But the subject was brought up to us, and to be quite honest with you sir. I'm kind of a little curious as to what was behind these animals first attacking the god damn Trump Tower myself, sir. I, like the Secretary of State, believe that the Vice President wasn't the main target of these bastards when they first attacked the building, sir. I believe she was there, and if she is a hostage of these bastards, it was a bonus for the terrorists to get their hands on her, dammit."

"With all due respect Mr. President Sir, giving this subject a bit more of a thought, I could come up with one reason I believe for the asses to be attacking the building Sir. I happen to know General Electric's keeping a vast sum of money stored inside the Trump Tower. It's their Union's entire retirement funds. I know anyone trying to get in that safe, might as well spit in the damn wind for all the good it'll do them. I was informed the vault was designed to take a direct hit from a nuclear explosion, and still remain intact. As good an idea as it might seem, I don't believe the asses would be so stupid as to try and break into that safe, or it was the reason for their attack, sir. Other than that Mr. President, I can't come up with any reason for these asses to be inside the building, unless they know something I don't, Mr. President Sir."

"Don't you think it'd be a good idea for you to try and find out what the hell these damn nuts might be up to inside that damn building, Director Raincloud Sir? Wouldn't it be a much easier job for us to defend against them, if we knew exactly what the hell they were doing, and what they might be up and what was the real reason for their attack on the damn building sir? What the hell they wanted from the damn Trump Tower from the start of this damn thing sir?" the again upset President asked, pissed off no one asked the question before now.

"It'd surely be an ideal situation to have that information available for our use at this point, Mr. President Sir. I'm terribly sorry to say sir that most likely, we'll find out what the hell they were up to inside the damn building, after we have destroyed them and we successfully have taken one or two of the damn terrorists in alive, sir."

"Okay everyone, we're getting a little off of the mark here I'm afraid." President Cole complained, and then he turned away from Director Raincloud, and the American Leader then looked at Director Hedemann and said in a quick tone of voice at him. "Director Hedemann Sir, are you absolutely positive that your Hostage Rescue people will be able to get my Vice President the hell out of the god damn building alive, sir? Before you answer that question I just placed before you sir. Allow me to explain why I feel it's so vitally important to get her out of there alive, Director. Director Hedemann Sir, the only reason no one has yet ever dared to try and kidnap the President of the United States, and have the balls to hold him or her hostage before this time. Is mainly because everyone believes it's simply impossible to get anywhere near any sitting President to pull a kidnapping of him off successfully for themselves, sir.

"Sure, there has been a few attempts on a past President before this latest attack, and I'm pleased to announce, only a few of them have met with any success. But if these rotten bastards are able to pull off what they're fucking planning here, using my god damn Vice President as their bargaining chip in this situation. The mystique once surrounding any powerful world leader, will have been removed and it'll be fair game on any seated Presidents, Vice Presidents, Senators and Representatives alike, from here on in. No Head of State will ever be safe again, no matter where they live, or the security surrounding them if we don't get my Vice President out of this mess alive, and we destroy these nuts in the process, sir. This is why it's absolutely necessary that we get the Vice President out of that damn building, and out alive, dammit. I'm appalled I'm forced to say what I'm about to offer and not have it burn my mouth while coming out of it. But I must get my point across to you in all possible terms, sir.

"Director Hedemann Sir, if you're only able to get one of the damn hostages out of that god damn Tower alive, that hostage absolutely must be the Vice President of the United States at all costs to all else involved in this fucking nightmare, sir. I'm shocked to hear these words coming from my mouth like this. But I don't care what happens to anyone else who might be forced to be left behind, if you're forced to leave the building with only the Vice President secured by your hostage rescue teams, sir. Director Hedemann Sir, I must ask you again sir. Are your people certain they're going to be able to get the Vice President out of this mess alive, sir?"

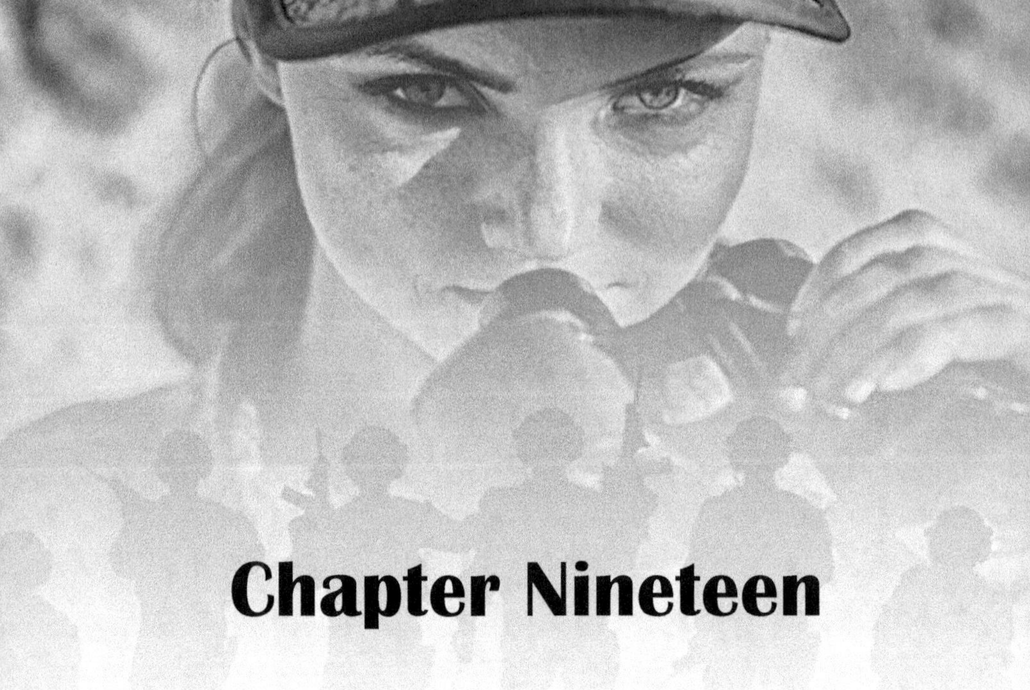

Chapter Nineteen

THE TRUMP INTERNATIONAL TOWER AND HOTEL,
NEW YORK CITY

As the elderly Fire Chief Addams slid his car to a stop near the Trump Tower's main entrance, he had to wait to hear why the FBI was suddenly interested in a fire in one of his buildings in New York. He held the radio as he stared at the masses of wildly acting civilians darting all around him and the area surrounding the Tower, without regard for themselves or any others trying to help them, or the traffic weaving in and out between the running civilians.

As he was about to leave his car, his radio suddenly burst into life on him. The young dispatcher was excited and he was actually yelling in his radio. "Chief, Chief Addams sir, it's all a farce sir, there's no fire inside the damn building, sir. The FBI just stated this mess is a hostage situation going down inside the Tower on us, Chief. They're ordering us to pull back our people well away from the building, the Feds want everyone out of the area so they can operate."

"That's a crock of hockey pucks if I have ever heard one said to me, mister. If this mess is a hostage situation then how come I have hundreds of civilians running all over the damn place like they're running away from a damn fire in the building? Can you answer me that sonny? No you can't, and neither can they. I received an alarm and it went from a three to a seven status. I have a mess of people running for their lives surrounding this damn building. You get your ass back on the damn horn with the FBI, and tell the chap I'm carrying out my duty as expected, and if he doesn't like it he can always get his can down here and fight this fire with me. I have to go, my trucks are starting to stack up on me. Keep me informed, I'm going to handheld now. Out." The Fire Chief cut off his communication with command and he prepared to leave his car.

The old man jumped out from his car, and he was instantly tackled by a crying woman half clothed. She knocked him down to the ground, and then she tripped over him as she scrambled to her feet. Looking over her shoulder, she continued to run as if the devil himself was chasing after her soul. Chief Addams got up and he started making for the first parked fire engine as his people piled out of the machine, and they started to fight with the heavy water hoses. Someone called out the positions of the local Johnny pumps in reference to their location by the Trump Tower. Chief Addams charged to the fire truck, intending to take command of their actions.

Inside the Trump Tower, Michael watched the maddening turmoil taking place just outside the Trump Tower in the streets with mild amusement. He grinned as he watched the woman crash into the old fireman and knock him down to the ground. But when he got up and headed for the parked fire truck, he decided to do something about his move. He knew he could not have a bunch of firemen trying to charge into the building on him. He fired in the ceiling again, and the remaining civilians dropped to the floor and they tried to protect themselves the best they could. The extremely upset leader of the terrorists figured there were no more than thirty people left on the floor in the lobby area of the building as he yelled at them.

"Stop! Everyone stop where you are! No more of you will be going out for the time being. The police arrived, and they're taking up firing positions against us. I think if you try to get out there now, you might be taken as troublemakers and fired on. It's for your own good you will wait until I let you go." He signaled the others, and they took control of the remaining civilians.

Outside the Trump Tower, Chief Addams froze in place as he began to yell at no one in particular. "What the hell was that shit I just heard, was that gun fire god dammit?"

His eyes narrowed as he lifted his weapon and then he drew a bead on the old man standing outside some twenty yards away from him like a statue. He carefully lined up his chest in his sights, and then he squeezed off a pair of rounds. Two 9 mm slugs instantly ripped into the old man's chest, sending him tumbling back until he landed on the ground with his head resting up against the front tire of the first fire truck to arrive on the scene. A number of firemen screamed to one another, as two of them rushed over to help the downed Fire Chief.

Michael decided to get things going a lot faster now. He emptied the weapon in the air, and also at the fire trucks parked just outside the Trump Tower. Slugs from his weapon bounced off the other buildings surrounding the main doors of the Trump Tower, sending firemen scattering and running from the building like the hordes of civilians were doing. The two firemen helping the downed Fire Chief, refused to leave his side and one of them tried CPR on the old man. No matter what they tried on the old man, they could not restart his heart.

Michael gave the two firemen time to make sure the old Chief was beyond their help, and then he slammed a second clip home, cocked the weapon while chambering a round, and then he sprayed the fire trucks over the firemen's heads with the small harbingers of death. It did not take more than that to get the remaining firemen to join the others quickly fleeing the area. The terrorist leader believed everyone understood the situation now, so he moved back deeper inside the building and slammed the door of the Tower behind him and secured the lock.

He turned to the remaining hostages and ordered them to go into the restaurant and wait there until he allowed them to leave the building. He was going to lock them all in it the restaurant, and then station a guard outside the doors to make sure everyone stayed put for him. But not before he checked for doors in the restaurant leading to the outside of the Tower. There was one service door, but it was covered by a steel grate lowered by Suarez, who was still on guard at the Security Center stationed in the basement of the massive building.

Many police squad cars started to stack up a block away from the Trump Tower. The officers were warned a unknown number of terrorists just took over the Trump Tower, and they were holding an unknown number of people hostage. The police were ordered to hold up that this operation was going to be commanded by the FBI, who were on route to the scene.

FBI HEADQUARTERS, NEW YORK CITY

When Director Hedemann issued orders to his Hostage Rescue Units to report for duty, orders were cut to have his people moved out to where they were needed. Placing the entire north eastern coast FBI squads on ready alert. The main point of contention was flashed to the FBI Units, and also to the FBI MCV, the Mobile Command Vehicle dispatched for the Trump International Hotel and Tower. The machine arrived at just about the same exact time as the first helicopter dispatched from Camp Smith that touched down at the old Brooklyn Navy Yard.

The FBI MCV pulled down Eighth Avenue and then the machine entered Central Park through Merchant's Gate and parked on West Drive in the very shadow cast by the Trump Tower. The first thing the Mobile Command Center did, was to raise its communication tower.

When this was accomplished, the Command Center began to open communications with the FBI Agents operating in the field and surrounding the Trump Tower, and helped coordinate all their efforts with the local police departments. The FBI Agents knew they needed the full cooperation of the local police and fire departments commanding Manhattan, if they were going to be successful dealing with the terrorists, and getting the hostages freed. Once the FBI center was fully operational, the Commander made direct contact with the FBI Headquarters in Washington, letting their Command Center know they were set in place, and ready to begin their operations against the terrorists now trapped inside the Trump Tower and free the hostages.

The worried President was listening attentively to Director Hedemann's words, when Peter came to the door of the Oval Office. He was standing with two papers in his hand, and silently slipped into the room as if he was a shadow, and he cautiously handed the pages to the President.

Director Hedemann continued with his conversation for the meeting, informing President Cole how his highly trained agents were going to make their initial assault on the Trump Tower, when the President turned away and took the papers from Peter. Peter whispered something in his ear, and President Cole quickly read the first report. He held up his hand to silence the FBI Director and announced. "Director Hedemann Sir, I want to take this time to inform you that your Mobile Command Vehicle has just arrived on the scene of this latest incident, and is currently broadcasting they're ready to begin their operations against the terrorists inside the building.

"I take it this is standard operating procedure for your Units, sir. I must remind you, your FBI Units haven't been given the job of securing my Vice President. I'm waiting to hear from you personally, your Hostage Rescue Teams will be able to get the Vice President out of that building alive. Mr. Hedemann Sir, I assure you none of your people are going to make a move against the damn terrorists or freeing the hostages until you give me this assurance." The President offered.

Director Hedemann drew in a deep breath, and he was just about ready to answer the President's question. When the President suddenly shoved himself away from his desk, almost knocking his chair over as he stood in a rush and then stared at the second report he held in his hand. The President shook with rage as he stared at the report. Fighting for control over his rampaging emotions, he turned to General White with pleading eyes.

The General thought something terrible happened just to the Vice President and he straightened his back, bracing himself for the words he feared and did not want to hear.

The fuming President could not speak, he was caught between shock, anger and contempt for the terrorists. President Cole reread the memo for a second time, to make certain he read what his mind did not want to acknowledge, as Peter moved a little closer to the

President's side to support him. He pulled away from Peter's grasp and snapped at his military officer. "Dammit to hell General White Sir! The sonofabitches just killed a Fire Chief responding to the emergency. I can't believe these bastards killed an old man whose only thought was to save lives.

"These fucking bastards had to prove to the world they were prepared to kill. I can't believe this, to kill a fireman or cop is like killing a priest, dammit. Why the hell would anyone want to kill a person who's only thought was to try and save lives? Christ sake, when these pricks started releasing some of the hostages, I thought they were only interested in getting something out of the damn building, or get us to deliver them a ton of cash and give them a way to leave the country. I really thought, well, I was hoping at least to get out of this damn mess without any loss of life. Now I see that's impossible, the sonofabitches had to kill for Christ sake." The President threw the paper across the room, it floated like a feather caught in a soft breeze. The American Leader's concern was for his Vice President, but he masked his emotions by allowing himself to overreact to the death of the elderly Fire Chief.

General White knew he had to say something to try and calm the President down a little, and he offered with concern. "Mr. President Sir, it could have been a helluva lot worse sir. The damn terrorists could've opened fire on the civilians fleeing the Trump Tower Sir."

"Thank you for that information I guess General White. That's a small comfort to me though, sir. Why the hell did they have to kill anyone during this fucking mess? Was it something they just had to do, to show us how desperate they truly are, dammit? Or was it they had to fulfill something that needed blood to quench its thirst for the bastards? I want these sonofabitches, and I want them real bad now, General White Sir. I want them worst than anything else I ever wanted in all my life, sir. Now, it's I who needs the taste of blood to satisfy my lust for revenge, sir. Their blood is what I demand, and it's up to you gentlemen who are the means to get that blood for me. Enough talking! Enough of everything dammit! I want the damn terrorist's hides."

The President's face was actually beet red as he raised his fist in the air and then shook it in sheer rage at the ceiling. He slowly regained his composure and rushed to the water cooler and filled a glass. He took two aspirins for the pounder of a headache he was suffering from, and then he returned to his desk after up-righting his chair. He sat down in a huff and removed a pad and quickly wrote as he spoke to General White at the same time.

"General White Sir, I know you're not going to need everyone of your troops where are they? I'm terribly sorry General, I don't remember where you stated they were stationed at this time, sir." The President offered as he looked up from the pad and he waited for the General's reply.

General White checked his watch and then he did a few quick calculations, and he offered to the American Leader. "Right about now Mr. President Sir, the Aircraft Carrier George Washington should be docking at Port Said in Egypt..."

"I know where the hell Port Said is General, thank you sir. I'm not a complete asshole you know sir! Err... I'm sorry, but this one's starting to really get to me, General White. I have to stop snipping at everyone around here, or risk not being a good leader during this time of trouble. I guess the fact the life of someone close and important and dear to me is on the line here, and it has me going a might I'm afraid. General White Sir, I'm giving you a direct order to have the elite soldiers you believe you'll need the most to carry out this operation against the damn terrorists, shipped back here to the States on the double quick, sir. I'm composing a letter to the French President as I speak with you sir, asking, no check that, begging then demanding to be allowed the use of the SST for an emergency flight here from Egypt, General White Sir.

"I'm quite certain a handwritten request coming directly from me, will be more than enough to get the French plane placed at your disposal by their President, General White. Dammit, I wish you had your people back here in the States where they should be, so they could handle this mess for us sir. I would've felt a whole lot more comfortable if your specialized troops were the ones preparing to storm this damn Tower, General White Sir."

The President's face blushed as he turned to Director Hedemann, and then he tried to soothe his ruffled feathers with kind words. "Director Hedemann Sir, please don't think for a second that I'm selling your outstanding Agents short by any means, sir. It's only I saw the General's troopers in action, and they did the job very well. I'm more than comfortable with his soldiers training and actions I sent to places I didn't even know existed before now. I'm terribly sorry to keep harping on this subject, Director. As of this moment, I haven't witnessed any of your Agents in action, sir. But all that's about to change I believe, Director Hedemann. I'm going to allow you to have your people set up to assault the Trump Tower, and get my Vice President free if and when I give you a green light to start your people in action against the damn terrorists, sir."

Turning back to General White, the President added to the military officer. "General White Sir, I know it's going to take your people some time to return to the States, and for them to get ready to do battle with these god damn animals hold up inside that building. That's why I'm going to allow Director Hedemann's Agents to make the first assault on the damn Tower. Win, lose, or draw General, I'm going to do something against the bastards until I get at them, and I'll snap their necks with my bare hands. Here's the letter for the French President, get your people moving home, General. I'm counting on your troops to save the life of my Vice President. God, I can believe this shit's happening right in the middle of the United States, General White."

The President moaned in a disgusted tone of voice as he took in a huge gulp of air to try and help steady down his nerves before continuing with his orders to the people in the room helping him. This time he was addressing everyone in the Oval Office. "People, I want Mary freed and freed alive and kicking, and I want everyone of these damn terrorists hanging by their damn gonads. I want their hides hanging on my office door by this time tomorrow morning. Arrr… you people know what the hell I want and what you people have to do to get the job done for me. So I better allow you people get on with what you have to do to get this thing handled."

The exhausted and extremely angry President stared at everyone in his office until one by one, they filter out of the Oval Office so they could carry out the orders the President issued them.

President Cole kept a close eye on the General while he left the Oval Office, and then he looked at FBI Director Hedemann and offered.

"Director Hedemann Sir, now General White's out of the office, I want you to remain so we can talk freely with you, sir. We're both intelligent men here, or we wouldn't be holding the offices we control sir. That's why I know you'll understand it's totally impossible for the General's troops to get back to the States in time, before this thing's over with and have a positive influence on the outcome of the situation, sir."

Hedemann nodded, feeling better the President understood the situation facing him.

"Fine, I see you know where I'm coming from, so I'll continue Director Hedemann Sir. I'm pleased I don't have to beat around the bush with you sir. Everything's coming down on your shoulders, Director. Your Agents are going to have to pull this thing off, or I'm going to lose my Vice President, and I won't stand for that for one second, sir. I trust you know what that means? How I'm going to be to deal with, if your Agents allow that to happen, Director Hedemann Sir."

"There's no need to go on with your warning Mr. President Sir." The Director offered to him.

"Fine, I can leave this subject then. Director Hedemann, as I just stated sir, the time for talking is over with. It ended the moment the damn terrorists killed the Fire Chief. How close are your people to getting involved in this damn thing, sir?"

"I believe it'll take me a few seconds to find that information out for you, Mr. President Sir. May I use your phone sir?" The FBI Director replied, and waited for the President's response.

"Please, help yourself Director Hedemann Sir." The President nodded towards the phone.

Director Hedemann made a call to his FBI headquarters in Washington. In a few seconds he was speaking to the Command and Control Center stationed in Central Park near the Trump Tower. The Director asked the agent on duty for the status on the HRU, and he was informed they were on board the helicopters, and they were just waiting word to lift off."

Director Hedemann covered the mouth piece and reported to the American Leader. "Mr. President Sir, my Agents are waiting for your word to go active sir."

The President winced as he did some quick soul searching. He found himself questioning if he might be overreacting to his anger, or was this the course of action to pursue. The more he thought about it, the more questions flooded his mind. He was worried about the Vice President, but knew he had to get her out of the Trump Tower and free from the terrorists. He could not allow her to remain a hostage to a terrorist group. As the President milled over these questions, he understood full well what he had to do, and he was only putting it off and marking time, in hopes the terrorists would go away. With a deep sigh he mumbled at the leader of the FBI.

"Director Hedemann Sir, there's no sense putting this damn order off for a moment longer. I'm giving your Agent Hostage Rescue Team the green light to proceed with this operation, get your Agents in the air, sir. And, may God help them, may God help me, and may God help all of us. This has to be the hardest order I have even issued in my entire life, Director Hedemann Sir. Wish your Agents the best of luck for me, I'll be praying for them and my Vice President, sir." The American Leader announced in an exhausted tone of voice.

Director Hedemann nodded back at the terribly shaken President, and then he spoke in the phone again. "Richard, get the Agents in the air sir."

"Consider them airborne Director Hedemann Sir." The agent on the phone informed him.

The FBI Commander hung up the phone, and then he glanced at the President as he remarked to the man. "The helicopters are airborne as of this moment Mr. President Sir."

"Fine, all we can do is sit tight and wait and pray your Agents are successful during this operation, sir. I wish there was an easier way we could have direct communication with your people in the field, Director." The President moaned as he stared at the FBI Director.

"Oh but there is a way to remain in constant communication with the assault teams as they begin their operation, Mr. President Sir. We can monitor the FBI console in the main building of the White House, sir. If you'd like to take an active part in this operation that is, sir."

"Of course I'd like to monitor the operation Mr. Hedemann, why the hell didn't I think of that, dammit." The President said while snapping his fingers. He headed for the door of the Oval Office with Director Hedemann trailing him. They both rushed down the corridor to the main section of the White House. Once in the hallway, the President lead the way to the offset room used by the FBI, involved with White House security. The communication center was constantly manned by two agents. Upon seeing the President enter the room, they both jumped up and stood at attention, while the President scanned the console. Not knowing what he was doing, he turned to Director Hedemann and asked him. "You know how to operate this damn mess, sir?"

"Yes sir, please Mr. President Sir allow me to set it up for you, sir."

THE TRUMP INTERNATIONAL HOTEL AND TOWER, NEW YORK CITY

Once the terrorist leader secured the hostages he was holding inside the plush restaurant, he decided to check in with Alexander, who he knew was busy setting up his people and weapons on the roof of the Trump Tower. He went to the service elevator and pushed the roof button. It felt like it took a short lifetime for the slow moving elevator to finally reach the roof area of the building, and when the doors opened he was surprised to see what was going on.

Alexander's people were doing a fine job with setting up all their defenses on the roof area of the building. The leader of the group was pleased to see the roof was ringed with a four foot high one foot thick parapet wall of poured concrete. The cold night air was very refreshing, and it instantly gave him a chill when the breeze hit his sweat soaked shirt.

Michael scanned the surrounding buildings, and came up with three structures that could be a threat against his people on the roof. The buildings were the only ones high enough to be used by snipers who would likely try to pick them off. He looked for Alexander, spotting him standing by the pair of Russian made AGS 17-30 mm grenade launchers, he headed right for him.

Twice he was forced to stop moving while someone moved a piece of equipment around on the roof in front of him. He moved forward again until he stood by Alexander's side, once there he pointed out the three buildings he wanted the Russian to pay close attention to, when Alexander and his people was ready to defend the roof area from assault from the police.

On the streets of Manhattan, sirens continued to fill the night air, as tens of police cars reported to the call for the emergency taking place at the Trump Tower. Every SWAT team throughout all of Manhattan, the Bronx, and Brooklyn, were now deployed in the surrounding area, ringing the Trump Tower with countless snipers ready to kill any terrorists they picked up in their sights. The terrorist leader heard the wail from the sirens, and looked over the side of the building to see what was going on below them, he was immediately roughly pulled back by the large Russian ex-soldier as he growled at the leader of the group.

"That bad fool mistake stupid big shot friend. We see American police take position in Park while go, leader. You believe weapon aim at build, and shooter wait one make mistake like you just do, Number One stupid man. Keep you stupid head in wall, or police shoot off for you good and proper, stupid leader." As if to prove his point, Alexander pointed out the black painted SWAT trailer parked on the road in Central Park, right next to an FBI command truck.

"Shit, you think you might be able to reach the trucks with grenades from this far a distance out, Alexander?" he asked the large Russian as he moved away from the concrete wall, as directed by the Russian. Once away from the side, they both leaned their heads together, so they could hear each other speaking over the roar from the wind this high on the building. He pointed out they had to be ready for a reaction from either the police, or FBI, and soon at that.

The Russian smiled at Michael, his mouth filled with rotten teeth and terrible breath, he groused. "You worry much about thing no concern you, big shot leader. Truck well in range of good Russian made grenade launch, but no shoot until last moment please. I control situation, let police try something against us. It end in their stupid death, Number One. I ready anything think of good. If police use helicopter, this beauty end bu'sheet but once for them please." Alexander picked up a reusable Russian SA-7, shoulder launched Grail anti aircraft missile, and he hoisted it on his shoulder and snapped the tracking radar on, to show him how the weapon worked.

"With good Russian made weapon like this I have. I take out poor America made helicopter, or aircraft any police use against us out but good and proper. I two weapon of these same kind at me disposal Number One, fifteen missile for weapon I have too please. No way American police can get on roof building and attack us and stay alive if they try do that." The large Russian jerked the weapon off his shoulder, and rested it up against the parapet wall, and left it there.

"That's all you need to defend the roof against any attack from the police, Alexander?" he asked, as he eyed the tallest building near the Trump Tower, which was on Columbus Avenue, about a good city block away from them. He knew they went over the list of weapons Alexander was going to employ during the attack, but he was fishing for reassurance from the large Russian, to convince him they would succeed. He could not believe his luck, he was expecting something to go wrong with his plan, but and as of yet everything has worked out as planned.

"Da! (Yes) Da please! But are no only weapon have defend position against police, my big shot friend of mine. I have AGS grenade launch work over other build surround this one please, everything prepared for us, Number One. I have two poor made America inferior machine gun spray build with please. I too have America made weapon LAW, they poor made and inferior anti tank weapon to same Russian type made weapon, and have hundred grenade we lob from roof keep police away. We ready anything come us way from outside build, Number One. You no worry no more about me and men and protect of roof this build, big shot leader you.

"One, we do what we agreed do for mission success, you make sure find everything worth in filthy America monument built by greed and lust, big shot leader you. I want be rich man at America expense, big time leader you be." Alexander allowed a hardy laugh before screaming at one of his men doing something wrong with setting up a piece of equipment.

"Horstmann! God dommit you anyhow, how many time tell no you place box ammunition for god dom gun under weapon, Christ sake Almighty stupid man you are." The angry ex-soldier stormed away from Michael, and he marched towards one of the machine guns. Shoving the stunned man he was angry with aside, Alexander then roughly pulled an ammunition box out from under one leg of the weapon, and then he shoved an empty box back in its place. Then the Russian placed the full box of ammunition behind the gun where the shooter could get at it easily as he roared again at the man who just made the mistake. "That where ammunition belong for weapon, dommit you. Christ sake, when you learn ever proper way to prepare for attack, stupid man? I no understand why put up with stupid man like you for so long now please."

Horstmann completely ignored the irate Russian, as he continued to prepare the weapon for firing. Each weapon was set up with the barrel sitting over the edge of the parapet wall, so it could easily fire over the barrier while the concrete offered the shooters the maximum protection from the police weapons. Everyone stationed on the roof area knew they would be fired on once they began their fire on the police positions on the streets below them.

The terrorist leader was caught up with the weapons and how The Russian and the rest of his people were setting them up for defense, and found himself helping anyone who needed a little extra help. Alexander did not mind the help from the leader of the group, he was minus a few men involved with helping Michael's people inside the Trump Tower. Everyone on the roof was freezing, it was cold with the night temperatures expected to drop to the low forties, but the wind was the major problem of the weather facing the terrorists on the roof of the Tower.

THE OLD BROOKLYN NAVY YARD

The pair of sleek black EH-60/A Blackhawk Quickfix helicopters, were spooling their motors just above idle speed to keep them hot and ready for immediate flight, when word came in for the agents to go active against the terrorists who took over command of the building. The helicopters began their assent in the night sky over New York City. Each attack helicopter was equipped with a three man crew, and eleven heavily armed FBI Agents specially trained in hostage rescue situations. Each agent was ready to go to work against the terrorists inside the building.

The helicopters rose nine hundred feet, and then they banked towards the northeast and went to full military power. The FBI hostage rescue team commanders got the men hot and gave them last minute instruction for their assault against the terrorists. Each agent knew they had one order to accomplish and that was to get the Vice President out of the building alive. Once they had her in control, a second team of agents were to return to the roof with the Vice President, and make sure she was on board a helicopter, and heading out of the area before the agents continued with their second part of the mission. The other FBI teams were to take up defensive positions inside the building, and then hunker down until they knew the Vice President was safe.

Once this was accomplished, the agents were then to concentrate their efforts on freeing the rest of the hostages, while taking out any terrorists they came across inside the building. The agents received orders to use lethal response against all the terrorists in the building. This was the first time any FBI Agents received orders to kill, rather than to try and take some prisoners. Each agent understood what they were supposed to do when they touched down on the roof of the Trump Tower, and they were chomping at the bit to begin their operation.

The two attack helicopters traveled at one hundred and twenty eight knots in a northeasterly direction, each air platform had a range of six hundred and seventy five nautical miles, with four and one half hours of flying time, before needing to refuel. A Mobile gas station large enough to land the helicopters and refuel them near the Trump Tower, was taken over by agents on the ground, standing by to refuel the helicopters in case the operation went much longer than was expected, and refueling of the helicopters was necessary.

Once Vice President Mary Hirshfield was safely on board one of the helicopters and heading out of the area. The pilot was instructed to make way for the USS Intrepid Aircraft Carrier, a floating Sea, Air and Space museum moored on the muddy waters of the Hudson River at 12th Avenue, in downtown Manhattan. A special squad of FBI Agents were waiting for the Vice President's arrival on board the well honored Aircraft Carrier, with orders to take her into protective custody, and protect her life until she could be removed from New York. It was decided to bring the Vice President to the Intrepid, because it was the closest military type structure in the area, and was the easiest to secure. The police blocked off all local traffic for a five block sector around the Intrepid, and two Coast Guard Cutters had taken up position at the stern of the old, proud warship, blocking water access to the threatening war machine.

All these strategies had been brought up to the concern President's attention, he had the final say on anything the FBI planned during this situation. The President agreed with getting the Vice President over to the Intrepid for safe keeping, until he could get her back to Washington.

The pair of Quickfix covert troop transport helicopters swiftly entered Manhattan from the East River side of the city, and they flew directly over the United Nations structure by way of 42nd street, actually using the building as their lineup position for their flight towards the Trump Tower. The black painted machines dropped down to two hundred feet, and they woven in and out of the structures higher than their flight path. The pilots took this route because they were using the buildings to hide their approach to the Trump Tower, in case the terrorists had placed a spotter on the roof of the building against them.

The co-pilot of the lead aircraft call out the streets they passed to the agents in the troop compartment, as they closed in on the Tower. "We're at Forty Seventh Street and Third Avenue. ETA to target is two minutes, I repeat Agents, two minutes to target. I don't like flying this low at this speed. It's playing kick ass on my damn electronics. I can't tell if any radar is zeroing in on us or not, sir. I might as well be flying blind for the good my electronics are doing me, sir."

One of the agents grunted loudly as he glanced at the cockpit and its two man crew, and then he barked at the pilot. "You have to stay flying as low as possible to the ground. We need the element of surprise on our side for this operation, if we plan to hit the damn building unobserved sir. Keep going pilot, what the hell would these subjects be doing with any god damn radar attack units, unless they had some anti aircraft missiles protecting them at the structure. This is a hostage situation, not a military engagement people. Okay, we have two minutes to target. Wake up and start chewing the fucking bark people. We have some work to do, guys."

In a few moments, the pilot announced their machine was just passing 437, the Madison Building. Then the pilot guided the helicopter through the Twin Towers of the magnificent Saint Patrick's Cathedral at fifty feet above the roof. Then they continued past the Olympic Tower, and the helicopter shot across Fifth Avenue. There was barely any civilian traffic below, and what there was, was mostly police cars or fire trucks responding to the Trump Tower situation.

The lead pilot stopped griping as the chopper darted through Six Fifty and Fifth Avenue. It was at this point the helicopter made its first flight correction at East 53rd Street, and Avenue of the Americans. This was accomplished while the helicopter traveled at one hundred twenty knots. At this point, the aircraft turned due north then set on a direct course for Central Park, neatly passing between the ABC building, and a taller structure to the right of the aged building.

Some of the FBI Agents sitting in the rear compartment of the two machines, felt the mounting excitement rapidly building in their bodies, and they yelled out old war calls, in an effort to match the anticipation in their churning guts. "Yeeeehhhhaaaa, what a fucking rush people." An agent screamed while cupping his hands around his mouth, in an attempt to amplify his scream over the roar coming from the motors of the helicopter.

FBI MOBILE COMMAND CENTER WEST DRIVE, CENTRAL PARK

When the FBI Mobil Command Center stationed in Central Park, was notified the helicopters were in flight and heading directly for the Tower. The Commander dispatched his snipers to the surrounding buildings of the Trump Tower, which would serve as a hide or nest for them to operate from. Possibly get some of the terrorist before the insertion teams arrived on scene. The snipers needed tall buildings to work from to get high enough, so they could get a bead on any terrorists who might be caught in the open on the roof area of the Tower. The buildings selected by the snipers as their hides, were the three tallest and the ones nearest to the Trump Tower.

Four of the snipers from the special FBI HRU teams moved into the forty five story structure of 21 Columbus Avenue, this building was constructed right behind the United States Post Office. The building was a mere block north of the Trump Tower, with an extremely clear view of the target and the surrounding area of their intended target building.

The FBI Agents/Snipers entered the chosen building and immediately headed to the roof of the structure, so they could set up their long range view finders and targeting scopes and weapons. The agents worked in teams, two snipers and two spotters to each team and the spotters used specially designed field glasses that marked off the distance of the subject target, and it also gave the windage and elevation and speed the target was moving at. The actual sniper/shooters had a powerful scope controlled by the spotter's glasses that automatically aimed the sniper's weapon mounted on top a tripod at their chosen targets.

A second team of FBI and New York police SWAT snipers and supporters, moved into the building at 75 Columbus Avenue, north of the target structure, and that building stood behind the old Bible Society structure, which was a much lower dwelling. The snipers did the same as the other teams at 21 Columbus Avenue, and they set up for their attack on the suspected terrorists.

A third team of snipers moved into the structure nearest the Trump Tower, at 1884 Broadway. These buildings were the only ones near enough to the Tower, to give the FBI and police snipers an effective angle and range to get a good shot off at any possible terrorists caught out in the open inside the building on top of the roof. The snipers had to be ready to take out any terrorists who might try and flee the building as well, if things started to go wrong with their attack.

A team of ten FBI Agents not connected with HRU Teams, entered 10 Columbus Circle. This structure offered a flat surface thirty five stories high for the officers to operate from. The agents were going to use this building as an advantage and observation platform, to help keep an eye on what was happening on the street around the Trump Tower, as well as giving the agents a place to set up their highly sensitive hearing and infrared targeting units. Which could practically see through the concrete walls of the Trump Tower, the agents needed the height, if they were to control the other agents and police on the streets, who took up positions around the Tower. The FBI was the controlling unit for the entire operation being waged against the terrorists.

Each of the sniper teams were notified in advance, and the second FBI Mobile Command Center was informed the pair of Blackhawk helicopters were on way to the target. The snipers moved more forward while holding fingers on the triggers of their weapons, trying to locate any possible terrorists in their field of vision. The only problems facing the sniper teams, was each building being used as observation positions, were lower than the Tower was tall. This problem decreased their line of vision, and it also hid the swarm of Alexander's men moving around on the roof of the Tower, while setting up their defensive weapons against any attack.

A few FBI Spotters diverted their eyes away from the target to peek at the skies above them. They were looking for the first sign of the pair of rapidly approaching helicopters. They knew once the agents on board the helicopters went in action, there should be many targets of opportunity moving around out in the open they could easily take out. Tensions mounted for the snipers and their assistants, and the pressure increased as the snipers waited for the choppers to enter the kill zone. All civilian helicopters and aircraft were ordered out of the area, for fear the terrorists might think they were an attack against them by the police.

Reporters flooded the area surrounding the Trump International Hotel and Tower, setting up their own communication vans and taping machines. Hundreds of lights were turned on, as hordes of cameras tried to get a long range glimpse of terrorists holding the Tower hostage, or the action taking place at the structure. No police or FBI Agents would comment on what was taking place, leaving the reporters begging for information. The stacked up reporters had no clue the Vice President was visiting the city that never sleeps, let alone a hostage in the Trump Tower.

Some of the agents and police sniper teams complained about the reporter's lights tracking, and possibly giving away their positions to the terrorists who might be able to pick them out because of the countless harsh lights exposing them. The lights were also disrupting and also interfering with the agent's infrared tracking and aiming units. So the ground agents ordered the reporters to shutdown their filming equipment until the operation was completed.

Other agents called the news stations while demanding they be a lot more careful about what they were broadcasting over the open airways over this terrorist situation. The concerned agents warned the stations they did not want the terrorists to pick up their strategy over radio or TV, or the steps the police and FBI were taking in defense against them. The agents pointed out they did not want the terrorists having any access to real time information being broadcasted by the careless reporters.

After a few minutes of arguing by FBI commanders and the producers of the programs, the news station finally relented, and they offered to broadcast what was happening in midtown Manhattan from far away from the Tower itself, after carefully editing the feeds to be aired.

However, this agreement did not happen until the FBI Command actually threatened to take a look into the stations FCC permits, and stop their reporters from following the FBI whenever a possible terrorist situation had to be handled by the agents. That was enough of a threat to bend the station thinking in favor of the FBI and their agents working out in the field.

Chapter Twenty

ON BOARD THE QUICK FIX HELICOPTER FLIGHT
ALFA, CHARLIE, FOXTROT 217

After this latest in flight correction was completed, the FBI HRU helicopters passed the Burlington Building, crossing West 53rd Street, and headed for the next upcoming in flight correction. The helicopters dropped closer towards the ground, using the shadows of the buildings to hide their advance against the Tower. While the helicopters were in flight, the co-pilot was constantly calling off the streets they past, on their way towards the target Tower.

"Say pilot, how the hell soon before we finally make it to the damn target zone." The senior controlling FBI Agent asked while making certain the helicopter was not falling behind its ordered schedule lot of time to start their attack on the building. According to the agent's watch, they were still just sixty five seconds away from the target building and terrorists, and unless things changed for them, they were right on schedule.

The co-pilot replied, after checking his watch and location once again. "Agent, I make it sixty three seconds away from target, sir. We'll keep you advised as to time on target, Agent."

"Roger that last, keep me advised sir." The agent snapped at the co-pilot.

ON THE ROOF OF THE TRUMP INTERNATIONAL TOWER AND HOTEL

Alexander finished setting up his last weapon of defense on the roof, ready to attack the less taller buildings surrounding the Tower, if they came under attack from the police. The Russian ex-soldier hesitated then picked up the SA-7 Grail shoulder missile system, and he flipped on the homing radar for no other reason than to make certain the weapon was in the proper working order. Instantly, a pair of fast moving dots appeared on the small radar tracking screen. He instantly flipped the narrow beam tracking radar off, and then rushed to the edge of the parapet wall, and began to search the sky for any sign of the two blimps he just picked up on his radar unit. He knew the police were going to try something against them, and he figured this was it.

Michael was still trying to be of some sort of help to the people operating on the roof when he noticed the large Russian move, and he rushed towards his side and asked him in an excited tone of voice. "What's wrong Alexander? Did you see something out there Twenty Seven?"

"Get down big stupid hot shot boss you! Build cross us crawl with police sniper, big fool you. I see something in radar tracking screen moment ago. I see two blimp on screen, they come after us, the fool police. I wait them come good please and we take out." The Russian then hoisted the shoulder launch missile system back on his shoulder again as knelt behind the concrete wall, and then he waited for what was coming to attack them from the blackness of the night sky.

Alexander drew in his breath and then he bellowed out at the other members from his group. "Everyone, stop what do please and get down for you protect worthless life. Company come at you, I want look like no one up here please. Take good cover, be ready by weapon in case we attack by America police fools. I make out two helicopters come at us now. They use downtown build cover approach against us. I detect them and I figure what up to. I have surprise wait them when come in range please. Get undercover now, big stupid people you be."

Alexander watched as his people rushed behind anything that would keep them from being spotted by approaching police officers riding inside the pair of rapidly approaching helicopters. It was good for them the Trump Tower was taller than most of the other buildings around it. It shielded his men from discovery by the police snipers. The Russian began to breathe when he could no longer see any of his men in the open. When he was satisfied he turned his attention to the area he was certain the helicopters would use to make their approach against the building.

He called out over his shoulder to one of the others from his group. "Twenty, Number Twenty you come here at once, god dommit you foolish person you I need here you."

The terrorist going by the Number Twenty went over to his leader crouched behind the concrete wall. Once by his side, Twenty waited for further orders. "Twenty, Ebershoff, you know how fire Russian good made SA-7 Russian missile, am I no right please, you big stupid you?"

"Yes I know how to operate the weapon, I was trained on it Twenty Seven. What do you want me to do with the weapon, Twenty Seven." Ebershoff asked the large Russian.

"This good for you be trained with weapon fool, be stand by me. I want you get SA-7 missile system, and take position right next me side this time now please. You wait final word from me before you fire weapon you stupid man. Then we spring up together and we both fire at god dom helicopter come at us please, and we knock them both out of god dom air..."

"Helicopters? Helicopters attacking us?" Ebershoff cried as he tried to see out in the darkness.

"Do no be big baby please, stupid man you. You knew United State police try mount some kind attack against us some time in future, you stupid man you be. This it please. I have pair police helicopter attack us position in few second. I believe they come at us from north side build, between those two build head us. You no turn track radar on until I do please. I no want warn stupid America police until too late them to react against us move against them. Get other SA-7 missile and take position to me up. Stay low please, we know police sniper in surround build, and wait shoot you good and dead. If you want ass shot off for you, walk no run stupid."

Alexander kept a close eye on everything Ebershoff was doing with the weapon as he quickly crawled across the opened area of the roof to the other shoulder launch missile system. He retrieved it and then he quickly scurried back to the Russian's side. Both missile armed terrorists then leaned up against the concrete wall and waited for the helicopters to arrive. The terrorist leader tried to hear the helicopters coming at them, he was unable to hear anything but the constant wail of the sirens below them, and the unsettling hollow of the wind above them. Michael marveled at how Alexander so easily detected the unbound police helicopters.

ON BOARD QUICK FIX HELICOPTER FLIGHT ALFA, CHARLIE, FOXTROT, 217

The flight engineer doing duty as the navigator on board the helicopter, doubled up as the weapons threat operator in the first helicopter. He was constantly monitoring the threat board when he thought he noticed a narrow radar burst suddenly tracking them while in flight. It was extremely short in duration, and with all the heavy interference he was receiving from the surrounding buildings and also the heavy ground clutter, the flight engineer could not swear it was someone using a tracking attack radar against them. This radar zone was usually used by military weapons such as the Stinger missile system, and most other portable shoulder type missile launch weapon systems. The flight engineer immediately called out to the pilot in an excited voice. "Err... Stan, I think I might have a major fucking problem on my hands, sir."

"Go Navigator, what's bugging ya ass buddy?" the pilot snapped at the navigator.

"I'm not positive about this, but I could swear we have just been probed by a low grade missile attack tracking radar system, sir. I could be mistaken about the probe though sir. It was only a momentary flash of radar energy I picked up, too short in duration to be absolutely positive about what might have just probed us, sir. Beside sir, I'm picking up so much damn ground clutter from all the damn buildings and granite, I can't be certain about anything at this point, sir."

"Flight Engineer, you think those birds might have a fucking shoulder launch missile weapon system with them, dammit? If they do, I'm aborting this fucking mission as of this moment!" The pilot warned the flight engineer, highly concerned over the possibility the terrorists might be armed with weapons that could easily destroy his helicopter while in flight at their disposal.

The flight engineer checked two more passes of his radar bounce, and when nothing showed up on the scope again. He shook his head and then grumbled at the pilot. "No way do these people have any missile systems at their disposal, Captain. These birds would be painting the shit out of us by now, if they had these weapons with them, sir. Maybe it was something I picked up from the flood of reporters down there. Christ sake, it could've been anything at this point sir. I'm picking up so much damn ground clutter Commander, I just don't know any longer sir."

"Did you pick up the report on the damn radar bounce a second time around Navigator? Talk to me man, I need your fucking input or I'm ending this damn thing as of now, man."

"Negatory on that last sir. My radar scopes clear as a bell right now Commander, except for the usual ground clutter constantly coming at us flying over Manhattan, sir."

"Then I take it as it was nothing to be concerned with. Look Flight Engineer keep your damn eyes glued to that fucking radar threat scope mister. If you pick up anything on it for a second time, and I mean anything that even looks like a god damn radar tracking and attack code to you. We're getting our asses the hell out of here so fast it's going to make your head spin man." The pilot warned his navigator as he turned to the controls of his helicopter.

The pilot keyed his internal intercom system, and then he warned the agents in the personnel compartment of his helicopter. "FBI Agents, be advised, we're presently passing over Carriegie Hall, next spot, Seventh Avenue, people. We'll be carrying out another in flight correction over Nine, Oh, One, Seventh Avenue shortly guys. Then we'll head north up West Fifty Seventh Street, until the next in flight correction completed for flight directly at the damn Trump Tower. I make it we're just about a few seconds away from the target at this time, gentlemen."

The second the Quick Fix helicopter made its next in flight correction, and the machine began to fly directly up 57th Street. The helicopter dropped down to power line height, flying merely fifty feet off the ground. The pilot slowed his speed down to just a hundred and twenty knots. The pilot was using the buildings as cover for their approach of the Tower, and it did not take him long to realize the speed he was traveling, was far too dangerous for the height he was at. He dropped his speed down to ninety knots, so he could better control his aircraft. The helicopter took West 57th Street to their third in flight correction point. This was the Catholic Apostolic Church between 9th and 10th Avenues, just about where the Trump Tower stood.

The final flight correction the aircraft had to discharged before it was aligned with the Tower, was to come in the middle of the forth block from the church. This correction was going to take place over the old Leon Lowenstein Center in Manhattan. From this last flight correction, the helicopters would travel due south, heading directly for the Trump Tower two blocks south of the final flight correction. The pilot was sweating as he held on to the stick as if it was a branch, and he was hanging over a cliff hundreds of feet high. His eyes strained and burned as he stared ahead of his aircraft into the pitch blackness of the night, while watching the buildings on either side as he headed his helicopter directly for his last in flight correction and then the Trump Tower.

"Flight Engineer! Any sign of that possibly attack tracking radar bounce you though you picked up a few minutes ago, man? I'm about to correct for final on the damn target sir, once I make this last correction then there's no turning back sir. You better make damn sure nothing out there is going to eat us a fucking live, or it's your ass when we get back to base mister."

"Stan, I'm clear on all radar scans of the entire area of concern at this time, sir. The scope's showing ground clutter and nothing else threatening us, Captain. I'd offer what I thought was a radar tracking signal was just some ground clutter clogging up my Unit on me, sir."

"Okay Flight Engineer, we're committing to the final correction. All Agents, we're making our final correction for the damn target. Eight seconds away from intended target people. You guys better be ready to repel out of the helicopter the second I go into hover mode over the roof of the damn Tower. I'll hover ten feet above the roof first out will secure the area before we touchdown on the roof, and then everyone bail out. Stand ready, we're correcting final at this moment."

The set of Blackhawk night attack equipped helicopters turned on their final approach towards the Trump Tower as one, and the two machines then quickly aligned their aircraft platforms with the Trump International Hotel and Tower now filling the windshields of both pilots and their helicopters as they continued their approach on the Tower.

FBI MOBILE COMMAND CENTER, WEST DRIVE, CENTRAL PARK

Countless numbers of FBI Agents and police officers flooding the ground area around the Trump Tower, were interviewing all the freed hostages. From the reports they gathered, the agents and officers got a pretty good picture of what was happening inside the Tower. The FBI knew there were hundreds of people still trapped on the upper floors of the building, and they were cut off by heavy fire doors closing off the floors they were on. They got a good count on the number of subjects inside the building, and they came up with eleven as their active number of terrorists. The agents had no idea of Alexander's attackers were stationed on the roof, or how many were involved in his team. The Feds got a good description of the terrorist leader, feeding the description into their computers, and it did not take long to put a face to the image.

The report read; Michael Van Kirk, age 31, last known address 1008 North Street, Newark, New Jersey. The rap sheet on him described the crimes he committed over the years, long and detailed. But as of yet, he was never convicted or even sent to jail for suspected crimes against society. The summary of this man's illegal activities, suggested Michael Van Kirk was a controlling factor in a known street gang involved in high return crimes mainly dealing with the very wealthy and unsuspecting citizens. It suggested he was more than capable of killing anyone who crossed him, and he has been known to be friends and worked with an extremely ruthless Russian ex-soldier the United States wanted to deport back to Russia, for crimes committed while living in the United States. The FBI Command Center stationed in Central Park, transferred the information down to Washington for the FBI Director's enlightenment.

THE OVAL OFFICE, THE WHITE HOUSE, WASHINGTON DC

President Cole waited while FBI Director Hedemann was brought up to speed on the events taking place in the heart of midtown Manhattan. It took ten minutes to have the communication console moved from the main section of the White House, over to the East Wing and Oval Office. The President was not about to stand in an uncomfortable small room while waiting for information on the helicopter attack against the Trump Tower. When the FBI Director finished with his field agent's report. The President snapped at the Director when he finished gathering the information they were in search of. "Well Mr. Hedemann, what do you have for me sir?"

"Mr. President Sir, we now at least know the identity of the leader of the terrorists. He's a big time perp named, Michael Van Kirk, known to pal around with a Russian paramilitary type, who goes by the name of Alexander. This Alexander fellow came here when the collapse of the communist regime was eminent. He entered the United States carrying a stack of top secret papers, and was granted political asylum in return for the wanted papers. Since arriving in the United States, this guy has been involved in the underground, and suspected in several different attacks against rival gangs working the New York dock area of the City. We've been looking for this one for over three months Mr. President Sir, but he hasn't surfaced. We can only hope this guy went back to Russia where we know he'll be dead within a week's time or less sir."

"Is there any chance this Russian might have teamed up with this Michael person for this operation, or whatever it is we're calling the damn thing, Director Hedemann?" the President asked with concern and then he added. "I'd hate like hell to be forced to go up against a military type, while we're trying to free the hostages, and weed out these pricks inside the Tower."

"It's not believed to have happened Mr. President Sir. As I have just informed you sir, we've been looking for this Russian ex-soldier for quite a while now in the States, sir. There's no way this Russian bastard can possibly be walking the streets of New York City without my knowing about it sir. If he's involved with these terrorists in the Trump Tower, I'm afraid many people are going to die. This Russian is plain, outright nuts, and he doesn't mind killing, he even enjoys it, sir. We also have a number fixed on the terrorists inside the building, Mr. President Sir.

"We've been able to place the number of terrorists at eleven strong. My Agents are reporting hundreds more civilians are still trapped on upper floors throughout the Tower, by means of the fire doors on each floor, Mr. President Sir. These doors were rigged to close in case of fire, containing the fire on the affected floor, and cutting it off from the rest of the Tower. The terrorists are using the fire doors as a means of controlling the civilians trapped inside. This narrows our avenue of attack. We have to be careful working over a floor, Mr. President."

The President stood and asked the FBI Director. "Good God Almighty Mr. Hedemann Sir, don't tell me Donald Trump and his family might be among those held hostages in the Tower."

"No Sir not at all Mr. President Sir, when I was informed of the terrorist attack on the Trump International Tower and Hotel, sir. I immediately established Mr. Trump and his family's whereabouts in the City, and I have been successful in locating him visiting his casino in Atlantic City sir. My people have branded him as the Ace of Trumps, because the man seems to always trump someone, and always coming out on top of the situation sir. In this case Mr. President Sir, it seems Mr. Trump beat these terrorists by not being home when they attacked the building." The FBI Director announced with relief lacing his tone of voice.

"Thank Christ Director Hedemann Sir, one day that man is going to be the President of this country. Well, at least you seem to have everything in order. When are your other Agents going to assault the Tower, Director?" the President moaned as he allowed himself to relax a little.

Director Hedemann checked his watch and then smiled as he announced. "It's time Sir!"

ON BOARD QUICKFIX HELICOPTER FLIGHT ALFA, CHARLIE, FOXTROT 2I7

The pair of twin helicopters completed their final in flight correction, and now they were heading directly for the Tower at ninety knots. The Hostage Rescue Agents inside the troop compartment of the machine, were preparing for the assault on the terrorists and building.

The agents who were scheduled to fast repel down the ropes from the helicopter to secure the roof area of the building, were already perched on the runners of the airframe, while their fellow agents hooked their ropes up to the overhead fasteners inside the helicopter. These agents riding outside the helicopter, gave the agents the thumbs up and then they slid back the breaches of their Heckler and Koch automatic weapons and chambered a round. Then they turned their attention towards the Trump Tower as they headed directly for it. The pilot was fighting the stick that was constantly being affected by the heavy head winds coming from the East River, as he climbed the helicopter until it was at level flight with the roof of the Trump Tower.

ON THE ROOF OF THE TRUMP INTERNATIONAL TOWER AND HOTEL

Alexander heard the roar from the helicopter's engines, moments before he was able to see them, as they charged at his position. The Russian held his location until the last possible moment, before jumping up to launch the missile at the oncoming helicopters. He glanced at Michael, who looked scared to death and then he grinned while turning to Ebershoff and hissing at him. "Big stupid person, you sure you know how use good Russian made weapon, fool?"

"Yes Alexander, I'm certain of it. I know what I'm doing with the damn thing, and I'll handle my part of this, Twenty Seven." Ebershoff offered the large Russian confidently.

"Prepare youself then stupid man you. Remember big fool you, do no arm track radar Unit until after stand and aim through site of weapon first please. Then arm you radar track system and wait for lock on tone then pull trigger of weapon. Is that simple stupid you. The missile do rest for you please. You ready, its time to fire at fool police helicopters, you big stupid man you. We kill both machine." Alexander ordered Ebershoff as he held him in his harsh glare.

"Yes Twenty Seven, I'm ready to hit the helicopters as they come in. You lead the way for me though?" Ebershoff announced cautiously as he placed the heavy shoulder launch missile system to its proper firing position resting on his shoulder, he then held his breath and waited.

"Always lead way. It way I live life all time, and be way I die, stupid you please." With that said, he jumped to his feet and brought the missile system up to his shoulder and wiggled it into the proper firing position. Then he looked into the aiming scope while flipping the tracking radar switch on with his thumb. He then waited for the tone to tell him to fire the weapon.

Ebershoff was on his feet just as quickly, and he also flipped the tracking unit on, and then he aimed the system at one of the black blurs heading directly at them. Twenty was sweating, even though it was so cold on the roof as he stared into the viewfinder and then zeroed the missile system right on the helicopter to the left of his system.

Instantly, the shoulder launch missiles acknowledged their target's position, because the two helicopters were so close to the launcher by this time. A loud tone and blinking red light filled their eyes and ears, informing the shooters their missiles were armed and ready for launching.

ON BOARD QUICK FIX HELICOPTER FLIGHT ALFA, CHARLIE, FOXTROT, 217

The pilot of the lead helicopter picked up the movement from the two men stationed on the roof of the building, at the same instant the flight engineer bellowed from the rear of the cockpit, and he knew something was wrong with their operation. The pilot tried to see what it was, but everything was happening so quickly, his mind was unable to register the threat facing him.

"Flight Engineer, holy shit Commander, I have a pair of fucking attack radar detection tracking the damn helicopter sir! I have a positive radar tracking warning signal being emitted from a portable shoulder launch missile systems, dammit! I have a positive missile lock on warning on our helicopter, sir. Jesus Christ Stan, you have to do something, God do something! Or they're going to kill us for the love of God! They have us zeroed in man! They're going to launch! God dammit, they're going to launch the fucking missiles and knock us out of the damn air, sir!"

The pilot's eyes grew as large as saucers, as he found himself staring right at a missile launching tube aimed directly at his helicopter from less than a city block away from his aircraft. Without thinking twice, the pilot immediately pulled back on the control stick, and then he threw his helicopter in a wild steep climb. Glaring warning lights screaming at him from the console informing the pilot he was about to stall out his helicopter, flashed in his eyes. The pilot ignored the warnings and the annoying warning beepers as he roared in his radio. "Two! One! I have a shoulder launch missile systems zeroing in on my platform, break off your damn attack and get the hell out of here! Take evasive maneuvers now man!"

The Commander of the lead helicopter continued to stare out his window at the man who looked larger than life while holding the shoulder launch missile system on his aircraft, as he tried to put more air between his aircraft and the missile launcher. The excited pilot cursed because he could swear he actually saw the shooter grinning back at him, as he did his best to get out of range of the missile and away from the Trump Tower and Hotel at the same time.

Outside the reacting helicopter, the four agents standing on the skids of the machine, were violently pitched off the skids into nothingness, as the helicopter did everything asked of it by the pilot and more. The violent shaking and harsh turning of the helicopter, made it impossible for the four agents to hold on, before being tossed away from the aircraft. Their three quarter inch thick lifelines instantly snapping under the tremendous torque the rapidly maneuvering helicopter placed on the nylon lines, as it tried to put as much distance between the machine and missile about to be launched at his machine. Out of the corner of the pilot's eye, he kept a look on the shooter still standing on the roof of the building, as he climbed into the darkness of night.

The pilot was praying, hoping the pitch blackness of the night would somehow swallow up his helicopter, and then make it totally impossible for the missile to locate and then destroy his aircraft. Then the pilot saw it, a red flash of flames along with the telltale streak of a missile charging right at his defenseless helicopter.

"Jesus Christ Commander! God dammit, I have a fucking missile launch! I'm tracking a pair of inbound missiles coming right at us sir! Commander! You have to do something, do something god dammmmmmit! I don't want to fucking dieeee in this machine!" The navigator cried out into his radio receiver as he held on for dear life.

"Arrrrrrrrrrrrrrrr!" the Commander of Alfa, Charlie, Foxtrot, Two, One, Seven helicopter screamed into the radio set, as he violently slammed his stick forward, putting his helicopter in a shake apart steep dive. The aircraft continued to shake viciously as it went in the steep dive, the windshield of the helicopter actually cracking under the tremendous pressure being placed on it, as the nearly out of control machine plunged towards the earth at breath robbing speed.

"Arrrrrrrrrrrrrrrr!" the pilot bellowed for a second time, knowing they were about to be killed by the missile charging right at his helicopter at mark speeds.

The anti-aircraft missile immediately zeroed in on the hot exhaust coming from the twin engines of the helicopter, and the blast was more than enough to rip apart the machine while still in flight. Flaming debris tumbled out of the black sky, landing on top of a number of buildings surrounding the Trump Tower, and also smashing onto the streets of midtown Manhattan below. The bodies of the FBI Agents and flight crew, fell to the streets below as numerous fires started by the burning rubble, as death found its resting place on the ground.

The second helicopter saw what just happened to the lead aircraft, and the pilot immediately tried desperately to get away from the Trump Tower in time to try and save everyone's life on board his helicopter. Ebershoff fired at the same instant Alexander did, and their two missiles actually crisscrossed while in flight on their way to their selected targets. The second helicopter erupted into a fireball with more force than the first one, sending large chunks of flaming debris from the rapidly breaking apart helicopter all over the streets of midtown Manhattan.

By the time the flaming debris littered the streets of midtown Manhattan, the first of the fire trucks moved in to start putting the numerous raging fires out. The firefighters were oblivious to the threat from the terrorists stationed on top of the Tower. They moved in to fight the fires, and possibly save lives of the wounded and dying agents. Fire hoses were laid out and in seconds, water was being trained on the roaring fires. Firemen fought not only the fires, but the hoses as they tried to jump out of their hands because of the pressure of the water in them.

FBI radios were filled with incoming calls and pleas for help from their Command Center and fellow agents out in the field. Many calls overlapping each other, as the FBI Agents informed headquarters of what was happening in the field.

"Jesus Christ Command, I have agents down all over the fucking place, god dammit! We need fucking help double quick over here Command." An agent from the FBI support team reported over his radio to his Command Center parked in Central Park.

Another call came in warning command. "I spotted an unknown number of subjects positioned on the roof of the Trump Tower. Subjects are firing shoulder launch missiles at the two incoming helicopters. Jesus Christ!" This agent's voice trailed off as he stared in stunned disbelief as the lead helicopter suddenly erupted into a ball of flames overhead.

The Commander manning the mobile center barked into his radio. "To all FBI Agents on the ground, you have green light to take out any subjects in your sights. Let's get it done people."

Another field report came in. "Weapon fire Command! We have a live fire situation on our hands at the Trump Tower! Hostages also believed to be involved in the action taking place at the structure. All Agents are to take out any subjects as ordered by Command, make your shots count on this one people. We have a messed up situation on our fucking hands. I want you people to…"

An overlapping report came in while drowning out the first report. "Agents down! Jesus Christ Almighty, we have numerous Agents down out here, dammit! We need medics on the double! I repeat, we have numerous Agents down and we need medical help out here immediately."

"Weapon's fire hot! The terrorists have just destroyed the two fucking HRU helicopters dammit!" Another agent reported to his Command Center.

The agents stationed inside the FBI Command Headquarters, stared at their radios in disbelief. This was the first time they had a hostage situation go sour on them, and causing the deaths of an unknown numbers of fellow officers, and possible hostages. Silence filled the Command Center.

The excited Russian ex-soldier actually punched the leader of the group in the arm, as he boasted proudly to him in a booming voice. "You see how I work, big shot leader you? I told you no one challenge me and me people ever, and live through foolish attempt please. If fool to try, they end like the fool who just tried attack us, burn to death in street big city."

Alexander waved his hand over his head as he bellowed above the roar of the wind. "All grenade launch, fire at target. I want every build use to by police, in fooking flame. Machine gun, work over build please. I no want any police near god dom build get shot off at us, god dommit. Fire at all build please. Shoot, shoot, shoot. Kill American police you see, dommit."

The grenade launchers started to pound out round after 30 mm round, at the three buildings nearest to the Trump Tower structure. The top of 21 Columbus Avenue was instantly turned into flaming rubble and twisted steel and broken windows, as the grenades ripped into the structure. One M-60 machine gun blew out many windows of the upper floors of the same building. The police snipers hiding inside this building, were killed in the opening volley and grenades fired at the building. The next building to feel the wrath of the terrorists, were the structures at Columbus Avenue and 62nd Street, soon terribly damaged by grenade and heavy machine gun fire.

The police snipers hiding inside this building suffered the same fate as their fellow agents from the helicopters. The next building to be turned on, was 1884 Broadway, here the FBI snipers got off the roof before coming under the attention of the terrorists. The Russian group did not stop once they turned the tallest buildings surrounding the Trump Tower into rubble and flames. The vast amount of weapons fire and grenades continued pouring out from the roof top of the Tower, as they searched for even more targets to attack below them.

Feuerman, the Nineteen man of the terrorist group, was the one operating one of the two grenade launchers, and he turned his weapon against the police SWAT trailer parked on West Drive in Central Park. He lobbed a number of rounds of grenades at the machine. As the grenades fell around the specialized machine, they ripped apart the trailer, and this sent the officers once inside the truck, scurrying away from the exploding vehicle.

Without waiting to fall under attack, the FBI Command Center vehicle started up, and then roared deeper into the Park, and well out of range of the terrorist's weapons, to avoid the terrible slaughter occurring on the streets of midtown Manhattan. All the while they were moving out, their radios were reporting a number of downed agents and automatic weapons fire in the field.

When the grenade launcher operator thought he done enough damage to the targets he was aiming at, he turned his attention against the next largest building in the area of the Trump Tower and his pick was the 10 Columbus Circle building. This building was being used as one of the observation and listening posts by a number of FBI agents pitted against the terrorists. As the grenades started to rip into the building, any agent who had not been killed in the initial attack, quickly made their way deeper inside this building, and the safety the interior of the structure afforded them. As soon as they were safe, the snipers tried to carry out their own counterattack aimed against the terrorist, but there was nothing much they could do from this position.

Moments after knocking the two Quickfix attack helicopters our of the sky, seven other buildings in the area of the Trump Tower and Hotel, including the NYPD SWAT trailer, were ripped apart and left burning. Just the upper floors of the picked out structures were being attacked, but the terrorists did not stop their assault on the city there.

Below in the streets of Manhattan, the firemen who braved the onslaught from the terrorists, as they began to fight the fires created by the downed helicopters, also continued working on the injured and dead. They found one agent who was standing on the skids of the helicopter, still alive. His rope tangled up in the overhead electrical wires, and his body never crashed to the ground. The firemen cut him free and shoved him inside a waiting ambulance, as they continued to fight the numerous fires started by the debris of the helicopters. The firemen's radios were being filled with the constant report of 'Ten forty Five, Code One', the fireman's code meaning they were coming across many dead bodies in their areas of responsibility.

As the terrorists stationed on the roof of the Tower continued to pound away at the other buildings of Manhattan with heavy weapons fire. The firefighters were forced to dodge falling chunks of cement and bricks being chipped off building from the rounds striking those structures. Many more fires were created by the weapon fire and exploding grenades. Nevertheless, the outstanding firemen continued their life saving work, but even they knew when they had to get out of harm's way, and they started to pull back away from the scene of all the carnage.

The still excited Russian slid a second box of hand grenades over to the concrete wall, and he savagely ripped off the top of the wooden box with his bare hands. He then pulled out a few grenades and tossed one to Michael as he pulled the pin on his grenade. He tossed the grenade over the side of the wall and it hit the street, bouncing once before exploding in a flash, sending a wave of hot shrapnel out at supersonic speed. Ripping into numerous parked cars, trucks, mailboxes, phone booths, newspaper stations, and a number of firemen busy fighting the many fires still raging on the streets, or still helping injured civilians and police officers.

Michael picked up what Alexander just done with his grenade, and he followed his lead and copied him. He pulled the pin and then tossed it over the side of the building. The Russian followed his grenade with his eyes all the way down to the ground, and he did not like the lack of destruction created by the weapon when it exploded. He picked up another grenade and pulled the pin, and then he counted to three, before tossing this weapon over the side of the building.

He followed this grenade all the way to the ground also, but when this one exploded twenty feet above the ground, and the explosion sent out a wide bloom of super heated, harden steel flying in all directions. He smiled to himself, because he was more than pleased with the idea of holding the grenade for those few seconds. He did the same with the next four grenades he tossed over the side of the building, ripping apart many parked cars, and shattering windows all the way up to the sixth floor of some of the buildings being hit by the exploding grenade fragments.

All firefighters, police, and remaining civilians, along with news reporters and anyone else in the vicinity. Dashed away from the area under attack by the terrorists on the roof of the Tower and Hotel, when the first grenades exploded above their heads, killing two people on the ground.

Both Michael and Alexander were not the only ones tossing the grenades off the roof of the Trump Tower. Eleven others of the Russian's group were also pitching their grenades off the Tower. The killing rain continued to fall from the roof area, until Alexander was positive all the police and firefighters had pulled well back to a much safer position further away from the Tower. When the Russian ex-soldier felt no one was left alive, or no one was near enough to the Tower to no longer be a very serious threat against them. He held up his hand and his people immediately stopped throwing grenades over the side of the building. However, the heavy M-60 machine guns continued to rip into the surrounding buildings though. The grenade launchers also stopped firing, to conserve the rest of their ammunition for possible future use.

The loud roar of echoing explosions soon faded in the huge caverns of midtown Manhattan, as Alexander cautiously looked over the parapet wall to the streets below him that were still hidden beneath a thick cloud of churning black smoke, and the numerous fires created by the crashing helicopters and the countless grenades exploding in the streets below.

The Russian stared over the side of the building until Broadway slowly came in the clear. The once well groomed street dividers of Broadway, the home to well manicured grass and a number of tall Maple trees and decorative plants and shrubs, had been torn apart, and the trees were knocked over and lying in the street. All victims of the grenades that rained down from above.

Alexander stared at the street below him and he noticed many destroyed cars and trucks, he also picked up a number of destroyed police cars along with two fire trucks also destroyed in his attack against the emergency responders and police officers. One civilian car was actually flipped over on its roof, and another one rested on its side, laying half on the sidewalk, and half in the all but destroyed street. The car on its roof was ablaze, and millions of tiny shards of shattered glass covered the once spotlessly clean Broadway street.

Alexander glared at the almost destroyed street until the smoke finally cleared away for him. Then, the full impact of his crime filled his eyes and mind. Lying helter-skelter right in the middle of the street were countless bodies of civilians, firemen, FBI Agents and police officers caught up in his deadly attack waged against them. The many dead and wounded were cut down right in the middle of their efforts to help their fallen co-workers and innocent civilians.

For a brief second, Alexander actually felt a slight twinge of pain because of the terrible carnage he had just created on the streets below him. But the flash of sparkling diamonds in his mind, quickly erased all the ill feelings he was suffering for the dead and dying below him.

Chapter Nineteen

THE OVAL OFFICE, THE WHITE HOUSE,
WASHINGTON DC

President Cole stood over FBI Director Hedemann's shoulder, while he was trying to find out how the helicopter attack against the Trump Tower went. The rather inpatient acting American President was hoping to hear that his Vice President had been freed, and she was on her way to the Aircraft Carrier moored in the Hudson River. The President had trouble fighting to keep the grin from his face. He liked the plan put forth by the FBI Director, and he had confidence in it.

Besides, the President was looking forward to putting it to the terrorists, who had dared to have the nerve to take his Vice President their hostage. President Cole kept repeating it was time they put it to the terrorists, rather than having it the other way around.

The deeply concerned President rested his hand lightly on the FBI Director's back, while he listened in on the report coming in. President Cole noticed the constant light, and the other one blinking when receiving a message. Under his hand, the President suddenly felt the Director's back tense up, and he put a little more pressure on his hand as the Director stood slowly. The stunned Hedemann's back was hunched over as if he had just been punched right in the guts as he struggled to his feet. His body actually shook from his anger and horror, as he kept the receiver glued to his ear. The Director's knuckles were white as he held a death grip on the receiver and sweat broke out on his forehead and it ran into his eyes. But he ignored the stinging as he continued to listen to the report coming in from his agent stationed in New York City.

"What's wrong with you, god dammit?" the President asked in a weak whisper.

The concerned Director Hedemann waved his hand at the President to silence him as he continued to listen to the report from his agent in the field. His strength drained from his body, and the Director suddenly dropped in his chair, and he allowed the receiver to fall from his hand to the floor. Peter moved in and he retrieved the receiver for the Director and placed it back in its cradle, he disappeared in the background as he waited to hear the Director report.

President Cole knew from the stunned look Director Hedemann just received terrible news. Jumping the gun, the President offered to the Director. "Please don't dare try and tell me my Vice President was killed in this rescue attempt Director. I won't stand for that for a minute mister."

"No Mr. President Sir, that's not the situation at all sir. I thank God for that much though, sir. That seems like the only thing that worked out in our favor this time. I'm certain the Vice President's still safe and sound where she's being held inside the Trump Tower, sir." The FBI Leader offered in a strained voice as he looked up and in the excited American Leader's face.

"Yes, thank God for that I believe, Director Hedemann Sir. Then what the hell has you so upset here, sir? Do you want me to send for a Doctor for you, Director? You don't look too good, are you sure you didn't just have a heart attack or something?" the worried President asked the FBI Director as he continued to stare at him, making sure he was alright.

"If only I were that lucky, if only I was that lucky. Errr... President Cole, I have some terrible news to report to you, sir. Both my helicopters were knocked out of the air by the terrorists who were obviously stationed on the roof of the Trump Tower. I'm sorry to inform you, but the Agents and crews are believed to be lost in the action." The Director reported to the President.

"Whatttt? How the hell is this possible for Christ sake? I can't believe this shit for a fucking minute, mister. You must be mistaken about this information. What the hell happened with your so called Hostage Rescue Teams, Director? Did they suffer a midair crash or worst? Talk to me man, dammit." The President roared at the obviously stunned man.

"No it was not a midair collision that has killed my Agents, Mr. President Sir. It seems we have underestimated the god damn terrorists, and their abilities and want to kill with such savagery, sir. It looks like the damn terrorists had some shoulder launch anti aircraft missiles set up on the roof of the Trump Tower, and they used the weapons to knock out our pair of aircraft as they approached the Tower to carry out their mission as ordered, Mr. President Sir."

ROOM 2012, THE TRUMP INTERNATIONAL TOWER AND HOTEL

Lieutenant Robert Walker and Sergeant Dorothy Ramirez heard the explosion that claimed the inbound helicopter. It was followed closely by a second but much larger explosion. Then the grenade launchers and M-60 machine guns started to fire from the roof of the Tower. The two young soldiers had no trouble identifying the weapon fire. Both elite soldiers hunkered down close to the floor, as they tried to figure out what was going on inside the Tower.

"This shit seems like fucking De Ja Va all over to me, baby. What the hell did we do, stumble into a stinking war zone right smack in the middle of the damn States!" the angry Lieutenant grumbled as he headed for the door to see if he could see anything going on in the hallway. Moments before the explosions, they both heard some rustling around outside their apartment, and he was about to check it out to try and find out what was happening outside his room.

Sergeant Dorothy Ramirez went to follow her soldier, but he stopped her and then waved her back as he held the butcher's knife locked in hand at the ready, and moved nearer towards the door. She got down on a knee and then prepared to leap into action if her soldier came under attack by whoever obviously invaded the Trump Tower.

ROOM STAR THREE, THE TRUMP INTERNATIONAL TOWER AND HOTEL

Once the terrorist leader was convinced Alexander and the rest of his people had everything under their control on the roof. He rested his hand on Alexander's back, and then informed him he was going back downstairs so he could check on the Vice President's condition, before mounting his assault against the diamond dealer's apartment. The leader of the group rushed to the service elevator and pushed the button and was soon on his way for the twenty second floor.

As he came out of the large service elevator, he nodded to the man he placed on station outside Room Star Three. The bodies of the two agents had been tossed down the open elevator shaft, to remove them from the middle of the hallway. He entered the Presidential Suite at the same instant Valentine stood hovering over the Vice President while staring at her nastily.

He heard Valentine's voice threatening, and he laughed as he checked in with Lizzie.

Valentine was straddling Ms. Hirshfield's legs, as he stood before her and hissed at the powerful politician. "You know pig, I never felt a Vice President's tits. I'm dying to know if they feel the same as the other pig's tits of this god dom country, bitch." With that said, he suddenly shoved his hand down the front of Hirshfield's blouse, and he grabbed her breasts harshly.

Not the slightest bit of being scared of the terrorist who held a loaded MP-5 machine gun across his chest with one hand, and the other hand stuffed down her blouse. She chomped down defiantly on his forearm, causing Valentine to scream out in pain as she purposely ground her teeth into the soft flesh of his arm. All the while she was biting, she glared in Valentine's eyes.

"Yeeeaaaoooowww! Let go bitch, before I blow your fucking head off you god dom shoulder, dammit." Valentine cried out in pain as he tried to free his arm from Mary's clamped on and grinding teeth. He pulled up on his arm, trying to get it free from her mouth and this move did not work, because the Vice President continued to hold on his arm with her teeth.

Ms. Hirshfield actually followed the pressure of his arm clamping down tighter on it, until she was standing. Valentine dropped his weapon and then he smashed the Vice President across the face with the back of his hand as hard as he could hit her. She released her grip, and then she staggered momentarily, almost knocking her chair over as she stepped back. It was the only thing that stopped her from falling over. Even though she was staggered, the fuming Vice President continued to fight, refusing to be intimidated by the extremely dangerous man. She retaliated by kicking him right between the legs as she growled, causing Valentine to double over in agonizing pain as he clutched at his crotch and then he sank to the floor and clamped his knees together.

Lizzie and Michael watched the scene being played out before them with amusement, until Valentine fell to the floor in pain. As his wits returned, he reached for his weapon on the floor next to him. He knew he was angry and was going to kill the Vice President if he did not step between them. He placed his hand against Mary's chest and then he shoved her backwards.

Ms. Hirshfield fell back in the chair and it tipped over under her weight. If it was not for Michael grabbing her arm and stead the chair at the same time, she would have tumbled over the chair. He could feel Valentine struggling to his feet and felt his anger, and he knew he had to do something to stop the inevitable from happening. He searched his mind as to what to do, and found his way out of the situation he knew would satisfy the seething Valentine.

Agent Edward Sweeney, who was still handcuffed to the chair, struggled against his restraints as he cursed Valentine for what he was doing to the Vice President. Valentine was trying to get around Michael to reach the obviously fuming Vice President, who refused to back down from either terrorist. He looped his weapon around Michael's hip, and he then tried to get a bead on Mary's chest. Michael roughly grabbed the barrel of his weapon and pulled it up until it pointed towards the ceiling of the apartment as he growled at his fellow terrorist angrily.

"Step back Two, you got what you asked for. This bitch has brass ovaries, not much sense, but nevertheless she has brass ovaries. I can't allow you to kill her over your own foolishness. Two, we need her alive to use as a shield to get out of here safely. However..." He then turned to Ms. Hirshfield and warned her angrily and in no uncertain terms. "I don't need any dumb cunt giving some backbone to any of these other hostages here and I can't allow you to attack my people either, without responding against your actions bitch.

"I know you understand we need you alive, and this knowledge gives you the guts to be what you are. So that forces me to do something drastic, to find another way to keep control over you and your god damn temper, missy. Since you know it's important for me to keep you alive, I'll give you that much alright. But on the other hand bitch, I don't need anyone else we have held here alive, as long as I have you. So..." He slowly removed his Glock 17 pistol, and then he aimed it right at Sweeney's head. Agent Sweeney stopped moving as he stared back into Michael's unblinking eyes, trying to will him from pulling the trigger against him.

Cathy saw what was going on behind her by craning her neck back, and she began to beg Michael for Sweeney's life. "Please don't do it, I'll keep the Vice President under control and make sure she don't cause any further trouble for you. You can't kill a defenseless man without reason. Please don't do it. I'll keep Mary from making any more trouble for..."

Lizzie moved to Cathy's side and she slammed her across the face with the back of her hand.

Ms. Hirshfield stood while trying to protest his threat to kill the helpless Sweeney. She did not believe this man would kill a defenseless man like he was threatening to do and be able to like with his actions. She could not allow herself to believe he would pull the trigger on the helpless agent, just because she was guilty of trying to defending herself against the other man's assault against her. She stared at the leader of the terrorists as he continued to aim his weapon with at Sweeney's head as if he was enjoying watching Sweeney staring back at him.

Valentine, the Number Two man of the group was standing before the Vice President again. He roughly shoved her back down in the chair. Then he pushed the barrel of his weapon in her face, and he dared her to try and stand again as he glared down at her.

The terrorist leader smiled at Sweeney staring at him with unblinking eyes, giving the special agent the illusion that he was not going to kill him. He smiles until Sweeney finally returned his grin. At that exact moment, he pulled the trigger on the agent. The slug nearly split Sweeney's head in two, sending brain matter, blood, and bone fragments flying over the back and hair of the female bodyguard, who roared with anger at the violent death just suffered by the brave young agent. "Nooooooo, you god damn sonofabitch you no. You killed him, you killed him you lousy bastard you. I'll see you burn in the fires of hell for all eternity for this murder, if it's the last thing I witness. I can't believe you just killed a completely defenseless man. I'll make sure…"

Michael grabbed her by the hair and he savagely bent her head against her neck, causing terrible pain to the helpless and extremely upset secretary. He shoved the still smoking weapon up against her cheek, the smoke actually burned her nostrils. As he hissed close enough to her face so the Vice President's secretary could actually smell his vile breath. "Bitch, I don't need you alive either you know! So unless you want to suffer the same fate as this other asshole. I suggest you be a little kinder with the words you address me with. I also suggest you sit still with your god damn mouth zipped shut! If you want to live to have any kids that is, bitch." He angrily gave Cathy's head a hard shove sideways with the barrel of his gun, to emphasize his warning against her. Then he shoved her head forward by her hair and finally released her.

Cathy's head slumped forward and rested on her chest as she sobbed softly. With Sweeney gone, she was the only other bodyguard left the Vice President had to protect her life.

Ms. Hirshfield was near hysterics, never before in her life had she ever witnessed such wanton violence displayed right before her eyes. She had been sheltered from the inner city strife all her life, and only knew of the disorder and death from what she read in the newspapers, and saw on the news. She never allowed herself to believe half of what the reporters said, thinking it was their way to hype their newspaper sales. Ms. Hirshfield cried for Sweeney's untimely death, one of the few men she really cared for. She cried for the feeling of helplessness, her body was full of rage for not being able to get at this man controlling her life. The fuming Vice President's head slumped forward as she cried softly, yet she refused to allow the angry terrorist to know he won a victory over her. She refused to look up at him, for fear of him understanding she had just given into his complete control over her body and actions.

The leader of the group moved a little closer to Ms. Hirshfield, and then he pulled her head up by the hair until their eyes met. He noticed the tears streaking her face and he snarled savagely at her. "You see bitch, you just learned a very valuable lesson on life here. So don't try and fuck with me again, and you and your other friend here just might live through this shit, bitch."

He noticed Ms. Hirshfield was slowly rolling some salvia around in her mouth, and he sneered rudely right in her face. "So I see you want to spit in my face then do you bitch? Well go ahead and do it, I dare you to try if you have the fucking guts to do so. I even warn you to try bitch, and see what happens to you and this other bitch right after you do." He then spun his weapon around in a high arch, making a big thing about aiming it right at the back of Cathy's head this time. Then he hissed again at Ms. Hirshfield as he continued to glare into the Vice President's eyes.

"Go ahead Miss high and fucking mighty and spit in my god damn face. I warn you bitch, anything you do against me, any further trouble you cause me or any of my other friends. Will cost another hostage their god damn life. You'll lose your sanity before I run out of fucking hostages to kill because of your stupid defiance. I repeat bitch, spit and see what happens to another one of your so called friends." Michael sneered at the Vice President's face.

With his thumb, he pulled back the hammer of the pistol, while still holding the weapon trained right on the back of Cathy's head. The gun barely wavered in his hand aimed at her head. Her bodyguard saw him aim the gun at her out of the corner of her eye, and she lowered her head and waited for death to visit her. Sweat rolled down Cathy's face, but she was not the least bit afraid of dying at this point. He stared at Ms Hirshfield, until she finally swallowed her salvia and he snapped at her. "That was very wise on your part, bitch! Now am I going to have any further trouble from you for the rest of the time I'm inside this god damn building, bitch?"

"No! You won't have any further trouble from me." Hirshfield said barely over a whisper.

"I didn't hear you, all important fucking bitch you." He snarled savagely right back at her.

"I said no! I'll not give you any further trouble." The Vice President said in a low voice.

"That's better." Michael snapped as he shook Ms. Hirshfield by the hair. He let go and turned to Lizzie with a sneer on his lips, acknowledging his dominated over the powerful woman.

THE OVAL OFFICE, THE WHITE HOUSE, WASHINGTON DC

FBI Director Hedemann relayed everything that just took place at and around the Trump International Tower and Hotel to the stunned President. From the helicopters being knocked out of the air, to the police and firefighters being slaughtered in the streets of Manhattan, while trying to aid the wounded and dying in midtown, and putting the numerous fires out as well.

The President, CIA Director Raincloud, and General White, and everyone else who mattered to the security of the United States, gathered in the Oval Office. All stared at the floor as they listened to everything the FBI Director said, as he counted off the staggering causalities of the failed attempted rescue operation for the Vice President. At the end of his speech, Director Hedemann turned to General White, and he pleaded more than said to the military officer.

"General White Sir, how the hell was I to know the bastards had such weapons at their disposal, dammit? I can't believe I was just the cause for so many brave men losing their lives in this botched attempt to free the Vice President, sir." Director Hedemann then turned away from the General to the President and he offered the man. "When this is over with, I'll turn in my resignation Mr. President Sir. After sending these brave Agents to their deaths, I don't deserve to hold office. Who could have known what my agents would be facing in this attack, dammit."

"Back off a little Mr. Hedemann Sir, because it's as you have just stated. Who the hell could have possibly known what the bastards had at their disposal during this terrorist attack. You can't blame yourself for this disaster sir. Even if we used General White's elite troops, they would've suffered the same fate as your brave Agents did. No one's going to quit around here unless I fire them. I'm the only one who'll lop off any heads if I feel anyone has let me down during this emergency, and I don't feel that way with you for a second, Director Hedemann Sir. I don't want anything but to get my Vice President out of that god damn building alive. Okay people, I'm open to any suggestions, and I want to know why the bastards are in this building in the first place, dammit." The President announced to all gathered in the Oval Office.

"I believe I might be able to answer that question for you, Mr. President Sir." "You Peter? How the hell would you know what the god damn terrorists are after inside the building?" the President replied as he turned in his chair, so he could see the young man's face.

"With all due respect Mr. President Sir, I have just received some information from a close friend in New York, sir. I called him when this terrorist thing first started, sir. If anything's happening in the Big City, I knew he'd know about it, Mr. President Sir. When I told him a group of terrorists hit the Trump Tower, he told me they were going after diamonds. I asked him what he meant by that remark, and he told me a number of Jewish diamond dealers were using the Trump Tower for the next few days to trade off, and to set the benchmark price for the diamond trade for the upcoming year. I asked him how much in diamonds he was talking about that these dealers had inside the building, and he told me somewhere around one half to one billion dollars of cut diamonds, are they were believed to be in the room with the diamond traders, sir."

The Secretary of Defense let his breath out in a rush as he offered. "No wonder the animals are willing to kill anyone they come across in the building for Christ sake. For a billion dollars in untraceable diamonds, I might be doing what they're doing to get away with a bundle like that."

The President gave the Secretary a queer look as he shook his head, and then the American Leader snapped at Peter. "You're positive about the diamonds being inside the building?"

"Positive Mr. President Sir, when I finished speaking with my friend, I called the head of the diamond trade market, at first he was unwilling to confirm or deny this information. But when I told the speaker who I was, and why I was calling, he talked rather freely with me after that. He hesitantly confirmed the presence of the diamonds and trader's meeting inside the Tower. He placed the value of diamonds nearer to three quarters of a billion dollars, Mr. President Sir."

"When you're talking in these crazy numbers, what's the difference in one half, three quarters, and one billion dollars, Peter. I seriously doubt I can even count that much money in my lifetime, dammit." The President grunted, feeling a little better with knowing what the terrorists were after in the trump Tower as he announced. "Okay, I need input. What I want has little to do with what we're speaking about now. But it's something I wanted cleared up for my peace of mind. Besides, it'll give you time to come up with your solutions to this situation, I need input people."

"Mr. President, I can always send in the Apache attack helicopters to get at the terrorists we now know are stationed on the roof of the Tower, sir." Director Hedemann offered lamely.

"And, do what with the god damn things, Mister? Blow up the god damn building and kill everyone inside the place? Those damn weapons are an all or nothing way out of this present mess. We can't possibly get at the terrorists, they're too well armed and entrenched inside the damn Tower for a successful mission to be carried out against them, dammit. We have to come up with another plan, one that'll get my Vice President the hell out of that damn place and in one piece mind you all here." The President grumbled at everyone gathered in the room.

"Mr. President Sir, I've been working on a scenario that might just do the trick for..."

"Thank God finally, okay General White, I'm all ears sir." The President announced.

"Mr. President Sir, we know there's no way in hell to successfully assault the damn terrorists stationed on the roof of the Tower armed as they are. Not with the weapons they have available at their disposal. So I suggest we hit the building from the mid section. My specialized Units have mountain climbing experts who can easily scale the side of the building, Mr. President Sir. My troopers can work their way to the floor where the Vice President's being held hostage, and they can breach it from that area, Mr. President Sir. Once my troops have breached..."

INSIDE ROOM 2012, THE TRUMP INTERNATIONAL TOWER AND HOTEL

Lieutenant Robert Walker stood ready to pounce on anyone he spotted at the door, he cracked the door open just far enough so he could see into the hallway. For the past few moments they heard someone prowling around on their floor. Looking outside, he instantly picked up an armed man standing in the hallway like he was on guard duty. While another man was rummaging through the apartment door they just forced opened. He checked out the other side of the hallway, and saw no one so he knew these two were working alone. The second guy came out of the room dragging a woman by the hair. She was crying and he shoved her rudely towards the stairway, while ordering her to go down to the lobby and wait there if she wanted to live and be free.

The terrified girl took off like a shot without looking back. The alert Lieutenant had no doubt in his mind the woman would not stop running until she did as told by this guy. The one who dragged the woman out of the apartment, smirked as he ducked back into the room, and Walker heard him ripping the place apart a second time. He knew these two were looking for anything of worth in the apartment. He looked at their weapons, both intruders carried the Heckler and

Koch 9 mm machine weapon, and they seemed like they knew how to handle themselves in a fight as well. He also spotted a Glock 9 mm pistol stuck in a holster on one of the invaders.

The Lieutenant looked at his weapon and shook his head, he knew they did not stand a snowball's chance in hell of going up against the automatic weapons and invaders the way they were armed, and the people who seemed to know how to handle them, just being armed with a butcher knife and broken table leg. It sounded like the guy rummaging around the apartment finished what he was doing. He carefully closed the door and tried to think of a way to get his hands on their weapons. He headed for Sergeant Ramirez who was still hiding in the kitchen, as he moved to her he came up with an idea. He knew it was only a matter of time before the two invaders forced their apartment door, and he had to be prepared to attack them when they did.

He got in Ramirez's face and snapped at her. "Raz, I've been thinking about you, little sister."

"Oh please I wish you wouldn't think of me, I might catch something hanging around in that filthy mind of yours, mister." She retorted to her lover and soldier with a smile.

"Ha, ha, funny girl, real funny sister. Look, I want you to get outta your fucking clothes!" he growled back at her, overlooking her failed attempt at being funny with him.

"What? Now is not the time for that kind of shit mister. We have a problem lover, and..."

"Cut the clowning around out and do what I just told ya for fuck sake. You're way off base. We have two stinking targets armed with MP-5s, and they seem to have some kinda military training, judging by the way they're carrying their fucking weapons and the way they stand. Now, they're checking out the uther apartments on this fucking floor, and sending anyone they find on the floor down to the fricking lobby area I guess. They're gonna be here any second now, and I don't trust the lousy bastards one bit. There's been too much shooting for me to believe they're gonna let anyone go alive from this stinking dump. There's too many weapons to believe this is a small operation going down here. Something big is going down, and I'll be dipped in shit if I can figure out what the hell it is, baby. We hafta get our hands on some real stinking weapons if we wanna getting out of this one with our skin. So get outta your stinking clothes will ya."

"All of them mister?" she asked as she pulled her tee shirt over her shoulders.

"All of them!" he griped as he moved behind her, and skillfully wove her knife in her hair while she struggled out of her jeans. By the time he finished hiding the knife in her hair, she was naked. He made certain the knife would slide freely out of her hair with slight pressure from her. It worked fine and he stepped back and surveyed her exquisite form, and then said to her. "Man, if this don't make the dopey shits drop their stinking guard down some so I can get the drop on the two assholes. Then they hafta be a pack of tail gunning turd pushing queer bastards."

"Well now you have me naked again, what the hell do you want me to do?" the Sergeant snapped as she placed her hands on her hips, and then she stared at the gawking Lieutenant.

"Listen up Raz, I want you to make like you were just coming outta the stinking bedroom when the dopey slugs come charging in our room. Keep your arms down at your side and let them order you around while they're getting a good look of ya. Act like you're scared shitless of the flaming assholes, and you're willing to do anything they want if they let you live. Then, the first chance you get I want you to act like you're even a little enchanted by their manly actions, play up to them some like you might even want to ball the shit outta them..."

"What? That's bullshit and bad manners mister! I'm not going to play up to the lousy bastards while I'm naked. I'll be totally helpless if they try something on me. This plan of yours is no good Walker, and I don't agree with it one bit, buster. You have to come up with another plan much better than this one, one that keeps my clothes on me for a change. Their manly actions, oh brother give me a fucking break will you please. Sometimes, I don't know how you think."

"C'mon, you know I'm not gonna allow the two asses to get familiar with you before I do them both in good and proper. Besides baby, I don't want you to actually ball the damn assholes. You know what I want, make it seem like you're awed by the way they entered your apartment, dammit. I'm going to be hiding by the damn planter over there." He pointed towards the planter with his chin as he went on with his plan for her. "You just hafta get the two idiots to move deeper into the damn apartment and past the planter. So I can get the jump on the two assholes from behind. I'll take out the guy on the left, and I'll make my move on the uther prick if I get half the chance to. If he's too fast for my ass, you're gonna hafta take him out with the stinking knife hidden in your hair. Understand baby? C'mon girl, they're almost here god dammit."

"Yeah yeah, I get the picture, get going mister. Consider these two birds putty in my hands, lover." The female Sergeant announced proudly to her soldier.

He rushed behind the large planter and pulled some leaves around his face, until Ramirez was even having some trouble seeing him. No sooner did he disappear in his makeshift jungle, than the lock on their apartment door unlatched, and the door swung open. The two men Alexander left behind to work the three floors clean, stood in the doorway with their weapons leveled at her naked body. Both of the young invaders sneered nastily at her as they stared at her body.

Even though the Sergeant expected this to take place with the two invaders, the sight of them appearing so suddenly inside her apartment scared her quite a bit. She froze in place and then she stared at the two goons with her mouth kind of slightly hanging open, as she felt any normal civilian would do in this type of situation. With having these two heavily armed men breaking into their room like they just did, and then aim their weapons at her.

"Whoa, will you look at what we just found ourselves in here buddy. You alone in this fucking apartment, bitch?" the first guy asked as he moved a little deeper into the room, and he quickly scanned the area before his eyes rested on her naked body again. He was thinking no one else was inside the apartment with this naked and good looking woman.

"Who the hell are you people? What the devil do you want in my apartment, the both of you? I'm going to call downstairs for security and have you two removed if you two guys don't leave my apartment immediately. Do you two fools hear me?" She yelled at the two gawking strangers glaring at her as if they were just daring her to move the wrong way on them.

"Relax a little will you sweetie, we are security for the damn building so there's no need to call for us, honey." The second invader snarled at her, as he moved his weapon to a more comfortable position and he repeated. "You were asked if you were alone in here once, now twice bitch. If I have to asked you for a third time, I'm going to blow your pretty little ass all the way to hell. Is there anyone else inside this god damn apartment with you bitch!"

"No, I'm alone, why do you ask? Who are you people? What the hell do you want in my room? I have no money, and my boyfriend doesn't make very much you know. So if you two are after some cash, oh brother have you two birds come to the wrong apartment I can tell ya." She tried to muster a smile, but it only ended up looking more like a sneer than a grin. She was truly scared of the two men, and she was fighting desperately to stop her body from trembling on her.

The second invader figured she was alone in the apartment and he smiled at the scared looking woman. The two invaders slowly relaxed their stance, and then they took a much softer stand with her. The first guy offered to the naked female in a commanding voice. "We're terrorists, and we have just taken over the entire fucking building, sweetie. Do you have any valuables hidden in here that we might be interested in taking? Man you look real fine there lady."

"I already told you two that I'm piss poor. Where are you going to move the building?" She asked while trying to be funny with the two invaders. When this did not work on them, she then placed her hands on her hips and thrust her chest out, making her breasts look larger than they were, and forcing them upwards in the same motion. The effect was absolutely perfect, and it forced the two to pay more attention to her body, than to what they were doing inside the apartment. She saw the bulge in the first guy's pants, and knew she had them where she wanted them as she purred. "So you two strong men are terrorists huh? Ooooh that excites me so much. Are you going to kill me?" the Sergeant asked as she ran her hands slowly over her breasts and then down the length of her exquisite body, until her hands ended up between her crotch.

The second man leaned a little closer to the other one and he interjected. "Man, this bitch is really cooking it up for us man. You think we have enough time for a little quickie with her before we do her little ass in, my friend?"

"Sure, why the hell not brother. Michael will never know we took this time to have a little fun with her, and if he does, the hell with him, who really cares what he thinks? I don't care, but I'm not going to pass a gift like this up for nothing, my friend. A chance like this comes along just once in a fucking lifetime. Here, hold my gun while I take firsties on the dumb bitch."

Hey man, that means I get stuck with sloppy seconds after you had your way with the damn bitch man. I don't want the leavings from you, I want to go first and you can have my leftovers for a change." The follower complained as he took the weapon and then he followed his partner more deeper into the apartment as he quickly closed in on the naked woman.

"Tough shit buddy, in case you don't understand your position around here, you're the low shit on the totem pole in the outfit, so get use to it man. I'm going first so like it buddy." The first guy griped as he quickly closed in on the slightly backing up Ramirez, who placed her hands behind her head, while rotating her hips seductively and rolling her shoulders at the excited man coming at her now. Her fingers carefully searching her hair for the hilt of the hidden knife in her hair. When she had the handle in her hand, she stopped backing up and waited for Walker to make his move on the two, while she continued to rotate her hips and stare at the man approaching her.

"That's it bitch, stir up that pretty little ass of yours real good and warm for me. Get it lubricated up real good for me, cause I'm coming for a piece of that little ass of yours, bitch." The first invader said with a sarcastic look on his face as he began to fumble with his pants.

Sergeant Ramirez picked up the movement out of the corner of her eye. It was her soldier making his move on the two, and she saw the trailing invader instantly sag locked in his arms, but not fall down to the floor. The first terrorist was still coming at her, his hands reaching for her slightly swaying breasts. Then from behind the one closing in on her, she heard.

"Shiitttttttt, hey stupid, over here fucker." The Lieutenant hissed at the man's back.

The terrorist stalking Ramirez, heard the slight whistle from behind him and he quickly turned around to see what his partner wanted from him. He was instantly startled when he came face to face with a taller, and much stronger looking and well built stranger holding both MP-5 machine weapons, one in each hand and he was aiming them both directly at his chest. The shocked terrorist mumbled at the wild looking stranger in an extremely angry voice as he stopped all his movement towards Ramirez and put all his concentration of this new threat.

"Who the fuck are you now, pal? Why the fuck are you butting your nose into something that doesn't concern you in the fucking least, pal? Why don't you do yourself a fucking favor here and drop my weapons and then turn around and head down to the fucking lobby and wait there to be freed from the damn Tower, my friend. I'm just going to tear me off a little piece of trim here, pal." The invader growled at Walker as he reached for his pistol tangled up in his bunched up pants sliding down his legs and gathering around his ankles.

"In case you don't recognize and realize it yet, I'm your worst fucking nightmare you ever had coming at your stinking ass, buddy. You're a fricking dead man, PAL." The Lieutenant mimicked the terrorist's word 'pal' back at him.

"You and what fucking Army is going to do me in, pal? You think for one second just because you have my weapons that this thing is over with? No way in hell is it over, not by a long shot I'm telling you, fella. You can't shoot me, not without hitting your little girlfriend standing directly in the line of fire right behind me, pal. Yes, I'm going to enjoy ripping you a new fucking asshole and then I'm going to work your girlfriend over real good and slow, pa... Awwww."

The terrorist's worthless threats were cut off as Ramirez's knife dug deep in his right lung, immediately taking the wind and strength from the terrorist's body. The terrorist's hands went over his head as they struggled to get a hold of the handle of knife sticking out of his back. He could not reach the blade or Sergeant Ramirez's face, he was clutching at. She pulled the knife out of his back and then she plunged the blade in his other lung, and then she actually turned the blade in the wound this time. The terrorist stopped fighting and slowly pitched forward, landing hard on his hands and knees, as he now concerned himself with the desperate struggle to try and breathe. The knife still sticking out of his back, and the invader's blood spurting from the gaping wounds in his rapidly dying body.

The terrorist looked at the grinning wild man standing before him but well out of his reach with both his weapons locked in his hands as any professional soldier would hold and aim them. He tried to speak but no words would come out of his mouth. The quickly dying terrorist listened as the stranger spoke at him in an extremely angry tone of voice. "Me, and that fucking Army, PAL." The grinning military officer pointed the best he could with the barrel of his weapon, shifting them towards the naked Sergeant, who moved around the dying terrorists to walk over to his side while she stared back at the man.

"I'm going to fucking kill you both nice and slow for this shit, mother fuckerrrrr." The terrorist suddenly fell forward, his last breath coming out of the gaping wound in his back and lungs.

"Cool job there I knew you could pull this thing off for me Raz. Okay little sister, you betta get dressed as quick as you can and then make sure you have a pair of stinking socks and shoes on your feet, baby. You know if your stinking feet get cold on ya, your whole fucking body won't wanna dance around any for us and we have a helluva way to go yet, baby."

"Got ya Robert, I have to get a move on it because I'm freezing my tits off standing here like this anyhow, Bobby. You want me to get you an over shirt as well, lover? I don't want you getting cold on me either, mister. What am I saying, I never seen you cold in your life, mister." She asked her soldier as she moved off to do what she was told.

"Yeah I'm always hot and ready to trot, and you betta get one for yourself while you're at it baby, where we're going next I think we're gonna need all the stinking warm we can possibly get for ourselves, Raz." Walker replied as he watched his lover head off for the bedroom as ordered.

"I guess you already have a plan all worked out in that sick twisted mind of yours on how we're going to get the hell out of here in one piece, right Bobby? I should have known you had something worked out for us already, Bobby." She asked and offered as she struggled into her clothes, and she handed him a flannel over shirt, and then she waited for his reply.

"Bet your little sweet ass I do baby, since when don't I know what the fucking I'm doing all the time baby. We're gonna make our fricking asses up for the stinking roof of this lousy dump, and then we're gonna wait there for the fucking cavalry to arrive and help us out some here. You know the damn the Feds gotta be planning some kinda god damn hit on this fucking place by now, and that has to come by way of the stinking roof area, baby. Let's get a stinking move on it girl. I feel extremely vulnerable standing here like this. Crap, I really wish the stinking Mutt was with us. We could sure use his damn help on this one, little sister." Walker griped as he skillfully padded down the first dead man's body. He removed any extra clips of bullets for the two automatic weapons, six were on each terrorist and he stuffed them in his pockets. Then he removed one Glock pistol, and shoved it in his belt and he tossed the other one to Ramirez.

He also found two extra clips for each pistol, and he gave them both over to the Sergeant, because his pockets were full of the clips for the heavier weapons they both had now. He was pleased each of the weapons took the same type of rounds for them, that way they could be used for either of the four weapons if and when needed. The Marine Lieutenant also found a small handheld radio on each of the two dead terrorists, and he took one and gave the other to Ramirez. One of the dead guys also had a candy bar on him which he shared with her. Once they had everything the dead men had on them, they both headed for the hallway again.

Outside their apartment, they did the standard action of working their way for the elevators. The Lieutenant moved out first, and he rushed towards a doorway and then he took a position there and he waited for the Sergeant to go over to the next door and do the same thing there. Then he sprang out of the doorway and went over to the next doorway ahead of her. Then he waits for her to pass him before moving out to the next doorway. He was the first one to reach the elevators and he pushed the button for the rooftop observation area. Nothing happened but the light blinking out of service. He tried the next two elevators and received the same message from them, and he complained at his girlfriend. "Christ sake sister, I don't know what the fuck gives around here, god dammit Raz. I know damn well I heard a fucking elevator working a few minutes ago. I guess it wasn't one of these two fucking things though baby."

"Maybe we should try the service elevator then? I'm sure one has to service this floor, they usually cover every floor of a building like this one, Bobby." She offered to her soldier.

"That's a damn good idea you got there little sister. I knew there was a damn good reason why I always had you hanging round me like this, little sister. Where the hell's the damn thing around here at for Pete's sake? I don't remember passing by any fricking service elevator on this stinking floor, baby. One of the damn things gotta be on this floor someplace. How else would the workers of this dump get any heavy furniture up to these expensive ass apartments they got inside this stinking dump, sister. They can't hump this heavy ass shit up the damn steps, they would die before they got any of that shit up this far into the damn building." The Lieutenant flashed his reassuring smile at her and then he waited for her reply.

The Sergeant pointed down the hall because that was the only area where the service elevator could possibly be at, and they both rushed for it. He found it and pushed the button, and it moved slowly from the fifth floor up to his.

Chapter Twenty Two

THE SECURITY COMMAND CENTER INSIDE
THE TRUMP INTERNATIONAL TOWER AND HOTEL

Suarez the Number Three terrorist of the group was annoyed and growing rather bored with watching the security monitors, fifteen screens in all. But the instant the service elevator started to move, it immediately registered on his security console. He knew it was something, because it moved without him being warned in advance by someone from the group that they were using the large and only still operating elevator in the entire building. He sat up and instantly placed a call out to the group's leader over his handheld radio. After he tried to stop the elevator from moving by throwing any switch labeled elevators inside the security room of the Tower.

"One, come in Number One. I think we have a slight problem on our hands, Number One."

"One here. What's the fucking problem now Three?" He growled into his handheld radio.

"One, where the hell you going in the service elevator man?" Three asked his leader.

"I'm not going anywhere in the damn thing. I'm not even using the damn service elevator, why do you ask me that Number Three?" he asked the other terrorist calmly.

"I didn't think you were using the damn thing because you didn't check in with me first, anyway it's moving Number One. Someone must have pushed the damn button for it."

"Can you stop the damn thing from there?" he snarled at his man in the security center.

"No can do from here One, I tried and I couldn't stop it from moving. The fire laws makes it impossible to control the service elevator from the security room, Number One. It's the only elevator that remains operational during any fire or other emergency situation inside the building. It's like that so the firefighters can get their equipment up to any floor of the building. I have no control over the damn thing from down here in the Security Command Post, Number One. Nothing I can do will possibly stop it from moving from down here."

"Where the hell's the damn car heading for Three?" the terrorist growled in his radio.

"Don't know for sure Number One, the elevator was sitting on the fifth floor, where it went automatically when you released it after using it to see what Twenty Seven was doing on the roof area. All I can tell you is it's heading towards the upper floors somewhere. If you wait a minute, I can tell what floor it stops at, Number One."

"Do that, I have to know where the hell it's heading for." He snarled at Three.

The elevator took forever moving up the interior of the Tower shaft. The second it stopped, Suarez came back on the radio. "Number One, the elevator went up to the twentieth floor for a minute, it stopped there and it's moving again. It looks like its heading for the roof area I believe. I think someone just got on it on that floor Number One. You want me to send Number Four after it and see if anyone's in it or if this is a fluke thing the elevator does once in a while?"

"Don't sweat it, I'll have Twenty Seven take care of the package from the roof." He broke off the communication with Suarez and then he switched the radio to Alexander's frequency.

"Twenty Seven, this is One. I need to speak to you, it's important, come in Twenty Seven."

"Da! This Twenty Seven, go head and speak big shot leader you please." The extremely dangerous Russian ex-soldier growled into the radio, upset Number One was bothering him.

He ignored the angry Russian's sarcasm as he replied to the man. "Twenty Seven, someone just got on the damn service elevator, and it's now heading for the roof area of the damn building. I want you to have a welcoming party waiting for him when he arrives in your area."

"That be pleasure of me to carry out for you Number One please. I wait package arrive, hope he make peace with maker by time I see his face, he greet him soon I promise you please." The large Russian snapped angrily as he broke off the communication with Michael.

Michael shook his head after he finished speaking with the Russian, and then he ordered Valentine to guard the Vice President and Cathy, who was constantly begging to be freed from Sweeney's dead body that she was still handcuffed to. Number One ignored her complaining as he headed to the twenty first floor to the diamond dealer's room. The Russian informed him the one who was assigned to blow the door open, was waiting for him there. Lizzie followed him as he took two steps at a time while running down the staircase towards the room.

Walker was out of breath as he stared at the numbers slowly flashing by his eyes. Ramirez had the wherewithal to turn on the radio they took from one of the invader to their apartment, and they both heard everything that was being said between the Russian and the leader of the group.

"What are we going to do now Bobby? You know they were talking about us on the radio just then. They know we're in here, and they're waiting for us to reach the roof. We're sitting ducks trapped inside this damn metal coffin." The Sergeant complained as she looped the MP-5 weapon over her shoulder with the barrel facing down, and she waited for the elevator to stop.

"Sitting ducks my fucking ass we are, little sister. I'm never a stinking sitting duck for anyone in this, or any uther stinking world I move around in, baby." The Lieutenant snapped at his girlfriend as he looped his weapon over his shoulder to get it out of his way. He then looked around the inside of the elevator until he found what he was looking for. He pointed towards the overhead trapdoor in the ceiling and snapped at his female Sergeant. "Up there fast, I'll help you get up there. Push open the fucking door with your arm, and then get on top of the car and wait for me. C'mon, we have some time left, but we gotta get a move on it, baby." He laced his fingers together, and she stepped in his hands and he easily hoisted her up as if she weighed nothing. She used her forearm to crash into the hatch which snapped open with little effort.

She ended up half in and half out of the elevator hatchway struggling for a handhold on top of the elevator car. Walker placed his hand against her rearend and then shoved up. She went flying and ended up on her hands and knees on top of the cab. She spun around and got on her knees as her weapon slid off her shoulder and clanked down on the top of the cab. She smiled down at her soldier and said. "Boy you'll do anything to cop a cheap feel from me, mister. You owe me one."

"Look out, I'm coming up." He leaped up and caught the lip of the cab, and he easily pulled himself through the narrow hatchway, using just the strength in his arms to easily handle his weight. His weapon slid all over his back as he struggled to get out of the hatchway. She tried to help him, but she only ended up being more in the way than anything else. When he was on top of the cab he slung his weapon over his shoulder, and looked for the hatch cover and replaced it. He looked up and saw the roof slowly coming at them and put an angry look on his face, because there was no place to hide on top of the cab or in the upper part of the elevator shaft.

"This is no fucking good baby. Those god damn jokers are gonna come in here hunting for fricking bear, and if they don't find us inside the damn cab, it's not gonna take them very long to figure out where the fuck we went." He checked out the both sides of the elevator shaft he could not see the bottom to, and spotted the metal ladder running the length of the shaft. It was used by the maintenance people working inside the shaft of the elevator. The cab was moving slow enough for them to easily grab hold of the ladder and get off the top of the cab. But before they got off the cab of the elevator, the Lieutenant explained to the Sergeant what he wanted her to do.

"Okay Raz, we gotta get off this god damn thing real quick like baby. We can't be caught hanging on the fucking ladder either when the lousy bastards come looking for our asses inside this damn thing. Once the birds don't find us in the cab, they're gonna search the top and if they don't find us up there, they're gonna look over the side of the damn thing. If we're caught hanging on the damn ladder by them, talk about being sitting fucking ducks sister."

"What the hell do we do now then Bobby? I'm scared to death, I wish we had a few more of our people with us dammit. I wouldn't be so damn afraid." She complained at her lover.

"Relax, this ain't nuthin but a stinking cake walk for us, baby. We've been through a helluva lot worse than this little bit of shit in Africa, Korea, and fucking Russia. We're gonna go over the side of this damn thing and get on the ladder and wait for the cab to pass us. Then we're gonna grab hold of the undercarriage and let it pull us to the top of the damn shaft. We're gonna hang there until these asses get tired of hunting for us. Simple enough act to follow, no baby?"

"That's fine, but then what are we going to do? We can't hang under there forever you know Robert. Sooner or later we're going to have to do something positive about this mess."

"No sweat there either baby, once the lousy pricks leave the damn cab, we're gonna get on the ladder and use it to get down to the fricking basement of this fucking dump, and see if we can find a damn fire door or some uther door down there leading to the outside of the stinking place. Maybe there's a garbage slide outta this damn dump. Something gotta lead to the outside the stinking building. Once we're outside this dump, we'll find the head honcho and offer him our observations, and see if he wants to put us to use. Whaddaya think about my plan so far baby?"

"Sounds like a winner to me, lover. Let's get going, I don't like standing here like I'm out of place." She grumbled as she went to the other side of the cab, and prepared to grab hold of the ladder of the elevator shaft. Suddenly, she was not so confident about herself as she reached for the metal rungs, which beat against her fingers as she reached to get a hold of one of them.

"C'mon, you gotta do it now, sister. We're fast running outta stinking time." Walker snapped.

She looked at her soldier and then she gave him a nasty look for a quick second. Then she pushed her hands out and grabbed hold of one of the rungs. One hand caught it, the other slapped her wrist by the passing rung before she grab it with her other hand. Her wrist was killing her and at first she thought she might have even broke it. But the pain was not bad enough for it to be a broken bone in her hand. She pulled herself off the cab and instantly flattened herself against the grease and grime covered ladder as the elevator slowly passed by her.

The amped up Marine Lieutenant jumped on the ladder with little if any trouble, and he flattened himself out on the ladder to wait for the elevator to pass by him as well. He was more confident then the Sergeant was, and his move was that much easier for him to accomplish.

As the elevator past her perched on the ladder, she noticed a few thick wires hanging from the bottom of the cab, and a wide flange I beam. A light under the cab lit the area up well. The light made it easier for her to see the hand grabs underneath, she turned to her side and reached out and grabbed the I beam. She actually allowed the cab of the elevator pull her off the ladder, and then she swung her lean, fit body under the cab. She moved hand over hand until she was about right in the center of the cab, in order to give Walker more room to grab on to the cab with.

Holding the weight of her body was not a problem, she only weighed one hundred and twenty two pounds soak and wet, and she was in fantastic shape. She worked out regularly with weights nearly her own weight, when she got to a gym. He smiled when he saw his lover grab hold of something under the cab, allowing it to pull her off the ladder, and then she disappears under it. "You okay baby?" The Lieutenant whispered at her as he prepared to grab the passing cab.

"No problem, there's plenty of room under here, and there's even a light so you can see where you're going, Robert." She offered over a whisper back to the waiting soldier.

"Good deal, watch out baby here I come." Before he left the ladder, he glanced above him and noticed someone just opened the elevator door on the roof and the elevator shaft was suddenly bathed in light from above. He looked to his side and saw the bottom of the cab and the Sergeant hanging below it. He took hold of the same I beam and then he allowed the cab to pull him free from the ladder as well. He moved in until he was hanging directly across from his girlfriend and fellow soldier. With his foot, he kicked out the light, because he was worried it would show his shadow on the wall, informing the terrorists where they were hiding from them.

The Lieutenant looked at the Sergeant and then asked her with concern. "Are you okay baby? If you want, I can help support some of your weight with my legs fur ya, if I wrap them around your waist, also be aware, the bastards are waiting for us. Someone just opened the stinking shaft doors, I saw a number of shadows before I moved. I saw some shadows of their weapons too."

"Shut up stupid, I think I hear some voices talking, we must be almost to the roof area, Walker." Just as she warned her soldier to be quiet, the elevator cab stopped with a jolting hop, almost shaking the both of them loose from beneath the cab. The cab rose above the floor a few inches for a brief moment, and then the elevator cab came down with a second hard jolt, as it came to rest perfectly even with the roof level of this stop.

"I guess we're at the fucking roof." He growled low as he tightened his grasp on the metal flange, and then he waited for the terrorists to do their act inside the elevator cab.

THE ROOF AREA OF THE TRUMP INTERNATIONAL HOTEL AND TOWER

The Russian ex-soldier Alexander had three of his men standing beside him by the doors leading into the large service elevator shaft. Where the cab structure went higher than the roof area inside the shaft, there was a steel structure sixteen feet higher, which housed the cables and mechanics controlling the heavy elevator system. The terrorist branded Twenty Seven had Izquierdo force open the sliding doors of the elevator shaft before the cab arrived at their stop. So they could easily check out and see if anyone was riding on top of the elevator car. The four terrorists were unable to see very much in pitch the dark of the deep shaft. Once the doors were open, the terrorists snapped the chamber of their weapons closed while setting a round in each of their weapons, and then they waited for the cab to arrive.

The large Russian took a step back as the cab stopped before him. The second the doors of the cab opened, the small group of terrorists fired wildly inside the cab. Flooding the interior of the entire compartment with metal ripping, steel jacketed rounds. Each man emptied their full clips into the empty cab, nearly ripping the insides out of it. Each man ejected the empty clips, and then slammed a full clip home and chambered a round in the weapon and then they waited. They held their fire as they quickly surveyed the interior of the car. The empty shells bouncing on the concrete floor, sounding like a ton of tiny bells rather than the harbingers of death they were.

The terrorists did not fire again as the Russian leader cautiously moved to the inside of the nearly destroyed elevator cab. He carefully checked for the bodies of those thought to be riding inside the cab. Not seeing a body on the floor he raised his eyes towards the top of the cab, and then he opened fire without warning the other terrorists working with him.

The cab's lights exploded as bullets shattered them, he stood in the middle of the sparks, insulation, and hundreds of torn metal fragments ripped from the ceiling of the car, as he continued to fire in the roof of the cab. Feeling anyone hiding on the roof was as good as dead then he waved Izquierdo in the cab with him as he slammed a third loaded clip into his weapon.

Izquierdo entered the nearly destroyed interior of the elevator car, thinking he was going to see a body lying on the floor. Not seeing anyone dead, he looked where the Russian was pointing with the barrel of his weapon, and then he shrugged at Russian as he waited for orders.

"Twelve! Think smartass hero type fool stupid hide top elevator cab please, you big stupid you. I want you up there quick pretty much, and check and see if anyone hide up there please. No worry big fool you, I keep cover okay from here, stupid man you. Get move on for me it please." Twenty Seven warned as he aimed his weapon at the cab's roof again and held it.

Izquierdo took in a breath as he shook his head in compliance with Alexander's orders. Then he leapt through the hatch, the cover blown away by weapon fire, and was nowhere to be seen. It was obviously blown free of the cab, and probably tumbled to the bottom of the elevator shaft.

The Russian allowed Number Twelve to use his shoulder as a step. This helped Twelve get through the small hatchway a little easier. Once he was on the roof of the elevator cab, he quickly scanned the area looking for a body, or someone prepared to attack him. His weapon was held at the ready, and he did not breathe properly again until he was certain no one was hiding on top of the cab. Izquierdo looked over his head, the roof of the shaft was still five feet above his head, with heavy steel support beams and motors and cables crisscrossing each other.

Twelve carefully searched all the little dark nooks and crannies of the heavy steel framework overhead. Finding no one hiding there, he looked over the side of the stalled cab. All he saw below was blackness, with an occasional light illuminating a certain floor, or a special airshaft below him. He went over to the other side of the elevator cab, and he discovered the ladder. He inched his way nearer to edge of the cab, while holding his weapon before him ready to fire. He looked down the endless ladder as far as he could see into the pitch black shaft.

There was plenty of light on this side of the shaft seeping in from the doors to the floors below, he could see far down the shaft and keeping the ladder in sight. Seeing no one hanging on the ladder, he smiled as he went to the hatch, and called down to the Russian who was still standing inside the elevator cab waiting for him to finish searching the top of the elevator cab.

"Hey Alexander, who told you someone was riding inside the damn cab? I didn't find anyone hiding or dead up here, and there's no trace of any fucking blood either. We hit no one! I think we were sent out on a wild goose chase." Twelve called from the top of the elevator car.

"Shut you stupid mouth up quick fast, big dummy you, and look second time for someone hide on you stupid ass. Someone up there I sure, and name Twenty Seven to you big dummy please. Remember all time, or I put bullet up ass, big stupid you. You no call by name, never, stupid man. I want you make sure no one hide up there. This elevator no move by own accord you believe true please. Someone push god dom button make car come up here, stupid you are man." Alexander growled at his fellow terrorist as he searched the interior of the cab a second time, for any signs of someone who might have been hiding in the elevator cab, before it made it up to the roof area of the Tower. Seeing nothing out of the ordinary but the destruction he caused. The Russian moved out of the car, and then he went on the roof to wait for Izquierdo to finish searching the top of the cab. He could not help but feel they were chasing shadows now.

Izquierdo gave a second look around on top of the cab, and he decided to count to fifty before daring to climb back inside the cab. When he was done counting he slid from the top of the car, get inside he looked at the Russian as announced. "Hey Alexander, err... Twenty Seven, I didn't find a fucking thing up there man. There's no one in or on top of the damn elevator cab. I saw no one, we hit no one and I found no bodies or even blood traces on top of the cab."

"Huh, big mouth hot dog Number One big shot leader Michael gave warn me someone no know to us ride elevator car, big stupid you." The Russian snarled at Izquierdo and then he added to his complaint at him. "If big shot leader think someone ride in god dom elevator please. We have act as if someone inside god dom cab, big stupid man you be. We done that, we act accord please. Big shot leader expect no more than that from us please. As far I concern, we done what we should do to protect each other up here. I have one more thing do before satisfied with situation please." Twenty Seven warned Twelve as he started to move inside cab again.

Izquierdo watched Alexander with questioning eyes. They all knew no one was either in, or on top of the elevator cab. The large Russian ex-soldier was acting like someone was still somehow inside the elevator cab. Izquierdo shrugged at the large Russian, and he relaxed his stance and allowed his weapon to lower a bit.

THE OVAL OFFICE, THE WHITE HOUSE, WASHINGTON D.C.

The current Chairman of the Joint Chiefs of Staff, General John White began to inform the President what he planned, once his people began their assault on the building. "With all due respect Mr. President Sir, when my troops breached the floor where the Vice President is believed being held hostage inside the building. They'll be instructed to fan out, and hit and take out any terrorist they spot in there. The soldier's weapons will be silenced, so they should be able to eliminate many terrorists they come across without alarming the others, until it's too late for them to react against my troop's intervention of the Trump Tower structure, Mr. President Sir.

"The troops then will go after the Vice President as their main objective of the operation, sir. After the soldiers secured the Vice President from the terrorists guarding her, Mr. President Sir. My troops will then take over a room inside the Tower, and they will protect her with their lives, while giving us word she's secured. Then the rest of my troops, FBI Agents and New York police, will enter the damn building and mop up the rest of the operation for us sir. Mr. President Sir, I'm positive my troops will assault the building from the floor we believed the Vice President is being held hostage. I believe we can clear out the lower floors of the structure..."

"Excuse me General White Sir, it seems Peter has something else he wants to give me sir. Up, there goes Director Hedemann's console now. General White, please remember where you left off in this conversation, while I find out what's on Peter's mind, sir. Mr. Hedemann, you'll use this time to find out what's coming in from your people as well, sir."

The President leaned over and Peter whispered to him. "Mr. President Sir, I have the latest update on the Trump Tower situation for you, sir. I just received word a shooting has taken place on the roof of the Trump Tower. Mr. President Sir, my contact doesn't know what all the shooting was about sir. But he suggests possibly some of the FBI Agents from the helicopters raid might have made it to the roof of the Tower alive, before they were destroyed. I don't believe this is at all possible though, Mr. President Sir. I know the two helicopters were hit too far away from the building to get anyone alive on to the roof of..."

"So who the hell do you think is doing all this damn firing inside the building then, dammit?" The President whispered back angrily at his young aide.

"Mr. President Sir, I really have no idea who might be doing the shooting, sir. The only thing I can come up with, is maybe someone staying inside the building, and somehow got his hands on some weapons and he's playing soldier, Mr. President Sir." Peter offered the American Leader.

"Yeah, I agree with that assumption Peter. There's no way in hell any of the Agents could have made it to the roof alive. It has to be someone inside the Tower giving the terrorists fits. Did your contact inform you how the outcome of this attack turned out?" the President asked.

"No Sire Mr. President Sir, he had no real idea who caused the weapon's fire on the roof of the Tower. He mention the terrorists were really cutting up the place with heavy weapons fire though, sir. I wish to hell I knew who this person that is mounting this counterattack on the terrorists is. If we knew who was operating independently inside the building. We could sure use his help to run some interference for us so we could've got the helicopters on the roof without them being hit the way they were attacked, Mr. President Sir." Peter moaned, and then he stopped speaking when he notices the FBI Director was waiting to speak to the President.

The President turned his attention to Director Hedemann, and then he offered to the lead FBI Agent as he mulled over all that was just told to him by his young aide. "Director Hedemann Sir, it seems someone has just attacked the terrorists stationed on the roof of the Trump Tower, sir. Do you know who this person might be sir? Are we going to continue calling these people terrorists, now we know they are nothing more than a pack of robbers?"

"No Mr. President Sir, but that's the same report I just received from my Command Post stationed in New York City sir. I must ask how you found out this information as quickly as I did, Mr. President Sir." The surprised FBI Director asked of the President with a smirk.

"I'm afraid that's privileged information at this time Director Hedemann Sir. I have to protect my sources you know, sir. I'll tell you all I know about this assault on the Tower. Director Hedemann Sir, someone has just mounted what we believe is a counterattack against the terrorists stationed on the roof of the Trump Tower sir, who are responsible for killing our two helicopters. We don't know who this, or these people might be, or where they might have come from. But there was certainly a firefight taking place moments ago on the roof of the Tower, Director." The President smiled, proud he one up the always smug acting FBI Director.

"Mr. President Sir, my Mobile Command Center stationed in Central Park, was forced to re-deployed much deeper inside Central Park, after the terrorists had opened fired on them. This is making it much harder for any of my Agents to amass any new information on this situation, sir." The FBI Director took a quick breath for himself, not liking the President was receiving vital information at the same time he was about the same situation going down at the Tower.

"With all due respect Mr. President Sir, what you've been informed about, is the same exact information that I had just received on the situation on the roof of the Trump Tower, sir. My spotters have reported they concluded there was no return fire from what we believe was a foiled counterattack leveled against the terrorist on the roof area of the building. I know exactly where the weapon's exchange took place, Mr. President Sir. It seems the elevator car, err... the service elevator was raised to the roof area, and the terrorists fired on whoever was riding inside the cab. We're not positive there was someone riding in the elevator at this point though, sir. But evidently, the terrorists thought that was a fact and they took action against what they might have perceived as a threat leveled against them, Mr. President Sir. That fact alone, makes us consider someone was, or is mounting a possible offensive against the perps inside the Tower, sir."

"Who do you think this person or persons might be, Director Hedemann Sir? Possibly one of your men who might have survived the helicopter operation?" Secretary of Defense, Jerry Levenhagen asked as he shifted his weight on the overstuffed couch.

"Beats the hell out of me, I can't say for certain there is or was someone working against the terrorists on the roof. I do know none of my people survived the attack on the helicopters. I have no confirming reports outside of this hard hitting firefight that seems to have been a more one sided affair, on the roof of the Tower, sir." Hedemann shot a smile at the Defense Secretary.

"If you were to venture a guess then, sir. Who do you think would be working against the god damn terrorists who attacked the damn building, Director Hedemann Sir?" The Security Director, Norman Griffin asked, pleased to have something to say or ask in the conversation.

"By a guess you mean what Secretary Griffin? I don't like to speculate on anything happening with the Trump Tower, Secretary Griffin Sir." Director Hedemann replied to the Secretary.

"Could this unknown person be a lone wolf police officer, or maybe even a fireman. Or a concerned citizen, maybe one of the guests from the Tower. Or someone visiting the Tower at the time of the assault, Mr. Hedemann Sir?" Director Griffin replied to Hedemann's question.

"Could be anyone, or all of them in fact at this point, Mr. Griffin Sir. I really don't know right now sir." Director Hedemann offered with a lot of stress lacing his tone of voice.

General White was so involved in formulating the plans for his troops to attack the Trump Tower. He was not paying close attention to the conversation going on between the FBI Director and National Security Secretary. Or he would have known who was grieving the terrorists. He continued to work over his thoughts, until he was drawn into the conversation by the Secretary of State Maria Hernandez, who suddenly asked him with much concern lacing her voice.

"Excuse me General White Sir, but I seem to remember hearing something about one, no correct that please General White, that two of your special operations soldiers were scheduled to linkup with the Vice President while she was visiting the Trump Tower, later on this weekend sometime sir. Am I correct with this assumption, General White Sir? If I'm correct, could it possibly be one or both of these soldiers giving the terrorists problems, sir?" Maria Hernandez had to sit back in her wheelchair and catch her breath, just speaking exhausted her lately.

General White looked at the disabled Secretary of State with puzzlement etched in his eyes as he offered her. "Excuse me please Ma'am, I was working on the other problem, and I'm afraid I wasn't paying very much attention to the conversation going on between everyone for a few moments, Ma'am. Would you mind repeating your question to me, Madam Secretary?"

"Well finally, at long last, an honest man. Very good, very refreshing General White Sir. But from here on in, I'd really appreciate it if you'd pay close attention to all conversations being carried out in this office, sir." The President snorted as he turned to the Secretary of State, to see if she was going to repeat her question to the concerned military officer.

"General White Sir, I just stated wasn't a pair of your specialized soldiers supposed to linkup with the Vice President in New York later on in the week sometime sir. Could these two soldiers be the ones who are going against the terrorists inside the Tower, sir."

"Jesus H. Christ, Walker!" General White roared as he flung his hands over his head and stood at the same time and then added. "It has to be him dammit, if anyone's giving anyone a problem, it has to be that crazy ass bastard, Ma'am. How the hell could I have been so damn sound asleep at the switch for crap sake. I should've known he'd find some way to get involved in this god damn mess, Ma'am. If anything going down against the terrorists, it has to be my two soldiers attacking them, dammit. Director Hedemann, what the hell's happening in the building, sir?"

A new surge of emotion instantly filled the members at the meeting in the Oval Office, as everyone felt they now had someone operating inside the building. Who were more than capable of getting to the Vice President, and then getting her out of harm's way alive, as Director Hedemann replied to the General's question of him. "General White Sir, it seems maybe one, or even both of your young soldiers just tried to use the service elevator to make their way to the roof of the Tower. Would this be something your people would consider doing while trapped inside the god damn Tower, General White Sir?"

"Yes! Yes of course they would! By all means it's exactly what they would and should do, Director Hedemann Sir. That's the first thing these two soldiers would seek to and were trained to do. To get high and make contact with us, and the best way to accomplish that feat, would be to get to the roof area of the god damn building, sir. Where Lieutenant Walker would know we'd make our first assault on the damn building. It had to be them two war wacky soldiers who just attacked the damn terrorists stationed on the roof, Director Hedemann Sir." The General proudly offered to the FBI Director as he stared to see if he was satisfied with his explanation.

"Do you think they were stopped by the terrorists when they opened fire on the elevator cab, General White Sir?" President Cole asked, hoping the pair of highly trained soldiers would not have been eliminated so easily by the terrorists.

"Not a chance in hell that war wacky bastard would've walked into an obvious trap laid out against them like that one was, Mr. President Sir." General White stopped speaking, and he checked his watch and then added to his words. "I'd say by now, both Lieutenant Walker and Sergeant Ramirez had successfully armed themselves, and they have taken out a number of terrorists by this time. I'd be willing to bet my retirement on it that they have also secured a radio, and knew the terrorists were waiting for them on the roof, and that's why there was no return fire from my soldiers. They were no longer in the damn thing when it arrived."

"What do you think the soldiers are up to in the building, General White Sir?" Griffin asked.

"Hmmm… I'd say they're more than likely heading for the basement of the building once they had discovered the terrorists were stationed on the roof. That'd be my guess of their actions. Lieutenant Walker was taught the first place to effect a successful E-vac, is the roof area of any building, and if this area was compromised he'd then make for the basement of said building. That area would have a number of escape routes open to him. Garbage dumpsters, mail slots, delivery stations, the list goes on. If anyone will find a way out of the building, it's him."

"What about the Vice President and this soldier of yours, General White Sir! Would this specially trained soldier be smart enough to affect her release on his own accord, sir? Before thinking about escaping the Tower, and saving his own ass in this god damn situation, General." President Cole asked, concerned the two soldiers might only think of getting out of the building.

"Right now, I don't think Lieutenant Walker's giving the Vice President a second thought, sir. His first and primary reaction, would and should be to get himself out of the compromised building as fast as possibly, and then find out what's going on around him, Mr. President Sir. Then he'd regroup and prepare for the next step in his actions with the other soldier with him. Once Lieutenant Walker receives orders from Command, in this case that would be me. He'd do anything in his power to get at the Vice President and then successfully affect her release from the terrorists, sir. I have to tell you Mr. President Sir, with Lieutenant Walker running around free inside the damn building along with Sergeant Ramirez, I'd say the Vice President's chances of getting out of this god damn situation alive has just dramatically increased for her, sir." The Chairman of the Joint Chiefs of Staff proudly boasted to the President of the United States.

"Is there any way we can communicate with this soldier? Errr… remind him to get the Vice President out of there." The suddenly invigorated American Leader asked of his military officer.

"At this point Mr. President Sir, there's no way in hell for us to successfully communicate with him. All we can do at this point is wait for him to finally surface, and he makes contact with us, Mr. President Sir. I know if he finds out the basement's a no go for him, his next move would be to get to some kind of communications, and then make contact with me…"

"Get in contact with you General White Sir?" FBI Director Hedemann asked, confused by the General's last statement as he added. "Why in Heaven's holy name, would this soldier try and get in contact with you, before making contact with the local police officials, General White Sir. Or the FBI if he really wanted to find out what's happening in that damn structure, General."

"Because Director Hedemann Sir, if this soldier found himself trapped in a terrorist situation, his most logical course of action would be to go on the offensive, and to do that he'd have to make contact with a control. Which as I have already stated happens to be me in this case, and I'd be the only one on God's green earth to tell him what to do next that he would listen to my orders, sir. That's the way we train these highly specialized and extremely dangerous soldiers, and that's the way he'll react sure as I'm standing here, Director Hedemann Sir. Like I just said, all we have to do is sit tight and wait. He'll get to me somehow and soon at that mind you, sir." The proud General said as he turned his attention back to the President.

"General White Sir, if this is fact as you have just stated then we better start make some plans on what we want this young soldier of yours to do, sir. I'll tell you right off the top of my head General White Sir. If this live wire of yours does make contact with you sir. I want you to stop him from doing anything to get himself and the other soldier with him out of the damn building, until he has the Vice President safely secured from the damn terrorists. I know damn well Ms. Hirshfield, and I know she'd rather go down fighting, than be a god damn hostage. I want this Lieutenant to get to the Vice President before he does anything else inside that god damn building, sir. Once he has her in his possession, he can then make good his escape from the building. Do I make myself perfectly clear on this subject with you, General White Sir?" President Cole snapped harshly at the powerful military officer.

"You make your point perfectly clear to me Mr. President Sir." The General replied as he slightly nodded at his Commander in Chief.

"Very well then General White Sir, I guess the first thing on the menu for us to try and solve, is for you to make contact with your office at the Pentagon. If you believe this young Lieutenant Walker is somehow going to try and communicate with you when he's able. I think you should have any incoming messages to your office immediately transferred over to the Oval Office, General. I'll make an open line available to these calls while you're in the White House with me, General White. Once your communication line is successfully established, we'll work on the countermeasures we plan to employ against these terrorists, sir. I guess we're going to continue to label these people as terrorists, even though we're aware they are just a bunch of robbers."

The President turned to his aide who was trying to make like wallpaper and stay out of sight of the powerful people meeting in the Oval Office and he offered to his favorite assistant. "Peter, it looks like we're going to get stuck being here for a little while. I think it might be a good idea if you were to get some food and plenty of coffee sent into the office for us. Make it simple though, sandwiches will do just fine for us. Once this mess is successfully over with then I'm taking everyone here out to supper on my dime and the sky is the limit."

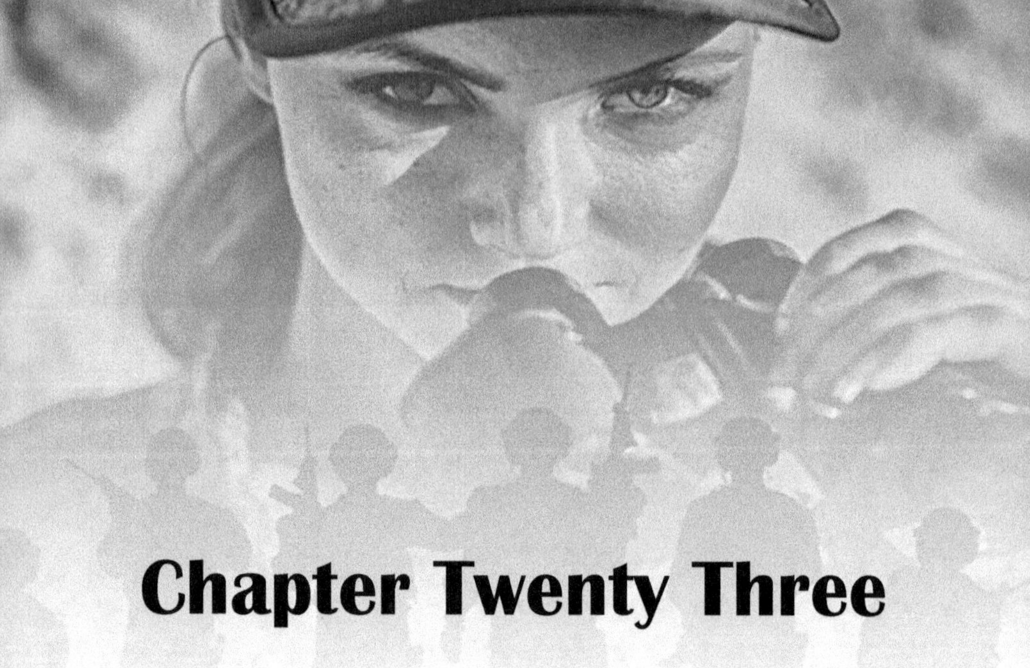

Chapter Twenty Three

THE TRUMP INTERNATIONAL TOWER AND HOTEL

Lieutenant Robert Walker's arms were aching him terribly, as he continued to hang on to the bottom of the elevator cab like he was a slab of meat hanging in a slaughter house. Only once did he dare to look below him, and that once was more than enough for him to never repeat that move again. He looked at Sergeant Dorothy Ramirez and smiled as he asked her with worry in his voice. "How you holding up baby? This is some shit we got our stinking asses involved in, god dammit. I wish to hell I knew what the fuck was going on around here, for crap sake."

"Bobby, I haven't heard a damn thing from my arms for quite a while now. They're numb as they can possibly be and I'm starting to getting a little weak in my arms as well! Can we please think about getting out of this damn place? Or are we going to spend the rest of our lives making like monkeys hanging in the trees? I'm about done with hanging onto this metal can for dear life like we have been doing for the last fifteen minutes, Robert."

He ignored Ramirez's witty remark as he replied. "Yeah, my stinking arms are killing me too, baby. I think it's about time we made our bird the fuck outta this damn dump. I'll go first, once I'm on the ladder, I'll hook on to you and pull you over to the ladder." He understood her arms were hurting worse than his, so he worked his way for the ladder. His first move let him know just how numb his arms truly were. He almost lost his grip when he let go of the I beam with one hand, and if it was not for a heavy cable wire hanging right next to his head, he would have tumbled into the blackness of the endless elevator shaft to his death. With speed he did not know he possessed, his other hand grabbed the wire then he got hold of the steel beam again. Once he had a good hold of it, he carefully worked hand over hand towards the ladder. It was amazing how fast his circulation came back in his arms when he almost fell from under the elevator cab.

When he was securely on the ladder covered in grease and filth, he shook his arms vigorously for a few moments in an effort to get the blood flowing again in them. Once he was sure he had most of his strength back in his arms, he held onto the ladder with one hand, and then he leaned out until he could actually grab hold of Ramirez by the shoulder with his other hand. When he had a good hold on her shirt, he barked at her. "It's time for you to move your purdy little ass towards me now baby. Don't worry, I got a great hold on you and I won't let you go."

Sergeant Dorothy Ramirez's arms did not want to respond to her orders, so she had to concentrate with all her might before her body finally move to her commands. Just the feel of her soldier's hand holding onto her shoulder, gave her the strength to get moving towards him. Slowly, hand over hand as the Lieutenant had done before her, she cautiously and slowly inched her way towards the ladder and Walker. Sweat burned her eyes, as her arms were assaulted with seething pains and threatened to cramp up on her at the same time.

"Oh my God, I'm afraid I'm not going to make it over to you, Bobby!" She suddenly cried out to her soldier as she stared at him.

"In a pig's fucking ass you won't make it over to my ass, little sister! I'll tell you what I'm gonna do if you don't make it, baby. I'm gonna split up your stuff with the other women from the Unit, and then I'm going to give the stinking Mutt the pictures of you giving me head under the god damn X-ray machine. You know how much he always wanted them, sister." The worried Lieutenant threatened, he would threatened her with anything to get her moving towards him.

The three pictures he was threatening her about, were taken when they were transporting a portable X-ray machine from one military base to another. It was loaded onto an unarmed slick helicopter, and when someone on board wondered how it would look if they took an X-ray of someone when he was getting head from a chick. Soon, one of the soldiers hooked up the power source from the helicopter to the machine. The then Corporal Ramirez was the only woman on board the aircraft, so naturally she was elected to do the deed for the other soldiers. The then Sergeant Walker was picked as the recipient of the deed.

She got him hard with her hand and mouth, and when he was ready to complete the act, she drew him into her mouth and the grinning technician on board the helicopter, happily took the X-ray of their sexual act in the process. Everyone on board the helicopter was disappointed on how poor the X-ray turned out. Because all they could see was her jaw open, but they could not easily tell what she had in her mouth. The soldiers could only deduce what she was doing if they employed their imagination, because they saw his hips so near her jaw.

The threat to give the Mutt the three X-rays, was more than enough to get her moving again, and when she was near enough to him, he immediately pulled her to him the rest of the way with only the strength in his arm. He held her tight up against the ladder and his body for a few moments, until she got most of her strength back in her body. Sergeant Ramirez was near tears as she desperately struggled to get the blood going in her arms again by also shaking them vigorously. When her strength returned, she took her weight off his arm that had locked her against the steel and oil slick ladder. Then she hung on and got her breathing under control.

"You okay sister?" he asked her while flashing a reassuring smile at her at the same time.

"Yeah, but I don't understand. I can't believe I couldn't hold my weight longer than I did."

"Don't be an ass baby sister, no one coulda held on to that damn I beam better than you did, even a man for Christ sake. Christ, you're only human you know baby. My arms were about to give out on me, and I believe I might be a little stronger than you are, baby girl."

"Yeah. Bobby, you weren't really going to give that pain in the ass Mutt those damn X-ray pictures were you? You told me you destroyed the damn things a coupla months ago. I can't believe I ever allowed myself be talked into doing something that damn stupid. I need my head examined sometimes, Robert." She moaned as she put her weight on the rungs of the ladder.

"Hey baby, remember that's what we were doing with that damn X-ray machine. Examining the way you give head." The Lieutenant retorted as he grinned at the beautiful Ramirez.

She could not help it and giggled at her soldier, knowing what he done was to get her moving as she asked her soldier. "You swear you're going to destroy them pictures when we get home?"

"Already done baby. Really, I destroy them when you told me to do it. I only used them as a threat to get your sissy little ass back in gear for ya. I swear it." He smiled at her.

"Ooooo you sonofabitch you. You just wait until I get you back to the room, lover. I'll fix you good mister." She threatened him with a smile that would have melted butter.

"Yeah yeah, whatdaya gonna do to me, baby girl?" he smirked, making like he was scared of her threat and he added. "Be gentle with me girl, I was once a virgin you know."

"I'm going to screw the living shit out of you for just saving my life."

"I didn't save nuthin. I only got your little ass back in gear, that's all baby. Besides sister, I ain't going anywhere near another fucking apartment in this stinking dump for as long as I live." The Lieutenant fired back at Sergeant Ramirez, he was serious about his last remark.

"Oh stop being such a baby will you please. What's our next move Bobby, we have to do something?" she asked as she shot a quick look at the roof of the Tower from the elevator shaft.

"Dunno for certain, I'm kinda outta fucking ideas here you know? You tell me what our next move is for a stinking change." The Lieutenant smirked as he looked around.

"I'll tell you this much Walker, we have to stop playing like monkeys under this damn elevator car, and get something accomplished. First thing we know we have to do, is get our feet on solid ground again. So we can then start making plans on our next moves against whatever is happening in this place." She offered as she checked her footing on the grease covered ladder.

"Huh, when our feet touch the fucking ground, I swear to God the first thing we're gonna do is get our stinking asses the fuck outta here lousy dump like our assholes are farting sparks. You wanna take the lead for a change, or do you want me to go first, Raz?" he asked his girlfriend as he kept a close eye on her, to make certain she was alright to move on the ladder.

"I don't even want to go second if I had my way about this mess, Robert. Hey Walker, we have to think of someone else who might be trapped inside this damn building, before we can possibly think about getting our asses the hell out of here." The Sergeant remarked as she moved to one side of the ladder to allow him to slip by her.

"Zat so? Who the hell's that you're so fucking worried about all of a sudden, Raz?" he demanded, confused by her remark as he started to move on the ladder.

"Did you forget the Vice President's also inside the building, and she could very well being held hostage by whoever took over this damn place?"

"Fuck the stinking Vice Pres. where she breathes from, Raz. She's probably good and safe with all the stinking slugs she has always protecting her stinking can all the damn time, twenty four seven, sister. Besides she never did anything for me you know. I'll tell you what I'm gonna do, I'm getting you the fuck outta this stinking dump first, before I even start thinking about anyone else who might be trapped inside this dump. Then, if the fucking bigwigs want her ass outta here they can clue me in on it, and I'll think about doing something about it then, baby. I'm not gonna do any fucking thing until I have your little ass the hell outside this fucking dump, and you're munching down a hot dog like you wanted to do when we first got here, baby."

"Walker..." She snapped but she was instantly cut off by his bitching at her.

"Walker fucking nuthin this time Raz! Don't you give me any of that stinking shit. I didn't come here to play hero for nuthin. I came here to dump on the stinking jerks running the damn United Nations dump. I'm done playing the stinking Rambo game for uther people's friggin benefit. As far as I know I'm plain old Joe blow fucking civilian, and that's what I'm gonna be. You outta here first and then we'll talk about the big shit lady in this fucking dump."

"Well, that's going to be a serious problem for you then, mister. Because I'm going to get the Vice President out of here with or without your help, and if you plan to get me out of this place. Then you're going to have to take the Vice President along with me, mister. Because that's the only way I'm leaving here without you forcing me to leave, Robert." She complained as she stared at the angry face looking up at her from below on the ladder.

"For fuck sake I don't mind telling you, you're starting to get to be one major pain in the fucking ass lately." The Lieutenant bitched, giving in to her over the Vice President's fate.

"If you remember right, the Vice President's apartment is on floor Twenty Two, Bobby. That's where I'm getting off this damn ladder lover. Are you coming with me, Rambo? I'll make it well worth your while if you do, Bobby dear." She sexily said and she fluttered her eyes at him, knowing this was the only way she was going to make him follow her to the gates of hell.

"Fuck you and the horse you rode in on!" The Lieutenant snapped back at her as he looked at his feet and continued his complaint. "You can purr all you fucking wanna, you're not getting your way this time around Raz. You out of here first then we'll talk about the stinking Veep."

"Please Walker, we can find another X-ray machine if you want."

"You're driving a pretty damn hard bargain here baby sister. You keep teasing me like that and I'm gonna take you up on that stinking offer. What stinking floor did you say she was on?" he asked her while still refusing to look at her, because she would have saw him smiling and know she could have her way with him any time she wanted it.

"The Twenty Second floor, Robert."

FLOOR TWENTY ONE, THE TRUMP INTERNATIONAL TOWER AND HOTEL

Michael rushed down the steps with Lizzie following. He exploded through the fire proof door, and ran down the hall to room 2145, where the diamond dealers were held up. He smiled when he saw the one Alexander informed him was waiting to blast their way into the heavily reinforced room, standing waiting for him. As he reached him, his handheld radio came on.

"Twenty Seven to big shot Number One Leader. Come in." The Russian growled angrily into his handheld radio.

"One here Twenty Seven." He said as he stopped by Fritch, Alexander's Number Eighteen man, and then he waited for the Russian to respond to him.

"Big shot Number One Leader you! You sent on goose wild chase against shadow of no one here, hot shot leader please. There no one in elevator when arrive roof, please. No package, nothing in cab dom thing! Next time waste time on someone, waste you time youself, big shot leader you. Where you present time at Number One?" the Russian snapped angrily.

"Are you positive no one was in the elevator, Twenty Seven? Someone made it go to the roof. Someone was heading up there, you must have missed him somehow, Twenty Seven. Did you check the top of the damn elevator car? If no one was up there, did you think to check out the sides of the cab to make sure that no one was hanging onto the damn elevator from the outside?"

"Believe me Number One big shot leader you please, I no miss anyone up here mista. If some stupid one in cab of elevator when way up, he disappeared in god dom air, big shot please. For no find one in or on top, or in support beam above elevator shaft, or on side god dom elevator, mister hot shot leader you. We look down ladder in shaft please, and we find no one hang on ladder, no. I ask you where you at present time please, big shot Number One Leader?" Twenty Seven repeated a second time in an angry voice as he waited for Michael to reply.

He did not pay any attention to what Fritch was doing to the reinforced door of the apartment they wanted to enter. He was too wrapped up in his conversation with the extremely dangerous Russian. He knew in his guts someone set the elevator in motion, and it was stupid for someone to do so without being in the elevator. It did not make very much sense otherwise to him. The leader of the terrorist group felt he had someone moving around the building, and he was trapped wondering if this guy was a cop, or just some nut wanting to play Rambo on him. Why else would this person be moving to the roof, instead of going to the ground floor to make his escape from the building? His mind was spinning over trying to figure out who was loose in the building, and was he planning to screw with him and the rest of his people? Suddenly, the once smooth running operation was going down its first bumpy road on him.

"Al... err... Twenty Seven, did any of your men check under the damn elevator cab? To see if anyone was hanging on to it from below?" Michael snapped, feeling the Russian had somehow missed the one who was riding in the elevator cab.

A slight hesitation prompted Michael to snap at the Russian. "I didn't hear that reply."

"Mudnya, (shit) svinaya idiyot, (fucking idiot) I be some time, Number One big shot leader you." Alexander cursed and then he admitted to the leader of his group. "I no check under elevator cab, god dommit. I no think human possible one hang on god dom cab below dom thing please, unless one in great physical shape, no please. But check bottom dom cab make you sure happy now big shot leader you. I big stupid man for not check on..."

"Forget about the damn elevator now and who might have been on his way up to the roof Twenty Seven. He's long gone by this time now. Look Twenty Seven, I want you to run a check on all your people, make sure no one's missing on you. I hope this asshole didn't find your people, and take them out to get their god damn weapons from them. That's all I need, some asshole running around who thinks he's a damn hero. Run that check for me please."

"All me people check in, no miss any no one from group please. I think you chase shadow again Number One. But I run check on me people make happy you, big shot leader you. I check bottom cab make self satisfied please, no. Where you Number One leader please?"

"I'm standing right at the door to the target apartment. Why?" he snapped at the Russian as he finally looked to see what Fritch was doing to the door to the apartment.

"Ha, this good for be there please, you see me man Eighteen?" Alexander asked.

"Yes, he's here. Why?" he questioned, growing a little peeved at Alexander for wasting time.

"Tell Number One big shot leader you see what he do to door of room?"

"Yeah, he's screwing around with the damn door to the apartment, Twenty Seven. What would I expect him to be doing for us? When is he going to blow the door out of our way? So we can get inside the room." He growled at the Russian, allowing his temper to get the best of him.

"Ha, you stupid big shot leader you. You really think I waste good man with stupid plan shoot fooking door down with god dom missile system, hurt all stand in hall please big shot leader you. I no have Eighteen use dangerous missile launcher blast door away for us please. You see you eyes own, he works with plastic explosive and he set against dom door of room to destroy. The fooking explosive work control explosion, by now should pack hinge side and dom door lock too also, Number One leader of group please. With plastic explosive, door come down without lose good man or destroy apartment and everything inside fooking room please, or destroy target of safe. How you feel now big, stupid jerk Number One Leader you." The large Russian was still upset with himself for not checking underneath the elevator cab.

"How soon before he blows the damn door, Twenty Seven?" Michael asked, still ignoring the Russian and the way he was speaking to him as he continued with his words. "To be quite frank with you Twenty Seven, I never did liked the idea of blasting the door down with a rocket."

"That how big stupid you are to be control us, big shot leader Number One. If you know like you say please, you know I no use fool tactic as blast door with dumb rocket, mista. I no amateur work with stupid you please. I professional like people are. You asked when Eighteen blow door open for you please. You better position know than me are. I tell what big shot leader, you stand with Eighteen and when he run, you run fast he do please. If not, you get experience on how forceful blast plastic explosive is, Number One Leader you please." Once again, the Russian laughed over the radio, and then he snapped at his man Fritch.

"Eighteen! Listen, three and two." Alexander gave another round of laughs over the radio.

'Keep laughing you big Russian asshole you, and we'll soon see who'll end up laughing at whom when this operation is over with, and we're out of the building. And, when your group's left behind to fight off the police for us, and everyone else who comes after you, wiseguy. Stupid huh, I'll be in the subway system laughing my ass off while you and the rest of your men are fighting for your lives in this building'. He thought as he disconnected communication with Alexander, and placed his attention on what Fritch was doing to the reinforced apartment door.

Fritch knew Alexander just told him in code that it was going to take him at least five minutes to reach them. Twenty Seven wanted him to stall for some extra time for him, so he could be there when they first entered the room. Fritch took more time than it should have taken him, to place the explosive charges against the door of the target apartment. Michael noticed how he slowed down his movements and wondered why it looked like he was stalling for some reason.

Number One knew he had to be extremely careful with Fritch, because he understood and spoke English, and he believed Alexander was a god, and was to be followed fanatically to the end of any mission he was on with the dangerous Russian. He moved a little closer to Fritch's side, and received a harsh glare from the sweating and concentrating man for his trouble.

Fritch ran a set of wires from the three different explosive charges to the one placed against the door, where he spliced the three red wires to themselves, and then to another red lead running down the length of the hallway. Number Eighteen then took three yellow wires and spliced them together to the yellow wire from the long lead. Once he had the wires connected to each other, he turned to Number One and snapped at him with an ugly sneer on his lips. "Kaboom!"

Michael smiled as he repeated the word back to Fritch. "Kaboom?"

Fritch checked his watch, and noticed he used up every second of the five minutes Alexander allowed him to set the charges against the door. He knew the Russian was about to arrive at their position, and he decided not to hang around the door, and replied to his remark. He ran down the hall as if someone was chasing him. It did not take Michael, or Lizzie long to figure out they should be right on Fritch's heels. Both of them took off, Lizzie ran alongside Michael and he complained bitterly to her. "I'd like to blast that asshole's head off his fucking shoulder."

"Fritch's?" Lizzie asked, stunned by his remark as she stared at him.

"No, Alexander's Lizzie. I really hate that fucking man with a god damn passion!" He snarled at her as they both ran down the hallway right behind Fritch.

"Oh, me too Michael, I really hate the big bastard because he's so damn arrogant and hard to work with and all he wants is to kill people, but don't worry, he'll get his soon enough I'm sure Michael." The two of them followed Fritch over to the slight bend in the long hallway where he set up the primer to the explosive charges. Alexander and Casolari were already standing there and both of them were grinning at the leader of the terrorists and his dangerous girlfriend.

Casolari, the Twenty Six man in Alexander's group, grinned nastily at Michael as he shouldered his weapon. He moved from behind the Russian and then waited.

Alexander smiled at Fritch as he spoke German. "You have charge set to go Fritch?"

Fritch nodded back to the Russian.

"This good hear Eighteen, you fire charge when set to please." He smirked at his man as he glanced down the long hallway to check on the wiring job Fritch done with the charges.

Fritch nodded again at the Russian.

Number One was fuming at the three members in Alexander's group. He did not like it in the least that the sneaky Russian was speaking a language he did not understand to the other man from his group. He did not trust the Russian, speaking in a language he could not understand did not make him feel any better, or what they were saying to each other in private. He found himself staring at Fritch's every move. He knew Lizzie was concentrating on the Russian and Casolari, so he did not worry too much about those two as a serious threat against him.

Lizzie moved behind Michael to protect him. The Russian easily detected the mistrust from his partners, and bellowed with laughter as he grunted at the leader. "Huh great and fearless big shot leader, I see you no trust me and my people, do you no please? When you learn please I on you side big shot leader, I no hidden agenda follow here against you, foolish man please?"

"That maybe so Alexander, but why the hell are you speaking German with this other guy for? Doesn't he understand any English, Twenty Seven?" He demanded to know from the large Russian, with Lizzie closing the distance between her and Michael a little.

"Da! That true, understands English pretty good okay big shot leader you."

"Then speak fucking English in front me and then I'll relax a little, Twenty Seven." He hissed hotly as he openly glared in the Russian's eyes.

"Huh, this I do especial for big shot leader you. I do no understand you so sensitive all time sudden. My friend, you learn relax please, and trust you friend for so long, Number One." He grinned at Michael, displaying he had no fear whatsoever of him, or from his girlfriend.

Number One knew he had to break the tension rapidly developing between the two of them. He understood he needed the Russian's group and until he was finished with them, he had to keep peace between Alexander's people and him and the rest of his people. His mind flashed to their conversation moments before, and he asked the Russian. "Say Twenty Seven, did you ever make contact with all your people like I asked you to do?"

Da, I do this you big shot Number One Leader please. Everyone check and they be fine. I wait to check, I no fear everyone okay Number One." The Russian turned to Fritch and growled at him. "Eighteen! Door off hinge please? Or I suppose do job? Push plunger you stupid you!"

Fritch flinched over the force in Alexander's bark, and he immediately set off the explosives placed against the reinforced door. Instantly, a mind deafening roar came from the three charges. Smoke, dust, shattered wood fragments, and countless chunks of concrete filled the hallway. The force of the explosion blew past Michael's face, depositing a thin layer of cement dust on it. Lizzie was trying to use his back to hide behind for some added protection from the blast.

"There have it you please, door to god dom apartment blown down, big shot Number One Leader you. We go and see anyone in apartment alive left, and help us with hide safe, big shot leader you?" The Russian asked as he pushed his way past Michael and Lizzie.

Before Michael trailed the Russian into the apartment, he decided to place a call down to the lobby and get some help up o him. "Number Five, you're needed on floor Twenty One. Drop what you're doing and get up here as fast as you possibly can. You can't used the service elevator because Twenty Seven just destroyed the damn thing, so have Eleven reactivate a second elevator by sticking one of the fuses back in the fuse box in for you, so you can get up here fast, Five."

Prochaska smiled as he clicked off the radio with Michael. Knowing he had just successfully breached the room they came to the Trump Tower to get into. He turned to the Eleven, and ordered him to activate one of the disabled elevators. Within a few seconds, Number Five was heading for the Twenty First Floor. All the while he was riding in the elevator he smiled.

The Russian kept moving his people around in an attempt to try and keep them on their toes, and alert for any possible attack from the police stationed all around outside the building. The Russian kept the bulk of his people stationed on the roof, just in case the police tried a second time to try and land a helicopter and attack them from that position.

Twenty Seven had no care in his mind where any of Michael's group were, or what they were doing either. He had his own plans for them when they had what they came to the Tower for, in their possession. He was going to kill Michael's crew once the diamonds were in their hands. The Russian could not wait to do Michael in, he never like the arrogant man from the get go.

He spoke on the radio as he followed Alexander down the littered hallway. The group stopped at the doorway and looked into the dust filled room. The door and part of the cement wall, were blasted in the room, killing three diamond dealers, as they tried to prepare to fight off the unknown attackers. Three other dealers were badly wounded, and two of them who made it safely to one of the bedrooms, were slightly dazed and confused, but they were mostly unhurt.

Number One was surprised to see so few of the diamond dealers in the nearly destroyed apartment, he expected to see a lot more of the dealers than these few. The angry Russian fired, killing the two badly wounded dealers, this served as a severe warning to the other two if they did not cooperate completely with him, their fate would be the same.

Both Fritch and Holzinger followed Alexander into the dust filled apartment, and they quickly took up defensive positions on the far wall, as the large and angry Russian rushed for the two stunned, still surviving elderly diamond dealers. Grabbing them both by their necks, the large Russian dragged them towards the overturned couch. He freed one of the dealers by roughly shoving him forward as he barked at the elderly dealer.

"You, turn over god dom couch please before I rip you fooking throat from you body, you big stupid man you." The Russian growled savagely at the one dealer, while he held the other in the painful neck grasp. When the couch was upright, Alexander shoved the diamond dealer to the couch as he ordered them both to sit on it and be still until they were asked questions.

INSIDE THE ELEVATOR SHAFT OF THE TRUMP TOWER

Lieutenant Robert Walker and Sergeant Dorothy Ramirez were making pretty good time with climbing down the never ending filth covered metal ladder inside the elevator shaft. When the Sergeant suddenly called out to her lover seven feet below her. "Hey Walker did you just hear that? It sounded like a small explosion just took place somewhere in the Tower. Damn, my arms are still killing me so badly, Bobby. I can't keep going on like you're doing. C'mon I need a few moments with my feet on the floor in order to rest, and to get some strength back in my arms or I might lose my grip and end up dropping down in the damn elevator shaft, Bobby. Please, I can't hold on much longer, can we stop somewhere for a few moments to rest."

"Yeah, I heard that shit and it was definitely some kinda stinking explosion in this fucking dump." The Lieutenant snorted as he looked down the shaft in an attempt to see if he could see any signs of where the explosion might have just occurred. He too was feeling the heavy strain of climbing down the ladder, and he had to admit he needed some time to rest for himself. From inside the shaft, he had access to all the floors from the basement to the roof of the structure. The service elevator was inside the secured fire door area of the structure. He had to move down another fifteen rungs, until he could tell what floor they were near. Written in black spray paint on the surface of the concrete wall, the number thirty four was clearly seen.

He called up to the Sergeant with exhaustion in his voice. "Hey Raz, we're on the stinking Thirty Fourth fucking floor of this damn dump. I think you're right, we should take a little break for ourselves, and maybe get something to drink. While we're resting, I'm gonna get to a fucking phone so I can make contact with someone in control, to find out what we have might have stumbled into, Raz. I'll pry open the damn door, can you make it down to me with no problem?"

"Yeah. But no further, please Robert. I have to rest my arms for a little while, I'm afraid if we don't rest for a little while, I might slip off the ladder." She begged him.

Walker hung on the ladder, wrapping his leg through the rung of the ladder so he would not slip off the ladder. This action made him able to free both his hands, and he worked his way nearer to the spring lever that held the elevator floor door closed. He checked out the mechanism for a few seconds to discover how it operated, and then he grabbed hold of the steel arm and gave it a good hard tug in the direction he hoped would free and open the door. The door instantly folded in on itself. The speed that the elevator door sprung opened, caught him by complete surprise, catching a chunk of skin from his index finger in the system. The once so dark elevator shaft was immediately bathed in a blinding light coming from the floor they were about to enter.

"Owe, god dammit! I can't believe that shit just happened to my stinking ass for crap sake. As if I didn't have enuf fucking little nicks and bruises beating up my fricking body on me, dammit." The Lieutenant bitched as he placed his filthy finger in his mouth, and then he sucked on it to try and stop the pain and to also stop it from bleeding at the same time.

"What's up? Did you hurt yourself, what happened? Do you need my help with the door? C'mon, I don't know how much longer I can hand on. My arms are killing me." She asked as she kicked him in the back of his head, she was a rung higher on the ladder than he was.

"Arrrr... I just caught my stinking shooting finger in the damn door mechanism, and it gave me a good bite dammit. It's bleeding a bit on me, baby. Give me a second to lick my wound will ya, and I'll get you onto the damn floor landing so you can rest." He bitched at his lady.

"Oh, you poor baby. Do you want me to kiss your little boo boo and make it feel all better for you, Robert?" she taunted him as she lightly kicked him in the back of his head again.

"I got something you can kiss and make feel a helluva lot better alright if you really wanna kiss something around here, wiseass." The Lieutenant snapped back at his grinning girlfriend.

"Ooooo, don't be so nasty and get in there will you please. I can't hold on much longer, this is getting real serious, Bobby." She kicked him in the head again to get him moving.

"Nag, nag, nag, that's all you do lately. Nag, nag, nag." He complained as he held on the ladder with one hand, and he swung his feet free and let go of the ladder at the same time, ending up landing on his rearend on the carpeted floor with a breath robbing thud.

Ramirez climbed down the ladder until she could touch the floor with her toe, and then she merely stepped off the ladder onto Floor Thirty Four, while staying on her feet. She looked at her soldier trying to catch his breath and sucking on his injured finger, and said. "Ta daa." She put her hands out and took a slight bow while smiling at her soldier as he struggling to his feet.

"I'll ta daa ya pretty little ass good and proper for ya." He growled at her as he stood and looked down the hallway. There were many civilians staring at him from the rooms located on the floor. None of them knew what was happening, or why they were trapped on their floor by the heavy fire doors. He could see some of the civilians tried to beat their way through the protective door, but they were unable to get through it with the tools they had at hand.

The Sergeant moved over to his side and she whispered to him. "Hey Walker, you have to say something to these poor souls. Look at their faces, they all look scared to death of us. I bet they think you're the cause of all this mess. You have to say something to them before they drop dead just from the sight of you and me. I told you that you had this kind of effect on people, and as you can see for yourself, I was right mister." The Sergeant then smiled at her man and tried to draw his attention towards the gathering civilians with a quick head movement.

"Ha fucking ha, you're getting to be a real funny girl there lately, little miss wiseass. Keep it up lady, and I'm gonna hop you right in that lovely little ass of yours, sister." He snapped at her, thinking she was just busting his horns again.

"I'm not kidding you lover. Just look at the poor people in the hallway, they look scared to death of us, and I think they feel we're the cause of all their problems, Robert. Say something to them will you please stupid, and say it nicely while you're at it and try not to scare them more than they are. They're innocent civilians." She gave him a slight shove on his back.

"Okay, okay, stop shoving me will ya, dammit. You know hate being fucking shoved like that when I'm trying to think." He bitched as he looked at a man standing in his apartment doorway while clutching a nine iron in his hands. The civilian stared at the two grime covered strangers with the automatic weapons slung over their backs as he spoke. "Hey pal, I'm one of the fucking good guys around here, like you man, I was just visiting this stinking dump."

The man with the nine iron did not move a muscle as he continued to just stare back at the bleeding man five feet in front of him.

Lieutenant Walker was a very frightening sight to behold, he was covered from head to toe with grime and grease from the interior of the filthy elevator shaft and ladder. He seemed to be bleeding from every part of his battered body as well. Most of the injuries happened because he was scratched up from the jagged edges of the destroyed elevator cab, where the bullets had ripped through the metal skin when they were hiding under it. He was also bleeding from his right thigh, where he was wounded from one of the ricocheting bullets fired at the cab by the terrorists. He stood before the old man with his MP-5 slung over his shoulder, the barrel facing down so nothing could fall into the barrel and jam the weapon on him.

His pockets were still stuffed full with the extra loaded clips of rounds for the weapons, and they made his pants hang wrong on his hips. The Glock 9 mm pistol was stuffed down the front of his pants, with the grease covered grip sticking out ominously. The extra clips for the pistol were stuffed in his pants, making them bulge out even further after he took the clips from the Sergeant before she climbed under the elevator cab. His hair was matted down to his head and grease covered and filthy, and a nice size cut over his left eye had blood flowing down the side of his face, and making him look like someone out of a late night horror movie.

He had wiped at the blood, smearing it down the side of his face and neck, and making him look like a wild man that had just escaped from an insane asylum. His once brand new and clean shirt was ripped to rags and hung from his shoulders and no longer looked new. His body stank from sweat, grease, and dried blood. Adding to this chilling apparition of the young soldier, was the way he stood in the center of the hallway just staring back at the group of scared civilians, like he was about to take their heads off their shoulders to anyone who said something to him.

Sergeant Ramirez did not look any better. She was suffering from her own number of minor cuts and abrasions, and the grease from the elevator shaft covered her clothes and coated her hair as well. She shoved him forward, and then said loud enough for the civilians to hear her words. "Walker, they're scared to death of you. They must think we're the terrorists who attacked the Tower. You have to talk to them before they go against us."

"Yeah, I told you to stop fucking pushing me like that, sister. God I hate when you do that shit to me." He bitched at his girlfriend without turning to look at her. He then smiled as he slowly spread his arms apart to show the guy holding the golf club he was no threat against him.

"You're in some shitty mood as usually, mister." She complained at her lover.

"What the hell can I tell you. This is my Sunday mood I'm using on these stinking people here. If you think this mood is bad you should see me for the rest of the fricking week, sister." The Lieutenant replied and then shut up because the man with the nine iron spoke to him

"I'm afraid you're hurt there young fella." The old golfer mumbled as he lowered his weapon, and then he pointed at Walker's leg with the club end of the stick. He heard Ramirez's words and decided to trust these two young kids standing in the hallway. He did not really have any other choice in the matter either, and he had to know what was happening around him.

"What's going on outside there sonny? Why are we trapped in here like this? I think I heard some sort of explosion in the building a little while ago, sonny." The old man griped as he relaxed his stance even more now and smiled at the young soldier.

"Hurt? You're hurt Bobby? Let me see the wound. How the hell did you get hurt, and why didn't you tell me you were hurt when we were hanging on the damn ladder, stupid? How many times do I have to tell you to not get hurt when we have to go through something like this shit, mister?" she cried as she grabbed his arm and turned him as she checked on his wound. Seeing the wound on his leg, she yelled at him. "Oh my God, you're wounded Bobby."

"It's nothing, just a scratch. I was hurt worse falling outta bed a coupla days ago." He mumbled as he tried to move her away from his hurting leg. But she was having none of it as she pull the cloth of his pant leg from the wound. She wanted to see how badly he was wounded.

From behind the guy holding the golf club, an elderly woman suddenly called at Walker. "Now you leave her alone young man. She's only worried about your health, and she has every right to be so, sonny. The wound has to be looked after and cleaned and attended to. You come in here and I'll look after it for you young man. I know first aid and how to dress a wound."

"Oh good, now I'm gonna be nagged by a little old lady I don't even know too I see, dammit. Man, when is this day ever gonna end for my stinking ass for crap sake?"

"I'm no lady, so you better get in here so I can have a look after your leg for you, young man." The woman growled at him as her husband moved to his left so the wounded soldier could enter the apartment and allow the elderly woman to look after his leg.

The guy with the golf club lowered it until he ended up using it as a sort of cane. The two grime covered soldiers did not look so much like terrorists, even though they were armed. They were too dirty and wounded for the civilians to believe they were involved on the wrong side of this thing. Many of the scared civilians came out of their apartments and rooms, and followed the two kids into Duane and Pat Calapp's apartment. The Lieutenant allowed the concerned woman to lead him over to their couch, and then she started undoing his pants.

"Whoa, whoa hold on there a sec lady. I ain't got any draws on." He mumbled as he took hold of her hands and tried to stop her from dropping his pants, so she could check his wound.

"Stop being such a big baby young man. I have to see the wound so I can look after it properly for you. I assure you son, I changed enough diapers in my life to know what they look like, sonny." Pat Calapp complained with a smirk as she continued to undo his pants, and then she pulled them down to his knees and checked out the wound. The bullet went clean through his thigh, it was an ugly wound but it did not hit any bones on his leg.

Ramirez slapped him on the back of his head and snapped at him at the same time. "Huh Mister Fearless, it seems like you might have just met your match there, mister. Why didn't you tell me you were wounded, stupid? I have to find this shit out for myself I guess, Bobby."

"C'mon Raz, you keep banging me on the back of my stinking noggin like that, you might end up scrambling my fricking brains more than they are on me, sister. In case you don't know it, I'm wounded here huh, so why don't ya lay off my stinking ass at least until I healed some. This old woman is killing me the way she's picking at my damn leg like she's doing honey."

The Sergeant laughed at her soldier as Pat continued to clean the bloody flesh wound to his leg. Once she had it cleaned of blood and dirt, she prepared to bandage the wound for him.

Duane spoke to Ramirez while his wife continued working on the stranger's leg. "I don't suppose you can tell us what's happening out there, young lady. We heard automatic weapons fire and a couple of explosions going off every now and then somewhere in the building. I know enough military crap to know when I hear hand grenades going off young lady."

"I take it you were you in the service sir?" Ramirez asked the old man politely.

"Yeah, but I'm sure you weren't even born when I was sailing around the world for the government young lady." The old man said with a smile as he looked back at her.

"The Navy sir?" she asked, figuring that was what he was in way back when.

"Yep. The Navy. I loved my service, Ma'am." The old man replied with a proud smile.

"Well sir..." The Sergeant went to offer, but she was cut off by the old man as he added.

"Please, Duane will do fine if you don't mind. Sir makes me feel so old." Duane said as he shot Ramirez a smile. Then he looked at his wife who was still working on the wounded soldier.

"Yes Sir Duane, we don't know what's taking place out there. We believe a pack of assholes attacked the building, and we feel they done this because of what might be hidden in the building someplace, sir. We got these weapons from a pair goons we stopped from looting our apartment. These buggers are heavily armed, and they seem to know how to do it and what they're doing..."

"Yes, we heard all gun fire going off a few moments ago. I felt whoever these people are, they must be killing everyone in the building they come across, because of the heavy weapon fire we heard now and then." Duane complained as he lit up a smoke, and then he offered one to Sergeant Ramirez who refused it with a simple wave of the hand. Then Duane offered a cigarette to the young Lieutenant who also waved it off as he watched what Pat was doing to his leg.

Chapter Twenty Four

Ibelieve most of that weapon fire was because of us, sir. Whoever attacked the stinking building was trying to kill us on the roof, sir. When we got us some weapons, we headed for the damn roof to wait for help to arrive fur us. We didn't know there was a helluva mess of fricking nuts up there waiting for us. When the elevator doors opened, they fired into the car hoping to kill us flat out, sir. We used the service ladder to escape their trap. We were heading for the Twenty Second Floor of this dump, to see if we could free the stinking Vice President who my main squeeze over there, believes she's being held by these flaming asses..."

"You mean to tell me that the Vice President of the United States was in the building, and now she might be one of the hostages these jaybirds took as their captives? If that don't beat it all to hell and back again, young man. Your Vice President being held a hostage just like us for Pete's sake." Someone from out in the hall called out to the people inside of the apartment.

"Yep, she's most likely being held hostage just like you guys." The Lieutenant replied matter of factly as he drew in his breath as the elderly woman used some liquid that burned his wound.

"Huh, now I don't feel so bad. If the Vice President's a hostage then we're going to get out of this thing in one piece. Someone will come in to get her out of here that much I can rely on." Another person from the hall offered to the strangers as he obviously let out his breath in a rush.

"C'mon give the poor kids a chance to tell us what they know. The kids can't even think with all you people pounding the hell out of them with all these questions." Duane complained at the nosy group of scared civilians, and then he asked a question of the two strangers staring at him as if he was protecting them. "Err... I'm sorry but I don't even know your name."

Ramirez was embarrassed because she did not take the time to introduce her and Walker to the group of civilians, as she offered to the elderly man. "Oh, sorry for not introducing ourselves to you, sir. Please forgive me, my name is Sergeant Dorothy Ramirez, and the wounded jerk over there, is Lieutenant Robert Walker, sir. We're from the Special Ops Forces stationed at..."

"Are you people from the Delta squad?" A voice asked from the group in the hallway.

"No it's the other way around I'm afraid, sir. The Delta Task Force, along with SEAL Team Six, and certain elements of the Rangers and Special Forces Green Berets, are part of our Unit. I'm afraid that's all the information I'm allowed to divulge to you." Ramirez offered to Duane.

"That's fine, but I'm more interested in finding out what your next move is. Rather than know what outfit you two soldiers belong to. I don't mind telling ya Ma'am, I'm as happy as hell to know we have two Special Forces soldiers trying to protect us from whatever the heck is happening inside this building we all thought was as secured at the White House. I have a gut feeling we might need your special training, before this thing's over with. Do you have a plan of action as to what to do against whoever has attacked the building, and taken the Vice President hostage?" Duane asked the pretty young female soldier with concern in his tone.

The Sergeant looked at the Lieutenant who was in the process of getting his thigh wrapped in a clean bandage by Duane's wife. Walker smiled at the elderly lady as he replied to the old man's question. "Well, the first thing I fucking intend to do, is make contact with my god damn Commanding Officer and see what the frig he want us to do during this stinking mess we stumbled into here, sir. According to Raz over there, we're going after the stinking Vice President, to get her purdy little ass the frick out of the stinking frying pan for her, sir."

"That sounds like a pretty good idea to me, young fella. But how the heck are you going to make contact with any of your people from here though, sir?" Duane asked as he shifted his nine iron from one hand to the other as he snuffed out his cigarette.

"I dunno fur sure, that's kinda impossible I guess. I believe Colonel Leadbetter's still cooling his fricking heels off over at Port Said in bumfuck Egypt at this time, sir. So there's no point with trying to make contact with his stinking ass, sir. He's too far away to be of any stinking help to me." The Lieutenant mumbled more to himself than to Duane who was still staring at him, as he searched his mind on who next was on his list to contact over this present emergency.

"Maybe you should try call the police from here, so you can find out what's happening here, sonny." Duane's wife said as she put the finishing touches on Walker's wounded leg.

"Huh, for Christ sake you fucking people, I woulda thought one of you guys woulda had the fricking smarts to have done that shit for yourselves, dammit. Didn't any of you people try to make contact with someone in Command for the love of God? I can't believe you fucking guys, man. What the hell were you guys waiting for Christ sake, for someone to come strolling in here and free your stinking asses from this shit?" the Lieutenant grumbled as he pulled his pants up, and then he placed his weight on his leg, and he continued to glare at the horde of scared looking civilians stuffed inside Duane's apartment, and stacked up out in the hallway.

"To be quite honest with you young man, no one wanted to dare use the telephone, for fear of letting whoever was killing everyone in the building, know we were trapped in here. We're kind of hoping the attackers would overlook us until they finished whatever the heck they came here to do, sonny. So we were all trying to stay as quiet as church mice in here, all the time we were trapped by the fire doors on this floor, young man." Duane offered matter of factly in his defense, feeling sorry he was scared to do anything about their present situation himself.

"Hummmm… I don't think that was a bad idea to follow after thinking about this shit for a moment. If you feel safe the way you're handling this mess then why would you wanna chance drawing any attention to yourselves, especially from the stinking terrorists, sir." The Sergeant offered the older man after noticing the gentleman's facial expression change to one of sadness. She wanted to make Duane feel like he made the right decision to remain quiet.

"Yeah, that's all fine, well, and okay for this pack of stinking civilians trapped in here, Raz. But I have to make contact with someone that knows what the fuck's going down around here, dammit. I hafta let someone know we're okay, and we're armed and ready to go to work if ordered to do so. I wish to hell I knew who to make contact with, Duane. Most of my stinking Command structure I usually deal with is overseas, sir." The surprised Lieutenant bitched as he tested his leg and then he offered. "Hey lady, it feels really great Ma'am."

"You do understand that you have to get medical treatment for the wound as soon as possible, young man. It's a serious injury I'm afraid. What I did was only a temporary fix, and it should serve you until you can have a Doctor check the wound for you. I think you'll live a long time, and go to Heaven when God calls you, for the good you did for your country and us, young man."

"Huh, that's a real switch Ma'am, this is the first time anyone ever suggested I'll go in that direction. Usually I'm told to head the uther way to hell, Ma'am." He replied with a smirk.

"Walker, how are you really doing, how many fingers am I holding up to you mister?" Ramirez asked her soldier while trying to make certain he was alright.

"One finger, and I'm taking it as being the middle finger you're aiming at my stinking ass, little sister. Everyone I know is always saluting me with their middle finger, or they're voting me Number One with the same fricking finger, baby. It's always the same, no one gives me anything but a dish of shit." He remarked while not taking the time to look up at Ramirez.

The Sergeant had to stifled a laugh over her soldier's last remark as she offered to the young Lieutenant. "How about you trying to make contact with someone in Washington, Robert? I'm sure someone there would be concerned about what's happening up here. I'm quite certain everyone in Washington was informed a terrorist situation was taking place in New York City with the Vice President of our country involved through no fault of her own, Bobby."

"Yeah, but who the hell do we make contact with those stinking stuff shirts down there for Pete's sake, and how the hell do we go about making contact with them assholes anyhow?" he grumbled in a hot tone as he stared at the Sergeant as he tried to formulate his ideas.

"I think you should try and make contact with the Pentagon. Someone there knows the deal about this damn place and what's happening here, Bobby. How about you trying to contact General White there, he's always been a square Joe whenever he had to deal with us. He seems like he wants to help us out of any minor scrapes we keep get ourselves in, Robert."

"Cool! That's a great idea there and I'm damn glad I thought of it, baby. But how do we get through to the General's ass from here, little sister?" the Lieutenant asked his better half.

"That seems like a simple chore to do son. Let the phone operator patch you through to this here General you're speaking about, sonny. I'm certain any operator would be able to patch you through to this General's office without very much trouble, if you feel he's the one who can help us out of this mess, Lieutenant. All I know is we have to do something now you pointed out we wasted too much time doing nothing for ourselves, young man." Duane offered with a grin.

The young military officer could not hide his grin as he replied to the old man still hanging on his golf club as if it was a walking cane or a weapon. "You got that right Homes. You have a stinking phone I can use to make contact with my Commanding Officer around here, friend?"

"Of course we have a phone. Right over here soldier." Duane handed him a cordless phone.

The Lieutenant grabbed it and stabbed the numbers in the phone as if he was angry at them then he waited for the call to be connected. He waited until he heard in the earpiece.

"New York City Directory, what city please?" the operator asked over the phone politely.

"Hey baby, I wanna speak to Washington D.C. You know, the stinking Pentagon, and put some gas in it for me will ya, honey." He snapped in the phone in a sharp tone of voice.

"I'm sorry sir, you need the Washington Information Center to retrieve that information, sir." The female operator replied to the excited man she was speaking to over the phone.

"Yeah, I dig that honey. How the hell do I get it from here?"

"One moment please and I'll help you sir. Here's the Washington's area code sir, that should get you through easy enough, sir." The operator repeated the area code a second time for the excited man on the other end of the phone, and then she disconnected on him.

He was so excited to get in contact with someone who could issue him some orders to follow during this terrorist situation. He had a little trouble punching in the numbers, and he ended up handing the phone over to Ramirez and she took over for him. When she had Washington's information on the line she handed the phone back to Walker.

"Yeah baby, I need the stinking number for the Pentagon, you know, it's over there someplace in Washington D.C. honey." He offered in an excited voice.

"You better watch how you speak to me sir, or you could find yourself talking to a dial tone sir. I know where the Pentagon is in Washington sir. Please hold the line while I get the number for you, sir. Almost instantly, a metallic sounding voice recited the number for the Pentagon, it repeated the number for a second time before breaking off the connection on him.

"I got the fucking number Raz." The military officer exclaimed in a victory tone.

"Well dial it man." Duane replied as he pointed to the phone with his golf club.

"Yeah puke, don't go fucking rushing me any, buddy." He bitched at the old man as he dialed the numbers just given to him by the operator. He had to wait a few seconds before someone at the Pentagon finally answered his call. Everyone milling about in the hallway, pressed a little forward into the apartment to hear what the soldier was saying on the phone.

"Pentagon main desk. Major William Lenken. How can I be of service please?"

"Yeah Major Lenken how are they hanging, sir. This is Lieutenant Robert Walker, sir. My Serial number is 045-313-7741 and I'm fricking stuck up here in New York fucking City, and I wanna speak to General White as soon as possible sir. It's a fucking emergency..." The Lieutenant was trying to be the wiseguy with the Major, but he was instantly cut off by the Major as he replied in an excited tone of voice to him.

"Lieutenant Robert Walker? You're up in New York City right sir? I mean at the Trump International thing in New York, Lieutenant?" the suddenly excited Major said as he looked in the phone like he was trying to see the face of the young soldier speaking to him.

"Yes sir, the one and only, man. I wanna speak to General White toot sweet, Major." He replied, feeling much better because he was speaking to someone who could help.

"Yes Sir Lieutenant, hold the line while I transfer your call over to General White, Lieutenant Walker, Sir. You're ordered to stay right where you are, Lieutenant. If we're disconnect for any reason whatsoever Lieutenant, you're ordered to call back immediately, sir. In fact Lieutenant, give me the damn phone number you're calling from, sir. I'll call you back if we accidently get disconnected for any reason, Lieutenant." The excited Major ordered Walker over the phone.

He quickly recited the number written down on the bottom of the receiver, and the Major wrote it as he replied. "Lieutenant Walker Sir, the General's been waiting for your call ever since this mess first started up there, sir. He's been sitting in the Oval Office with the President, and every other bigwig running our country ever since the attack first began, sir. You will hold the line open, Lieutenant. That is a direct order sir!"

"Yes Sir Major."

A series of loud ear splitting screeches, whines, and clicks assaulted his ear to the point where he had to move the phone a little away from his ear, to avoid the annoying noise.

THE OVAL OFFICE, THE WHITE HOUSE, WASHINGTON DC

The Chairman of the Joint Chiefs of Staff, General John White just finished his third cup of coffee, while sitting in the Oval Office with the President of the United States, and the select number of his other Cabinet members and special advisors when the light on his phone blinked. The General almost jumped out of his chair, as he lifted the received and then barked into it. "Yeah Lieutenant Walker, General White here, son. It's about fucking time you decided to get in touch with me mister! Where the hell are you exactly mister and what are you doing sir?"

"Sorry General White, this is Major Lenken at the Pentagon. I have your Lieutenant Walker waiting to speak with you, sir. Hold on while I connect you to his call, General White Sir."

General White glared at the phone, knowing he just made an ass of himself, and the Major allowed him to walk into it with both feet. President Cole got General White's attention by waving his hand and mouthing words silently at him. "It that Lieutenant Walker?"

General White nodded in the affirmative to the American Leader.

The line was connected and General White heard the voice of his young warrior. "General White Sir, I'm sorry for bugging your ass like this sir. But I'm stuck here in New York fucking City as ordered sir. There's something funky happening in the stinking building, sir. I wanted to make contact with Colonel Leadbetter, but he's in bumfuck Egypt sucking up the sun and frigging suds, sir. I wanna report we were attacked by an unknown number of possible terrori..."

"Shut up and pay attention to my words, soldier! Where the hell are you at present, mister?"

"I'm in an apartment on the Thirty Fourth Floor of the stinking dump, making contact with you as orders dictate, sir." He smirked, knowing he was busting the General's horns.

"Keep fucking pushing me like this Lieutenant Wiseass, and you'll find your ass counting fucking polar bears at the North Pole for your next mission, soldier. Am I to take it you're free to move around the building at will, Lieutenant?" the General asked while holding his breath, fearing the only reason for this call, was to make the terrorists demands known to him.

"Yeah, I'm free as a stinking bird in this friggin dump sir."

"Thank God for that much Lieutenant." General White grunted as he let out his breath and then added to his orders for the young military officer. "Okay Lieutenant listen to my questions, and answer them with a one word reply if at all possible, mister. Unless asked to do otherwise. Are you armed, and if so, what type of weapons do you have at your disposal, mister?"

"We're hot and ready to rock General White Sir." He said in the phone confidently.

Another relieving breath as the General asked. "With what I asked you Lieutenant?"

"We got a pair of MP-5s and two stinking Glock pistols, sir. We took them offa a coupla of the stinking terrorists we dispatched when they were stupid enuf to try and invade our stinking apartment against us, General. A serious mistake on their part I can tell ya sir."

"By your response, am I to take it that Sergeant Ramirez is with you, Lieutenant? And she's likewise armed and ready to do battle with you, Lieutenant?" the General snorted.

"Yes sir. She's cocked, locked and ready to fucking rock as well, sir."

"Outstanding, fucking outstanding Lieutenant. Do you have an accurate number on the terrorists operating inside the building, Lieutenant?" the General asked with concern.

"Negative on that last sir. As I stated, their numbers are less by two at this time sir."

"You only took out two sonofabitches in the time you been running all over that building, Lieutenant? Are you slipping on me mister? By the length of time this terrorist action is taking, I'd think by now both you and Ramirez would have capped them all, and you're reporting the terrorist threat is over with, mister." The General roared at the Lieutenant over the phone.

"Yes sir, but that ain't to say we're not going to get more of the stinking slugs in due time sir."

"Okay, you and Ramirez did real well so far, Lieutenant. Listen up to these next questions, and answer them quickly, mister. Times of the essence here Walker. Do you know where the Vice President's being held captive in the Tower, son? We know she was taken by these terrorists through a number of radio communications we picked up as the terrorists first attack the Special Agents protecting her life, sir." The General demanded from the young Lieutenant.

"Yes Sir General White Sir, I believe she's being held in the original room Star Three on the Twenty Second Floor of this fucking building, sir. I have no friggin idea if she's being held hostage by the terrorists at this time though, sir. I have no communications with her."

"I'm telling you Lieutenant Walker, my god damn Vice President's being held hostage by these damn terrorists mister. Do you think you can get to her, and free her from them if ordered to do so, Lieutenant Walker?" a new voice demanded of him.

"Who is this? Identify your fucking self, or I'm breaking off this frigging connection, bud! Then you're gonna find yourself talking to a god damn dial tone on this damn thing, buster." Walker demanded to know from the new voice suddenly baking at him, fearing a terrorists might have just broken into his conversation on them.

"I'm the god damn President of the United States Lieutenant Walker, and I want a god damn answer to my last question, mister. I want my Vice President freed from the damn terrorists ten minutes ago, sir." President Cole snapped nastily into the phone at Walker.

"Yes Sir Mr. President Sir, sorry for not recognizing your voice right off, sir. Yes Sir, I should be able to get at the Vice President and free her from the stinking terrorist's easy enuf I believe, sir. That's what I was trained for sir." The young Lieutenant offered to the American Leader.

General White waved his hand to silence the President, as he continued to speak to his Lieutenant. "Walker, you think you can get and free her without putting her life, check that shit, everyone inside that fucking place is in danger, mister. I'm not going to beat around the bush with you on this one, Lieutenant. I want to know if you feel confident enough to get to the Vice President, and get her out of the terrorist's control, safely at that mister. Don't fuck around on me with this one mister. It's too important Lieutenant. Only answer yes if you're positive you can carry out this mission, if I give you the green light to go get her, Lieutenant Walker Sir."

After a few seconds of hesitation while Lieutenant Walker checked with Sergeant Ramirez, and he received a positive nod from her. Only then did he finally answer the concerned General's question. "Yes Sir General White, we're positive of it sir!"

"Out fucking standing Lieutenant. If you pull this thing off, I'll make it up to you Lieutenant. Get to the Vice President, free her and make it to the apartment you're using to speak with me for your safe base to operate from, mister. When you get back with her, I want you to hunker down and protect her life with everything you have at your disposal, sir. When you let me know the Vice President's safe and in your control, we're going to move in with every asset we have at our command. Then we're going to rip the bastard's new assholes, Lieutenant. Even the President wants a lesson taught to these god damn nuts. Fuck with the States and you're going to die."

Drawing in a breath, the General continued with his orders to the Lieutenant without missing a beat. "What about the civilians you with you Lieutenant? Any of them able to lend you any support assistance? I'm giving you authority to draft anyone you need to help you accomplish this mission, Lieutenant Sir. I'm glad you're armed, damn glad son. I knew I could count on you and Ramirez to do the right thing here. I'm damn glad you're in that damn building mister.

"God must be looking over my shoulder, by allowing me to have the foresight to have sent both your and Ramirez's asses over to New York at this critical time, Lieutenant. Walker, I can't impress upon you how fucking important this mission is to the leaders of our country. You free the Vice President then we can seek revenge on these bastards for killing the FBI Agents who attempted to storm the Tower, in a failed attempt to free the Vice President, sir. Walker, you're the only chance we have to gain her freedom alive. It's believed when the bastards pull out of the Tower, they intend to kill all the damn hostages they have command over, mister. You have to get at the Vice President before this can happen to her as well, soldier."

"Yes sir, I read you loud and clear General White Sir. We'll get her alright sir."

"Outstanding Lieutenant, leave this line open all the while you're on your mission. I don't care about the damn expense to the owner. Tell whoever owns it I'll pay for his entire phone bill out of pocket for the entire fucking month. Is there anyone you can leave to monitor the damn phone while you' re carrying out your orders, Lieutenant?" the General asked his soldier.

"Yes sir, I got the right man for the stinking job standing right next to me, General."

"Outstanding Lieutenant, that's what you'll do then, sir. Leave whoever you have in mind to man the phone for you, so we have real time updates on your act in there, mister. I swear, the second you return with the Vice President in hand, we'll get the bastards. Walker, I don't want you screwing around on this one. It's far too important you get the Vice President out of the terrorist's hands alive. I don't want you or the Sergeant playing Rambo or Pambo in there, mister. Only go in if you feel you can control the situation, and get her out of there alive. I don't care how you accomplish your damn orders. Just get her out alive, soldier. Everyone's expendable, including you and Sergeant Ramirez on this fucking mission, do you catch my drift, Lieutenant?"

"Understood as ordered and received sir." He grunted into the phone.

"I knew you would, Trooper. That's why you were trained. Any help I can give you from this end, ask and it'll be at your disposal. I don't care what it is. You ask for it and it'll be waiting for you. Walker, this is important, I want this, the President wants this, every American wants this. You must free the Vice President and get her out alive.

Do you understand my orders, mister? I can't impress on you how important this mission is for our country. I wish I had more of your people in there with you, Lieutenant. I hope you can pull this one off for us as ordered son."

"Too easy, no sweat with my orders or the outcome of those orders either, General White Sir. As long as I have Sergeant Ramirez working on my side sir, there's no fricking mountain I can't move outta the stinking way, or carry out my orders successfully, General White Sir. We'll get the Vice President out alive, or we'll both die trying and you can bank on that sir."

"You'll do no such thing Lieutenant. You'll not die, not on this mission you won't mister. That's a direct order, Lieutenant! You'll free the Vice President, and then you will get her the hell out of the god damn building alive, or you'll be butting heads with me, soldier." The President snorted at Lieutenant Walker over the phone, cutting off the General's words.

"Yes sir, I read you loud and clear Mr. President Sir." The young soldier replied, knowing who was warning him this time over the phone.

"Very good then Lieutenant Walker Sir, I repeat, once you have the Vice President under your control, you'll return to this god damn apartment, and then you will use the damn room as a bunker until we can work our way to your position there, Lieutenant. Give me the damn apartment number you'll be using as this god damn safe house once you have the Vice President in your control, Lieutenant." General White demanded of his young officer.

The Lieutenant looked at the old man who was busy lighting up a second cigarette while still holding onto the golf club tucked under his arm. Duane looked at Walker and then announced. "The number is One, One, Seven on the Thirty Forth Floor of the Trump Tower, sonny."

Walker repeated the number for his General and Commanding Officer.

"Okay Lieutenant, you have a job to do so get it done for us, soldier. Don't forget, leave this line open at all times, Lieutenant. I want the damn phone number to this room, in case we get disconnected for any reason, Walker. Who the hell are you leaving to man the phone, Walker?"

"General White Sir, I'm leaving a Mr. Duane Calapp, he's an ex Navy puke, and I guess he owns the stinking apartment I'm in, sir. He's a real cool dude, and his wife fixed my leg up pretty damn good for me, sir." Walker replied to the General as he glanced at the old man for a second.

"Never mind any of that candy ass crap, soldier. You have a fucking job to complete as ordered mister, so I suggest you get it done double quick, Lieutenant. I'll be waiting to hear from you sir. I warn you soldier, don't make me wait too fricking long to have a positive response from you over this order mister. Before I let you go, how is it really going in there, Lieutenant?" General White snarled at the trooper as he waited for Lieutenant Walker's reply.

"Yes Sir General White Sir, one thing I can tell you for certain sir, it ain't hell, but you can sure see it from where I'm standing, General." The young officer snapped as he handed the phone over to Duane, and then he headed for the door along with Sergeant Ramirez in tow. Every civilian standing in the hallway, immediately made a path while patting the two young Eagles on their backs, as they both headed off to carry out their orders.

INSIDE ROOM 2145, THE TRUMP INTERNATIONAL TOWER AND HOTEL

Alexander enjoyed slapping the elderly diamond dealers around in the apartment, when his radio suddenly beeped on him. The ex-Russian soldier stepped away from the stubborn old man, who still was refusing to tell him the location of safes. The terrorists located five of seven safes, and rather than rip the apartment apart and waste time. The terrorists decided to beat the Jew for the information they needed from him. It was getting them nowhere because the Jew refused to speak or give up the last two hidden safes in the apartment.

"Yes, this Twenty Seven. What you want from me please? I busy now big stupid man you. I have work I do for you stupid people, god dommit." The angry Russian hissed into his radio.

"Twenty Seven, this is Twenty One, Thirteen and Twenty Four haven't responded to the request they check in with me immediately. They're well overdue getting back to me as ordered. What do you want us to do about the two missing people, Twenty Seven?" The worried terrorist reported to his Commander over the radio.

"Where they work when disappear you sight please, stupid man you? What floor they assign check out for you please?" Alexander barked savagely at him over the handheld radio.

"Twenty Seven, the two of them were ordered to operate and clear out Floor Twenty for us. The two were supposed to make certain that everyone was off that floor, just in case we needed that floor to gain entry into the target room from below the fortified apartment." Twenty One reported to Twenty Seven with his voice dripping with concern for the two missing people.

"Where you stand at now please in this god dom building stupid man you?" the suddenly angry Russian growled again as he placed his attention on the radio.

"I'm on Floor Fifteen, Twenty Seven. We're still working on moving some of the hostages we want to keep to this floor. Everyone we want, is on their way over here except for the hostage that you have in your possession on floor Twenty Two."

"That idea you carry out me please big stupid you are. Leave one man behind keep good eye other hostage we want keep. Then you get down Floor Twenty and you check for two missing stupid men please. If I know two stupid people, they probably find filthy American woman and have way with her, and they no answer radio for you, god dommit. If this true, you send them up me and I straighten out but in good hurry up please, Twenty One. Go stupid you, and let know what go when find out about two miss fools, please. I fix then but good, dommit!"

The report on the missing men sent Alexander in a blind rage, he glared at the old Jew he was questioning, before being interrupted by

Twenty One's report. Fuming he still would not answer his questions, the fuming Russian grabbed him around the neck, and then he dragged him near the window. With his right foot, Alexander slammed it against the plate glass, it bounced off the hardened glass. Twice he slammed his foot hard and wildly against the glass, until it finally shattered under his harsh assault. He then dragged the Jew and hung him out of the shattered window as he roared at him. "I no time bargain any longer with you fool, stupid man. You tell now where safe are, or I let go neck please. Speak or die, stupid man you! Safe no worth stupid life, dumb man you." Alexander shoved him a little further out of the broken window, until he was actually balancing on the very end of the Russian's arm and window edge at the same time.

"I don't know who told you there were that many safes in the room. There aren't seven safes in this apartment, I swear. I don't know who told you there were seven safes, there are not. You found all the safes there is in the apartment. Whoever told you there were more safes, was wrong. Please don't kill me, I have a wife and family, I'm their only support. Don't kill me please." The scared elderly Jew begged for his life, as he stared into the wild eyes of the Russian ex-soldier.

"You must think me big dumb jerk, no stupid man you? I know dom well seven safe in room please. Since you value diamond more than family, and worthless life. You take diamond with you to death." With that said, Alexander simply opened his hand and the Jew tumbled out of the window, and fell twenty one floors to his death below. He screamed until he finally hit the concrete overhead of the building on the second floor.

The Russian then marched over to the last diamond dealer still alive, and he roughly grabbed him around the neck, and dragged him over to the shattered window. Even before the Russian could hang him out the window, he begged for his life. "No don't kill me, I'll show you where the other two safes are hidden in the apartment. Please don't kill me please."

Alexander released the death grip he had on the Jew's neck, and then he barked at him as he glared at the man. "You open safe for me if value you fool life?"

"Yes, yes, please don't kill me. I'll open the safes for you if you allow me to live. I'll do anything you want and I'll show you where the safes are hidden in the room."

Twenty Seven turned to Michael who nodded back at him. The Russian roughly shoved the Jew forward, and he immediately headed for the master bedroom of the apartment. The Jew crossed the room and went right over to a support column, he fumbled around with it until he found the hidden panel and slid it out of the way. A small safe was instantly exposed. He played with the combination, and in seconds the safe opened for the small group of terrorists.

Number One smiled, knowing they would have never found this safe the way it was hidden so well inside the column. When it opened, he grabbed the Jew and yanked him out of the way, and then he looked into the safe. Inside were five red velvet bags jam packed with many unset diamonds. Each bag held different size diamonds. He poured the first bag out over his hand on the window sill, and then whistled as he stared at the glittering stones. He immediately realized he was looking at over fifteen million dollars worth in cut stones. He gathered the stones and carefully poured them back in the bag. He did not pour anymore of them out, he just opened up the other bags and peeked inside them. The smallest bag of diamonds were more than a karat and a half in size. Number One turned and showed the bags to Twenty Seven, who refused to react to the vision. Michael then leaned over to the Russian and whispered to him.

"Twenty Seven, we're rich beyond on wildest dreams because of what's in this one safe alone. There are enough of these fucking diamonds to make everyone set for life here Twenty Seven. Look at these babies will you please." Michael was beaming from ear to ear at the Russian.

"I see god dom thing, but still one safe miss in god dom apartment please, big shot leader you. I want all safe opened before happy am I be, Number One please."

He stared at the large Russian and then he shook his head as he snapped at him. "You know you're absolutely right Twenty Seven. You want to make this one show you where the last safe is hidden in this damn apartment for us, so you can finally be happy for once in your life?"

Without responding to his words, the Russian took hold of the Jew's neck again and he squeezed it with all his might. The old man's face turned bright red as he struggled to breathe. His hands frantically tried to pull Twenty Seven's hands free of his neck. The large Russian kept the pressure up, until he felt most of the strength leave the elderly Jew's body. Then he finally released him by shoving him back. The diamond dealer tumbled back and landed hard on the floor after tripping over his own feet. He rolled over on to his side and then rubbed his neck with one hand, while steadying his body with the other, as he labored to get air into his starving lungs. Gasping for air, the old man tried to stand after the large Russian kicked him in the side. He was unable to stand, he was too weak from the lack of air and too scared to move.

Twenty Seven roughly grabbed the Jew by the collar of his shirt, and then he hoisted him up to his feet and snarled in his face. "You only half home big stupid fool you. There one more safe want know is where hide please in apartment please. You job no finish until show me where last safe hide, and open remain safe for me if you know what good you, big stupid you." The Russian let him go and the diamond dealer almost fell as he growled at him again.

"It very wise you no waste me time by fall again fool. My patience run thin with you please. I want know where last safe locate in god dom room, stupid man you be." He barked at the man as he moved a little closer to the diamond dealer in an effort to scare him further.

The Jewish merchant put his hands in front of his face to help fend off what he thought was going to be a blow from the large Russian man. He back peddled out the room, turning when he reached the door of the master bedroom. He actually ran from this part of the apartment, and he dashed over to the living room and made it across the room quickly until he reached the other end of the room. There was a thick corner support beam caddie cornered there. It looked massive and obviously made of solid concrete. Again, the diamond merchant fumbled around with the thick column until he located the unseen edge of a panel. Even the panel looked to be made of cement, and it slid sideways with a little effort from the scared old man. The elderly diamond dealer waited to be ordered to open the safe for the terrorists in the room.

Number One knew if it had been left up to his people, they would have never located the two safes without destroying the entire apartment first. He had to give the devil his do, and he turned to the Russian and offered to him. "Twenty Seven, if you didn't make this one show us where these two safes were hidden inside this damn apartment. We would never have found the damn things no matter how hard we looked for them in here. Good work Alexander."

"Da, da, this smart you understand this please big shot leader you. I know never find safe without help from stupid Jew man, please. That why kill other Jew in front this stupid one please. It effective way conduct interrogation against some no want help us, no please thank you? It works in Russia all time when employ. I see work in gutless United States just as well, Number One." The large Russian did not take his eyes off the old Jew while he spoke with Michael.

Michael then turned his back on Twenty Seven, pissed off he was such a crude and extremely dangerous man as he watched the old Jew carefully remove the panel. In the hole was the safe. "Open it!" He hissed as he moved to the Jew's side. While he had his back to Alexander, Lizzie covered the Russian with her weapon. She skillfully worked her way behind him, and she carefully unslung her weapon and held it at a relaxed readiness. She was just daring the Russian to make a move on Michael's back. But he never did make a move on the leader of the group.

Instead, the Russian looked over the Jew's shoulder as he rapidly worked the combination on the small safe, and when the door opened Michael pulled him away from it by his shirt. The Jew fell back and tripped over a chair, causing him to fall to the floor again.

Like a huge stalking cat, the angry Russian was right on top of the old man before he even stopped falling. The large Russian had the Jew's head locked in his powerful hands, and with a hard and rapid jerk sideways, along with a fast yank up. He easily snapped the Jew's neck with a sickening sound. Then Alexander maintained his tight grasp on the Jew's neck until he was certain he was dead and he finally allowed the old man to slip out of his arms.

Lizzie quickly moved between Alexander and Michael with his back to the Russian. She took a defensive stance and stared at the Russian. She did not make any pretense of her actions, this time her weapon was held at the ready. She looked at Casolari and Fritch, and they both put their hands up to show they had no interest in what she was about to do with Alexander. They knew if Lizzie killed him, or vice-a-versa, or the best possible case scenario. They both killed each other, then their share of the take would increase dramatically for them.

Lizzie caught Geofferson, Michael's man in her glare, and then she took her eyes off him when he put his hands up, and then flinched so slightly she almost missed the movement all together. He was offering no resistance to her threat, she put her attention back on the large Russian and then waited for her chance to react against him.

The Russian released the pressure on the Jew's neck. He was slumped over the old man's body like a huge bear, and he happened to look up to see Lizzie aiming her weapon right at him. He slowly straightened up as he let the Jew's body fall to the floor and he glared at her.

"What this about stupid woman, dommit? Is you go betray trust in Number One and kill me? I no understand you threat against me with fooking weapon? I place trust Michael. I no threat you, I know not to trust you two. Is it how you split share what found in fooking room? Where treachery end for you stupid woman? Will end only when you kill everyone, and have all money youselve? What happen next then? Who kill last one so he or she have all loot we find please?" Alexander stood tall, expanding his chest even larger to give Lizzie an easier target to fire on.

"Go head do you worse to me, stupid bitch you. I prepare die always please. I, like all good Russia soldier, always prepare die all time, dommit. Alexander no afraid die no time, he no afraid anything, he welcome death come please. hoot this what real want do against me."

Hearing what the Russian just said, Michael took his eyes out the safe and turned to see what was happening behind him. He was stunned to see Lizzie threatening his ally with her weapon. He was not ready to kill Alexander just yet, he still needed him to control his group of crazy killers until he and the others he wanted, to save escaped the building. Once outside, he did not care what happened to the Russian and the rest of his bunch. They would have served their purpose, and of no further use to him. He still needed the Russian alive for the time being. He moved until he could see Lizzie's eyes and then he grumbled at her. "What the hell are you doing here, Lizzie? Twenty Seven's our friend dammit. Put up your damn weapon Lizzie."

'Not now' the Russian thought to himself, but wait until we are ready to move against you and the others of your friends. Then I will kill you and have my pleasure with your ugly body, bitch. When I tire, I toss you out the window just like the Jews to ground below me.

Lizzie barely took any notice of Number One or what he was saying to her as she kept her weapon trained right on the Russian's large chest as she replied to his words. "I didn't like how Twenty Seven was looking at you, Number One. I felt he was going to kill you with your back turned to him. I don't trust him on this heist in the least, Number One."

"I'm sure he doesn't trust you either Lizzie. But we're a group, and we can't go at each other's haunches, especially when we're so close to leaving this building rich beyond our dreams. We need each other if we want to get out of here alive. Put up your weapon. If we have to worry about each other attacking one another then we might as well give up to the police. None of us will get out of here without the other's help." He turned to the Russian and asked him. "Twenty Seven, you're still part of this thing right? Or do you have other intentions in your mind? Tell me now, so I know how to deploy the rest of my people, and continue with this heist."

Chapter Twenty Five

Alexander slowly spread his hands apart as he offered in totally submission to the elected leader of the group of terrorists. "Big shot leader you, I here protect you back and enjoy spoil of United States fools, please. I no claim anything else from anyone please. You stupid woman here jump, mistake of intention make, it must be time month for her, no Number One?"

The Russian's rude remark made Lizzie see red as her finger tightened on the trigger of her weapon, and she openly glare back at the extremely dangerous Russian ex-soldier.

Number One put up his hand to stop Lizzie from firing at the Russian as he snapped at her. "You see, I told you Twenty Seven's still part of the group. Put up your weapon. Right now!"

The concerned Russian's radio suddenly beeped on him but he did not answer it as he continued to stare at Lizzie's unwavering weapon and glaring eyes. Fear slowly crept into his body, as he worried if this woman was insane, and if she was truly going to kill him.

The leader of the group's stare sharpened as he growled at her for a second time. "Lizzie, I don't have the fucking time for this kind of crap. Twenty Seven's not our enemy here dammit. Our enemy's are waiting outside this building, waiting to kill us. We need everyone we have, if we want to get out of this with the diamonds and our skins. Back off."

"You really trust this big animal to do what he was supposed to do and protect us while we get these diamonds, One?" Lizzie snarled at Michael as she glare at the Russian grinning at her. Once he told her to put her weapon up, Alexander knew she was not going to shoot him.

"I trust everyone from the group. If I can't rely on everyone then we're not going to make it."

Alexander's handheld radio continued to beep, letting him know someone was trying to raise him on it. But he was forced to ignore the call.

"You really trust this Russian slob, One?" Lizzie asked Michael again.

"Yes!" He replied as he grabbed Lizzie's weapon and forced the barrel towards the floor. Lizzie relented and allowed the pressure to guide her weapon away from Alexander's body.

Michael shook his head and then he turned to Alexander and told him to try and calm down the situation taking place between him and the only female member of their group. "Twenty Seven, take a look at what's inside this damn safe and then see if you can remain angry at Lizzie. We hit the mother lode here my friend. This one's full with beautiful glass Twenty Seven."

The Russian ignored the constant beeping of his handheld radio, while he looked at what Michael was bragging about. He moved nearer to the safe and looked inside. It was stuffed full to overflowing with a number of red velvet bags, containing all different sizes of unset diamonds. There were twenty bags packed in the small tight space. Michael removed one of the bags and it felt like it weighed ten pounds in his hands. It was a struggle to get the overstuffed bag out of the safe. The bags were so jammed into the safe, he had to actually tugged on the bag before it finally came free of the safe. He carried the bag over to a small corner table and dumped the glittering contents on it. Diamonds, hundreds of unset diamonds poured out on the table. There were too many to count, and everyone from the bag was almost the size of his thumb nail.

There was a thousand diamonds stuffed in the bag. Hundreds spread out across the table in a wave of glittering wealth. The sight made the ill feeling disappear from them, as both Lizzie and Alexander fingered the fine gems with care. The Russian lifted one of the diamonds to the light, and he rolled it slowly between his fingers, enjoying the glitter the light caused as it shone through the small glass globe. He smiled as he put the diamond in his pocket and patted it.

The leader of the group noticed the Russian's move, but he let it go. Alexander saw the look and knew he saw him take a diamond, and he smiled at the leader of the group as he groused at him. "I take fooking little beauty show people why part of action please big shot leader. When see size and worth of dom thing please, they happy be here then I tell you." He again patted his pocket gently, letting everyone know he took one of the gems.

He relaxed as he nodded to the Russian, approving of the reason why he took one of the diamonds. Beside there were so many, one or two would not be missed by anyone.

The small radio stopped beeping, and Alexander forgot about the call.

The leader of the group saw enough of the diamonds as he quickly scooped up the diamonds and replaced them in the bag, and then he secured it. Then he summarized in his mind what the dealers tried to do inside the apartment against them. In the first five safes, they barely found enough diamonds to make it interesting for their efforts of attacking the building. Then when the elderly Jew lead them over to the sixth safe, there was enough diamonds hidden inside it to make them happy. But when they got to the seventh small safe, they became rich beyond their fondest hopes and wildest dreams.

"Twenty Seven, you do see what the damn Jew diamond dealer tried to do against us, right? He tried to offer us the first five safes in hopes we would take what we found and leave. When he saw we weren't going to give up. The bastard lead us over to the sixth safe, and hoped we'd be satisfied with what we found hidden inside that one while he continued to hold out the real bulk of diamonds from us. The bastard he was Twenty Seven. I can't believe he tried to screw us over like that. When that guy saw we weren't going to back off on our search until we had all the diamonds in here, he lead us over to this safe where they had the mother lode stored. Damn, we would've never found this safe, no matter how long we looked for it in the apartment. It was very wise on your part to make the bastard lead us to the other two safes, my friend."

The Russian smiled over the complement from Michael. In Russia, no one was ever given any compliments, just threats of death and severe punishment. He was not unhappy he killed the last Jew before he opened the safes, he knew Geofferson would open the safes as easy as he opened the door of his home. The safes the last Jew opened were different though. Geofferson took a look at the construction, and then he offered he would have had to use explosives on that safe to open it. They were specially constructed, and if he did not find the combination, there was no way they were going to open the safe short of using explosives against it. This would have scattered the diamonds all over the large room. Losing many of the diamonds in the process, and forcing them to waste more time trying to pick up the scattered gems.

Michael removed the rest of the red velvet bags of diamonds, taking the time to glance into each one of the bags before laying them out on the table before the other members of his group. Every time he looked in the bags, he whistled and got more excited over the vastness of their take. Everyone inside the room gathered around the bags, staring at them in awe as Michael piled them one on top of the other before them. There were twenty five bags in all piled in the safe, with each one weighing seven pounds or more, and each was packed to capacity with unset diamonds. Millions of dollars worth were piled on top of the marble table.

He removed his backpack and then poured the loose diamonds from the bags in it. The diamonds disappeared in the form fitting pack. He put the diamonds from ten bags in his pack. Then Michael called Lizzie over to his side and opened her pack and poured five bags in hers. He then waved Alexander over to him and repeated the procedure, pouring five bags of diamonds in his backpack. Geofferson was given five bags in his backpack also. The remaining bags from the other safes of diamonds were poured into his pack which was the largest of them all, after he placed it securely on his back. This was to force the diamonds to take the shape of his back and actually disappear on his body.

When the diamonds disposed of inside the backpacks on the few chosen terrorists, Michael turned to the Russian and offered to him. "We have enough to carry, we did it Twenty Seven, that's it, we better make plans to get out of this building in one piece, Twenty Seven."

"Huh, it see all sudden you make decision for all group on you own, me friend. How come sudden you know we too much carry out of build big shot leader you? My people on roof nothing carry them with please out of here. There many other can carry more weight. I say we go after other safe in build no matter take long time please." The Russian snarled nastily.

He actually allowed his anger to get the best of him as he snapped at the large Russian. "Twenty Seven, we have enough loot to make us happy for the rest of our lives. My people are more than satisfied with what we have on our backs now. If you want more then give me the diamonds you have, and you can go after anything you want left in the building, Twenty Seven. You know where we're suppose to meet and split up what we have. Show up and you'll get your shares and you can split it with the rest of your group however you want to split it up.

"Hmmm... I'll go one step further with you at that, Twenty Seven. If you loot this place like you want to do. You and your people can keep everything you get and still have an equal share in what we have on our backs, my friend. I have no intention of holding you back from anything you might want to do in here. All you have to do is make damn sure we get out of here as to our original bargain, and then you're free to do whatever the hell you want in here."

The leader of the group took a breath and noticed Alexander was considering his proposal. He decided to kept pressing, in hopes the Russian would be foolish enough to remain, and cover his and his people's escape while looting the building. It would make his plan of screwing Alexander out of his share of diamonds much easier to accomplish. He was smart enough to make the Russian believe it was his idea, rather than something he placed in his mind.

"Twenty Seven, I don't want to hold you back in anything you might want to do inside the building, my friend. But I seriously think you'd be a very foolish man to stay when the rest of us leave here. You know if we split up our two groups before the action has been completed, we give the cops the advantage against all of us, and we reduce our chances of escaping safely from the building. I say the hell with the damn building and cash, cash can be traced you know, Twenty Seven. We have enough worth on our backs to make us very happy for the rest of our lives." He tapped his backpack to add power to his complaint before continuing with his words. "C'mon Twenty Seven, let's just stay with the original plan..."

"Original plan agree break in apartment and remove much cash as carry everyone in group, big shot leader you. It you change action as you call please, not me big shot leader you." The angry Russian snapped harshly back at Michael.

"I know I said that Twenty Seven, I didn't need you to remind me what I said. But it's stupid to go after the rest of the damn building. I say we have enough of what we came into this building for, and we should be happy with what we have Twenty Seven. We have to get the hell out of this damn building and then head for our safety place, and wait there until some of the heat dies down some for..." His words were cut off in by the sound of a radio going off.

Alexander's radio beeped and the sound caused Michael to stop speaking, to allow the Russian to reply to the incoming message, as he watched him raise the radio and reply. "Da! Who it, what you want me from please? I very busy here, god dommit you stupid man."

"Twenty Seven, Twenty One, I just found the two missing men. I have the two of them down, Thirteen and Twenty Four are out for the count, and their weapons are missing too, and so are their handheld..."

"What you mean Thirteen and Twenty Four out for count, what they count for you big stupid you? If stupid fools down, how get down and out of it you say me, big stupid fool you?"

"They're down for the count, somebody did them in, they're both dead, Twenty Seven. I don't know how Twenty Four was killed, I think his neck might be broken. Thirteen was done in by a knife, Twenty Seven. He's has two deep wounds in his back, both to his lungs. Whoever did this to Thirteen really knew what the hell he was doing with his attack on our man, if he was able to take out Thirteen this easily, Twenty Seven."

"You think attack cop, maybe military type?" Alexander snorted in the radio.

"Judging by the way they both were killed, military trained definitely, Twenty Seven."

"Dommit! That all I need screw up bad day already, military type America Rambo play hero against us in here, stupid man you. How many people think took kill two good men I lost to operate?" the upset Russian snarled as he shifted the radio to the other hand.

"I'd figure two at least, maybe even three attackers, Twenty Seven. I think Thirteen went in this apartment, and Twenty Four stayed behind him. I see someone, or ones hiding behind them, and when our people moved deeper into the room. The one behind them, must have jumped Twenty Four and did him in, while who Thirteen was going after in the apartment. Jumped him from behind when he turned to help Twenty Four out, and that other person stabbed him in the back. I'm not positive that's the way it happened, but all the signs point to that type of action, Twenty Seven. What the hell do you want me to do Twenty Seven?"

"God dommit you! You feel people who kill our men, military trained then, huh?"

"Absolutely Twenty Seven. If anyone got the jump on Twenty Four and snapped his neck, he had to be military. I believe he might be special military trained at that, Twenty Seven."

"Special military trained you say to me please? What that mean special military trained please, you stupid man you?" Twenty Seven asked, confused by Twenty One's last remark.

"I think they were Special Forces, you know what I mean Twenty Seven. Delta, SEAL, or some other special American Military Units they have operating for this country. I don't really know which one it was, but they definitely had to be special military trained, Twenty Seven."

A thought suddenly entered the Russian's mind as he suddenly shouted in the radio. "Twenty One, get up to Floor Twenty Two by

American Vice President of this god dom country. If soldier true fooking Amirikanskaya soldiers like you think they trained. Their first thought be free god dom Vice President of this miserable country please. I on way up there to help with special train fooking soldier, dommit. Are other hostages guarded you well please?"

"Yes Twenty Seven. They're well secured and controlled Twenty Seven."

"Get up room Star Three, big stupid man you. I join quick soon please." Twenty Seven turned to face the leader of the group, and then he snarled at him. "You won fooking argument big shot leader you. I no waste time go after other god dom apartment, thing break down for I like please. I think you be right Number One big shot leader you. We have get out build before overcome by fooking Amirikanskaya police and military type from outside this god dom build."

The angry Russian looped the nylon backpack off his shoulder, and he swung it around in one swift movement and handed it to Michael as he announced. "You take and protect for me please. I no need bulk slow down any my move on me. If have engage Special Force soldier. It be most interesting me do battle fine train soldier from this god dom country. It time see who be better military train, worthless Amirikanskaya soldier, or great Russia warrior." Before letting go the his backpack of diamonds, he angrily warned Michael in no uncertain terms.

"I force trust you all diamond with please, big shot leader. You where suppose be when come time split take please, you no there I get there. I hunt down end earth and kill you bad, real painful like my stupid friend you. I help Dunagan with big shot Vice President woman of this god dom country please. Once sure custody okay, move down with you and make keep her in you sight please. I order people on roof start second round destruction Tower back police off us please. I no want think might forgot them minute outside, no big shot leader you." The Russian let go of the backpack, and then he chambered a round in his weapon, and headed off in a rush for the staircase. But not before giving one last warning to the leader of the group.

"Big shot leader, you better wait at meet place when time come split take from here please, or I hunt down and hurt real bad, promise you this big shot leader. You no like one bit what I do you body if I force hunt you down, Number One big shot. It take long time you die by me hand, if dare cross Alexander please." Twenty Seven's last words were heard as his large body turned the corner of the apartment, and he rushed out in the hallway while heading for the staircase.

Fritch followed Casolari over to the other stairwell as ordered, while the Russian headed for the staircase to enable him to come at room Star Three from the other end of the long hallway. In hopes of trapping the unknown American soldiers Twenty Seven was positive were in the building, and at this time were trying to free the Vice President from them.

Michael turned to Lizzie and grinned now they were free of Twenty Seven and all his threats. "Well, that was much easier than I first expected. Come on Lizzie, we'll collect Suarez and the others in the security room, and then we'll get out of this damn building while the stupid Russian fool and the rest of his people defend our escape against the cops for us."

Lizzie smiled as happily as she fell in step behind him.

THE OVAL OFFICE, THE WHITE HOUSE, WASHINGTON DC

The Chairman of the Joint Chiefs of Staff, General John White, made no bones about taking over the operation to free the Vice President from the FBI Director and the rest of his HRU teams. This was easy, because two of his specially trained soldiers were running around free inside the compromised Trump building, and they were ready to go in action against the terrorists, and secure the Vice President's freedom. The powerful General turned to Director Hedemann and barked at the man. "Director, I'm deploying the Apaches helicopters..."

"Hold on a moment there, General White." The President snapped abrasively and then added angrily. "I'm afraid you're jumping the gun a bit here, sir. Your people don't have the Vice President in custody, and you're calling in the heavy weapons against the terrorists already, sir. Do you mind telling me why you want to move in the Apache helicopters,

General White Sir? I thought that would be one of our last moves to be carried out against the terrorists, sir. Once we're certain the Vice President was in the control of our people, General White."

"With all due respect Mr. President Sir, I intend to move the fast attack Apache helicopters to a lot closer position nearer the Trump Tower, sir. They can remain airborne up to four hours before needing refueling. I'll have the helicopters move in, refuel from the gas station we had taken over for just this purpose and have them hover in their ordered standoff positions, until we have need of them in this action, Mr. President Sir. The instant we hear from Lieutenant Walker and Sergeant Ramirez they have the Vice President in their custody. I'll have the Apaches move in on the assholes stationed on the roof. At the same time the Apache's open up on those terrorists, I'll have the main doors leading into the Tower lobby blown, and the Agents and police will pour in heavy numbers, and take back the building from the terrorists Mr. President Sir.

"I have to be ready to move the instant my people get control of the Vice President, if we don't jump off right away, sir. The god damn terrorists will surely use this slack time to pursue my soldiers along with the freed VP, and possibly retake her as hostage while killing my two soldiers at the same time. Mr. President, I have to get my support assets set in position ahead of the jump off time, and ready to attack the damn terrorists at a moment's notice. I can't have Lieutenant Walker sitting on his finger, while waiting for us to support him sir."

The President held up his hand to silence the complaining military officer. "Calm down a little please, General White Sir. You're getting a little too excited. I was only asking why you felt you needed to move the Apache helicopters from the Brooklyn Navy Yard to Manhattan before they were needed, that's all sir. I thought the helicopters were better off sitting where they are. Rather having them moving around, and possibly be detected by the terrorist's, and having them react against their presence. That's all I was questioning, by the way General I take exception to the way you refer to Ms. Hirshfield, it's the Vice President and not the VP if you don't..."

"Mr. President." General White repeated heatedly, refusing to back down now he felt he held the upper hand in this situation, and he totally ignored the President's grumble aimed at him as he added to his words. "The Apaches won't be detected by anyone until it's too late for the god damn terrorists to react to their presence on the scene, sir. My Apaches can fly in at ground level, using the wider streets of midtown Manhattan to get around, and they can approach the final streets in whisper mode, flying close to the ground as the buildings will allow them. Mr. President Sir, when the Apaches attack the Tower, any terrorists won't know the helicopters are there until they're actually eye level with the bastards, and firing death and destruction at them from two sides of the compromised building, Mr. President Sir."

"I see where you're coming from now, General White Sir. After thinking about this thing a little further, I believe I'm going to agree with your suggestions, and give you the green light to move the Apaches to where you think they'll better serve your soldiers and this situation. Err... General White Sir, I'm giving you the go ahead to use whatever will assure you of getting my Vice President out of the damn building alive. As I said General White, both your young warriors are expendable under these orders, sir. They only have to live long enough to keep Mary alive, until our reinforcements can get inside the building to her. She's the only one I'm interested in getting out of that god damn building safely. Once she's out of the building, you can worry about the other hostages. Is this clear to your people inside the Tower, General White Sir?"

"Yes sir, I understand your demands sir. Thank you very much Mr. President Sir."

"Fine, now I'm certain that's understood by you, General White Sir. I'm giving you permission to pull up a number of tanks from armories in Manhattan, or anywhere else in New York for that matter. I believe there's aircraft stationed at the old Floyd Bennett Airfield in Brooklyn, and there are also other aircraft being held at the Air Reserve Unit at the Westchester Airport if I'm not mistaken sir. I guess what I'm trying to say General White is, anything you need is yours to be used, sir. I want my Vice President the hell out of this mess, and I want her out of it alive, dammit." The President roared as he pounded his fist down heavily on the desk.

"That's exactly what I'm planning to do, Mr. President Sir." General White barked, knowing time was fast running out on him and his two soldiers inside the Tower.

President Albert Cole glared angrily at his General, and then he allowed himself to calm down as he replied. "Okay General White Sir, let's get your Apaches in the air then, sir."

General White nodded and then he picked up the phone and dialed the Brooklyn Navy Yard.

THE OLD BROOKLYN NAVY YARD

Even though the Brooklyn Navy Yard had officially been closed for a little more than ten years now, the Navy never burned its bridges completely at the site. They maintained a small section of the once Naval Base operational to store outdated or mothballed military equipment. The Apache helicopters ordered from Camp Smith sat on the main driveway of the base. The high tech machines were armed, as waited to be called to duty. Each platform was equipped with twelve hellfire missiles, one pod on each side, with two pods of hydra 70 2.75 inch rockets, and the destructive fire power of its extremely deadly 30 mm M-230 chain gun that finished its armor.

The four pilots were hanging around their machines taking a little time for themselves. A number of armed Shore Patrol guards surrounded each of the air platforms while the pilots ate and rested some. There was a security mobile communication vehicle parked on the side of the first helicopter. It was being manned by more Shore Patrol Officers. The Navy Lieutenant sat half in and half outside the gray painted Humvee when the call from the President's office came in. The phone buzzed and the Lieutenant nearly jumped out of his skin as he reached for the phone and then responded. "Yes Lieutenant Kokolis here sir."

"Lieutenant Kokolis, this is General John White, Chairman of the Joint Chiefs of Staff, sir."

"Yes Sir General White!" Kokolis replied smartly to the Commander with pride in his voice.

"Lieutenant, I want to speak to the Commander of the lead Apache helicopters, sir." The Chairman of the Joint Chiefs of Staff ordered the Lieutenant.

"Yes Sir General White Sir, right away sir. He's getting something to eat, sir. It'll take me a few moments to have the Commander get over to the radio for you, sir." The Lieutenant covered the receiver and then he stuck his head outside the Humvee and yelled out. "Commander, Hey Commander, I have the Four Star on the horn, and he wants you A-SAP sir."

The Commander tossed his half eaten hot dog in the shitter, and then he dashed over to the Humvee and he took the receiver and offered. "Yes Sir General White Sir, this is Commander Strole, sir. Is it time for us to get some payback, General White Sir?"

"Commander Strole, I want your two birds in the air by the time I hang up, sir. Get your ass to the Trump Tower covertly, mister. Use the buildings of the City to cover your approach to the structure. I have a gas station standing by for refueling possibilities at Zero, One, Three, on your map, Commander. When you reach that position, I want you to top off your fuel supply, sir. Then you'll make to coordinates One, Seven, Seven and touchdown and wait further orders, sir.

"You'll keep the engines of your helicopters spooling at all times while on the ground until your machines are needed, I'm going to send a flash message out on your Q-Seven receiver, Commander. When you receive that tone, you'll take out all soft targets stationed on the roof of the god damn structure without hesitation, sir. Be advise Commander, the terrorists on the roof are armed with Russian Grail, shoulder launched anti-aircraft missile, and also AGS 17-30 mm grenade launchers. If they send enough of them out, they might get lucky and damage one of your aircraft, sir. They're also armed with a pair of heavy machine guns. The terrorists made use of a number of small arms which are automatic, and we have no total on the exact number of damn terrorists stationed on top of the damn thing at this time, sir. I want you to make..."

"Good God Almighty General White Sir. What the hell's going on at this god damn building you want us to neutralize for you, sir? Are we going in on an all out attack against a civilian target right smack dab in the heart of New York City with weapons blazing, General White Sir?" The stunned Army pilot of the lead Apache helicopter grumbled, not believing what he was hearing coming from his Commanding Officer's mouth.

"You're hearing me correctly Commander Strole, you and your backup helicopter are going in to kill all soft targets stationed on the roof of a civilian building, as you just put it, right in the heart of New York City. I don't want you to let up on the soft targets until you're positive everyone of those bastard's are making their way to hell. I'm not going to screw around with you on this one Commander Strole. I want everything on that damn roof taken out by your weapon systems, sir. You know who they're holding hostage so I don't have to go over that part of this operation with you again, sir. I don't need those pricks surviving and making it back inside the god damn building, so they could go after the Vice President once we established her free..."

"I take it you have operatives positioned inside of the building under your Command, General White Sir." The concerned Commander of this flight of Apaches asked the General.

"Commander Strole! If you interrupt me once more during this briefing, you'll not be flying helicopters for a living any longer, sir. You'll be cleaning out the god damn fuel tanks of the damn things from the inside for the rest of your enlistment, sir. You don't ask god damn questions in this conversation! You just listen up and carry out your orders as received, Commander. Do you understand me and my orders and your position in this briefing, sir!"

"Yes Sir General White! I understand my orders as received General White Sir." Commander Strole snapped back at his Commanding Officer this time.

"Fine, listen up then Commander. Once you have erased all soft targets on the roof of the building. You're instructed to drop down the east side of the building, until you're hovering around the thirty fourth floor of the structure, and be ready hovering there. I'll have my people on that floor, and if they come under attack from any remaining terrorists operating inside the building. I'll expect you to break the backs of said attackers with controlled weapons fire, sir. Your only duty Commander after you have cleared the roof, is to protect that floor at all costs. The Vice President will be there, along with a number of other god damn civilians and my people. So you'll have to be extremely careful on how you attack the damn area in question if needed sir. If you have any questions, now is the time to ask them Commander. I want you to make certain you understand everything expected of you. Questions Commander?"

"Yes Sir General White Sir, just one sir. How am I going to know if your people need any help from where I'll be positioned with my choppers while hovering near the thirty fourth floor of the structure in question, General White Sir?"

"That's simple Commander Strole. Glad you brought up that question to my attention, Commander. As of this moment, we're holding open a link to the room we plan to place the Vice President in for safe keeping until our ground forces can get to her side. Our two operatives are equipped with radio communications that has a number of channels available to them. When the time comes for you to go operational on the second part of your assignment, and my operative has the Vice President in his custody. He's going to switch to channel CB Fifteen, and broadcast on the open channel. I understand you're capable of monitoring all civilian radio bands with your equipment on board your Apache airframe, Commander?"

"Yes sir, that's a positive on that response General White Sir." The Commander offered.

"Commander Strole, the moment you finish your attack on the roof against the terrorists stationed there, you're ordered to switch over to Civilian Channel Fifteen, and allow my operatives to control your weapons fire, sir."

"Roger that last General White Sir." The pilot offered to the General. "Fine, get your ass in the air and head for your ordered standoff position, sir. Good luck with your orders Commander. Before you go, my operative will identify himself as Mother Hen." The General ordered the pilot.

"Mother Hen, General White Sir." The Commander broke off the connection, and he dashed for his machine of war. The other crew was already manning their aircraft. The Commander buckled in, and increased power and in less than a heartbeat, the two jet black, sleek, and dangerous fast attack helicopters ripped their way through the night air for New York City.

FLOOR THIRTY FOUR, THE TRUMP INTERNATIONAL TOWER AND HOTEL

After Lieutenant Robert Walker was finished speaking with the Chairman of the Joint Chiefs of Staff, he slapped the old man on his back and then announced he was going after the Vice President. "Hey baby, you ready to get some payback on these stinking tent pegs, Raz?"

"All you have to do is lead the way for me, and I'll take it from there, Robert." Sergeant Dorothy Ramirez replied proudly as she stood and then chambered a round in her weapon as she asked her soldier. "Your leg okay Bobby?"

"Yep, she did a dynamite job of fixing it up fur me. It feels near as good as new for me." Lieutenant Walker then foolishly stomped his foot on the floor to prove his point, and he paid the price with a bone jarring pain stabbing him from his wound.

"Just how are you going to get to the Vice President's floor from here, young man?" Duane asked the confident young soldier standing in front of him.

"The same way we got here sir, through the stinking elevator shaft and ladder, sir."

"Are you going to drag the female Vice President of the United States up the ladder in the elevator shaft, young man?" the old man asked the soldier, surprised by his last statement.

"If I hafta, I'll put her ass over my fricking shoulder and carry her to get her ass up here. I don't think she'll care what we have to do to or with her, and what she has to do once we get her away from the stinking asses." He smirked as he left the overcrowded apartment, and went towards the elevator. He looked at the doors and chose the ones that would allow him to come out in the off side hallway, where they wouldn't be seen by the terrorists guarding Hirshfield. The Lieutenant looked at the flat stainless steel set of doors, not knowing how to get them open. He rested his hands against them and then he tried to manhandle the doors open, the doors would not budge an inch for him. He turned to the horde of civilians staring at him and asked. "Do any of you fucking guys know how the fuck to open up these damn things?"

"Yeah sonny, I know how to open them." A man who looked like a thousand years old piped up, and then added. "I saw a maintenance man working on the doors a few days ago, sonny. He used a special key to open them. He allowed me to look at the tool. It was a piece of metal that went in straight, and when turned, the key arm bent down. Then the doors sprang open."

"Can you make one of the damn things up, err..?" the Lieutenant asked the old man.

"Mclaughin, John Mclaughin, sonny. Sure thing young fella, I can make one of the keys for you sonny. All I need is a narrow piece of metal that'll fit in that hole in the corner of the elevator door there sonny." The old man pointed to the hole drilled in the door in the upper corner.

Walker looked at the small hole in the door, it looked like three eighths of an inch in diameter and he snapped. "I need a fucking radio aerial. Does anyone of you guys have a fucking portable radio, or a set of god damn rabbit ears on their TV I can use?"

"Yes young man I have one, I'll get it for you right away soldier." A Spanish woman replied as she darted back into her apartment, and then she brought out a portable radio and handed it to the young soldier as she looked him in the eyes.

He smiled at her, and then he attacked and ripped the small radio apart like it was his enemy. He easily snapped the aerial in two and then handed it over to the old man. The old man took the areal and bent the shaft about an inch and a half over and then handed it back to Walker as he said to the young soldier. "There it is, now young fella all you have to do is stick it in that there hole and give it a good turn and then watch the doors pop open for you, sonny. That simple young man." Mclaughin offered to the Lieutenant with a smile on his lips.

The soldier grabbed the bent shaft and stretched on his toes and manhandled the aerial into the narrow hole. It was a bit of problem to get the bent section in the hole, but once it finally slipped through the hole, he spun the shaft until the bent end hit something resisting it behind the door. He glanced back at the old man and told him he wanted him to stand guard by the elevator opening, and make sure no one fell into the soon to be opened shaft. He also told the old man to jam something in the elevator door, so it would not automatically shut on them, trapping them inside the elevator shaft.

"That's it, you got it in the right place sonny, now all you have to do now is give it a good hard twist and the doors should spring open automatically for you if you hit the right spot that is, sonny." The old man said proudly after he acknowledged the Lieutenant's orders with a nod. He was beaming over the fact his makeshift tool was going to work for the soldier.

The Lieutenant put pressure on the aerial shaft, it bent some in his hands. Just as he thought it was not going to work, something let go inside the door, and the elevator doors folded in on themselves. Yanking the shaft out of his hand, as the doors disappeared in the side of the shaft. He had to step back for fear he might stumble into the now open shaft. Many hands instantly grabbed him by the arms and back, and they pull him away from the shaft. Some women shouted when the doors sprang open. He struggled out of the civilian hands, and then carefully inched his way back to the opened shaft until he could look into it. He whistled as he spat down it. Then he turned to his right and saw the ladder pinned to the concrete wall. It was an easy grab, he looked at the female Sergeant and asked her. "You ready to do our stinking act, sister?"

"Ready, willing, and more than able Bobby. You want to go first, soldier?"

"Hell, I don't even wanna go second for crap sake." He mumbled as he used the same phase she used on him an hour ago.

He then turned to Duane and reminded him by offering. "Mr. Calapp Sir, you have to get back in the apartment and man the damn phone for me, sir. I don't want anyone looking for me from my Command Center, and not knowing where the fuck I went in this lousy dump, sir."

"No problem there sonny." Duane quickly disappeared back in his apartment.

The Lieutenant moved over to the elevator shaft and then he took up a position near the opening and he offered his hand to the Sergeant as he explained to her. "Once you're in the fricking shaft, I want you to go up the ladder high enuf so I can get on the damn thing with ya. I wanna lead the way on this one Raz. When we're both on the stinking ladder, you'll follow me down the damn thing and we'll go get the damn Veep. If we run into any of the stinking assholes holding her, we'll both do them in nice and easy, Raz."

"My mother didn't raise no fools that lived and I'm no hero either, Bobby. You lead if you want to. I'm more than willing to bring up the rear for you, lover."

The horde of civilians gathered in the hallway chuckled as Ramirez moved to her soldier's side, and then she stepped out in the pitch blackness of the shaft. With her toe stretched out as far as it would go, she searched for the first rung of the metal ladder. Touching it with her foot, she then grabbed the ladder with her left hand, while Walker supported most of her weight with his arms. When she had both feet and one hand on the grime covered ladder, the Lieutenant let go and she grabbed hold of the ladder with both hands. She then climbed up nine rungs, until she felt he had enough room to get on the ladder safely.

Before he tried to get on the ladder, he turned and looked at the civilians staring so intensely at him, and he smiled at them. He saluted the group as a whole and then reached into the darkness. He took hold of the ladder and easily used the strength in his arms to pull his body to it.

There was a collective gasp from some of the civilians stacked up in the hallway, as the Lieutenant instantly disappeared into the pitch blackness of the shaft. None of them were brave enough to get any closer to the opened elevator shaft than they were standing. Another old man moved the nearest to the doors, and he suddenly waved his hands at everyone. Then he started to push everyone away from the opening. John Mclaughin beamed with pleasure over the fact the soldier gave him this great responsibility to look after.

A second civilian rushed out of his apartment armed with a flat screw driver, and he bent down and jammed it underneath the elevator door, locking it open in place. It did not take very long for the horde of gathered civilians to get bored with just staring at the open elevator shaft door, and one by one they slowly started to drift back to their apartments.

Chapter Twenty Six

THE OVAL OFFICE, THE WHITE HOUSE, WASHINGTON DC

When General White finished speaking with the Commander of the two fast attack Apache helicopters, he went over to the phone that was open to the apartment in the Trump Tower and he barked into it. "Walker! Where the hell are you, mister!"

"Sorry sir, the young soldier you want to speak with sir, has just went into the elevator shaft along with the female soldier with him. They're both heading to where the Vice President is being held captive in the building, sir." Duane replied to the General's call.

"Who the hell am I'm speaking with for Christ sake, mister?" General White growled angrily into the phone at the voice on the other end.

"I'm Duane Calapp sir, your soldier left me in charge of the phone line for him, sir." The civilian replied to the Chairman of the Joint Chiefs of Staff.

"Oh yeah Mr. Calapp, I remember the Lieutenant telling me about you, sir. Sorry for biting your head off juts then sir. You said my people just entered the god damn elevator shaft so they could carry out my orders, sir?" the General asked the civilian with concern in his voice.

"That's correct General." Duane offered with pride in his tone.

"How was Lieutenant Walker, sir? What was his frame of mind when he left you, Mr. Calapp Sir?" the General questioned the obviously elderly civilian.

"It was real fine sir. He seemed very confident to carry out his order for you, General. He positively made me believe there was no doubt in his mind whatsoever, he was going to free the Vice President and then get her here safely, General, err...?"

"White sir. General White, and I'll be the only person communicating with you on this damn phone, until my soldiers return with the Vice President in tow. Mr. Calapp Sir, here's what I want you to do for me until my soldiers return with the Vice President, sir."

Sergeant Ramirez complained as they entered the elevator shaft that it was a long way down, forcing the Lieutenant to think of this ladder as the so called Stairway to Heaven obstacle from the training base. The Stairway to Heaven was a four story structure of telephone poles, all soldiers on base had to climb by means of wooden slats in a certain amount of time, if they wanted to be part of the specialized unit of elite soldiers. He slowly made his way down the never ending slippery ladder. The air inside the shaft was stale and it stank and he kept looking for the floor numbers painted on the grim covered concrete wall. Rung by rung, they slowly made it down to the twenty second floor of the building. Sweat rolled in his eyes as he strained climbing down the never ending ladder. The two soldiers were moving as fast as they dared. They had no idea three terrorists were also working their way to the same floor at the same time.

Halfway down the ladder, Sergeant Ramirez asked him. "Hey Walker, how's the leg doing?"

"It's hurting like two muthafucka's banging their heads together in a stinking closet. Thank you very much for reminding me of the damn thing, baby."

She looked down at her lover, and then questioned. "What the hell does that mean Bobby?"

"It means it hurts like fricking hell, and I don't need you reminding me about the damn thing."

The two elite Special Forces soldiers had a good head start on Alexander and his two other people heading for the Vice President's apartment. The Russian was employing caution heading for the twenty second floor of the Trump Tower, which slowed his progress down dramatically. The slow progress of the terrorist's ensured both Walker and Ramirez would reach the Vice President's apartment, well ahead of the three terrorists in the Tower.

Feeling time was rapidly running out on them, he increased his pace a little moving down the ladder, and only slowed when he saw the number twenty three painted on the wall in silver spray paint. He stopped and called up to the Sergeant. "Hey Raz, the next floor's the one we want."

Blood was oozing from his leg wound through the bandages.

"I know, have you given any thought as to how you're going to get inside the apartment once we reach the floor? I'm not taking my clothes off again for forget that." She looked at her lover.

"Yeah, we know the two asses we did in were going by the number Thirteen and Twenty Four. We also know the one running this stinking freak show, is going by the stinking number Twenty Seven, and he didn't give out the alarm on us. It was lucky you were listening in on their damn communications, so we know what the fuck's going on around us. I'm planning to rap on the door and say I'm Twenty Four, and I was instructed by Twenty Seven to relieve the creep guarding the Veep. I hope these stinking slugs don't know each other, from what I'm picking up over the radio, it seems there are two different group of nuts running this damn show. Anyway, I'm hoping the tent peg in the room opens the door, and I'll take it from there slick as snot."

"Why do you think the one going by Twenty Seven didn't sound the alarm that two of his friends were done in by us, Walker? I'd think he would've wanted everyone in his group to know some of his people are down and out for the count on him."

"Yeah, I think I know how the dopey motherfucker thinks. If I was him, right now I'd be making for the stinking staircase in hopes of cutting us off." He replied to her.

"You think he knows we're soldiers coming to rescue the Vice President, Walker?" she asked as she followed him down the final few steps of the ladder.

"You bet your sweet little ass on it, baby. This fricking geek seems like he knows what's going on around his stinking ass pretty much all the damn time. I'd say we have a few minutes at most to get the damn Veep outta their hands before this lousy prick shows up, along with some of his stinking friends, and they try to do us in like we did to his fucking friends. C'mon Raz, we gotta create some fucking violence around here, little sister. I want some fucking payback."

"We're going to win this damn thing, right Bobby?" Sergeant Ramirez asked with concern as she watched her soldier working on the closed elevator doors to floor twenty two now.

"We gotta win this damn thing, you know what they always taught us, 'winning isn't everything, it's the only fucking thing' baby. Besides, I was never brought up to be a stinking looser, good, bad or fucking otherwise, Raz. Coming in second place, only means that you're the first to fucking lose, and I don't lose nuthin in my stinking life."

"Just make sure you don't get killed on me. I'll not talk to you again if that happens mister. I'll be angry with you buster." She warned as she shot him one of her best smiles.

"You know how it goes, what don't kill me only serves to piss me off real fucking bad, sister." Lieutenant Walker retorted with a smirk as he snapped the handle to the spring that held the elevator doors closed in place on this floor. He used his foot this time to stop the doors from springing open too quickly on them, and having them slamming loudly against the wall and possibly alerting the terrorists in the Vice President's apartment. He remembered the racket the other elevator doors made when they first opened on the thirty forth floor.

Using the strength in his hands and arms, the excited Lieutenant allowed the elevator doors to open quietly and slowly. He had his right leg woven between the rungs of the ladder, to enable him to be able to use both his hands on the doors. When the doors were open, he pulled his leg out of the rung, and then he stretched it to the landing. Getting a foothold, he pushed off the ladder and ended up on the floor standing. He looped his weapon off his shoulder and held it at the ready, as he immediately checked out the hallway. Seeing no one around, he ducked his head back in the elevator shaft and announced. "The coast is clear, we gotta get a move on it Raz."

Ramirez took hold of his hand, and she allowed him to actually pull her off the ladder. The instant her feet touched the floor, she immediately swung her MP-5 machine pistol from around her shoulder, and then she took a defensive stance of a hunting soldier. She looked in her soldier's bloodshot eyes, and smiled and then she looked at his leg and complained.

"Gees Walker your leg's bleeding pretty bad again. You want me to look at it for you?"

"My leg's fucking fine, let it go will ya for fuck sake. We're gonna pay these sonofabitches in Star Three a stinking visit. C'mon, but I want you to stay outta sight, until I take care of the dick at the fricking door. Raz, if this Richard Cranium (slang for Dick Head) finds us running around out here and takes me out. It's gonna be up to you to finish the mission for us. Remember, the big guy back in Washington said get the Veep's ass outta this mess to the exclusion of all else, baby." The young soldier offered as he moved towards the splintered oak doors of the apartment.

"I know what General White told you he wanted, and I don't particularly care he thinks us as if we were the walking dead on this one, Robert. You just take it easy please, I want to live through this shit storm, Walker." She seethed at him as she held him in her gaze.

"Raz, you know what the other grunts say bout me. 'I'm too wild to be mild'. In case you didn't notice it baby, this crap comes with the stinking turf. We always end up with our dicks stuck in the fricking grinder, and our asses thought expendable by the damn top brass. In your case, your tits baby." Walker corrected and then smirked as he turned the corner on the floor and stopped dead in his tracks. The surprised Lieutenant was staring at the shattered, once exquisitely carved red oak doors ripped apart by the machine gun fire from Michael and Lizzie.

The Lieutenant glanced back at Sergeant Ramirez, knowing she would be kind of upset by the condition of the doors to the apartment. He knew she really liked the female Vice President, and understood she was going to be pissed if anything happened to her on his watch.

The Sergeant stood three paces behind the Lieutenant, staring at the ripped apart doors, her eyes wide and anger in her heart. It did not help to see the two large blood stains marring the fine carpeting in the middle of the hallway just outside the doors of the plush apartment.

He noticed the elevator door near the entrance to Star Three was wedged open, and he knew where the bodies of the dead agents ended up. He figured the guy going by the number Twenty Seven more than likely ordered the bodies tossed down the elevator shaft, to get them out of the way. He knew it was a shitty end for a few brave men who gave their lives in the line of duty he thought as he stepped in front of the crumbling door. He gave a quick look back at the Sergeant who nodded, and then she hoisted her weapon up until the stock was pressed tightly against her shoulder, prepared to fire. He took in a deep breath and then he tapped on the door, causing more of the splintered wood to fall free of the shattered doors.

Inside Apartment Star Three, the terrorist guarding the hall was taking a leak. The other one, Valentine stood in the center of the gallery keeping a close eye on the Vice President and her female bodyguard, while also watching the doors leading into the apartment. The terrorist had his gun haphazardly tucked under his arm, while holding it against his chest and pointing out with his arm. He was enjoying a cold Bud when he heard the tapping on the door. Dropping the beer to the floor, he lifted his weapon to a firing position, and then he aimed it at the double doors while calling out to whoever was on the other side of the door.

"Yeah? Who's there, and what the hell do you want in here?" the voice demanded.

The other terrorist taking a leak immediately rushed out of the bathroom while zippering his fly, when he heard Valentine call out to someone. Valentine gave him a quick head nod, and the second man took up a firing position standing nearby him. They both held their weapons at the ready while staring at the shattered front doors of the apartment.

"Hey inside, Twenty Seven felt you guys needed some relief. He wants you to report up to the roof, and I'm to take over guard positions until we're relieved by someone else." The Lieutenant held his weapon ready as he waited for someone to open the door from inside for him.

Valentine looked at the other man and then shrugged as the second man whispered at him. "Valentine, I'm certain he didn't mean you were to report up to the roof. I believe he was only talking about me. I remember the crazy ass Russian saying he was going to rotate us every once in a while, to keep us on guard and better alert for him. This is okay, I'm certain of it."

"Then why didn't Twenty Seven notify me before sending this one down here to relieve us?"

"Damn Valentine, you expect some consideration from that big Russian prick? If you are I have a bridge in Brooklyn for sale I'd like to sell ya man." The second terrorist replied.

Valentine stared at his partner, and then laughed as he realized what his partner just said to him. He knew this was something Alexander would pull on them. Especially after the slight confrontation they went through a short while ago. This had to be another one of his pressure plays. He shook his head and then lowered his weapon as he moved his head, and the other man headed for the door to open it for the man standing in the hallway waiting to be allowed into the apartment, while shouldering his weapon in the same motion.

Before they left the old man's apartment on the upper floor, Walker and Ramirez were given clean shirts, and they made certain they washed their hands and faces in an effort to pull off the Lieutenant's plan. But they did not take the time to wash their hair because he felt the wet hair might send a warning signal to the terrorists he planned to kill inside the Vice President's apartment. He knew they would expect their friends to get dirty during their operation in the Trump Tower, but not have washed hair. He did not know what they might think about that. They did combed their hair trying to get as much of the elevator filth out of it as possible.

When the two soldiers made their way down the filthy elevator shaft, the grease and grime coating the ladder for years, caked on their clean shirts. The dangerous trip down the ladder covered them with grease again, almost to the point of being unrecognizable as humans. Knowing he was unable to do anything about the grime, he decided to take a new look at this plan. He felt the grime might better serve a purpose, he hoped the terrorists might think what happened on the roof was a mess, and that was why the leader sent them down to the apartment. To give them a break from the action. The wise Lieutenant cautiously shifted his weapon around his battered body while still trying to hold it at the ready, yet making the terrorists think he was just suffering from totally exhaustion, and he could not hold the weapon any other way.

The young military officer heard someone heading for the double doors, and he immediately put the saddest and exhausted look on his face he could possibly muster. He was saying a silent prayer, hoping what he was attempting to do was going to work out for him, and they would get the jump on the unknown number of jerks inside the room holding the Vice President hostage. He heard the chair set up against the doors being moved away and he could see that much through the countless holes ripped into the heavy wood doors. Try as he might, he could not get a good fix on how many terrorists were inside the room with the Vice President.

Walker warned the Sergeant he was going to signal her if he could get a count on the terrorists in the room before going in action. Slowly, the door on the left opened, and he heard the door dragging pieces of shattered wood and other debris with it across the floor.

The man on loan from Alexander to Michael's people, found himself staring at a filth covered person he did not recognized. The grime did not serve to alarm the terrorist, and Walker doubted even his mother would not have recognized him in his condition. The blood covering his leg did not interest the terrorist in the least either. The way he knew the one in the hallway was part of their mission, was because of the weapon he carried. Each weapon had a series of strips of black tape strapping clips together for fast reloading. Three loaded clips were taped together, giving the weapon ninety rounds before being forced to get other clips for the weapon.

The terrorist nodded slightly to the Lieutenant while studying his face. He figured the Russian had the people on the roof use dirt for face covering or camouflage. He smiled as he felt dealing with the crazy Russian, no one knew how he was going to act, or what he might make his people do for the mission. The terrorist stepped aside to allow Walker to enter the room.

When the door was open enough for him to see into the apartment, he noticed the terrorist opening the door. Then he spotted another target further in the shambled room. He scanned the layout of the interior, and saw some broad he knew was not the Vice President, sitting in a chair back to back with a man slumped over and obviously dead. It looked like they had been handcuffed together, because the female had her hands pulled out to her sides, and when she moved, the dead guy along moved with her. The female looked a real mess there, sitting in the chair while holding her fingers apart and locked outwards, almost as if they were burning her. Or maybe she was afraid to allow them to touch for some reason he did not know. He had no idea why she was doing this, nor did he real care at this point.

Cathy's fingers were held out straight and painfully, because her hands and fingers were soaked with Agent Edward Sweeney's blood and brain matter that splattered over them when he was shot in the head by the leader of the terrorists. She sat bolt upright in the chair while staring at the red mess threatening to rob her of her sanity. The female agent refused to allow her fingers to touch together, all she could think about doing was washing her hands, her face, and her hair, and then change into some clean clothes. She did not care if she had to go around naked, as long as she was able to get Sweeney's blood off her body.

He tried to get a location on where the Vice President was being held inside the apartment, as he took his first step into the interior of the large room. Before moving in, the Lieutenant let go of his weapon with his right hand, and then he brought it up to his face and scratched the tip of his nose, twice. This was to serve as a warning to Sergeant

Ramirez that he had detected two terrorists inside the room, and both of them were standing to his right side.

As silently and stealthily as a large hunting cat, Ramirez moved as close to the set of doors as she dared, to support her man as he entered the room. The Lieutenant brought his hand up to the weapon, and wove his fingers around the implement of death, as he marveled this asshole staring so closely at him, did not notice he just placed his finger on the trigger of his weapon.

"Alexander must have you guys jumping through fucking hoops up there on the roof. Was it as bad as it looks like it was up there when the police attacked you guys up there? Was the crazy ass Russian fool able to stop the helicopters from attacking you guys up there, pal?" the terrorists asked Walker with concern in his voice.

"Yeah, he nailed it good, and it was real rough when the helicopter attacked us, pal." He did not know there were two helicopters that tried to land on the roof, so he used a singular response to the terrorist's question. He also used the word pal he heard a number of the terrorists using over his radio every now and then, as he added to his words. "I don't want to live through anything like that ever again it was that bad, pal." The Lieutenant grunted, trying to pick up the accent he detected from the one speaking to him. His thoughts and actions were interrupted by the second man, who took a more threatening stance against him.

"What the hell's going on the roof? What are you doing bothering us like this, pal? And, what's wrong with that stupid Russian up there anyhow? He should know better than to just send anyone down here to relieve us without notifying me first, dammit! Who the hell are you pal? I don't recognize you, and why are you carrying your weapon like that? Are you threatening me with the damn thing, pal?" Valentine roared as he moved his weapon around to get it in a better firing position for himself, not liking this guy who he did not recognize. His move was stopped dead in his tracks before he got set against the intruder to the plush room.

The wise soldier evaluated the threatening situation, and he assumed Valentine was more of a danger to him than the other jerk standing abreast of him, and he decided to take Valentine out first.

He hoped Ramirez was quick enough to take out the other terrorist before he did him in. The young military officer jerked his weapon up and fired, sending five bullets ripping into Valentine's chest. While he fired Walker dropped down to the floor, trying to make himself a much harder target for the other guy, in case she was unable to get at him quick enough.

Valentine's body went flying up and then backwards, his weapon went tumbling away from his hand in the opposite direction his body tumbled off in. The once extremely threatening terrorist was dead before his body came to rest crumbled up on the floor, half leaning against the far wall of the living area. When Valentine's body stopped rolling on the floor, the Lieutenant immediately called out to Sergeant Ramirez. "Clear on the left."

This was to let her know no other targets were to her left side, if she charged in the room. The female Sergeant was as quick as she needed to be, to back the Lieutenant and support his actions inside the apartment. In less time than it took for the second terrorist to realize this stranger was a serious threat against him, and even before he was able to place his other hand on his weapon. The Sergeant appeared in the doorway while aiming her weapon right at the other man.

Without thinking about it for a second she fired, sending a short burst of seven rounds ripping into the second terrorist's body. He like his partner, was dead before his body stopped dancing across the floor from the bullets slamming into him. The second she fired, she dashed into the apartment and then she rolled to her right as instructed by Walker. She quickly scanned her surroundings, seeing no one threatening them in her field of vision, she bellowed back to the out of breath Lieutenant. "Clear on the right!"

The automatic weapons fire made Cathy try to raise her hands to her ears, in an attempt to try and cover them as she screamed almost hysterically. The shock of seeing Sweeney killed so close to her, was having a terrible effect on her fighting ability and sanity at the same time. She could not move her hands to her ears because of the way she was still handcuffed to Sweeney's body, so she screamed instead. She screamed out of fright, resentment, of anger and rage held against the terrorist who so callously killed someone she held so dear. She was outraged the terrorists were holding the Vice President hostage, and not treating her with the greatest of respect demanded of a person of her outstanding position and abilities.

The Vice President's female bodyguard cursed for allowing herself to become so helpless in this deadly situation threatening the life of her ward. She was scared to death these new terrorists were there to take over the mission for the others, and they were going to kill everyone inside the apartment. She refused to look up while trying to work out some sort of attack in her mind to get herself free, and then get to the Vice President and release her and make their escape from the Tower and the other terrorists still running around inside the structure.

From behind her she heard Hirshfield screaming in fear for her life over the violent intrusion on their apartment. Not knowing if this person was a terrorist added to her anger which took over her thoughts and fears. Cathy was steaming with rage she was unable to get to Ms. Hirshfield's side to protect her like she was trained to do over the years of her service. Suddenly, her head snapped up and her eyes flew open as her mind registered the words these new terrorists said.

Walker pushed himself off the floor and then he walked up to the screaming woman and bellowed at her. "Hey bitch, in case you don't know it yet baby. I'm one of the fucking good guys. Who the hell are you baby? You look sorta familiar to my ass. Do I know you baby?"

The Sergeant pushed herself off the floor as well and she rushed over to the Vice President. The second Vice President Mary Hirshfield saw the grime covered but smiling face looking at back at her, she instantly stopped screaming and returned her smile. Mary breathed out a great sigh of relief as she whispered softly after recognizing the female warrior. "Sergeant Ramirez? Is that really you, I pray God it's you young lady?"

"Yes it is Ma'am. It's me and the grunt over there is Lieutenant Walker, Ma'am. Are there any other terrorists inside the apartment, Ma'am?" she asked with concern as she flipped the chair containing the Vice President over on its side, and then she placed a protective knee in the small of her back while using the chair to protect her. Ms. Hirshfield was not handcuffed, so she sprawled out on the floor, making it easier for her to hover over and protect the Vice President.

"No, those two were the only ones still inside the apartment, Sergeant. Your friend's hurt, how did you two ever get up here without being captured by the other terrorists in the building, Sergeant Ramirez?" Ms. Hirshfield asked as she struggled to roll on to her side, so she could see the Sergeant's face a little better. When Ramirez removed her knee from the small of her back, she realized they killed the only two terrorists in the once magnificent room.

"Don't tell him about the wound because he's rather sensitive about it I'm afraid, Ma'am." The Sergeant offered as she again smiled at the Vice President.

Cathy looked into the eyes of the wild looking man hovering so near her and smiling. He was in a relaxed state, because he overheard Ms. Hirshfield tell the Sergeant the two dead men, were the only terrorists still in the room with them. The secretary was a real mess. The Lieutenant, who had not paid very much attention to her when she first visited the two soldier's room the night before, did not recognize her. Her face was contorted in such a mask of sheer horror and anger, it completely changed her once beautiful features. He slowly recognized the woman he was staring so intensely at, and then he said with a smirk to her. "Cathy?"

"Don't just stand there like the big dumb lout that you are, stupid! Get me out of this god damn thing will you please, stupid!" she hissed hotly at the grinning elite soldier.

"Hey baby, you keep going on like that and you might end up hurting my stinking feelings on me, pretty lady. I don't like to have my feelings hurt you know, baby." He replied and then he went over to the guy he hit and started to search through the pockets of the terrorist. The Lieutenant noticed a slight fresh wound on the terrorists forearm, and thought it might have been caused by a round he fired. He did not recognize the wound had been inflicted on his arm by a pair of human teeth. He smiled when he located the missing keys he was searching for, and he held them up triumphantly for Cathy to see, she was unimpressed as she barked nastily at him.

"Get over here and get me the hell out of this god damn handcuffs I told you, stupid."

His neck straightened as his eyebrows arched slightly over the angry words she used so harshly against him. He shrugged and then moved over to her side as he said to her in a grunt.

"Huh, there you go again baby, trying to hurt my stinking feelings on me I see, baby. Hey baby, read my stinking licks. You betta calm down some before you go and hurt yourself, baby. Think of your fucking blood pressure for a stinking minute will ya huh, baby. I don't need you hurting yourself and then I gotta get stuck carrying your friggin slack ass all over this stinking building. I need you to help protect the Veep with me, baby."

She was still glaring at Lieutenant Walker as she snarled so angrily at him again. "C'mon, C'mon you stupid ass you! You're moving as slow as shit coming out of a coke bottle for the love of God. Get these damn things off me now, dammit! Before I plant a kick on your dumb ass on you, buster! I need to take a damn shower and feel clean again, stupid!"

"Hey bitch, you're using some of the fucking grunt slang there, baby. You got someone in the stinking service, baby?" he asked as he freed her first hand from the handcuffs.

"Fuck you stupid, just get your ass moving and get me free of these damn handcuffs like I just told you, mister!" The female bodyguard roared as she moved her free hand over to her other hand, trying to massage the terrible pain pounding away on her wrist.

"Hey baby, don't go try and apologize to me now sister. It's too late for that kinda shit, baby. Hang on while I free your uther hand, will you stop wiggling around so much, dammit!" He groused at her while trying to be funny, as he continued to fumble around with the handcuffs on her wrist. The second he freed her other hand, she was on her feet in a flash and ripping at her blood soaked clothes, tearing them from her body as she stormed towards her bathroom.

He knelt on a knee and settled in to enjoy the strip show she was putting on, as she tugged at her blood stained filthy clothes. Then he offered with a smirk to the angry young woman. "Hey baby, as much as I'd dearly like to rip me off a little piece of trim right about now. I'm really sorry to tell ya baby, we don't have the time for that type of thing to go down at this time, baby. I hafta get the Veep the hell outta this stinking dump before more of these bad guys show up, and we hafta party with the lousy slugs before we can get the heck outta here to safety, baby."

The female bodyguard suddenly spun on her heels and she placed her hands on her hips, naked except for her panties and the small hidden weapon. She glared angrily at the grinning soldier as she growled at him. "I don't give a good god damn what the fuck you have to do right now, stupid. I'm not going anywhere until I wash Sweeney's blood off of my damn body, buster. And, if you call me baby once more stupid. You'll not need to worry about anything else for the rest of your wasted life, fella." With this said to the soldier, she turned and headed to the bathroom. Instantly, they heard the water in the shower running at full blast.

The Lieutenant smiled as he watched her move to the bathroom and then he grumbled, even though he knew she would not hear any of his words. "Err... yeah, right, okay, sure thing there baby, anything you say baby. But you better make your shower real quick, sister. We don't have the fucking time to waste with hanging round here any longer then we hafta, baby." He retorted with a smirk as he relaxed, and then he decided to wait until she was done in the shower. Then, as if an afterthought, he mumbled at no one in particular in the room. "Man, I never saw a woman working so damn hard at trying to hurt my stinking feelings on me like she's doing."

Sergeant Ramirez helped Vice President Hirshfield to her feet as she turned to her soldier and complained. "C'mon, you haven't heard anything from your feelings since I've known you mister. We did it Walker, we got the Vice President away from the terrorists and she's unhurt."

"Go ahead and pile it up on the big dumb jerk I see sister. What's all this shit about, pick on poor old Walker day or something round here Raz?" he griped back at her.

In the stairway leading up to the twenty second floor, Alexander charged up the last few steps in a rush. The moment he heard the automatic weapons fire from that floor, he immediately knew where it was coming from. He stopped his forward movement so fast he nearly slid on the smooth concrete stairwell landing, and almost fell. He then dropped down to a knee and moved in slowly. He slowed down in hopes Fritch and Casolari did not hear the weapon's fire, and they came storming onto the floor and drawing the fire from whoever was trying to free the Vice President and other hostage left in the room. Thus allowing him to get the jump on the would be heroes before they realized he was behind them.

Carefully, the wise Russian moved his foot onto the landing, and then he slumped low as he cautiously worked his way over to the shattered window of the heavy fireproof door. The window was blown out by the special agent guarding the Vice President's apartment, when he fired at Michael when the group started their assault on the building. From his vantage point, the large Russian could make out the shattered doors of the apartment. He saw no one around them, he heard voices from the room though, and knew they were not coming from any of his people. He was sure the Vice President had been freed by whoever attacked his people, and someone with military or police background was fighting them. The Russian terrorist cursed under his breath, wishing he knew how many attackers were involved in this move to free his hostages.

There was a sudden crash, followed by a loud bang from the other end of the hallway, and he smiled. Knowing his people made the fatal mistake of charging right on the floor without displaying caution or smarts in their actions. He was not the only one who heard the racket.

Inside the Presidential suite of the Trump International Tower and Hotel, Lieutenant Robert Walker jumped to his feet, and he immediately readied his weapon when he heard the sudden noise coming from the hallway. Sergeant Dorothy Ramirez immediately grabbed Ms. Mary Hirshfield by the arm, and she roughly dragged her to her bathroom. She not so politely shoved the Vice President into the bathtub, and then she ordered her to stay low for her own protection. The Sergeant felt this was the safest place in the entire apartment to deposit her ward, and she wanted her there in case they got involved in a firefight with whoever just entered their floor.

Neither Walker nor Ramirez was fooling themselves into thinking whoever was outside the apartment, was there to help them with their rescue of the Vice President. The Lieutenant moved like the warrior he was on the hunt for enemy towards the shattered doors. Sergeant Ramirez was off to his left supporting his rear flank. He reached the door and looked out of the damaged frame in both directions, trying to see whoever it was moving around on the floor.

The large Russian peeked through the blown out window, just as Lieutenant Walker went in action against his two people outside the room. He easily picked up the soldier moving, and he ducked back behind the door and then waited. He decided to allow Fritch and Casolari to shoulder the weight of the upcoming battle, while he came at this stranger from behind and killed the invader. Before he had a chance to mount a defense against his attack.

The Lieutenant did not notice the movement in the window from the Russian as he ducked behind the door. This door was the only one he was able to see from where he was standing in the doorway, not seeing anyone from that section, he deduced where the attack would be mounted against him from. He turned to his left and heard more noise from that direction.

He ducked back inside the apartment, and then signaled the Sergeant with his hands where the targets he just located were in the hallway. Just then, Cathy walked out of her bathroom topless while still drying her hair with a towel. She immediately stopped what she was doing and stared at the soldier who was kneeling on the floor in a perfect attack position. He was staring outside the room like he was waiting for someone to attack him. She instantly dropped to the floor out of instinct and her many years of special service training, and she slipped the clean shirt she had looped over her shoulder on her. She had a pair of blue jeans on, and mouthed silently at the grime covered military man. "What's going on out there Walker? Someone coming at us?"

He mouthed back at her while trying to keep his eyes trained on the outside. "I have an unknown number of targets working towards us from the left side of the stinking hallway, baby. We have the Veep safely tucked in the bathtub in her room. I don't need her getting tagged on my fucking watch here. I want you to get in there and protect her ass while we do in these new assholes. Don't allow anyone in the god damn bathroom under no circumstances Raz. We'll take care of these slugs who think we don't know they're making a move on us, baby."

The Vice President's female bodyguard understood most of what the soldier said to her by reading his lips, and what she did not picked up, she figured out for herself. She nodded back at the soldier and then she headed for Ms. Hirshfield's bathroom not before stopping by the body of Valentine. She bends down and yanked the Glock pistol from his belt, and then in a rage and a want for some form of vengeance against him or his body. She savagely kicked him right in the lifeless face. Then she straightened up and headed for the Vice President hiding in the bathroom in the master bedroom of the apartment.

She entered the bathroom and quickly checked on Mary's condition, finding she was okay she took over guard duty of her by the door leading out of the bedroom into the main section of the large apartment. Then she settled down and waited for the next move to come by the new batch of terrorists trying to attack them from outside the apartment. She took up a perfect defensive position inside the room that gave her the best possible protection and advantage point on anyone who might try and get into the bathroom against her.

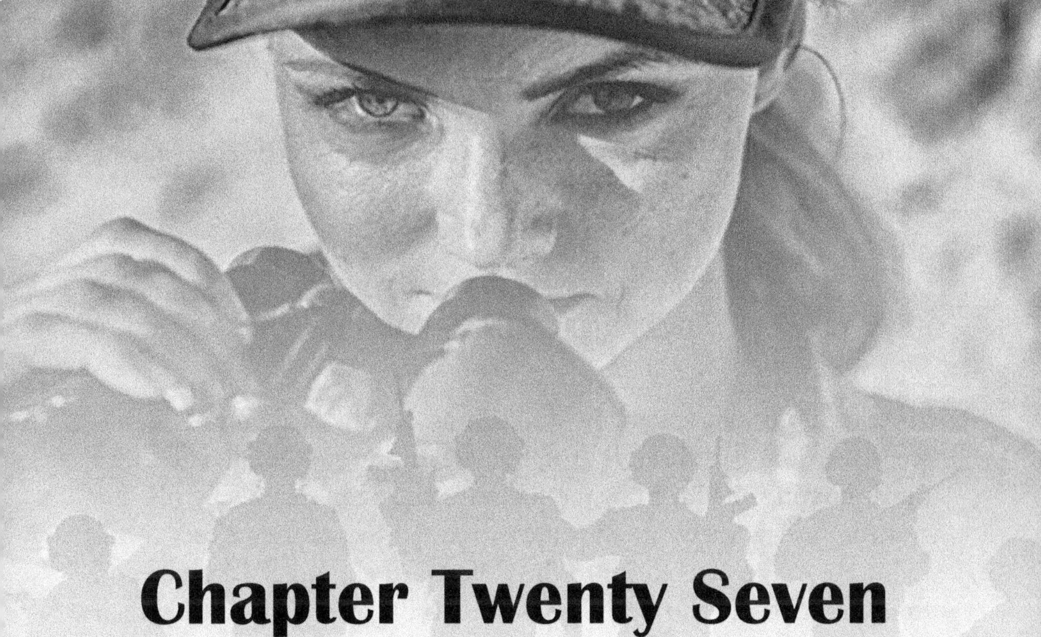

Chapter Twenty Seven

THE OVAL OFFICE, THE WHITE HOUSE,
WASHINGTON DC

When the Chairman of the Joint Chiefs of Staff, General John White was informed by Duane, that his Lieutenant Walker and the female soldier were heading down the elevator shaft to get the Vice President. The General immediately ordered the two Apache fast attack helicopters airborne. Both aircraft were fueled, and the second they got the go ahead to begin their mission. The pair of machines lifted off and moved for the Trump Tower. The twin helicopters headed for the structure, until they were within a block of it, and then they hovered and waited for the final attack order. The set of war machines hovered ten feet off the ground, one in Central Park, the other spooled on 58th Street behind 10 Columbus Circle. The two Apaches helicopters came in from Ninth Avenue, and both were less than three seconds away from their assigned target.

General White paced in the Oval Office in a blind rage, his hands were locked behind his back while he waited for the first reports the helicopters got to their ordered standoff positions. The second the attack helicopters arrived at the stations, the pilots checked in with their Commander. Then, and only then did the General breathe properly again.

THE TWENTY SECOND FLOOR OF THE TRUMP INTERNATIONAL TOWER

The moment Lieutenant Walker was certain Ms. Hirshfield was secured in the bathroom by her bodyguard, he moved after the new threat coming at him from the hallway. The Sergeant was by his side and the instant they moved out, he pointed to a service closet to his right. He wanted her to get to the closet and take a defensive position from inside it. He had two reasons for this the important one being, it would place her out of harm's way when the shooting started against the terrorist. Just in case they got the upper hand on them, and they had to engage in an all out firefight in the hallway. The other reason was; from this vantage point, he hoped she would be able to see further down the hall, and line up her attack on their approaching targets.

From the other stairwell, the Russian picked up everything taking place beyond the fireproof door from the landing onto the floor He smiled as he watched the well trained Americans work towards his unsuspecting people. He could tell there was two enemy and the strangers definitely had military training, by the way they were moving against his people at the other end of the hall. While the two moved down the hall, he studied their moves. It didn't take long to figure out these strangers were better trained in the military arts of warfare than Fritch and Casolari.

He decided his two people were going to be killed by these two strangers, and he could only hope one of his people were quick enough to take out at least one of them, before he had to engage them from their flanks. He grinned again, thinking how good it will be to take out one, or both of these young American warriors. He felt there was not an American soldier alive that could match wits and skills against his Russian honed military training.

Lieutenant Walker waited before moving out against this new threat coming at him. He was giving Sergeant Ramirez the time she needed to force open the closet and get inside it. She ingeniously worked her way into the narrow closet, and then she jammed the door open with something she found lying on the floor. Then she leaned on her back and stretched her neck out until she was able to see further down the hallway as her soldier planned. There was a slight bend at one point about midway down the hall, and from her position she could see around it. She turned to the Lieutenant and gave him the thumbs up, and mouthed 'no MOE' informing him she did not have a Mark One Eyeball, or visual contact on any of the targets coming at them.

The Lieutenant put on a disgusted look and shook his head, he hoped Sergeant Ramirez was at a point where she could detect the targets moving in the hallway. So she could tell him where they were, and how many there was of them. He hated to make a move on anyone he could not see clearly. The Lieutenant's move would end up giving the targets the upper hand against him if he had to charge blindly at them. So slowly, he cautiously inched his way towards the bend in the hallway, hoping the unseen targets would move far enough up for Sergeant Ramirez to detect their numbers, and from what direction and how they were coming at him.

Inside the Vice President's apartment, there was activity. Cathy made certain Hirshfield was safe in the bathtub, she handed her the small automatic pistol she carried for self protection. She then told Hirshfield she was going to leave and see if she could help the soldiers as they worked their way down the hallway. Hirshfield, who did not like being a defenseless hostage, gave Cathy her blessing. She fingered the ice cold pistol locked in her hands, knowing in her mind she would never use it against another human being, but just holding it gave her some piece of mind.

Then Cathy moved with all the grace of a ballet dancer as she checked around the disheveled apartment until she had a clear view of the front doors. She moved close to the pair of shattered oak doors, and took up her new position and settled down to wait for the outcome of the deadly confrontation going on in the hallway twenty feet from where she taken her defensive position. Although she had no intention of getting involved in any action with the terrorists, she was going to make certain no one but the two young soldiers were going to enter the apartment again.

Lieutenant Walker sat on the carpet floor using the strength of his legs to slowly push himself towards the bend in the hall. There was a sudden movement down the hallway that instantly froze him in place. He tried, but he could not see in that section of the hallway from his position.

Sergeant Ramirez detected the slight movement and she immediately trained her eyes on the area. She saw someone moving in the shadows and she waved her hand before her until she got his attention, and then she tapped the right side of her nose. Then held it in front of her and moved it around. She then moved her hand down to her waist, and brought it swiftly across her belly. Informing Lieutenant Walker their target she just picked up was about halfway down the walkway, and he was positioned on the right side of the hall.

The Lieutenant understood one target was on the right side of the hall about halfway down. Being the soldier he was, it did not take long for him to figure out there had to be a second guy the Sergeant was unable to detect at this point, coming from the left side of the hallway. He knew if these two movers were not military trained, there was a possibility they were moving parallel to one another. A stupid move on their part, because anyone working towards a target always worked their way in a staggered but standard attack position. That way one could protect the other while they moved forward to engage their intended targets.

He made a couple quick hand signals at Sergeant Ramirez who understood the silent language of the elite soldiers, and she knew he thought there was a second target on the other side of the hallway, just out of their sight. She moved in the confining closet until she could get a bead on the unseen target. She understood the detected target was as good as dead, and her duty was to protect him from the unseen one, when he made his move on the target they discovered.

The Lieutenant pushed off the floor using his leg power, and then he cautiously inched his way a little closer to the slight bend in the hallway. He leaned forward and then picked up the target Fritch in his line of sight. The second he detected the terrorist, he pulled back so as not to be seen by him or the other target he was certain was working with this one he picked up. Seeing Fritch, he knew he was right, there were at least two terrorists in the hall, because the one he spotted was looking to his side, and he seemed to be speaking to someone he could not see.

It was the only reason why he was not spotted by the terrorist when trying to peek at him. He leaned up against the wall, and he tried to get his breathing under control. He knew he had to be perfect on attacking the two terrorists, because he and Ramirez were the only ones standing between them and the Vice President and Cathy and their safety. He also knew General White would take a shit on his head if he was to allow Hirshfield to become hostage a second time in the same day. He gave one last look to the Sergeant, and held up two fingers and wiggled them around in the air, showing her he was positive there were two targets coming at them.

The concerned female Sergeant nodded and then she shifted her body until she felt she was in the right position to fire at her target, while lying nearly flat on the tile floor inside the narrow closet. She leaned forward, knowing the blackness of the small closet completely shielded her from the view of the terrorist she had a good bead on. She lined her weapon up on the terrorist crouching in the hallway, and then she waited for her soldier to make his dash across the hall to pick off the other terrorist they could not see clearly from their current positions.

The cautious Russian watched from his position as the pair he took to be American soldiers, skillfully worked their way toward a position affording them the ability to take out Fritch and Casolari. He did not mind losing Fritch, but Casolari proven himself to him more than once, and he was sorry he was about to lose him in the engagement with the two American soldiers. The large Russian ex-soldier judged what the male soldier was attempting to do, and understood he was getting the upper hand on Fritch. He shrugged over the prospect of losing Casolari, and felt if he was as good as he thought he was. Then Casolari should be able to react in time to do in the male, who looked like he was setting up to spring across the hallway against his people.

He felt this was the correct move, if the soldiers wanted to end the threat from his people. He quietly opened the heavy fire door, and then he slid hid body on the landing behind the two working soldiers. He did not breathe until he was sure they had not detected his move.

When the Russian was positive his moves were carried off unobserved, he slid along the floor until his back touched the wall. Then, using his neck muscles, the Russian inched his way up the wall, until he was standing. He flattened out against the wall and worked behind the two soldiers.

The Lieutenant had no idea someone was working behind him, his thoughts were directed at the two terrorists he knew were in the hallway, and nothing was going to draw his attention away from this present and clear threat aimed against him. He stood, and then crouched low as he bounced up and down on the balls of his feet a couple of times, to get his muscles ready to react in a flash. When he felt he was good to go, he suddenly sprang out and propelling his body across the opening in the hallway. Only stopping when he crashed his body hard against the opposite wall of the hallway. He smashed into the wall with such power, he actually crushed the two layers five eights inch thick fireproof sheetrock, actually caving it in on itself. All the while he moved, he fired towards where he was certain the one terrorist he could not detect, was lurking.

Casolari picked up the large shadow run yards before him, and he tried to pick his weapon up to a firing position. Before he could pull the trigger on the shadow, he was forced to drop flat to the floor to avoid the wall of lead coming from Walker's weapon. At the same instant he fired at Casolari, Sergeant Ramirez opened fire on the second target she had dead in her sights. Fritch's head splattered like an overripe melon as the slugs from her weapon ripped into his head. The terrorist went flying back, dead before his body stopped twitching the dance of death.

Casolari got low to the floor to try and avoid most of the soldier's wildly fired rounds. He got tagged on the back of his right leg that he left dangling in the air as he dropped down to the floor and cover himself. He did not have a clear line of fire on this threat across from him, but he fired blindly up the hallway where he was sure he saw the shadow end up lying on the floor.

The Lieutenant allowed himself to slid down the crumbling wall, and then he dropped flat on the floor as he returned almost controlled fire on Casolari now, as he started to get control of his actions and weapon. His clip emptied and he ejected the empty clip and slammed a full one home. He slid the action and chambered the round and held the trigger as he sprayed a wall of lead down the lower section of the hall with the entire clip before letting up on the trigger.

Casolari was trapped out in the open while lying as flat as possible on the floor, he could not lift his head enough to get a clear shot off at the stranger. He held his weapon out, and fired blind at his target using one hand to try and control his wildly jumping weapon. The force of bullets exploding in the weapon forced his hand this way and that and up and down, stopping him from getting a good bead on his target. No rounds from Casolari's weapon were coming even close to the Lieutenant. Casolari's free arm was stretched out before his head as he tried to shield it from the bullets ripping into the floor just inches before his face and closing in on him.

Quickly, the line of rounds fired from Walker's weapon worked their way at him, and soon they found their mark as the excited Lieutenant got better control over his outstretched arm and weapon. Two rounds smashed into Casolari's forehead, forcing his body up and then back almost folding his body over on himself. The second he saw the movement of the body, he took the time to aim and emptied the rest of his clip into Casolari's tumbling body on the floor.

When he fired at Casolari, the Russian moved at his back. He shoved off the wall with his shoulders and quickly moved down the hall, until he ended up standing a few feet away from the prone Walker's back. Neither he nor Ramirez noticed the Russian coming at them until it was too late for either of them to react against his attack on Walker. Alexander had him locked up dead in his sights, and he rapidly closed in on the trapped American soldier preparing to fire at him.

Sergeant Ramirez had emptied her weapon on Fritch, and was trapped in the midst of flipping the tapped clips in her hands, and slamming the loaded clip back in her weapon, when she noticed the Russian coming down the hall heading right for Walker's back. She rushed trying to place the clip in her weapon. She pushed the clip home with all her might, her hands trembled so much it caused the clip to seat improperly in the weapon. When she pulled back on the action of the weapon to chamber the round, the hammer picked up the bullet wrong and jammed almost sideways in the weapon. The soldiers called this type of a jam a stovepipe round.

She understood what happened to her weapon, and she cursed herself for causing the miss loading as she tried to free the messed up round from the chamber and then reseat the clip properly. Using all her strength, she could not dislodge the sideways and slightly bent unspent round from her weapon. She looked up at the same time she struggled with her jammed stove piped round. She could do nothing in time to save his life but scream out at him.

"Walkerrrrr! Behind you god dammit! Behind you!" Sergeant Ramirez roared at her soldier.

She screamed his name out in hopes of drawing the threat to his life away from him, even if her call meant drawing the attacker's attention to her, and causing him to kill her instead of her soldier. She wanted him to live above everything else in her life. But to her dismay, the attacker completely ignored her screaming, and he kept moving against him. The terrorist did not flinch when Sergeant Ramirez screamed Walker's name out. All she could see in her mind, was her soldier lying in a pool of blood as she continued to wrestle with her jammed weapon.

The soldier was bewildered by Sergeant Ramirez's scream, and he turned just as his weapon clicked empty for the second time. He found himself staring at the huge, lurking figure of a man standing so near him, and still charging him with his weapon aimed right at his face. He dumped his empty weapon and then went fishing for the side arm he had tucked in the belt of his pants. It was buried under his weight, and by the time he was able to get a good grip on the handle of the sidearm, the advancing Russian stopped walking at him and was preparing to fire.

"Walkerrrrr!" Ramirez desperately screamed out a second time, as she struggled to get to her feet to make an unarmed charge at the terrorist threatening to kill her soldier right before her eyes. Tears of anger and frustration were streaming down her face as she got on a knee and then she prepared to launch herself at the massive figure preparing to kill her soldier. The tightness of the closet hampered her movement, adding to her frustration and anger as she actually threw the empty gun at the lurking figure. All the while she stared at the Russian's sneering face in pure hatred. She suddenly froze in place as she heard the first round fired off from the terrorist's weapon at her soldier. She screamed again at the top of her lungs at her man.

"Walkerrrrr! Noooooo! Not you too god dammit! I'm not going to fucking lose you this time! That's not going to happen on this fucking day, mister." Sergeant Ramirez wailed as she turned to look at her soldier, fearing she was going to see him shot to death right before her eyes.

The way the terrorist was taking his time while firing at the soldier, proved he was enjoying killing her lover the way he was doing it. Instead of firing his weapon on automatic to kill him fast. He was delighting in pulling the trigger one round at a time in a controlled and slow manner, but as fast as he could pull the trigger on the weapon on her soldier.

The Lieutenant did the only thing he could think of doing, he covered his head with both arms, when he heard the first round fired at him. He was shocked, there was no pain in his body and at first he thought he was instantly killed by the round, and he was beyond feeling any pain. When the second then third round was fired at him and he was still feeling no pain. He thought the terrorist was a bad shot, and missed him with the rounds he was firing at him. When the fourth and fifth round was fired and there was still no pain to his body, he dared to think Sergeant Ramirez fired and got the terrorist before he was able to kill him.

The Lieutenant drew his eyes out from under his arms in time to see the large Russian come crashing down to his knees. Alexander's weapon falling from his hands as he fell forward, landing hard on his knees. A trace of blood came from the side of his mouth and his eyes glazed over with the look of death as it wrapped its icy fingers around him, as they gradually closed on the terrorist. Blood was streaming from the corner of his mouth as he exhaled, and then his body fell from his knees to flat on the floor. His body hit the ground with a sickening thud, and then rolled on his side and stopped moving. The ugly sound of the death rattle came from his air starved lungs, as they continued to struggle for oxygen and life. The stunned Lieutenant could swear he saw the dying man smile at him for a brief moment as his eyes closed their final time.

Sergeant Ramirez was on her feet and rushed out of the closet and stepped on Alexander's twitching body as she hurried to his side, while he was trying to get to his feet. She helped him the rest of the way up as Walker struggled, and stood on shaky legs as they and he leaned against the broken wall. Both he and Ramirez tried to figure out how the terrorist was just killed.

"Are you alright? Oh dear God in Heaven, please tell me you're okay Robert. God help me I thought that sonofabitch was going to kill you. Are you sure you're okay?" she nearly shouted as she quickly examined his body from head to toe for wounds. Just the injured leg was visible to her inspection of his rock hard and still trembling body. She could not take her hands off his body, she did not know it, but her mind was forcing her hands to stay on his body, so they could be certain he was alive and breathing.

"Yeah yeah, I'm fucking fine. It was a good thing you were able to get the fucking drop and did the mutherfucker in before he did me in, Raz. You saved my life. Thanks baby." The Lieutenant said through quivering lips as he continued to struggle to get control of himself. His body shook violently from the overwhelming fear of almost being killed by the dead man lying on the floor in the middle of the hallway almost blocking it on them his frame was so large.

"Christ Almighty Raz, I can't believe this mutherfucker was able to get up on me without my seeing his stinking ass coming at me, and doing the pecker in before he came so close to getting my fucking ass for crap sake. Thanks again for getting him for me baby. He had me dead to fucking rights, and there wasn't a god damn thing I could've done about it."

"I didn't do him, my weapon jammed up on me and I couldn't do anything with the damn thing. I thought you got the jump on the bastard before he did you, Bobby. If you didn't kill him, and I didn't do him, who the hell did him?" Sergeant Ramirez moaned as she continued to touch his rock hard body all over. The second she said that, their eyes went towards the Vice President's suite. The Lieutenant breathed in a deep sigh of relief when he noticed the Vice President's bodyguard standing half in the hallway and half in the apartment with the Glock pistol still locked in her shaking hands, and the weapon still being held in the firing position.

Ramirez broke away from her soldier and she rushed down the hall to Cathy, locking her up in a breath robbing hug and almost knocking the both of them to the floor she cried at her. "You saved his life, I love you. Oh God, I'm so glad you backed us up like you did. I'll never forget you for this. I love that man so much, and I don't think I could've went on without him in my life." She kissed Cathy on her tear stained cheek as she continued to hug her body to hers.

Cathy dropped the pistol in the hall and allowed her body to sag in Ramirez's strong arms. She stopped Cathy from falling when she noticed she was going down, by catching her in her arms.

While Cathy hid inside the apartment, she was in position to notice Alexander rush past the doors, and she knew the terrorist she saw when the invaders attacked their apartment, was trying to get behind Walker and Ramirez to kill them. She did not engage him, because he showed no interest in entering the apartment. Her first duty was to protect the Vice President's life at the cost of all else. To engage the terrorist might have very well placed Ms. Hirshfield in danger. She had no intention of drawing attention to herself, or to the Vice President.

When the terrorist past the door and disappeared down the hallway, she realized if the terrorist killed the two soldiers, he would then turn his attention on them and try to take Ms. Hirshfield hostage again. She understood she had to do something to stop him, so she did the only thing she was trained to do. She cautiously came out from behind the overturned table, and then she hurried to the main doors of the apartment. With a quick glance back to where the Vice President was in the bathroom and seeing no sign of her. She used the door and wall to protect her body, as she leaned out in the hallway with just the upper part of her body. Then she carefully aimed her weapon at the back of the large terrorist who just darted past the destroyed doors.

She leaned in the hall with half her body and aimed at the Russian's back, and held her breath as she prepared to fire. She rushed herself, because she saw the terrorist had the soldier in his sights, and he was ready to slaughter the young soldier in cold blood. She also heard

Ramirez screaming his name out from someplace, but she could not see her and this added to her haste.

This was the first time in her life she had to actually think about killing a human being, but she did not waste time struggling with her consciousness. She recognized the terrorist as the one she hated the most. She knew this one was called Twenty Seven and Alexander, and he was the most dangerous one who attacked the Tower, and she had to kill this man before he killed the soldiers.

She pulled the trigger, her first and hardest time. She watched the back of the terrorists as she fired at his back and noticed his body jump slightly from the bullet ripping into his back. But the man did not fall. So she continued to fire at his body until he began to tumble forwards, and Sergeant Ramirez came flying out from the darkness of the closet. The reason she stopped firing at his body, was for fear of hitting the Sergeant who unexpectedly ran right in her line of fire. Or she would have emptied the entire clip in her weapon in the Russian's back before he died. She hated the man that much for Agent Edward Sweeney and the other agent's death.

Lieutenant Walker continued to lean against the wall until he was able to get his legs under him again then he walked towards the two hugging and crying women. He got alongside Cathy, and then he held out his fist to her and waited.

She did not know the reason for this action, but when Sergeant Ramirez reached out and banged his fist with hers. She knew what he wanted from her, and she reached out a trembling hand and pounded his fist with hers. Then she smiled at him with tears in her eyes.

The Lieutenant smiled at the badly shaken female bodyguard as he offered her. "You did real good there trooper. You just saved my fucking ass back there, baby. Anytime you wanna leave this cushy fucking desk job you got here and tackle a real stinking job for a change, baby. You come look me up Boot, and I'll find a place for your little ass in my outfit, baby. We can always use another female with brass ovaries and a steady hand and guts in the outfit. You just proved yourself to me today, sister." Then he continued walking until he disappeared in the apartment.

"Is he always like this?" Cathy asked the Sergeant as she stared at his wide back.

"Whaddaya mean? Like what?" the Sergeant asked, confused by her last words.

"So damn hard nose and non caring. You think he would've taken a few seconds to get himself back together, Sergeant. If I was so close to dying, it'd take me at least a week before I could stand, let alone walk and talk again." She offered with a half smile to Ramirez.

"That's because he's all man, and he has just paid you one helluva huge compliment whether you know it or not, by offering to get you into his outfit, Cathy. You have to be one helluva person for him to offer that deal to you. But I'll tell you this much though. If Bobby didn't offer it to you, I surely would've for saving his life for me, Cathy. I would've died if that pig had killed my soldier. C'mon Cathy, we better get back to the Vice President and get her out of here, before any of the other terrorists come up to find out what all the shooting was about." Sergeant Ramirez said as she turned and then she headed for the apartment.

Lieutenant Walker rushed to the bathroom where he deposited the Vice President. Ms. Hirshfield still laid on her side in the tub, with both her hands covering her ears and sobbing softly. He looked at the badly shaken politician and then warned her. "C'mon Ma'am, we gotta get the hell outta this stinking piss hole in a fast hurry it up."

He took Ms. Hirshfield's hand and pulled Mary out of the bathtub. He then lead her out of the apartment towards the blocked open elevator shaft. Sergeant Ramirez and the bodyguard joined the two standing by the elevator shaft. Cathy was still slightly sobbing from the traumatic experience of killing a man for the first time in her life.

"Ma'am, we gotta use this fricking thing to get our asses up to the Thirty Forth Floor of this stinking dump where I have a number of uther people waiting to help us. It's gonna be an extremely dangerous climb for you. But we'll get you through this fucking shit easy enuf, Ma'am. I'll have Raz get on the fucking ladder first, and then I'll help you on it from here, Ma'am. Once you're on the ladder, I'll get Cathy out on the damn thing, and then I'll follow her up it, Ma'am. You're gonna hafta climb as fast as you possibly can, I don't wanna get caught in the shaft if any of the uther terrorists come up to the old room, Ma'am. The big guy's waiting to know we have you in custody, and then he wants us to get payback with these stinking slugs who took you hostage, Ma'am." The soldier warned the Vice President as he stared at her.

"The big guy?" Ms. Hirshfield asked, a little puzzled as she allowed herself to be led closer to the elevator shaft where Sergeant Ramirez had moved to the lead and she cleared up Lieutenant Walker's words for her. "He means the President, Ma'am. Are you afraid of heights, Ma'am?"

"No, not at all. I liked climbing when I was a child. I was always climbing the trees back at home, Sergeant Ramirez." Ms. Hirshfield replied as she smiled at the young female Sergeant.

"That's great Ma'am, just think of this as a tree then. I'll go first and I'll lean out and help pull you onto the ladder with me, Ma'am. Then I'll get above you and lead the way for you Ma'am. Walker will take care of Cathy and our rear, Ma'am."

Ms. Hirshfield nodded at the Sergeant who stepped out in the wall of darkness in the shaft, and then she called to the Vice President. "Ma'am, I'm on the ladder and ready for you to come out to me, Ma'am. Be very careful and I'll help you all the way Ma'am, all you have to do is look in the shaft to see where I am at, Ma'am. Then put your hand out and I'll take it and then pull you out onto the ladder Ma'am. I won't allow you to fall Ma'am."

The grime covered Lieutenant Walker took the Vice President's hand that made it much easier for her to lean out into the elevator shaft. Once Ms. Hirshfield was able to look into the shaft, she noticed Sergeant Ramirez smiling at her as she hung onto the metal ladder with one hand, and then she reached out to her with the other. There was plenty of light in this area from the open door to the floor. Ms. Hirshfield gave out with a deep sigh and then she reached out, allowing Sergeant Ramirez to instantly grab her hand and then she actually pull her out on the ladder.

Lieutenant Walker maintained a death like grip on Mary's arm, and he nearly supported her full weight on his one outstretched arm. The second Mary's foot touched the tip of the rung, she pulled herself the rest of the way onto the ladder mostly by herself.

Sergeant Ramirez quickly climbed above the Vice President, after she was certain Ms. Hirshfield was comfortable with her footing and hold on the ladder. Then she continued further up the ladder, followed slowly by the steady female Vice President.

The Lieutenant took hold of the ladder next, and when he was comfortable he leaned back towards the floor opening while reaching his hand out to the young woman on the floor. Cathy took hold of his hand, and he pulled her onto the ladder with mostly the power in his arm. He snapped at the upset looking woman. "You betta shake your stinking tail a little baby for me and head up the fucking ladder, and I'll take up the rear and make sure you're alright, baby."

The female bodyguard nodded at the military officer and then she started to climb up the ladder one hand over the other. Although she was not very afraid of heights, she did not like climbing the filthy and slippery metal ladder. Especially without being able to see where she was going. She climbed slowly, fighting slipping on the grease coating metal rungs.

Walker was getting pissed at her slow pace and he reached up with a paw and slammed it on her rearend, and then he gave her a good shove up. He did this because she was moving so slowly, he was getting very concerned the other terrorists might be coming on the floor behind them, and find them trapped in the elevator shaft. The push caused the female bodyguard to gripe angrily at him from above and she glared down at him as she stopped moving on the ladder.

"Hey you big stupid sod you. You better watch where the hell you're putting your god damn hands on me, buster. Before I rip the damn things out of their sockets, and beat you to death with the bloody ends, mister. I don't like this shit one fucking bit and pushing me like that is only going to cause me to slow down even more, buster." She snapped angrily at Lieutenant Walker, turning while trying to see his face in the pitch blackness of the elevator shaft.

"Hey bitch, if you don't get a fucking move on it baby. I'm gonna climb up behind you, and then I'm gonna stick my god damn dick right up your stinking ass fur you and see if that'll make you move any fucking faster than you're moving now, baby. You're moving like old people fuck for crap sake. We gotta get a stinking move on it double quick, or we're gonna end up as a pile of friggin shit in here, dammit. Move it will ya, baby!" He roared at her this time.

She knew the soldier was right, and she picked up her pace a little as she bitched at him again. "Okay, okay, just don't shove me like that again buster. I don't like that crap one bit Lieutenant Walker. I'm not very happy with doing this shit you know, mister."

MICHAEL AND LIZZIE

After Michael and Lizzie deposited the Russian's share of the diamonds in with theirs, they both left the diamond dealer's apartment with grins plastered on their faces and in great moods. Once they were satisfied they had everything of worth they wanted from in the suite. They rushed from the room towards the east side stairwell, and then they ran down the steps to the security complex stationed in the basement of the building.

The leader of the group planned to set a number of explosive charges in certain areas of the basement, where he knew the IRT subway tunnel ran close to the Trump Tower basement. He believed the police would be so involved with trying to attack them from the street or roof of the building, they would not think to check the basement area out like he did before his group attacked the structure. At least this thought was what he was banking on, as he continued charging down the countless steps heading for the basement of the building.

Michael was further banking on the police not being aware of the nearness of the train tunnel to the basement of the Trump Tower. He had Suarez carry enough explosives with him to blow a hole through the concrete wall, opening it up to the subway where he and the others planned to make their escape from the compromised building. The leader of the group planned to take his few people, leaving the Russian who he had no idea was just killed by the Vice President's bodyguard, and the rest of his group behind to fight off the police and FBI Agents when they made their move against the building. Once they blew an opening they were going to walk through the tunnel, and come up in

New York far away from the Trump International Hotel and Tower, and all the mayhem they created, so as not to draw any undue attention to themselves.

They both ran down the stairs leading to the basement. Completely out of breath, Michael took the corner and nearly stumbled over his own feet when he saw Suarez and Purvis standing inside the security center waiting for them. They both looked like they were in an arcade game room, with all the reflections from the number of screens, filled the center with an eerie glow.

Lizzie lagged a little behind him, this was because she was much smaller in stature than he was, and she had less lung capacity. This allowed him to pull away from her on their trek to the basement. This was not the only reason she was lagging a bit behind him. She did not like the way things were shaping up on their plans, and taken time to formulate her own plan on how she was going to escape the trap she felt was rapidly closing in on her. She believed if some of them separated, there might stand a much better chance some of them would get out of the building.

Suarez came out of the plywood security building the moment he noticed Michael come around the corner from the staircase, and he called out to him. "Hey, what the hell's going on up there for Christ sake? I keep hearing automatic weapons fire going off. Then I see your people running all over the place, and they seem like they're attacking shadows, Michael. Are we breaking down? Are things going sour on us? Have the police breached the building Mike?"

"Don't be so damn stupid Suarez, everything's going according to plan. The Russian is off playing his little war games in the building, and I don't care where he is now. We have all the diamonds with us, and the only ones I care about getting out of this place in one piece, are with me right now and ready to go. The only thing that happened I didn't count on is, someone from inside the building is running around playing hot shot soldier against us. Evidently, someone involved with the Armed Forces was visiting the damn Trump Tower, and he somehow armed himself and is screwing with us. As bad as that might sound, it's working out better in our favor.

"With these guys causing some problems with attacking Alexander's people. The crazy ass Russian was left with no other choice but to give up his share of the diamonds, and then he went off to defeat these other assholes. I thank God for the Russian's belief of constantly being better than everyone else. It's clouding his mind, and he's out there trying to prove his stupid ideals to the world. This screwed up belief of superiority was the controlling factor that made the dumb ass rush off and give up his share of the loot to us. He's so damn predictable all the damn time. Do you have the explosives ready?" he snapped at Suarez, just as Lizzie turned the corner.

"Sure do Michael, they're stored in the security center with Purvis, who's still monitoring the security monitors, so we know mostly of what's going on inside the building, Mike? I was picking up some of the fighting going on, and that's how we knew of all the gunfire going off in the building. I was getting really worried about it. I guess the Russian is out of it then?"

"Yes he's out of it, and Purvis is wasting his time with still watching those damn things. Whatever's happening upstairs no longer concerns any of us, it's over and the only thing we have to concern ourselves with now, is getting the hell out of here in one piece. We have to blast an escape hole into the train tunnel then we'll be home free and clear. Call Purvis out of there and have him take the explosives with him." The leader ordered as he turned to Lizzie who was acting exhausted and sitting down on a curb, trying to catch her breath.

"Are you alright? You look like you're going to pass out on me Lizzie."

"Yes, I'm okay I guess Michael. But I'm not going with you through the basement escape route though. I have other plans in mind that just might work out a little better to enable me to get out of the building in one piece, Michael. I hope you don't mind if I pull out on you and make my own way out of here." Lizzie said between her huge gasps for air.

"What the hell are you talking about Lizzie? You've been hanging around that crazy ass Russian bastard too much. He's beginning to rub off on you a little. Enough of this crap, you're coming with us and that's all there is to it, Lizzie. What the hell are you going to do here alone?"

"Michael, I've been doing a lot of thinking lately, and I feel I stand a much better chance of escaping the building using my plan, rather than yours. I'm not trying to stop you and the others from going your own way out of here. I feel my plan is a good one though Michael, and it'll work out very well for me, and I might as well take advantage of it. Besides Michael, if we split up here, maybe some of us will get out of this place in one piece."

"Are you going to give up your share of the diamonds to me if you're going to go off on your own, Lizzie?" he smirked at her as he stared at Lizzie, waiting for her response.

"No way in hell will I give up my share of the diamonds to you, Michael. Why the hell would I do that, I'm not that stupid you know. I'll carry my share of the loot with me as we had originally planned and agreed to, Michael. Please don't worry about it will you, you know damn well you can trust me with your life no matter what. I'll meet you where we had agreed after this thing is over, and then we can make an even split of the diamonds between the remaining survivors, Michael." Lizzie offered as she tried to smile, but she was too out of breath to carry it off.

He stared at Lizzie for a long moment and then he snapped at her in an angry tone of voice. "Okay Liz, if you feel this strong about your plan to escape this place, and you feel this is a good idea for you to take. Then I'm not going to stand in your way, I have more than enough diamonds with me to make us extremely wealthy for the rest of our lives. We'll make it out of here okay so don't worry about us any. So if you think you can make it out of here successfully using your plan then good luck with you. We'll meet in three week's time at the second place we discussed, without any of Alexander's people showing up I might add. I don't feel like bumping into him or any of his god damn crazy ass soldiers if they're lucky enough to get out of here alive.

"Okay Lizzie, from here on in you're on your own, good luck to ya. Remember, I'll see you in three week's time, and you better be there." He kissed her on the side of her cheek, and then patted her rearend lightly as Purvis joined them carrying the explosives in his arms.

Purvis looked at Lizzie still sitting down on the curb desperately gasping for air, and he was concerned about her and he asked Michael.

"What the hell gives with her my friend? She looks like she's just about out of it on us, Mike. Are we going to leave the dumb bitch behind not that I wouldn't mind leaving her behind, Michael? But I really don't want to leave anyone behind to possibly identify us to the police if they're caught once we're out of here."

"Don't worry about her Purvis. She can take good care of herself alright. She's going to stay behind and escape the building in a way she has in mind. She'll get out of here okay because she's that good, so let's get going so we can get out of here before the police break into the building against us. I can't help but feel that the damn cops are quickly closing in on us from all side." The rest of the terrorists fell in behind him as they all except for Lizzie, headed one level below where they were standing in the basement area of the building.

Lizzie remained sitting on the curb for several moments longer, watching as the three men quickly disappeared into the darkness of the basement as they headed for the floor below where she was seated. Once the group was out of sight, she instantly jumped to her feet and went into action. Along with the diamonds hidden in her backpack, was a high fashion dress neatly folded. She looped the body fitting backpack off her back, and then she quickly emptying the contents out on the floor in a clean area. Once she had everything out of the backpack, she stripped.

Naked, she took the diamonds and carefully poured them into a thin leather money belt she brought with her. When she had all that would fit in the belt, she then looped it around her waist. Then she neatly flattened it out with her hands until it blended in perfectly with her waist to where it was nearly invisible on her exquisite body.

Then she struggled into the free flowing pale blue dress that could easily double as a gown on her body. She used the reflection of herself in the glass of the Security Command Center as a mirror, to help her dress properly to make it look as if she was one of the visitors to the Tower, and she was somehow caught up in all the mayhem that took place inside the building. She had a slight bit of trouble getting into the tight fitting dress, mainly because her body was covered with sweat, and it was stopping the fine silk fabric from sliding easily over her beautiful body.

She quickly neatened the dress out on her body by using her hands to get many of the folds out of the fine fabric. When she was satisfied, she looked as good as she was going to look under the circumstances. She then opened the pocketbook and poured the rest of the diamonds loosely in it. She then snapped her pocketbook shut after burying the diamonds under all the other items she had inside the pocketbook, and then she cautiously walked towards the lobby of the building a few floors above where she felt the police would soon surely arrive inside the damaged building.

All the while Lizzie cautiously moved up the steps towards the lobby area of the Trump Tower, she continued to keep smoothing out her hair and dress with her dirty hands. Reminding herself to move like one of the scared and stunned guests from the building as she carefully climbed the stairs. As she walked up the countless steps, her body movements took the rest of the folds out of her dress, until it looked almost perfect on her body.

She even remembered to place a stunned look on her face and held it, and then she acted like she was scared to death while waiting for someone to tell her where to go. When she finally reached the lobby area of the building, she waited inside the stairwell actually hiding behind the heavy fire door to the main lobby area of the structure. She was sure the police were about to come charging into the building at any moment now. She planned to walk right out among them and allow the police to direct her where to go from the building, while acting confused over what was happening around her. Once she was outside the building, she would then use all the confusion and quickly disappear like a bad memory from the area.

Chapter Twenty Eight

SUBWAY TUNNEL TEN, THE IRT,
TWENTY FEET BELOW GROUND

The New York City police were made aware of the tamper sensors poured into the walls of the Trump Tower when it was under recent modernization. The police understood if they severed any of the sensor wires, they would immediately set off a number of alarms inside the Security Command Center stationed in the basement of the building. The officers were sent to where the train tunnel wall was actually part of the Trump Tower foundation. There the officers set up a number of explosive charges against the wall, when it was announced they would storm the building the moment they knew the Vice President of the United States was rescued by a number of people who were working inside the building to free her from the terrorists. The police gathered in the same exact place where Michael and his two friends intended to place their own explosive charges on the other side of the wall.

Twenty police officers dressed in heavy body armor and black hoods, stood in the cramped, almost smothering tight area of the train tunnel, waiting for the signal to blow the hole through the wall. So they could attack the terrorists inside the Trump Tower from the basement area of the building. The air inside the tunnel was sour and stale at best, filled with a cloud of dust, and many other foul odors assaulting the officer's noses. The officers were coughing and farting, not making the conditions of the dim tunnel any better to breath in. They took the odors, bad air and cramped space in stride as long as they were part of the retaliation attack being mounted against the terrorists. The officer's had one thought in mind to get even with the ones who killed so many of their fellow police officers in the grenade and rocket attack against them.

INSIDE THE TRUMP INTERNATIONAL
TOWER AND HOTEL

The leader of the group of terrorists along with the last two members of his original group who he wanted to save, rushed down the remaining stairs leading to the second basement level bordering the train tunnel they needed to get to inside the structure. It took the group five minutes to get down there. Suarez was armed with the blueprints of the Trump Tower basement, he removed from the Security Command Center. After his inside man the turn coat security guard informed him where they were stored in the room that housed the security guards who conducted the security work for the Trump Tower.

Suarez used the blueprints to help guide them towards the wall until they found the exact location he was searching for. When the group finally reached the area they wanted, Suarez placed his ear up against the concrete wall, and then he listened until he heard the first train speed by their position. Then he announced to the others with him in an excited voice. "This is the spot we're searching for, Michael. I just heard a train going by on the other side of the wall. Dammit, we're going to pull this thing off like we planned." Suarez remarked with a grin on his face.

The concrete was marked as eighteen inches thick at this section of the wall, and the blueprints stated there were two layers of reinforcing bars weaved in the cement to help support the tremendous weight load of the Trump Tower. Michael knew the amount of explosive charges they would need to blow a good size hole in the wall, but was not going to be powerful enough to harm the integrity of the structure. They did not need the entire building come crumbling down on their heads before they could escape the structure. He planned to only pop a hole just wide enough for them to squeeze through then escape through the train tunnel system of the Big City.

Michael believed it would take the police more than six hours before they discovered the hole and realize a number of the attackers had successfully escaped the Trump Tower. The spot where they were going to blast through the wall, was resting right in the center between two massive supporting columns that would remain unaffected by the number of small explosive charges they were planting against the wall of the foundation of the building.

The leader of the group watched attentively as Suarez carefully planted the number of explosive charges against the wall of the Tower. He lightly tapped his toe on the floor while watching the other terrorists worked their magic with the set of explosive charges. When he was pleased with the placement of the explosive charges against the wall, and they were wired in the correct sequence to get the best possible effect from the small explosions. He turned to Michael and then he gave him a slight nod.

"Are the charges ready to go Suarez?" he asked with worry in his voice.

Suarez grinned back at him as he shook his head in the positive.

"Don't we have to get far away from the charges than where we're standing so near them, Suarez? I never been this close to an explosive charge in my entire life. This is a first time so I don't know how far away from the damn charges we have to be, to remain safe when they go off for us." Michael asked, concerned they were standing much too near the charges, and they might get hit by some of the displaced concrete, and metal support bars.

"Yes, we have to move a little further away from the charges if you don't want to get hurt by the fragments the explosion will displace, Michael. Unless you relish the thought of maybe picking some concrete chunks out from your teeth with a nail." Suarez smirked as he gave him a look that informed him he was stupid, if he wanted to stand this close to the charges.

"Where the hell's a safe spot for us to stand then when you set off the charges, Suarez?" he snapped as he glared at Suarez.

Suarez looked around the dimly lit parking area, until he spotted another heavy support column some twenty yards away from their charges. He pointed at the column, and then he made a mad dashed towards it for the protection the thick column of concrete would offer them from the explosion. Suarez carefully rolled out the rest of the wire leads to the charges behind him, as he ran along with the rest of the exhausted terrorists. Purvis ran over to a parked car in the lower section of the garage, and he instantly shattered the driver's window with his elbow, and then he reached in and popped the hood to the motor area of the car.

Purvis then twisted and pulled on the wires to the battery, snapping one cable in the process. Then he went to work on the second wire still attached to the battery, he twisted it up so bad that the pressure actually broke the terminal and edge on the battery off. Once the battery was free of the car, he lugged it over to where the other two terrorists were waiting for him. When Suarez saw the condition of the battery he glared angrily at Purvis as he growled at him at the same time. "Dammit, I hope I can still get the damn spark I need from the damn thing, you animal you. Couldn't you have been a little more careful with getting the battery out of the car for me? This thing is the only way I have to get the spark I need to set off the damn charges, stupid."

"Hey man, keep talking at me like that and see where it gets you, buddy. I didn't have any god damn tools to work with, and I had to manhandle the damn thing out of the car with my bare hands. I'd like to see what the battery would look like if you went after the damn thing, using nothing but just your damn hands as tools. If this battery doesn't work, I can easily go to another car and get you that battery for you." Purvis complained at the upset Suarez.

Suarez just shook his head at the other man slowly.

"Stop your damn griping all the time and get back there with Michael behind the support column and keep your damn head low, before it gets knocked off that stump during the explosion." Suarez barked at Purvis, refusing to get locked in a battle of wits with the always complaining man. He hooked the wires from the plunger used to set off the explosives to the mangled terminals of the nearly destroyed car battery. The one with the car wire still attached to the terminal was easy to hook up his wire to. The broken terminal posed a bit of a problem to him. Every time he tried to thread the thin stripped end of the wire into the gaping hole in the battery, the wire would not stay put. He quickly realized he was going to be forced to actually hold the wire set in place in the battery with his hands, while Michael turned the plunger to set off the explosive charges for him.

He offered they should get another battery to use.

Suarez thought about sending Purvis out to locate a second battery for him. He glanced at his watch and felt they were fast running out of time, and he decided to try and get the spark from the destroyed battery. Still having a problem with holding the wire secured to the broken end of the terminal, he waved Michael over to his side. He quickly showed him what he wanted with the plunger of the charger while he tried to hold the wire set in place in the battery.

Michael nodded after understanding what Suarez wanted him to do with the plunger, when he was positive what he was supposed to do with the box with an arm attached to it. The leader of the group waited for Suarez to give him the okay to turn the arm to set off the explosive charges. He continued to try and hook up the end of the wire to something inside the broken end of the battery where he could steal an electrical charge from. But nothing he could do with the battery would work out, so he resided himself to actually holding the wire in place with his fingers. He found the right place to hold the wire against to get the spark from it. When he got the wire set in place, he nodded to Michael and he instantly turned the key to the plunger.

INSIDE THE ELEVATOR SHAFT OF THE TRUMP INTERNATIONAL TOWER

Lieutenant Robert Walker kept a close eye on the thoroughly exhausted and slow moving female bodyguard, as she so slowly climbed the grease covered ladder, while Sergeant Dorothy Ramirez went as fast as she could, while watching Vice President Mary Hirshfield's surprisingly fast progress on the ladder below her. When the Sergeant finally reached floor thirty four, she went groping with her foot for the floor landing. A rush of hands suddenly grabbed her leg, and they helped her out of the dark elevator shaft onto the concrete ledge. The still concerned and scared residents of the Tower trapped on this floor were still milling around in the hall, waiting for the two young soldiers to return with the Vice President of the United States in their charge.

Sergeant Ramirez was literally dragged from the ladder by the horde of civilians still milling about in the hallway of their floor. She actually had to pull herself free of their grasp, to assist the Vice President out of the elevator shaft onto the floor. Lieutenant Walker saw the Sergeant shove off the ladder, and he quickly moved up, climbing past Cathy by hanging off the side of the ladder to get around her. As he past her he told her he was going to move up to help Ms. Hirshfield get off the ladder safely. He climbed up until he was hanging right by the Vice President's side, as she waited hanging on the rung for the Sergeant's help from the landing.

Sergeant Ramirez reached out the same time as Ms. Hirshfield did. Lieutenant Walker was by her side and he wrapped around the rungs with his legs again, and then he use his hands to help the Vice President off the ladder, putting painful stress on his wounded leg at the same time.

When Ms. Hirshfield was safely on the landing, he told Cathy to move up to him. He was concerned about the strength left in the smallish woman's arms and legs. He did not know how strong she was, or what was left of her strength. On the floor above them, the civilians gathered so tightly around the hand shaking and smiling but filthy Vice President. Sergeant Ramirez was beginning to feel slightly threatened by the group of overzealous civilians gathering around the exhausted Vice President and herself. She called out Mary's name as she pushed through the crowd of civilians. She then grabbed hold of Ms. Hirshfield's arm, and roughly shoved her way through the gathered people, leading the Vice President to Duane's apartment. Once inside the room, she barked at Duane to shove the other people out of his apartment.

Duane nodded and grinned at Sergeant Ramirez, as he went in the hall and bellowed at his neighbors to go back to their rooms. His words fell on deaf ears as they all wanted to catch a glimpse of the Vice President. The Sergeant made certain Hirshfield was comfortable then she rushed outside to help Walker and Cathy get onto the landing. She closed the door to Duane's apartment behind her, securing Ms. Hirshfield in the room. She smiled as she saw the old man struggling to move his neighbors in the hall. Again, she had to shove her way through the milling people to get back to the elevator. When she did, she saw Walker helping Cathy by him.

"Is she ready to come across yet?" Ramirez asked her soldier.

"Yeah, but she's fucking beat out real bad on me Raz. You betta be real fucking careful with her coming to you. I think she's probably so damn tired she's about to give it up. I don't think she has anymore gut left in her stinking pussy ass body. I'll pass her over to you, but I'll lean way out with her like I did with the Veep. Make damn sure she don't pull me the fuck offa the god damn ladder, or you into the stinking elevator shaft if she loses her grip on you."

"You got it Bobby. I'm ready to receive her." Ramirez replied to his words.

Lieutenant Walker looked at the terrified looking Cathy, and snapped at her. "Well baby, it's all up to your stinking ass now. If you're tired of fucking living, just let go of the damn ladder and it'll be over for you in a second, and you'll end up just another stinking chalk mark on the floor of this fucking shaft, baby. If you wanna continue to live, you betta find some fucking strength left in that pussy ass sissy body of yours baby, and make it to that landing, Baby!"

Lieutenant Walker knew very well what he was doing and unless he missed his guess, this strong minded woman was every bit as strong willed as Sergeant Ramirez was, and she was not going to allow him to get away with calling her a pussy ass, or doubting the strength she possessed by her body much longer, and get away with the baby remark to her again either.

The bodyguard's face turned red as a beet and she snarled in his face a few inches away from hers. "Now you look here stupid. I told you before not to call me 'baby', and I won't repeat myself again to you mister. If you do it again, it'll cost you big time buster. When this crap is over, it's you and me, one on one and we'll see how good you think you really are, mister."

"On the fucking mats baby? You got it baby." He asked and offered, confused and amused at the same time by her threat just aimed at him.

"No stupid, you and me between the damn sheets. If you're man enough to try and take me up on the challenge, soldier boy." She retorted angrily at the grinning soldier whose grime covered face was mere inches away from hers.

"I'm man enuf to do you real good and proper. You got yourself a stinking deal there, baby."

"Didn't I just tell you not to call me baby, arrr... fuck you stupid! You'll never learn will you, thickhead?" she hissed as she reached out with surprising strength, and she locked hold of Sergeant Ramirez's arm and allowed the strong female soldier to pull her free of the ladder and onto the landing. Again, the two women hugged once Cathy was safely on the landing and then Sergeant Ramirez said with a smile to him.

"You know something Cathy, if you try and take the big lug on one on one between the sheets. You're going to lose real bad to him little sister, hmmm... unless you..." She offered as she thought for a moment.

"Unless what Sergeant Ramirez? It looks like I could use all the help I can get with him I'm afraid." The bodyguard asked the grinning female Sergeant.

"Unless you get him all amped up using your mouth, so he can't control himself before letting him between your legs. If he dives right in there he's going to rag your ass raw until you can't stand up any longer, little sister. He has some stamina for a man when he wants to take his time with the lady he's with. He makes sure she came all she wanted before he finally pops off." Sergeant Ramirez said with a sarcastic grin then she gave Cathy a quick wink of her eye.

"You don't mind my being with your man in a bed, Sergeant? It's the only way I could possibly think of thanking him for saving the Vice President's life. I love him for that Sergeant Ramirez." She replied while looking Sergeant Ramirez in her eyes.

"Hey, I love him always Cathy, and in case you don't realize it, he saved your life also, sister. But if you remember right, you also saved his life and I'll love you always for that, Cathy. And hell no little sister, I don't mind you being with him in bed. Hell girl, it'll give me a break, and it'll give him a chance to thank you privately for saving his life. Now sister, I think we better move away from the doorway, and give Bobby room to get over here himself." They both moved a little further away from the opening to the elevator shaft, just as the young soldier jumped from the ladder and landed lightly on the floor nearly right in front of them.

"Where the hell's the damn Veep at, Raz?" Walker growled angrily over not seeing the Vice President in the hallway as he was instantly swamped by the excited horde of civilians still hanging around in the hallway. Some of the civilians patted him on the back, while others tried to shake his hand or just touch the two young soldiers who saved the Vice President's life. He looked at Sergeant Ramirez and then snarled at her. "What in the name of unholy hell are all these flaming assholes still doing hanging around out here, dammit? Don't any of these fucking twits know it's fucking dangerous to be out here like this for crap sake?"

"I tried to get them to disperse Bobby, but they won't listen to me at all I'm afraid. I can't get them to go back to their damn apartments." She snapped at her soldier as she moved close to him, and then wiggled herself under his arm. He hugged her briefly as he hissed.

"Oh... they won't fucking listen to you will they, well we'll hafta see about that sack of bullshit." The Lieutenant then raised his hands and screamed out at the mess of civilians looking at him. "People, people, people, listen up people. You guys hafta get the fuck outta this stinking hallway right this god damn moment. I know some of the fricking tent pegs that attacked this damn building, are following us up here and there's gonna be one helluva a mini fucking war played out right in the god damn middle of this stinking hallway in a few moments. You people hafta get the hell out of the fuc..."

It was like someone just threatened the civilians with a gun, many of them screamed as they turned and made a mad dash for the protection of their rooms. The sound of doors slamming shut, and furniture being dragged against doors filled the vacated hallway. Sergeant Ramirez looked at lieutenant Walker and she mumbled at him while displaying an exhausted smile. "Whew, you sure do know how to kill a good party, Bobby. Must be your body odor mister."

"Fucking A right I do, dammit. Where the hell's the damn Veep at Raz? I wanna make certain she's secured and well looked afta." He asked Sergeant Ramirez for a second time.

"She's safe and sound in Duane's room. He's protecting her. Err... I think it might be a good idea if you stop calling her Veep though. She's going to hear you one of these times, and she's liable to slam her big toe up your ass for it, Bobby."

"Aw... C'mon Raz, you think she's that fucking sensitive?" he asked as he followed her, Cathy and Duane back to his apartment. Inside, Ms. Hirshfield sat comfortably on a couch, and Duane's wife was serving her a cup of tea, after Mary washed up and rested a little. When Ms. Hirshfield saw both Walker and Ramirez enter the apartment, she stood and offered him her hand.

The grime covered Lieutenant put out his hand, but instead Ms. Hirshfield cupped his head in her hands, and she kissed him on his grime covered cheek as she asked him. "You don't mind if I kiss you, do you soldier? You saved my life and I thank you so much for that, soldier. I only wish you came to us a lot sooner, maybe more of my entourage could have survived, Lieutenant."

"Naw, knock your socks off and help yourself, Ma'am. I like it when chicks kiss me Ma'am." He replied feeling slightly uncomfortable though.

Ms. Hirshfield kissed him a second time and then added. "Thank you so much for saving my life, soldier. You're a fearless and very proud soldier, Lieutenant Robert Walker." The Vice President was a sight to behold herself, her dress torn and tattered and covered with grease and dirt from the ladder. Her body was covered with a number of minor nicks and cuts, some of them were still bleeding. Her hair a mess, filthy and matted down to her head. She stood with one shoe on, one foot bare. She lost her other shoe while climbing up the ladder. Her hands were filthy, even though she tried to clean them, and her fingernails were chipped and cracked.

The exhausted Lieutenant smiled as he looked at the Vice President's face, she had a thick grease smudge on her right cheek, as he mumbled in a calm and pleasing tone at her. "Arrrr... you disappointed me a little Ma'am. I thought you were kissing me because you found me irresistible." He smiled again over his wise remark aimed at the powerful female Vice President of the United States, feeling a helluva lot better now he freed her successfully from the terrorists.

"Jesus Walker, you don't know when to quite!" Ramirez snapped at her soldier as she rushed to his side, stopping him from saying anything that might insult the overjoyed Vice President.

Ms. Hirshfield overlooked Lieutenant Walker's attempt at being funny as she added. "You saved my life, and for that I'm entirely in your debt, Lieutenant Walker. The people of the United States are in your debt." Mary let go of his head, and she then moved to Sergeant Ramirez's side and she did the same thing to her, kissing her on the side of the cheek and repeating the same words to her. Then she looked at the two soldiers, and announced. "When this is all over, I want you to come over to the White House. So the people, and President and I, can thank you properly for what you two have accomplished for me and their country. We have to thank you properly for the lives of the other hostages you saved as well, Lieutenant Walker, Sergeant Ramirez."

The Lieutenant did not inform Ms. Hirshfield that he and Sergeant Ramirez were operating under direct orders from the President of the United States to save her life only, and the President was not interested in any other hostages until the police took over what he was doing. At that point, he would have the luxury of thinking of the other civilians still trapped in the building. When Ms. Hirshfield finished her little speech, she turned to her bodyguard and she shook her hand, and then she returned the pistol to her, the lone survivor of her entire security people.

"Gees Vice President Hirshfield Ma'am, I can't believe you held on to my weapon all this time, Ma'am." The bodyguard replied as she took her weapon, and held on to it for no other reason than she did not have any place to put it.

"It's your weapon and I didn't want to be responsible for losing it on you, Cathy. I happen to know the amount of paperwork involved if you lose a weapon while on duty, young lady." Ms. Hirshfield replied as she suddenly smiled warmly at her bodyguard and secretary.

Duane heard someone scream over the phone and he picked up the receiver and placed it to his ear. He paid dearly for that mistake. General White was fuming as he listened to the commotion going on in the civilian's apartment. The General screamed in the receiver for someone to talk to him. Duane heard him shouting words he never heard before, as the military officer ran down his complete itinerary of swear words. The old man tried to get a word in edgewise, but the fuming General was popping off and not allowing him to interrupt his tirade.

The Lieutenant noticed the old man struggling with the phone held away from his ear and said. "Oh crap, I forgot all about the stinking General on the damn horn. If I know the General, he's probably trying to pull Duane's head through the god damn phone with his bare hands."

Cathy leaned over to Ms. Hirshfield and whispered to her. "I'm terribly sorry about Sweeney's death. I really liked that poor man, Mary."

Tears instantly built up in her eyes as she thought of the horrifying way Agent Sweeney was slaughtered right before her eyes. This was the first time she had a chance to even think about him and his terrible death, since he was slaughtered so savagely by the leader of the terrorists. Ms. Hirshfield knew she was going to cry for his death, but now was not the time for that soul saving indulgence. She would save it for her private time, and she nodded to her bodyguard while biting her lower lip to try and stop herself from crying.

Everyone laughed for the first time since the terrorists had entered the Trump Tower over the Lieutenant's gripe, as he took the phone from the old man. He slammed his hand down on Duane's back as he offered the old man. "Here you go man. Let me take it from here for you sir. You did damn good for a stinking Navy puke you know, sir. Glad to have you on board with me and Sergeant Ramirez sir. I really needed your stinking help on this one sir."

Duane gladly handed the receiver over to the young Lieutenant. He was overjoyed to be called a Navy puke by such a brave young modern day soldier as this warrior was.

The soldier tried to place the receiver next to his ear, but the General was still raging to beat the band. Only when he whistled loudly into the receiver, did the General finally calm down some and he grumbled. "Who the fuck's whistling in my god damn ear? I'll snap your fucking pencil neck for whistling in my damn ear like that. Who the hell are you and why the fuck..."

"Err, excuse me General White, Lieutenant Walker, sir." He mumbled in the phone.

"Walker!!! It's about fucking time you got back to me, you little fuck head you! You took your ever loving time getting back to me over this damn situation you were ordered to handle. Half a million screaming Chinese babies were born in the fucking time it took you two shitbirds to carry out one tit sucking milk run operation I sent your two asses out on. I trust you have the Vice President in your possession, and she's in A number one shape, and you have successfully completed the mission I sent you two on? You better not tell me otherwise if you know what's fucking good for you and your damn girlfriend, Lieutenant Walker."

"Yes Sir General White Sir! We have successfully completed our mission as ordered, and the Vice President's with me sir and she's in tip top shape, sir."

"Out fucking standing Walker, that's outstanding. You earned your keep for the fucking day, Lieutenant. Err... huh... here... no wait a sec will you please... hold on a second, for Christ sake, dammit. Walker, the President's having a fricking puppy, he wants to speak to his Vice President pronto. Before I let him have the damn horn, get outside with Ramirez and guard those fire doors, Lieutenant. Jam the doors closed and put something in the fold so they can't be pried open on you. Just in case any of these buggers try to get on your floor the same way you did.

"Then Lieutenant Walker, both you and Sergeant Ramirez are ordered to defend the damn doors which should be no problem for you two, son. If you have to, draft some of the... Huh... yeah, I know you want to speak to her, hold your damn water until I give orders to my soldiers, will ya please sir." General White snapped at the President, before he realized who he was speaking to. To his surprise, the President smiled and then he merely folded his arms across his chest and then waited for the General to finish with his troops.

"Jesus Christ sir, that wasn't the stinking Boss you just barked at like that, was it General?" he asked when he was sure the General was with him again on the phone.

"You bet your ass it was, sonny. No one fucks with me while I'm speaking to one my boys, not even the Big Cheese. As I said, you're ordered to defend the fire doors which gives you two points of responsibility. I don't care if you have to draft some of the damn puke civilians to get the job done, Lieutenant. Now you have the Vice President in your hands, you have to protect her life with everything at your disposal mister. Is this understood Lieutenant Walker Sir?"

"Yes sir, your orders are as clear as a fucking bell General White Sir." He offered calmly.

"Out fucking standing soldier, you did one helluva job and I'm damn proud of you and Sergeant Ramirez, Lieutenant Walker Sir. Now get this last part of your mission done and then you're home free and I'll buy the first rounds. I'm going to commit my people as of this moment Lieutenant. Keep your ass low and your eyes open. Good luck Lieutenant Walker."

"Yes sir, I'll do as ordered sir." The Lieutenant offered as he handed the phone to the Vice President, and called Sergeant Ramirez over to his side. He told her to follow his lead.

THE OVAL OFFICE, THE WHITE HOUSE, WASHINGTON DC

When the Chairman of the Joint Chiefs of Staff, General John White broke off the communications with Lieutenant Walker, and he gave the phone to the President, he jumped at the other phone and barked into it. "Commander, this is General White." He already forgot the Commander's first name, and he did not care to try and remember it.

"Go General White Sir. This is the Face Lift Commander, sir." The pilot replied to his Commanding Officer.

"Commander, go get them sonabitches for me mister. It's payback time for everyone involved in this god damn mess. I want you to sterilize that roof area and then get down to the Thirty Forth Floor, and run protection for my people stationed on that floor, sir."

"Roger that last General White Sir, payback's a coming knocking. We'll get them for you sir, hell's coming for supper! Beginning our attack as of this moment, General White Sir."

Both sleek fast attack Apache helicopters moved out as one, each attacking the roof of the Trump Tower from two opposite ends of the building. The two Apache airframes rose ominously in the darkness and smoke filled night air hanging heavily over Manhattan. All street and lights of the surrounding buildings in Manhattan were shot out or turned off by the General's order, and the black outline of the Apache night attack war machines were nearly impossible to detect, or hear coming as they were placed in the whisper mode. Until it was too late for any terrorists to defend themselves against the invading machines of war.

As the two helicopters reached attack altitude, along with the attack angle, they both opened fire on the building at the same time, beginning with the 30 mm rapid fire chain machine gun. Adding the destructive power from the Hydra missile pods, when they detected a possible radar signature or other possible threat aimed against them. With the heat of battle increasing, the pilots resorted more on the 2.75 inch rockets, until they were fired off from the helicopters. Machine gun fire from the helicopters wracked over every inch of the roof, ripping apart the massive air-conditioner units, the concrete structure once housing the service elevator, sending the cab tumbling down the fifty seven story shaft to the basement.

In less than a heartbeat, the entire rooftop area of the Trump International Hotel and Tower was ripped asunder by the heavy armor piercing rounds, and M255A1 Flechette warhead rocket power of the two Apache helicopters. The one thousand, one hundred and seventy nine grains of sharp, super hard, red hot Flechettes from the exploding Hydra rockets, ripped to shreds anything or one caught in the open on the roof of the Tower.

It took just that long for the group of terrorist stationed of the roof of the Trump Tower to be eliminated by the wall of death hurtled at them from the M-261 launchers on each of the war machines of death. Thirty eight rockets in all fired from the lead helicopter did more damage than estimated on the building. The other thirty eight rockets from the trailing helicopter, were overkill. Fires raged out of control in many areas on the roof of the Trump Tower from the exploding rockets and munitions the terrorists carried to the roof with them. The hotel equipment stored on the roof by maintenance crews, exploded in fireballs when it came under direct fire from the twin helicopters. Death and destruction were dealt out swiftly, the terrorists did not have a chance to grab any of their anti-aircraft weapons and fire them at the war machines.

The Trump Tower was not the only building in the surrounding area to suffer from the wrath of the two attack helicopters. A number of the surrounding buildings near the attack zone, were also damaged by rounds and rockets that overshot their intended target. The top floor of the building directly across from the Trump Tower to the north was set ablaze, destroyed by a series of detonations as air-conditioning units and electrical power exchanges caught fire and exploded on this building's roof. Nearly every window in the building was shattered down to the tenth floor. Other buildings in the area suffered shattered windows and burning debris striking the buildings from the exploding Trump Tower and rockets.

The Trump Tower's exclusive penthouse supporting the roof of the structure, was ripped apart with both eight million dollar apartments totally destroyed, as their supporting walls crumbled in on themselves from the heavy attack on the building. Destroyed also was the many pieces of fine antique furniture and paintings that once adorned the extravagant rooms. The occupants of these two apartments were still being held hostage inside the restaurant in the lobby area of the structure. The floors below the penthouse were also destroyed by the heavy weapon and rocket fire from the helicopters and the crumbling walls of the building. Roaring fires were raging and consuming everything on the upper three floors of the Trump Tower.

The streets below the Trump Tower were once again being showered by a rain of flaming chunks of blown apart, tar covered concrete and other burning materials, along with ricocheting rounds and exploding rockets heads from the twin gunships, along with body parts from the number of terrorists once stationed on the roof of the Trump Tower.

The surrounding buildings received more damage than the Tower, by the overshooting helicopter rounds and rockets and explosions taking place on the structure roof.

When the lead pilot realized there was no return fire coming from anyone who was once stationed on the roof of the Trump Tower, he ordered his Wingman to remain high and erase anyone on what was left of the roof, while he dropped down to the thirty forth floor to carry out his further orders from General White to protect the Vice President's life. He warned the other pilot anyone on the roof was to be classified as hostile, and taken out until their orders were changed. The standby pilot was to use controlled fire to minimize any further collateral damage to the surrounding buildings, and civilians, police, and firefighters operating on the streets below. The lead pilot would be the one who flew cover for whoever was attacking the terrorists from inside the Tower, and working under the General's orders.

Inside the Tower, the two exhausted and beat up soldier, Lieutenant Robert Walker and Sergeant Dorothy Ramirez ran out in the deserted hallway, and they jammed the three elevator doors closed, using pieces of furniture, wood, or whatever else they could get their hands on. Then the two Special Forces soldiers split up and ran for the two sets of heavy fire doors stationed at each end of the floor, where they plopped down in front of the metal coated doors, and then they both took up defensive positions before them and waited. Then the two exhausted soldiers began their long wait for anyone foolish enough to try and challenge them, or for the police to arrive and relieve them of their duties. The Lieutenant jammed a finely carved wood chair he found in the hall up against the fire door, stopping it from being forced open from the other side. He ordered Sergeant Ramirez to do the same thing with her door.

Lieutenant Walker then dumped the one extra clip he still had for the MP-5 machine gun on the floor at his feet. He then laid his pistol down on the floor right next to the extra clip, along with the one extra clip he had for the pistol as well. Then the two specialized soldiers settled down in front of the fire doors to wait for help from the outside world to arrive and relieve them of any further responsibility for the Vice President's life.

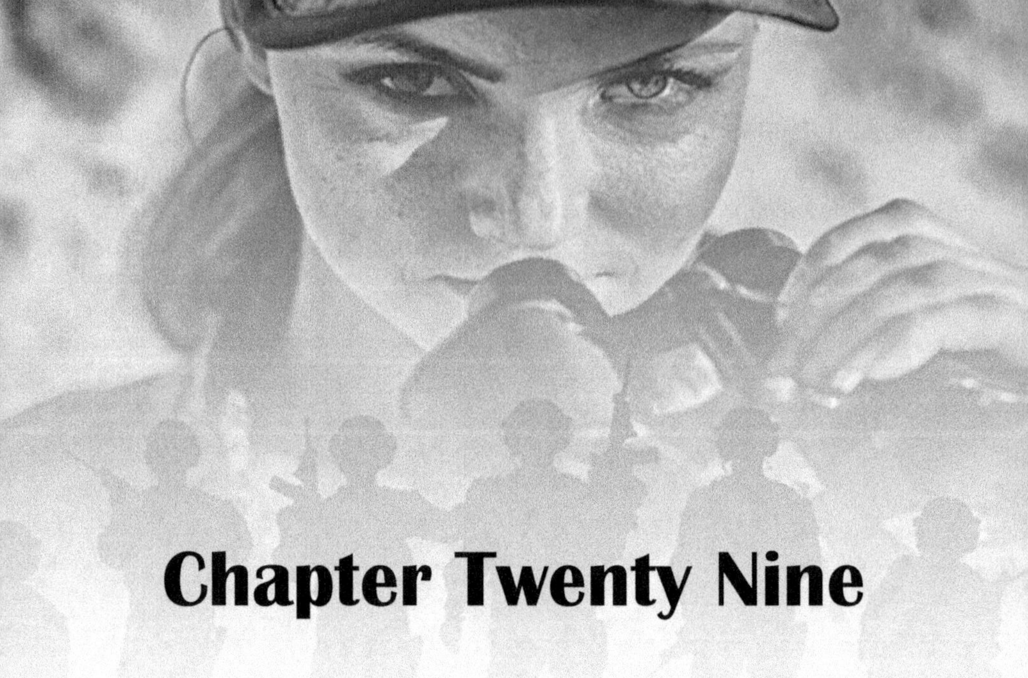

Chapter Twenty Nine

THE BASEMENT AREA OF THE TRUMP
INTERNATIONAL TOWER

Michael was having a serious problem with trying to turn the key for the plunger to set off the explosive charges set in the concrete wall. The arm of the detonator seemed to be stuck in one position, and it would not move no matter what he tried. Angry, he cursed Suarez and in return, Suarez cursed Purvis for making a mess of the car battery. The three terrorists had no idea a force of police officers were gathered on the other side of the concrete wall.

The excited officer who manned the radio for the specialized unit of police officers huddled up in the IRT Tunnel Ten, got the go ahead signal to blast his way into the Trump Tower basement, and he immediately offered to his Commanding Officer. "Commander, I just received the Green Chip order from Command, sir. Yes sir, that's a go, we have the green light to begin our attack on the Trump Tower and the god damn terrorists, sir."

The Green Chip signal had been chosen by the police to honor Donald Trump.

The Commander smiled as he nodded to his ordinance explosive team, and they immediately fired off their explosive charges.

When the larger than expected explosion occurred, both Michael and Suarez assumed it was their charges going off. But with a roar much larger than Suarez had expected, he was momentarily stunned by the sheer force of the powerful explosion. Chunks of concrete and rubble went flying with deadly force at where they were hiding. This was strange, because most of the charges he set should have been directed away, and not at them. He looked at the leader of the group with concern, and then he growled at the man.

"Dammit, you could have fucking warned me you were going to pop the damn thing off when you did, Suarez. I wasn't ready for the blast and I got hit with half of that crap from the damn explosion. Will you look at this mess. I don't understand, I thought you told me that the..."

His angry words were cut off when a wave of police officers suddenly rushed through the five by five foot hole slammed through the side of the concrete wall from the train tunnel side. Some of the officers stumbled over the rubble littering the floor, as they bent the metal rebar out of their way and then the officers rushed into the Trump Tower's basement from the tunnel side of the hole. The police did not know what might be waiting for them on the other side of the wall, so they entered the Trump Tower basement ready for bear. The second they saw the three men gathered behind the concrete column, the specialized group of police officers immediately opened fire on the three while waiting to ask questions later.

Michael, Suarez, and Purvis were instantly torn apart by the heavy automatic weapons fire aimed at them from the large group of police officers suddenly piling into the Trump Tower basement area, when they saw the three men hiding by the wide support column. The three terrorists were dead before they could even begin to react to the police suddenly surrounding them. Officers circled the three bodies lying on the floor, and they moved the weapons away from their bodies in case they were not dead. The Commander looked at the dead men and said to the other officer standing next to him. "Yep, it looks like we just got us some of the bastards who attacked this place, thank God for that much. The asses, okay people let's get up to the lobby area and see what the hell we find waiting for us up there."

Mixed in with the scattered cement chunks and other building rubble, were thousands of shiny small glass dots of glistening lights. When the police opened fire on the three terrorists, their bullets ripped into Michael's backpack, sending millions of dollars worth of diamonds flying in all directions, mixing in with the rubble covering on the floor. When one of the police officers happened to pick up one of the glass nuggets, he showed it to the Commander.

The Commander knew immediately what it was and he left some of the other officers behind to gather up as many of the gems as they could find all in the mess. The Commander then ordered the rest of his officers to follow him and he headed right for the stairway with the rest of the rushing police officers falling in line behind him.

THE MAIN DOORS TO THE TRUMP INTERNATIONAL TOWER AND HOTEL

Smoke hung heavy on Broadway, burning the eyes of the gathered rescue workers as police and FBI Agents prepared to breach the Trump Tower from the main doors of the structure. Firefighters risked taking their lives in their hands again by coming out of their cover, to start fighting the many fires raging in the streets of midtown Manhattan surrounding the Trump Tower. Some of the buildings were burning out of control and they had to be brought under control before they fully got out of hand on the horde of firefighters.

The ornamental brass main doors of the Trump Tower facing Columbus Circle, were the next area to be attacked by the horde of gathered police and special agents massed on the street before the Tower. Agents from the FBI ran this part of the operation, and when they received the go ahead from their Commanders to hit the building, they fired a low charge AT4CS BDM, a military Bunker Defeating Munitions weapon, that was a light weight fire once and throw away item commonly referred to by the soldiers as the Bunker Buster. The charge was lightened up to where the agents figured it would only blow apart the decorative brass and glass doors of the building, and not do much more damage than that to the lobby.

The instant the charge shattered the brass doors, both FBI and New York City police officers charged as one into the building. Three agents lead the way for the rest, and when they picked up Jurado and Jaureque hiding behind the massive lobby desk. The officers immediately took them for terrorists and the agents dropped to the floor and then opened fire on them.

The two terrorists were ready for the assault, and they returned fire on the attacking agents on the floor. More agents and police protected by body armor, piled into the lobby area, and they immediately added their fire power to the agents who first entered the building first. Their weapon fire was more than enough to turn the tide on the two terrorists.

The reservation's desk and part of the lobby and terrorists hiding behind the desk, were ripped apart. The agents and officers then quickly fanned out, and stopped when weapons fire came out of the restaurant to their right. No officers returned fire, they heard many screams from inside the restaurant, and they knew hostages were trapped in the eatery, along with the shooter or shooters. One agent tried to talk the terrorist inside the restaurant into giving up.

Some of the officers and agents stopped entering the building, and they took up defensive positions around the restaurant other doors from outside the lobby of the Tower. Other agents and officers continued to enter the building, and they fanned out in the lobby on the ground floor. They were looking for any other possible terrorists, hostages, or guests roaming around the area.

Still hiding inside the stairwell leading up to the lobby of the building from the basement levels. Lizzie found herself hiding behind the heavy fireproof door leading to the lobby. She was unarmed and looked every bit like a visitor to the Trump Tower, who was merely caught up in this nightmare, as it continued to play out before her eyes. She was scared to death, and this added to her appearance as she stared at the flood of police officers pouring into the lobby area of the Trump International Hotel and Tower from the outside.

Lizzie moved away from the heavy fire door when she thought an officer might have noticed her through the window as he rushed past it. She let out her breath in a rush as she rested against the cool wall, closing her eyes and putting her head back for an exhausted moment to gather her strength. She knew what she had to do, she forced herself to be strong, and walk out in all the mayhem still taking place in the lobby area of the building, as if a visitor to the Tower caught up in this mess. She quickly regained her strength and was just about to make her move. But something stopped her from going out to the lobby.

Her sharp mind placed her eye on what was bothering her. Her troubling thoughts warned her someone out there might recognize her as being one the terrorists who had attacked the building. Her strength argued with her mind, as it pointed out she was dressed in the fine dress, and no one was going to recognize her as a terrorist threatening them with a weapon just hours before. She opened her eyes and then shook her hands while trying to get herself moving again. She looked at her dress, suddenly it did not look so nice on her. The hem of the expensive dress, was covered with dirt and grease from where it had dragged along the floor of the filthy parking garage. There was a wide dark greasy smudge that ran from her right side by her rearend, and crossed around the front of the dress and ended under her right breast.

She cursed herself for failing to notice where she picked the smudge up from. She tried to wipe some of the dirt off her dress, but it was a greasy grime that would not come off with just her hands, and her action only served to make the smudge even worse. Giving up on the stain, she moved nearer to the wire reinforced glass panel of the fire door, and she used the reflection of herself to check her face and hair. To her horror, she had a smudge of dirt on her face at the edge of her chin. She spat on her fingers and swiped at the dirt which disappeared.

The only female robber again tried to straighten her hair, but this was impossible to accomplish with just her hands. The dirt and dust had taken its toll, and she looked like she just stumbled out of bed. She was so caught up with trying to repair her appearance that she had failed to notice the horde of police officers coming up behind her from the basement area, until one of the officers smirked at her from the steps.

"Well will you look at what we just found hiding up here. This here high priced hooker's more worried about her god damn looks than she is with getting her lovely little ass the hell out of here in one fucking piece." One of the almost out of breath officers moaned as he stared at the stunningly good looking young woman, and then he moved further up the staircase the officers were bunching up on behind him.

She was shocked and caught off guard as she spun around, and then she came face to face with three police officers standing on the landing with her. She looked behind them and noticed a sea of black uniforms and masks on more police officers who were obviously staring at her on what she was able to see of their looks.

"Man, if I knew something like this little thing here was waiting to be saved in this fucking dump by us. I would've broken my neck a little harder to get my ass up here a whole lot sooner, Captain." A second officer called out from the stairwell, as he tried to get a better look at the beautiful woman the other police officers were talking about.

The Commander moved to the lead of the group of officers, and he snapped at them in an angry tone. "Okay you bunch of fucking children, you had your little fun and games with the lady, can the crap while I see what the fuck's going on out there, dammit. Relax a little until I see what's going down." The Commander moved over to Lizzie's side, and he took a quick look out of the small reinforced window. He saw the confrontation taking place in front of the restaurant between his fellow officers, and an unseen and number of terrorists.

The Commander pulled back and then he stared at Lizzie for a moment before he offered to her and the rest of his officers. "It's fucking nuts out there. I don't blame you for hiding in here where you think it's safe. I might do the same thing for a little while myself, until things calm down a might out there. You visiting the building or you a resident here, young lady?" the Commander asked, his instincts taking over as he started to question the beautiful woman. In his mind, he had no doubts she was not working with the terrorists who attacked the building, but he still wanted to know what she was doing there anyhow.

The police officer's remarks about her being a high class hooker gave her an idea which she immediately capitalized on, as she shifted her weight and shied away from answering the police officer's questions. Prompting him to offer in a more angry tone at her. "Look, I don't give a good god damn what the hell you were doing inside this fucking building before I got here, young lady. I didn't catch you doing your act, and I don't work for fucking Vice either. So right now, you're cool with me. But I'd like to know what the hell you were doing here, and if you can give me a possible number on the amount of terrorists still hiding in this fucking building. Look lady, you're not in any trouble with me, so you can level with me without any fear."

"Well, I was kind of visiting a sick friend here, sir. When these mad men suddenly burst into the apartm..." She began to offer until she was stopped by the police officer.

"Who were you visiting in the building if you don't mind my asking you, young lady?" the Commander interrupted while continuing to fish around for some more information from her.

"Well, if you don't mind sir. I don't think I'd care to mention his name." She replied shyly as she looked at the floor, and then she moved her foot like she was caught doing something wrong.

"I bet you don't want to fucking tell us who he was. He's probably married." Another officer called out from the stairwell area, causing the rest of the police officers to chuckle at his words he just aimed at the young lady.

The Commander glared at the officers gathered on the stairs and popping off at the scared girl, and they immediately quieted down again. Then he continued his interrogation of the young woman standing before him. "How come you don't want to tell me his name young lady?"

"Well it's like this sir, you see sir, this sick friend of mine kind of comes with a little extra luggage, sir." She said as she again looked at her foot as she wiggled it on the filthy floor.

"What the hell are you talking about young lady?" the Commander snapped back at her, he did not like the game he thought she was playing against him. He was used to having his questions answered promptly, especially from a high priced midtown hooker.

"Well Mr. Officer Sir, you see this sick friend is kind of married, sir." She offered a second time shyly as she stared into the eyes of the angry looking police officer.

"I told you Commander, she's doing some fucking married guy in this dump. She's nothing more than just a high price hooker, sir." The same officer called out again.

"Ohhhhh... I see what you're saying to me young lady. I don't blame you for wanting to keep his name secret, young lady. Look, it's like I told you before, I don't have any gripe with you or your profession. Just as long as you keep off my fucking beat while you make your living in my City. Okay lady, my men and I are going to get out there and help out our people with these assholes. Right now lady, anyone we free from the building is expected to assemble in the Circle. You'll see a number of people already gathered where you have to go out there.

"Once you're out of the building, I want you to wait there until we get a chance to interview you about what you might know or seen, on has taken place inside the Tower. When we get your information from you, you'll be free to be on your way. You're instructed to follow the last man out of this stairwell, and he'll get you outside the doors to the street. Make certain you get yourself over to the Circle and wait there until we had a chance to speak with you. Don't leave the area before we interviewed you, do you understand what I'm telling you to do, young lady?" the Commander looked her dead in her eyes for a long moment.

"Yes Sir Mr. Officer, I'm to go over to the Circle and wait there until you, or someone from the department speaks to me first, sir. Yes Officer, I understand what you want me to do and I'll do as you have ordered me, sir." She offered as she flashed her sexiest smile and swayed her hips slightly at the police officer.

"You read me all wrong here young lady. I won't be the one conducting any of the interviews with the civilians from the Tower out there, Miss. I have a more important job than that shit to do in here. Someone from the department will be assigned to carry out the interviews. Ma'am, don't forget to follow my last man out of this fucking place for your own safety."

The female robber nodded at the concerned officer as she allowed herself to be moved away from the heavy fire door, and lead to the back of the group of officers gathered on the landing. Someone called out, suggesting the Commander get her name and address, so they can use her and her services at the next policeman's ball. All the police officers laughed as some shoved each other on the stairs when they made a hole for the beauty to walk to the rear of their group.

"I already told you bunch of fucking clowns once. The next time I have to talk to you pack of god damn children, I'm going to do it with the end of my boot. I said to can the crap or else. This isn't a fucking game we're playing here, we have a mess of bad guys active out there. Who are trying to cap our asses, and it's up to us to put a stop to it, and start saving the lives of civilians caught up in this mess, and that's what we're going to do. Let's get ready children, it's time to get involved in the action." The Commander took hold of the doorknob of the stairwell door as a female Sergeant moved over to his side, and then she offered barely over a whisper to him.

"Say Billy, you don't really think this lady of the night is going to follow your orders, do you sir? You know the instant that honey hits the air outside, she's going to make like a ghost and disappear, sir. Tell you true, if I found myself in her shoes, that's what I'd do as soon as I was out of here." The Sergeant smiled at her Commanding Officer as she waited his reply.

"Yep, I gathered that crap for myself, Sergeant. Who the hell gives a fuck anyhow. I know she don't know a damn thing that'd help us out with this mess anyhow. Look at her, she's shaking like a leaf, and I don't blame her. I'm scared to death myself, dammit. There's no telling how long the poor kid's been hiding in here, and judging by her chosen profession, she's not about to offer us up anything that'd force her to come to court, and testify against any of these flaming assholes anyhow, Sergeant. Besides, there'll be plenty of other people waiting to be interviewed we can get any useful information from. I don't want to hold her on anything, and if she can disappear in this mess and put this bad dream behind her. I say good luck to her. You ready to go Sergeant? We have a more important thing to do rather than worry about her."

The female Police Officer Sergeant nodded at the Commander and then she flung open the heavy fireproof door. Then the police unit piled into the mayhem taking place in the lobby area of the Trump hotel. The last cop out of the staircase area, dragged Lizzie behind him and he roughly manhandled her over to the shattered front brass doors of the Tower. He unceremoniously shoved her out the doors as he barked at her. Reminding her to get over to the Circle, and wait there to be interviewed by one of the other police officers there.

She nodded at the angry acting police officer as she ran down the littered covered marble steps as fast as the tight fitting dress allowed her to run, and then she rushed onto the rubble covered sidewalk surrounding the burning upper floors of the Trump Tower. Many more police officers charged past her on their way into the Trump Tower, without paying very much attention to her presence on the street as they ran by her.

Standing on the point of the once beautiful triangle the Trump Tower was constructed on, she looked in all directions before committing to her next course of action. She looked down 60th Street which had the least number of police and people running around, and she headed down that block. She walked at a fast pace, but not too fast as to draw any attention to herself. As she tried to act like she did not know what was going, and she allowed herself to be directed out of the area by other police officers trying to take command over this section of midtown Manhattan. Anytime she was asked by an officer if she was inside the Tower at the time of the attack, she replied no, and then she continued walking. She kept walking down the block as she tried to ignore the horde of people frantically running wildly around in all directions.

The once female terrorist/robber walked out of the area and then up 60th Street, until she crossed Eighth Avenue, and then she hailed a cab she noticed parked by the side of a curb. She smiled because she was swift enough to remembered to stuff some cash in her backpack when they first attacked the Trump Tower, which she carried buried beneath the mound of diamonds loose in her pocketbook. She opened it while making certain not to spill any of the diamonds out, as she dug through the inches of unset diamonds to find the five twenty dollar bills on the bottom of the bag. Finding them she allowed herself a quick smile.

The cab driver tried his best to engage his fair in conversation, in an attempt to try and find out a little something about what was happening just down the block. He was there for ten minutes trying to find a fair. She completely ignored all the driver's very bothersome questions as she ordered him to head for Grand Central Station, where she intended to board a train and let it bring her out to her mother's home in Brooklyn. Once she was in Bergen Beach, she would change her clothes, and then take a relaxing and long hot bath. She had many of her old clothes still stored at her mother's home, so she could use them until she brought new ones later on. Then she would disappear from the United States forever.

So she could begin her new life living in South America, as an extremely wealthy and unattached young woman. She did not deceive herself in the least, because she realized when she saw all the police officers coming up from the basement area behind her in the building. She understood, Michael and the others with him were more than likely dead.

The cab slowly pulled away from the curb with the driver still bitching as he weaved his car in and out of the heavy flow of traffic being diverted from the lower streets of the city to where he was driving, and they were terribly clogging up the roads he was using.

Again she completely ignored the upset acting cab driver's rude remarks and flood of curses as she smiled in victory over what she was able to accomplish. Happy she paid close attention when Michael told them where they were going to dump the unset diamonds they were going to steal from the diamond dealers when they hit the Tower.

She was going to make contact with Michael's fence man, and sell him the diamonds she escaped the Tower with, for whatever she could possible get for them. Then she would beat it down to South America and disappear from the United States for the rest of her life, and start her life anew acting as a very wealthy European woman on vacation. She took in a deep breath and then she let it out slowly, trying to calm down her rattled nerves.

The wave of New York City police officers and FBI Agents, along with a horde of special agents usually assigned to protect the leaders of the United States, were flooding into the overcrowded lobby of the Trump International Hotel and Tower, in almost uncountable numbers and completely taking over the lower section of the building. Some of the police officers breached the restaurant doors, attacking them in force and instantly killing the lone terrorist hiding inside. Unfortunately, he was able to kill three of the hostages who tried to take matters into their own hands, by rushing him when they heard the police officers trying to talk the terrorist out of the restaurant.

Other police officers were left at the security structure stationed in the basement of the Tower, with orders to open up all the fire doors throughout the Tower when called to do so. The police were going to use the doors to help try and control the civilians they were going to free from the upper floors of the building, and then get them out of the Tower in an orderly fashion. The officers were going to release one floor at a time to better control the known to be frightened civilians still trapped inside the Tower.

The police wanted everyone hanging around outside the structure until they knew for certain they had all the terrorists in the building captured or killed, and there were no explosive charges set to go off after the terrorists left the building. Bomb squads from the FBI and local police departments entered the building next, and they were quickly put to work making certain there were no surprises waiting to go off later on against them.

The FBI and special agents had one thing on their minds as they continued to pour into the lobby of the hotel, and that was to make it to the Vice President's apartment, and then form an impenetrable ring of security around her. There was a mix of secret service agents assigned to protect the President and his staff, entering the building along with many FBI Agents. They were rushing up the stairs towards the thirty forth floor. Although it was known one of the five elevators was still operational, the officers did not chance using it. In case the terrorists might have planted some explosives in or on top of the cab. No one trusted anything still operating inside the building, until the bomb squad had a chance to check out the structure, and they gave their approval the building was classified as safe and free of any possible explosive charges. It was decided to take the Vice President down the staircase for safety and protection for her.

As a large number of agents and police rush up to the twenty second floor where it was discovered there were suspected terrorists still free on the fifteenth floor. Most of the special and FBI Agents continued on towards the thirty forth floor, while the police who followed them stopped on the fifteenth floor and went after the reported terrorists.

Unknown to the scrambling police, there was only one terrorist still active on the floor, and he was involved with guarding a number of hostages chosen before Michael discovered they had the Vice President of the United States in their possession.

Twelve SWAT team police officers wearing black protective body armor and masks, quickly surrounded Apartment 1531 from the hall. Inside the room they heard people talking at the same time. The squad leader raised the megaphone to his mouth and ordered everyone inside the room to come out with their hands over their heads. The angry sounding voice warned if everyone in the room did not come out, they were going to come in after them. Panic cries from the civilians came from the apartment, when one voice was heard above the others. He was ordering everyone in the apartment to shut up while he tried to think of what he was going to do next.

The police realized they were dealing with only one terrorist operating inside the room after hearing him order the others to be quiet, and this terrorist was holding many hostages in the room with him. The squad leader tried to negotiate with the scared sounding man. He called out for the terrorist to make it easier on himself and the others with him, by giving up and then freeing the hostages and come out of the apartment with his hands over his head.

Lavarack, the last terrorist still alive inside the Trump Tower, was scared to death and acting like a wild man inside the apartment. He understood he was trapped in a no win situation along with the hostages. He realized the police and hostages were just waiting for him to make a mistake so they could all jump him. His attention was torn between the police officer out in the hallway yelling at him, and the harsh glares and threatening actions from the hostages in the room with him. He listened to the police and turned his back on the hostages.

McKinney was a rough and tumble man, and the second he picked up his chance to act against the radical, he rushed the back of the terrorist. Grabbing his weapon with one powerful hand he forced the barrel of the weapon towards the ceiling as Lavarack pulled the trigger, sending a stream of lead ripping into the ceiling of the room. With his other hand, McKinney looped it around the terrorist's neck, and then he pulled him back and bending him over his knee. A sickening cracking sound filled the air as the terrorist's weapon fell to the floor, and his body slumped over while still wrapped up in the older man's arm.

The second the police gathered in the hallway heard the weapon fire coming from the apartment. They immediately assaulted the door with the ramrod and their own body weight. With two heavy hits from the ramrod and bodies, the metal and wood door went flying from its hinges. The police poured into the room and found themselves staring at a large man clutching the body of a dead man in his hands who they knew was the terrorist. Some of the officers aimed their weapons at the large man staring back at them with a stunned look on his face.

Upon seeing the flood of police officers threatening him, McKinney let go of the limp body, and then he raised his hands as he called out to the officers. "Hey, whoa, hold on there a minute there friends. I'm not one of them dopey asses who created all this mess. I live in the Tower, have been since it first opened for business. I'm sorry to say, but I believe I might have just killed this little punk holding us against our will, sirs."

The old man stepped aside and allowed himself to be shoved roughly up against the wall by excited officers, and then roughly searched as the rest of the officers poured into the room. When the squad leader was sure the only terrorist was dead and the hostages set free, he made contact with his Command, and the leader announced the building was classified as secured.

The FBI and secret agents still charging up the stair, started to dwindle down some, with a number of officers dropping out of the charge from exhaustion caused by the unending steps they were rapidly climbing. The FBI Agents were the first ones to make it to the floor where the Vice President was suppose to be waiting for them. The agents found themselves blocked by the set of heavy fire doors, and a secret agent called down via radio and ordered the fire door on this floor to be released by the security console in the basement now being manned by New York City police officers. The locks were flipped opened but the door refused to move.

The Field Commander knew of Lieutenant Walker and his female partner's presence behind the fire doors, and he called out to him. "Lieutenant Robert Walker, and your fellow soldier Sergeant Dorothy Ramirez. This is Special Agent Harry Mayberry on the other side of this damn door, sir. Look Lieutenant, we have secured the entire building and all terrorists are classified as dead, or in police custody as of this moment, and I'm now ordering you to open up this damn door immediately, soldier. Listen up Lieutenant, the building's burning and we have to get the Vice President out of here A-SAP, sir. You hear me in there Lieutenant?"

Lieutenant Walker heard the agent yelling at him, but he was taking nothing for granted, not after all he and Ramirez went through to get the Vice President away from the terrorists. He was in an extremely bad mood, and he was exhausted and his body was killing him from being beaten up from the feet up, and his leg was also killing him. He had the Vice President and her secretary under his protection, and it was his ass the General was going to beat on if he screwed up this late in the game. He cupped his hand to his mouth and called back to the special agent on the other side of the door.

"Hey fucking big mouth! How the fuck do I know you are who the hell you say you fucking are, buster? You gotta come up with something a whole lot betta than that little bit of bullshit you're trying to spoon feed me, before I believe anything you gotta say to my stinking ass, and I let this fucking door move any, you fucking asshole you. I warn you fuckers, if any of you dumb shits try to move that fricking door on your own. I'll send a wall of lead against ya, and you'll be sucking in air through ya fricking ribs, man. Whatdaya have to say to that, fella?"

Agent Mayberry smiled over the threat coming from the elite soldier because knew Lieutenant Walker was correct and he called out to him. "Okay Lieutenant Walker, how the hell am I going to convince you I am who I say I am, sir. How about I make contact with your General White back in Washington, and have him order you to open this damn door for me, Lieutenant."

"That makes my fucking boat float fella, there's no fricking cook book for this god damn mess you know, buddy. You gotta do what the fuck you gotta do to prove to my stinking ass you are who you say you are, and I open this fucking door for you bunch of pricks out there." He shot back nastily at the officers on the other side of the fire door as he glared at the door.

Agent Mayberry knew this young kid was just following his instincts and judgment protecting the Vice President's life. The agent waved his radio operator over to his side, and then he placed the call back to Washington to what he believed was his headquarters. But instead he found himself speaking directly with a military officer on the radio. Once he spoke to General White and told him his man would not open the fire door for them, the General knew what he had to do. General White spoke to Duane who was still sort of manning the phone in his apartment. The General told him to have Lieutenant Walker open the fire door.

Duane dropped the phone and rushed to the door of his apartment and stuck his head out in the hallway so he could see the exhausted Lieutenant kneeling on the floor with his weapon held at the ready and aimed at the closed fire door, and he called out to him. "Hey Lieutenant Walker, I just heard from your boss back in Washington, Lieutenant. You know, he's the one who tried to eat my head off when you were in my apartment a little while ago, sir. He just told me to tell you it was okay sir, and you were ordered to open the fire door for the people on the other side of the damn thing, Lieutenant. Your General also told me everything's cool, and you were to step down now son. Hey Lieutenant, did you hear what I just said kid?"

Duane watched as the exhausted young warrior waved back at him without bothering to turn to see his face, and he slowly stood on shaky legs and then he held his weapon in one hand as he pulled the chair away from the fire door with the other. Instantly, a rush of excited agents and FBI personnel barged through the opening, forcing Duane to drop back in his apartment, and he lock the door to better protect his ward, the Vice President.

Agent Harry Mayberry came charging through the door first as soon as there was enough room for him to get through the opening, and he looked at the beat up Lieutenant Walker. Then he reached out and snapped at the young warrior. "I'll take charge of that weapon for you, sir! Your part of this frackis is over with as of this time, Lieutenant

Walker Sir. You and your female partner did good son, real good Lieutenant." The agent did not want anyone armed so close to the Vice President and themselves as well.

"In a pig's fucking ass you'll take my fucking weapon away from me buster! No one's gonna get my stinking weapon from me until I know everything's fucking secured, and the stinking Veep's in good fucking hands, buddy." Lieutenant Walker growled angrily at the concerned looking agent, as he actually leveled his weapon right at the older man's chest, and then he just dared him to try and take his piece away from him.

General White took the time to speak with Vice President Hirshfield on the phone while Duane was speaking to Lieutenant Walker out in the hallway, and when she found out the cavalry was on the other side of the fire doors, and the Lieutenant was stopping them from getting to her. She ordered Duane to open the door to his apartment, she then cautiously looked out in the hallway and when she saw the confrontation taking place between Lieutenant Walker and the special agent, she called out to him. "Lieutenant Walker, it's all right sir. They're our friend's sir. Lieutenant Walker, you done your job, and it's time to allow someone else to take over for you for a change. I'm ordering you to give that Agent your weapon right this minute, mister. Now, do you hear me, god dammit Lieutenant!"

The Lieutenant took a quick glance over his shoulder, and when noticed it was the Vice President ordering him to put up his weapon, he finally relented and did as she ordered. Slowly while drawing in his breath in a deep sigh, he finally relaxed his weapon from a firing stance and allowed it to slide slowly through his cramping, sweat covered hands. Actually forcing Agent Mayberry to reach and catch it, before the weapon fell to the floor. Once Mayberry had his weapon, he slapped the Lieutenant on the shoulder as he told the exhausted and battered warrior he done a super human job. Then Agent Mayberry headed for the smiling Vice President and her secretary who was standing protectively right next to Mary Hirshfield who offered her hand to him. Agent Mayberry wanted to check on their condition, and to see if either of the two young women needed any emergency medical assistance.

Sergeant Dorothy Ramirez put up her weapon and then she rushed for her soldier's side like he was the only man left on the face of the earth, as he slowly slid down the side of the wall with his back leaning against it. He ended up sitting on his rearend on the floor with his legs crossed under him. She fell into his arms on the floor, and kissed him on his grime covered, scratched up face as she smiled and continued to kiss him.

Cathy stood by the Vice President's side, and she smiled as she witnessed the two lovers kissing, and she turned to Vice President Hirshfield and then announced in a flat tone of voice.

"IT'S OVER..."